# A DOCUMENTARY HISTORY OF

# The Negro People in the United States

# A DOCUMENTARY HISTORY

## OF

# The Negro People
# in the
# United States

*Edited by*
HERBERT APTHEKER

*Preface by*
W. E. B. Du Bois

I Vol. 1

FROM COLONIAL TIMES THROUGH THE CIVIL WAR

A Citadel Press Book
PUBLISHED BY CAROL PUBLISHING GROUP

First Carol Publishing Group Edition 1990

Copyright © 1951, 1979 by Herbert Aptheker

A Citadel Press Book
Published by Carol Publishing Group

Editorial Offices
600 Madison Avenue
New York, NY 10022

Sales & Distribution Offices
120 Enterprise Avenue
Secaucus, NJ 07094

In Canada: Musson Book Company
A division of General Publishing Co. Limited
Don Mills, Ontario

Citadel Press a registered trademark of
Carol Communications, Inc.

Manufactured in the United States of America
ISBN 0-8065-0168-5

Carol Publishing Group books are available at special discounts
for bulk purchases, for sales promotions, fund raising, or
educational purposes. Special editions can also be created to
specifications. For details contact: Special Sales Department,
Carol Publishing Group, 120 Enterprise Ave., Secaucus, NJ 07094

20  19  18  17  16  15  14  13

# Preface

It is a dream come true to have the history of the Negro in America pursued in scientific documentary form. When the attempt was made in the 19th century by Nell, Wells Brown and George W. Williams, the results were received with tolerance, but with little sympathy or serious comprehension. Historians were not prepared to believe that Africans even in America had any record of thought or deed worth attention. Then came the long hammering of Carter Woodson, the series of researches by a continuous line of students, black and white; and especially the painstaking and thorough scholarship of Herbert Aptheker.

At long last we have this work which rescues from oblivion and loss, the very words and thoughts of scores of American Negroes who lived slavery, serfdom and quasi-freedom in the United States of America from the seventeenth to the twentieth century. For fifteen years Dr. Aptheker has worked to find and select 450 documents to make an authentic record and picture of what it meant to be a slave in the Land of the Free, and what it meant to be free after the Emancipation Proclamation.

Historical scholarship has done all too little of this sort of research. We have the record of kings and gentlemen ad nauseum and in stupid detail; but of the common run of human beings, and particularly of the half or wholly submerged working group, the world has saved all too little of authentic record and tried to forget or ignore even the little saved. With regard to Negroes in America, in addition to the common neglect of a society patterned on assumed aristocracy, came also the attempt, conscious or unconscious, to excuse the shame of slavery by stressing natural inferiority which would render it impossible for Negroes to make, much less leave, any record of revolt or struggle, any human reaction to utter degradation.

Many of us for years have known of the existence of wide literature which contradicted such assumptions and efforts. I hasten to greet the day of the appearance of this volume, as a milestone on the road to Truth.

W. E. B. Du Bois

# Contents

## III. THE ABOLITIONIST ERA

CONTENTS

CONTENTS

CONTENTS

## IV. THE CIVIL WAR

*A Documentary History of the Negro People in the United States*
FROM THE RECONSTRUCTION ERA TO 1910
will include the index for both volumes

# Introduction

THIS WORK attempts, within the limits of half a million words, to present the essence of the first three hundred years of the history of the American Negro people. This is done through the words of Negro men, women and children themselves.

"Too long have others spoken for us." So began, in 1827, the first editorial in the first Negro newspaper, well-titled *Freedom's Journal*. Here the Negro speaks for himself. These are the words of participants, of eye-witnesses. These are the words of the very great and the very obscure; these are the words of the mass. This is how they felt; this is what they saw; this is what they wanted.

And that is history. It is what the masses endure, how they resist, how they struggle that forms the body of true history. It is the coming into being, the bringing forth of the new—including the old, but the old as it is pregnant with the new—that is the heart of true history.

A Jim Crow society breeds and needs a Jim Crow historiography. The dominant historiography in the United States either omits the Negro people or presents them as a people without a past, as a people who have been docile, passive, parasitic, imitative. This picture is a lie. The Negro people, the most oppressed of all people in the United States, have been militant, active, creative, productive.

When John R. Lynch, Negro Congressman from Mississippi, said in 1882: "The impartial historian will record the fact that the colored people of the South have contended for their rights with a bravery and a gallantry that is worthy of the highest commendation," he spoke truly. And when the National Association of Colored Men declared in 1896 that "the American Negro has at no time in the past been either unmindful or indifferent to or failed to assert and contend for his own rights," the Association spoke the truth.

The Negro people have fought like tigers for freedom, and in doing so have enhanced the freedom struggles of all other peoples. Their history demonstrates that no matter what the despoilers of humanity may do—enslave, segregate, torture, lynch—they cannot *destroy* the people's will to freedom, their urge towards equality, justice and dignity, for without these things there is no decent life, there is no joy, there is no peace. To work in this history, to see the defiance of slaves, the courage of martyrs, the resistance of the plain people, and to study the great human documents they left behind is a most rewarding experience.

Moreover, the Negro people's history demonstrates the essential identity of needs of all the common peoples of the earth—of all colors and all nationalities—so that, in the words of the Rev. J. L. Moore, of the Florida Colored Farmers' Alliance, in 1891, "the laboring colored man's interests and the laboring white man's interests are one and the same."

This *Documentary History* is offered in the hope that it may contribute, in however limited a fashion, to the realization in the United States and in our time of full equality and unity for all men and women.

Some particular aspects of this work require explanation. The editor has not sought to include material on the cultural history of the Negro people and for this would refer the reader to such anthologies as that on Negro poetry by Arna Bontemps and Langston Hughes, on Negro literature by Sylvestre C. Watkins, and *The Negro Caravan* by Sterling A. Brown, Arthur P. Davis and Ulysses Lee.

The work also has a chronological limitation since it ends in 1910. We halt here for the first decade of the twentieth century brings us to the threshold of the modern period of American Negro history. We come to the founding of the National Association for the Advancement of Colored People; to the consolidation of great monopolies, the beginnings of the "New South," and the development of imperialism.

The next ten year period sees a new era begin: the First World War; the passing of Booker T. Washington; the growth of the N.A.A.C.P. and of the National Urban League; the shift in Negro population characteristics from about one-quarter urban in 1910 to over one-third urban in 1920; the leap forward of Southern-born Negroes in the North by over 320,000 between 1910 and 1920, more than the entire number in the preceding forty years and five times the average of the previous decade; and with all this, the beginnings of mass Negro entry into industry. A subsequent volume is now in preparation bringing the story through World War II.

In an undertaking of this sort space considerations were of very great importance. Originally the editor's collated documents totalled some two million words, and more than that had been discarded at first reading. The editor has striven to avoid repetitiousness in the documents. Historical significance and typicality were primary considerations in the selecting of documents, and an effort has been made to illuminate the many-sidedness and richness of Negro history.

The editor has labored for brevity in his documentary introductions and has tried to keep the explanatory footnotes to a minimum consistent with providing sufficient information to place the documents in their time. Some documents because of their transcendent historic quality, as Booker T. Washington's Atlanta Speech of 1895 and the original 1905 declaration of the Niagara Movement, are presented in their entirety, but generally documents have been extracted, limited by the aim of getting across their essence and something of their flavor.

With each document is given its source and, normally, the library, archive or repository where this source was consulted. Where no library is indicated, the New York Public Library was used. Unless otherwise stated all newspapers were examined in the microfilm division of the Schomburg Collection, 135th Street Branch, New York Public Library.

All footnotes are the editor's and all bracketed words are his, unless stated otherwise. In no case have words themselves been changed, except in Document 120[d], where the reason for the change is given. Misspellings and grammatical errors have been corrected if they occurred in printed sources and clearly were typographical mistakes. The word "Negro" has been capitalized throughout in accordance with correct usage.

All words in the documentary text itself come from Negroes with rare and immediately apparent exceptions, as in publishing testimony before investigating bodies the questions posed by white people are given; and all documents are of a contemporaneous nature, except Numbers 42 and 58 where participants tell of the events some years after their occurrence.

It is hoped that the rather complete table of contents, the numerous running heads and the detailed index will make readily accessible any particular item the reader may desire.

Many debts of gratitude have been accumulated in the course of preparing this work. The staffs of the following institutions have been very helpful: the Public Libraries of Brooklyn, Boston, Chicago, Detroit, New York, Raleigh and Richmond; and of the Schomburg Collection already mentioned; the State Archives, Historical Societies and Historical Commissions of California, Connecticut, Georgia, Iowa, Maryland, Massachusetts, Minnesota, Mississippi, New York, North Carolina, Pennsylvania, South Carolina, Virginia and Wisconsin; the Library of Congress and the Ridgway Library Company of Philadelphia; the libraries of Columbia University, Harvard University, Howard University and the Universities of California, Minnesota, North Carolina, South Carolina and Wisconsin; the National Archives, the American Antiquarian Society, the Boston Athenaeum and the Jefferson School of Social Science.

The writings, published and unpublished, of many historians and biographers have been essential and several of these are acknowledged within the body of the text itself. Here the editor wishes to mention specifically his indebtedness to the work of Jack Abramowitz, James S. Allen, Frederic Bancroft, Horace M. Bond, Arna Bontemps, Benjamin Brawley, Helen T. Catterall, Earl Conrad, Elizabeth Donnan, Helen G. Edmonds, Arthur H. Fauset, John H. Franklin, E. Franklin Frazier, Shirley Graham, Lorenzo J. Greene, Bella Gross, Harry Haywood, Luther P. Jackson, James H. Johnston, Sidney Kessler, Elizabeth Lawson, Benjamin Quarles, L. D. Reddick, W. Sherman Savage, A. A. Taylor, Ridgely Torrence, Charles H. Wesley and Harvey Wish.

Various sections of this work were kindly read, prior to publication, by Lloyd L. Brown, Louis Burnham, John Pittman and Doxey A. Wilkerson and valuable comments and criticisms resulted. The entire manuscript was read by Philip S. Foner, distinguished labor historian and editor of the writings of Frederick Douglass, and his suggestions were most helpful. Great assistance was rendered the editor by Miss Myrtle Powell and Mrs. Madeline Lawrence, and for this he is grateful.

The life and work of the late Dr. Carter G. Woodson constantly inspired the editor. His writings, his advice and his friendship were among the most precious influences in the editor's life.

As will be obvious to the reader, without the encouragement, guidance and gracious kindness of Dr. William Edward Burghardt Du Bois this work would not have appeared. He opened to the editor his priceless library and his enormous mass of correspondence, and many times he shared his unrivaled learning thus opening paths that the editor but dimly discerned. The editor finds it impossible to adequately express his profound appreciation to Dr. Du Bois.

Whatever failings, errors or shortcomings this work may have are the fault of the editor, and his alone is the responsibility for views and interpretations offered.

Finally, to Fay—and to Bettina—thank you.

HERBERT APTHEKER

July, 1951

# I

# Through the Revolutionary Era

## 1

## EARLY NEGRO PETITIONS FOR FREEDOM,
### 1661–1726

Individual Negroes quite frequently petitioned governmental bodies for freedom prior to the American Revolution. Three examples of such petitions are given below. The first, dated 1661, was in Dutch and was addressed to the colony of New Netherlands (later New York). Its prayer was granted. The second, dated 1675, was the work of a Virginia Negro and what decision was made in regard to it does not appear. The third petition, dated 1726, was addressed to the North Carolina General Court and was denied.

### [a]

#### *New Netherlands Petition, 1661*

To the Noble Right Honorable Director-General and Lords Councillors of New Netherlands

Herewith very respectfully declare Emanuel Pieterson, a free Negro, and Reytory, otherwise Dorothy, Angola, free Negro woman, together husband and wife, the very humble petitioners of your noble honors, that she, Reytory, in the year 1643, on the third of August, stood as godparent or witness at the Christian baptism of a little son of one Anthony van Angola, begotten with his own wife named Louise, the which aforementioned Anthony and Louise were both free Negroes; and about four weeks thereafter the aforementioned Louise came to depart this world, leaving behind the aforementioned little son named Anthony, the which child your petitioner

1

out of Christian affection took to herself, and with the fruits of her hands' bitter toil she reared him as her own child, and up to the present supported him, taking all motherly solicitude and care for him, without aid of anyone in the world, not even his father (who likewise died about five years thereafter), to solicit his nourishment; and also your petitioner [i.e., Emanuel] since he was married to Reytory, has done his duty and his very best for the rearing . . . to assist . . . your petitioners . . . very respectfully address themselves to you, noble and right honorable lords, humbly begging that your noble honors consent to grant a stamp in this margin of this [document], or otherwise a document containing the consent and approval of the above-mentioned adoption and nurturing, on the part of your petitioner, in behalf of the aforementioned Anthony with the intent [of declaring] that he himself, being of free parents, reared and brought up without burden or expense of the [West Indian] Company, or of anyone else than your petitioner, in accordance therewith he may be declared by your noble honors to be a free person: this being done, [the document] was signed with the mark of Anthony Pieterson.

Manuscript in New York State Library, Albany. The editor is indebted to Professor Margaret Schlauch formerly of New York University and Professor Adriaan Barnouw of Columbia University for the translation. Ellipses indicate illegible portions of the document; bracketed words are the editor's.

## [b]

### *Virginia Petition, 1675*

To the R^T Hon^ble Sir William Berkeley, Knt., Gover^r and Capt. Genl. of Virg^a, with the Hon. Councell of State.

The Petition of Phillip Corven, a Negro, in all humility showeth: That yo^r pet^r being a servan^t to M^rs Anny^e Beazley, late of James Citty County, widdow, de^ed. The said M^rs Beazley made her last will & testament in writing, under her hand & seal, bearing date, the 9th day of April, An. Dom. 1664, and, amongst other things, did order, will appoint that yo^r pet^r by the then name of Negro boy Phillip, should serve her cousin, Mr. Humphrey Stafford, the terme of eight yeares, then next ensueing, and then should enjoy his freedome & be paid three barrels of corne & a sute of clothes, as by the said will appears. Sonne after the makeing of which will, the said M^rs Beazley departed this life, yor pet^r did continue & and abide with the said M^r Stafford, (with whome he was ordered by the said will to live) some yeares, and then the said Mr. Stafford sold the remainder of yo^r pet^r time to one Mr. Charles Lucas, with whom y^or pet^r alsoe continued, doeing true & faithfull service; but the said Mr. Lucas, coveting yo^r pet^r's service longer then of right itt was due, did not att the expiracon of the said eight yeares, discharge y$^{or}$ pe$^{tr}$ from his service, but compelled him to serve three years longer than the time set by the said Mrs. Beazley's will, and then not being willing y$^{or}$ pe$^{tr}$ should enjoy his freedome, did, contrary to all honesty and good conscience with threats & a high hand, in the time of yo$^r$ pe$^{tr's}$ service with him, and by his confederacy with some persons compel yo$^r$ pe$^{tr}$ to sett his hand to a writeing, which the said M$^r$ Lucas now saith is an Indenture for twenty yeares, and forced yo$^r$ pe$^{tr}$ to acknowledge the same in the County Court of Warwick.

Now, for that itt please yo$^r$ Hon$^r$, yo$^r$ pe$^{tr}$, who all the time of the makeing the said forced writing, in the servicee of the said Mr. Lucas, and never discharged from the same, the said M$^r$ Lucas alwaies unjustly pretending that yo$^r$ pe$^{tr}$ was to serve him three yeares longer, by an order of Court, w$^h$ is untrue, which pretence of the said Mr. Lucas will appeare to yo$^r$ hon$^s$ by y$^e$ testimony of persons of good creditt

Yo$^r$ Pe$^{tr}$ therefore most humbly prayeth yo$^r$ hon$^{rs}$ to order that the said M$^r$ Lucas make him sattisfaction for the said three yeares service above his time, and pay him corne & clothes, with costs of suite.

And yo$^r$ pe$^{tr}$ (as in duty bound) shall ever pray, &c.

Wm. P. Palmer, ed., *Calendar of Virginia State Papers*, I (Richmond, 1875), pp. 9–10.

[c]

## North Carolina Petition, 1726

To the Honoble Christopher Gale Esqr Chief Justice of the General Court February the third one thousand Seven hundred & twenty Six

The Complaint and petition of peter Vantrump a free Negro Sheweth that yor Complainant being a free Negro and at his own voluntary disposall & hath hired himself to Service Sundry times particularly in New York and other places and being at St Thomas's this Summer past one Captain Mackie in a Brigantine from thence being bound (as he reported) to Europe Your Honors Complainant agreed to go with him in Order to gett to Holland but instead of proceeding the Sayd Voyage the Sayd Mackie came to North Carolina where combining with one Edmund porter of this province and fearing the Sayd Mackie not to be on a lawfull Trade Yor Complainant was desirous to leave him and the Sayd porter by plausible pretences gott Your Complainant to come away from the Sayd Mackie with him although Your Complainant often told the Sayd porter that he was not a Slave but a free man Yet nevertheless the Sayd porter now against all right now pretends Your Complainant to be his Slave and hath held and used him as

Such wherefore Your Complainant prays he may be adjudg$^d$ & declar$^d$ free as in Justice he ought to be & Sign$^d$ Peter Vantrump.

Wm. Saunders, ed., *The Colonial Records of North Carolina*, II (Raleigh, 1886), pp. 702–03.

## 2

# STATEMENTS OF SLAVE REBELS, 1741

The history of American Negro slavery was marked by very many conspiracies and revolts on the part of the Negroes. The colonial period was no exception to this. The New York City slave plot of 1741, during which many buildings were destroyed by fire, was one of the major events of this character. It provoked hysteria leading to exaggeration of the extent of the actual conspiracy, but that one existed is clear. To obtain direct statements from contemporary Negroes themselves concerning these events is not easy. Below appear the confessions of two Negroes made in New York City on the afternoon of May 30, 1741, while chained to stakes before a howling, impatient mob. Following these confessions, the slaves were burned alive. In addition, twenty-nine other Negroes were executed as were four whites including, among the latter, two women.

The recorder of the slaves' confessions takes us to the scene of the execution.

Mr. Moore, the deputy secretary, undertook singly to examine them both, endeavoring to persuade them to confess their guilt, and all they knew of the matter, without effect, till at length Mr. Roosevelt came up to him, and said he would undertake Quaco, whilst Mr. Moore examined Cuffee; but before they could proceed to the purpose, each of them was obliged to flatter his respective criminal that his fellow sufferer had begun, which stratagem prevailed; Mr. Roosevelt stuck to Quaco altogether, and Mr. Moore took Cuffee's confession, and sometimes also minutes of what each said; and afterwards upon drawing up their confessions in form from their minutes, they therefore intermixed what came from each.

Quaco's confession at the stake. He said—

1. That Hughson was the first contriver of the whole plot, and promoter of it; which was to burn the houses of the town; Cuffee said, to kill the people.

2. That Hughson brought in first Caesar, Varack's; then Prince, Auboyneau's; Cuffee, Philipse's; and others, amongst whom were old Kip's Negro; Robin, Chambers'; Cuffee, Gomez's; Jack, Codweis's, and another short Negro, that cooks for him.

3. That he (Quaco) did fire the fort; that it was by a lighted stick taken out of the servant's hall, about eight o'clock at night; that he went up the

back stairs with it, and so through Barbara's room, and put it near the gutter, betwixt the shingles and the roof of the house.

4. That on Sunday afternoon, a month before the firing of the fort, over a bowl of punch, the confederates at Hughson's (amongst whom were the confederates above named, Albany and Tickle, *alias* Will, Jack and Cook, Comfort's; old Butchell, Caesar, and Guy, Horsfield's; Tom, Van Rant's; Caesar, Peck's; Worcester, and others voted him, (Quaco), as having a wife in the fort, to be the person who should fire the fort; Sandy and Jack, Codweis's; Caesar and Guy, Horsfield's; were to assist him in it.

5. That Hughson desired the Negroes to bring to his house what they could get from the fire, and Hughson was to bring down country people in his boat to further the business, and would bring in other Negroes.

6. That forty or fifty to his knowledge were concerned, but their names could not recollect. (The mob pressing and interrupting.)

7. That Cuffee, Gomez's; and Caesar, Peck's, fired Vant Zant's storehouse.

8. That Mary Burton had spoke the truth, and could name many more.

9. Fortune, Wilkins's, and Sandy, had done the same; and Sandy could name the Spaniards, and say much more, which Cuffee particularly confirmed.

10. Being asked what view Hughson had in acting in this manner? he answered, to make himself rich.

11. That after the fire was over, Quaco was at Hughson's house, Jack, Comfort's, a leading man, Hughson, wife, and daughter present, and said the job was done, meaning the fire; that he went frequently to Hughson's house, and met there Tickle and Albany.

12. Quaco said his wife was no ways concerned, for he never would trust her with it; and that Denby knew nothing about the matter. [The wife was the governor's cook; Denby his domestic.]

13. Jamaica, Ellis's not concerned that he knew of, but was frequently at Hughson's with his fiddle.

14. Said he was not sworn by Hughson, but others were.

Daniel Horsmanden, *The Negro Conspiracy in the City of New York, in 1741* (N.Y., 1851), pp. 87–89.

3

# SLAVES PETITION FOR FREEDOM DURING THE REVOLUTION, 1773–1779

The ferment preceding and accompanying the Revolutionary War stimulated many Negro people, collectively and individually, to make public pleas against slavery and to point out to the less than two and a half million American white people the incongruity and the danger of shouting "Liberty or Death" while enslaving 750,000 human beings. There follow five examples of such statements covering the years from 1773 through 1779.

[a]

Province of the Massachusetts Bay To His Excellency Thomas Hutchinson, Esq; Governor; To The Honorable His Majesty's Council, and To the Honorable House of Representatives in General Court assembled at Boston, the 6th Day of *January,* 1773.

The humble PETITION of many Slaves, living in the Town of Boston, and other Towns in the Province is this, namely

That your Excellency and Honors, and the Honorable the Representatives would be pleased to take their unhappy State and Condition under your wise and just Consideration.

We desire to bless God, who loves Mankind, who sent his Son to die for their Salvation, and who is no respecter of Persons; that he hath lately put it into the Hearts of Multitudes on both Sides of the Water, to bear our Burthens, some of whom are Men of great Note and Influence; who have pleaded our Cause with Arguments which we hope will have their weight with this Honorable Court.

We presume not to dictate to your Excellency and Honors, being willing to rest our Cause on your Humanity and Justice; yet would beg Leave to say a Word or two on the Subject.

Although some of the Negroes are vicious, (who doubtless may be punished and restrained by the same Laws which are in Force against other of the King's Subjects) there are many others of a quite different Character, and who, if made free, would soon be able as well as willing to bear a Part in the Public Charges; many of them of good natural Parts, are discreet, sober, honest, and industrious; and may it not be said of many, that they are virtuous and religious, although their Condition is in itself so unfriendly to Religion, and every moral Virtue except *Patience.* How many of that Number have there been, and now are in this Province, who have had every Day of their Lives imbittered with this most intollerable Reflection, That, let their Behaviour be what it will, neither they, nor their Children to all Generations, shall ever be able to do, or to possess and enjoy any Thing, no, not even *Life itself,* but in a Manner as the *Beasts that perish.*

We have no Property! We have no Wives! No Children! We have no City! No Country! But we have a Father in Heaven, and we are determined, as far as his Grace shall enable us, and as far as our degraded contemptuous Life will admit, to keep all his Commandments: Especially will we be obedient to our Masters, so long as God in his sovereign Providence shall *suffer* us to be holden in Bondage.

It would be impudent, if not presumptuous in us, to suggest to your Excellency and Honors any Law or Laws proper to be made, in relation to our unhappy State, which, although our greatest Unhappiness, is not our *Fault;* and this gives us great Encouragement to pray and hope for such Relief as is consistent with your Wisdom, Justice, and Goodness.

We think Ourselves very happy, that we may thus address the Great and General Court of this Province, which great and good Court is to us, the best Judge, under God, of what is wise, just-and good.

We humbly beg Leave to add but this one Thing more: We pray for such Relief only, which by no Possibility can ever be productive of the least Wrong or Injury to our Masters; but to us will be as Life from the dead.

Signed,

**FELIX**

*The Appendix: or, some Observations on the expediency of the Petition of the Africans, living in Boston, &c., lately presented to the General Assembly of this Province. To which is annexed, the Petition referred to. Likewise, Thoughts on Slavery with a useful extract from the Massachusetts Spy, of January 28, 1773, by way of an Address to the Members of the Assembly. By a Lover of Constitutional Liberty.* (Boston, E. Russell, n.d.) pp. 9–11. Copy in the Boston Athenaeum.

## [b]

Boston, April 20th, 1773

Sir, The efforts made by the legislative of this province in their last sessions to free themselves from slavery, gave us, who are in that deplorable state, a high degree of satisfaction. We expect great things from men who have made such a noble stand against the designs of their *fellow-men* to enslave them. We cannot but wish and hope Sir, that you will have the same grand object, we mean civil and religious liberty, in view in your next session. The divine spirit of *freedom*, seems to fire every humane breast on this continent, except such as are bribed to assist in executing the execrable plan.

We are very sensible that it would be highly detrimental to our present masters, if we were allowed to demand all that of *right* belongs to us for past services; this we disclaim. Even the *Spaniards*, who have not those sublime ideas of freedom that English men have, are conscious that they have no right to all the services of their fellow-men, we mean the *Africans*, whom they have purchased with their money; therefore they allow them one day in a week to work for themselves, to enable them to earn money to purchase the residue of their time, which they have a right to demand in such portions as they are able to pay for (a due appraizement of their services being first made, which always stands at the purchase money.) We do not pretend to dictate to you Sir, or to the Honorable Assembly, of which you are a member. We acknowledge our obligations to you for what you have already done, but as the people of this province seem to be actuated by the principles of equity and justice, we cannot but expect your house will again take our deplorable case into serious consideration, and give us that ample relief which, *as men,* we have a natural right to.

But since the wise and righteous governor of the universe, has permitted our fellow men to make us slaves, we bow in submission to him, and determine to behave in such a manner as that we may have reason to expect the divine approbation of, and assistance in, our peaceable and lawful attempts to gain our freedom.

We are willing to submit to such regulations and laws, as may be made relative to us, until we leave the province, which we determine to do as soon as we can, from our joynt labours procure money to transport ourselves to some part of the Coast of *Africa,* where we propose a settlement. We are very desirous that you should have instructions relative to us, from your town, therefore we pray you to communicate this letter to them, and ask this favor for us.

In behalf of our fellow slaves in this province, and by order of their Committee.

Peter Bestes,
Sambo Freeman,
Felix Holbrook,
Chester Joie.

For the Representative of the town of Thompson.

Printed leaflet, original in library of New York Historical Society; photostat in Boston Public Library. The last word in this leaflet—Thompson—was written in ink.

[c]

*To his Excellency Thomas Gage Esq. Captain General and Governor in Chief in and over this Province.*
*To the Honourable his Majestys Council and the Honourable House of Representatives in General Court assembled* May 25 1774

The Petition of a Grate Number of Blackes of this Province who by divine permission are held in a state of Slavery within the bowels of a free and christian Country

Humbly Shewing

That your Petitioners apprehind we have in common with all other men a naturel right to our freedoms without Being depriv'd of them by our fellow men as we are a freeborn Pepel and have never forfeited this Blessing by aney compact or agreement whatever. But we were unjustly dragged by the cruel hand of power from our dearest frinds and sum of us stolen from the bosoms of our tender Parents and from a Populous Pleasant and plentiful country and Brought hither to be made slaves for Life in a Christian land. Thus we are deprived of every thing that hath a tendency to make life even tolerable, the endearing ties of husband and wife we are strangers to for we are no longer man and wife than our masters or mistresses thinkes proper marred or onmarred. Our children are also taken from us by force and sent maney miles from us wear we seldom or ever see them again there to be made slaves of for Life which sumtimes is vere short by Reson of Being dragged from their mothers Breest Thus our Lives are imbittered to us on these accounts By our deplorable situation we are rendered incapable of shewing our obedience to Almighty God how can a slave perform the duties of a husband to a wife or parent to his child How can a husband leave master to work and cleave to his wife How can the wife submit themselves to there husbands in all things How can the child obey thear parents in all things. There is a great number of us sencear . . . members of the Church of Christ how can the master and the slave be said to fulfil that command Live in love let Brotherly Love contuner and abound Beare yea onenothers Bordenes How can the master be said to Beare my Borden when he Beares me down whith the Have chanes of slavery and operson against my will and how can we fulfill our parte of duty to him whilst in this condition and as we cannot searve our God as we ought whilst in this situation. Nither can we reap an equal benefet from the laws of the Land which doth not justifi but condemns Slavery or if there had bin aney Law to hold us in Bondage we are Humbely of the Opinion ther never was aney to inslave our children for life when Born in a free Countrey. We therfor Bage your Excellency and Honours will give this its deer weight and consideration and that you will accordingly cause an act of the legislative to be pessed that we may obtain our Natural right our freedoms and our children be set at lebety at the yeare of twenty one for whoues sekes more petequeley your Petitioners is in Duty ever to pray.

*Collections, Massachusetts Historical Society*, 5th Series, III (Boston, 1877) pp. 432–37 for above and the following petition.

## [d]

*To the Honorable Counsel & House of [Representa]tives for the State of Massachusetts Bay in General Court assembled, January 13, 1777*

The petition of A Great Number of Blackes detained in a State of slavery in the Bowels of a free & Christian Country Humbly sheweth that your

Petitioners apprehend that they have in Common with all other men a Natural and Unaliable Right to that freedom which the Grat Parent of the Unavers hath Bestowed equalley on all menkind and which they have Never forfeited by any Compact or agreement whatever—but that wher Unjustly Dragged by the hand of cruel Power from their Derest friends and sum of them Even torn from the Embraces of their tender Parents—from A populous Pleasant and plentiful country and in violation of Laws of Nature and off Nations and in defiance of all the tender feelings of humanity Brough hear Either to Be sold Like Beast of Burthen & Like them Condemnd to Slavery for Life—Among A People Profesing the mild Religion of Jesus A people Not Insensible of the Secrets of Rational Being Nor without spirit to Resent the unjust endeavours of others to Reduce them to a state of Bondage and Subjection your honouer Need not to be informed that A Live of Slavery Like that of your petioners Deprived of Every social privilege of Every thing Requisit to Render Life Tolable is far worse then Nonexistence.

[In imitat]ion of the Lawdable Example of the Good People of these States your petitiononers have Long and Patiently waited the Evnt of petition after petition By them presented to the Legislative Body of this state and cannot but with Grief Reflect that their Sucess hath ben but too similar they Cannot but express their Astonishment that It have Never Bin Consirdered that Every Principle from which Amarica has Acted in the Cours of their unhappy Dificultes with Great Briton Pleads Stronger than A thousand arguments in favours of your petioners they therfor humble Beseech your honours to give this petion its due weight & consideration & cause an act of the Legislatur to be past Wherby they may be Restored to the Enjoyments of that which is the Naturel Right of all men—and their Children who wher Born in this Land of Liberty may not be heald as Slaves after they arive at the age of twenty one years so may the Inhabitance of this Stats No longer chargeable with the inconsistancey of acting themselves the part which they condem and oppose in others Be prospered in their present Glorious struggle for Liberty and have those Blessing to them, &c.

### [e]

To the Honbl. General Assembly of the State of Connecticut to be held at Hartford on the Second Thursday of Instant May [1779]—The Petition of the Negroes in the Towns of Stratford and Fairfield in the County of Fairfield who are held in a State of Slavery humbly sheweth—

That many of your Petitioners, were (as they verily believe) most unjustly torn, from the Bosom of their dear Parents, and Friends, and without any Crime, by them committed, doomed, and bound down, to perpetual Slavery; and as if the Perpetrators of this horrid Wickedness, were conscious (that we poor Ignorant Africans, upon the least Glimering Sight, derived from a Knowledge of the Sense and Practice of civilized Nations) should Convince them of their Sin, they have added another dreadful Evil, that of holding us in gross Ignorance, so as to render Our Subjection more easy and tolerable. may it please your Honours, we are most grievously affected, under the Consideration of the flagrant Injustice; Your Honours who are nobly contending, in the Cause of Liberty, whose Conduct excites the Admiration, and Reverence, of all the great Empires of the World; will not resent, our thus freely animadverting, on this detestable Practice; altho our Skins are different in Colour, from those whom we serve, Yet Reason & Revelation join to declare, that we are the Creatures of that God, who made of one Blood, and Kindred, all the Nations of the Earth; we perceive by our own Reflection, that we are endowed with the same Faculties with our masters, and there is nothing that leads us to a Belief, or Suspicion, that we are any more obliged to serve them, than they us, and the more we Consider of this matter, the more we are Convinced of our Right (by the Laws of Nature and by the whole Tenor of the Christian Religion, so far as we have been taught) to be free; we have endeavoured rightly to understand what is our Right, and what is our Duty, and can never be convinced that we were made to be Slaves. Altho God almighty may justly lay this, and more upon us, yet we deserve it not, from the hands of Men. we are impatient under the grievous Yoke, but our Reason teaches us that it is not best for us to use violent measures, to cast it off; we are also convinced, that we are unable to extricate ourselves from our abject State; but we think we may with the greatest Propriety look up to your Honours, (who are the fathers of the People) for Relief. And we not only groan under our own burden, but with concern, & Horror, look forward, & contemplate, the miserable Condition of our Children, who are training up, and kept in Preparation, for a like State of Bondage, and Servitude. we beg leave to submit, to your Honours serious Consideration, whether it is consistent with the present Claims, of the united States, to hold so many Thousands, of the Race of Adam, our Common Father, in perpetual Slavery. Can human Nature endure the Shocking Idea? can your Honours any longer Suffer this great Evil to prevail under your Government: we entreat your Honours, let no considerations of Publick Inconvenience deter your Honours from interposing in behalf of your Petitioners; we ask for nothing, but what we are fully persuaded is ours to Claim. we beseech your Honours to weigh this matter in the Scale of Justice, and in your great Wisdom and goodness, apply such Remedy as the Evil does

require; and let your Petitioners rejoice with your Honours in the Participation with your Honours of that inestimable Blessing, *Freedom* and your Humble Petitioners, as in Duty bound shall ever pray &c.
dated in Fairfield the
11th Day of May A D 1779—

>                        prime a Negro man
>                        servant to Mr.
>                    Vam A. Sturge
>                        of Fairfield
>                        his
>                    Prince   X   a Negro man
>                        mark
>                    servant of Capt. Stephen Jenings
>                        of Fairfield ——

Signed in Presence of                    in Behalf of themselves and
    Jonth Sturges.                        the other  Petitioners

Photostat of original document in Archives, Connecticut State Library. Dr. Lorenzo J. Greene, of Lincoln University, Jefferson City, Missouri, very kindly lent this photostat to the editor.

# 4

# GAINING FREEDOM DURING THE REVOLUTION, 1779–1784

The Revolution itself made it possible for many Negroes to gain their freedom in a number of ways. Two such methods, one stemming from the flight of a Tory master and the other from faithful service by the Negro in the Revolutionary Army, are illustrated in the two documents below of the years 1779 and 1784. The second method, service in the Revolutionary Army, was a very common one, since some five thousand Negroes fought in that Army, of whom many were slaves.

## [a]

To the Honble the General Assembly of the Governor and Company of the State of Connecticut Now Sitting at Hartford in said State—

The memorial of Pomp a Negro man Slave belonging to the Estate of Jeremiah Leaming late of Norwalk in the County of Fairfield in said State— Clerk now absconded and with the Enemy at open war with the United States of America and under their protection humbly shewith—

That on the 11th Day of July last past the said Jeremiah Leaming with his Family Voluntarily join'd the British Troops in said Norwalk and with them then went over to Long Island and New York and hath ever since their [sic] continued under their protection—

That your Honors Memorialist being unwilling to go with his said master over to the Enemy made his Escape from him while the said Troops were in said Norwalk and is held and Considered as a part of the Estate of his said Master and forfeited to the said State of Connecticut—

That the said Jeremiah Leamings Estate hath been a Special County Court held at Fairfield with and for the County of Fairfield on the 4th Tuesday of September last past Declared and adjudged forfeit to said State and since Administration hath been granted thereon to Samuel Gruman of Sd. Norwalk who is now about to Inventory the same wherein your Honors Memorialist must be included and considered a part of his master('s) Estate as your Honors Memorialist is advised notwithstanding your Honors Memorialist at the Time of his Sd. Master(')s Joining the Enemy veryly tho't and believed by his remaining in said Norwalk and preventing by his Escape as aforesd. his masters taking him with him over to the Enemy he should have obtained his Freedom from Slavery and that your Honors Memorialist is about Thirty Years of Age and of a firm and healthy Constitution and able to well-provide for himself and a Wife and Child and that his Wife is a free woman and your Honors Memorialist is advised that he cannot be Emancipated without your Honors Consent as he is now become the property of the Sd. State altho the Selectmen of Sd. Norwalk Judge your Honors Memorialist a proper Subject of Freedom—Wherefore your Honors Memorialist humbly prays your Honors to take his Case into your wise Consideration and resolve that he be freed from his State of Slavery or in such other way grant him such relief in the premises as your Honors in your great Wisdom shall Judge proper and he as in Duty Bound shall Ever pray Dated at Norwalk the 20th Day of October A.D. 1779

his<br>
Pomp   X<br>
mark

Archives, Connecticut State Library. Photostat kindly provided the editor by Dr. Lorenzo J. Greene.

## [b]

**To The General Assembly of the State of North Carolina**

The Petitioner of Ned Griffin a Man of mixed Blood Humbley Saieth that a Small space of Time before the Battle of Gilford a certain William Kitchen then in the Service of his Countrey as a Soldier Deserted from his line for which he was Turned in to the Continental Service to serve as the Law Directs—Your Petitioner was then a Servant to William Griffin and was purchased by the said Kitchen for the purpose of Serving in His place, with a Solom Assurance that if he your Petitioner would faithfully serve the Term of Time that the said Kitchen was Returned for he should be a free Man— Upon which said Promise and Assurance your Petitioner Consented to enter in to the Continental Service in said Kitchens Behalf and was Received by Colo: James Armstrong At Martinborough as a free Man Your Petitioner furter saieth that at that Time no Person could have been hired to have served in said Kitchens behalf for so small a sum as what I was purchased for and that at the Time that I was Received into Service by said Colo: Armstrong said Kitchen Openly Declaired me to be free Man—The Faithfull purformance of the above agreement will appear from my Discharge,— some Time after your Petitioners Return he was Seized upon by said Kitchen and Sold to a Certain Abner Roberson who now holds me as a Servant— Your Petitioner therefore thinks that by Contract and merit he is Intitled to his Freedom I therefore submit my case to your Honourable Body hoping that I shall have that Justice done me as you in your Wisdom shall think I am Intitled to and Desarving of & Your Petitioner as in duty bound Will Pray

N Carolina

Edgecomb County

April 4th 1784

                        his

Ned   X   Griffin

         mark

MS. in archives of the North Carolina Historical Commission, Raleigh, North Carolina. Photostat in editor's possession. Published by the editor in *The Negro History Bulletin*, November, 1949.

## 5

# NEGROES PROTEST AGAINST TAXATION WITHOUT REPRESENTATION, 1780

Seven Negroes of Dartmouth, Massachusetts, including Paul Cuffe and his brother John, protested on February 10, 1780, in a petition to the revolutionary legislature of their state, against the fact that they were subjected to taxation without the right to vote. In 1783, by court decision, Negroes subject to taxation were declared to be entitled to the suffrage.

The Paul Cuffe involved in this petition became a successful ship captain and merchant. In 1815 he pioneered in the actual colonization of West Africa by American Negroes, transporting at his own expense thirty-eight Negroes for this purpose.

To The Honouerable Councel and House of Representives in General Court assembled for the State of the Massachusetts Bay in New England—March 14th A D 1780—

The petition of several poor Negroes & molattoes who are Inhabitant of the Town of Dartmouth Humbly Sheweth—That we being Chiefly of the African Extract and by Reason of Long Bondag and hard Slavery we have been deprived of Injoying the Profits of our Labouer or the advantage of Inheriting Estates from our Parents as our Neighbouers the white peopel do haveing some of us not long Injoyed our own freedom & yet of late, Contrary to the invariable Custom & Practice of the Country we have been & now are Taxed both in our Polls and that small Pittance of Estate which through much hard Labour & Industry we have got together to Sustain our selves & families withal—We apprehand it therefore to be hard usag and [one word is illegible here—ed.] doubtless (if Continued will) Reduce us to a State of Beggary whereby we shall become a Berthan to others if not timely prevented by the Interposition of your Justice & power & yor Petitioners farther sheweth that we apprehand ourselves to be Aggreeved, in that while we are not allowed the Privilage of freemen of the State having no vote or Influence in the Election of those that Tax us yet many of our Colour (as is well known) have cheerfully Entered the field of Battle in the defence of the Common Cause and that (as we conceive) against a similar Exertion of Power (in Regard to taxation) too well Known to need a recital in this place—

That these the Most honouerable Court we Humbley Beseech they would to take this into Considerration and Let us aside from Paying tax or taxes or cause us to Be Cleaired for we ever have Been a people that was fair from all these thing ever since the days of our four fathers and therefore we take it as aheard ship that we should be so delt By now in these Difficulty times for their is not to exceed more then five or six that hath a cow in this town and theirfore in our Distress we send unto the peaceableness of thee people and the mercy of God that we may be Releaved for we are not alowed in voating in the town meating in nur to chuse an oficer Neither their was not one ever heard in the active Court of the General Asembly the poor Dispised miserable Black people, & we have not an equal chance with white people neither by Sea nur by Land therefore we take it as a heard ship that poor old Negroes should be Rated which have been in Bondage some thirty some forty and some fifty years and now just got their Liberty some by going into the serviese and some by going to Sea and others by good fortan and also poor Distressed mungrels which have no larning and no land and also no [one word illegible—ed.] Neither where to put their head but some shelter them selves into an old rotten but which thy dogs would not lay in

Therefore we pray that these may give no offence at all By no means But that thee most Honouerable Court will take it in to consideration as if it were their own case for we think it as to be a heard ship that we should be assessed and not be a lowed as we may say to Eat Bread therefore we Humbley Beg and pray thee to plead our Case for us with thy people O God; that those who have the rule in their hands may be mercyfull unto the poor and needy give unto those who ask of thee and he that would Borrow of thee turn not away empty: O God be mercyfull unto the poor and give unto those who give ought unto the poor therefore we return unto thee again: most honouerable Court that thou wouldst Consider us in these Difficut times for we send in nur come unto thee not with false words Neither with lieing Lips therefore we think that we may be clear from being called tories tho some few of our Colour hath Rebelled and Done Wickedly however we think that their is more of our Collour gone into the wars according to the Number of them into the Respepiktive towns then any other nation here and [one word illegible—ed.] therefore We most humbley Request therefore that you would take our unhappy Case into your serious Consideration and in your wisdom and Power grant us Relief from Taxation while under our Present depressed Circumstances and your poor Petioners as in duty bound shall ever pray &c

Manuscript in Archives Division, Massachusetts Historical Society; photostat in editor's possession.

# II

# The Early National Period

---

## 6

## A PIONEER NEGRO SOCIETY, 1787

A Negro society was formed in Philadelphia in 1787. Shortly afterwards similar societies were formed elsewhere, as in Newport, Boston and New York. These maintained a steady correspondence and members exchanged visits, thus serving as something of a link between centers of the Northern free Negro population of the post-Revolutionary generation. The insurance features of this Philadelphia society served, too, as the beginnings of a major modern Negro business—the Negro insurance companies. The preamble of the Philadelphia Free African Society, dated April 12, 1787, and the financial rules adopted by the Society on May 17, 1787, follow.

### [a]

### *The Society's Preamble*

Whereas Absalom Jones and Richard Allen, two men of the African race, who, for their religious life and conversation have obtained a good report among men, these persons, from a love to the people of their complexion whom they beheld with sorrow, because of their irreligious and uncivilized state, often communed together upon this painful and important subject in order to form some kind of religious society, but there being too few to be found under the like concern, and those who were, differed in their religious sentiments; with these circumstances they labored for some time, till it was proposed, after a serious communication of sentiments, that a society should be formed, without regard to religious tenets, provided, the persons lived

17

an orderly and sober life, in order to support one another in sickness, and for the benefit of their widows and fatherless children.

Wm. Douglass, *Annals of the First African Church, in the United States of America, now styled The African Episcopal Church of St. Thomas, Philadelphia* . . . (Phila., 1862), p. 15.

## [b]

### *The Society's Financial Rules*

We, the Free Africans and their descendants of the City of Philadelphia in the State of Pennsylvania or elsewhere do unanimously agree for the benefit of each other, to advance one shilling in silver, Pennsylvania currency, monthly and after one year's subscription from the date hereof then to hand forth to the needy of this society, if it should require, the sum of three shillings and nine-pence per week of said money; provided this necessity is not brought on them by their own imprudence. And it is further agreed that no drunkard or disorderly person be admitted as a member, and if they should prove disorderly after having been received, the said disorderly person shall be disjoined from us, if there is not an amendment. by being informed by two of the members, without having any of his subscription money returned to him. And if any should neglect paying his monthly subscription for three months and no sufficient appearing for such neglect, if he do not pay the whole at the next ensuing meeting, he shall be disjoined from us by being informed by two of the members as an offender, without having any of his subscription money returned. Also, if any persons neglect meeting every month, for every omission he shall pay 3 pence, except in case of sickness or other complaint that should require the assistance of the society, then, and in such case, he shall be exempt from the fines and subscriptions during said sickness. Also, we apprehend it to be just and reasonable that the surviving widow of a deceased member should enjoy the benefits of this society as long as she remains his widow, complying with the rules thereof, excepting the subscriptions. And we apprehend it to be necessary that the children of our deceased members be under the care of the society so far as to pay their schooling, if they cannot attend the free school; also to put them out as apprentices to suitable trades or places if required. Also that no member shall convene the society together but it shall be the sole business of the committee and that only, on special occasions and to dispose of money in hand to the best advantage and use of the society after they are granted the liberty as the Monthly Meeting and to transact all other business whatever except that of Clerk and Treasurer. And we unanimously agree to choose Joseph Clark to be our Clerk and Treasurer; and whenever another shall succeed him, it is always understood that one of the people called Quakers, belonging to one of the three Monthly Meetings in Philadelphia is to be chosen to act as Clerk and Treasurer of this useful institution. The following persons met viz., Absalom Jones, Richard Allen, Samuel Boston, Joseph Johnson, Cato Freeman, Caesar Cranchell and James Potter, also William White whose early assistance and useful remarks were found truly profitable.

R. R. Wright, *The Negro in Pennsylvania* (Phila., 1918, Univ. of Pa.), p. 31.

# 7

# NEGROES ASK FOR EQUAL EDUCATIONAL FACILITIES, 1787

The Negro's effort to obtain equal educational rights has its beginnings in the 18th century. One of the first evidences of this comes from Boston and took the form of a petition to the State Legislature dated October 17, 1787, whose prayer was not granted. The leader behind this petition was Prince Hall, who was born in Barbados in 1748 and came to Massachusetts when seventeen years old. He served in the Revolutionary Army and became a Methodist Minister in Cambridge after the War. He was the founder of the Negro Masonic Order in the United States (a charter was granted his lodge from London in 1787) and an early spokesman against the slave trade and slavery. At his home was established, in 1798, a school for Negro children.

To the Honorable the Senate and House of Representatives of the Commonwealth of Massachusetts Bay, in General Court assembled.

The petition of a great number of blacks, freemen of this Commonwealth, humbly sheweth, that your petitioners are held in common with other freemen of this town and Commonwealth and have never been backward in paying our proportionate part of the burdens under which they have, or may labor under; and as we are willing to pay our equal part of these burdens, we are of the humble opinion that we have the right to enjoy the privileges of free men. But that we do not will appear in many instances, and we beg leave to mention one out of many, and that is of the education of our children which now receive no benefit from the free schools in the town of Boston, which we think is a great grievance, as by woful experience we now feel the want of a common education. We, therefore, must fear for our rising offspring to see them in ignorance in a land of gospel light when there is provision made for them as well as others and yet can't enjoy them, and for not other reason can be given this they are black . . .

We therefore pray your Honors that you would in your wisdom some

provision may be made for the education of our dear children. And in duty
bound shall ever pray.

Manuscript in Massachusetts Historical Society.

8

## PROTEST AGAINST KIDNAPPING AND THE SLAVE TRADE, 1788

The kidnapping and sale into slavery of free Negroes was a recurrent tragedy.
Printed below is an early mass petition protesting against this—and the African
slave trade—which was presented under Prince Hall's leadership, to the Massachusetts legislature on February 27, 1788. Many whites also protested against the
incident which provoked this petition. In April, 1788, word reached Boston that
these particular kidnapped Negroes had been sold into slavery at the French
colony of Martinique, but that they had refused, though severely beaten, to work
as slaves. Governor John Hancock of Massachusetts protested to the Governor
of the island and that summer the Negroes were returned, amidst celebrations, to
Boston. Meanwhile, the incident and the protests from Negroes and whites which
it had produced, led to the passage by the state, March 26, 1788, of a strict anti-
slave-trade act with provisions for recovery of damages by any victim of a kidnapper.

To the Honorable the Senit and House of Riprisentetives of the comon
Welth of Massachsetts bay in general court assembled February 27 1788:
The Petition of greet Number of Blacks freemen of this common welth
Humbly sheweth that your Petetioners are justly Allarmed at the enhuman
and cruel Treetment that Three of our Brethren free citizens of the Town
of Boston lately Receved; The captain under a pertence that his vessel was
in destres on a Island belo in this Hearber haven got them on bord put them
in irons and carred them of, from their Wives & children to be sold for
slaves; This being the unhappy state of these poor men What can your Petetioners expect but to be treeted in the same manner by the same sort of
men; What then are our lives and Lebeties worth if they may be taken a way
in shuch a cruel & unjust manner as these; May it pleas your Honnors, we
are not uncensebel that the good Laws of this State forbedes all such base
axones: Notwithstanding we can aseuer your Honners that maney of our
free blacks that have Entred on bord of vessles as seamen *and* have ben sold
for Slaves & sum of them we have heard from but no not who carred them
away; Hence is it that maney of us who are good seamen are oblidge to stay

at home thru fear and the one help of our time lorter about the streets for want of employ; wereas if they were protected in that lawfull calling thay might get a hanceum livehud for themselves and theres: which in the setturation thay are now in thay cannot. One thing more we would bege leve to Hint, that is that your Petetioners have for sumtime past Beheald whith greef ships cleared out from this Herber for Africa and there they ether steal or case others to steal our Brothers & sisters fill there ships holes full of unhappy men & women crouded together, then set out to find the Best markets seal them there like sheep for the slarter and then Returne near like Honest men; after haven sported with the Lives and Lebeties fello men and at the same time call themselves Christions: Blush o Hevens at this.

These our Wattey greevences we cherfully submeet to your Honores Without Decttateing in the lest knowing by Experence that your Honers have and we Trust ever will in your Wisdom do us that Justes that our Present condechon Requires as God and the good Laws of this commonwelth shall [one word illegible—ed.] you—as in Deutey Bound your Petetioners shall ever pray.

MS., Harvard College Library.

## 9

## SLAVES OF A FUGITIVE TORY GAIN THEIR FREEDOM, 1789

The flight of Tories during the American Revolution produced many property entanglements. Not least among these was that represented by the slaves of these royalist refugees. An example of this is indicated in a petition for freedom presented by two Negroes to the legislature of Connecticut in January, 1789, printed below in its officially summarized form. It will be observed that the prayer was granted.

Upon the Petition of Cesar a Negro and Lowis his Wife both of Hebron in the County of Tolland Shewing to this Assembly that by the Laws of this State they were Slaves to the Rev$^d$ Samuel Peters late of said Hebron but now of the City of London in Great Britain who left said Hebron in Septemb$^r$ 1774 and hath ever since remained in the Kingdom of Great Britain, and that the Petitioners have during the absence of the said Peters been at Liberty to provide for themselves, and that the Petitioners now have eight Children, which they have by their Industry maintained in a decent Manner, and the

Petitioners in April 1784, wrote to the said Peters then at London requesting that he would give to the Petitioners and their Children their Freedom And that the said Peters in answer to the request of the Petitioners on the 26th Day of July 1784 Wrote a Letter to the Petitioners declaring his willingness to grant the request of the Petitioners if it was in his Power, but supposed that the Petitioners were Claimed by the State of Connecticut as forfeited by the said Peters to said State, and that some Persons have lately been endeavouring to sell the Petitioners and their Children out of this State, and that the Petitioners are in continual fear of being secretly taken with their Children and sold out of this State to some foreign Country. Praying that they and their said eight Children may be emancipated and declared free from the said Peters as per Petition on File, And upon the Tryal of said Cause and a full hearing of the said Petition and the Evidence produced to support the same, it appears that the said Peters by his Letter dated at London the 26th Day of July 1784, to the Petitioners in answer to their request that he has in said Letter declared that he is willing to emancipate the Petitioners and their Children, and that he would do all in his Power to effect the same.

Whereupon *it is Resolved by this Assembly* that the Petitioners and their said eight Children be and they are hereby emancipated and declared free from the said Peters and all others from by or under his former Claim to the Petitioners and their said eight Children as Slaves.

Leonard W. Labaree, ed., *The Public Records of the State of Connecticut* . . . VI (Hartford, 1945), pp. 531–32. James Brewster, director of the Connecticut State Library, informed the editor (letter dated September 8, 1947) that the original of this petition could not be located.

## 10

## BENJAMIN BANNEKER'S LETTERS, 1790–1791

One of the most remarkable figures of 18th century America was the Maryland free Negro, Benjamin Banneker (1731–1806). Mechanical and mathematical aptitude combined to produce in this man a noteworthy American scientific pioneer. His *Almanacs* were widely used throughout the United States in the 1790's and he was one of a team of three who planned and surveyed the site for the present city of Washington. Published below are a letter he wrote May 6, 1790 to a close friend, Major Andrew Ellicott, in connection with astronomical calculations and another written a year later to Thomas Jefferson, then Secretary of State, enclosing the manuscripts of the first edition of his *Almanac*. The letter and manuscript impressed Jefferson and he sent the latter to Condorcet, Secretary of the Academy of Sciences at Paris.

## [a]

### *To Andrew Ellicott*

I have at the request of several Gentlemen, calculated an Ephemeris for
the year 1791 which I presented unto Mr. Hayes printer in Baltimore, and
he received it in a very polite manner, and told me, that he would gladly
print the same, provided the calculations came any ways near the truth, but
to satisfy himself in that, he would send it to Philadelphia to be inspected
by you, and at the reception of an answer he should know how to proceed—
and now Sʳ:, I beg that you will not be too severe upon me, but as favourable
in giving your approbation as the nature of the case will permit, knowing
well the difficulty that attends long calculations, and especially with young
beginners in Astronomy, but this I know that the greater, and most useful
part of my Ephemeris is so near the truth, that it needs but little correction,
and as to that part that may be somewhat deficient, I hope that you will
be kind enough to view with an eye of pity, as the Calculations was made
more for the sake of gratifying the curiosity of the public, than for any
view of profit, as I suppose it to be the first attempt of the kind that ever
was made in America by a person of my complexion—

I find by my calculation there will be four Eclipses for the ensuing year,
but I have not yet settled their appearances, but am waiting for an answer
from your Honour to Mr. Hayes in Baltimore;—So no more at present, but
am Sr:

Your very humble and most obedient Servt:

B BANNEKER

MS. in New York Historical Society.


## [b]

### *To Thomas Jefferson*

I am fully sensible of that freedom, which I take with you in the present
occasion; a liberty which seemed to me scarcely allowable, when I reflected
on that distinguished and dignified station in which you stand, and the almost general prejudice and prepossession, which is so prevalent in the world
against those of my complexion.

I suppose it is a truth too well attested to you, to need a proof here, that
we are a race of beings, who have long labored under the abuse and censure
of the world; that we have long been looked upon with an eye of contempt;
and that we have long been considered rather as brutish than human, and
scarcely capable of mental endowments.

Sir, I hope I may safely admit, in consequence of that report which hath reached me, that you are a man less inflexible in sentiments of this nature, than many others; that you are measurably friendly, and well disposed towards us; and that you are willing and ready to lend your aid and assistance to our relief, from those many distresses, and numerous calamities, to which we are reduced.

Now Sir, if this is founded in truth, I apprehend you will embrace every opportunity, to eradicate that train of absurd and false ideas and opinions, which so generally prevails with respect to us; and that your sentiments are concurrent with mine, which are, that one universal Father hath given being to us all; and that he hath not only made us all of one flesh, but that he hath also, without partiality, afforded us all the same sensations and endowed us all with the same faculties; and that however variable we may be in society or religion, however diversified in situation or color, we are all in the same family and stand in the same relation to him.

Sir, if these are sentiments of which you are fully persuaded, I hope you cannot but acknowledge, that it is the indispensable duty of those, who maintain for themselves the rights of human nature, and who possess the obligations of Christianity, to extend their power and influence to the relief of every part of the human race, from whatever burden or oppression they may unjustly labor under; and this, I apprehend, a full conviction of the truth and obligation of these principles should lead all to.

Sir, I have long been convinced, that if your love for yourselves, and for those inestimable laws, which preserved to you the rights of human nature, was founded on sincerity, you could not but be solicitous, that every individual, of whatever rank or distinction, might with you equally enjoy the blessings thereof; neither could you rest satisfied short of the most active effusion of your exertions, in order to the promotion from any state of degradation, to which the unjustifiable cruelty and barbarism of men may have reduced them.

Sir, I freely and cheerfully acknowledge, that I am of the African race, and in that color which is natural to them of the deepest dye; and it is under a sense of the most profound gratitude to the Supreme Ruler of the Universe, that I now confess to you, that I am not under that state of tyrannical thraldom, and inhuman captivity, to which too many of my brethren are doomed, but that I have abundantly tasted of the fruition of those blessings, which proceed from that free and unequalled liberty with which you are favored; and which, I hope, you will willingly allow you have mercifully received, from the immediate hand of that Being, from whom proceedeth every good and perfect Gift.

Sir, suffer me to recall to your mind that time, in which the arms and tyranny of the British crown were exerted, with every powerful effort, in order to reduce you to a state of servitude: look back, I entreat you, on the variety of dangers to which you were exposed; reflect on that time, in which every human aid appeared unavailable, and in which even hope and fortitude wore the aspect of inability to the conflict, and you cannot but be led to a serious and grateful sense of your miraculous and providential preservation; you cannot but acknowledge, that the present freedom and tranquility which you enjoy you have mercifully received, and that it is the peculiar blessing of Heaven.

This, Sir, was a time when you clearly saw into the injustice of a state of slavery, and in which you had just apprehensions of the horror of its condition. It was now that your abhorrence thereof was so excited, that you publicly held forth this true and invaluable doctrine, which is worthy to be recorded and remembered in all succeeding ages: 'We hold these truths to be self-evident, that all men are created equal; that they are endowed by their Creator with certain unalienable rights, and that among these are, life, liberty, and the pursuit of happiness.'

Here was a time, in which your tender feelings for yourselves had engaged you thus to declare, you were then impressed with proper ideas of the great violation of liberty, and the free possession of those blessings, to which you were entitled by nature; but, Sir, how pitiable is it to reflect, that although you were so fully convinced of the benevolence of the Father of Mankind, and of his equal and impartial distribution of these rights and privileges, which he hath conferred upon them, that you should at the same time counteract his mercies, in detaining by fraud and violence so numerous a part of my brethren, under groaning captivity, and cruel oppression, that you should at the same time be found guilty of that most criminal act, which you professedly detested in others, with respect to yourselves.

I suppose that your knowledge of the situation of my brethren, is too extensive to need a recital here; neither shall I presume to prescribe methods by which they may be relieved, otherwise than by recommending to you and all others, to wean yourselves from those narrow prejudices which you have imbibed with respect to them, and as Job proposed to his friends, 'put your soul in their souls' stead'; thus shall your hearts be enlarged with kindness and benevolence towards them; and thus shall you need neither the direction of myself or others, in what manner to proceed herein.

And now, Sir, although my sympathy and affection for my brethren hath caused my enlargement thus far, I ardently hope, that your candor and generosity will plead with you in my behalf, when I make known to you, that it was not originally my design; but having taken up my pen in order to direct to you, as a present, a copy of my Almanac, which I have calculated for the succeeding year, I was unexpectedly and unavoidably led thereto.

This calculation is the product of my arduous study, in this most advanced stage of life; for having long had unbounded desires to become acquainted with the secrets of nature, I have had to gratify my curiosity herein through my own assiduous application to Astronomical Study, in which I need not recount to you the many difficulties and disadvantages which I have had to encounter.

And although I had almost declined to make my calculation for the ensuing year, in consequence of that time which I had allotted therefor, being taken up at the Federal Territory, by the request of Mr. Andrew Ellicott, yet finding myself under several engagements to Printers of this State, to whom I had communicated my design, on my return to my place of residence, I industriously applied myself thereto, which I hope I have accomplished with correctness and accuracy; a copy of which I have taken the liberty to direct to you, and which I humbly request you will favorably receive; and although you may have the opportunity of perusing it after its publication; yet I choose to send it to you in manuscript previous thereto, that thereby you might not only have an earlier inspection, but that you might also view it in my own hand writing.

*Copy of a Letter from Benjamin Banneker to the Secretary of State* (Philadelphia, 1792).

11

# SOUTH CAROLINA NEGROES DENOUNCE JIM CROW JUSTICE, 1791

Until the end of the Civil War free Negroes suffered from severe legal disabilities. Amongst the most onerous of these were laws—existing throughout the South and in many Northern states, too—forbidding Negroes the privilege of testifying under oath in a court, and prohibiting them from instituting suit in any case whatsoever. A very early protest against this was presented to the legislature of South Carolina by Charleston free Negroes in January, 1791. The memorial, which was rejected, is printed below:

To the Honorable David Ramsay Esquire President and to the rest of the Honorable New Members of the Senate of the State of South Carolina

The Memorial of Thomas Cole Bricklayer P. B. Mathews and Mathew Webb Butchers on behalf of themselves & others Free-Men of Colour. Humbly Sheweth

That in the Enumeration of Free Citizens by the Constitution of the United States for the purpose of Representation of the Southern States in Congress Your Memorialists have been considered under that description as part of the Citizens of this State. Although by the Fourteenth and Twenty-Ninth clauses in an Act of Assembly made in the Year 1740 and intitled an Act for the better Ordering and Governing Negroes and other Slaves in this Province commonly called The Negro Act now in force Your Memorialists are deprived of the Rights and Privileges of Citizens by not having it in their power to give Testimony on Oath in prosecutions on behalf of the State from which cause many Culprits have escaped the punishment due to their atrocious Crimes, nor can they give their Testimony in recovering Debts due to them, or in establishing Agreements made by them within the meaning of the Statutes of Frauds and Perjuries in force in this State except in cases where Persons of Colour are concerned, whereby they are subject to great Losses and repeated Injuries without any means of redress.

That by the said clauses in the said Act, they are debarred of the Rights of Free Citizens by being subject to a Trial without the benefit of a Jury and subject to Prosecution by Testimony of Slaves without Oath by which they are placed on the same footing.

Your Memorialists shew that they have at all times since the Independence of the United States contributed and do now contribute to the support of the Government by chearfully paying their Taxes proportionable to their Property with others who have been during such period, and now are in full enjoyment of the Rights and Immunities of Citizens Inhabitants of a Free Independent State.

That as your Memorialists have been and are considered as Free-Citizens of this State they hope to be treated as such, they are ready and willing to take and subscribe to such Oath of Allegiance to the States as shall be prescribed by this Honorable House, and are also willing to take upon them any duty for the preservation of the Peace in the City or any other occasion if called on.

Your Memorialists do not presume to hope that they shall be put on an equal footing with the Free white citizens of the State in general they only humbly solicit such indulgence as the Wisdom and Humanity of this Honorable House shall dictate in their favor by repealing the clauses the act aforementioned, and substituting such a clause as will efectually Redress the grievances which your Memorialists humbly submit in this their Memorial but under such restrictions as to your Honorable House shall seem proper.

May it therefore please your Honors to take your Memorialists case into tender consideration, and make such Acts or insert such clauses for the purpose of relieving your Memorialists from the unremitted grievance they now Labour under as in your Wisdom shall seem meet.

And as in duty bound your Memorialists will ever pray

MS. in South Carolina Historical Commission Library, Memorial Building, Columbia, S.C.; published by editor in *The Journal of Negro History*, XXXI (Jan. 1946), pp. 97–98.

## 12

## A LETTER FROM AND TO SLAVE REBELS, 1793

The postal service was not open to slaves, and laws forbade that they be taught how to read or write. The result is that letters from or to slaves are exceedingly rare. And a rarity among rarities is a letter from and to Negro slave rebels. Records of a few such, however, exist and the first among these, found early in August, 1793, on a street in Yorktown, Virginia follows:

Dear Friend—The great secret that has been so long in being with our own color has come nearly to a head tho some in our Town has told of it but in such a slight manner it is not believed, we have got about five hundred Guns aplenty of lead but not much powder, I hope you have made a good collection of powder and ball and will hold yourself in readiness to strike whenever called for and never be out of the way it will not be long before it will take place, and I am fully satisfied we shall be in full possession of the whole country in a few weeks, since I wrote you last I got a letter from our friend in Charleston he tells me he has listed near six thousand men, there is a gentleman that says he will give us as much powder as we want, and when we begin he will help us all he can, the damn'd brutes patroles is going all night in Richmond but will soon cill [kill—ed.] them all, there an't many, we will appoint a night to begin with fire clubs and shot, we will kill all before us, it will begin in every town in one nite Keep ready to receive orders, when I hear from Charleston again I shall no and will rite to you, he that give you this is a good friend and don't let any body see it, rite me by the same hand he will give it to me out his hand he will be up next week don't be feared have a good heart fight brave and we will get free, I had like to get each [one word is illegible here—ed.] but God was for me, and I got away, no more now but remain your friend—Secret Keeper Richmond to secret keeper Norfolk.

MS., South Carolina Historical Commission, Columbia, S.C.

## 13

# A NEGRO INFORMER WRITES THE
# GOVERNOR OF SOUTH CAROLINA, 1793

The story of Judas is an ancient one. All people have had their traitors and the Negro people are no exception. As the preceding document demonstrated, insurrectionary plans were in existence in 1793 and the disclosure of some of these was made by a free Negro of Charleston to the Governor of South Carolina in a letter which reached that official on October 10, 1793.

Altho I am one of those too unpopular characters here, a free black, yet tis my love to a people among whom I have been all my life, would urge me to tell you personally what I do in this way was I not certain that my only being seen talking to your Excellency would be attended with my destruction. But Sir we in the secret are watched and that more by some of your colour than our own, be on your guard against certain strangers, dont let your attention be directed to French men alone * you and I believe in our situation we also have enemies to the Northward give the most particular orders to your Patrols in every part of the State; keep up the military duty till after the 10th of January next at least, dont be lulled by the seeming humility of those about you. For Gods sake Sir show this to no body, but make use of its contents as coming from one, who is contented with his Situation, and has no other view in this, then saving the blood of his fellow creatures as I know that will be all that can be got from this bad advice that has been given to A Black.

MS., South Carolina Historical Commission, Columbia, S.C.

## 14

# NEGROES PROTEST AGAINST POLL TAX,
## 1793–1794

In 1760, the first capitation or poll tax was levied upon free Negroes in South Carolina. In 1787 the poll tax law was altered so that all free Negroes, female as well as male, from the ages of 16 through 50 were required to pay nine shillings and four pence, whether or not they had already been subjected to other types

* It was widely charged at this time that the revolutionary government of France had sent agents into the South to stir up slave rebellion.

of taxation. And in 1789 a law was passed—to become effective in 1791—requiring each free Negro—of any age or sex—to pay, in addition, a yearly tax of twenty-five cents per individual for the ensuing ten years.

These enactments represented a very considerable economic burden to the already fearfully harassed free Negroes of South Carolina. Two petitions from them to the state legislature protesting these laws are printed below. Both are undated, but the first reached the legislature in December, 1793, and the second in April, 1794. The first was signed by twenty-three free Negro men and women from Camden; the second by thirty-four Negro men and women of Charleston. Each document was accompanied by another, numerously signed by white neighbors, urging favorable action. Neither won this, although in 1809 the poll tax law was amended to exclude Negroes physically incapable of earning a livelihood.

[a]

To the Honourable David Ramsay Esquire President of the Honourable Senate, and to the others the Honourable the Members of the same—

The Petition of John Morris William Morris and other Inhabitants of Camden District in behalf of themselves and others who come under the description of Free Negroes Mulattoes and Mustizoes—
Humbly Sheweth

That with submission your Petitioners beg leave to observe that they conceive their ancestors merited the Publick confidence and obtained the Title of a Free People by rendering some particular Services to their Country, which the Wisdom & goodness of Government thought just and right to notice and to reward their Fidelity with Emancipation, & other singular Privileges.

That before the War, and till very lately your Petitioners who were Freeholders or Tradesmen, paid a Tax only for their Lands, trades, and other Taxable property in common with others the Free White Citizens of the State, and in consequence of their paying the same, was Exempted from paying a Pole-Tax for any of their children while under their Jurisdiction.—

That in March 1789, an Ordinance was passed that a Tax of One fourth of a Dollar per head per Annum be Imposed upon all Negroes Mustizoes & Mulattoes: the same to commence in February 1791, and from thence continue for the space of Ten years.—

That by a Subsequent Act, Intitled an Act for raising Supplies for the year of our Lord One thousand seven hundred and ninety two, past the 21st day of December last past, your Petitioners besides paying a Tax for their Lands & other Taxable property are made liable & have accordingly paid the sum of Two Dollars per head for themselves—the same sum per head for their Wives—and the same sum per head for each of their Children above Sixteen Years of age, who are under their Jurisdiction:

That your Petitioners are generally a Poor needy People; have frequently large Families to maintain; and find it exceeding difficult and distressing to support the same, and answer the large demands of the Publick; which appears to them considerably more than double what was formerly Exacted from them; In consequence of which they conceive their Situation in life but a small remove from Slavery; that they are likely to suffer continued inconvenience & disadvantages; and in the end to be reduced to poverty and want itself.—

In confidence therefore of the high Opinion we entertain of your Honours Veracity, and readiness to redress every Grievance which may appear really such, We do most humbly Pray, That your Honours would condescend to take the distressed Case of your Petitioners into your wise Consideration, and Vouchsafe to Grant them such relief as your Honours in your Wisdom shall see meet.—

And your Petitioners as in duty bound shall ever Pray &c

## [b]

To the honorable, the Representatives of So Carolina the Petition of the
          People of Colour of the state aforesaid who are under the act
intitled an Act for imposing a poll tax on all free Negroes, Musteez and Mulatoes.—
          most humbly sheweth
that whereas (we your humble petitioners) having the honor of being your Citizens, as also free and willing to advance for the support of Government anything that might not be prejudicial to us, it being well known that we have not been backward on our part in performing any other public duties that hath fell in the compass of our knowledge,

We therefore, being sensibly griev'd at our present situation, also having frequently discovered the many distresses, occasion'd by your Act imposing the poll tax, such as widows with large families, & women scarcely able to support themselves, being frequently followed & payment extorted by your tax gatherers—

These considerations on our part hath occasioned us, to give you this trouble, requesting your deliberate body, to repeal an Act so truly mortifying to your distress'd petitioners—for which favor your petitioners will ever acknowledge & devoutly pray.

MSS. in South Carolina Historical Commission Library, Memorial Building, Columbia, S.C.; published by the editor in *The Journal of Negro History* XXXI (April, 1946), pp. 131–39.

15

# TWO NEGRO LEADERS REPLY TO SLANDERS— AND DENOUNCE SLAVEHOLDING, 1794

From the days of the Revolution to those of the Civil War, Philadelphia had the largest number of Negroes of any Northern city. These Negro people were a well-organized, militant and highly-articulate group.

When a cholera epidemic swept the city, in 1793, they played, under the leadership of two pioneers of the Negro church, Richard Allen and Absalom Jones, an outstanding part in public assistance work. Misrepresentations concerning this work brought from Messrs. Allen and Jones, in 1794, a reply, abstracts from which follow.

The Negro leaders could not resist the temptation of appending to their pamphlet refuting these slanders a brief but closely reasoned statement on the evil of slaveholding which is also reprinted below.

[a]

### Refuting Misrepresentations

In consequence of a partial representation * of the conduct of the people who were employed to nurse the sick, in the late calamitous state of the city of Philadelphia, we are solicited, by a number of those who feel themselves injured thereby, and by the advice of several respectable citizens, to step forward and declare facts as they really were; seeing that from our situation, on account of the charge we took upon us, we had it more fully and generally in our power, to know and observe the conduct and behavior of those that were so employed.

Early in September [1793], a solicitation appeared in the public papers, to the people of colour to come forward and assist the distressed, perishing, and neglected sick; with a kind of assurance, that people of our colour were not liable to take the infection. Upon which we and a few others met and consulted how to act on so truly alarming and melancholy an occasion. After some conversation, we found a freedom to go forth, confiding in him who can preserve in the midst of a burning fiery furnace, sensible

---

* Reference here is to *A Short Account of the Malignant Fever, lately prevalent in Philadelphia* . . . by Mathew Carey (2nd. ed., Phila., 1793), especially pp. 76–77, which reads: "At an early state of the disorder, the elders of the African Church met, and offered their services to the mayor . . . Their offers were accepted . . . The great demand for nurses afforded an opportunity for imposition, which was eagerly seized by some of the vilest of the blacks . . . Some of them were even detected in plundering . . . But it is wrong to cast a censure on the whole for this sort of conduct . . . The services of Jones, Allen, and Gray . . . demand public gratitude."

that it was our duty to do all the good we could to our suffering fellow mortals. We set out to see where we could be useful. The first we visited was a man in Emsley's alley, who was dying . . . We visited upwards of twenty families that day—they were scenes of woe indeed! The Lord was pleased to strengthen us, and remove all fear from us, and disposed our hearts to be as useful as possible.

In order the better to regulate our conduct, we called on the mayor next day, to consult with him how to proceed, so as to be most useful. The first object he mentioned was a strict attention to the sick, and the procuring of nurses. This was attended to by Absalom Jones and William Gray; and, in order that the distressed might know where to apply, the mayor advertised the public that upon application to them they would be supplied. Soon after, the mortality increasing, the difficulty of getting a corpse taken away, was such, that few were willing to do it, when offered great rewards. The black people were looked to. We then offered our services in the public papers, by advertising that we would remove the dead and procure nurses. Our services were the production of real sensibility;—we sought not fee nor reward, until the increase of the disorder rendered our labour so arduous that we were not adequate to the service we had assumed. The mortality increasing rapidly, obliged us to call in the assistance of five—hired—men, in the awful discharge of interring the dead. They, with great reluctance, were prevailed upon to join us. It was very uncommon, at this time, to find any one that would go near, much more, handle, a sick or dead person.

Mr. Carey . . . has observed, that, "for the honor of human nature, it ought to be recorded, that some of the convicts in the gaol, a part of the term of whose confinement had been remitted as a reward for their peaceable, orderly behavior, voluntarily offered themselves as nurses to attend the sick at Bush-hill; and have, in that capacity, conducted themselves with great fidelity," etc. Here it ought to be remarked, (although Mr. Carey hath not done it) that two thirds of the persons, who rendered these essential services, were people of colour, who, on the application of the elders of the African church, (who met to consider what they could do for the help of the sick) were liberated, on condition of their doing their duty of nurses at the hospital at Bush-hill; which they as voluntarily accepted to do, as they did faithfully discharge, this severe and disagreeable duty.—May the Lord reward them, both temporally and spiritually.

When the sickness became general, and several of the physicians died, and most of the survivors were exhausted by sickness or fatigue; that good man, Doctor [Benjamin] Rush, called us more immediately to attend upon the sick, knowing we could both bleed; he told us we could increase our utility, by attending to his instructions, and accordingly directed us where to procure medicine duly prepared, with proper directions how to administer them, and at what stages of the disorder to bleed, and when we found ourselves incapable of judging what was proper to be done, to apply to him, and he would, if able, attend them himself, or send Edward Fisher, his pupil, which he often did; and Mr. Fisher manifested his humanity, by an affectionate attention for their relief.—This has been no small satisfaction to us; for, we think, that when a physician was not attainable, we have been the instruments, in the hand of God, for saving the lives of some hundreds of our suffering fellow mortals.

We feel ourselves sensibly aggrieved by the censorious epithets of many, who did not render the least assistance in the time of necessity, yet are liberal of their censure of us, for the prices paid for our services, when no one knew how to make a proposal to any one they wanted to assist them. At first we made no charge, but left it to those we served in removing their dead, to give what they thought fit—we set no price, until the reward was fixed by those we had served. After paying the people we had to assist us, our compensation is much less than many will believe.

We do assure the public, that *all* the money we have received, for burying, and for coffins which we ourselves purchased and procured, has not defrayed the expence of wages which we had to pay those whom we employed to assist us. [A detailed financial statement follows—ed.] From this statement, for the truth of which we solemnly vouch, it is evident, and we sensibly feel the operation of the fact, that we are out of pocket . . . We feel ourselves hurt most by a partial, censorious paragraph, in Mr. Carey's second edition, of his account of the sickness . . . where he asperses the blacks alone, for having taken advantage of the distressed situation of the people. That some extravagant prices were paid, we admit; but how came they to be demanded? the reason is plain. It was with difficulty persons could be had to supply the wants of the sick, as nurses . . . It was natural for people in low circumstances to accept a voluntary, bounteous reward; especially under the loathsomeness of many of the sick, when nature shuddered at the thoughts of the infection, and the task assigned was aggravated by lunacy, and being left much alone with them. Had Mr. Carey been solicited to such an undertaking, for hire, Query, "what would *he* have demanded?" but Mr. Carey, although chosen a member of that band of worthies who have so eminently distinguished themselves by their labours, for the relief of the sick and helpless—yet, quickly after his election, left them to struggle with their arduous and hazardous task, by leaving the city. 'Tis true Mr. Carey was no hireling, and had a right to flee, and upon his return, to plead the cause of those who fled; yet, we think, he was wrong in giving so partial and injurious an account of the black nurses; . . .

The bad consequences many of our colour apprehend from a partial relation of our conduct are, that it will prejudice the minds of the people in general against us—because it is impossible that one individual, can have knowledge of all, therefore at some future day, when some of the most virtuous, that were upon most praiseworthy motives, induced to serve the sick, may fall into the service of a family that are strangers to him, or her, and it is discovered that it is one of those stigmatized wretches, what may we suppose will be the consequence? Is it not reasonable to think the person will be abhored, despised, and perhaps dismissed from employment, to their great disadvantage, would not this be hard? and have we not therefore sufficient reason to seek for redress? . . .

Mr. Carey pays William Gray and us a compliment; he says; our services and others of their colour, have been very great. &c By naming us, he leaves these others, in the hazardous state of being classed with those who are called the "vilest" . . . We have many unprovoked enemies, who begrudge us the liberty we enjoy, and are glad to hear of any complaint against our colour, be it just or unjust; in consequence of which we are more earnestly endeavouring all in our power, to warn, rebuke, and exhort our African friends, to keep a conscience void of offence towards God and man; and, at the same time, would not be backward to interfere, when stigmas or oppression appear pointed at, or attempted against them, unjustly; and, we are confident, we shall stand justified in the sight of the candid and judicious, for such conduct.

Mr. Carey's first, second, and third editions, are gone forth into the world, and in all probability, have been read by thousands that will never read his fourth—consequently, any alteration he may hereafter make, in the paragraph alluded to, cannot have the desired effect, or atone for the past; therefore we apprehend it necessary to publish our thoughts on the occasion. Had Mr. Carey said, a number of white and black Wretches eagerly seized on the opportunity to extort from the distressed, and some few of both were detected in plundering the sick, it might extenuate, in a great degree, the having made mention of the blacks . . .

It is even to this day a generally received opinion in this city, that our colour was not so liable to the sickness as the whites. We hope our friends will pardon us for setting this matter in its true state.

The public were informed that in the West Indies and other places where this terrible malady had been, it was observed the blacks were not affected with it. Happy would it have been for you, and much more so for us, if this observation had been verified by our experience.

When the people of colour had the sickness and died, we were imposed upon and told it was not with the prevailing sickness, until it became too notorious to be denied, then we were told some few died but not many. Thus were our services extorted *at the peril of our lives,* yet you accuse us of exorting *a little money from you.*

The bill of mortality for the year 1793, published by Matthew Whitehead, and John Ormrod, Clerks, and Joseph Dolby, sexton, will convince any reasonable man that will examine it, that as many coloured people died in proportion as others. In 1792 there were 67 of our colour buried, and in 1793 it amounted to 305; thus the burials among us have increased more than fourfold, was not this in a great degree the effects of the services of the unjustly vilified black people?

[b]

*Denouncing Slavery*

The judicious part of mankind will think it unreasonable, that a superior good conduct is looked for, from our race, by those who stigmatize us as men, whose baseness is incurable, and may therefore be held in a state of servitude, that a merciful man would not deem a beast to; yet you try what you can to prevent our rising from the state of barbarism, you represent us to be in, but we can tell you, from a degree of experience, that a black man, although reduced to the most abject state human nature is capable of, short of real madness, can think, reflect, and feel injuries, although it may not be with the same degree of keen resentment and revenge, that you who have been and are our great oppressors, would manifest if reduced to the pitiable condition of a slave. We believe if you would try the experiment of taking a few black children, and cultivate their minds with the same care, and let them have the same prospect in view, as to living in the world, as you would wish for your own children, you would find them upon the trial, they were not inferior in mental endowments.

We do not wish to make you angry, but excite your attention to consider, how hateful slavery is in the sight of that God, who hath destroyed kings and princes, for their oppression of the poor slaves; Pharaoh and his princes with the posterity of King Saul, were destroyed by the protector and avenger of slaves. Would you not suppose the Israelites to be utterly unfit for freedom, and that it was impossible for them to attain to any degree of excellence? Their history shews how slavery had debased their spirits. Men must be wilfully blind and extremely partial, that cannot see the contrary effects of liberty and slavery upon the mind of man; we freely confess the vile habits often acquired in a state of servitude, are not easily thrown off;

the example of the Israelite shews, who with all that Moses could do to reclaim them from it, still continued in their former habits more or less; and why will you look for better from us? Why will you look for grapes from thorns, or figs from thistles? It is in our posterity enjoying the same privileges with your own, that you ought to look for better things.

When you are pleaded with, do not you reply as Pharaoh did, "wherefore do ye Moses and Aaron, let the people from their work, behold the people of the land, now are many, and you make them rest from their burdens?" We wish you to consider, that God himself was the first pleader of the cause of slaves.

That God who knows the hearts of all men, and the propensity of a slave to hate his oppressor hath strictly forbidden it to his chosen people, "thou shalt not abhor an Egyptian, because thou wast a stranger in his land. Deut. xxiii. 7." The meek and humble Jesus, the great pattern of humanity, and every other virtue that can adorn and dignify men, hath commanded to love our enemies, to do good to them that hate and despitefully use us. We feel the obligations, we wish to impress them on the minds of our black brethren, and that we may all forgive you, as we wish to be forgiven; we think it a great mercy to have all anger and bitterness removed from our minds; we appeal to your own feelings, if it is not very disquieting to feel yourselves under the dominion of a wrathful disposition.

If you love your children, if you love your country, if you love the God of love, clear your hands from slaves, burden not your children or country with them. Our hearts have been sorrowful for the late bloodshed of the oppressors, as well as the oppressed, both appear guilty of each others blood, in the sight of him who said, he that sheddeth man's blood, by man shall his blood be shed.

Will you, because you have reduced us to the unhappy condition our colour is in, plead our incapacity for freedom, and our contented condition under oppression, as a sufficient cause for keeping us under the grievous yoke? We have shewn the cause of our incapacity, we will also shew, why we appear contented; were we to attempt to plead with our masters, it would be deemed insolence, for which cause they appear as contented as they can in your sight, but the dreadful insurrections they have made, when opportunity has offered, is enough to convince a reasonable man, that great uneasiness and not contentment, is the inhabitant of their hearts.

God himself hath pleaded their cause, he hath from time to time raised up instruments for that purpose, sometimes mean and contemptible in your sight; at other times he hath used such as it hath pleased him with whom you have not thought it beneath your dignity to contend, many add to your numbers, until the princes shall come forth from Egypt and Ethiopia stretch out her hand unto God.

*A Narrative of the Proceedings of the Black People, during the late awful calamity in Philadelphia, in the year 1793* . . . by A.J. and R.A. [Absalom Jones and Richard Allen] (Phila., 1794).

16

## RULES OF AN EARLY NEGRO SOCIETY, 1796

Negro organizations were first formed in the eighteenth century, and one of the earliest of these was the Boston African Society, established in 1796. The Rules of this benevolent society were published by the group itself in 1802, at which time it listed forty-four Negro men as its membership.

*1st.* We, the African Members, form ourselves into a Society . . . for the mutual benefit of each other, which may from time to time offer; behaving ourselves at the same time as true and faithful Citizens of the Commonwealth, in which we live; and that we take no one into the Society, who shall commit any injustice or outrage against the laws of the country.

*2d.* That before any person can become a Member of the Society, he must be presented by three of the Members of the same; and the person, or persons, wishing to become Members, must make application one month at least beforehand, and that at one of the monthly, or three monthly meetings. Person, or persons if approved of shall be received into the Society. And, that before the admittance of any person into the Society, he shall be obliged to read the rules, or cause the same to be read to him; and not be admitted as a member unless he approves them.

*3d.* That each Member on admittance, shall pay one quarter of a Dollar to the Treasurer; and be credited for the same, in the books of the Society; and his name added to the list of Members.

*4th.* That each Member shall pay one quarter of a Dollar per month to the Treasurer, and be credited for the same on the book; but no benefit can be tendered to any Member, untill he has belonged to the Society one year.

*5th.* That any Member, or Members, not able to attend the regular meetings of the Society, may pay their part by appointing one of their brothers to pay the same for them . . .

*6th.* That no money shall be returned to any one, that shall leave the Society; but if the Society should see fit to dismiss any one from their community, it shall then be put to a vote, whether the one, thus dismissed shall have his money again . . .

*7th.* That any Member, absenting himself from the Society, for the space of one year, shall be considered as separating himself from the same . . .

*8th.* That a committee, consisting of three or five persons, shall be chosen by the members every three months; and that their chief care shall be, to attend to the sick, and see that they want nothing that the Society can give . . .

*9th.* That all monies, paid into the Society shall be credited to the payers . . .

*10th.* When any Member, or Members of the Society is sick, and not able to supply themselves with necessaries, suitable to their situations; the committee shall then tender to them and their family whatever the Society have, or may think fit for them. And should any Members die, and not leave wherewith to pay the expenses of his funeral, the Society shall then see that any, so situated, be decently buried. But it must be remembered, that any Member, bringing on himself any sickness, or disorder, by intemperance, shall not be considered, as entitled to any benefits, or assistance from the Society.

*11th.* Should any Member die, and leave a lawful widow and children, the Society shall consider themselves bound to relieve her necessities, so long as she behaves herself decently, and remains a widow; and that the Society do the best in their power to place the children so that they may in time be capable of getting an honest living.

*12th.* Should the Society with the blessing of heaven acquire a sum, suitable to bear interest, they will then take into consideration the best method they can of making it useful.

*13th.* The Members will watch over each other in their Spiritual concerns . . .

*14th.* That each Member traveling for any length of time; by Sea or Land, shall leave a Will . . .

*Laws of the African Society, instituted at Boston . . . 1796* (Boston, 1802, printed for the Society). Copy in the Boston Athenaeum.


# 17

# THE EARLIEST EXTANT NEGRO PETITION TO CONGRESS, 1797

In 1775 the revolutionary state of North Carolina passed a law forbidding the manumission of slaves, except for meritorious services as judged and approved by a county court. Nevertheless, as the preamble to a law of 1778 declared, "divers evil-minded persons, intending to disturb the public peace, did liberate and set free their slaves," and this provoked the courts of Perquimans and Pasquotank to order these Negroes captured and sold to the highest bidder. The act of 1778 approved this, but warned that no Negro who had gained his liberty by faithful service in the Revolutionary Army was to be re-enslaved.

Ten years later the North Carolina legislature passed another act on this question because, despite the law of 1775, "divers persons from religious motives [mostly Quakers—ed.], in violation of the said law, continue to liberate their slaves, who are now going at large to the terror of the people of this State." This act of 1788 provided for the apprehension of all such illegally manumitted Negroes, with twenty percent of the sale price going to the informer. Something like a reign of terror descended upon many free Negroes and quite a few fled the State. On January 23, 1797, four of these Negroes, named Jacob Nicholson, Jupiter Nicholson, Joe Albert and Thomas Pritchet, residing in Philadelphia, petitioned Congress through Representative John Swanwick of Pennsylvania for a redress of their grievances. On January 30, 1797, the question as to whether or not to accept a petition from fugitive slaves was debated in Congress and rejected by a vote of fifty to thirty-three. In the course of the debate, Representative William Smith, of South Carolina, declared: "The practice of a former time, in a similar case, was that the petition was sealed up and sent back to the petitioners." This petition of 1797 appears to be the first from Negroes to Congress, however, that is still extant.

*To the President, Senate, and House of Representatives.* The Petition and Representation of the under-named Freemen, respectfully showeth:—

That, being of African descent, late inhabitants and natives of North Carolina, to you only, under God, can we apply with any hope of effect, for redress of our grievances, having been compelled to leave the State wherein we had a right of residence, as freemen liberated under the hand and seal of humane and conscientious masters, the validity of which act of justice, in restoring us to our native right of freedom, was confirmed by judgment of the Superior Court of North Carolina, wherein it was brought to trial; yet, not long after this decision, a law of that State was enacted, under which men of cruel disposition, and void of just principle, received countenance and authority in violently seizing, imprisoning, and selling into slavery, such as had been so emancipated; whereby we were reduced to the necessity of separating from some of our nearest and most tender connexions, and of seeking refuge in such parts of the Union where more regard is paid to the public declaration in favor of liberty and the common right of man, several hundreds, under our circumstances, having in consequence of the said law, been hunted day and night, like beasts of the forest, by armed men with dogs, and made a prey of as free and lawful plunder. Among others thus exposed, I, Jupiter Nicholson, of Perquimans county, N.C., after being set free by my master, Thomas Nicholson, and having been about two years employed as a seaman in the service of Zachary Nickson, on coming on shore, was pursued by men with dogs and arms; but was favored to escape by night to Virginia, with my wife, who was manumitted by Gabriel Cosand, where I resided about four years in the town of Portsmouth, chiefly employed in sawing boards and scantling; from thence I removed with my wife to Philadelphia, where I have been employed, at times, by water, working along shore, or sawing wood. I left behind me a father and mother, who were manumitted by Thomas Nicholson and Zachary Dickson; they have since been taken up, with a beloved brother, and sold into cruel bondage.

I, Jacob Nicholson, also of North Carolina, being set free by my master, Joseph Nicholson, but continuing to live with him till, being pursued night and day, I was obliged to leave my abode, sleep in the woods, and stacks in the fields, &c, to escape the hands of violent men who, induced by the profit afforded them by law, followed this course as a business; at length, by night, I made my escape, leaving a mother, one child, and two brothers, to see whom I dare not return.

I, Joe Albert, manumitted by Benjamin Albertson, who was my careful guardian to protect me from being afterwards taken and sold, providing me with a house to accommodate me and my wife, who was liberated by William Robertson; but we were night and day hunted by men armed with guns, swords, and pistols, accompanied with mastiff dogs; from whose violence, being one night apprehensive of immediate danger, I left my dwelling, locked and barred, and fastened with a chain, being at some distance from it, while my wife was by my kind master locked up under his roof. I heard them break into my house, where, not finding their prey, they got but a small booty, a handkerchief of about a dollar value, and some provisions; but, not long after, I was discovered and seized by Alexander Stafford, William Stafford, and Thomas Creesy, who were armed with guns and clubs. After binding me with my hands behind me, and a rope around my arms and body, they took me about four miles to Hartford prison, where I lay four weeks, suffering much from want of provision; from thence, with the assistance of a fellow-prisoner, (a white man) I made my escape and for three dollars was conveyed, with my wife, by a humane person, in a covered wagon by night, to Virginia, where, in the neighborhood of Portsmouth, I continued unmolested about four years, being chiefly engaged in sawing boards and plank. On being advised to move northward, I came with my wife to Philadelphia, where I have labored for a livelihood upwards of two years, in Summer mostly, along shore in vessels and stores, and sawing wood in the Winter. My mother was set free by Phineas Nickson, my sister by John Trueblood, and both taken up and sold into slavery, myself deprived of the consolation of seeing them, without being exposed to the like grievous oppression.

I, Thomas Pritchet, was set free by my master Thomas Pritchet, who furnished me with land to raise provisions for my use, where I built myself a house, cleared a sufficient spot of woodland to produce ten bushels of corn; the second year about fifteen, and the third, had as much planted as I suppose would have produced thirty bushels; this I was obliged to leave about one month before it was fit for gathering, being threatened by Holland Lockwood, who married my said master's widow, that if I would not come and serve him, he would apprehend me, and send me to the West Indies; Enoch Ralph also threatening to send me to jail, and sell me for the good of the country; being thus in jeopardy, I left my little farm, with my small stock and utensils, and my corn standing, and escaped by night into Virginia, where shipping myself for Boston, I was, through stress of weather landed in New York, where I served as a waiter for seventeen months; but my mind being distressed on account of the situation of my wife and children, I returned to Norfolk in Virginia, with a hope of at least seeing them, if I could not obtain their freedom; but finding I was advertised in the newspaper, twenty dollars the reward for apprehending me, my dangerous situation obliged me to leave Virginia, disappointed of seeing my wife and children, coming to Philadelphia, where I resided in the employment of a waiter upward of two years.

In addition to the hardship of our own case, as above set forth, we believe ourselves warranted, on the present occasion, in offering to your consideration the singular case of a fellow-black now confined in the jail of this city, under sanction of the act of General Government, called the Fugitive Law, as it appears to us a flagrant proof how far human beings, merely on account of color and complexion, are, through prevailing prejudice, outlawed and excluded from common justice and common humanity, by the operation of such partial laws in support of habits and customs cruelly oppressive. This man, having been many years past manumitted by his master in North Carolina, was under the authority of the aforementioned law of that State, sold again into slavery, and, after serving his purchaser upwards of six years, made his escape to Philadelphia, where he has resided eleven years, having a wife and [f]our children; and, by an agent of the Carolina claimer, has been lately apprehended and committed to prison, his said claimer, soon after the man's escaping from him, having advertised him, offering a reward of ten silver dollars to any person that would bring him back, or five times that sum to any person that would make due proof of his being killed, and no questions asked by whom.

We beseech your impartial attention to our hard condition, not only with respect to our personal sufferings, as freemen, but as a class of that people who, distinguished by color, are therefore with a degrading partiality, considered by many, even of those in eminent stations, as unentitled to that public justice and protection which is the great object of Government. We indulge not a hope, or presume to ask for the interposition of your honorable body, beyond the extent of your constitutional power or influence, yet are willing to believe your serious, disinterested, and candid consideration of the premises, under the benign impressions of equity and mercy, producing upright exertion of what is in your power, may not be without some salutary effect, both for our relief as a people, and toward the removal of obstructions to public order and well-being.

If, notwithstanding all that has been publicly avowed as essential principles respecting the extent of human right to freedom; notwithstanding we have had that right restored to us, so far as was in the power of those by whom we were held as slaves, we cannot claim the privilege of representation in your councils, yet we trust we may address you as fellow-men, who, under God, the sovereign Ruler of the Universe, are intrusted with the distribution of justice, for the terror of evil-doers, the encouragement and protection of the innocent, not doubting that you are men of liberal minds, susceptible of benevolent feelings and clear conception of rectitude to a catholic extent, who can admit that black people (servile as their condition generally is throughout this Continent) have natural affections, social and domestic attachments and sensibilities; and that, therefore, we may hope for a share in your sympathetic attention while we represent that the unconstitutional bondage in which multitudes of our fellows in complexion are held, is to us a subject sorrowfully affecting; for we cannot conceive this condition (more especially those who have been emancipated and tasted the sweets of liberty, and again reduced to slavery by kidnappers and man-stealers) to be less afflicting or deplorable than the situation of citizens of the United States, captured and enslaved through the unrighteous policy prevalent in Algiers. We are far from considering all those who retain slaves as wilful oppressors, being well assured that numbers in the State from whence we are exiles, hold their slaves in bondage, not of choice, but possessing them by inheritance, feel their minds burdened under the slavish restraint of legal impediments to doing justice which they are convinced is due to fellow-rationals. May we not be allowed to consider this stretch of power, morally and politically, a Governmental defect, if not a direct violation of the declared fundamental principles of the Constitution; and finally, is not some remedy for an evil of such magnitude highly worthy of the deep inquiry and unfeigned zeal of the supreme Legislative body of a free and enlightened people? Submitting our cause to God, and humbly craving your best aid and influence, as you may be favored and directed by that wisdom which is from above, wherewith that you may be eminently dignified and rendered conspicuously, in the view of nations, a blessing to the people you represent, is the sincere prayer of your petitioners.

*Annals of the Congress of the United States*, 4th Cong., 2nd Session, VI (Washington, 1849), pp. 2015–2018.

## 18

## A "DISQUIETING" NEGRO PETITION TO CONGRESS, 1800

The second day of the new century witnessed the presentation to Congress, by Representative Robert Waln of Pennsylvania, of a petition directed against the slave trade, the fugitive slave act of 1793 and the institution of slavery itself. The petition came from the free Negroes of Philadelphia headed by the Reverend Absalom Jones. It precipitated a heated and extended debate and was referred to a committee, where it died, only after the House expressed the opinion that portions of the petition had "a tendency to create disquiet and jealousy."

The petitioners, after mentioning their sense of the bounties of Providence in their freedom, and the happiness they felt under such a form of Government, represent that they cannot but be impressed with the hardships under which numbers of their color labored, who they conceived equal objects of representation and attention with themselves or others under the Constitution. That the solemn compact, the Constitution, was violated by the trade of kidnapping, carried on by the people of some of the Southern States on the shores of Maryland and Delaware, by which numbers were hurried into holes and cellars, torn from their families and transported to Georgia, and there inhumanly exposed to sale, which was degrading to the dignified nature of man. That by these and other measures injurious to the human species, there were 700,000 blacks now in slavery in these States. They stated their application to Congress to be, not for the immediate emancipation of the whole, knowing that their degraded state and want of education would render that measure improper, but they ask an amelioration of their hard situation. They prayed that the act called the fugitive bill, which was very severe on that race of people, might be considered; also that the African slave trade might be put a stop to.

*Annals of the Congress of the United States*, 6th Cong., X (Washington, 1851), pp. 229–230.

## 19

## GABRIEL'S CONSPIRACY, 1800

The chosen leader of a very extensive slave conspiracy was a twenty-four year old man standing six feet two inches, answering to the name of Gabriel and legally the property of Thomas Henry Prosser of Henrico County, Virginia.

Several thousand Negroes were involved in this bid for freedom which occurred in the summer of 1800. It was nipped in the bud because of betrayal on the day set for the outbreak (August 30) and because of a tremendous storm and flood which made military operations impossible. Gabriel and about thirty-five other slaves rebels were executed during the months of September and October.

No direct statement from Gabriel himself survives. When he was questioned by the one-time revolutionist, James Monroe, then Governor of Virginia, he, according to Mr. Monroe, "seemed to have made up his mind to die, and to have resolved to say but little on the subject of the conspiracy." From the records of the trial of Gabriel, held October 6, 1800 (he was hanged the next day) and the trial of his confederate, Jack Bowler, held on October 9, 1800, are published the statements of several Negroes:

### [a]

### *October 6th*

*Prosser's Ben:* Gabriel was appointed Captain at first consultation respecting the Insurrection, and afterwards when he had enlisted a number of men was appointed General. That they were to kill Mr. Prosser, Mr. Mosby, and all the neighbors, and then proceed to Richmond, where they would kill everybody, take the treasury, and divide the money amongst the soldiers; after which he would fortify Richmond and proceed to discipline his men, as he apprehended force would be raised elsewhere to repel him. That if the white people agreed to their freedom they would then hoist a white flag, and he would dine and drink with the merchants of the city on the day when it should be agreed to.

Gabriel enlisted a number of Negroes. The prisoner went with the witness to Mr. Young's to see Ben Woolfolk, who was going to Caroline to enlist men there. He gave three shillings for himself and three other Negroes, to be expended in recruiting men.

The prisoner made the handles of the swords, which were made by Solomon. The prisoner shewed the witness a quantity of bullets, nearly a peck, which he and Martin had run, and some lead then on hand, and he said he had ten pounds of powder which he had purchased. Gabriel said he had nearly 10,000 men; he had 1,000 in Richmond, about 600 in Caroline, and nearly 500 at the coal pits, besides others at different places, and that he expected the poor white people would also join him, and that two Frenchmen had actually joined, whom he said Jack Detcher knew, but whose names he would not mention to the witness. That the prisoner had enlisted nearly all the Negroes in town as he said, and amongst them had 400 Horsemen. That in consequence of the bad weather on Saturday night, an agreement was made to meet at the Tobacco House of Mr. Prosser the ensuing night. Gabriel said all the Negroes from Petersburg were to join him after he had commenced the Insurrection.

*Mr. Price's John:* He saw the prisoner at a meeting, who gave a general invitation to the Negro men to attend at the Spring to drink grog. That when there he mentioned the Insurrection, and proposed that all present should join them in the same, and meet in 3 weeks for the purpose of carrying the same into effect, and enjoined several of the Negroes then present to use the best of their endeavors in enlisting men, and to meet according to the time appointed.

*Ben Woolfolk:* The prisoner was present at the meeting at Mr. Young's, who came to get persons to join him to carry on the war against the white people. That after meeting they adjourned to the Spring and held a consultation, when it was concluded that in 3 weeks the business should commence. Gabriel said he had 12 dozen swords made, and had worn out 2 pair of bullet moulds in running bullets, and pulling a third pair out of his pocket, observed that was nearly worn out. That Bob Cooley and Mr. Tinsley's Jim was to let them into the Capitol to get the arms out. That the lower part of the Town towards Rocketts was to be fired, which would draw forth the citizens (that part of the town being of little value); this would give an opportunity to the Negroes to seize on the arms and ammunition, and then they would commence the attack upon them. After the assembling of the Negroes near Prosser's, and previous to their coming to Richmond, a company was to be sent to Gregorie's Tavern to take possession of some arms there deposited. The prisoner said, at the time of meeting the witness at Mr. Young's, that he had the evening before received six Guns—one of which he had delivered to Col. Wilkinson's Sam. That he was present when Gabriel was appointed General and Geo. Smith second in command. That none were to be spared of the whites except Quakers, Methodists, and French people. The prisoner and Gilbert concluded to purchase a piece of silk for a flag, on which they would have written "death or Liberty," and they would kill all except as before excepted, unless they agreed to the freedom of the Blacks, in which case they would at least cut off one of their arms. That the prisoner told the witness that Bob Cooley had told him if he would call on him about a week before the time of the Insurrection he would untie the key of the room in which the arms and ammunition were kept at the Capitol and give it to him, or if he did not come, then on the night of the Insurrection being commenced, he would hand him arms out as fast as he could arm his men, and that he had on a Sunday previous to this, been shown by Cooley every room in the Capitol.

### [b]

### *October 9th*

*Prosser's Ben:* The witness deposes that Gabriel informed him that the prisoner was the first person from whom he received information of the insurrection intended by the Negroes, which was to centre at William Young's. The prisoner said at the Blacksmith shop, in which the witness worked, that he would raise and enlist men and contend for command with Gabriel.

The prisoner came to the shop at sundry times, and had frequent conversations and mentioned at repeated times there, that he had procured six or seven pounds of powder for the purpose of fighting the white people. The prisoner agreed (in hearing of the witness) together with Gabriel and Solomon, to commence the fight with scythe blades, until they could procure arms from the white people. He saw the prisoner at his Master's great-house on the Saturday night appointed for the commencement of the insurrection, in company with Gabriel and Solomon, who said and concluded that the excessive bad weather would prevent the people from meeting that night, and appointed the ensuing Sunday night as the time of meeting at his Master's tobacco house; he also saw them together on the Sunday morning following.

*Mrs. Price's John:* I saw the prisoner at Mr. Young's spring, in company with Gabriel: he enlisted with Gabriel and engaged to get as many men to join as he could, and meet in three weeks from that time for the purpose of fighting the white people. Prosser's Tavern being appointed the place of Rendezvous, the prisoner enquired of Gabriel what he was to do for arms: the prisoner applied to many who had agreed to engage in the insurrection, to give him the voice for General. But upon the votes being taken, Gabriel had by far the greater number. Whereupon, it was concluded that the prisoner should be second in command, to-wit, a captain of light horse. The prisoner and Gabriel had secret conversations. That the meeting was interrupted by the appearance of Mr. Young's overseer, and thereupon the people dispersed, having previously agreed to meet at Mr. Moore's school-house, where a final conclusion on the business should be had.

*Prosser's Sam:* This witness was a runaway at the time of the affair was to have happened: On the Tuesday night of the week appointed for the meeting of the Negroes, the prisoner fell in company with a Negro by name Frank: the prisoner enquired of the deponent if he had heard that the Negroes were going to rise in arms and fight for their liberty. (being the first knowledge he had of the insurrection,) and the prisoner said the business would certainly commence on Saturday night then next ensuing, if it did not rain hail stones. The prisoner said they intended to seize on some arms deposited at Priddy's Tavern: a Negro by name Charles, having promised to conduct them to the spot where they were kept. In a conversation with the prisoner in the corn field, he remarked that he had procured as much ammunition as two persons could carry, and throwing his arms around Lewis, another Negro present, said we have as much right to fight for our liberty as any men: and that on Saturday night they would kill the white people; that they would first kill Mr. Prosser and the neighbors, and then proceed to Richmond.

H. W. Flournoy, ed., *Calendar of Virginia State Papers*, IX (Richmond, 1890), pp. 159–60, 164–65.

## 20

## PHILANTHROPY, 1800

During the Revolution the organization of separate Negro churches began. First among these were Negro Baptist churches which appeared in Virginia by 1776 and in Georgia by 1779, the latter being founded by George Liele. Liele shortly left for Jamaica and Andrew Bryan succeeded him as leader of the Georgia Negro Baptists. Despite some persecution, Bryan persisted in his religious work and by 1800, seven hundred Negroes were members of his church in Savannah. He had by this time purchased the freedom of his wife and was himself the owner of eight slaves. In response to a gift from an English philanthropist, the Rev. Dr. Rippon, he sent the following letter from Savannah on December 23, 1800:

*My Dear and Reverend Brother,* After a long silence occasioned by various hindrances, I sit down to answer your inestimable favour by the late dear Mr. White, who I hope is rejoicing, far above the troubles and trials of this frail sinful state. All the books mentioned in your truly condescending and affectionate letter, came safe, and were distributed according to your humane directions. You can scarcely conceive, much less than I describe, the gratitude excited by so seasonably and precious a supply of the means of knowledge and grace, accompanied with benevolent proposals of further assistance. Deign, dear sir, to accept our united and sincere thanks for your great kindness to us, who have been so little accustomed to such attentions. Be assured that our prayers have ascended, and I trust will continue to ascend to God, for your health and happiness, and that you may be rendered a lasting ornament to our holy Religion and a successful Minister of the Gospel.

With much pleasure, I inform you, dear sir, that I enjoy good health, and am strong in body, tho' sixty-three years old, and am blessed with a pious wife, whose freedom I have obtained, and an only daughter and child who is married to a free man, tho' she, and consequently, under our laws, her seven children, five sons and two daughters, are slaves. By a kind Providence I am well provided for, as to worldly comforts, (tho' I have had very little given me as a minister) having a house and lot in this city, besides the land on which several buildings stand, for which I receive a small rent, and a fifty-six acre tract of land, with all necessary buildings, four miles in the country, and eight slaves; for whose education and happiness, I am enabled thro' mercy to provide.

But what will be infinitely more interesting to my friend, and is so much more prized by myself, we enjoy the rights of conscience to a valuable extent, worshiping in our families and preaching three times every Lord's day, baptizing frequently from ten to thirty at a time in Savannah, and administering the sacred supper, not only without molestation, but in the presence, and with the approbation and encouragement of many of the white people. We are now about seven hundred in number, and the work of the Lord goes on prosperously. . . .

Another dispensation of Providence has much strengthened our hands, and increased our means of information; Henry Francis, lately a slave to the widow of the late Colonel Leroy Hammond, of Augusta, has been purchased by a few humane gentlemen of this place, and liberated to exercise the handsome ministerial gifts he possesses amongst us, and teach our youth to read and write. He is a strong man about forty-nine years of age, whose mother was white and whose father was an Indian. His wife and only son are slaves.

Brother Francis has been in the ministry fifteen years, and will soon receive ordination, and will probably become the pastor of a branch of my large church, which is getting too unwieldy for one body. Should this event take place, and his charge receive constitution, it will take the rank and title of the 3rd Baptist Church in Savannah.

*The Baptist Annual Register, 1798–1801,* in *The Journal of Negro History,* I (1916), pp. 86–88.

21

# A CALL TO REBEL, AND AN INFORMER'S LETTER, 1802

The corpses of Gabriel and his comrades had barely turned cold when reports of other slave plots began to appear. Printed below are the recruiting speech of a Negro rebel named Arthur, slave of William Farrar of Henrico county, Virginia, as recorded in the spring of 1802; and a letter written on June 7, 1802 by an anonymous slave informer to one Mr. Mathews of Norfolk.

## [a]

### *The Rebel*

Black men if you have now a mind to join with me now is your time for freedom. All clever men who will keep secret these words I give to you is life. I have taken it on myself to let the country be at liberty this lies upon my mind for a long time. Mind men I have told you a great deal I have joined with both black and white which is the common man or poor white people, mulattoes will Join with me to help free the country, although they are free already. I have got 8 or 10 white men to lead me in the fight on the magazine, they will be before me and hand out guns, powder, pistols, shot and other things that will answer the purpose . . . black men I mean to lose my life in this way if they will take it.

## [b]

### *The Informer:*

White pepil be-ware of your lives, their is a plan now forming and intend to put in execution this harvest time—they are to commence and use their Sithes as weapons until they can get possession of other weapons; their is a great many weapons hid for the purpose, and be you all assured If you do not look out in time that many of you will be put to death. the sceam is to kill all before them, men, women, and children. their has been expresses going In Every direction for some days to see all the Negroes they could this holladay, to make the arrangements and conclud what time it was to commence and at what plasis they are to assemble. watch they conduc of your Negroes and you will see an alteration. I am confident of the leaders and can not give you my name. I am also a greater friend to some of the Whites, and wish to preserve their lives. I am a favorite Servant of my Master and Mistis, and love them dearly.

MSS., Virginia State Archives, Richmond; published in H. Aptheker, *American Negro Slave Revolts* (Columbia Univ. Press, 1943), pp. 229–30, 233–34.

## 22

# EARLY ORGANIZED ANTI-SLAVERY WORK BY NEGROES, 1808–1809

Among the very earliest forms of organized anti-slavery activity was that conducted by Negroes themselves within and through their own societies. Three examples of this type of agitation follow: the first consists of extracts from an address delivered by the Reverend Peter Williams, Jr., in the New York African Church on January 1, 1808, the day when the federal law barring the African slave trade went into effect; the second, delivered the same year, is by an anonymous member of the Boston African Society; the third was delivered in New York City on January 2, 1809, the speaker being William Hamilton, a Negro pioneer Abolitionist and an organizer of subsequent nation-wide Negro conventions.

### [a]

Oh, God! we thank thee, that thou didst condescend to listen to the cries of Africa's wretched sons; and that thou didst interfere in their behalf. At thy call humanity sprang forth, and espoused the cause of the oppressed: one hand she employed in drawing from their vitals the deadly arrows of injustice; and the other in holding a shield, to defend them from fresh assaults: and at that illustrious moment, when the sons of 76 pronounced these United States free and independent; when the spirit of patriotism, erected a temple sacred to liberty; when the inspired voice of Americans first uttered those noble sentiments, "we hold these truths to be self-evident, that all men are created equal; that they are endowed by their Creator with certain unalienable rights; among which are life, liberty, and the pursuit of happiness"; and when the bleeding African, lifting his fetters, exclaimed, "am I not a man and a brother"; then with redoubled efforts, the angel of humanity strove to restore to the African race, the inherent rights of man . . .

May the time speedily commence, when Ethiopia shall stretch forth her hands; when the sun of liberty shall beam resplendent on the whole African race; and its genial influences, promote the luxuriant growth of knowledge and virtue.

Peter Williams, Jr., *An Oration on the Abolition of the Slave Trade; delivered in the African Church, in the City of New York, January 1, 1808* (N.Y., 1808).

## [b]

Men have exercised authority over our nation as if we was their property, by depriving us of our freedom, as though they had a command from heaven thus to do. But, we ask, if freedom is the right of one nation; why not the right of all the nations of the earth? . . .

Some men that we are conversant with, however, are ready to say, that a black man, or an African, ought never to be free. But this assertion is groundless, since it is founded on so shallow a foundation as to scarcely bare bringing up to remembrance as an argument, that because many are slaves they all ought to be. . . .

Did not America think it was a privilege truly desirable to be enjoyed, when her mother nation was about to invade her land, and bring her under her dominion; did she not greatly regret the thought of a deprivation of her freedom when she asked the assistance of her sister nation, France, to vindicate her cause against Britain with her? If desirable, I say, to America under such circumstances, why not to any or all the nations of the earth? I answer, equally desirable to all. . . .

Slavery hath ever had a tendency to spread ignorance and darkness, poverty and distress in the world. Although it hath advanced a few, yet many have been the sufferers; it was first invented by men of the most malicious dispositions, and has been carried on by men of similar character. . . .

Freedom is desirable; if not, would men sacrifice their time, their property, and finally lose their lives in the pursuit of it? If it was not a thing that was truly valuable, should we see whole nations engaged in hostility, to procure it for their country, wives and children? Yea, I say there is something so dreadful in slavery that some had rather die than experience it.

*The Sons of Africa: An Essay on Freedom. With observations on the origin of slavery.* By a member of the African Society in Boston (Boston, 1808, printed for the Society). Copy in the Boston Athenaeum.

## [c]

The proposition has been advanced by men who claim a pre-eminence in the learned world, that Africans are inferior to white men in the structure both of body and mind; the first member of this proposition is below our notice; the reasons assigned for the second are, that we have not produced any poets, mathematicians, or any to excel in any science whatever; our being oppressed and held in slavery forms no excuse, because, say they, among the Romans, their most excellent artists and greatest scientific characters were frequently their slaves, and that these on account of their ascendant abilities, arose to superior stations in the state; and they exultingly tell us that these slaves were white men.

My Brethren, it does not require a complete master to solve this problem, nor is it necessary in order like good logicians to meet this argument, that we should know which is the major and the minor proposition; and the middle and extreme terms of syllogism, he must be a wilful novice and blind intentionally, who cannot unfold this enigma.

Among the Roman's it was only necessary for the slave to be manumitted, in order to be eligible to all the offices of state, together with the emoluments belonging thereto; no sooner was he free than there was open before him a wide field of employment for his ambition, and learning and abilities with merit, were as sure to meet with their reward in him, as in any other citizen. But what station above the common employment of craftsmen and labourers would we fill did we possess both learning and abilities; is there ought to enkindle in us one spark of emulation; must not he who makes any considerable advances under present circumstance be almost a prodigy: although it may be true we have not produced any to excel in arts and sciences, yet if our situation be properly considered, and the allowances made which ought to be, it will soon be perceived that we do not fall far behind those who boast of a superior judgment, we have produced some who have claimed attention, and whose works have been admired, yes in despight of all our embarresments our genious does sometimes burst forth from its incumbrance.

William Hamilton, *An Address to the New-York African Society, for Mutual Relief, delivered in the Universalist Church, January 2, 1809* (N.Y., 1809). Copy in Boston Athenaeum.

## 23

## LETTER TO A SLAVE REBEL, 1810

As already stated, letters to and from slave rebels are a great rarity. In March, 1810, two such communications were discovered on a road in Halifax county, North Carolina. One was from a slave in Greene County, Georgia to another slave, named Cornell Lucas of Martin county, North Carolina; another, likewise to and from slaves, had been sent from Tennessee and was intended for Brunswick county, Virginia. Contemporaries declared both letters to be similar, but only one, that to Cornell Lucas, appears to be extant. It reads as follows:

Dear Sir— I received your letter to the fourteenth of June, 1809 with great freedom and joy to hear and understand what great proceedance you have made, and the resolution you have in proceeding on in business as we have undertook, and hope you will still continue in the same mind. We have spread the sense nearly over the continent in our part of the country, and have the day when we are to fall to work, and you must be sure not to fail on that day, and that is the 22d April, to begin about midnight, and do the work at home first, and then take the armes of them you slay first, and that will strengthen us more in armes—for freedom we want and will have, for we have served this cruel land long enuff, & be as secret convaing your nuse as possabel, and be sure to send it by some cearfull hand, and if it happens to be discovered, fail not in the day, for we are full abel to conquer by any means.—Sir, I am your Captain James, living in the state of Jorgy, in Green county—so no more at present, but remaining your sincer friend and captain until death.

N.Y. *Evening Post,* April 30, 1810; published in H. Aptheker, *American Negro Slave Revolts* (Columbia University Press, 1943), p. 245.

## 24

## BUYING ANOTHER'S FREEDOM, 1810–1811

In 1806 the state of Virginia required all Negroes who might be manumitted in the future to leave the State, unless permission to the contrary was granted by the legislature. As a result Negroes who had purchased relatives with the intent of liberating them—a fairly common practice throughout the South—immediately began to petition the legislature for the necessary permission. Two such petitions follow—the first dated December 20, 1810; the second, December 9, 1811.

### [a]

To the Honble. Speaker and other members of the Genl. Assembly of Virginia.

The Petition of Henry Birch most respectfully represents, that he is a free man of Colour. That he has long resided in the County of Hanover, and uniformly supported the character of an Honest, sober and industrious man. That he has two sons who are slaves, whom he purchased of Mr. Wm. Dandridge Claiborne Esq. of King William County, with the view of procuring their freedom. Your Petitioner therefore humbly prays that a law may be passed authorizing his sons John Birch and Bond Birch to reside within the Commonwealth, and will ever pray, etc.

### [b]

To the Honorable, the Speaker & house of Delegates of the General Assembly of Virginia.

The Petition of Jemima Hunt (a free woman of color) of the County of Southampton, humbly sheweth—that sometime in the month of November, in the Year 1805—Your petitioner entered into a contract with a certain Benjamin Barrett of said county for the purchase of Stephen a Negro man Slave, the property of said Barrett, & husband to your petitioner, for the sum of ten pounds annually for ten years, and the said Barrett farther bound himself to take the sum of ninety pounds if paid within five years & at the expiration of that time to make a complete bill of sale for the said Negro Stephen, which will appear by reference being made to the obligation entered into between the said Barrett and your petitioner. Your petitioner farther states that she has paid the full amount of the purchase money and has obtained a bill of sale for the said Negro Stephen; who (being her husband) she intended to emancipate after she had complyed with her contract,—but in some short time after as your petitioner has been informed an act of Assembly was passed, prohibiting slaves, being emancipated after the law went into operation, from residing in the state—Your petitioner farther states she has a numerous family of Children by the said Stephen, who are dependent upon the daily labor of herself & husband for support, & without the assistance of her husband Stephen they must suffer or become burthensome to their county.

Therefore your petitioner humbly prays that the legislature would take her case into consideration & pass a law to permit the said Negro Stephen to reside in the State after emancipation, and to enjoy all the privileges that other free people of colour are entitled to & as in duty bound Your petitioner will ever pray, etc.

J. H. Johnston, Jr., in *Journal of Negro History*, XIII (1928), pp. 90–91.


## 25


# CONFESSION OF A VIRGINIA REBEL, 1812

In 1812 slave unrest in Virginia again reached the stage of organized conspiracy and several evidences of this reached the Governor. Among these was the confession of a slave forwarded in a letter dated April 10, 1812 by Henry Edmondson and John Floyd, the latter destined to be Governor of Virginia and thereafter Secretary of War in Buchanan's cabinet.

Confession made before John Floyd and Henry Edmondson, Justices of the peace for the County of Montgomery, on the 2nd of April, 1812, by a Negro man now in the jail of said County, who calls himself Tom, and says he is the property of John Smith of the County of Henry in this State, who he (Tom), murdered on Monday, the 23rd day of March last past as he confesses, being instigated thereto by a woman the property of said Smith by the name of Celia.

*Question:* Have you any knowledge of other Negroes other than the woman before mentioned who are disposed to rise in order to kill their masters?

*Answer of Tom:* I know of a great many—thirty or forty who appear to be instigated to kill their masters by a Negro man in the County of Rockingham, N. Carolina, by the name of Goomer, who is called by the Negroes a conjurer. A Negro man Jack, the property of the widow Wit, told me to kill my master; that I could not be hurt for it, and that Goomer would conjure me clear, and that when they got fixed they intended to rise and kill the white people. That George Harsten of Henry was to be poisoned by himself (Jack), the poison to be furnished by Goomer. That W. Hill was to be waylaid and shot by Tom, boy, the property of (master not known to him), and one of Goomer's men; and he was to be paid 200 lbs. of Hemp for it by W. Hill's Hannah. Major Redd of Henry was to be poisoned by Jack, the poison to be furnished by Goomer.

Celia told me that the widow Penn's Jim of P.C.,* who has a wife at Mr. Staples in Henry, that if he was in my place he would not serve my master any longer, but wait till he could meet him coming home drunk and kill him, but that he must not kill him in the plantation. The Negroes in the neighborhood said that these British people was about to rise against this Country, and that they intended to rise sometime in next May. That they were buying up guns for the purpose. That they said they were not made to work for the white people, but they (the white people), made to work for themselves; and that they (the Negroes), would have it so. That the plan in that neighborhood was first to break open Ned Staples' store in order to get the Guns, Powder, &c out of it—that they would then raise an army, Goomer was to be one of their head men, and George Powell's Harry another. Mrs. Wit's Jack said he would make haste and learn all he could (being at the time nearly equal to Goomer in conjuration), and get as high as he could. The Negroes in the neighborhood said they were glad that the people were burnt in Richmond,† and wished that all the white people had been burnt with them. That God Almighty had sent them a little Hell for the white people, and that in a little time they would get a greater. That the Negroes in his neighborhood had sent word by ——, a Negro waggoner for Mr.

* Point Comfort, Virginia.
† Reference here is to a disastrous fire in a Richmond theatre in 1811.

Staples, of their plans to the Negroes at Lynchburg and received for answer to be ready in May next. The plan was to rise about the middle of May in the night and do all the mischief they could before they were found out. That I said when he was in Lynchburg the white people were draughting and exercising, but what was that—it would do no good, and that when the Negroes rose they would put a stop to it. That there were ten Negroes for one white man.

*Question:* Did you ever hear them say whether they intended to murder the white women and children, or not?

*Answer of Tom:* I never heard them say.

*Question:* How did you hear that the British were about to rise against this country[?]

*Answer:* It was heard from the poor people in the neighborhood, and by hearing the newspapers read.

He further stated that he was to have killed his master some time before. That on Saturday he was to kill him, and that he and his master passed two or three miles together, but he could not. That he and the Negro woman (Celia) had a further conversation about it on Sunday night, and the next day about 1 o'clock he killed him. That when he returned to the house on the evening, the Negro woman (Celia) asked him if he had killed his master. He told her he had. She told him to take a horse and clear himself. He told her he did not wish to go then, that they would think he had killed his master. She told him he must not stay there, that if he did she would be brought in with him; on which he started, and that he met with a Negro woman of a Mr. Hall's in Franklin. That he told her he was a runaway, and that he had killed his master. Also that the Negroes were shortly to rise against the white people. She said they could not rise too soon for her, as she had rather be in hell than where she was.

H. W. Flournoy, ed., *Calendar of Virginia State Papers,* X (Richmond, 1892), pp. 120–23.

## 26

## DENYING NEGRO INFERIORITY, 1813

The following extracts from an address by George Lawrence, a free Negro of New York, delivered January 1, 1813, on the fifth anniversary of the illegalization by the United States of the African slave trade, illustrate not only the leadership offered by Negroes themselves in the struggle against slavery but also their early attacks upon the concept of Negro inferiority.

My brethren, the land in which we live gives us the opportunity rapidly to advance the prosperity of liberty. This government founded on the principles of liberty and equality, and declaring them to be the free gift of God, if not ignorant of their declaration, must enforce it; I am confident she wills it, and strong forbodings of it is discernable. The northern sections of the union is fast conceding, and the southern must comply, although so biased by interest, that they have become callous to the voice of reason and justice; yet as the continual droppings of water has a tendency to wear away the hardest and most flinty substance, so likewise shall we, abounding in good works, and causing our examples to shine forth as the sun at noon day, melt their callous hearts, and render sinewless the arm of sore oppression. My brethren, you who are enroled and proudly march under the banners of the Mutual Relief, and Wilberforce Societies, consider your important standings as incorporated bodies, and walk worthy of the name you bear, cling closely to the paths of virtue and morality, cherish the plants of peace and temperance; by doing this you shall not only shine as the first stars in the firmament, and do honor to your worthy patrons, but immortalize your names. Be zealous and vigilent, be always on the alert to promote the welfare of your injured brethren; then shall providence shower down her blessings upon your heads, and crown your labors with success. It has been said by your enemies, that your minds were not calculated to receive a sufficient store of knowledge, to fit you for beneficial or social societies; but your incorporation drowned that assertion in contempt; and now let shame cover their heads, and blushes crimson their countenances. In vain they fostered a hope that our unfavorable circumstances would bear them out in their profane insinuations. But is that hope yet alive? No; or do we know where to find it? If it is to be found, it must be in the dark abysses of ignorance and folly, too little, too trifling for our notice.

There could be many reasons given, to prove that the mind of an African is not inferior to that of an European; yet to do so would be superfluous. It would be like adding hardness to the diamond, or lustre to the sun. There was a time whilst shrowded in ignorance, the African was estimated no higher than beasts of burthen, and while their minds were condensed within the narrow compass of slavery, and all their genius damped by the merciless power of cruel masters, they moved in no higher sphere. Their nature was cramped in infancy, and depraved in riper years, vice was showed them for virtue, and for their labor and industry, the scourge was their only reward. Then did they seem dead to a better state, but it was because they were subject to arbitrary power; and then did their proud oppressors assert, though against their better judgment, that they were destined by nature to no better inheritance. But their most prominent arguments are lighter than vanity, for vacuous must the reasons of that man have been, who dared to assert that genius is confined to complexion, or that nature knows difference in the immortal soul of man: No! the noble mind of a Newton could find room, and to spare, within the tenement of many an injured African.

My brethren, the time is fast approaching when the iron hand of oppression must cease to tyrannize over injured innocence, and very different are the days that we see, from those that our ancestors did; yet I know that there are thousands of our enemies who had rather see us exterminated from off the earth, than partake of the blessings that they enjoy; but their malice shall not be gratified; they will, though it blast their eyes, still see us in prosperity. Our day star is arisen, and shall perform its diurnal revolutions, until nature herself shall change; and my heart glows with the idea, kindles with joy, as my eye catches its radient beams dispersing the dark clouds of ignorance and superstition. The spring is come, and the autumn nigh at hand, when the rich fruits of liberty shall be strewed in the path of every African, or descendant. and the olive hedge of peace encompass them in from their enemies. . . .

And, O! thou father of the universe and disposer of events, thou that called from a dark and formless mass this fair system of nature, and created thy sons and daughters to bask in the golden streams and rivulets contained therein; this day we have convened under thy divine auspices, it's not to celebrate a political festivity, or the achievement of arms by which the blood of thousands were spilt, contaminating thy pure fields with human gore! but to commemorate a period brought to light by thy wise counsel, who stayed the hands of merciless power, and with hearts expanded with gratitude for thy providences, inundated in the sea of thy mercies we farther crave thy fostering care. O! wilt thou crush that power that still holds thousands of our brethren in bondage, and let the sea of thy wisdom wash its very dust from off the face of the erth; let LIBERTY unfurl her banners, FREEDOM AND JUSTICE reign triumphant in the world, universally.

George Lawrence, *An Oration on the Abolition of the Slave Trade, delivered on the First Day of January, 1813, in the African Methodist Episcopal Church* (N.Y., 1813).

## 27

# A PHILADELPHIA NEGRO CONDEMNS
# DISCRIMINATORY PROPOSALS, 1813

In 1813 *A Series of Letters by A Man of Color* was published in Philadelphia. Its author was James Forten, a well-to-do free Negro of that city, a veteran of the

Revolutionary War and one who was to play a leading role in the early Negro convention movement and the Abolitionist movement. The proposed legislation against which James Forten here directs his pen entailed the registration of Negroes. It was not passed.

We hold this truth to be self-evident, that God created all men equal, is one of the most prominent features in the Declaration of Independence, and in that glorious fabric of collected wisdom, our noble Constitution. This idea embraces the Indian and the European, the savage and the Saint, the Peruvian and the Laplander, the white man and the African, and whatever measures are adopted subversive of this inestimable privilege, are in direct violation of the letter and spirit of our Constitution, and become subject to the animadversion of all, particularly those who are deeply interested in the measure.

These thoughts were suggested by the promulgation of a late bill, before the Senate of Pennsylvania, to prevent the emigration of people of color into this state. It was not passed into a law at this session, and must in consequence lay over until the next, before when we sincerely hope, the white men, whom we should look upon as our protectors, will have become convinced of the inhumanity and impolicy of such a measure, and forbear to deprive us of those inestimable treasures, liberty and independence. This is almost the only state in the Union wherein the African race have justly boasted of rational liberty and the protection of the laws, and shall it now be said they have been deprived of that liberty, and publicly exposed for sale to the highest bidder? Shall colonial inhumanity that has marked many of us with shameful stripes, become the practice of the people of Pennsylvania, while Mercy stands weeping at the miserable spectacle? People of Pennsylvania, descendants of the immortal Penn, doom us not to the unhappy fate of thousands of our countrymen in the Southern States and the West Indies; despise the traffic in blood, and the blessing of the African will forever be around you. Many of us are men of property, for the security of which we have hitherto looked to the laws of our blessed state, but should this become a law, our property is jeopardized, since the same power which can expose to sale an unfortunate fellow creature, can wrest from him those estates, which years of honest industry have accumulated. Where shall the poor African look for protection, should the people of Pennsylvania consent to oppress him? We grant there are a number of worthless men belonging to our color, but there are laws of sufficient rigor for their punishment, if properly and duly enforced. We wish not to screen the guilty from punishment, but with the guilty do not permit the innocent to suffer. If there are worthless men, there are also men of merit among the African race, who are useful members of Society. The truth of this let their benevolent institutions and the numbers clothed and fed by them witness. Punish the guilty man of color to the utmost limit of the laws, but sell him not to slavery! If he is in danger of becoming a public charge, prevent him! If he is too indolent to labor for his own subsistence, compel him to do so; but sell him not to slavery. By selling him you do not make him better, but commit a wrong, without benefiting the object of it or society at large. Many of our ancestors were brought here more than one hundred years ago; many of our fathers, many of ourselves, have fought and bled for the independence of our country. Do not then expose us to sale. Let not the spirit of the father behold the son robbed of that liberty which he died to establish, but let the motto of our legislature be: "The law knows no distinction. . . ."

Those patriotic citizens, who, after resting from the toils of an arduous war, which achieved our independence and laid the foundation of the only reasonable republic upon earth, associated together, and for the protection of those inestimable rights for the establishment of which they had exhausted their blood and treasure, framed the Constitution of Pennsylvania, have by the ninth article declared, that "All men are born equally free and independent, and have certain inherent and indefeasible rights, among which are those of enjoying life and liberty." Under the restraint of wise and well administered laws, we cordially unite in the above glorious sentiment, but by the bill upon which we have been remarking, it appears as if the committee who drew it up mistook the sentiment expressed in this article, and do not consider us as men, or that those enlightened statesmen who formed the constitution upon the basis of experience, intended to exclude us from its blessings and protection. If the former, why are we not to be considered as men? Has the God who made the white man and the black left any record declaring us a different species? Are we not sustained by the same power, supported by the same food, hurt by the same wounds, wounded by the same wrongs, pleased with the same delights, and propagated by the same means? And should we not then enjoy the same liberty, and be protected by the same laws? We wish not to legislate, for our means of information and the acquisition of knowledge are, in the nature of things, so circumscribed, that we must consider ourselves incompetent to the task; but let us, in legislation be considered as men. It cannot be that the authors of our Constitution intended to exclude us from its benefits, for just emerging from unjust and cruel emancipation, their souls were too much affected with their own deprivations to commence the reign of terror over others. They knew we were deeper skinned than they were, but they acknowledged us as men, and found that many an honest heart beat beneath a dusky bosom. They felt that they had no more authority to enslave us, than England had to tyrannize over them. They were convinced that if amenable to the same laws in our actions we should be protected by the same laws in our rights and privileges. Actuated by these sentiments they adopted the glorious fabric of our liberties, and declaring "all men" free, they did not particularize white and black, because they never supposed it would be made a question whether *we were men or not*. Sacred be the ashes, and deathless be the memory of those heroes who are dead; and revered be the persons and the characters of those who still exist and lift the thunders of admonition against the traffic in blood. And here my brethren in color, let the tear of gratitude and the sigh of regret break forth for that great and good man, who lately fell a victim to the promiscuous fury of death, in whom you have lost a zealous friend, a powerful and herculean advocate; a sincere adviser, and one who spent many an hour of his life to break your fetters, and ameliorate your condition—I mean the ever to be lamented Dr. Benjamin Rush. . . .

Let us put a case, in which the law in question operates peculiarly hard and unjust.—I have a brother, perhaps, who resides in a distant part of the Union, and after a separation of years, actuated by the same fraternal affection which beats in the bosom of a white man, he comes to visit me. Unless that brother be registered in twenty-four hours after, and be able to produce a certificate of that effect, he is liable, according to the second and third sections of the bill, to a fine of twenty dollars, to arrest, imprisonment and sale. Let the unprejudiced mind ponder upon this, and then pronounce it the justifiable act of a free people, if he can. To this we trust our cause, without fear of the issue. The unprejudiced must pronounce any act tending to deprive a free man of his right, freedom and immunities, as not only cruel in the extreme, but decidedly unconstitutional both as regards the letter and spirit of that glorious instrument. The same power which protects the white man, should protect the black.

The evils arising from the bill before our Legislature, so fatal to the rights of freemen, and so characteristic of European despotism, are so numerous, that to consider them all would extend these numbers further than time or my talent will permit me to carry them. The concluding paragraph of my last utterance, states a case of peculiar hardship, arising from the second section of this bill, upon which I cannot refrain from making a few more remarks. The man of color receiving as a visitor any other person of color, is bound to turn informer, and rudely report to the Register, that a friend and brother has come to visit him for a few days, whose name he must take within twenty-four hours, or forfeit a sum which the iron hand of the law is authorized to rend from him, partly for the benefit of the Register. Who is this Register? A man, and exercising an office, where ten dollars is the fee for each delinquent, will probably be a cruel man and find delinquents where they really do not exist. The poor black is left to the merciless gripe of an avaricious Register, without an appeal, in the event, from his tyranny or oppression! O miserable race, born to the same hopes, created with the same feeling, and destined for the same goal, you are reduced by your fellow creatures below the brute. The dog is protected and pampered at the board of his master, while the poor African and his descendant, whether a Saint or a felon, is branded with infamy, registered as a slave, and we may expect shortly to find a law to prevent their increase, by taxing them according to numbers, and authorizing the Constables to seize and confine every one who dare to walk the streets without a collar on his neck!—What have the people of color been guilty of, that they more than others, should be compelled to register their houses, lands, servants and *children?* Yes, ye rulers of the black man's destiny, reflect upon this: our *children* must be registered, and bear about them a certificate, or be subject to imprisonment and fine. You, who are perusing this effusion of feeling, are you a parent? Have you children around whom your affections are bound, by those delightful bonds which none but a parent can know? Are they the delight of your prosperity, and the solace of your afflictions? If all this be true, to you we submit our cause. The parent's feeling cannot err. By your verdict will we stand or fall—by your verdict, live slaves or freeman. It is said that the bill does not extend to children, but the words of the bill are, "Whether as an *inmate, visitor, hireling, or tenant, in his or her house or room.*" Whether this does not embrace every soul that can be in a house, the reader is left to judge; and whether the father should be bound to register his child, even within the twenty-four hours after it is brought into the world, let the father's feelings determine. This is the fact, and our children sent on our lawful business, not having sense enough to understand the meaning of such proceedings, must show their certificate of registry or be borne to prison. The bill specifies neither age nor sex—designates neither the honest man or the vagabond—but like the fretted porcupine, his quills aim its deadly shafts promiscuously at all.

For the honor and dignity of our native state, we wish not to see this bill pass into a law, as well as for its degrading tendency towards us; for although oppressed by those to whom we look for protection, our grievances are light compared with the load of reproach that must be heaped upon our commonwealth. The story will fly from the north to the south, and the advocates of slavery, the traders in human blood, will smile contemptuously at the once boasted moderation and humanity of Pennsylvania! What! That place, whose institutions for the prevention of slavery, are the admiration of surrounding states and of Europe, becomes the advocate of mancipation and wrong, and the oppressor of the free and innocent!—Tell it not in Gath!

publish it not in the streets of Askelon! lest the daughters of the Philistines rejoice! lest the children of the uncircumcised triumph.

It is to be hoped that in our Legislature there is patriotism, humanity, and mercy sufficient to crush this attempt upon the civil liberty of freemen, and to prove that the enlightened body who have hitherto guarded their fellow creatures, without regard to the color of the skin, will still stretch forth the wings of protection to that race, whose persons have been the scorn, and whose calamities have been the jest of the world for ages. We trust the time is at hand when this obnoxious Bill will receive its death warrant, and freedom still remain to cheer the bosom of a man of color. . . .

I proceed again to the consideration of the bill of *inalienable* rights belonging to black men, the passage of which will only tend to show that the advocates of emancipation can enact laws more degrading to the free man, and more injurious to his feelings, than all the tyranny of slavery, or the shackles of infatuated despotism. And let me here remark, that this unfortunate race of humanity, although protected by our laws, are already subject to the fury and caprice of a certain set of men, who regard neither humanity, law nor privilege. They are already considered as a different species, and little above the brute creation. They are thought to be objects fit for nothing else than lordly men to vent the effervescence of their spleen upon, and to tyrannize over, like the bearded Mussulman over his horde of slaves. Nay, the Mussulman thinks more of his horse than the generality of people do of the despised black!—Are not men of color sufficiently degraded? Why then increase their degradation? It is a well known fact, that black people, upon certain days of public jubilee, dare not be seen after twelve o'clock in the day, upon the field to enjoy the times; for no sooner do the fumes of that potent devil, Liquor, mount into the brain, than the poor black is assailed like the destroying Hyena or the avaricious Wolf! I allude particularly to the *Fourth of July!*—Is it not wonderful, that the day set apart for the festival of liberty, should be abused by the advocates of freedom, in endeavoring to sully what they profess to adore. If men, though they know that the law protects all, will dare, in defiance of law, to execute their hatred upon the defenceless black, will they not by the passage of this bill, believe him still more a mark for their venom and spleen?—Will they do not believe him completely deserted by authority, and subject to every outrage brutality can inflict—too surely they will, and the poor wretch will turn his eyes around to look in vain for protection. Pause, ye rulers of a free people, before you give us over to despair and violation—we implore you, for the sake of humanity, to snatch us from the pinnacle of ruin, from that gulf, which will swallow our rights, as fellow creatures; our privileges, as citizens; and our liberties, as men!

There are men among us of reputation and property, as good citizens as any men can be, and who, for their property, pay as heavy taxes as any citizens are compelled to pay. All taxes, except personal, fall upon them, and still even they are not exempted from this degrading bill. The villainous part of the community, of all colors, we wish to see punished and retrieved as much as any people can. Enact laws to punish them severely, but do not let them operate against the innocent as well as the guilty. Can there be any generosity in this? Can there be any semblance of justice, or of that enlightened conduct which is ever the boasted pole star of freedom? By no means. This bill is nothing but the *ignus fatuus* of mistaken policy! . . .

By the third section of this bill, which is its peculiar hardship, the police officers are authorized to apprehend any black, whether a vagrant or a man of reputable character, who cannot produce a certificate that he has been registered. He is to be arrayed before a justice, who is thereupon to commit him to prison!—The jailor is to advertise a Freeman, and at the expiration of six months, if no owner appear for this degraded black, he is to be *exposed to sale,* and if not sold to be confined at hard labor for seven years!!— Man of feeling, read this!—No matter who, no matter where. The constable, whose antipathy generally against the black is very great, will take every opportunity of hurting his feelings!—Perhaps he sees him at a distance, and having a mind to raise the boys in hue and cry against him, exclaims, "Halloa! Stop the Negro!" The boys, delighting in the sport, immediately begin to hunt him, and immediately from a hundred tongues is heard the cry—*"Hoa, Negro, where is your Certificate!"*—Can anything be done more shocking to the principles of civil liberty! A person arriving from another state, ignorant of the existence of such a law, may fall a victim to its cruel oppression. But he is to be advertised, and if no owner appear—how can an owner appear for a man who is free and belongs to no one!—if no owner appear, he is exposed for sale!—Oh, inhuman spectacle: found in no unjust act, convicted of no crime, he is barbarously sold, like the produce of the soil, to the highest bidder, or what is still worse, for no crimes, without the inestimable privilege of a trial by his peers, doomed to the dreary walls of a prison for the term of seven tedious years!—My God, what a situation is his! Search the legends of tyranny and find no precedent. No example can be found in all the reigns of violence and oppression, which have marked the lapse of time. It stands alone. It has been left for Pennsylvania to raise her ponderous arm against the liberties of the black, whose greatest boast has been that he resided in a state where civil liberty, and sacred justice were administered alike to all.—What must be his reflection now, that the asylum he had left from emancipation has been destroyed, and that he is left to suffer, like Daniel of old, with no one but his God to help him! Where is the bosom that does not heave a sigh for his fall, unless it be callous to every sentiment of humanity and mercy?

The fifth section of this bill is also peculiarly hard, inasmuch as it prevents freemen from living where they please.—Pennsylvania has always been a refuge from slavery, and to this state the Southern black, when freed, has flown for safety. Why does he this? When masters in many of the Southern states, which they frequently do, free a particular black, unless the black leaves the state in so many hours, any person resident of the said state, can have him arrested and again sold to slavery:—The hunted black is obliged to flee, or remain and be again a slave. I have known persons of this description sold three times after being first emancipated. Where shall he go? Shut every state against him, and, like Pharaoh's kine, drive him into the sea.—Is there no spot on earth that will protect him! Against their inclination, his ancestors were forced from their homes by traders in human flesh, and even under such circumstances the wretched offspring are denied the protection you afford to brutes.

It is in vain that we are forming societies of different kinds to ameliorate the conditions of our unfortunate brethren, to correct their morals and to render them not only honest but useful members to society. All our efforts by this bill are despised, and we are doomed to feel the lash of oppression:— As well may we be outlawed, as well may the glorious privileges of the Gospel be denied us, and all endeavors used to cut us off from happiness hereafter as well as here! The case is similar, and I am much deceived if this bill does not destroy the morals it is intended to produce.

I have done. My feelings are acute, and I have ventured to express them without intending either accusation or insult to any one. An appeal to the heart is my intention, and if I have failed, it is my great misfortune not to have had a power of eloquence sufficient to convince. But I trust the eloquence of nature will succeed, and that the law-givers of this happy Commonwealth will yet remain the Blacks' friend, and the advocates of Freemen.

C. G. Woodson, ed., *Negro Orators and their Orations* (Washington, 1925, Associated Publishers), pp. 42–51.

# 28

## BUYING FREEDOM, 1815

Documents illustrative of the practice of free Negroes purchasing relatives in order to emancipate them have already been presented. At times, too, slaves accumulated sufficient funds to buy their own freedom—given of course agreement from the master. A petition to the Virginia legislature, dated Washington county, December 9, 1815, indicative of this practice, follows:

To the Honorable the Legislature of Virginia.

The petition of Burke a free man of Colour humbly represents. That about the year 1811 he purchased from his then master William P. Thoppson, Esqr. his freedom for the sum of four hundred dollars. That he was born in the State of Virginia where he has a wife and children in slavery, that although he is a person of colour, he has attachments and affections, perhaps as strong as if it had pleased heaven to give him a white skin. That from documents accompanying this petition, he hopes to satisfy your honorable body, that he would be as usefull perhaps a valuable Citizen. That if your petitioner is compelled to remove from his native Country in order to preserve the blessing of liberty which he has acquired, he must necessarily separate from his wife family. He humbly trusts that the Legislature of his Country will not compell him to adopt an alternative so distressing to his feelings; that they will not insist on maintaining a policy very questionable in its character, and so subversive of humanity. Your petitioner feels confident that all those who know him, wish him to continue his residence in this state, that they apprehend no mischief from his residence amongst them, and that however dangerous or inconvenient a population of the class to which he belongs, may be to the Eastern section of this State where that population is abundant; the same causes of apprehension do not exist in the Western part of the State, where the black population is very small and where labour is scarce and difficult to be procured. The prayer therefore of your petitioner is that he have leave to remain in this Commonwealth free from any penalty whatever, that a law be passed for that purpose, and your petitioner will, etc.

J. H. Johnston, Jr., in *Journal of Negro History*, XIII (1928), pp. 94–95.

29

## THE NEGRO CHURCH ACHIEVES
## INDEPENDENCE, 1816

As has already been observed separate Negro churches were formed in the eighteenth century. These, however, remained within the jurisdictional control of higher all-white religious bodies until legal separation—including full control over property—was achieved by the African Methodist Episcopal Church in January, 1816. The extemporaneous remarks of the Rev. Daniel Coker, minister of the

Bethel Church in Philadelphia, made at a meeting held on January 21, 1816, in honor of the event, graphically describe the issues and supply much additional information. Coker was elected the first Bishop of the A.M.E. church in 1816, but soon resigned to serve as a missionary in Africa and was succeeded by Richard Allen.

. . . The Jews in Babylon were held against their will. So were our brethren. But how, it will be asked, were your brethren bound?

1. By the deed. 2. By the charter of their church. (To whom were they bound? To the conference. For how long were they bound? Answer. It was supposed by the ecclesiastical expounders of the law, that it would be till the last trump should sound!) But it will be asked, were they not at liberty to go from under the controul of the conference when they thought proper? In answering this we shall disclose a paradox, viz. The conference (as I have understood) have said repeatedly, that the coloured societies was nothing but an unprofitable trouble; and yet, when the society of Bethel Church unanimously requested to go free, it was not granted, until the supreme court of Pa said, it should be so. But again, it will be asked, who could stop them, if they were determined to go. None—Provided they had left their church property behind; to purchase which, perhaps many of them had deprived their children of bread.—And this in my opinion, would have been about equal to captivity!

2. Those Jews as above stated, had not equal privileges with the Babylonians, although they were governed by the same laws, and suffered the same penalties. So our brethren were governed by the same church law, or discipline, and suffered all its penalties. But it is evident, that there was a difference made between the coloured members and those of a superior colour (vulgarly so called) in point of church privileges; and it is evident that all this distinction was made on account of the complexion. Is this denied[?] . . . .

And how many of you, (I had like to have said) have acted the hypocrite, and mocked God. For while you have prayed that Ethiopia might stretch out her hands unto God, now when God seems to be answering your prayers, and opening the door for you to enjoy all that you could wish, many of you rise up and say, the time is not yet come; and it is thought by some a mark of arrogance and ostentation, in us who are embracing the opportunity that is now offered to us of being free. May the time speedily come, when we shall see our brethren come flocking to us like doves to their windows. And we as a band of brethren, shall sit down under our own vine to worship, and none to make us afraid.

MINISTERS belonging to the *African Bethel Church,* who have withdrawn from under the charge of the Methodist Bishops and Conference, but are still Methodists:—

## IN PHILADELPHIA

Richard   Allen, ordained by bishop Asbury
James Champin, ordained by bishop Asbury
Jacob   Tapsico, ordained by bishop Asbury
Jeffrey   Bulah, ordained by bishop Asbury

And five or six local preachers, and about fourteen hundred members, who are now, by the decision of the Supreme Court, placed under the charge of Richard Allen.

## IN BALTIMORE

Daniel Coker, ordained by bishop Asbury
Richard Williams, Local Preacher
Henry Harden,   Local Preacher
Abner Coker,    Local Preacher
Charles Pierce,   Local
James Towson,   Local
James Coal,    Local

And several hundred members.
At Elkridge we have a Church and a growing Society.
*N.B.* Contrary to the predictions of many, we have found to our great consolation, that the wholesome and friendly laws of our happy country will give us protection in worshipping God according to the dictates of our own conscience.

And my prayer is, that we, the descendants of Africa, may enjoy, and not abuse our glorious privileges: and always retain a high sense of our obligation of obedience to the laws of our God, and the laws of our land.

*Sermon Delivered Extempore in the African Bethel Church in the City of Baltimore, on the 21st of January, 1816, to a numerous concourse of people, on account of the Coloured People gaining their Church (Bethel) in the Supreme Court of the State of Pennsylvania, by the Rev. D. Coker, Minister of said Church. To which is annexed a list of the African Preachers in Philadelphia, Baltimore, &c who have withdrawn from under the charge of the Methodist Bishops and Conference,* (BUT ARE STILL METHODISTS). (n.d., n.p.)

30

# THE NEGRO'S RESPONSE TO COLONIZATION, 1817–1818

In December, 1816 the American Colonization Society was formed by prominent white people, including several slaveholders. Its object was to transport free Negroes to Africa on the plea that they were incapable of serving useful lives in the United States; and the Society informed slaveholders that the removal of free Negroes would make more secure the institution of slavery. The Society and the ideas it represented generally met determined opposition from the Negro people, though in the South itself public expressions of such opposition were framed, necessarily, in a veiled and ambiguous manner. Examples of this appear in the statements coming from two meetings of Negro people held in January, 1817; one in Richmond, Virginia, the other in Philadelphia.

Where the idea of colonization did appeal to Negroes it did so on the basis of possibly offering a practical alternative to a life of continual humiliations. Indicative of this minority sentiment is the letter written by Abraham Camp, an Illinois free Negro, on July 13, 1818, to Elias B. Caldwell, Secretary of the Colonization Society.

[a]

At a meeting of a respectable portion of the free people of color of the city of Richmond, on Friday, January 24, 1817, William Bowler was appointed chairman, and Lentey Craw, secretary. The following preamble and resolution were read, unanimously adopted, and ordered to be printed.

Whereas a Society has been formed at the seat of government, for the purpose of colonizing, with their own consent, the free people of color of the United States; therefore, we, the free people of color of the city of Richmond, have thought it advisable to assemble together under the sanction of authority, for the purpose of making a public expression of our sentiments on a question in which we are so deeply interested. We perfectly agree with the Society, that it is not only proper, but would ultimately tend to the benefit and advantage of a great portion of our suffering fellow creatures, to be colonized; but while we thus express our approbation of a measure laudable in its purposes, and beneficial in its designs, it may not be improper in us to say, that we prefer being colonized in the most remote corner of the land of our nativity, to being exiled to a foreign country—and whereas the president and board of managers of the said Society have been pleased to leave it to the entire discretion of Congress to provide a suitable place for carrying these laudable intentions into effect—Be it therefore

Resolved, That we respectfully submit to the wisdom of Congress whether it would not be an act of charity to grant us a small portion of their territory, either on the Missouri river, or any place that may seem to them most conducive to the public good and our future welfare, subject, however, to such rules and regulations as the government of the United States may think proper to adopt.

William Lloyd Garrison, *Thoughts on African Colonization: or an impartial exhibition of the Doctrines, Principles & Purposes of the American Colonization Society. Together with the Resolutions, Addresses & Remonstrances of the Free People of Color.* (Boston, 1832), Pt. II, pp. 62–63.

[b]

Philadelphia, January 1817.

At a numerous meeting of the people of color, convened at Bethel church, to take into consideration the propriety of remonstrating against the contemplated measure, that is to exile us from the land of our nativity; James Forten was called to the chair, and Russell Parrott appointed secretary. The intent of the meeting having been stated by the chairman, the following resolutions were adopted, without one dissenting voice.

Whereas our ancestors (not of choice) were the first successful cultivators of the wilds of America, we their descendants feel ourselves entitled to participate in the blessings of her luxuriant soil, which their blood and sweat manured; and that any measure or system of measures, having a tendency to banish us from her bosom, would not only be cruel, but in direct violation of those principles, which have been the boast of this republic.

Resolved, That we view with deep abhorrence the unmerited stigma attempted to be cast upon the reputation of the free people of color, by the promoters of this measure, "that they are a dangerous and useless part of the community," when in the state of disfranchisement in which they live, in the hour of danger they ceased to remember their wrongs, and rallied around the standard of their country.

Resolved, That we never will separate ourselves voluntarily from the slave population in this country; they are our brethren by the ties of consanguinity, of suffering, and of wrong; and we feel that there is more virtue in suffering privations with them, than fancied advantages for a season.

Resolved, That without arts, without science, without a proper knowledge of government, to cast into the savage wilds of Africa the free people of color, seems to us the circuitous route through which they must return to perpetual bondage.

Resolved, That having the strongest confidence in the justice of God, and philanthropy of the free states, we cheerfully submit our destinies to the guidance of Him who suffers not a sparrow to fall, without his special providence.

Resolved, That a committee of eleven persons * be appointed to open a correspondence with the honorable Joseph Hopkinson, member of Congress from this city, and likewise to inform him of the sentiments of this meeting, when they in their judgment may deem it proper.

W. L. Garrison, *op. cit.*, part II, pp. 9–10.

## [c]

I am a free man of colour, have a family and a large connection of free people of colour residing on the Wabash, who are all willing to leave America whenever the way shall be opened. We love this country and its liberties, if we could share an equal right in them; but our freedom is partial, and we have no hope that it ever will be otherwise here; therefore we had rather be gone, though we should suffer hunger and nakedness for years. Your honour may be assured that nothing shall be lacking on our part in complying with whatever provision shall be made by the United States, whether it be to go to Africa or some other place; we shall hold ourselves in readiness, praying that God (who made man free in the beginning, and who by his kind providence has broken the yoke from every white American) would inspire the heart of every true son of liberty with zeal and pity, to open the door of freedom for us also. I am, &c.

Abraham Camp.

C. G. Woodson, *The Mind of the Negro as revealed in letters written during the Crisis, 1800–1860* (Washington, 1926, Associated Publishers), p. 2.

31

# AN EARLY NEGRO EDUCATIONAL SOCIETY,
## 1818

The Negro people have formed many social, literary, debating, educational and welfare societies to service their own particular needs and desires. Typical of these was the "Pennsylvania Augustine Society, for the education of people of colour" established by prominent Philadelphia free Negroes in 1818, including the Reverend John Gloucester, James Forten, Russell Parrott, Robert Douglass,

* Consisting of Rev. Absalom Jones, Rev. Richard Allen, James Forten, Robert Douglass, Francis Perkins, Rev. John Gloucester, Robert Gorden, James Johnson, Quamoney Clarkson, John Summersett, Randall Shepherd.

Samuel Cornish and Joseph Cassey. Here is the preamble of this society's constitution.

We the Subscribers, persons of colour of the city of Philadelphia, in the State of Pennsylvania, sensibly impressed with the high importance of education, towards the improvement of our species, in an individual as well as a social capacity; and fully persuaded, that it is to the prominently defective system of instruction, as it now exists among us, that we must in a great measure attribute the contemptible and degraded situation which we occupy in society, and most of the disadvantages under which we suffer; and viewing, with serious concern, the formidable barriers that prejudices, powerful as they are unjust, have reared to impede our progress in the paths of science and of virtue, rendering it almost impossible to obtain for our offspring such instruction as we deem essentially necessary to qualify them for the useful walks of society: We therefore are convinced, that it is an unquestionable duty which we owe to ourselves, to our posterity, and to our God, who has endowed us with intellectual powers, to use the best energies of our minds and of our hearts, in devising and adapting the most effectual means to procure for our children a more extensive and useful education than we have heretofore had in our power to effect; and now, confidently relying upon the zealous and unanimous support of our coloured brethren, under the protection of divine providence, have resolved to unite and form ourselves into a society, to be known by the name of "The Augustine Education Society of Pennsylvania," for the establishment and maintenance of a Seminary, in which children of colour shall be taught all the useful and scientific branches of education, as far as may be found practicable, under the following regulations:— . . .

*An Address, delivered at Bethel Church, Philadelphia; on the 30th of September, 1818 . . . . by Prince Saunders* (Phila., 1818). Copy in Ridgway Branch, Library Company of Philadelphia.

## 32

# A NEGRO RESISTS THE KIDNAPPERS, 1820

On December 14, 1820, two white men forcibly entered the home of a Negro in Kennet Township, Pennsylvania. Both were killed by the Negro. The white men— named Griffith and Shipley—were seeking to return the Negro to slavery. With their bodies were found pistols, handcuffs, a whip and a rope. The Negro, John Read, was tried for the murder of Griffith—the master—and acquitted; but when tried for the death of the agent, Shipley, he was convicted of manslaughter and sentenced to nine years' imprisonment. The state, however, had sought the death penalty. The court's record of the Negro's testimony follows:

Read, the prisoner, a Negro, two or three years before came into Pennsylvania from Maryland and represented that, although he was free, an attempt had been made to hold him in slavery, frequently declared himself afraid of kidnappers, and often went armed. He married in Pennsylvania and had one child; hired a house in Kennet Township and worked about the neighborhood. On the night of the 14th of December, 1820, his wife was from home; he lay down, but felt uneasy and could not sleep, and then got up and made a fire. About midnight he thought he heard persons walking around the house,—one at length rapped smartly at the door. He asked what was wanted; the person answered they had a search-warrant for stolen goods. Read told them to go away; he believed them to be kidnappers, and if they were not, he had no stolen goods, and if they would wait until morning they might search the house. Soon after they began to force the door. He rolled a barrel of cider against it, and told them if they attempted to come in he would kill them. They pried the door off the hinges, and it fell over the cider barrel; at the instant he heard the click of a pistol, and called out, "It is life for life!" One of the persons said, "Rush on, Shipley; damn the Negro, he won't shoot." A person attempted to enter, he shot him; another attempted to come in, he struck him with a club, the man fell on his knees, and as he arose Read struck him once or twice. Seizing his gun he ran to a neighbor's and told him that the kidnappers had attacked his house; that he had killed two, and asked for more powder, as he was afraid they would pursue him. He made no attempt to escape, and was arrested.

*The Pennsylvania Magazine of History and Biography* (1889) XIII, pp. 106–09.

33

## THE VESEY CONSPIRACY, 1822

One of the most extensive slave conspiracies in American history was that led in 1822 by Denmark Vesey of Charleston, South Carolina. Active organizational work was begun late in 1821. Slaves were enlisted not only from Charleston but also from its surrounding area to a distance of about eighty miles. Thousands were involved, though since almost all the leaders "died silent"—as one of them, Peter Poyas, had urged—it is not possible to be more precise as to the numbers involved.

First word of the plot came to the slaveholders on May 30, 1822 when Peter (also called Devany), a "favorite and confidential slave," to quote the court record, of a Col. J. C. Prioleau, having been approached five days earlier to join the movement, told his master of this. The arrests of two leading rebels—Peter, slave of James Poyas, and Mingo, slave of William Harth—followed, but both men behaved in so deceptive a manner that they were released. Spies were put on their trails, however, and then two other informers appeared, and complete exposure followed.

One hundred and thirty-one Negroes, and four whites, were arrested. The whites, convicted of sympathy for the rebels, were fined and jailed. Of the Negroes, thirty-seven were hanged while the others were variously punished.

Below follow the remarks made by the first informer in May, and the statement finally elicited in court from one of those executed, Rolla, a slave of Governor Bennett of South Carolina.

## [a]

### *The Informer*

On Saturday afternoon last (my master being out of town) I went to market; after finishing my business I strolled down the wharf below the fish market, from which I observed a small vessel in the stream with a singular flag; whilst looking at this object, a black man, (Mr. Paul's William) came up to me and remarking the subject which engaged my attention said, I have often seen a flag with the number 76 on it, but never with 96, before. After some trifling conversation on this point, he remarked with considerable earnestness to me. Do you know that something serious is about to take place? To which I replied no. Well, said he, there is, and many of us are determined to right ourselves! I asked him to explain himself—when he remarked, why, we are determined to shake off our bondage, and for this purpose we stand on a good foundation, many have joined, and if you will go with me, I will show you the man, who has the list of names who will take yours down. I was so much astonished and horror struck at this information, that it was a moment or two before I could collect myself sufficient to tell him I would have nothing to do with this business, that I was satisfied with my condition, that I was grateful to my master for his kindness and wished no change. I left him instantly, lest, if this fellow afterwards got into trouble, and I had been seen conversing with him, in so public a place, I might be suspected and thrown into difficulty. I did not however remain easy under the burden of such a secret, and consequently determined to consult a free man of colour named —— * and to ask his advice. On conferring with this friend, he urged me with great earnestness to communicate what had passed between Mr. Paul's man and myself to my master, and not lose a moment in so doing.

* The free Negro was named Pencell. He was rewarded by the state of South Carolina with $1,000. The informer himself was freed and given an annual pension of $50, which was raised in 1857 to $200.

I took his advice and not waiting, even for the return of my master to town, I mentioned it to my mistress and young master. On the arrival of my master, he examined me as to what had passed, and I stated to him what I have mentioned to yourselves.

## [b]

### Rolla's Statement

I know Denmark Vesey. On one occasion he asked me what news, I told him none; he replied we are free but the white people here won't let us be so, and the only way is to rise up and fight the whites. I went to his house one night to learn where the meetings were held. I never conversed on this subject with Batteau or Ned—Vesey told me he was the leader in this plot. I never conversed either with Peter or Mingo. Vesey induced me to join; when I went to Vesey's house there was a meeting there, the room was full of people, but none of them white. That night at Vesey's we determined to have arms made, and each man put in 12½ cents toward that purpose. Though Vesey's room was full I did not know one individual there. At this meeting Vesey said we were to take the Guard-House and Magazine to get arms; that we ought to rise up and fight against the whites for our liberties; he was the first to rise up and speak, and he *read to us from the Bible, how the Children of Israel were delivered out of Egypt from bondage.* [Italics in original.] He said that the rising would take place, last Sunday night week, (the 16th June) and that Peter Poyas was one.

*An Official Report of the Trials of Sundry Negroes, charged with an attempt to raise an insurrection in the State of South-Carolina . . . prepared and published at the request of the Court,* by Lionel H. Kennedy and Thomas Parker, members of the Charleston bar and the Presiding Magistrates of the Court (Charleston, 1822), pp. 48–51, 66–67. Original court records are located in the Memorial Building, South Carolina Historical Commission, Columbia, S.C.

## 34

## A FAVORITE SERVANT REQUESTS A FAVOR, 1822

This petition from a free Negro of Goochland County, Virginia, dated December 18, 1822, prays for the right to remain in the State. It contains interesting details concerning the responsibilities imposed upon favorite slaves as well as concerning one of their prime duties—that of serving as informers. Accompanying Moses' petition was a note from Thomas Peers, his former owner, urging the prayer be granted for "it would be policy in the legislature to do so, when it is taken into consideration the opportunities that such characters have of access to information, that the whites are deprived of, when dangerous plots might be agitated by Negroes." The prayer was granted.

To the Legislature of Virginia

The petition of Moses a Free Man of Colour humbly representeth to your honorable body that He was born in your State a slave, and has served in perpetual bondage till about two years ago, a period of about forty five years; when He became emancipated, in a way he begs leave to present to the consideration of the Legislature; your Petitioners original owner died many years ago leaving him in the possession of his Widow Judith Peers who also died about ten years past: and your petitioner solemnly declares that He faithfully performed the duties of a Servant while in the service of both of his Owners to the best of his knowledge and ability, and to their satisfaction, He always believed. In addition to the performance of the ordinary duties of a slave, part of his time he acted as a Manager for his Mistress having the direction of the hands & charge of the plantation, stock and crops and sometimes carrying the crops to market. A great part of his time He acted as a Miller in a Mill employed in grinding for Neighborhood purposes, as well as Manufactoring Flour for market; he believes with general satisfaction to those concerned. Nor did He ever during all the time spoken of or since he was very young drink a drop of ardent spirits; and He begs leave with humility to mention that on one occasion his mistress's house was on fire at a late hour of the night when all the Family were asleep. He discovered it, gave an alarm and with great personal danger rushed to the fire, extinguished the flames, and rescued the family, who otherwise probably would have perished. Your Petitioner begs leave to say that He has always been watchful to detect and desirous to suppress those mischiefs and vices in slaves and free Persons of Colour which He is informed rendered it necessary that the Legislature should enact the law prohibiting free Persons of Colour remaining in the state.

After the death of his Mistress your Petitioner was transfered to her son Doctr. Thomas Peers for the payment of her debts; and for that purpose He was hired to the Reverend Joel Cross deceased, to conduct a Toll and manufactoring Mill; From his deportment in Mr. Cross's service, He proposed to your Petitioner and those to whom He belonged to purchase him and permit your Petitioner at reasonable and stipulated wages to serve him a time sufficient to reimburse the purchase money as a ransom of his subsequent liberty: This was agreed on by all concerned; He was purchased by Mr. Cross at the price of Four hundred and fifty Dollars. The time of his servitude for raising the money and interest expired about two years ago, when by the will of the said Reverend Joel Cross he was entitled to his freedom. Since that time, exclusive of supporting himself, He has honestly accumulated about one hundred and fifty Dollars by his labour, principally on the James River Canal. Your Petitioner made application last summer to the County Court of Goochland to remain in the State a Free Man, but from scruples relating to the construction of the law a few, perhaps two of the Court, that leave was denied him, as no act of extraordinary merit was specified your Petitioner has been informed by a Member of that Court altho' his general Character was unimpeached, and but for those scruples the Court would with sincere willingness have given its unanimous assent; some of the Court and able Counsel have advised this appeal to your Honorable body. Your Petitioner has been informed and believes that if the following fact had been made known the Court would cheerfully accorded its assent to his remaining the State. Your Petitioner ventures humbly to beg leave to mention the following circumstance, In times when there were frequent alarms of insurrections of the Blacks, in the neighborhood, where there number was great being near large estates and extensive coal mines your Petitioner has more than once secretly made known to his Mistress the whispers of such plots being agitated and concerning them He was always distressed and anxious to make discoveries. Your Petitioner trusts the Legislature will consider such conduct sufficiently entitled to the character of extraordinary merit, to obtain permission to remain in the State, and prays that your Honorable Body will relieve him from the trying dilemma of choosing whether to return to slavery, or retain his liberty, already purchased by his labour, by an involuntary exile, the remainder of his life, from his wife and children and the land of his nativity. And your Petitioner with humility & reverence will ever pray &c

Moses.

Errata. Wherever the word Joel Cross is used it should be Joseph Cross

Virginia State Archives, Richmond.

35

# A KIDNAPPED NEGRO ASKS FOR HELP, 1823

The kidnapping of free Negroes both within and outside the South, and their sale into slavery was, as we have seen, a regularly recurring crime until emancipation. Letters, however, from the victims of this practice are exceedingly rare. One such was dated Charleston, S.C., October 21, 1823 and was sent to Dr. James Rush, the distinguished physician of Philadelphia and son of the renowned Dr. Benjamin Rush.

Dear Sir,

I take the liberty of righting thease few lines to you and will thank you for to look at the re[c]ording-office and get a coppy of my free papers and send them on to me as I am made a slave heair for [illegible] Back and as I wish to return to my native place and I will pay you for your kindness to ordes [towards] me for so doing I have sent you the names of persons that well noes me to be free Borne in that state

| | |
|---|---|
| Miss Mary Stockton | Mr James Ray Jr |
| Mr Rich^d Stockton | Mr James Duncanson |
| Miss Susan Stockton | Mr Joseph Lance |
| Mr Harris Do —— | Mr Todd |
| Miss Abby Do —— | Dr Smith |
| Dr Bailey | |

Dear Sir,

I was Borne in the family of Thomas Cox

I remain your Humble Servant
Phillis Cox

MS. Correspondence of Dr. James Rush, I, p. 177 in Ridgway Branch, Library Company of Philadelphia.

## 36

## A NEGRO INFORMER SEEKS PEACE, 1824

In the unique document published below a Negro informer named Lewis Bolah explains to the Virginia legislature, in a petition dated December 6, 1824, the circumstances under which he betrayed a conspiracy involving slaves, free Negroes and some white men. The hatred that this earned him from the Negro people is indicated in the petition. Bolah's prayer was supported in writing by several distinguished white Virginians, and the legislature granted it.

To the Senate and House of Delegates of the Commonwealth of Virginia—

Your Petitioner Lewis Bolah now a free man of colour but formerly a Slave asks permission most respectfully to represent to the Legislature of Virginia —That he is a Native of this State and resided in the vicinity of the City of Richmond the greater part of his life. That some years past in consequence of the pecuniary embarrassments of his former owner he was sold and transported to the State of Louisiana and became the property of Mr. Waters Clarke of the City of New Orleans with whom he lived for some time. During the year 1812 the slaves and free persons of colour in the City of New Orleans and the surrounding Country connected with a few abandoned and lawless white persons who were bent on rapin and plunder meditated and planed a Plot of Treason and Insurrection which if it had been carried into operation would have presented one general scene of conflagration, murder and robbery & the City of New Orleans and the sorrounding Country if possible would have exhibited a spectacle of ruin and desolation exceeding anything which formerly transpired in St Domingo. This horrible conspiracy was communicated to him, he was invited to join in it, was offered the post of Captain in the operations and assured of being rewarded by freedom and Wealth. Shocked by the proposition and being much attached to his master and family who had treated him most humanely your Petitioner resolved to pursue such a course of conduct as was calculated to prevent the effusion of blood, to bring the ringleaders to trial and punishment and thereby save the lives not only of the whites but the misguided persons of his own colour who might be persuaded to join the nefarious conspiracy and subject themselves to retributive justice and the vengeance of offended Law. He therefore immediately communicated the intelligence which he had received to the Civil Authorities of New Orleans who adopted such plans as caused the apprehension of the ringleaders of the insurrection when assembled in counsel on the very eve of the execution of their Plot and they were condemned and executed—

In February 1813 the Legislature of Louisiana being pleased to consider the conduct of your Petitioner & some others as useful and meritorious passed an act to purchase and emancipate them and the Treasurer of the State having paid to his Master Mister Waters Clark the sum of $800, he was regularly manumitted by an instrument under the hand of Wm C C Claiborne Governor & the Seal of the State. Immediately after being emancipated, feeling himself unsafe your Petitioner entered into the service of the United States then at War with Great Britain and joined the squadron of Commodore John Shaw, with whom he continued 'till April 1814—

Your Petitioner will further represent that being born and raised in the vicinity of the City of Richmond, all his attachments, all that can render life desirable to him are only to be found by him in the State of Virginia. In Louisiana he could not remain with safety as he had every reason to believe that he might be the victim of disappointed Treason. He has sometimes contemplated going to Hayti and again to Messurado [?], but is convinced that from his deportment in New Orleans he would be an object of persecution in any Society governed by persons of colour and in any part of the United States (having no family) he would be perfectly isolated and could have none of those attachments which contribute to the happiness of men so that the Liberty which has been granted him so far from being the greatest boon which could have been bestowed, has as yet only caused him to be an unhappy wanderer. Some short time past he was about to Petition the Hustings Court of the City of Richmond for permission to remain in this State but was informed that though the Member of that honourable body wished to grant the indulgence that they had not the power in consequence of the operation of the Law prohibiting the migration of free persons of colour to this State. He therefore humbly prays the Legislature to pass an act authorizing and permitting him to remain and reside within this Commonwealth And your Petitioner will ever pray &c &c

Archives, Virginia State Library, Richmond.

# III

# The Abolitionist Era

---

## 37

## THE FIRST NEGRO NEWSPAPER'S OPENING EDITORIAL, 1827

The first Negro newspaper, *Freedom's Journal,* owned and edited by Samuel Cornish and John B. Russwurm, appeared in New York City on March 16, 1827. Its first editorial, stressing the fight against slavery and discrimination, is published here in full. It will be observed that this newspaper appeared four years before Garrison's *Liberator.*

TO OUR PATRONS

In presenting our first number to our Patrons, we feel all the diffidence of persons entering upon a new and untried line of business. But a moment's reflection upon the noble objects, which we have in view by the publication of this Journal; the expediency of its appearance at this time, when so many schemes are in action concerning our people—encourage us to come boldly before an enlightened publick. For we believe, that a paper devoted to the dissimination of useful knowledge among our brethren, and to their moral and religious improvement, must meet with the cordial approbation of every friend to humanity.

The peculiarities of this Journal, renders it important that we should advertise to the world our motives by which we are actuated, and the objects which we contemplate.

We wish to plead our own cause. Too long have others spoken for us. Too long has the publick been deceived by misrepresentations, in things which concern us dearly, though in the estimation of some mere trifles; for though there are many in society who exercise towards us benevolent feelings; still (with sorrow we confess it) there are others who make it their business to enlarge upon the least trifle, which tends to the discredit of any person of colour; and pronounce anathemas and denounce our whole body for the misconduct of this guilty one. We are aware that there are many instances of vice among us, but we avow that it is because no one has taught its subjects to be virtuous; many instances of poverty, because no sufficient efforts accommodated to minds contracted by slavery, and deprived of early education have been made, to teach them how to husband their hard earnings, and to secure to themselves comfort.

Education being an object of the highest importance to the welfare of society, we shall endeavour to present just and adequate views of it, and to urge upon our brethren the necessity and expediency of training their children, while young, to habits of industry, and thus forming them for becoming useful members of society. It is surely time that we should awake from this lethargy of years, and make a concentrated effort for the education of our youth. We form a spoke in the human wheel, and it is necessary that we should understand our pendence on the different parts, and theirs on us, in order to perform our part with propriety.

Though not desiring of dictating, we shall feel it our incumbent duty to dwell occasionally upon the general principles and rules of economy. The world has grown too enlightened, to estimate any man's character by his personal appearance. Though all men acknowledge the excellency of Franklin's maxims, yet comparatively few practise upon them. We may deplore when it is too late, the neglect of these self-evident truths, but it avails little to mourn. Ours will be the task of admonishing our brethren on these points.

The civil rights of a people being of the greatest value, it shall ever be our duty to vindicate our brethren, when oppressed; and to lay the case before the publick. We shall also urge upon our brethren, (who are qualified by the laws of the different states) the expediency of using their elective franchise; and of making an independent use of the same. We wish them not to become the tools of party.

And as much time is frequently lost, and wrong principles instilled, by the perusal of works of trivial importance, we shall consider it a part of our duty to recommend to our young readers, such authors as will not only enlarge their stock of useful knowledge, but such as will also serve to stimulate them to higher attainments in science.

We trust also, that through the columns of the FREEDOM'S JOURNAL, many practical pieces, having for their bases, the improvement of our brethren, will be presented to them, from the pens of many of our respected friends, who have kindly promised their assistance.

It is our earnest wish to make our Journal a medium of intercourse between our brethren in the different states of this great confederacy: that through its columns an expression of our sentiments, on many interesting subjects which concern us, may be offered to the publick: that plans which apparently are beneficial may be candidly discussed and properly weighed; if worth, receive our cordial approbation; if not, our marked disapprobation.

Useful knowledge of every kind, and everything that relates to Africa, shall find a ready admission into our columns; and as that vast continent becomes daily more known, we trust that many things will come to light, proving that the natives of it are neither so ignorant nor stupid as they have generally been supposed to be.

And while these important subjects shall occupy the columns of the FREEDOM'S JOURNAL, we would not be unmindful of our brethren who are still in the iron fetters of bondage. They are our kindred by all the ties of nature; and though but little can be effected by us, still let our sympathies be poured forth, and our prayers in their behalf, ascend to Him who is able to succour them.

From the press and the pulpit we have suffered much by being incorrectly represented. Men whom we equally love and admire have not hesitated to represent us disadvantageously, without becoming personally acquainted with the true state of things, nor discerning between virtue and vice among us. The virtuous part of our people feel themselves sorely aggrieved under the existing state of things—they are not appreciated.

Our vices and our degradation are ever arrayed against us, but our virtues are passed by unnoticed. And what is still more lamentable, our friends, to whom we concede all the principles of humanity and religion, from these very causes seem to have fallen into the current of popular feeling and are imperceptibly floating on the stream—actually living in the practice of prejudice, while they abjure it in theory, and feel it not in their hearts. Is it not very desirable that such should know more of our actual condition; and of our efforts and feelings, that in forming or advocating plans for our amelioration, they may do it more understandingly? In the spirit of candor and humility we intend by a simple representation of facts to lay our case before the public, with a view to arrest the progress of prejudice, and to shield ourselves against the consequent evils. We wish to conciliate all and to irritate none, yet we must be firm and unwavering in our principles, and persevering in our efforts.

If ignorance, poverty and degradation have hitherto been our unhappy lot; has the Eternal decree gone forth, that our race alone are to remain in this state, while knowledge and civilization are shedding their enlivening rays over the rest of the human family? The recent travels of Denham and Clapperton * in the interior of Africa, and the interesting narrative which they have published; the establishment of the republic of Hayti after years of sanguinary warfare; its subsequent progress in all the arts of civilization; and the advancement of liberal ideas in South America, where despotism has given place to free governments, and where many of our brethren now fill important civil and military stations, prove the contrary.

The interesting fact that there are FIVE HUNDRED THOUSAND free persons of colour, one half of whom might peruse, and the whole be benefitted by the publication of the Journal; that no publication, as yet, has been devoted exclusively to their improvement—that many selections from approved standard authors, which are within the reach of few, may occasionally be made—and more important still, that this large body of our citizens have no public channel—all serve to prove the real necessity, at present, for the appearance of the FREEDOM'S JOURNAL.

It shall ever be our desire so to conduct the editorial department of our paper as to give offence to none of our patrons; as nothing is farther from us than to make it the advocate of any partial views, either in politics or religion. What few days we can number, have been devoted to the improvement of our brethren; and it is our earnest wish that the remainder may be spent in the same delightful service.

In conclusion, whatever concerns us as a people, will ever find a ready admission into the FREEDOM'S JOURNAL, interwoven with all the principal news of the day.

And while every thing in our power shall be performed to support the character of our Journal, we would respectfully invite our numerous friends to assist by their communications, and our coloured brethren to strengthen our hands by their subscriptions, as our labour is one of common cause, and worthy of their consideration and support. And we most earnestly solicit the latter, that if at any time we should seem to be zealous, or too pointed in the inculcation of any important lesson, they will remember, that they are equally interested in the cause in which we are engaged, and attribute our zeal to the peculiarities of our situation; and our earnest engagedness in their well-being.

*Freedom's Journal* (N.Y.), March 16, 1827 (Microfilm in N.Y. Pub. Lib.).

* Dixon Denham, *Narratives of travel and discoveries in northern and central Africa* . . . (Boston, 1826); Hugh Clapperton, *Journal of a second expedition into the interior of Africa* . . . (Phila., 1829).

## 38

# A NEGRO NEWSPAPER REPORTS A LYNCHING,
## 1827

The first newspaper account of a lynching of a Negro, so far as is known, appeared in the *Freedom's Journal* for August 3, 1827. The news item itself was dated Tuscaloosa, Alabama, June 20, and was as follows:

*Horrid Occurrence.*—Some time during the last week one of those outrageous transactions—and we really think, disgraceful to the character of civilized man, took place near the north east boundary line of Perry, adjoining Bibb and Autanga counties. The circumstances we are informed by a gentleman from that county, are—That a Mr. McNeily having lost some clothing or some other property, of no great value, the slave of a neighboring planter was charged with the theft. McNeily, in company with his brother, found the Negro driving his master's wagon, they seized him, and either did or were about to chastise him, when the Negro stabbed McNeily, so that he died in an hour afterwards; the Negro was taken before a Justice of the Peace, who, after serious deliberation, waived his authority—perhaps through fear, as the crowd of persons from the above counties had collected to the number of seventy or eighty, near Mr. People's (the justice) house. He acted as President of the mob, and put the vote, when it was decided he should be immediately executed by being *burnt to death*—then the sable culprit was led to a tree and tied to it, and a large quantity of pine knots collected and placed around him, and the fatal torch was applied to the pile, even against the remonstrances of several gentlemen who were present; and the miserable being was in a short time consumed to ashes. An inquest was held over the remains and the Sheriff of Perry county, with a company of about twenty men, repaired to the neighborhood where this barbarous act took place, to secure those concerned, but with what success we have not heard, but we hope he will succeed in bringing the perpetrators of so highhanded a measure to account to their country for their conduct in this affair. This is the second Negro who has been thus put to death, without Judge or Jury in that county.

39

# NEW YORK NEGROES HAIL EMANCIPATION,
## 1827

On July 4, 1827 slavery was officially and finally ended in New York State. In honor of this event many celebrations were held by the Negro people. Typical of these and of the sentiments the occasion evoked were the services held in Albany, and the address delivered there on July 5, by the Reverend Nathaniel Paul, pastor of the first African Baptist Society in that city. The Reverend Mr. Paul was later a close friend of William Lloyd Garrison and an outstanding Abolitionist.

We look forward with pleasing anticipation to that period, when it shall no longer be said that in a land of freemen there are men in bondage, but when this foul stain will be entirely erased, and this, worst of evils, will be forever done way. The progress of emancipation, though slow, is nevertheless certain: It is certain, because that God who has made of one blood all nations of men, and who is said to be no respecter of persons, has so decreed; I therefore have no hesitation in declaring from this sacred place, that not only throughout the United States of America, but throughout every part of the habitable world where slavery exists, it will be abolished. However great may be the opposition of those who are supported by the traffic, yet slavery will cease. The lordly planter who has his thousands in bondage, may stretch himself upon his couch of ivory, and sneer at the exertions which are made by the humane and benevolent, or he may take his stand upon the floor of Congress, and mock the pitiful generosity of the east or west for daring to meddle with the subject, and attempting to expose its injustice: he may threaten to resist all efforts for a general or a partial emancipation even to a dissolution of the union. But still I declare that slavery will be extinct; a universal and not a partial emancipation must take place; nor is the period far distant. The indefatigable exertions of the philanthropists in England to have it abolished in their West India Islands, the recent revolutions in South America, the catastrope and exchange of power in the Isle of Hayti, the restless disposition of both master and slave in the southern states, the constitution of our government, the effects of literary and moral instruction, the generous feelings of the pious and benevolent, the influence and spread of the holy religion of the cross of Christ, and the irrevocable decrees of Almighty God, all combine their efforts and with united voice declare, that the power of tyranny must be subdued, the captive must be liberated, the oppressed go free, and slavery must revert back to its original chaos of darkness, and be forever annihilated from the earth. Did I believe that it would always continue, and that man to the end of time would be permitted with impunity to usurp the same undue authority over his fellow, I would disallow any allegiance or obligation I was under to my fellow creatures, or any submission that I owed to the laws of my country; I would deny the superintending power of divine providence in the affairs of this life; I would ridicule the religion of the Saviour of the world, and treat as the worst of men the ministers of an everlasting gospel; I would consider my Bible as a book of false and delusive fables, and commit it to the flames; nay, I would still go farther; I would at once confess myself an atheist, and deny the existence of a holy God. But slavery will cease, and the equal rights of man will be universally acknowledged. Nor is its tardy progress any argument against its final accomplishment. But do I hear it loudly responded,—this is but a mere wild fanaticism, or at best but the misguided conjecture of an untutored descendant of Africa. Be it so. I confess my ignorance, and bow with due deference to my superiors in understanding; but if in this case I err, the error is not peculiar to myself; if I wander, I wander in a region of light from whose political hemisphere the sun of liberty pours forth his refulgent rays, around which dazzle the star-like countenances of Clarkson, Wilberforce, Pitt, Fox and Grenville, Washington, Adams, Jefferson, Hancock and Franklin; if I err, it is their sentiments that have caused me to stray. . . . We do well to remember, that every act of ours is more or less connected with the general cause of emancipation. Our conduct has an important bearing, not only on those who are yet in bondage in this country, but its influence is extended to the isles of India, and to every part of the world where the abomination of slavery is known. Let us then relieve ourselves from the odious stigma which some have long since cast upon us, that we were incapacitated by the God of nature, for the enjoyment of the rights of freemen, and convince them and the world that although our complexion may differ, yet we have hearts susceptible of feeling; judgment capable of discerning, and prudence sufficient to manage our affairs with discretion, and by example prove ourselves worthy the blessings we enjoy.

*An address, delivered on the celebration of the abolition of slavery, in the State of New-York, July 5, 1827, by Nathaniel Paul (Albany, 1827), pp. 15–20.*

40

# A NEGRO WOMAN ON WOMEN'S RIGHTS, 1827

The following anonymous contribution to *Freedom's Journal,* August 10, 1827, represents an early expression of a "women's rights" viewpoint. It is the first such, expressed by a Negro, to be seen by the editor.

Messrs. Editors,

Will you allow a female to offer a few remarks upon a subject that you must allow to be all important? I don't know that in any of your papers, you have said sufficient upon the education of females. I hope you are not to be classed with those, who think that our mathematical knowledge should be limited to "fathoming the dish-kettle," and that we have acquired enough of history, if we know that our grandfather's father lived and died. 'Tis true the time has been, when to darn a stocking, and cook a pudding well, was considered the end and aim of a woman's being. But those were days when ignorance blinded men's eyes. The diffusion of knowledge has destroyed those degraded opinions, and men of the present age, allow, that we have minds that are capable and deserving of culture. There are difficulties, and great difficulties in the way of our advancement; but that should only stir us to greater efforts. We possess not the advantages with those of our sex, whose skins are not coloured like our own, but we can improve what little we have, and make our one talent produce two-fold. The influence that we have over the male sex demands, that our minds should be instructed and improved with the principles of education and religion, in order that this influence should be properly directed. Ignorant ourselves, how can we be expected to form the minds of our youth, and conduct them in the paths of knowledge? There is a great responsibility resting somewhere, and it is time for us to be up and doing. I would address myself to all mothers, and say to them, that while it is necessary to possess a knowledge of cookery, and the various mysteries of pudding-making, something more is requisite. It is their bounden duty to store their daughters' minds with useful learning. They should be made to devote their leisure time to reading books, whence they would derive valuable information, which could never be taken from them. I will not longer trespass on your time and patience. I merely throw out these hints, in order that some more able pen will take up the subject.

MATILDA

41

# TWO MILITANT PAMPHLETS BY NEGROES, 1829

Two significant pamphlets written by Negroes were published in 1829. The first of these was written by a New York free Negro, Robert Alexander Young, of whom very little is known. His work appeared in February and struck, in a peculiar and mystical fashion, a bitter note of foreboding and militance. It was entitled *The Ethiopian Manifesto, Issued in Defence of the Blackman's Rights, in the scale of Universal Freedom,* and was published by the author himself in New York City.

The second, and by far the more important of the two works, was the work of David Walker and its full title was: *Walker's Appeal, in Four Articles: Together with a Preamble, to the Coloured Citizens of the World, but in particular, and very expressly, to those of the United States of America, written in Boston, State of Massachusetts, September 28, 1829.*

Of Walker himself it is known that he was born of a free mother in Wilmington, North Carolina on September 28, 1785. Disgust with slavery led him to leave the South when he was about thirty or thirty-five years old. He settled in Boston and earned his living as a dealer in old clothes. He immediately became active in anti-slavery work and was a leader in Boston's Colored Association. He served as that city's agent for *Freedom's Journal* and occasionally contributed to it.

Late in 1829 he published his *Appeal,* and from then until his mysterious death sometime in 1830, supervised the distribution and reprinting of his booklet, which during the last year of his life went into its third edition, from which the extracts here published are taken.

The *Appeal* created great excitement throughout the nation, especially in the slave South. The Governors of Georgia and North Carolina expressed alarm over this work as did city officials in Richmond, Savannah, New Orleans, Wilmington and elsewhere, while free Negroes and slaves and at least one white man, a printer in Milledgeville, Georgia, were found to be actively distributing it.

As will be observed, the stirring contents of this *Appeal* justified the slave-holders' alarm.

## [a]

### *Robert Alexander Young*

. . . Ethiopians! open your minds to reason; let therein weigh the effects of truth, wisdom, and justice, (and a regard to your individual as general good,) and the spirit of these our words, we know full well, cannot but produce the effect for which they are by us herefrom intended. Know, then, in your present state or standing, in your sphere of government in any nation within which you reside, we hold and contend you enjoy but few of your rights of government within them. We here speak of the whole of the Ethiopian people, as we admit not even those in their state of native simplicity, to be in an enjoyment of their rights as bestowed to them of the great bequest of God to man.

The impositions practiced to their state, not being known to them from the heavy and darksome clouds of ignorance which so wofully obscures their reason, we do, therefore, for the recovering them, as well as establishing to you your rights, proclaim, that duty—imperious duty, exacts the convocation of ourselves in a body politic; that we do, for the promotion and welfare of our order, establish to ourselves a people framed unto the likeness of that order, which from our mind's eye we do evidently discern governs the universal creation. Beholding but one sole power, supremacy, or head, we do of that head, but hope and look forward for succour in the accomplishment of the great design which he hath, in his wisdom, promoted us to its undertaking.

We find we possess in ourselves an understanding; of this we are taught to know the ends of right and wrong, that depression should come upon us or any of our race, of the wrongs inflicted on us of men. We know in ourselves we possess a right to see ourselves justified therefrom, of the right of God; knowing, but of his power hath he decreed to man, that either in himself he stands, or by himself he falls. Fallen, sadly, sadly low indeed, hath become our race, when we behold it reduced but to an enslaved state, to raise it from its degenerate sphere, and instill into it the rights of men. are the ends intended of these words; here we are met in ourselves, we constitute but one, aided, as we trust, by the effulgent light of wisdom to a discernment of the path which shall lead us to the collecting together of a people, rendered disobedient to the great dictates of nature, by the barbarity that hath been practised upon them from generation to generation, of the will of their more cruel fellow-men. Am I, because I am a descendant of a mixed race of men, whose shade hath stamped them with the hue of black, to deem myself less elligible to the attainment of the great gift allotted of God to man, than are any other of whatsoever cast you please, deemed from being white, as being more exalted than the black? . . .

Beware! know thyselves [slaveholders] to be but mortal men, doomed to the good or evil, as your works shall merit from you. Pride ye not yourselves in the greatness of your worldly standing, since all things are but moth when contrasted with the invisible spirit, which in yourself maintains within you your course of action: That within you will, to the presence of your God, be at all times your sole accuser.

Weigh well these my words in the balance of your consciencious reason, and abide the judgment thereof to your own standing, for we tell you of a surety, the decree hath already passed the judgment seat of an undeviating

God, wherein he hath said, "surely hath the cries of the black, a most persecuted people, ascended to my throne and craved my mercy; now, behold! I will stretch forth mine hand and gather them to the palm, that they become unto me a people, and I unto them their God." Hearken, therefore, oh! slaveholder, thou task inflicter against the rights of men, the day is at hand, nay the hour draweth nigh, when poverty shall appear to thee a blessing, if it but restore to thy fellow-man his rights; all worldly riches shall be known to thee then but as a curse, and in thine heart's desire to obtain contentment, when sad reverses come upon thee, then shalt thou linger for a renewal of days, that in thine end thou might not curse the spirit which called thee forth to life. Take warning, again we say, for of a surety from this, God will give you signs to know, in his decrees he regards the fallen state of the sons of men. Think not that wisdom descries not from here your vanity. We behold it, thou vain bloated upstart worldling of a slaveholder, laugh in derision of thy earthly taught and worldly sneer; but know, on thee we pronounce our judgment, and as fitting thee, point out to thy notice this our sign. Of the degraded of this earth, shall be exalted, one who shall draw from thee, as though gifted of power divine, all attachment and regard of thy slave towards thee. Death shall he prefer to a continuance of his race:—being doomed to thy vile servitude, no cohabitation shall be known between the sexes, while suffering under thy slavery; but should ungovernable passion attain over the untaught mind an ascendancy, abortion shall destroy the birth. We command it, the voice of imperative justice, though however harsh, must be obeyed. Ah! doth your expanding judgment, base slaveholder, not from here descry that the shackles which have been by you so undeservingly forged upon a wretched Ethiopian's frame, are about to be forever from him unlinked. Say ye, this can never be accomplished? If so, must indeed the power and decrees of Infinity become subservient to the will of depraved man. But learn, slaveholder, thine will rests not in thine hand: God decrees to thy slave his rights as a man. This we issue forth as the spirit of the black man or Ethiopian's right, established from the Ethiopian's Rock, the foundation of his civil and religious rights, which hereafter will be exemplified in the order of its course. Ethiopians, throughout the world in general, receive this as but a lesson presented to you from an instructive Book, in which many, many are therein contained, to the vindication of its purpose. As came John the Baptist, of old, to spread abroad the forthcoming of his master, so alike are intended these our words, to denote to the black African or Ethiopian people, that God has prepared for them a leader, who awaits but his season to proclaim to them his birthright. How shall you know this man? By indubitable signs which cannot be controverted by the power of mortal, his marks being stamped in open visage, as equally so upon his frame, which constitutes him to have been particularly regarded in the infinite work of God to man. . . .

Peace and Liberty to the Ethiopian first, as also all other grades of men, is the invocation we offer to the throne of God.

## [b]

### David Walker

I am fully aware, in making this appeal to my much afflicted and suffering brethren, that I shall not only be assailed by those whose greatest earthly desires are, to keep us in abject ignorance and wretchedness, and who are of the firm conviction that Heaven has designed us and our children to be slaves and *beasts of burden* to them and their children. I say, I do not only expect to be held up to the public as an ignorant, impudent and restless disturber of the public peace, by such avaricious creatures, as well as a mover of insubordination—and perhaps put in prison or to death, for giving a superficial exposition of our miseries, and exposing tyrants. But I am persuaded, that many of my brethren, particularly those who are ignorantly in league with slave-holders or tyrants, who acquire their daily bread by the blood and sweat of their more ignorant brethren—and not a few of those too, who are too ignorant to see an inch beyond their noses, will rise up and call me cursed—Yea, the jealous ones among us will perhaps use more abject subtlety, by affirming that this work is not worth perusing, that we are well situated, and there is no use in trying to better our condition, for we cannot. I will ask one question here.—Can our condition be any worse?— Can it be more mean and abject? If there are any changes, will they not be for the better, though they may appear for the worst at first? Can they get us any lower? Where can they get us? They are afraid to treat us worse, for they know well, the day they do it they are gone. But against all accusations which may or can be preferred against me, I appeal to Heaven for my motive in writing—who knows that my object is, if possible, to awaken in the breasts of my afflicted, degraded and slumbering brethren, a spirit of inquiry and investigation respecting our miseries and wretchedness in this *Republican Land of Liberty! ! ! ! ! !* . . . .

### Our Wretchedness In Consequence of Slavery

My beloved brethren: The Indians of North and of South America—the Greeks—the Irish, subjected under the king of Great Britain—the Jews, that ancient people of the Lord—the inhabitants of the islands of the sea—in fine, all the inhabitants of the earth, (except however, the sons of Africa) are called *men*, and of course are, and ought to be free. But we, (coloured people) and our children are *brutes!!* and of course are, and *ought to be* SLAVES to the American people and their children forever!! to dig their mines and work their farms; and thus go on enriching them, from one generation to another with our *blood* and our *tears! ! ! !* ....

O! that the coloured people were long since of Moses' excellent disposition, instead of courting favour with, and telling news and lies to our *natural enemies,* against each other—aiding them to keep their hellish chains of slavery upon us. Would we not long before this time, have been respectable men, instead of such wretched victims of oppression as we are? Would they be able to drag our mothers, our fathers, our wives, our children and ourselves, around the world in chains and hand-cuffs as they do, to dig up gold and silver for them and theirs? This question, my brethren, I leave for you to digest; and may God Almighty force it home to your hearts. Remember that unless you are united, keeping your tongues within your teeth, you will be afraid to trust your secrets to each other, and thus perpetuate our miseries under the *Christians! ! ! !* ....

Never make an attempt to gain our freedom or *natural right,* from under our cruel oppressors and murderers, until you see your way clear *—when that hour arrives and you move, be not afraid or dismayed; for be you assured that Jesus Christ the King of heaven and of earth who is the God of justice and of armies, will surely go before you. And those enemies who have for hundreds of years stolen our *rights,* and kept us ignorant of Him and His divine worship, he will remove. Millions of whom, are this day, so ignorant and avaricious, that they cannot conceive how God can have an attribute of justice, and show mercy to us because it pleased Him to make us black—which colour, Mr. Jefferson calls unfortunate!!!!!! As though we are not as thankful to our God, for having made us as it pleased himself, as they, (the whites,) are for having made them white. They think because they hold us in their infernal chains of slavery, that we wish to be white, or of their color—but they are dreadfully deceived—we wish to be just as it pleased our Creator to have made us, and no avaricious and unmerciful wretches, have any business to make slaves of, or hold us in slavery. How would they like for us to make slaves of, and hold them in cruel slavery, and murder them as they do us?—

* It is not to be understood here, that I mean for us to wait until God shall take us by the hair of our heads and drag us out of abject wretchedness and slavery, nor do I mean to convey the idea for us to wait until our enemies shall make preparations, and call us to seize those preparations, take it away from them, and put every thing before us to death, in order to gain our freedom which God has given us. For you must remember that we are men as well as they. God has been pleased to give us two eyes, two hands, two feet, and some sense in our heads as well as they. They have no more right to hold us in slavery than we have to hold them, we have just as much right, in the sight of God, to hold them and their children in slavery and wretchedness, as they have to hold us, and no more. . . . [Note in original.]

Fear not the number and education of our *enemies,* against whom we shall have to contend for our lawful right; guaranteed to us by our Makers; for why should we be afraid, when God is, and will continue, (if we continue humble) to be on our side?

The man who would not fight under our Lord and Master Jesus Christ, in the glorious and heavenly cause of freedom and of God—to be delivered from the most wretched, abject and servile slavery, that ever a people was afflicted with since the foundation of the world, to the present day—ought to be kept with all of his children or family, in slavery, or in chains, to be butchered by his *cruel enemies*. . . . ˙

## Our Wretchedness In Consequence Of Ignorance

. . . . if you commence, make sure work—do not trifle, for they will not trifle with you—they want us for their slaves, and think nothing of murdering us in order to subject us to that wretched condition—therefore, if there is an *attempt* made by us, kill or be killed. Now, I ask you, had you not rather be killed than to be a slave to a tyrant, who takes the life of your mother, wife, and dear little children? Look upon your mother, wife, and children, and answer God Almighty; and believe this, that it is no more harm for you to kill a man, who is trying to kill you, than it is for you to take a drink of water when thirsty; in fact, the man who will stand still and let another murder him, is worse than an infidel, and, if he has common sense, ought not to be pitied. . . .

I pray that the Lord may undeceive my ignorant brethren, and permit them to throw away pretensions, and seek after the substance of learning. I would crawl on my hands and knees through mud and mire, to the feet of a learned man, where I would sit and humbly supplicate him to instil into me, that which neither devils nor tyrants could remove, only with my life— for colored people to acquire learning in this country, makes tyrants quake and tremble on their sandy foundation. Why, what is the matter? Why, they know that their infernal deeds of cruelty will be made known to the world. Do you suppose one man of good sense and learning would submit himself, his father, mother, wife and children, to be slaves to a wretched man like himself, who, instead of compensating him for his labours, chains, hand-cuffs and beats him and family almost to death, leaving life enough in them, however, to work for, and call him master? No! no! he would cut his devilish throat from ear to ear, and well do slave-holders know it. The bare name of educating the coloured people, scares our cruel oppressors almost to death. But if they do not have enough to be frightened for yet, it will be, because they can always keep us ignorant, and because God approbates their cruelties, with which they have been for centuries murdering us. The whites shall have enough of the blacks, yet, as true as God sits on his throne in Heaven. . . .

### Our Wretchedness In Consequence Of The Colonizing Plan

. . . Let no man of us budge one step, and let slave-holders come to beat us from our country. America is more our country, than it is the whites—we have enriched it with our *blood and tears*. The greatest riches in all America have arisen from our blood and tears:—and will they drive us from our property and homes, which we have earned with our *blood?* They must look sharp or this very thing will bring swift destruction upon them. The Americans have got so fat on our blood and groans, that they have almost forgotten the God of armies. But let them go on. . . .

Remember Americans, that we must and shall be free and enlightened as you are, will you wait until we shall, under God, obtain our liberty by the crushing arm of power? Will it not be dreadful for you? I speak Americans for your good. We must and shall be free I say, in spite of you. You may do your best to keep us in wretchedness and misery, to enrich you and your children, but God will deliver us from under you. And wo, wo, will be to you if we have to obtain our freedom by fighting. Throw away your fears and prejudices then, and enlighten us and treat us like men, and we will like you more than we do now hate you, and tell us no more about colonization, for America is as much our country, as it is yours.—Treat us like men, and there is no danger but we will all live in peace and happiness together. For we are not like you, hard hearted, unmerciful, and unforgiving. What a happy country this will be, if the whites will listen. What nation under heaven, will be able to do any thing with us, unless God gives us up into its hand? But Americans, I declare to you, while you keep us and our children in bondage, and treat us like brutes, to make us support you and your families, we cannot be your friends. You do not look for it, do you? Treat us then like men, and we will be your friends. And there is not a doubt in my mind, but that the whole of the past will be sunk into oblivion, and we yet, under God, will become a united and happy people. The whites may say it is impossible, but remember that nothing is impossible with God.

The Americans may say or do as they please, but they have to raise us from the condition of brutes to that of respectable men, and to make a national acknowledgement to us for the wrongs they have inflicted on us. As unexpected, strange, and wild as these propositions may to some appear, it is no less a fact, that unless they are complied with, the Americans of the United States, though they may for a little while escape, God will yet weigh them in a balance, and if they are not superior to other men, as they have represented themselves to be, he will give them wretchedness to their very heart's content. . . .

If any are anxious to ascertain who I am, know the world, that I am one of the oppressed, degraded and wretched sons of Africa, rendered so by the avaricious and unmerciful, among the whites. If any wish to plunge me into the wretched incapacity of a slave, or murder me for the truth, know ye, that I am in the hand of God, and at your disposal. I count my life not dear unto me, but I am ready to be offered at any moment. For what is the use of living, when in fact I am dead. But remember, Americans, that as miserable, wretched, degraded and abject as you have made us in preceding, and in this generation, to support you and your families, that some of you, (whites) on the continent of America, will yet curse the day that you ever were born. You want slaves, and want us for your slaves!!! My colour will yet, root some of you out of the very face of the earth!!!!!!

. . . Now, Americans! I ask you candidly, was your sufferings under Great Britain, one hundredth part as cruel and tyrannical as you have rendered ours under you? Some of you, no doubt, believe that we will never throw off your murderous government and "provide new guards for our future security." If Satan has made you believe it, will he not deceive you? * Do the whites say, I being a black man, ought to be humble, which I readily admit? I ask them, ought they not to be as humble as I? or do they think that they can measure arms with Jehovah? Will not the Lord yet humble them? or will not these very coloured people whom they now treat worse than brutes, yet under God, humble them low down enough? Some of the whites are ignorant enough to tell us, that we ought to be submissive to them, that they may keep their feet on our throats. And if we do not submit to be beaten to death by them, we are bad creatures and of course must be damned, &c. If any man wishes to hear this doctrine openly preached to us by the American preachers, let him go into the Southern and Western sections of this country—I do not speak from hear say—what I have written, is what I have seen and heard myself. No man may think that my book is made up of conjecture—I have travelled and observed nearly the whole of those things myself, and what little I did not get by my own observation, I received from those among the whites and blacks, in whom the greatest confidence may be placed.

The Americans may be as vigilant as they please, but they cannot be vigilant enough for the Lord, neither can they hide themselves, where he will not find and bring them out.

* The Lord has not taught the Americans that we will not some day or other throw off their chains and hand-cuffs, from our hands and feet, and their devilish lashes (which some of them shall have enough of yet) from off our backs. [Note in original.]

42

# THE PIONEER NATIONAL NEGRO
# CONVENTION, 1830

The year 1830 marks the beginnings of the annual national conventions of the
Negro people which have been held from that time to the present, with few in-
terruptions.

To explain the background for this first convention and as a description of the
event itself, we publish an article on the subject which appeared in the New York
Negro magazine, *The Anglo-African,* for October, 1859. The piece was printed
anonymously, but it was based upon an interview with Hezekiah Grice, a founder
of the convention movement.

Following this, appear a contemporary account of a preliminary Philadelphia
meeting held in February and the minutes of the Convention itself held in the
same city in September, 1830.

[a]

### *The Anglo-African*

On the fifteenth day of September, 1830,* there was held at Bethel Church,
in the city of Philadelphia, the first Convention of the colored people of these
United States. It was an event of historical importance; and, whether we
regard the times or the men of whom this assemblage was composed, we find
matter for interesting and profitable consideration.

Emancipation had just taken place in New York, and had just been arrested in Virginia by the Nat Turner rebellion † and Walker's pamphlet.
Secret sessions of the legislatures of the several Southern States had been
held to deliberate upon the production of a colored man who had coolly
recommended to his fellow blacks the only solution to the slave question,
which, after twenty-five years of arduous labor of the most hopeful and noble-
hearted of the Abolitionists, seems the forlorn hope of freedom to-day—insurrection and bloodshed. Great Britain was in the midst of that bloodless
revolution which, two years afterwards, culminated in the passage of the
Reform Bill, and thus prepared the joyous and generous state of the British
heart which dictated the West India Emancipation Act. France was rejoicing in the not bloodless *trois jours de Juliet.* Indeed, the whole world seemed
stirred up with a universal excitement, which, when contrasted with the

---
* The actual date was September 20, 1830.
† This is an error; the Turner Revolt occurred in 1831.

universal panics of 1837 and 1857, leads one to regard as more than a philo-
sophical speculation the doctrine of those who hold the life of mankind
from the creation as but one life, beating with one heart, animated with
one soul, tending to one destiny, although made up of millions upon millions of molecular lives, gifted with their infinite variety of attractions and
repulsions, which regulate, or crystallize them into evanescent substructures
or organizations, which we call nationalities and empires and peoples and
tribes, whose minute actions and reactions on each other are the histories
which absorb our attention, whilst the grand universal moves on beyond
our ken, or only guessed at, as the astronomers shadow out movements of our
solar system around or towards some distant unknown centre of attraction.

If the times of 1830 were eventful, there were among our people, as well
as among other peoples, men equal to the occasion. We had giants in those
days! There were Bishop Allen, the founder of the great Bethel connection
of Methodists, combining in his person the fiery zeal of St. Francis Xavier
with the skill and power of organizing of a Richelieu; the meek but equally
efficient [Christopher] Rush (who yet remains with us in fulfilment of the
scripture), the father of the Zion Methodists, [Nathaniel] Paul, whose
splendid and stately eloquence in the pulpit, and whose grand baptisms in
the waters of Boston Harbor, are a living tradition in all New England;
the saintly and sainted Peter Williams, whose views of the best means of
our elevation are in triumphant activity to-day; William Hamilton, the
thinker and actor, whose sparse specimens of eloquence we will one day
place in gilded frames as rare and beautiful specimens of Etruscan art—
William Hamilton, who, four years afterwards, during the New York riots,
when met in the street, loaded down with iron missiles, and asked where he
was going, replied, "to die on my threshold!"; [William J.] Watkins, of
Baltimore, Frederick Hinton, with his polished eloquence, James Forten,
the merchant prince, William Whipper, just essaying his youthful powers,
Lewis Woodson and John Peck, of Pittsburgh, Austin Steward, then of
Rochester, Samuel E. Cornish, who had the distinguished honor of reasoning Gerrit Smith out of colonizationism, and of telling Henry Clay that he
would never be president of anything higher than the American Colonization Society, Philip A. Bell, the born *sabreur*, who never feared the face of
clay, and a hundred others, were the worthily leading spirits among the
colored people.

And yet the idea of the first Colored Convention did not originate with
any of these distinguished men: it came from a young man of Baltimore,
then, and still, unknown to fame. Born in that city in 1801, he was in 1817
apprenticed to a man some two hundred miles off in the South-east. Arriving
at his field of labor, he worked hard nearly a week and received poor fare

in return . . . Early nightfall found him on his way to Baltimore . . .

In 1824 our young friend fell in with Benjamin Lundy, and in 1828–29, with Wm. Lloyd Garrison, editors and publishers of the "Genius of Universal Emancipation;" a radical anti-slavery paper—whose boldness would put the "National Era" to shame—printed and published in the slave State of Maryland. In 1829–30, the colored people of the free States were much excited on the subject of emigration: there had been an emigration to Hayti, and also to Canada, and some had been driven to Liberia by the severe laws and brutal conduct of the fermenters of colonization in Virginia and Maryland. In some districts of these States, the disguised whites would enter the houses of the free colored men at night, and take them out and give them from thirty to fifty lashes, to get them to consent to go to Liberia.

It was in the spring of 1830, that the young man we have sketched, Hezekiah Grice, conceived the plan of calling a meeting or convention of colored men, in some place north of the Potomac, for the purpose of comparing views and of adopting a harmonious movement either of emigration, or of determination to remain in the United States; convinced of the hopelessness of contending against the oppressions in the United States, living in the very depth of that oppression and wrong, his own views looked to Canada; but he held them subject to the decision of the majority of the convention which might assemble.

On the 2nd of April, 1830, he addressed a written circular to prominent colored men in the free States, requesting their opinions on the necessity and propriety of holding such convention, and stated that if the opinions of a sufficient number warranted it, he would give notice of the time and place at which duly elected delegates might assemble. Four months passed away, and his spirit almost died within him, for he had received not a line from an one in reply. When he visited Mr. Garrison in his office, and stated his project, Mr. Garrison took up a copy of Walker's Appeal, and said, although it might be right, yet it was too early to have published such a book.

On the 11th of August, however, he received a sudden and peremptory order from Bishop Allen, to come instantly to Philadelphia, about the emigration matter. He went, and found a meeting assembled to consider the conflicting reports on Canada of Messrs. Lewis and Dutton; at a subsequent meeting held the next night, and near the adjournment, the Bishop called Mr. Grice aside, and gave him to read a printed circular, issued from New York city, strongly approving of Mr. Grice's plan of a convention, signed by Peter Williams, Peter Vogelsang and Thomas L. Jinnings. The Bishop added, "my dear child, we must take some action immediately, *or else these New Yorkers will get ahead of us!* . . ." Mr. Grice introduced the subject of the convention; and a committee consisting of Bishop Allen,

Benjamin Pascal [Paschall], Cyrus Black, James Cornish, and Junius C. Morel, were appointed to lay the matter before the colored people of Philadelphia. This committee, led, doubtless, by Bishop Allen, at once issued a call for a convention of the colored men of the United States, to be held in the city of Philadelphia on the 15th September, 1830.

. . . . On the fifteenth of September, Mr. Grice landed in Philadelphia, and in the fulness of his expectation asked every colored man he met about the Convention; no one knew anything about it; the first man did not know the meaning of the word, and another man said, "who ever heard of colored people holding a convention—convention, indeed!" Finally, reaching the place of meeting, he found, in solemn conclave, the five gentlemen who had called the Convention, and who had constituted themselves delegates: with a warm welcome from Bishop Allen, Mr. Grice, who came with credentials from the people of Baltimore, was admitted as delegate. A little while after, Dr. Burton, of Philadelphia, dropped in, and demanded by what right the six gentlemen held their seats as members of the Convention. On a hint from Bishop Allen, Mr. Pascal [Paschall] moved that Dr. Burton be elected an honorary member of the Convention, which softened the Doctor. In half an hour, five or six tall, grave, stern-looking men, members of the Zion Methodist body in Philadelphia, entered, and demanded by what right the members present held their seats and undertook to represent the colored people. Another hint from the Bishop and it was moved that these gentlemen be elected honorary members. But the gentlemen would submit to no such thing, and would accept nothing short of full membership, which was granted them. . . .

The main subject of discussion was emigration to Canada; Junius C. Morel, Chairman of a Committee on that subject, presented a report, on which there was a two days' discussion; . . . The Convention recommended emigration to Canada, passed strong resolutions against the American Colonization Society, and at its adjournment appointed the next annual Convention of the people of color to be held in Philadelphia, on the first Monday in June, 1831.

At the present day, when colored conventions are almost as frequent as church-meetings, it is difficult to estimate the bold and daring spirit which inaugurated the Colored Convention of 1830. It was the right move, originating in the right quarter and at the right time. Glorious old Maryland, or, as one speaking in the view that climate grows the men, would say, Maryland-Virginia region, which has produced Benjamin Banneker, Nat. Turner, Frederick Douglass, the parents of Ira Aldridge, Henry Highland Garnet, and Sam. Ringgold Ward, also produced the founder of colored conventions, Hezekiah Grice! . . .

In looking to the important results that grew out of this Convention, the independence of thought and self-assertion of the black man are the most remarkable. Then the union of purpose and union of strength which grew out of the acquaintanceship and mutual pledges of colored men from the different States. Then the subsequent conventions, where the great men we have already named, and others, appeared and took part in the discussions with manifestations of zeal, talent and ability, which attracted Garrison, the Tappans, Jocelyn, and others of that noble host, who, drawing no small portion of their inspiration from their black brethren in bonds, did manfully fight in the days of anti-slavery which tried men's souls, and when, to be an Abolitionist, was, to a large extent, to be a martyr. . . .

## [b]

### Meeting of February, 1830

At a public meeting of the respectable people of colour, of the city and county of Philadelphia, held in the first coloured Wesley Methodist Church, on the 16th instant, PETER GARDNER, was called to the chair; and JUNIUS C. MORRELL [also commonly spelled Morel—ed.], was appointed secretary.

The object of the meeting being stated, the following resolutions were adopted.

Resolved, 1st. That we do most cordially rejoice that the bond of brotherhood, which rivets a nation together in one indissoluble chain, has collected so large a portion of our people together to sympathize and commiserate the condition of our brethren recently from Ohio, now in Canada.*

Resolved, 2d. That while the laws of this country permit the freedom of expression, and cease to muzzle the press, we shall cheerfully vindicate the cause of our oppressed people.

Resolved, 3d. That we view with deep interest the disposition and transactions of our brethren in Ohio, so far as relates to their emigration to Canada, the noblest design and patriotic achievement ever performed by our people in this country.

Resolved, 4th. That the Colony, in Canada, not only merits the appro-

---

* By 1829 about 2,200 Negroes lived in Cincinnati, many of them fugitives from the South. That year city authorities by proclamation demanded that all Negroes obey, within 60 days, an Ohio law of 1807, hitherto dormant, requiring the registering and bonding, in the sum of $500, of every Negro. The Negroes in mass meeting requested an additional thirty days and sent a delegation to Canada to prepare for migration. The time extension was not granted, and a mob attacked the Negro quarter for three days. The Negroes fought back and finally drove the mob away. When the Canadian deputation returned with a favorable answer, about one thousand Negroes left Cincinnati and established Wilberforce Settlement, near London, Ontario.

bation and esteem of every philanthropist, but of every man whose sable skin divests him of his freedom, and impairs his usefulness in this country.

*Resolved, 5th.* That we view it as an asylum from oppression, and a generous invitation for our people to dwell in a land where they can breathe the pure air of liberty, and where every opportunity is held out for us to occupy that space, and enjoy those rights in the moral world, which God, in his wisdom has destined us to fill as rational beings.

*Resolved, 6th.* That we view with charity the national policy of the American Colonization Society; as one necessary to the interests of the white inhabitants of this country.

*Resolved, 7th.* That we recommend that philanthropic association to turn its attention to Canada, where it can complete much, with less means, and more convenience; and in a climate more congenial to the health and prosperity of its colonists, and already under the influence of civilization.

*Resolved, 8th.* That we return gratitude to those philanthropists who have enacted laws to ameliorate our condition; and also, shall ever reverence those who may yet promote our interests, and especially Pennsylvania, under whose laws it is our happy lot to remain subject but we solemnly deprecate such laws as those in Ohio, which have completed the banishment of our brethren in these United States.

*Resolved, 9th.* That we do cordially and earnestly wish for the prosperity of that neighboring nation (without the most distant idea of revolting against the laws of our country) for her benevolence in opening a door for the oppressed whose only crime or transgression was the unalterable colour of their skin.

*Resolved, 10th.* That the thanks of this meeting be tendered to the benevolent citizens of Philadelphia; who, being informed of the situation of these unfortunate people, afforded much pecuniary aid towards alleviating its wants.

*Resolved, 11th.* That if any of the sentiments contained in the above resolutions shall prove offensive to the American people, we sincerely hope that their knowledge of our ignorance will be a sufficient apology while we declare that our intentions are pure and the only event that gave rise to our present sentiments was the oppression of our brethren, in a country whose republican constitution declares, *"that all men are born free and equal."*

Samuel Hazard, ed., *The [Weekly] Register of Pennsylvania* . . . (Philadelphia) V, February 27, 1830.

[c]

*Minutes of the Convention*

At a Convention held by adjournments from the 20th day of September, to the 24th of the same inclusive, 1830, in accordance with a public notice issued on behalf of the coloured citizens of Philadelphia, and addressed to their brethren throughout the U. States, inviting them to assemble by delegation, in Convention, to be held in the city of Philadelphia, on the 20th day of September, 1830, and signed on behalf, by the Rev. Bishop *Allen, Cyrus Black, Junius C. Morel, Benjamin Paschall,* jr., & *James Cornish*—

The delegation accordingly met in Bethel church, on the 20th of September, at 10 o'clock A. M. and after a chaste and appropriate prayer by the venerable Bishop *Allen,* the Convention was organized by electing

> Rt. Rev. Richard Allen, President.
> Dr. Belfast Burton, of Philadelphia,⎫ Vice Presidents
> Austin Steward of Rochester, N.Y.    ⎭
> Junius C. Morel, of Philadelphia, Secretary and
> Robert Cowley, of Maryland, Assistant Secretary.

On motion it was *Resolved,* That this Convention do recommend the formation of a Parent Society; and that immediately after its organization, to appoint a general corresponding Agent, to reside at or near the intended purchase in Upper Canada.

On motion it was *Resolved,* That this Convention enjoins and requires of each of its members to use their utmost influence in the formation of societies, *auxiliary* to the Parent Society about being established in the city of Philadelphia; and also to instruct the auxiliary societies when formed, to send delegates to the next General Convention.

On motion it was *Resolved,* That the next General Convention shall be composed of delegates appointed by the Parent Society and its auxiliaries: provided always, that the number of delegates from each society, shall not exceed *five,* and all other places, where there are no auxiliaries, are hereby invited to send one delegate.

On motion it was *Resolved,* That this Convention address the Free People of Colour throughout the United States, and publish in one of the daily papers of this city.

On motion it was *Resolved,* That the Convention do adjourn at the invitation of one of the managers of the Lombard-street Free School for colored children. The Convention were highly gratified at the order, regularity and improvement discoverable in the various departments, among a collection of children, Their specimens in writing, needle-work, &c. &c made a deep impression on the Convention, with a desire that the People of Colour may availingly appreciate every extended opportunity for their improvement in the various situations where they may reside.

On motion, the House adjourned *sine die.*

Rt. Rev. Richard Allen, President

Junius C. Morel, Secretary

The following Delegates composed the Convention, viz.

*Pennsylvania*—Rev. Richard Allen, Dr. Belfast Burton, Cyrus Black, Junius C. Morel, Benjamin Paschall, jr., James Cornish, Wm. S. Whipper, Peter Gardiner, John Allen, James Newman, Charles H. Leveck, Frederick A. Hinton.

*New-York*—Austin Steward, Jos. Adams, George L. Brown.

*Connecticut*—Scipio C. Augustus.

*Rhode Island*—George C. Willis, Alfred Niger.

*Maryland*—James Deavour, Hezekiah Grice, Aaron Willoon, Robert Cowley.

*Delaware*—Abraham D. Shad.

*Virginia*—Arthur M. Waring, Wm. Duncan, James West, jr.

Honorary Members.

Robert Brown, William Rogers, John Bowers, Richard Howell, Daniel Peterson, Charles Shorts, of Pennsylvania; Leven Williams, of New-York; James P. Walker, of Maryland; John Arnold, of New-Jersey; Sampson Peters, of New-Jersey; Rev. Anthony Campbell, of Delaware; Don Carolos Hall, of Delaware.

CONVENTION OF PEOPLE OF COLOUR

As much anxiety has prevailed on account of the enactment of laws in several States of the Union, especially that of Ohio, abridging the liberties and privileges of the Free People of Colour, and subjecting them to a series of privations and sufferings, by denying them a right of residence, unless they comply with certain requisitions not exacted of the Whites, a course altogether incompatible with the principles of civil and religious liberty.

In consideration of which, a delegation was appointed from the states of Connecticut, New York, Pennsylvania, Delaware, and Maryland, to meet in Convention in Philadelphia, to consider the propriety of forming a settlement in the province of Upper Canada, in order to afford a place of refuge to those who may be obliged to leave their homes, as well as to others inclined to emigrate with the view of improving their condition.

The said Convention accordingly met in Bethel Church, city of Philadelphia, on the 20th of September, 1830; and having fully considered the peculiar situation of many of their brethren, and the advantages to be derived from the proposed settlement, adopted the following

### ADDRESS

### To the Free People of Colour of these United States

Brethren, Impressed with a firm and settled conviction, and more especially being taught by that inestimable and invaluable instrument, namely, the Declaration of Independence, that all men are born free and equal, and consequently are endowed with unalienable rights, among which are the enjoyments of life, liberty and the pursuits of happiness.

Viewing these as incontrovertable facts, we have been led to the following conclusions; that our forlorn and deplorable situation earnestly and loudly demands of us to devise and pursue all legal means for the speedy elevation of ourselves and brethren to the scale and standing of men.

And in pursuit of this great object, various ways and means have been resorted to; among others, the African Colonization Society is the most prominent. Not doubting the sincerity of many friends who are engaged in that cause; yet we beg leave to say, that it does not assist in this benevolent and important work.

To encourage our brethren earnestly to co-operate with us, we offer the following, viz. 1st. Under that government no invidious distinction of colour is recognized, but there we shall be entitled to all the rights, privileges and immunities of other citizens. 2d. That the language, climate, soil, and productions are similar to those in this country. 3d. That land of the best quality can be purchased at the moderate price of one dollar and fifty cents per acre, by the one hundred acres. 4th. The market for different kinds of produce raised in that colony, is such as to render a suitable reward to the industrious farmer, equal in our opinion to that of the United States. And lastly, as the erections of buildings must necessarily claim the attention of the emigrants, we would invite the mechanics from our large cities to embark in the enterprise; the advancement of architecture depending much on their exertions, as they must consequently take with them the arts and improvements of our well regulated communities.

It will be much to the advantage of those who have large families, and desire to see them happy and respected, to locate themselves in a land where the laws and prejudices of society will have no effect in retarding their advancement to the summit of civil and religious improvement. There the diligent student will have ample opportunity to reap the reward due to industry and perseverance; whilst those of moderate attainments, if properly nurtured, may be enabled to take their stand as men in the several offices and situations necessary to promote union, peace, order and tranquility. It is to these we must look for the strength and spirit of our future prosperity.

Before we close, we would just remark, that it has been a subject of deep regret to this convention, that we as a people, have not availingly appreciated every opportunity placed within our power by the benevolent efforts of the friends of humanity in elevating our condition to the rank of freemen. That our mental and physical qualities have not been more actively engaged in pursuits more lasting, is attributable in a great measure to a want of unity among ourselves; whilst our only stimulus to action has been to become domestics, which at best is but a precarious and degraded situation.

It is to obviate these evils, that we have recommended our views to our fellow-citizens in the foregoing instrument, with a desire of raising the moral and political standing of ourselves; and we cannot devise any plan more likely to accomplish this end, than by encouraging agriculture and mechanical arts: for by the first, we shall be enabled to act with a degree of independence, which as yet has fallen to the lot of but few among us; and the faithful pursuit of the latter, in connection with the sciences, which expand and ennoble the mind, will eventually give us the standing and condition we desire.

To effect these great objects, we would earnestly request our brethren throughout the United States, to co-operate with us, by forming societies *auxiliary* to the Parent Institution; about being established in the city of Philadelphia, under the patronage of the General Convention. And we further recommend to our friends and brethren, who reside in places where, *at present,* this may be impracticable, so far to aid us, by contributing to the funds of the Parent Institution; and, if disposed, to appoint one delegate to represent them in the next Convention; to be held in Philadelphia the first Monday in June next, it being fully understood, that organized societies be at liberty to send any number of delegates not exceeding *five.*

Signed by order of the Convention,

Rev. Richard Allen, *President,*
Senior Bishop of the African Methodist Episcopal Churches.
Junius C. Morel, *Secretary*

*Constitution of the American Society of Free Persons of Colour, for improving their condition in the United States; for purchasing lands; and for the establishment of a settlement in Upper Canada, also The Proceedings of the Convention, with their Address to the Free Persons of Colour in the United States.* (Phila., 1831) Copy in Ridgway Branch, Library Company of Philadelphia.

43

# THE NEGRO PEOPLE AND GARRISON'S
## *LIBERATOR,* 1830

William Lloyd Garrison wrote on December 15, 1830 to the Philadelphia Negro Abolitionist, James Forten, giving him information concerning the forthcoming *Liberator*. Forten's reply, dated December 31, 1830, printed below, is typical of the substantial assistance rendered by Negroes to Garrison and his newspaper throughout the paper's existence. Without this aid the publication would not have lasted, as Garrison himself stated, pointing out that of its four hundred and fifty subscribers during its first year fully four hundred were Negroes, and that as late as 1834 out of a total of 2,300 subscribers, about 1,700 were Negroes.

I am extremely happy to hear that you are about establishing a paper in Boston. I hope your efforts may not be in vain; and may the "Liberator" be the means of exposing, more and more, the odious system of Slavery, and of raising up friends to the oppressed and degraded People of Colour, throughout the Union. Whilst so much is doing in the world, to ameliorate the condition of mankind, and the spirit of Freedom is marching with rapid strides, and causing tyrants to tremble, may America awake from the apathy in which she has long slumbered. She must, sooner or later, fall in with the irresistible current. Great efforts are now making in the cause of Liberty: the people are becoming more interested and determined on the subject.

Although the Southern States have enacted severe laws against the Free People of Colour, they will find it impossible to go in opposition to the Spirit of the Times. We have only to hope, that many such Philanthropists, as Mr. [Benjamin] Lundy and yourself, will come forward, to plead our cause; we can never feel sufficiently grateful to our long tried, faithful and zealous friend Mr. Lundy. He has indeed laboured for us, through evil and good report, and under many disadvantages & hardships—may he hereafter receive his rewards.

I learn with the greatest regret, that so much prejudice exists in the Eastern States, but may the "Standard you are about to erect in the Eyes of the Nation" be the means of dispersing those clouds of errors, and of bringing many advocates to our cause.

I would have answered your letter earlier, had it not been owing in the first place, to a multiplicity of business, which prevented me from soliciting subscribers to your Paper. I herewith enclose you the money for twenty seven subscribers, and their names and places of abode, you will also herewith receive. I would request you to send on a few extra papers, that I may hand them to my friends.

Garrison MSS., Boston Public Library.

## 44

## DENOUNCING COLONIZATION, 1831

A New York branch of the American Colonization Society was formed in January, 1831. As a result a mass meeting of Negroes was held in New York City on January 25, under the leadership of Samuel Ennals and Philip A. Bell. Here an "address to the citizens of New York" was broadcast as follows:

We solemnly protest against that Christian philanthropy which, in acknowledging our wrongs, commits a greater by vilifying us. The conscientious man would not kill the animal, but cried, "mad dog," and the rabble dispatched him . . . A difference of color is not a difference of species. Our structure and organization are the same, and not distinct from other men; and in what respects are we inferior? . . . We are content to abide where we are. We do not believe that things will always continue the same. The time must come when the Declaration of Independence will be felt in the heart, as well as uttered from the mouth, and when the rights of all shall be properly acknowledged and appreciated. God hasten that time. This is our home, and this is our country. Beneath its sod lie the bones of our fathers; for it, some of them fought, bled, and died. Here we were born, and here we will die.

*The Liberator* (Boston) February 12, 1831.

## 45

## PROSPECTUS OF A FORGOTTEN NEGRO NEWSPAPER, 1831

After *Freedom's Journal* and its continuator, *Rights of All*, both published in New York City by Samuel E. Cornish, the next Negro newspaper was *The African Sentinel and Journal of Liberty*. This was edited in Albany, New York, by John E. Stewart. The prospectus for the paper was dated January 26, 1831, and four monthly numbers of the paper appeared through August, 1831. From September, 1831 until March, 1832 it seems to have appeared as a weekly; thereafter no reference to it has been seen. No copy of the paper has been found.

## PROPOSALS
*For publishing in the city of Albany, N.Y.,*
A paper under the title of
THE AFRICAN SENTINEL
AND
JOURNAL OF LIBERTY

For the general advancement and improvement of the people of color.

Feeling deeply sensible of the great utility of such a work to the colored community, the subscriber, flattering himself of its success, has made every arrangement necessary for its publication, with a gentleman whose facilities in connection with his mechanical abilities, will render it a Journal of as respectable an appearance as any in the State. We are not indifferent, however, as to the responsibilities attending so arduous an undertaking, when we reflect that men of greater attainments, both in a literary and natural point of view, have preceded us in this heretofore unsuccessful undertaking as has been demonstrated by the recent failures of the "FREEDOM'S JOURNAL" and "RIGHTS OF ALL:" which, through the neglect, and not inability of the colored people of the United States, were suffered to go down from the proud eminence which they were attaining through the watchful zeal, talents and exertions of their Editor and Proprietor, MR. S. E. CORNISH. Notwithstanding such powerful considerations to cope with, we have resolved to enter the field, and *"stand the hazard of the die."* And should we succeed, where others have failed, the praise will redound more to the credit, patriotism and liberality of OUR COUNTRYMEN, than to our limited exertions. Still we trust our efforts, feeble as they may be, will be duly appreciated by our friends, and meet with a cordial support from every man whose bosom flows with the least spark of love of liberty and equality, and who believes as we do, and as is set forth in the Declaration of American Independence, "that all men are created free and equal" and "endowed by their Creator with certain unalienable rights, among which, are life, liberty, and the pursuit of happiness." In order to promote that happiness, so desirable to all, it is necessary, and indispensably so, that there should be *at least* one public Journal, conducted by a colored man, and devoted to the interests of the colored population throughout this country, for the purpose of diffusing such information of passing events as may be calculated both to instruct and amuse, and for the general communicating of our thoughts and sentiments upon such subjects, as are frequently agitated in the world, touching our condition as a part of the great family of man: And more particularly here, where the arts, sciences and literature, are as accessible to the humble peasants as to the more proud and opulent,—here, where the people of every clime, save Africa, are hastening to enjoy the benefits of those Institutions so congenial to the cultivation of every science and of every art.

Descendants of Africa!—Will you not arise with the dignity of MEN, and each proclaim "AM I NOT A MAN AND A BROTHER?" and with one accord establish and support a Paper, the aim of which shall be to destroy that hydra-headed canker-worm of prejudice, encourage education, Temperance and Morality, and urge the distribution of equal justice and equality? It is anxiously hoped that the colored community will give the subject that impartial consideration which the abject state of the mass of the colored population demands.

We trust, with our exertion, together with the promised aid of a few ready pens, to present our patrons with a Journal corresponding with the wishes of every friend to Equal Rights. And ere we conclude, we humbly solicit the patronage and support of those philanthropic and general citizens, who sympathize and wish for the amelioration of the condition of the long benighted sons and daughters of Africans, that a liberal public will enable THE AFRICAN SENTINEL to take a firm stand upon the ramparts of his NATION'S RIGHTS, and establish the fame of his JOURNAL OF LIBERTY.

THE AFRICAN SENTINEL and JOURNAL OF LIBERTY, will also be devoted to the dissemination of the news of the day, but more particularly to that relating to the colored population; both Foreign and Domestic, and will be published in a quarto form consisting of eight pages for the first four months, at the rate of $1.50 cents per year; and should patronage warrant, it will after that time, be continued semi-monthly at the rate of $2.00 per year, until arrangements can be made for its publication weekly.

*The Liberator*, March 12, 1831.

## 46

## NEGRO SOCIETIES IN PHILADELPHIA, 1831

Organization of social and charitable groups among Negroes has been a widespread and tenacious phenomenon. An early and highly informative detailing of the facts concerning this phase of Negro life, for the single city of Philadelphia, dated March 1, 1831, appeared as an advertisement in that city's *Gazette*. It will be observed that several of the societies were named in honor of anti-slavery leaders like Anthony Benezet, William Granville and Thomas Clarkson.

TO THE PUBLIC

Whereas, we believe it to be the duty of every person to contribute as far as is in their power towards alleviating the miseries, and supplying the wants, of those of our fellow beings who, through the many misfortunes and calamities to which human nature is subject, may become fit objects for our charity. And, whereas, from the many privations to which we as people of colour are subject, and our limited opportunity of obtaining the necessaries of life, many of us have been included in the number dependent on those provisions made by law, for the maintenance of the poor; therefore, as we constitute a part of the public burden, we have deemed it our duty to use such means as was in our reach to lessen its weight, among which, we have found the forming of institutions for mutual relief, the most practicable and best calculated to effect our object. To these institutions, each member pays a sum varying from one to eight dollars as an initiation fee, and from twelve and a half of twenty-five cents monthly. The funds are exclusively appropriated to the relief of such of its members, as through sickness or misfortune, may be unable to work; to the interments of deceased members, and to the relief of their widows and orphans, & Therefore, by contributing a trifling sum to these funds while in prosperity, we not only secure to ourselves a pension in sickness and adversity, but also contribute to the relief of our distressed brethren; and as these societies are incorporated and bodies politic in law, each member is sure of such benefits as are guaranteed by their constitutions. But as the public are not acquainted with the manner of distributing these benefits, nor the amount distributed, many have mistaken our object, and doubted the utility of these institutions—have thought them incentive to extravagance and dissipation, and formed merely to gratify our ostentatious desire, in consequence of which, the societies have thought it necessary, for the satisfaction of the public, to publish a statement of their expenses for charitable purposes during the last year; which, as we believe, will convince every candid person, that the above named opinions are erroneous, as most of the objects of these charities are persons whose daily earnings are scarcely adequate to their daily wants; and, many of them having large families, without some such aid they would necessarily become objects of public charity; whereas, by belonging to one or more of these institutions, they receive such aid as enables them to live, and in case of their death to be decently interred without increasing the public expense.

We, the subscribers, being appointed a committee to lay before the public a statement of the expenses of each society, for the year 1830, together with the dates of their formation, do certify the following to be correct.

## MALE SOCIETIES

| | Formed | Paid out from 1830 to 1831 |
|---|---|---|
| The African Friendly Society of St. Thomas | 1795 | $ 76.50 |
| Sons of Africa | 1810 | 222.00 |
| Benezet Philanthropic | 1812 | 415.19 |
| Benevolent Sons of Zion | 1822 | 116.99 |
| Sons of St. Thomas | 1823 | 43.12 |
| Harrison Benevolent | 1823 | 56.06 |
| Coachman's Benevolent | 1825 | 212.12½ |
| United Sons of Wilberforce | 1827 | 308.68 |
| Tyson Benevolent | 1824 | 93.38 |
| Beneficial Phil. Sons of Zoar | 1826 | 38.50 |
| United Brethren | 1829 | 159.00 |
| Humane Mechanics | 1828 | 38.00 |
| Union Ben't Sons of Bethel | 1828 | 178.61 |
| United Shipley Beneficial 1829 | 1829 | 97.07½ |
| Citizen Sons of Philadelphia | 1830 | 18.40 |
| Library Benevolent | 1830 | 70.35 |
| | | $2202.71¾ |

## FEMALE SOCIETIES

| | Formed | Paid out from 1830 to 1831 |
|---|---|---|
| The Female Benevolent Society of St. Thomas | 1793 | 80.84 |
| Female Benevolent Whitesonian | 1816 | 80.12 |
| African Female Band Benevolent Society of Bethel | 1817 | 428.50 |
| Female Benezet Society | 1818 | 196.12½ |
| Daughters of Aron | 1819 | 61.12½ |
| Female Granville Society | 1821 | 161.22½ |
| Daughters of Africa's Society | 1821 | 149.97 |
| Female African Benevolent | 1822 | 212.55½ |
| Daughters of Zion Angolian Ethiopian Society | 1822 | 103.67 |
| Daughters of St. Thomas Society—Feb. 1 | 1822 | 250.72 |
| Daughter of Absalom, April 5 | 1824 | 360.33 |
| Daughters of Ethiopia | 1825 | 131.30 |
| Female Tyson Society | —— | 132.75 |
| Daughters of Hosea | 1825 | 109.77 |
| Female Methodist Assistance Soc. | 1827 | 32.50 |
| United Daughters of Wesley | 1827 | 144.78 |

FEMALE SOCIETIES (*continued*)

|  | Formed | Paid out from 1830 to 1831 |
|---|---|---|
| Free Daughters of Shipley | 1827 | 108.72 |
| Daughters of Isaiah | 1828 | 73.72½ |
| Daughters of Gideon | 1828 | 189.65 |
| Female Clarkson Society | 1828 | 90.00 |
| United Sister's Society | 1828 | 208.75 |
| Union Daughters of Industry | 1829 | 39.50 |
| Female Harrison Benevolent Soc. | 1829 | 97.25 |
| Female Beneficial Philanthropic Society of Zoar | 1826 | 42.21 |
| Benevolent Daughters of Zion | 1826 | 75.50 |
| Daughters of Noah of Bethel Church | 1822 | 40.00 |
| Citizen Daughters of Philadelphia | 1830 | 15.00 |
|  |  | $3616.58½ |
|  | Total of male societies | 2202.71¾ |
| Total of male and female societies |  | $5819.29¼ |

There are several societies of the same kind, that have not made their returns to be published, for reasons unknown to us.

> John Bowers,
> William C. West,
> James Cornish,
> Robert C. Gordon, Sr.
> Benjamin Paschall,
> Committee

*Hazard's Register,* March 12, 1831, VII, pp. 163–64.

## 47

## FIRST ANNUAL NEGRO CONVENTION, 1831

The first annual Negro convention was held in Philadelphia, June 6–11, 1831. Present were fifteen delegates from New York, Pennsylvania, Delaware, Maryland and Virginia. Of its address to the nation, printed below, explanation is required only of the proposal for a manual labor (or, as we would say now, vocational education) school. The idea was put forth in 1827 by Samuel Cornish and was taken up with vigor two years later by an anti-slavery white minister of New Haven, the Rev. S. S. Jocelyn. In meetings with New York Negroes this was discussed and the Rev. Jocelyn was invited to participate (along with other white men including Garrison, Arthur Tappan and Benjamin Lundy) in the 1831 convention. As the address shows, the idea was accepted by this convention. Committees were formed to implement the decision and the appeal of one of them, dated September 5, 1831, is also printed below. The city government of New Haven, aided and stimulated by most of the press of the nation—Negro-hating and pro-slavery as it was—prevented, however, the establishment of the institution.

## [a]

### Convention Address

Respected Brethren and Fellow Citizens—

In accordance with a resolution of the last Convention, we have again assembled in order to discharge those duties which have devolved upon us by your unanimous voices.

Our attention has been called to investigate the political standing of our brethren wherever dispersed, but more particularly the situation of those in this great Republic.

Abroad, we have been cheered with pleasant views of humanity, and the steady, firm, and uncompromising march of equal liberty to the human family. Despotism, tyranny, and injustice have had to retreat, in order to make way for the unalienable rights of man. Truth has conquered prejudice, and mankind are about to rise in the majesty and splendour of their native dignity.

The cause of general emancipation is gaining powerful and able friends abroad. Britain and Denmark have performed such deeds as will immortalize them for their humanity, in the breasts of the philanthropists of the present day; whilst, as a just tribute to their virtues, after ages will yet erect unperishable monuments to their memory. (Would to God we could say thus of our own native soil!)

And it is only when we look to our own native land, to the birthplace of our *fathers,* to the land for whose prosperity their blood and our sweat have been shed and cruelly extorted, that the Convention has had cause to hang its head and blush. Laws, as cruel in themselves as they were unconstitutional and unjust, have in many places been enacted against our poor unfriended and unoffending brethren; laws, (without a shadow of provocation on our part,) at whose bare recital the very savage draws him up for fear of the contagion—looks noble, and prides himself because he bears not the name of a Christian.

But the Convention would not wish to dwell long on this subject, and it is one that is too sensibly felt to need description.

We would wish to turn you from this scene with an eye of pity, and a breast glowing with mercy, praying that the recording angel may drop a tear, which shall obliterate forever the remembrance of so foul a stain upon the national escutcheon of this great Republic.

This spirit of persecution was the cause of our Convention. It was that first induced us to seek an asylum in the Canadas; and the Convention feel happy to report to their brethren, that our efforts to establish a settlement in that province have not been made in vain. Our prospects are cheering; our friends and funds are daily increasing; wonders have been performed far exceeding our most sanguine expectations; already have our brethren purchased eight hundred acres of land—and two thousand of them have left the soil of their birth, crossed the lines, and laid the foundation for a structure which promises to prove an asylum for the coloured population of these United States. They have erected two hundred log houses and have five hundred acres under cultivation.

And now it is to your fostering care the Convention appeal, and we appeal to you as to men and brethren, yet to enlarge their borders.

We therefore ask of you, brethren—we ask of you, philanthropists of every colour, and of every kindred, to assist us in this undertaking. We look to a kind Providence, and to you, to say whether our desires shall be realized, and our labours crowned with success.

The Convention has done its duty, and it now remains for you, brethren, to do yours. Various obstacles have been thrown in our way by those opposed to the elevation of the human species; but, thanks to an all-wise Providence, his goodness has yet cleared the way, and our advance has been slow but steady. The only thing now wanted, is an accumulation of funds, in order to enable us to make a purchase agreeably to the direction of the first Convention; and, to effect that purpose, the Convention has recommended, to the different Societies engaged in that cause, to persevere and prosecute their designs with doubled energy; and we would earnestly recommend to every coloured man, (who feels the weight of his degradation) to consider himself in duty bound to contribute his mite towards this great object. We would say to all, that the prosperity of the rising generation mainly depends upon our active exertions.

Yes, it is with us to say whether they shall assume a rank and standing among the nations of the earth, as men and freemen, or whether they shall still be prized and held at market price. Oh, then, by a brother's love, and by all that makes man dear to man—awake in time! Be wise! be free! Endeavour to walk with circumspection; be obedient to the laws of our common country; honour and respect its lawmakers and lawgivers; and, through all, let us not forget to respect ourselves.

During the deliberations of this Convention, we had the favour of advising and consulting with some of our most eminent and tried philanthropists —men of unblemished character and of acknowledged rank and standing. Our sufferings have excited their sympathy; our ignorance appealed to their humanity; and, brethren we feel that gratitude is due to a kind and benevolent Creator, that our excitement and appeal have neither been in vain. A plan has been proposed to the Convention for the erection of a College for the instruction of young men of colour, on the manual labour system, by which the children of the poor may receive a regular classical education, as well as those of their more opulent brethren, and the charge will be so regulated as to put it within the reach of all. In support of this plan, a benevolent individual has offered the sum of one thousand dollars, provided that we can obtain subscriptions to the amount of nineteen thousand dollars in one year.

The Convention has viewed the plan with considerable interest, and after mature deliberation, on a candid investigation, feel strictly justified in recommending the same to the liberal patronage of our brethren, and respectfully solicit the aid of those philanthropists who feel an interest in sending light, knowledge, and truth, to all of the human species.

To the friends of general education, we do believe that our appeal will not be in vain. For, the present ignorant and degraded condition of many of our brethren in these United States (which has been a subject of much concern to the Convention) can excite no astonishment, (although used by our enemies to show our inferiority in the scale of human beings;) for, what opportunities have they possessed for mental cultivation or improvement? Mere ignorance, however, in a people divested of the means of acquiring information by books, or an extensive connexion with the world, is no just criterion of their intellectual incapacity; and it has been actually seen, in various remarkable instances, that the degradation of the mind and character, which has been too hastily imputed to a people kept, as we are, at a distance from those sources of knowledge which abound in civilized and enlightened communities, has resulted from no other causes than our unhappy situation and circumstances.

True philanthropy disdains to adopt those prejudices against any people which have no better foundation than accidental diversities of colour, and refuses to determine without substantial evidence and incontestible fact as the basis of her judgment. And it is in order to remove these prejudices, which are the actual causes of our ignorance, that we have appealed to our friends in support of the contemplated Institution.

The Convention has not been unmindful of the operations of the American Colonization Society, and it would respectfully suggest to that august body of learning, talent, and worth, that, in our humble opinion, strengthened, too, by the opinions of eminent men in this country, as well as in Europe, that they are pursuing the direct road to perpetuate slavery, with all its unchristianlike concomitants, in this boasted land of freedom; and, as citizens and men whose best blood is sapped to gain popularity for that Institution, we would, in the most feeling manner, beg of them to desist; or, if we must be sacrificed to their philanthropy, we would rather die at home. Many of our fathers, and some of us, have fought and bled for the liberty, independence, and peace which you now enjoy and, surely, it would be ungenerous and unfeeling in you to deny us a humble and quiet grave in that country which gave us birth!

In conclusion, the Convention would remind our brethren that knowledge is power, and to that end, we call on you to sustain and support, by all honorable, energetic, and necessary means, those presses which are devoted to our instruction and elevation, to foster and encourage the mechanical arts and sciences among our brethren, to encourage simplicity, neatness, temperance, and economy in our habits, taking due care always to give preference to the production of freemen wherever it can be had. Of the utility of a General Fund, the Convention believes there can exist but one sentiment, and that is for a speedy establishment of the same. Finally, we trust our brethren will pay due care to take such measures as will ensure a general and equal representation in the next Convention.

Signed—

Belfast Burton, ⎫
Junius C. Morel, ⎬ *Publishing Committee*
William Whipper, ⎭

*The Liberator*, October 22, 1831.

## [b]

### *Appeal from Philadelphia Committee for a Manual Labor School*

The undersigned committee appointed by a general convention held in this city, to direct and assist the conventional agent, the Rev. Samuel E. Cornish, in soliciting funds for the establishment of a COLLECTIVE SCHOOL, on the Manual Labor system, beg leave to call the attention of the enlightened and benevolent citizens of Philadelphia and its vicinity to the important subject. In doing which they deem it unnecessary in this enlightened country, and at this enterprising era, to adduce arguments, or multiply words by way of appeal. The contrast between enlightened and barbarous natives, between the educated, and the vulgar, is the plainest demonstration of the utility of their plan and importance of their appeal. The colored citizens of the United States, assembled by delegation in this city, June last, alive to the interests of their brethren and community generally, resolved at whatever labor or expense to establish, and maintain an institution in which their sons of the present and future generation may obtain a classical education and the mechanic arts in general.

Believing that all who know the difficult admission of our youths into seminaries of learning, and establishments of mechanism—all who know the efficient influence of education in cultivating the heart, restraining the passions, and improving the manners—all who wish to see our colored population more prudent, virtuous, and useful will lend us their patronage, both in money and prayers. The committee, in conclusion, would respectfully state, that the amount of money required to erect buildings, secure apparatus and mechanical instruments, is $20,000; of this sum the colored people intend to contribute as largely as God has given them the ability, and for the residue they look to the Christian community, who know their wants, their oppression and wrongs—and more particularly to the inhabitants of this city, celebrated for its benevolence, and in which so many preceding steps, taken for the advancement of our oppressed people, have had their origin. They would further state, that all monies collected by the principal agent, Rev. Samuel E. Cornish, who is now in this city, and whom they recommend to the confidence of all to whom he may appeal, will be deposited in the United States Bank, subject to the order of Arthur Tappan, Esq. of New York, their generous patron and friend; and in the event of the institution not going into operation, to be faithfully returned to the several donors. The contemplated Seminary will be located at New Haven, Conn., and established on the self supporting system, so that the student may cultivate habits of industry, and obtain useful mechanical or agricultural profession, while pursuing classical studies.

Signed in behalf of the Convention by

James Forten
Joseph Cassels
Robert Douglass
Robert Purvis
Frederick A. Hinton

Provisional Committee of Philadelphia

*Hazard's Register*, September 24, 1831, VIII, pp. 195–96.

## 48

## NAT TURNER'S OWN STORY, 1831

The best known of all American Negro slave revolts was that which broke out on August 21, 1831 in Southampton county, Virginia. under the leadership of Nat

Turner. It was the climax of a three year period of great slave unrest throughout the South, and had significant repercussions upon pro- and anti-slavery thought.

In the uprising approximately sixty whites were killed, while in the suppression at least one hundred Negroes died. Thirteen slaves and three free Negroes were arrested immediately, tried and hanged. Nat Turner was not captured until October 30, and was executed—going calmly to his death, according to newspaper reports—on November 11, 1831.

An autobiographical statement made by Nat Turner while a prisoner is here reprinted:

. . . I was thirty-one years of age the second of October last, and born the property of Benjamin Turner, of this county. In my childhood a circumstance occurred which made an indelible impression on my mind, and laid the groundwork of that enthusiasm which has terminated so fatally to many, both white and black, and for which I am about to atone at the gallows. It is here necessary to relate this circumstance. Trifling as it may seem, it was the commencement of that belief which has grown with time; and even now, sir, in his dungeon, helpless and forsaken as I am, I cannot divest myself of. Being at play with other children, when three or four years old, I was telling them something, which my mother, overhearing, said it had happened before I was born. I stuck to my story, however, and related some things which went, in her opinion, to confirm it. Others being called on, were greatly astonished, knowing that these things had happened, and caused them to say, in my hearing, I surely would be a prophet, as the Lord had shown me things that had happened before my birth. And my mother and grandmother strengthened me in this my first impression, saying, in my presence, I was intended for some great purpose, which they had always thought from certain marks on my head and breast. . . .

My grandmother, who was very religious, and to whom I was much attached—my master, who belonged to the church, and other religious persons who visited the house, and whom I often saw at prayers, noticing the singularity of my manners, I suppose, and my uncommon intelligence for a child, remarked I had too much sense to be raised, and, if I was, I would never be of any service to any one as a slave. To a mind like mine, restless, inquisitive, and observant of everything that was passing, it is easy to suppose that religion was the subject to which it would be directed; and, although this subject principally occupied my thoughts, there was nothing that I saw or heard of to which my attention was not directed. The manner in which I learned to read and write, not only had great influence on my own mind, as I acquired it with the most perfect ease,—so much so, that I have no recollection whatever of learning the alphabet; but, to the astonishment of the family, one day, when a book was shown me, to keep me from crying, I began spelling the names of different objects. This was a source of wonder to all in the neighborhood, particularly the blacks—and this learning was constantly improved at all opportunities. When I got large enough to go to work, while employed I was reflecting on many things that would present themselves to my imagination; and whenever an opportunity occurred of looking at a book, when the school-children were getting their lessons, I would find many things that the fertility of my own imagination had depicted to me before. All my time, not devoted to my master's service, was spent either in prayer, or in making experiments in casting different things in moulds made of earth, in attempting to make paper, gunpowder, and many other experiments, that, although I could not perfect, yet convinced me of its practicability if I had the means.*

I was not addicted to stealing in my youth, nor have ever been; yet such was the confidence of the Negroes in the neighborhood, even at this early period of my life, in my superior judgment, that they would often carry me with them when they were going on any roguery, to plan for them. Growing up among them with this confidence in my superior judgment, and when this, in their opinions, was perfected by Divine inspiration, from the circumstances already alluded to in my infancy, and which belief was ever afterwards zealously inculcated by the austerity of my life and manners, which became the subject of remark by white and black; having soon discovered to be great, I must appear so, and therefore studiously avoided mixing in society, and wrapped myself in mystery, devoting my time to fasting and prayer.

By this time, having arrived to man's estate, and hearing the Scriptures commented on at meetings, I was struck with that particular passage which says, "Seek ye the kingdom of heaven, and all things shall be added unto you." I reflected much on this passage, and prayed daily for light on this subject. As I was praying one day at my plough, the Spirit spoke to me, saying, "Seek ye the kingdom of heaven, and all things shall be added unto you." *Question.* "What do you mean by the Spirit?" *Answer.* "The Spirit that spoke to the prophets in former days,"—and I was greatly astonished, and for two years prayed continually, whenever my duty would permit; and then again I had the same revelation, which fully confirmed me in the impression that I was ordained for some great purpose in the hands of the Almighty. Several years rolled round, in which many events occurred to strengthen me in this my belief. At this time I reverted in my mind to the remarks made of me in my childhood, and the things that had been shown me; and as it had been said of me in my childhood, by those by whom I had

* When questioned as to the manner of manufacturing those different articles, he was found well informed. [Footnote in original.]

been taught to pray, both white and black, and in whom I had the greatest confidence, that I had too much sense to be raised, and if I was I would never be of any use to any one as a slave; now, finding I had arrived to man's estate, and was a slave, and these revelations being made known to me, I began to direct my attention to this great object, to fulfil the purpose for which, by this time, I felt assured I was intended. Knowing the influence I had obtained over the minds of my fellow-servants—(not by the means of conjuring and such-like tricks—for to them I always spoke of such things with contempt), but by the communion of the Spirit, whose revelations I often communicated to them, and they believed and said my wisdom came from God,—I now began to prepare them for my purpose, by telling them something was about to happen that would terminate in fulfilling the great promise that had been made to me.

About this time I was placed under an overseer, from whom I ran away, and after remaining in the woods thirty days, I returned, to the astonishment of the Negroes on the plantation, who thought I had made my escape to some other part of the country, as my father had done before. But the reason of my return was, that the Spirit appeared to me and said I had my wishes directed to the things of this world, and not to the kingdom of heaven, and that I should return to the service of my earthly master—"For he who knoweth his Master's will, and doeth it not, shall be beaten with many stripes, and thus have I chastened you." And the Negroes found fault, and murmured against me, saying that if they had my sense they would not serve any master in the world. And about this time I had a vision—and I saw white spirits and black spirits engaged in battle, and the sun was darkened—the thunder rolled in the heavens, and blood flowed in streams—and I heard a voice saying, "Such is your luck, such you are called to see; and let it come rough or smooth, you must surely bear it."

I now withdrew myself as much as my situation would permit from the intercourse of my fellow-servants, for the avowed purpose of serving the Spirit more fully; and it appeared to me, and reminded me of the things it had already shown me, and that it would then reveal to me the knowledge of the elements, the revolution of the planets, the operation of tides, and changes of the seasons. After this revelation in the year 1825, and the knowledge of the elements being made known to me, I sought more than ever to obtain true holiness before the great day of judgment should appear, and then I began to receive the true knowledge of faith. And from the first steps of righteousness until the last, was I made perfect; and the Holy Ghost was with me, and said, "Behold me as I stand in the heavens." And I looked and saw the forms of men in different attitudes; and there were lights in the sky, to which the children of darkness gave other names than what they really were; for they were the lights of the Saviour's hands, stretched forth from east to west, even as they were extended on the cross on Calvary for the redemption of sinners. And I wondered greatly at these miracles, and prayed to be informed of a certainty of the meaning thereof; and shortly afterwards, while laboring in the field, I discovered drops of blood on the corn, as though it were dew from heaven; and I communicated it to many, both white and black, in the neighborhood—and I then found on the leaves in the woods hieroglyphic characters and numbers, with the forms of men in different attitudes, portrayed in blood, and representing the figures I had seen before in the heavens. And now the Holy Ghost had revealed itself to me, and made plain the miracles it had shown me; for as the blood of Christ had been shed on this earth, and had ascended to heaven for the salvation of sinners, and was now returning to earth again in the form of dew,—and as the leaves on the trees bore the impression of the figures I had seen in the heavens,—it was plain to me that the Saviour was about to lay down the yoke he had borne for the sins of men, and the great day of judgment was at hand.

About this time I told these things to a white man (Etheldred T. Brantley), on whom it had a wonderful effect; and he ceased from his wickedness, and was attacked immediately with a cutaneous eruption, and blood oozed from the pores of his skin, and after praying and fasting nine days he was healed. And the Spirit appeared to me again, and said, as the Saviour had been baptized, so should we be also; and when the white people would not let us be baptized by the church, we went down into the water together, in the sight of many who reviled us, and were baptized by the Spirit. After this I rejoiced greatly, and gave thanks to God. And on the 12th of May, 1828, I heard a loud noise in the heavens, and the Spirit instantly appeared to me and said the Serpent was loosened, and Christ had laid down the yoke he had borne for the sins of men, and that I should take it on and fight against the Serpent, for the time was fast approaching when the first should be last and the last should be first. *Ques.* "Do you not find yourself mistaken now?"—*Ans.* "Was not Christ crucified?" And by signs in the heavens that it would make known to me when I should commence the great work, and until the first sign appeared I should conceal it from the knowledge of men; and on the appearance of the sign (the eclipse of the sun, last February *), I should arise and prepare myself, and slay my enemies with their own weapons. And immediately on the sign appearing in the heavens, the seal was removed from my lips, and I communicated the great work laid out for me to do, to four in whom I had the greatest confidence (Henry, Hark, Nelson, and Sam). It was intended by us to have begun the work of death on the

* An event which caused much alarm throughout the nation.

4th of July last. Many were the plans formed and rejected by us, and it affected my mind to such a degree that I fell sick, and the time passed without our coming to any determination how to commence—still forming new schemes and rejecting them, when the sign appeared again, which determined me not to wait longer.

Since the commencement of 1830 I had been living with Mr. Joseph Travis, who was to me a kind master, and placed the greatest confidence in me; in fact, I had no cause to complain of his treatment to me. On Saturday evening, the 20th of August, it was agreed between Henry, Hark, and myself, to prepare a dinner the next day for the men we expected, and then to concert a plan, as we had not yet determined on any. Hark, on the following morning, brought a pig, and Henry brandy; and being joined by Sam, Nelson, Will, and Jack, they prepared in the woods a dinner, where, about three o'clock, I joined them.

*Q.* Why were you so backward in joining them?

*A.* The same reason that had caused me not to mix with them years before,

I saluted them on coming up, and asked Will how came he there. He answered, his life was worth no more than others, and his liberty as dear to him. I asked him if he thought to obtain it. He said he would, or lose his life. This was enough to put him in full confidence. Jack, I knew, was only a tool in the hands of Hark. It was quickly agreed we should commence at home (Mr. J. Travis') on that night; and until we had armed and equipped ourselves, and gathered sufficient force, neither age nor sex was to be spared— which was invariably adhered to. We remained at the feast until about two hours in the night, when we went to the house and found Austin. . . .

I took my station in the rear, and, as it was my object to carry terror and devastation wherever we went, I placed fifteen or twenty of the best armed and most to be relied on in front, who generally approached the houses as fast as their horses could run. This was for two purposes—to prevent their escape, and strike terror to the inhabitants; on this account I never got to the houses, after leaving Mrs. Whitehead's, until the murders were committed, except in one case. I sometimes got in sight in time to see the work of death completed; viewed the mangled bodies as they lay, in silent satisfaction, and immediately started in quest of other victims. Having murdered Mrs. Waller and ten children, we started for Mr. Wm. Williams',—having killed him and two little boys that were there; while engaged in this, Mrs. Williams fled and got some distance from the house, but she was pursued, overtaken, and compelled to get up behind one of the company, who brought her back, and, after showing her the mangled body of her lifeless husband, she was told to get down and lay by his side, where she was shot dead.

The white men pursued and fired on us several times. Hark had his horse shot under him, and I caught another for him as it was running by me; five or six of my men were wounded, but none left on the field. Finding myself defeated here, I instantly determined to go through a private way, and cross the Nottoway River at the Cypress Bridge, three miles below Jerusalem, and attack that place in the rear, as I expected they would look for me on the other road, and I had a great desire to get there to procure arms and ammunition. After going a short distance in this private way, accompanied by about twenty men, I overtook two or three, who told me the others were dispersed in every direction.

On this, I gave up all hope for the present; and on Thursday night, after having supplied myself with provisions from Mr. Travis', I scratched a hole under a pile of fence-rails in a field, where I concealed myself for six weeks, never leaving my hiding-place but for a few minutes in the dead of the night to get water, which was very near. Thinking by this time I could venture out, I began to go about in the night, and eavesdrop the houses in the neighborhood; pursuing this course for about a fortnight, and gathering little or no intelligence, afraid of speaking to any human being, and returning every morning to my cave before the dawn of day. I know not how long I might have led this life, if accident had not betrayed me. A dog in the neighborhood passing by my hiding-place one night while I was out, was attracted by some meat I had in my cave, and crawled in and stole it, and was coming out just as I returned. A few nights after, two Negroes having started to go hunting with the same dog, and passed that way, the dog came again to the place, and having just gone out to walk about, discovered me and barked; on which, thinking myself discovered, I spoke to them to beg concealment. On making myself known, they fled from me. Knowing then they would betray me, I immediately left my hiding-place, and was pursued almost incessantly, until I was taken, a fortnight afterwards, by Mr. Benjamin Phipps, in a little hole I had dug out with my sword, for the purpose of concealment, under the top of a fallen tree.

During the time I was pursued, I had many hair-breadth escapes, which your time will not permit you to relate. I am here loaded with chains, and willing to suffer the fate that awaits me.

Thomas R. Gray, [ed.,] *The Confessions of Nat Turner, the leader of the late insurrection in Southampton* [County], *Va.* . . . (Baltimore, 1831). Copy in Virginia State Library, Richmond.

49

## A NEGRO LIBERATOR, 1831

Some free Negroes devoted much of their lives and earnings to buying and then freeing other Negroes. Outstanding in this regard were women like Aletheia Turner and Jane Minor and men like John C. Stanly and John Updike. Indicative of this process is the manumission paper of one Rhueben Rhenalds as prepared by Updike in November, 1831:

Know all men by these presents that I John Updike (a free man of color) of the town of Petersburg in the State of Virginia have manumitted, emancipated, and set free, and do by these presents manumit, emancipate, and set free a certain Negro man named Rheuben Rhenalds, lately purchased by me from Shadrach Brander, so that the said Rheuben Rhenalds shall be and remain free from this time henceforth forever. In testimony whereof, I have hereto set my hand and affixed my seal and delivered to the said Rheuben Rhenalds this his deed of emancipation this 17th day of November, one thousand eight hundred and thirty-one.

Luther P. Jackson, ed., "Manumission Papers of Petersburg, Virginia" in *The Journal of Negro History*, XIII (1928), p. 534.

50

## THE NEGROES OF PHILADELPHIA SPEAK, 1832

A proposal of discriminatory legislation in Pennsylvania led many Philadelphia Negroes, under James Forten, William Whipper and Robert Purvis, to assemble and draft a petition of protest together with a factual appendix on the condition of the free Negro in that state. The meeting occurred and the petition was presented in January, 1832:

*To the Honorable the Senate and House of Representatives of the Commonwealth of Pennsylvania:*
 The memorial of the people of color of the city of Philadelphia and its vicinity, respectfully showeth:
 That they have learned with deep regret that two resolutions have passed the House of Representatives of this commonwealth, directing the committee of the judiciary to inquire—First, into the expediency of passing a law

to protect the citizens of this commonwealth against the evils arising from the emigration of free blacks from other states into Pennsylvania—and, secondly, into the expediency of repealing so much of the Acts of Assembly passed on the 27th of March, 1820, and the 25th of March, 1826, as relates to fugitives from labor from other states, and of giving full effect to the act of Congress of the 12th of February, 1793, relative to such fugitives.

At the same time that your memorialists entertain the most perfect respect for any expression of sentiment emanating from so high a source as one of the legislative bodies of Pennsylvania, they cannot but lament, that at a moment when all mankind seem to be struggling for freedom, and endeavoring to throw off the shackles of political oppression, the constituted authorities of this great state should entertain a resolution which has a tendency to abridge the liberties heretofore accorded to a race of men confessedly oppressed. Our country asserts for itself the glory of being the freest upon the surface of the globe. She wrested that freedom, while yet in her infancy, by force of arms, at the expense of infinite blood and treasure, from a gigantic and most powerful adversary. She proclaimed freedom to all mankind—and offered her soil as a refuge to the enslaved of all nations. The brightness of her glory was radiant, but one dark spot still dimmed its lustre. Domestic slavery existed among a people who had themselves disdained to submit to a master. Many of the states of this union hastened to wipe out this blot: and foremost in the race was Pennsylvania. In less than four years after the declaration of independence by the act of 1st March, 1780, she abolished slavery within her limits, and from that time her avowed policy has been to enlarge and beautify this splendid feature in her system—to preserve unimpaired the freedom of all men, whatever might be the shade of complexion with which it may have pleased the *Almighty* to distinguish them. *"All men,"* says our declaration of *rights*, "are born equally free and independent"—and "have certain inherent and indefeasible rights, among which are those of enjoying and defending life and liberty, of acquiring and protecting property and reputation; and of pursuing their own happiness." *"All men* have a natural and indefeasible right to worship Almighty God according to the dictates of their own conscience." "The people shall be secure in their persons, houses and possessions, from unreasonable searches and seizures. No person shall be proceeded against criminally by information. No person shall be put twice in jeopardy of life or limb. Every man shall have a remedy of due course of law." Where, in this forcible epitome of man's indefeasible rights, promulgated nine years after the African had been elevated to freedom—where, in this declaration of the people of this commonwealth, assembled in convention, do we find a distinction drawn between the man whose skin is white, and him whose skin is dark? Where, in the legislative acts of this commonwealth, under the constitution, and subsequent to this declaration, do we find such a distinction? On what page of our statute book does it appear? It is confidently asserted that in Pennsylvania it does not exist—and has been repudiated and banished from her code. "It is not for us to enquire," says the beautiful preamble to the act of 1780, "it is not for us to enquire, why, in the creation of mankind, the inhabitants of the several parts of the earth were distinguished by a difference in feature or complexion—it is sufficient for us to know that all are the work of an Almighty hand." And from that day to the present, Pennsylvania has acted upon a principle, that among those whom the same Almighty hand has formed, the hand of man should not presume to make a difference. And why, we respectfully ask, is this distinction now to be proclaimed for the first time in the code of Pennsylvania? Why are her borders to be surrounded by a wall of iron, against freemen, whose complexions fall below the wavering and uncertain shades of white? For this is the only criterion of admission or exclusion which the resolutions indicate. It is not to be asked, is he brave—is he honest—is he just—is he free from the stain of crime—but is he black—is he brown—is he yellow— is he other than white?

This is the criterion by which Pennsylvania, who for fifty years has indignantly rejected the distinction, who daily receives into her bosom all men, from all nations, is now called upon to reject from her soil, such portions of a banished race of freemen, born within view of her own mountains, as may seek within her limits a place of rest. We respectfully ask, is not this the spirit of the first resolution? And why, we repeat, shall this abandonment of the principles of your honorable forefathers *now* first take place in Pennsylvania? Have the rights we now possess been abused? The domestic history of Pennsylvania answers these questions in the negative. Who can turn to the page in that history which exhibits a single instance of insurrection or violation of the peace of society, resulting from the residence of a colored population in this commonwealth. The story of *their* wrongs may be read in the most eloquent productions of our *law givers*. The story of the injuries which the people of Pennsylvania have sustained from *them,* cannot be found because it does not exist. Your memorialists are aware that prejudice has recently been exalted against them by unfounded reports of their concurrence in promoting servile insurrections. With the feeling of honest indignation, inspired by conscious innocence, they repel the slander. They feel themselves to be citizens of Pennsylvania. Many of them were descended from ancestors, who were raised with yours on this soil, to which they feel bound by the strongest ties. As children of the state, they look to it as a guardian and a protector, and in common with you feel the necessity of maintaining law and order, for the promotion of the common-weal. Equally unfounded is the charge, that this population fills the alms-houses with paupers—and increases, in an undue proportion, the public burdens. We appeal to the facts and documents which accompany this memorial, as giving abundant refutation to an error so injurious to our character.

Unsupportable as your memorialists conceive the first resolution to be, the second, which proposes the repeal of so much of the laws of 1820 and 1826, as relates to fugitives from labor, is still more abhorrent to their feelings. What, let us ask, is the substance of these portions of the acts in question? Simply to take from aldermen and justices of the peace, the power of de-ciding upon the liberty or slavery of a man. The power is still reserved to them to issue a warrant, and cause the arrest of a suspected fugitive from labor. But the determination of his fate, a question almost as momentous as that of life or death, is referred to the intelligence and discretion of judges. And is this a defect in our laws? Is it a defect, that before a man, a husband, a father, shall be torn from the bosom of his family and consigned to chains—and doomed to hopeless slavery, he shall be heard before a judge? Is this provision of our laws a stain upon our statute book? Rather let us ask, was it not derogatory to the character of the commonwealth of Pennsylvania, that she should ever have prized liberty so lightly, as to per-mit officers, whom to this day she does not suffer to pass upon matters of property beyond one hundred dollars, (and even then subject to the right of appeal,) whose powers were formerly limited to one fifth of that sum—to decide by their voice the permanent and irrevocable fate of a human being? Now that this enormity has ceased to overshadow the land, we can scarcely credit that it ever existed. We can with difficulty persuade ourselves to be-lieve that in this free and powerful state, it ever could have been, that a man should be seized without a warrant, dragged to the office of any magistrate whom the oppressor might choose to select—and from thence, at his bidding, be consigned to slavery—such was the law—such, we earnestly pray, may it never be again. Pennsylvania has revolted from the flagrant injustice. She has taken one step in advance. She has said, a justice of the peace shall not pass upon the liberty of a man; a justice of the peace shall not bear a freeholder from his house, a father from his family. No authority less than that of a judge shall inflict this blow. And is this not enough? Is it not enough that there are more than one hundred individuals in this com-monwealth, the single voice of any one of whom is competent to decide the fate of a human being? Can the most hardened trafficker in human agony desire or demand more than this? Is it not, we respectfully ask, far too great a concession to the spirit of slavery, that we should suffer even our judges to officiate as the instruments for the assertion of her claims? Compare the condition of a judge in this commonwealth, with that of a judge of the very nation from which we have wrested our own liberties. Let a man of the deepest jet be brought before him, and it is the glorious prerogative of that judge to exclaim, "Your feet are on English soil—therefore you are free!"

While here, in this republican land, which has again and again proclaimed the equality of rights of all men, the judge, the American judge, the Pennsylvania judge, himself a freeman, is bound by our laws, tied down hand and foot, obliged to stifle the beatings of his own heart, to keep down his own indignant spirit, and sentence a fellow being to chains and to the lash. Is not this a sufficient sacrifice at the altar of slavery? Would it not be just, is it not due to the honor of the state, do not the constitution of the state and the declaration of rights demand, that instead of the retrograde step now proposed, another be made in *advance,* and that the decision *of a jury* should be required upon so high a question as the liberty of a man? We respectfully submit it to your honorable bodies, that if the authorities of this state are to be employed in such unhappy matters they should be obliged to call to their aid the same means of attaining to a rightful decision, as are secured to us in all other transactions of life, *a jury of twelve men*— and why should this not be? Should the most elevated individual in this community demand of the humblest and lowliest black man, five hundred and thirty-four cents, that humble and lowly man may place his cause under the protection of a jury. Then shall he be denied this privilege, when that which is dearer to him than his life, is demanded by his adversary? Your memorialists do not ask you to interfere with those rights of property which are claimed under the constitution, by our fellow citizens of other states. They simply and most respectfully ask, that if the aid of the officers of this commonwealth be invoked, if the judiciary of this state be called upon to enforce what is termed the right of property in human beings, that they shall be permitted to lend their aid only under such checks and guards, as are consistent with the feelings of this state, with the spirit and letter of her constitution, and with the whole tenor of our code of laws.

In conclusion, your memorialists most earnestly pray, for the sake of humanity, for the honor of the community, in the name of freedom, they most earnestly pray, that your honorable bodies will reject, if offered for your adoption, any measures such as those which appear to be contemplated by the resolutions referred. And your memorialists will ever pray, &c

Signed in behalf of a numerous meeting of the people of color, held in the city of Philadelphia, on the —— day of January, 1832.

William Whipper, ⎱ *Secretaries.*                    JAMES FORTEN, *Chairman*
Robert Purvis,   ⎰

In connexion with the foregoing memorial, we beg leave to offer the following statement of facts for the information of all who desire to be correctly informed on the subjects to which they relate.

1. By a statement published by order of the guardians of the poor in 1832, it appears that out of 549 outdoor poor relieved during the year, only 22 were persons of color, being about 4 per cent of the whole number, while their ratio of the population of the city and suburbs exceeds 8¼ per cent. By a note appended to the printed report of the guardians of the poor, above referred to, it appears that the colored paupers admitted into the almshouse for the same period, did not exceed 4 per cent of the whole number.

2. In consequence of the neglect of the assessors, to distinguish, in their assessment, the property of people of color from that of others, it is not easy to ascertain the exact amount of taxes paid by us. But an attempt has been made to remedy this defect by a reference to receipts kept by tax-payers. The result thus obtained must necessarily be deficient, and fall short of the amount really paid by people of color; because it is fair to presume that we could not find receipts for all the money paid in taxes, and because no returns have been made except where receipts were found. From these imperfect returns, however, it is ascertained that we pay not less than 2500 dollars annually, while the sum expended for the relief of our poor, out of the public funds has rarely, if ever, exceeded $2000 a year. The amount of rents paid by our people, is found to exceed $100,000 annually.

3. Many of us, by our labor and industry have acquired a little property; and have become freeholders. Besides which, we have no less than six Methodist meeting houses, two Presbyterian, two Baptist, one Episcopalean, and one public hall, owned exclusively by our people, the value of which, in the aggregate, is estimated to exceed $100,000. To these may be added, two Sunday schools, two tract societies, two Bible societies, two temperance societies, and one female literary institution.

4. We have among ourselves, more than fifty beneficent societies, some of which are incorporated, for mutual aid in time of sickness and distress. The members of these societies are bound by rules and regulations, which tend to promote industry and morality among them. For any disregard or violation of these rules,—for intemperance or immorality of any kind, the

members are liable to be suspended or expelled. These societies expend annually for the relief of their members when sick or disabled, or in distress, upwards of $7000, out of funds raised among themselves for mutual aid. It is also worthy of remark, that we cannot find a single instance of one of the members of either of these societies being convicted in any of our courts. One instance only has occurred of a member being brought up and accused before a court; but this individual was acquitted.

5. Notwithstanding the difficulty of getting places for our sons as apprentices, to learn mechanical trades, owing to the prejudices with which we have to contend, there are between four and five hundred people of color in the city and suburbs who follow mechanical employments.

6. While we thankfully embrace the opportunity for schooling our children, which has been opened to us by public munificence and private benevolence, we are still desirous to do our part in the accomplishment of so desirable an object. Such of us as are of ability to do so, send our children to school at our own expense. Knowing by experience the disadvantages many of us labor under for want of early instruction; we are anxious to give our children a suitable education to fit them for the duties and enjoyments of life. In making the above statement of facts, our only object is, to prevent a misconception of our real condition; and to counteract those unjust prejudices against us, which the prevalence of erroneous opinions in regard to us, is calculated to produce.

We know that the most effectual method of refuting, and rendering harmless, false and exaggerated accounts of our degraded condition, is by our conduct; by living consistent, orderly and moral lives. Yet we are convinced that many good and humane citizens of this commonwealth, have been imposed upon, and induced to give credit to statements injurious to our general character and standing. At this important crisis, pregnant with great events, we deem it a duty we owe to ourselves and to our white friends, and to the public in general, to present to their candid and impartial consideration, the above statements. We ask only to be judged fairly and impartially. We claim no exemption from the frailties and imperfections of our common nature. We feel that we are men of like passions and feelings with others of a different color, liable to be drawn aside by temptation, from the paths of rectitude. But we think that in the aggregate we will not suffer by a comparison with our white neighbors whose opportunities of improvement have been no greater than ours. By such a comparison, fairly and impartially made, we are willing to be judged.

We have been careful in our exhibit of facts, to produce nothing but what may be sustained by legal evidence; by which we mean such facts as are susceptible of proof in a court of law. We have submitted our statements, with the sources whence they are drawn, to some of the intelligent citizens of Philadelphia who can testify to their substantial accuracy.

All of which is respectfully submitted to a candid public.

*The Liberator,* April 14, 1832, for the memorial and *Hazard's Register,* June, 1832, IX, pp. 361–62 for the appendix.

51

## SECOND ANNUAL NATIONAL NEGRO CONVENTION, 1832

The second annual Negro convention was again held in Philadelphia, June 4–13, 1832. This time there were twenty-nine delegates from eight states; Maryland, Delaware, New Jersey, Pennsylvania, New York, Connecticut, Rhode Island and Massachusetts. The convention resolved to raise money for Negro refugees in Canada, to form Negro temperance societies, to boycott slave-made products, to petition state and national legislatures against slavery and discrimination, to employ a Negro lecturer on the question of Negro rights, and to continue the efforts for an industrial school. It arranged and heard a debate on colonization between Garrison and the Rev. R. R. Gurley, secretary of the American Colonization Society, as a result of which was reaffirmed the Negro people's opposition to emigration schemes. Henry Sipkins and Philip A. Bell of New York, were the President and Secretary, respectively, of this Convention.

*To The Free Colored Inhabitants of these United States:*
Fellow Citizens:

We have again been permitted to associate in our representative character, from the different sections of this Union, to pour into one common stream the afflictions, the prayers, and sympathies of our oppressed people; the axis of time has brought around this glorious, annual event. And we are again brought to rejoice that the wisdom of Divine Providence has protected us during a year, whose autumnal harvest, has been a reign of terror and persecution; and whose winter has almost frozen the streams of humanity, by its frigid legislation. It is under the influence of times and feelings like these we now address you. Of a people situated as we are, little can be said, except that it becomes our duty, strictly to watch those causes that operate against our interests and privileges; and to guard against whatever measures will either lower us in the scale of being, or perpetuate our degradation in the eyes of the civilized world.

The effects of Slavery on the bond, and Colonization on the free: Of the first we shall say but little, but will here repeat the language of a high minded Virginian in the Legislature of that state, on the recent discussion of the slave question before that honourable body, who declared, that man could not hold property in man and that the master had no right to the slave, either by a law of nature or a patent from God, but by the will of society; which we declare to be an unjust usurpation of the rights and privileges of men.

But how beautiful must the prospect be to the philanthropist, to view us, the children of persecution, grown to manhood, associating in our delegated character, to devise plans and means for our moral elevation, and attracting the attention of the wise and good, over the whole country, who are anxiously watching our deliberations!

We have here to inform you, that we have patiently listened to the able and eloquent arguments produced by the Rev. R. R. Gurley, Secretary of the American Colonization Society, in behalf of the doings of said Society, and William Lloyd Garrison, Esq., in opposition to its action.

A more favourable opportunity to arrive at truth seldom has been witnessed, but while we admire the distinguished piety and christian feelings, with which he so solemnly portrayed the doctrines of that institution; we do now assert that the result of the same, has tended more deeply to rivet our solid conviction, that the doctrines of said Society, are at enmity with the principles and precepts of religion, humanity and justice, and should be regarded by every man of color in these United States, as an evil for magnitude, unexcelled, and whose doctrines aim at the entire extinction of the free colored population and the riveting of Slavery.

We might here repeat our protest against that institution, but it is unnecessary, your views and sentiments have long since gone to the world, the wings of the wind have borne your disapprobation to that institution. Time itself cannot erase it. You have dated your opposition from its beginning, and your views are strengthened by time and circumstances, and they hold the uppermost seat in your affections. We have not been unmindful of the compulsory laws which caused our brethren in Ohio, to seek new homes in a distant land, there, to share and suffer all the inconveniences of exiles in an uncultivated region, which has led us to admire the benevolent feelings of a rival government in its liberal protection to strangers, which has induced us to recommend to you, to exercise your best endeavors to collect monies to secure the purchase of lands in the Canadas, for those who may by oppressive legislative enactments, be obliged to move thither.

In contributing to our brethren that aid which will secure them a refuge in a storm, we would not wish to be understood, as possessing inclination to remove, nor in the least to impoverish that noble sentiment which we rejoice in, exclaiming—

This is *Our* own,

Our native land.

All that we have done, humanity dictated it, neither inclination nor alienated feelings to our country prescribed it, but that power which is above all other considerations, viz: The law of necessity.

We yet anticipate in the moral strength of this nation, a final redemption from those evils that have been illegitimately entailed on us as a people. We yet expect by due exertions on our part, together with the aid of the benevolent philanthropists of our country, to acquire a moral and intellectual strength, that will unshaft the calumnious darts of our adversaries, and present to the world a general character, that they will feel bound to respect and admire.

It will be seen by a reference to our proceedings, that we have again recommended the further prosecution of the contemplated college, proposed by the last convention, to be established at New Haven, under the rules and regulations then established. A place for its location will be selected in a climate and neighborhood, where its inhabitants are less prejudiced to our rights and privileges. The proceedings of the citizens of New Haven with regard to the erection of the college, were a disgrace to themselves, and cast a stigma on the reputed fame of New England and the country. We are unwilling that the character of the whole country shall sink by the proceedings of a few. We are determined to present to another portion of the country not far distant, and at no very remote period, the opportunity of gaining for them the character of a truly philanthropic spirit, and of retrieving the character of the country, by the disreputable proceedings of New Haven. We must have Colleges and high Schools on the Manual Labor system, where our youth may be instructed in all the arts of civilized life. If we ever expect to see the influence of prejudice decrease, and ourselves respected, it must be by the blessings of an enlightened education. It must be by being in possession of that classical knowledge which promotes genius, and causes man to soar up to those high intellectual enjoyments and acquirements, which places him in a situation, to shed upon a country and a people, that scientific grandeur which is imperishable by time, and drowns in oblivion's cup their moral degradation. Those who think that our primary schools are capable of effecting this, are a century behind the age, when to have proved a question in the rule of three, was considered a higher attainment, than solving the most difficult problem in Euclid is now. They might have at that time performed, what some people expect of them now, in the then barren state of science, but they are now no longer capable of reflecting brilliancy on our national character which will elevate us from our present situation. If we wish to be respected we must build our moral character, on a base as broad and high as the nation itself—our country and our character demand it—we have performed all the duties from the menial to the soldier—our fathers shed their blood in the great struggle for independence. In the late war between Great Britain and the United States, a proclamation was issued to the free colored inhabitants of Louisiana, September 21st, 1814, inviting them to take up arms in defence of their country, by Gen. Andrew Jackson. And in order that you may have an idea of the manner in which they acquitted themselves on that perilous occasion, we will refer you to the proclamation of Thomas Butler, Aid-de-Camp.*

You there see that your country expects much from you and that you have much to call you into action, morally, religiously and scientifically. Prepare yourselves to occupy the several stations to which the wisdom of your country may promote you. We have been told in this Convention, by the Secretary of the American Colonization Society, that there are causes which forbid our advancement in this country, which no humanity, no legislation and no religion can control. Believe it not. Is not humanity susceptible of all the tender feelings of benevolence? Is not legislation supreme—and is not religion virtuous? Our oppressed situation arises from their opposite causes. There is an awakening spirit in our people to promote their elevation, which speaks volumes in their behalf. We anticipated at the close of the last Convention, a larger representation and an increased number of delegates; we were not deceived, the number has been ten fold. And we have a right to expect that future Conventions will be increased by a geometrical ratio; until we shall present a body, not inferior in numbers to our state legislature, and the *phenomena* of an *oppressed people*, deprived of the rights of citizenship, in the midst of an enlightened nation, devising plans and measures for their personal and mental elevation, by *moral suasion alone.*

In recommending you a path to pursue, for our present good and future elevation, we have taken into consideration the circumstances of the free colored population, so far as it was possible to ascertain their views and sentiments, hoping that at a future Convention, you will all come ably represented, and that your wishes and views may receive that deliberation and attention, for which this body is particularly associated.

Finally—Before taking our leave, we would admonish you, by all that you hold dear, beware of that bewitching evil, that bane of society, that curse of the world, that fell destroyer of the best prospects and the last hope of civilized man,—INTEMPERANCE.

Be righteous, be honest, be just, be economical, be prudent, offend not

* The statements referred to may be found most conveniently in C. G. Woodson, *The Negro in Our History* (Washington, 1941), pp. 200–02.

the laws of your country—in a word, live in that purity of life, by both precept and example—live in the constant pursuit of that moral and intellectual strength, which will invigorate your understandings, and render you illustrious in the eyes of civilized nations, when they will assert, that all that illustrious worth, which was once possessed by the Egyptians, and slept for ages, has now arisen in their descendants, the inhabitants of the new world.

*The Liberator*, September 22, 1832.

## 52

## THE AMERICAN NEGRO'S FOURTH OF JULY, 1832

About ten per cent of the American people did not officially celebrate the Fourth of July until after the Emancipation Proclamation. The Negro population held an observance, rather, on July 5 and used the occasion to reiterate their demand for equality. Typical is the address of a leading Connecticut Negro, Peter Osborne, delivered July 5, 1832, in the New Haven African Church.

Fellow-Citizens—On account of the misfortune of our color, our fourth of July comes on the fifth; but I hope and trust that when the Declaration of Independence is fully executed, which declares that all men, without respect to person, were born free and equal, we may then have our fourth of July on the fourth. It is thought by many that this is impossible to take place, as it is for the leopard to change his spots; but I anticipate that the time is approaching very fast. The signs in the north, the signs in the south, in the east and west, are all favorable to our cause. Why, then, should we forbear contending for the civil rights of free country-men? What man of national feeling would slumber in content under the yoke of slavery and oppression, in his own country? Not the most degraded barbarian in the interior of Africa.

If we desire to see our brethren relieved from the tyrannical yoke of slavery and oppression in the south, if we would enjoy the civil rights of free countrymen, it is high time for us to be up and doing. It has been said that we have already done well, but we can do better. What more can we do? Why, we must unite with our brethren in the north, in the south, and in the east and west, and then with the Declaration of Independence in one hand, and the Holy Bible in the other, I think we might courageously give battle to the most powerful enemy to this cause. The Declaration of Independence has declared to man, without speaking of color, that all men are born free and equal. Has it not declared this freedom and equality to us too?

What man would content himself, and say nothing of the rights of man, with two millions of his brethren in bondage? Let us contend for the prize. Let us all unite, and with one accord declare that we will not leave our own country to emigrate to Liberia, nor elsewhere, to be civilized nor christianized. Let us make it known to America that we are not barbarians; that we are not inhuman beings; that this is our native country; that our forefathers have planted trees in America for us, and we intend to stay and eat the fruit. Our forefathers fought, bled and died to achieve the independence of the United States. Why should we forbear contending for the prize? It becomes every colored citizen in the United States to step forward boldly, and gallantly defend his rights. What has there been done within a few years, since the union of the colored people? Are not the times more favorable to us now, than they were ten years ago? Are we not gaining ground? Yes—and had we begun this work forty years ago, I do not hesitate to say that there would not have been, at this day, a slave in the United States. Take, courage, then, ye Afric-Americans! Don't give up the conflict, for the glorious prize can be won.

*The Liberator,* December 1, 1832.

# 53

# A NEGRO LIBRARY IS FOUNDED, 1833

Among the numerous types of organizations formed by Negroes themselves because of the Jim Crow social pattern were library societies. Leading in this regard was the Philadelphia Negro library formed in February, 1833, by such men as Robert Purvis, James Needham, Frederick A. Hinton, Thomas Butler and William S. Gordon.

We, the people of color of this city, being deeply impressed with the necessity of promoting among our rising youth, a proper cultivation for literary pursuits and the improvement of the faculties and powers of their minds, deem it necessary to state for the information of our friends wherever situated, that we have succeeding in organizing an institution under the title of "the Philadelphia Library Company of Colored persons."

It will be perceived that this is not a mere fractional effort, the design of any single society among us, of which we are proud it can with truth be said there are many, all having originated for our mutual benefit and improvement; neither is it sectarian, but its features are such as to embrace the entire population of the City of Philadelphia, as its name imports.

In accordance with which we most respectfully appeal to the friends of science and of the people of color, for such books or other donations as will facilitate the object of this institution.

*Hazard's Register* (Phila.), March 16, 1833, XI, p. 186 (page is numbered incorrectly in original; it should be 176).

## 54

## A NEGRO CARRIES THE ABOLITIONISTS' MESSAGE TO EUROPE, 1833

Negro refugees from Cincinnati settled near London, Ontario in 1830 and named their community Wilberforce in honor of the English Abolitionist (see footnote to document 42b). In 1832 these men and women appointed the Rev. Nathaniel Paul, Negro Abolitionist and friend of Garrison, as their agent in England to raise money for them. While abroad, Paul did effective anti-slavery work as this letter to Garrison, dated Bristol, England, April 10, 1833, suggests:

Having an opportunity of sending to America, I improve it in writing you a few lines. I have much to say, and I hardly know what to say first; but I will begin with that subject which, next to the salvation of the soul, I know lies nearest your heart—viz. the liberation of the helpless slave, and the elevation of the people of color from that state of degradation that they have so long been in. . . .

I have been engaged, for several months past, in travelling through the country and delivering lectures upon the system of slavery as it exists in the United States, the condition of the free people of color in that country, and the importance of promoting the cause of education and religion generally among the colored people. My lectures have been numerously attended by from two to three thousand people, the Halls and Chapels have been over-flown, and hundreds have not been able to obtain admittance. I have not failed to give Uncle Sam due credit for his 2,000,000 slaves; nor to expose the cruel prejudices of the Americans to our colored race; nor to fairly exhibit the hypocrisy of the Colonization Society, to the astonishment of the people here. And is this, they say, republican liberty? God deliver us from it.

And now, to contrast the difference in the treatment that a colored man receives in this country, with that which he receives in America, my soul is filled with sorrow and indignation. I could weep over the land of my

nativity! I would ask those hypocritical pretenders to humanity and religion, who are continually crying out, "What shall we do with our black
and colored people?" Why do ye not do them justice? What! are you better
than Englishmen? Admit them to equal rights with yourselves; this is all
that they ask, this is all that is needful to be done. What hinders you from
doing this? Is it any thing but the pride of your hearts? Here, if I go to
church, I am not pointed to the "Negro seat" in the gallery; but any gentleman opens his pew door for my reception. If I wish for a passage in a stage,
the only question that is asked me is, "Which do you choose, sir, an inside
or an outside seat?" If I stop at a public inn, no one would ever think here
of setting a separate table for me; I am conducted to the same table with
other gentlemen. The only difference that I have ever discovered is this, I
am generally taken for a stranger, and they therefore seem anxious to pay
me the greater respect.

I have had the pleasure of breakfasting twice with the venerable
[William] Wilberforce, and have now a letter in my pocket that I received from him, a few weeks since, which I would not take pounds for.
Once I have been in the company of the patriotic [Thomas] Clarkson. I
must say I viewed them both as Angels of Liberty. God bless and reward
them.

In regard to the object that brought me to this country, I would say, that,
considering the peculiar state of the country, I have been quite as successful
as I could expect. The object has met with the most decided approbation
from all classes of people. I do not hold out the delusive idea that the whole
of the colored people are going to Canada; but have invariably said, that in
spite of all that will ever remove there, or to any other part of the world
they will continue to increase in America. It is only to open the door for all
such as choose to go, or that prefer Canada to the United States.

When I shall return, I cannot at present say; but I think that it will not
be under several months.

Farewell, in the name of the Lord. Let us trust and persevere to the end.

*The Liberator,* June 22, 1833.

## 55

## THE NEGRO PHOENIX, 1833

A powerful social organization was formed among Negroes of New York in April,
1833 under the title of the Phoenix Society. Leaders in this group were the Rev.
Christopher Rush, the Rev. Theodore S. Wright, Thomas L. Jinnings, Benjamin

F. Hughes and Peter Vogelsang. Arthur Tappan assisted it financially. Its constitution thus expressed its purpose:

This Society will aim to accomplish the following objects:—

   To visit every family in the ward, and make a register of every colored person in it—their name, sex, age, occupation, if they read, write and cypher—to induce them, old and young, and of both sexes, to become members of this Society, and make quarterly payments according to their ability—to get the children out to infant, Sabbath, and week schools, and induce the adults also to attend school and church on the Sabbath—to ascertain those persons who are able to subscribe for a newspaper that advocates the cause of immediate abolition of slavery and the elevation of the colored population to equal rights with the whites—to encourage the females to form Dorcas Societies; to help to clothe poor children of color, if they will attend school—the clothes to be loaned, and to be taken away from them if they neglect their schools, and to impress on the parents the importance of having the children punctual and regular in their attendance at school—to establish circulating libraries, formed in each ward, for the use of people of color, on very moderate pay—to establish mental feasts, and also lyceums for speaking and for lectures on the sciences—and to form moral societies—to seek out young men of talents and good moral character, that they may be assisted to obtain a liberal education—to report to the Board all mechanics who are skillful and capable of conducting their trades to procure places at trades, and with respectable farmers, for lads of good moral character—giving a preference to those who have learned to read, write and cypher—and in every other way to endeavor to promote the happiness of the people of color, by encouraging them to improve their minds and to abstain from every vicious and demoralizing practice.

*The Liberator,* June 29, 1833.


56

## THIRD ANNUAL NATIONAL NEGRO
## CONVENTION, 1833

The third annual convention of the Negro people met in Philadelphia, June 3–13, 1833, with sixty-two members from the same eight states represented in the 1832 convention. The presidency was given to Abraham D. Shadd of Pennsylvania. The address prepared by this convention is similar to the preceding one, though a new note is struck in the bitter denunciation levied against the presence of anti-Negro prejudice in the north.

### To the free Coloured inhabitants of the United States
#### Brethren and Fellow Citizens

It is a matter of high congratulation that, through the providence of Almighty God, we have been enabled to convene, for the fourth time, as the representatives of the free people of colour of eight of the States of the Union, for the purpose of devising plans for our mutual and common improvement, in this the land of our nativity.

To that important object the entire attention of the Convention has been directed; but to effect it, as might be expected, a very considerable diversity of sentiment as to the best means, existed. Various circumstances growing out of our local situations operate to produce a great difference of feeling, as well as of judgment, in the course best calculated to insure our advancement in prosperity. Our brethren at the south are subject to many very cruel and oppressive laws, to get clear of which they will consent to go into exile, as promising to them enjoyments from which they are cut off in the land of their birth. Gratitude to the bountiful Bestower of all good, compels us to rejoice in the acknowledgement that the lot of many has fallen in a happier and fairer portion of the land, to separate ourselves from which, or to promulgate a wish to do so, without better prospects of improvement before us than has yet come to our knowledge, would be suicidal to the vital interests of the coloured people of the free states, and would justly draw upon us the execration of the thinking part of the slave states.

Ours is a defensive warfare; on our domicil we meet the aggressor, and if we move, or give our consent to move, and bid them to follow before we are driven, forcibly driven, from our lodgements—which, Heaven be praised, is not probable—their denunciations would be fit.

The Canadian Reports, as published in the minutes of this Convention, may be regarded as the unequivocally expressed sentiments of the coloured people of the free states, viz: improvement, but without emigration, except it be voluntary.

By an attentive perusal of the minutes and proceedings of the Convention, it will be apparent how deeply we sympathize in the distresses of our more unfortunate brethren, and the interest we willingly take, to the extent of our power, to mitigate their sufferings. We feel confident that the course pursued, as presented in this address, will receive the approbation of our constituents, and of those of our fellow citizens who are solicitous that our moral, religious, civil, and political condition should be improved in the United States. To promote our welfare, a great and increasing interest is manifesting itself in various parts of the Union; and we feel assured that we shall receive the hearty concurrence and support of our brethren, in the measures herein recommended for our general benefit. We supplicate the intercession of Jehovah, to extend this interest to the most remote parts of our country. We think that we cannot make a stronger or more effectual appeal to your judgements to secure your active cooperation in the plans suggested, than by exhibiting to you a brief outline of the efforts making by your friends to elevate the character and condition of the man of colour.

With a view that we may the more clearly understand the duties that now devolve upon us, it may be necessary to advert to times gone by, when in a state of slavery, ignorance, and misery, with scarcely sufficient intellect remaining to wish for freedom: such is the deterioriating effect of the slave system, carried to the extent that it has been and now is in America; there arose a number of philanthropists, who espoused our cause, and by their continued exertions have effected the entire liberation of the slaves in some of the states; and the salutary influence of those principles has been felt, in some degree, in every part of the United States, and once bid fair to make every citizen of our country proud of the distinguished appellation of an American. But it is lamentable that a deep and solemn gloom has settled on that once bright anticipation, and that monster, *prejudice,* is stalking over the land, spreading in its course its pestilential breath, blighting and withering the fair and natural hopes of our happiness, resulting from the enjoyment of that invaluable behest of God to man—FREEDOM.

It is not to be expected that we would enter into a disquisition, with a view to satisfy the minds of those who fancy they are interested in prolonging the miseries of their fellow men; on that subject, it is presumed the greatest stretch of human reason has been employed to elucidate its repugnance to the precepts of the Gospel; its infringement on the natural rights of man; its injury to the interests of those who cleave to it on the score of supposed interest, and its repugnance to the happiness, as well as to the interests of society in general. From these considerations, the conviction is forced upon us that they willingly and wilfully shut their eyes against the clearest evidences of reason. In that state of helplessness in which we were, schools were erected for our improvement, and from them great benefit has resulted. Schools have been erected by philanthropists, and many of us have been educated without so much as knowing when, or by whom, the edifices have been reared. But the manifest improvement we have made, loudly demands we should employ the talents we possess in assisting the philanthropists of the present time in their endeavors for our further advancement. A host of benevolent individuals are at present actively engaged in the praiseworthy and noble undertaking of raising us from the degradation we are now in, to the exalted situation of American freemen. Their success eminently depends upon the succour and encouragement they receive from our united efforts to carry into effect those plans recommended for the government of our conduct. With a strong desire for our improvement in morality, religion, and learning, they have advised us strictly to practise the virtues of temperance and economy, and by all means early to instruct our children in the elements of education. The Convention being perfectly convinced of the impossibility of our moral elevation without a strict adherence to these precepts, has conceived it to be its duty earnestly to call upon our brethren to give their aid and influence in promoting an object so desirable. In conformity to the recommendation of the former Convention, we are happy to have it in our power to state, that several temperance societies have been formed in most, if not in all, the states represented. In the course of the proceedings, will be found an elaborate report on the subject of temperance, to the careful perusal of which we invite the especial attention of our brethren. That societies for mental improvement, particularly among the females, have been established in several places, and a manifest improvement has marked their progress. Some diligence has also been employed in extending the benefits of education to a considerable number of children, who had been before neglected, and mental feasts have been held, of mixed companies of males and females, in some of the cities, on the recommendation of our very worthy friend, the Rev. Simeon S. Jocelyn, of New Haven.

From these promising beginnings we eagerly anticipate a speedy and extensive spread of those principles so justly calculated to dignify human nature; and earnestly hope a universal imitation of those salutary examples, without which the best endeavors of our friends must prove abortive.

The resolution passed at the last Convention, that the auxiliary societies obtain all the information possible relative to the number and state of the schools in their respective sections; the branches of education taught in each, with the number of scholars, and make returns of the same through their delegates, to this Convention, has not been fulfilled to the extent desired; but a general report will be found attached to the proceedings.

A circumstance that we would particularly introduce to the serious consideration of our brethren in general, is, the great efforts that are making by our friends, for the establishment of manual labour schools, for the improvement of our youth in the higher branches of education; for the report on which subject we refer the reader to the minutes. It is not, however, thought to be improper here to state, that in the city of New York efforts are making to establish, in that state, a school of this description. In the state of Pennsylvania, a benevolent (deceased) has bequeathed ten thousand dollars for, or towards, the erection of a similar school. And the New England A.S. [Anti-Slavery] Society, (which has laid a broader base for philanthropic exertion in the cause of the man of colour, than any benevolent institution that has preceded it,) has, in addition to its various other methods to raise the character and condition of the free people of colour, promoted addresses and discussions, oral and written, defending us from the unjust aspersions of our enemies; has opened a subscription, with a determination to raise funds sufficient to establish manual labour schools in New England for the instruction of coloured youth. This most meritorious institution, in the vindication of the natural, civil, and political rights of the coloured people, ought, and we trust does, occupy a distinguished place in the feelings and affections of our people. The more perfectly and securely to carry into effect that part of their plan relating to schools, they deemed it necessary to send our very worthy and highly talented advocate and defender, W. L. Garrison, to England, to endeavour to raise funds to aid in that enterprise, but not less to unfold the manifold misrepresentations respecting the people of colour, by Mr. Elliot Cresson, an agent of the American Colonization Society, in his addresses to the British people.

On the subject of the American Colonization Society, the expression of public sentiment has been frequently and clearly given. . . . We cannot, however, brethren, pass over this inept cause of much of our debasement, without informing you that we have arrived at that point in the examining of the duties submitted for our consideration; that we must necessarily leave the confined borders of our own view of natural, civil and political rights, growing out of immemorial prescriptive usage, that birth constitutes citizenship. Theories, perfectly new and multiform, are offered for adjudication. We shall decline a decision until we have examined their several merits. We shall first call your attention to the most important of those theories, that of the American Colonization Society, not only because it pursues, by its dependent agents, the most irrational course to effect the object they profess to have in view, as unfolded by them to the people of the North, but that the supporters of the system at the South are among the most talented and respectable of their citizens; how these men should advocate a cause so incommensurate to produce the avowed desired effects, seems involved in impenetrable mystery. But it is worse than idle, when the address is made to the common sense of the common men, to ask whether a child or person born in the United States of America can be considered a native of England. The philanthropists of this association have endeavoured to establish, as a primary belief, that the coloured child, that is, the child not white, no matter how many generations he may be able to trace in a lineal ascent, is an African, and ought to be sent to the land of his forefathers—Africa. When they have worked up the fancy of their hearers to that pitch that they really believe us to be Africans, it becomes an easy matter to excite their sympathy so that they readily loose their purse strings, and voluntarily contribute to the beneficent scheme of the Society to restore us to the land of our nativity. The show of seeming seriousness in combatting so ludicrous a position, if it was not upheld by a very respectable portion of the intelligence of the country, might create a doubt of the intent.

But this society has most grossly vilified our character as a people; it has taken much pains to make us abhorrent to the public, and then pleads the necessity of sending us into banishment. A greater outrage could not be committed against an unoffending people; and the hypocrisy that has marked its movements, deserves our universal censure. We have been cajoled into measures by the most false representations of the advantages to be derived from our emigration to Africa. The recommendation has been offered as presenting the greatest and best interests to ourselves. No argument has been adduced, other than that based on prejudice, and that prejudice founded on our difference of colour. If shades of difference in complexion is to operate to make men the sport of powerful caprice, who can pretend to determine how long it may be before, on this principle, the colonists may be again compelled to migrate to the land of their fathers in America.

The conduct of this institution is the most unprincipled that has been realized in almost any civilized country. Based and supported as it was, by some men of the greatest wealth and talent that the country boasts, under the sanction of names so respectable, the common sense of the community was led astray, little imagining that any thing more was designed than appeared on the surface, viz: the improvement of the condition of the people of colour, by their removal to Africa, and the evangelizing of that continent. The hidden insidious design in our removal, political expediency, was confined to the few that organized the society; its secret purposes have been kept as close as possible. But Southern inquisitiveness demanded a development of the secret, with which they were satisfied, and it received their support—while the North, prompted by sentiments of benevolence towards us, entered heartily into the scheme. But the real objects being now manifest many have withdrawn their support from it, from their conviction of its insufficiency to perform what was expected, and the want of good faith on the part of the society, as to its real object in awakening their sympathy. The deception is discovered, and it is hoped that before long, the man of colour will be reinstated in his natural rights. . . .

*Minutes and proceedings of the third annual convention for the improvement of the free people of colour* . . . (N.Y., 1833, published by order of the convention).

57

# A NEGRO WRITES A BIGOTED OFFICIAL, 1833

It will be recalled that the attempt in 1831 to establish a school for Negro youth in New Haven failed. Shortly thereafter a Quaker lady, Prudence Crandall of Canterbury, Connecticut, admitted a Negro girl to her academy. White patrons then boycotted it and so she welcomed Negroes alone. As a result, the building was damaged by a mob and the lady was imprisoned, the sentencing magistrate being one Andrew T. Judson. To the latter, the Rev. Nathaniel Paul, Negro Abolitionist, addressed the following letter dated London, England, August 29, 1833:

Sir—Through the medium of the American newspapers, I have seen your name, and the names of your worthy coadjutors, and have read your noble and praiseworthy deeds, in regard to the establishment of a school in your town, conducted by one Miss Prudence Crandall, for the instruction of young ladies of color! And believing that acts so patriotic, so republican, so Christian-like in their nature, as yours, against the unpardonable attempts of this fanatical woman, should not be confined to one nation or continent, but that the WORLD should know them, and learn and profit thereby;—I have thought proper to do all in my power to spread your fame, that your works may be known at least throughout this country. Nor will you marvel at my magnanimity when I inform you that I am, myself, a native of New-England, and consequently *proud* of whatever may emanate from her sons, calculated to exalt them in the eyes of the world.

And as I have been for some months past and still am engaged in travelling and delivering lectures upon the state of slavery as it exists in the United States, and the condition of the free people of color there, it will afford me an excellent opportunity of making this whole affair known; nor shall I fail to improve it. Yes, sir, Britons shall know that there are men in America, and whole towns of them, too, who are not so destitute of true heroism but that they can assail a helpless woman, surround her house by night, break her windows, and drag her to prison, for the treasonable act of teaching females of color to read!!!

Already is the State of Connecticut indebted to me for my gratuitous services since I have been in this country, in her behalf; especially the city of *New-Haven,* and its worthy Mayor. Their magnanimous conduct in regard to the establishment of a college for colored youth in that place, I have spread from "Dan to Beersheba;"—and Dennis Kimberly [Mayor of New Haven] may rest assured that the name of Benedict Arnold does not stand higher in the estimation of the American people than *his* does in England! It is my intention, sir, to give you an equal elevation.

I shall make no charge for the service I may render you. Nevertheless, if you think I am truly deserving, and ought to have a compensation, whatever you may feel it your duty to give, you will please to hand it over to the Treasurer of the "American Colonization Society," of which, I understand, you are a member and an advocate.

*The Liberator,* November 23, 1833.

## 58

## FREDERICK DOUGLASS AND THE SLAVE-BREAKER, 1834

In 1834 a man was being steeled for future struggles by the ministrations of a professional slave-breaker in Maryland. Frederick Douglass tells us of this experience:

If at any one time of my life, more than another, I was made to drink the bitterest dregs of slavery, that time was during the first six months of my stay with this man Covey. We worked all weathers. It was never too hot, or too cold; it could never rain, blow, snow, or hail too hard for us to work in the field. Work, work, work, was scarcely more than the order of the day than of the night. The longest days were too short for him, and the shortest nights were too long for him. I was somewhat unmanageable at the first, but a few months of this discipline tamed me. Mr. Covey succeeded in *breaking* me—in body, soul, and spirit. My natural elasticity was crushed; my intellect languished; the disposition to read departed, the cheerful spark that lingered about my eye died out; the dark night of slavery closed in upon me, and behold a man transformed to a brute!

Sunday was my only leisure time. I spent this under some large tree, in a sort of beast-like stupor between sleeping and waking. At times I would rise up and a flash of energetic freedom would dart through my soul, accompanied with a faint beam of hope that flickered for a moment, and then vanished. I sank down again mourning over my wretched condition. I was sometimes tempted to take my life and that of Covey, but was prevented by a combination of hope and fear. My sufferings, as I remember them now, seem like a dream rather than like a stern reality.

Our house stood within a few rods of the Chesapeake bay, whose broad bosom was ever white with sails from every quarter of the habitable globe.

Those beautiful vessels, robed in white, and so delightful to the eyes of free men, were to me so many shrouded ghosts, to terrify and torment me with thoughts of my wretched condition. I have often, in the deep stillness of a summer's Sabbath, stood all alone upon the banks of that noble bay, and traced, with saddened heart and tearful eye, the countless number of sails moving off to the mighty ocean. The sight of these always affected me powerfully. My thoughts would compel utterance; and there, with no audience but the Almighty, I would pour out my soul's complaint in my rude way with an apostrophe to the moving multitude of ships. . . .

I shall never be able to narrate half the mental experience through which it was my lot to pass, during my stay at Covey's. I was completely wrecked, changed, and bewildered; goaded almost to madness at one time, and at another reconciling myself to my wretched condition. All the kindness I had received at Baltimore, all my former hopes and aspirations for usefulness in the world, and even the happy moments spent in the exercises of religion, contrasted with my then present lot, served but to increase my anguish.

I suffered bodily as well as mentally. I had neither sufficient time in which to eat, or to sleep, except on Sundays. The overwork, and the brutal chastisements of which I was the victim, combined with that ever-gnawing and soul-devouring thought—*"I am a slave—and a slave for life—a slave with no rational ground to hope for freedom"*—rendered me a living embodiment of mental and physical wretchedness.

*Life and Times of Frederick Douglass written by himself* (N.Y., 1941, Pathway Press), pp. 139–41.

59

## A NEGRO REPLIES TO AN ANTI-ABOLITIONIST, 1834

In the summer of 1834 a New York physician, Dr. David M. Reese, issued a pamphlet entitled *A Brief Review of the First Annual Report of the American Anti-Slavery Society*, in which he insisted the Abolitionists were anti-American since they threatened law and order. Dr. Reese proved, also, to his own satisfaction, the inexpediency if not impossibility of emancipation and concluded by remarking that his work would extinguish abolitionism. This drew from a young New York Negro bookseller and Abolitionist, David Ruggles, a pamphlet published by himself in 1834, entitled *The "Extinguisher" Extinguished! or David M. Reese, M. D. "Used Up."* Now David Ruggles speaks:

Abolitionists do not wish "amalgamation:" I do not wish it, nor does any colored man or woman of my acquaintance, nor can instances be adduced where a desire was manifested by any colored person; but I deny that "inter-marriages" between "whites and blacks are unnatural," and hazard nothing in giving my opinion that if *"amalgamation"* should become popular Dr. R. would not be the last to vindicate it, practically too if *expedient*. How utterly vain and futile are the following remarks, "The fact that no white person ever did consent to marry a Negro without having previously forfeited all char-acter with the whites, and that even profligate sexual intercourse between the races, everywhere meets with the execration of the respectable and virtuous among the whites, as the most despicable form of licentiousness; is of itself irrefragable proof that *equality* in any aspect in this country, is neither practicable nor desirable. Criminal amalgamation may and does exist among the most degraded of the species, but Americans (what a pa-triot!) will never yield the sanction of law and religion to an equality so incongruous and unnatural."

Now "that no white person never did consent to marry a Negro without having previously forfeited all character with the respectable and virtuous among the whites," *is not true*, unless it is true that a man's "character" depends upon the color of his skin; if it does, which of the two races would "forfeit all character" by intermarrying, the white or the colored? The whites have robbed us (the blacks) for centuries—they made Africa bleed rivers of blood!—they have torn husbands from their wives—wives from their husbands—parents from their children—children from their parents—brothers from their sisters—sisters from their brothers, and bound them in chains—forced them into holds of vessels—subjected them to the most unmerciful tortures: starved and murdered, and doomed them to endure the horrors of slavery! Still, according to Dr. Reese's logic, the whites have virtuous "characters" and we are *brutes!*

> "Deem our nation brutes no longer,
>   Till some reason you can find,
>   Worthier to regard, and stronger,
>   Than the color of our kind!
>   Slaves of gold! whose sordid dealings
>   Tarnish all your boasted powers,
>   Prove that *ye* have human feelings,
>   *Ere* ye proudly question ours!"

. . . . "Would you be willing to marry a black wife," is a question often asked by colonizationists to members of the A.S. [Anti-Slavery] Society. Were I a white man, or was the question reversed and put to me, my reply would be—you had better put your question to colonizationists at the south, who have been so long in a process of training. Why insult gentlemen with a silly, "quirkish," nonsensical interrogative, loped off from the fag ends of extremity. Every man that can read and has sense sufficient to put two ideas together without losing one, knows what the Abolitionists mean when they speak of elevating us "according to our equal rights." But why is it that it seems to you so "repugnant" to marry your sons and daughters to colored persons? Simply because public opinion is against it. *Nature* teaches no such "repugnance," but experience has taught me that education only does. Do children feel and exercise that prejudice towards colored persons? Do not colored and white children play together promiscuously until the white is taught to despise the colored? . . . .

My dear brother, Rev. Bishop Reese, M.D. closes his famous exigesis by submitting his conclusions to the citizens and christians of America, pretty sure that no "sophistry can evade them." I now submit my criticism to the same candid public, entirely regardless whether *sophistry* evade them or not, but challenging the truth to search them. If there be anything of importance in the review which I have not noticed, it was not because the thing itself was impregnable, nor because I was not equal to the seige, but, as I stated before, because my limits did not permit a comment upon every error in my brother's deviating course. But as it is, I submit it to the candor of a generous public, and should *public sentiment* condemn the work, should it be thought out of place and *inexpedient* by any of my friends—should it gain for me frowns and reproaches instead of laurels—one thing I know, posterity will requite my wrongs, and when the "extinguisher" of Dr. David M. Reese shall itself have been extinguished in death, and sunk down— down—in the long eternal sleep of oblivion, my little book, pregnant with truth, shall survive the revolution of ages, and give even Dr. Reese himself a reluctant IMMORTALITY!

## 60

## NEGRO YOUTH LEADERS, 1834

Negro youth leaders, Henry Highland Garnet, William H. Day and David Ruggles, who were to become men of national renown, formed The Garrison Literary and Benevolent Association of New York in March, 1834. At their first meeting one hundred and fifty Negro youth, not over twenty years of age, gathered in a public school, but a city official told them they would have to choose a different name for their society if they wanted to continue using public facilities. The young men decided to retain their name and rent a meeting place. The preamble to the constitution of this organization reads:

If acting conformably to the will of our Creator,—if promoting the welfare of our fellow creatures around us,—and if securing our own happiness, are objects of the highest moment, we are loudly called upon to cultivate and extend the great interests of religion, virtue and literature. Feeling ourselves obligated to God for His mercies towards us, we think it our duty to begin, in early life, to assist each other to alleviate the afflicted. And whereas we believe the downfall of prejudice, slavery, and oppression, and the moral and intellectual improvement of the rising generation of our race depend on early improvement; and whereas faithful philanthropists have engaged in our cause, through the press and otherwise, we think it would encourage them with persevering energy to vindicate our cause, to see the youth of color distinguish themselves by their good conduct and intellectual attainments:—we believe, therefore, that the forming ourselves into an associated body will be the means of spreading information and diffusing knowledge, and we hope to do good to soul and body; we therefore, looking to Heaven for direction, do form ourselves into an association. . . .

*The Liberator*, April 19, 1834.

61

## TO THE CHAIN GANG, 1834

Under the tyrannical maritime laws of the nineteenth century the seaman's life was a bitter one, but Negroes, many of whom served aboard ships, had a particularly difficult time of it. A letter from one such seaman, John Tidd of Boston, dated New Orleans, April 6, 1834, to a Negro friend, Mr. Arthur Jones of his home city, is indicative of this. The Captain involved here was one Crosby of the brig *Union*, but the result of Tidd's appeal has not been learned.

Mr. Arther Jones i know take my pen in hand to in form you that I am well and hope this few lines will find you the same my Captin has put me in the Chan gan and has left me hear—and has carrid of my papers and clothing and by the information i can git he want to sall me and further more I want you to stop him Thair when he arives and make him scend for me and have me relievd from the presson The reason of this bee caus I was a little belaited with my supper and he gain to jaw me and i told him if he did not like et he might get somboday alse and Captin and offerses and two Pasangers and draidy [?] me acrows the decks one of The Mr. Balay and the Other haskar [?] and I want you to draw et of as you thin propper and

gow to a lawyer and have them all stoped thair in tell I return that I can
get recompence from the all and I want you to have this Attend to and I
will sattisfy you when I Return I have nothing more to write to you know
love to all inquaring friends

                    And my Sincer friendship take to your self
                                                        John Tidd

Garrison MSS., Boston Public Library.


## 62


## MORE KIDNAPPING OF NEGROES, 1834

Several of the documents already quoted dealt with the practice of kidnapping
free Negroes for sale as slaves. This was a continuing and terrible grievance of the
Negro people. At the May, 1834 convention of the New England Anti-Slavery
Society, a leading Negro Abolitionist of Boston, James G. Barbadoes, referred to
five such cases within his own knowledge, including that of his own brother.


About eighteen years ago, Robert H. Barbadoes was kidnapped in New
Orleans, imprisoned, handcuffed and chained, for about five months or
longer, and deprived every way of communicating his situation to his parents. His [seamen's] protection was taken from him, and torn up. He was
often severely flogged to be made submissive, and deny that he was free
born. He was unluckily caught with a letter wrote with a stick, and with
the blood drawn from his own veins, for the purpose of communicating to
his father his situation; but this project failed, for the letter was torn
away from him and destroyed and he was very severely flogged. He then lost
most every hope; but at length the above Peter Smith [one of other four
victims] was kidnapped again in this garden of paradise of freedom,
and being lodged in the same cell with him, he communicated to Smith the
particulars of his sufferings. At the examination of Smith, he was found
to have free papers, signed by the Governor; in consequence of which, he
was set at liberty. He then wrote to Barbadoes' parents, and likewise arrived
in Boston as soon as the letter. Free papers were immediately obtained, and
signed by his father and Mrs. Mary Turel, Mr. ———— Giles, and Mr.
Thomas Clark, town clerk; and by the Governor of this state, demanding
him without delay, he was returned to his native town, Boston, where all
these other persons belonged.

*The Liberator*, June 7, 1834.

63

# FOURTH ANNUAL NATIONAL NEGRO
# CONVENTION, 1834

The speech of William Hamilton, of New York, as chairman of the fourth annual convention of the Negro people, is of great interest for its clear presentation of the reasons for the gathering, and its lucid analysis of the need for unity among all opposing slavery. The convention was held in New York City, June 2–13, 1834 and was attended by 50 delegates from Pennsylvania, New York, New Jersey, Connecticut, Massachusetts, Rhode Island, Maryland and Ohio as well as two visitors from Canada and Haiti.

Gentlemen, It is with the most pleasing sensations, that I, in behalf of my coloured fellow citizens of New York, tender you of the Delegation to this Convention, a hearty welcome to our city. And in behalf of the Conventional Board, I repeat the welcome. And, gentlemen, with regard to myself, my full heart vibrates the felicitation.

You have convened to take into consideration what may be best means for the promotion of the best interest of the people of colour of these United States, particularly of the free people thereof. And that such Convention is highly necessary, I think a few considerations will amply show.

First, the present form of society divides the interest of the community into several parts. Of these, there is that of the white man, that of the slave, and that of the free coloured man. How lamentable, how very lamentable, it is that there should be, any where on earth, a community of castes, with separate interests! That society must be the most happy, where the good of one is the common good of the whole. Civilization is not perfect, nor has reason full sway, until the community shall see that a wrong done to one is a wrong done to the whole; that the interest of one is or ought to be the common interest of the whole. Surely that must be a happy state of society where the sympathies of all are to all alike.

How pleasing, what a compliment to the nation, is the expression of Mons Vallier, a celebrated traveller in Africa, where, speaking of the Hottentots, he says, "There none need to offer themselves as objects of compassion, for all are compassionate." Whatever our early-tutored prejudice may say to the contrary, such a people must be happy. Give me a residence in such a society, and I shall fancy myself in a community the most refined.

But alas for the people of colour in this community! Their interest is not identified with that of other men. From them, white men stand aloof. For them the eye of pity hath scarcely a tear.

To them the hand of kindness is palsied, to them the dregs of mercy scarcely are given. To them the finger of scorn is pointed; contumely and reproach is continually theirs. They are a taunt, a hissing, and a byword. They must cringe, and crouch, and crawl, and succumb to their peers. Long, long, long has the demon of prejudice and persecution beset their path. And must they make no effort to throw off the evils by which they are beset? Ought they not to meet to spread out their wrongs before one another? Ought they not to meet to consult on the best means of their relief? Ought they not to make one weak effort; nay, one strong, one mighty moral effort, to roll off the burden that crushes them?

Under present circumstances it is highly necessary the free people of colour should combine, and closely attend to their own particular interest. All kinds of jealousy should be swept away from among them, and their whole eye fixed, intently fixed, on their own peculiar welfare. And can they do better than to meet thus; to take into consideration what are the best means to promote their elevation, and after having decided, to pursue those means with unabating zeal until their end is obtained?

Another reason why this Convention is necessary, is, that there is formed a strong combination against the people of colour, by some who are the master spirits of the day, by men whose influence is of the strongest character, to whom this nation bow in humble submission, and submit to their superior judgment, who turn public sentiment whichever way they please.

You cannot but perceive that I allude to the Colonization Society. However pure the motives of some of the members of that society may be, yet the master spirits thereof are evil minded towards us. They have put on the garb of angels of light. Fold back their covering, and you have in full array those of darkness.

I need not spread before you the proof of their evil purposes. Of that you have had a quantity sufficient; and were there no other good reason for this Convention; the bare circumstance of the existence of such an institution would be a sufficient one. I do hope, confidently hope, that the time will arrive, and is near at hand, when we shall be in full possession of all the rights of men.

But as long at least as the Colonization Society exists, will a Convention of coloured people be highly necessary. This society is the great Dragon of the land, before whom the people bow and cry, Great Jehovah, and to whom they would sacrifice the free people of colour. That society has spread itself over this whole land; it is artful, it suits itself to all places. It is one thing at the south, and another at the north; it blows hot and cold; it sends forth bitter and sweet; it sometimes represents us as the most corrupt, vicious, and abandoned of any class of men in the community. Then again we are kind, meek, and gentle. Here we are ignorant, idle, a nuisance, and a drawback on the resources of the country. But as abandoned as we are, in Africa we shall civilize and christianize all that heathen country. And by thus preaching continually, they have distilled into the minds of the community a desire to see us removed.

They have resorted to every artifice to effect their purposes, by exciting in the minds of the white community, the fears of insurrection and amalgamation; by petitioning State legislatures to grant us no favours; by petitioning Congress to aid in sending us away; by using their influence to prevent the establishment of seminaries for our instruction in the higher branches of education.

And such are the men of that society that the community are blind to their absurdities; contradictions and paradoxes. They are well acquainted with the ground and the wiles by which to beguile the people.

It is therefore highly necessary we should meet, in order that we may confer on the best means to frustrate the purpose of so awful a foe.

I would beg leave to recommend an attentive consideration to this matter. Already you have done much toward the enervation of this giant: he begins to grow feeble; indeed he seems to be making his last struggle, if we may judge from his recent movements. Hang around him, assail him quickly. He is vulnerable. Well pointed darts will fetch him down, and soon he breathes no more.

Cheer up my friends! Already has your protest against the Colonization Society shown to the world that the people of colour are not willing to be expatriated. Cheer up. Already a right feeling begins to prevail. The friends of justice, of humanity, and the rights of man are drawing rapidly together, and are forming a moral phalanx in your defence.

That hitherto strong-footed, but sore-eyed vixen, prejudice, is limping off, seeking the shade. The Anti-Slavery Society and the friends of immediate abolition, are taking a noble, bold and manly stand, in the cause of universal liberty. It is true they are assailed on every quarter, but the more they are assailed the faster they recruit. From present appearances the prospect is cheering, in a high degree. Anti-Slavery Societies are forming in every direction. Next August proclaims the British dominions free from slaves.

These United States are her children, they will soon follow so good an example. Slavery, that Satanic monster, that beast whose mark has been so long stamped on the forehead of the nations, shall be chained and cast down into blackness and darkness for ever.

Soon, my brethren, shall the judgment be set. Then shall rise in glory and triumph, reason, virtue, kindness and liberty, and take a high exalted stand among the sons of men. Then shall tyranny, cruelty, prejudice and slavery be cast down to the lowest depths of oblivion; yea, be banished from the presence of God, and the glory of his power for ever. Oh blessed consummation; and devoutly to be desired!

It is for you, my brethren, to help on in this work of moral improvement. Man is capable of high advances in his reasoning and moral faculties. Man is in the pursuit of happiness. And reason, or experience, which is the parent of reason, tells us that the highest state of morality is the highest state of happiness. Aside from a future day of judgment and retribution, there is always a day of retribution at hand. That society is most miserable that is most immoral—that most happy that is most virtuous. Let me therefore recommend earnestly that you press upon our people the necessity and advantage of a moral reformation. It may not produce an excess of riches, but it will produce a higher state of happiness, and render our circumstances easier.

You, gentlemen, can begin here. By managing this conference in a spirit of good will and true politeness; by constantly keeping in view and cultivating a spirit of peace, order and harmony, rather than satire, wit, and eloquence; by putting the best possible construction on each other's language, rather than charging each other with improper motives. These dispositions will bespeak our character more or less virtuous and refined, and render our setting more or less pleasant. I will only now add, that the report of the Conventional Board will be submitted at your call; and my earnest hope is that you may have a peaceful, pleasant sitting.

*Minutes of the Fourth Annual Convention, for the improvement of the free people of colour . . . (N.Y., 1834, pub. by order of the convention).*

## 64

## NEGRO CHILDREN SPEAK, 1834

In March 1834 was opened the first school for Negroes in Cincinnati, paid for by themselves. The city had then about twelve hundred Negroes. The great demand for education led, within a year, to the opening of three more schools, with white and Negro teachers, for adults as well as children. Late in 1834 youngsters at these schools were asked to write on: "What do you think *most* about?" Five answers have survived, and here they are:

*1st.* Dear school-mates, we are going next summer to buy a farm and to work part of the day and to study the other part if we live to see it and some home part of the day to see our mothers and sisters and cousins if we are got any and see our kind folks and to be good boys and when we get a man to get the poor slaves from bondage. And I am sorrow to hear that the boat of Tiskilwa went down with two hundred poor slaves from up the river. Oh how sorrow I am to hear that, it grieves my heart so that I could faint in one minute.

——— ———, aged seven years.

*2d.* Dear school-master, I now inform you in these few lines, that what we are studying for is to try to get the yoke of slavery broke and the chains parted asunder and slave holding cease for ever. O that God would change the hearts of our fellow men.

——— ———, aged twelve years.

*3d.* In my youthful days dear Lord, let me remember my creator, Lord. Teach me to do his will. Bless the cause of abolition—bless the heralds of the truth that we trust God has sent out to declare the rights of man. We trust that it may be the means of moving mountains of sin off all the families. My mother and stepfather, my sister and myself were all born in slavery. The Lord did let the oppressed go free. Roll on the happy period that all nations shall know the Lord. We thank him for his many blessings.

——— ———, aged eleven years.

*4th.* Dear Sir.—This is to inform you that I have two cousins in slavery who are entitled to their freedom. They have done everything that the will requires and now they wont let them go. They talk of selling them down the river. If this was your case what would you do? Please give me your advice.

——— ———, aged ten years.

*5th.* Let us look back and see the state in which the Britons and Saxons and Germans lived. They had no learning and had not a knowledge of letters. But now look, some of them are our first men. Look at king Alfred and see what a great man he was. He at one time did not know his a, b, c, but before his death he commanded armies and nations. He was never discouraged but always looked forward and studied the harder. I think if the colored people study like king Alfred they will soon do away the evil of slavery. I cant see how the Americans can call this a land of freedom where so much slavery is.

——— ———, aged sixteen years.

*Report on the condition of the people of color in the state of Ohio; proceedings of the Ohio Anti-Slavery Convention, held at Putnam . . . April, 1835* (n.d., n.p.). Copy in Columbia University Library.

65

## FIFTH ANNUAL NATIONAL NEGRO CONVENTION, 1835

The fifth annual convention of the Negro people met in Philadelphia, June 1–5, 1835. Present were thirty-five delegates from six states and the District of Columbia. This proved to be the last of the regular yearly conventions that had begun in 1830, although thereafter each year witnessed many local, state and regional Negro conferences. Prominent at this convention were Robert Purvis, William Whipper, Stephen Smith, and, destined to be a leader among Washington Negroes for many years, John F. Cook. The most significant resolutions adopted here follow:

*Resolved,* That this convention recommend to the free people of color throughout the United States, the propriety of petitioning Congress and their respective State legislatures to be admitted to the rights and privileges of American citizens, and that we be protected in the same. . . .

*Resolved,* That the free people of color are requested by this convention, to petition those state legislatures that have adopted the Colonization Society, to abolish it. . . .

*Resolved,* That we recommend as far as possible, to our people to abandon the use of the word "colored," when either speaking or writing concerning themselves; and especially to remove the title of African from their institutions, the marbles of churches, and etc. . . .

*Resolved,* That our duty to God, and to the principles of human rights, so far exceeds our allegiance to those laws that return the slave again to his master, (from the free states,) that we recommend our people to peaceably bear the punishment those inflict, rather than aid in returning their brethren again to slavery. . . .

*The Liberator,* August 1, 1835.

66

## A NEGRO DESCRIBES A KIDNAPPING, 1836

The following letter by David Ruggles, detailing the facts concerning the kidnapping of a free Negro in New York City on July 23, 1836, originally appeared in the New York *Sun* and was then widely reprinted:

It is too bad to be told, much less to be endured!—On Saturday, 23d instant, about 12 o'clock, Mr. George Jones, a respectable free colored man, was arrested at 21 Broadway, by certain police officers, upon the pretext of his having "committed assault and battery." Mr. Jones, being conscious that no such charge could be sustained against him, refused to go with the officers. His employers, placing high confidence in his integrity, advised him to go and answer to the charge, promising that any assistance should be afforded to satisfy the end of justice. He proceeded with the officers, accompanied with a gentleman who would have stood his bail—he was locked up in Bridewell—his friend was told that "when he was wanted he could be sent for." Between the hours of 1 and 2 o'clock, Mr. Jones was carried before the Hon. Richard Riker, Recorder of the City of New York. In the absence of his friends, and in the presence of several notorious kidnappers, who preferred and by oath sustained that he was a runaway slave, poor Jones, (having no one to utter a word in his behalf, but a boy, in the absence of numerous friends who could have borne testimony to his freedom,) was by the Recorder pronounced to be a SLAVE!

In less than three hours after his arrest, he was bound in chains, dragged through the streets, like a beast to the shambles! My depressed countrymen, we are all liable; your wives and children are at the mercy of merciless kidnappers. We have no protection in law, because the legislators withhold justice. We must no longer depend on the interposition of Manumission or Anti-Slavery Societies, in the hope of peaceable and just protection; where such outrages are committed, peace and justice cannot dwell. While we are subject to be thus inhumanly practised upon, no man is safe; we must look to our own safety and protection from kidnappers, remembering that "self-defence is the first law of nature."

Let a meeting be called—let every man who has sympathy in his heart to feel when bleeding humanity is thus stabbed afresh, attend the meeting; let a remedy be prescribed to protect us from slavery. Whenever necessity requires, let that remedy be applied. Come what, any thing is better than slavery.

*The Liberator*, August 6, 1836.

## 67

## "UNSPEAKABLE HAPPINESS" OF NEGRO PARENTS, 1836

Free Negroes frequently raised by public appeals the money necessary for the buying of a loved one's freedom. The following advertisement, dated Portland,

Maine, December 16, 1836, appeared in the Abolitionist press as the result of the success of one such effort:

George Potter and Rosella his wife, would take this opportunity to express their gratitude to God, and under him, to the benevolent individuals, who generously contributed in aiding them to redeem their two children from Slavery. They have the unspeakable happiness of informing the generous donors that, on the 12th inst. they received their children, aged eleven and seven years, raised from the degradation of Slavery to the rank of Freemen.

*The Liberator,* January 2, 1837.

## 68

## REPORT OF A NEGRO VIGILANCE COMMITTEE, 1837

New York City Negroes formed a vigilance committee on November 20, 1835. Its function, like similar organizations elsewhere, was to prevent the kidnapping of Negroes and to assist fugitive slaves. The first anniversary of this committee was celebrated at the church of the militant Negro Abolitionist, the Rev. Theodore S. Wright, on January 16, 1837. Here is the official report of this meeting:

The meeting was called to order by the Reverend Theodore S. Wright.
Prayer was offered by Rev. John J. Miter.
An abstract of the annual report was read by Mr. William Johnston.
On motion of G. R. Barker, of New York, *Resolved,* That the report be accepted and approved.
On motion of J. J. Miter, *Resolved,* That the present Committee of Vigilance be continued.
On motion of John T. Reymond, *Resolved,* That we commend the Vigilance Committee to the confidence, co-operation, and prayers of the friends of oppressed humanity.
  ' In support of this resolution, Mr. Reymond spoke with great feeling on the force of prejudice. He himself had felt its keen edge. In the course of his remarks, he related the following fact. In the year 1832, he addressed a large meeting of colored people, in this city, in relation to the Wilberforce colony in Canada. His speech was noticed in one of the city papers, and found its way to his native place, Norfolk, Va. A copy was sent to the Mayor of the city, who caused a writ to be issued immediately, for the arrest of Mr. Reymond's person. Before, however, he visited Norfolk, the Mayor died; but the writ was still in the possession of the officer. When Mr. Reymond

returned, the then mayor sent a request for him to come to the court-house. There the inquiry was made whether he had been absent from the State more than a year. He told them he had. Orders were then given for his imprisonment, and without the privilege of being heard in his own defence, he was locked up in jail for twenty-four hours. He was afterwards released, on condition that he would leave the city and State forthwith. Said Mr. Reymond, "the address, delivered at the above named meeting was the sole cause of my being thus, unceremoniously, *banished from my native State!*"

In conclusion, he said, "his voice should ever be lifted to plead the rights of oppressed—bleeding humanity. He was ready to jeopard his life, his all, in defence of this sacred cause. If he must fall a victim to the wrath of the oppressor, he should make the sacrifice willingly—but he pledged himself to that meeting, and to God, to use every lawful means to rescue his brother from the grasp of unbridled tyranny."

As the Rev. Mr. Ludlow rose to offer a resolution, the Secretary of the Committee [David Ruggles] presented to the audience the afflicted wife of Peter John Lee, (a colored man who was recently kidnapped from Rye, Westchester county, and hurried into hopeless bondage, by the minions of slavery) and her two worse than fatherless, little sons. The affecting sight melted the whole meeting into tears. There stood a mother and her two little boys beside her, arrayed in something more than the habiliments of widowhood. A most appalling spectacle of the fiendish spirit of American slavery. At this moment of thrilling interest, Mr. Ludlow offered the following:

*Resolved,* That in view of the exertions of this Committee during the past year, and for their operations in future, we pledge ourselves to raise the sum of three thousand dollars.

After a most appropriate and deeply affecting address from Mr. Ludlow, the resolution was unanimously adopted.

Mr. H. Dresser, Esq., next addressed the meeting on the following resolution:

*Resolved,* That as the trial by jury is the great bulwark of the liberties of freemen, it is RIGHT that the privileges of the same be extended to all persons claimed as fugitive slaves.

Mr. Dresser exposed the danger of investing an interested magistracy with power to decide in all cases affecting the freedom of our citizens, independent of an *impartial* jury. He established the doctrine of the resolution by an appeal to the highest judicial authorities, as well as by reference to the alarming facts which had fallen under his own observation in this city, and which were detailed in the Report.

The exercises continued until a late hour in the evening, while a large audience manifested their interest by listening with profound attention until the close of the meeting. The benediction was pronounced by the Rev. Dr. Raymond, and the meeting adjourned.

T. S. Wright, *Chairman.*

David Ruggles, Secretary New York Committee of Vigilance

### EXECUTIVE COMMITTEE

William Johnston, (Treasurer)

David Ruggles (Secretary)

James W. Higgins (Chairman)

Theodore S. Wright

George R. Barker

Thomas Vanrensselaer

Robert Brown

Samuel E. Cornish

### Receipts in aid of the Committee of Vigilance

Total Receipts .......................................$ 839.52

General Expenditure ................................. 1228.71

Balance against the Treasury......................... 389.19

The total number of persons protected from slavery by the Committee of Vigilance to January 16, 1837, is THREE HUNDRED AND THIRTY FIVE.

It is with pleasure we state, that the principal part of the subscriptions raised by the exertions of the general committee, has been obtained by the efforts of the Ladies, who collect from their friends one penny a week. It is also worthy of remark that the sum of $12.50 and two trunks of clothes were given to the committee by George Jones,* who was dragged to slavery by an order from our City Recorder.

*The First Annual Report of the New York Committee of Vigilance, for the year 1837 . . . (N.Y., 1837).*

## 69

## A NEWLY-FOUNDED NEGRO NEWSPAPER, 1837

A Negro newspaper, *Weekly Advocate,* was established by a New York Abolitionist, Philip A. Bell, in January, 1837. It was edited by the same Rev. Samuel E. Cornish who had edited *Freedom's Journal,* and continued, under the name, *The Colored American,* (adopted in March, 1837) until 1841. Its first editorial, appearing in the issue dated January 7, 1837, follows:

The addition of another Paper to the list of those already before the Public, may be, and is probably considered, by some persons of common

* See document 66.

observation and superficial reflection, as unnecessary and uncalled for; but numerous, however, as we freely allow them to be, it is believed by many of our people, that there is still a vacancy to be supplied, a chasm to be filled up; and that there is NOW a clear opening for one of a different character, which shall be devoted to the moral improvement and amelioration of our race. After the most mature deliberation we have commenced the noble enterprise. Our paper, though somewhat small in size, will be found valuable in contents. The advantages of the present undertaking are not to be estimated by words, they are incalculable. If the Press, a "FREE PRESS," be a foe to the tyrant—if its blessings be so great and innumerable, the Question naturally presents itself, why may we not have one of our own? . . .

We need scarcely say, we are opposed to colonization . . . We shall advocate Universal Suffrage and Universal Education, and we shall oppose all Monopolies, which oppress the Poor and laboring classes of society. . . .

We need not say, that our entire dependence for support is upon the colored portion of this great community, when we tell them that the ADVOCATE IS THEIR PAPER, in every sense of the word—that it will advocate their just claims and rights—sustain them in every proper appeal to manly generosity and justice. And as the cause of IMMEDIATE EMANCIPATION is based on incontrovertible right, we shall at all times, take it up with resolution, and defend it with firmness . . .

## 70

## A POLITICAL AND CIVIL RIGHTS MEETING OF NEGROES, 1837

Typical of the persistent, organized efforts of the Negro people to obtain full political and civil rights was the meeting held in New York City on February 20, 1837. The report of the meeting is taken from an extra issued two days later by the N.Y. *Weekly Advocate*. Following this appears a letter from David Ruggles to the editor of a New York newspaper, *Zion's Watchman*, dated August 7, 1837, which explains the first demand raised at the above meeting.

### [a]

On Monday evening last a very large meeting of our people was held at Phenix Hall, in Chapel Street. Henry Davis was called to the chair, and Philip A. Bell and Edward V. Clark appointed Secretaries.

The object of the meeting, in accordance with the notice previously given, was stated to be to get up petitions for the Legislature of this State now in session in Albany.

1st. For the repeal of the laws authorizing the holding of a person to service as a Slave in this State.

2d. To grant a *trial by jury* for their liberty to persons of color within this State arrested and claimed as fugitive slaves.

3d. For an alteration of the Constitution, so as to give the right of voting to all the male citizens of the State on the same terms without distinction of color.*

Three petitions, one for each of the objects specified, were then presented, considered and adopted. A large number of signatures was obtained on the spot. Indeed the crowd was so great, that *all* present could not get an opportunity to give in their names.

The subject therefore of giving a further opportunity to all who may wish to sign these petitions was referred to a committee; and it is understood that to this end one or more of their number will be in waiting at Phenix Hall every day for a few days, from 3 o'clock till 9 in the evening to receive the names of such as desire to add them to the petitions.†

## [b]

### *David Ruggles' Letter*

Mr. Editor: I suppose, not one in a thousand of your readers can be aware of the extent to which slavery prevails even in the so-called free state of New York.

Within the last four weeks, I have seen not less than eleven different persons who have recently been brought from the south, and who are now held as slaves by their masters in this state; as you know the laws of this state allow any slaveholder to do this, nine months at a time; so that when the slave has been here nine months, the master has only to take him out of the state, and then return with him immediately, and have him registered again, and so he may hold on to the slave as long as he lives! Some of the slaves whom I have recently seen are employed by their masters, some are loaned, and others hired out; and each of the holders of these slaves whom I have seen are professors of religion!! One of these professors is Mr. David Stanford, of Brooklyn; he is a member, I am told, of the Methodist Episcopal Church!

*The Liberator,* October 13, 1837.

---

* The New York Constitution of 1821 provided that Negro male residents twenty-one years of age or older might vote if they possessed property to the value of at least $250.
† *The Colored American,* March 11, 1837, reported that the first petition was signed by 605 men and 271 women; the second by 489 men and 272 women; the third by 620 men. These, together with a petition from Brooklyn signed by 232 Negroes, were presented to the State legislature on March 5, and rejected by a vote of 71 to 24.

71

## "FOUNDED IN AVARICE . . . ," 1837

An early and fairly extended analysis by a Negro of the roots of Negro oppression was that produced in March, 1837 by the Rev. Hosea Easton of Massachusetts, an active participant in the early convention movement. Extracts from this work follow:

It is with diffidence that I offer this treatise to the public; but an earnest desire to contribute my mite, for the benefit of my afflicted brethren, is my only apology. The subject is one of peculiar difficulty; especially as it is one in which I am deeply interested.

To speak or write on a subject relating to one's self, is peculiarly embarrassing; and especially so, under a deep sense of injury. As an apology for the frequent errors that may occur in the following pages, I would remark: It cannot be reasonably expected, that a literary display could adorn the production of one from whom popular sentiment has withheld almost every advantage, even of a common education.

If this work should chance to fall into the hands of any whose minds are so sordid, and whose hearts are so inflexible, as to load it, with its author, with censure on that account merely, I would only say to them, that I shall not be disposed to envy them in the enjoyment of their sentiments, while I endeavor to content myself in the enjoyment of a consciousness of having done what I could to effect the establishment of righteousness and peace in the earth. . . .

Excuses have been employed in vain to cover up the hypocrisy of this nation. The most corrupt policy which ever disgraced its barbarous ancestry, has been adopted by both church and state, for the avowed purpose of withholding the *inalienable rights* of one part of the subjects of the government. Pretexts of the lowest order, which are neither witty nor decent, and which rank among that order of subterfuges, under which the lowest of ruffians attempt to hide, when exposed to detection, are made available. Indeed, I may say in candor, that a highwayman or assassin acts upon principles far superior, in some respects, in comparison with those under which the administrators of the laws of church and state act, especially in their attempts to hide themselves and their designs from the just censure of the world, and from the burning rays of truth. I have no language to express what I see, and hear, and feel, on this subject. Were I capable of dipping my pen in the deepest dye of crime, and of understanding the science of the

bottomless pit, I should then fail in presenting to the intelligence of mortals
on earth, the true nature of American deception. There can be no appeals
made in the name of the laws of the country, of philanthropy, or humanity,
or religion, that is capable of drawing forth anything but the retort,—*you
are a Negro!* If we call to our aid the thunder tones of the cannon and the
arguments of fire arms, (vigorously managed by black and white men, side
by side,) as displayed upon Dorchester Heights, and at Lexington, and at
White Plains, and at Kingston, and at Long Island, and elsewhere, the
retort is, *you are a Negro*—if we present to the nation a Bunker's Hill, our
nation's altar, (upon which she offered her choicest sacrifice,) with our
fathers and brothers, and sons, prostrate thereon, wrapped in fire and
smoke—the incense of blood borne upward upon the wings of sulphurous
vapor, to the throne of national honor, with a hale of national glory echoing
back, and spreading and astonishing the civilized world;—and if we present the thousands of widows and orphans, whose only earthly protectors
were thus sacrificed, weeping over the fate of the departed; and anon, tears
of blood are extorted, on learning that the government for which their lovers
and sires had died, refuses to be their protector; if we tell that angels weep
in pity, and that God, the eternal Judge, "will hear the desire of the humble,
judge the fatherless and the oppressed, that the man of the earth may no
more oppress,"—the retort is, YOU ARE A NEGRO! If there is a spark of
honesty, patriotism, or religion, in the heart or the source from whence such
refuting arguments emanate, the devil incarnate is the brightest seraph in
paradise. . . .

The injury sustained by the colored people, is both national and personal;
indeed, it is national in a twofold sense. In the first place, they are lineally
stolen from their native country, and detained for centuries, in a strange
land, as hewers of wood and drawers of water. In this situation, their blood,
habits, minds, and bodies, have undergone such a change, as to cause them
to lose all legal or natural relations to their mother country. They are no
longer her children; therefore, they sustain the great injury of losing their
country, their birthright, and are made aliens and illegitimates. Again, they
sustain a national injury by being adopted subjects and citizens, and then
be denied their citizenship, and the benefits derivable therefrom—accounted
as aliens and outcasts, hence, are identified as belonging to no country—
denied birthright in one, and had it stolen from them in another—and, I had
like to have said, they had lost title to both worlds; for certainly they are
denied all title in this, and almost all advantages to prepare for the next.
In this light of the subject, they belong to no people, race, or nation; subjects of no government—citizens of no country—scattered surplus remnants
of two races, and of different nations—severed into individuality—rendered

a mass of broken fragments, thrown to and fro, by the boisterous passions of this and other ungodly nations. Such, in part, are the national injuries sustained by this miserable people. . . .

The arguments founded on these premises, are many. Cotton, rice, indigo, tobacco, and sugar, are great blessings to the world, say they, and they may as well be made to produce them as not; for they are a lazy crew at the best, and if they are not made to work for us, they will not work at all, &c. But to come to the truth, the whole system is founded in avarice. I believe the premises to be the production of modern philosophy, bearing date with European slavery; and it has been the almost sole cause of the present prevailing public sentiment in regard to the colored population. It has given rise to the universal habit of thinking that they were made for the sole end of being slaves and underlings. There could be nothing more natural, than for a slaveholding nation to indulge in a train of thoughts and conclusions that favored their idol, slavery. It becomes the interest of all parties, not excepting the clergy, to sanction the premises, and draw the conclusions, and hence, to teach the rising generation. What could accord better with the objects of this nation in reference to blacks, than to teach their little ones that a Negro is part monkey?

"The love of money is the root of all evil;" it will induce its votaries to teach lessons to their little babes, which only fit them for the destroyers of their species in this world, and for the torments of hell in the world to come. When clergymen, even, are so blinded by the god of this world, as to witness the practice of the most heinous blasphemy in the house, said to be dedicated to God, for centuries, without raising their warning voice to the wicked, it would not be at all surprising if they were to teach their children a few lessons in the science of anatomy, for the object of making them understand that a Negro is not like a white man, instead of teaching him his catechism.

The effect of this instruction is most disastrous upon the mind of the community; having been instructed from youth to look upon a black man in no other light than a slave, and having associated with that idea the low calling of a slave, they cannot look upon him in any other light. If he should chance to be found in any other sphere of action than that of a slave, he magnifies to a monster of wonderful dimensions, so large that they cannot be made to believe that he is a man and a brother. Neither can they be made to believe it would be safe to admit him into stages, steam-boat cabins, and tavern dining-rooms; and not even into meeting-houses, unless he have a place prepared on purpose. Mechanical shops, stores, and school rooms, are all too small for his entrance as a man; if he be a slave, his corporeality becomes so diminished as to admit him into ladies' parlors, and into small private carriages, and elsewhere, without being disgustful on account of his deformity, or without producing any other discomfiture. Thus prejudice seems to possess a magical power, by which it makes a being appear most odious one moment, and the next, beautiful—at one moment too large to be on board a steam-boat, the next, so small as to be convenient almost any where.

H. Easton, *A Treatise on the Intellectual Character, and Civil and Political Condition of the Colored People of the United States* . . . (Boston, 1837), pp. 33–34, 43–44. Copy in Columbia Univ. Library.

## 72

## A NEGRO DENOUNCES PREJUDICE WITHIN THE ABOLITIONIST MOVEMENT, 1837

At the convention of the New York State Anti-Slavery Society, held in Utica, September 20, 1837, the Rev. Theodore S. Wright made the following dramatic speech directed against the white supremacist thinking present within the Abolitionist movement:

Mr. President: All who have heard the [annual] report which has been presented are satisfied it needs no eulogy. It supports itself. But, sir, I would deem it a privilege to throw out a few thoughts upon it—thoughts which arise on beholding this audience. My mind is involuntarily led back a few years to the period prior to the commencement of this great moral effort for the removal of the giant sin of oppression from our land. It is well known to every individual who is at all acquainted with the history of slavery in this land, that the convention of 1776, when the foundations of our government were laid, proclaimed to the world the inalienable rights of man; and they supposed that the great principles of liberty would work the destruction of slavery throughout this land. This remark is sustained by an examination of the document then framed, and by the fact that the term "slavery" is not even named. The opinion that slavery would be abolished—indeed, that it had already received a death-blow, was cherished by all the reformers.—This spirit actuated Woolman, Penn, Edwards, Jefferson, and Benezet, and it worked out the entire emancipation of the North.

But it is well known that about 1817 a different drift was given—a new channel was opened for the benevolence which was working so well. The principle of expatriation, like a great sponge, went around in church and state, among men of all classes, and sponged up all the benevolent feelings which were then prevalent, and which promised so much for the emancipa tion of the enslaved and down-trodden millions of our land. That, sir, we call the dark period.. Oh, sir! if my father who sits beside me were to rise up and tell you how he felt and how men of his age felt, and how I felt (though a boy at that time), sir, it would be seen to have been a dark period. Why, sir, the heavens gathered blackness, and there was nothing cheering in our prospects. A spirit was abroad, which said "this is not your country and home," a spirit which would take us away from our firesides, tear the freeman away from his oppressed brother. This spirit was tearing the free father away from his children, separating husband and wife, sundering those cords of consanguinity which bind the free with the slave. This scheme was as popular as it possibly could be. The slaveholder and the pro-slavery man, the man of expanded views, the man who loved the poor and oppressed of every hue and of every clime, all united in this feeling and principle of expatriation.

But, sir, there were hundreds of thousands of men in the land who never could sympathize in this feeling; I mean those who were to be removed. The people of color were broken-hearted; they knew, sir, there were physical impossibilities to their removal. They knew, sir, that nature, reason, justice and inclination forbade the idea of their removing; and hence in 1817, the people of color in Philadelphia, with James Forten at their head—(and I envy them the honor they had in the work in which they were engaged), in an assembly of three thousand, before high heaven, in the Presence of Almighty God, and in the midst of a persecuting nation, resolved that they never would leave the land. They resolved to cling to their oppressed brethren. They felt that every ennobling spirit forbade their leaving them. They resolved to remain here, come what would, persecution or death. They determined to grapple themselves to their enslaved brethren as with hooks of steel. My father, at Schenectady, under great anxiety, took a journey to Philadelphia to investigate the subject. This was the spirit which prevailed among the people of color, and it extended to every considerable place in the North and as far South as Washington and Baltimore. They lifted up their voice and said, this is my country, here I was born, here I have toiled and suffered, and here I will die. Sir, it was a dark period. Although they were unanimous, and expressed their opinions, they could not gain access to the public mind: for the press would not communicate the facts in the case—it was silent. In the city of New York, after a large meeting, where protests were drawn up against the system of colonization, there was not a single public journal in the city, secular or religious, which would publish the view of the people of color on the subject. . . .

Ought I not this afternoon to call upon my soul, and may I not ask you to call upon *your souls* to bless the Lord for His unspeakable goodness in bringing about the present state of things? What gratitude is called for on our part, when we contrast the state of things developed in your report with the dark period when we could number the Abolitionists, when they were few and far between? Now a thousand societies exist, and there are hundreds of thousands of members. Praise God and persevere in this great work. Should we not be encouraged? We have everything to hope for, and nothing to fear. God is at the helm. The Bible is your platform—the Holy Spirit will aid you. We have everything necessary pledged, because God is with us. Hath he not said—"Break every yoke, undo the heavy burdens, and let the oppressed go free"?—"Remember them that are in bonds, as bound with them"? Why do I see so many who minister at the sacred altar— so many who have everything to lose and nothing to gain, personally, by identifying themselves with this cause? Nothing but the spirit of Almighty God brought these men here.

This cause, noble though persecuted, has a lodgment in the piety of our countrymen, and never can be expatriated. How manifest has been the progress of this cause! Why, sir, three years ago, nothing was more opprobious than to be called an "Abolitionist" or "antislavery man"!

Now you would be considered as uncharitable towards pro-slavery men, whether editors of newspapers, presidents of colleges or theological seminaries, if you advance the idea that they are not Abolitionists or antislavery men. Three years ago, when a man professed to be an Abolitionist, we knew where he was. He was an individual who recognized the identity of the human family. Now a man may call himself an Abolitionist and we know not where to find him. Your tests are taken away. A rush is made into the abolition ranks. Free discussion, petition Anti-Texas, and political favor converts are multiplying. Many throw themselves in, without understanding the breadth and depth of the principles of emancipation. I fear not the annexation of Texas. I fear not all the machination, calumny and opposition of slaveholders, when contrasted with the annexation of men whose hearts have not been deeply imbued with these high and holy principles. Why, sir, unless men come out and take their stand on the principle of recognizing man as man, I tremble for the ark, and I fear our society will become like the expatriation society; everybody an Abolitionist. These points which have lain in the dark must be brought out to view. The identity of the human family, the principle of recognizing all men as brethren—that is the doctrine, that is the point which touches the quick of the community. It is an easy thing to ask about the vileness of slavery at the South, but to call the dark man a brother, heartily to embrace the doctrine advanced in the second article of the constitution, to treat all men according to their moral worth, to treat the man of color in all circumstances as a man and brother—that is the test.

Every man who comes into this society ought to be catechized. It should be ascertained whether he looks upon man as man, all of one blood and one family. A healthful atmosphere must be created, in which the slave may live when rescued from the horrors of slavery. I am sensible I am detaining you, but I feel that this is an important point. I am alarmed sometimes when I look at the constitutions of our societies. I am afraid that brethren sometimes endeavor so to form the constitutions of societies that they will be popular. I have seen constitutions of abolition societies, where nothing was said about the improvement of the man of color! They have overlooked the giant sin of prejudice. They have passed by this foul monster, which is at once the parent and offspring of slavery. Whilst you are thinking about the annexation of Texas—whilst you are discussing the great principles involved in this noble cause, remember this prejudice must be killed or slavery will never be abolished. Abolitionists must annihilate in their own bosoms the cord of caste. We must be consistent—recognize the colored man in every respect as a man and brother. In doing this we shall have to encounter scorn; we shall have to breast the storm. This society would do well to spend a whole day in thinking about it and praying over it. Every Abolitionist would do well to spend a day in fasting and prayer over it and in looking at his own heart. Far be it from me to condemn Abolitionists. I rejoice and bless God for this first institution which has combined its energies for the overthrow of this heaven-daring—this soul-crushing prejudice.

The successors of Penn, Franklin and Woolman have shown themselves the friends of the colored race. They have done more in this cause than any other church and they are still doing great things both in Europe and America. I was taught in childhood to remember the man of the broad-brimmed hat and drab-colored coat and venerate him. No class have testified more to the truth on this subject. They lifted up their voices against slavery and the slave-trade. But, ah! with but here and there a noble exception, they go but halfway. When they come to the grand doctrine, to lay the ax right down at the root of the tree, and destroy the very spirit of slavery—there they are defective. Their doctrine is to set the slave free, and let him take care of himself. Hence, we hear nothing about their being brought into the Friends' Church, or of their being viewed and treated according to their moral worth. Our hearts have recently been gladdened by an address of the Annual Meeting of the Friends' Society in the city of New York, in which they insist upon the doctrine of immediate emancipation. But that very good man who signed the document as the organ of that society within the past year, received a man of color, a Presbyterian minister, into his house, gave him his meals alone in the kitchen, and did not introduce him to his family. That shows how men can testify against slavery at the South, and not assail it at the North, where it is tangible. Here is something for Abolitionists to do. What can the friends of emancipation effect while the spirit of slavery is so fearfully prevalent? Let every man take his stand, burn out this prejudice, live it down, talk it down, everywhere consider the colored man as a man, in the church, the stage, the steamboat, the public house, in all places, and the death-blow to slavery will be struck.

*The Colored American* (N.Y.), October 4, 1837; published in C. G. Woodson, ed., *Negro Orators*, pp. 86–92.

## 73

# THE NEGRO'S POLITICAL TACTICS, 1837

Many of the characteristic features of Negro political tactics, as these have evolved during generations of oppression, were expressed at a meeting of New Bedford, Massachusetts Negroes held late in October or early in November, 1837. Among the men prominent upon this occasion, in addition to the two mentioned in the document, were William P. Powell and Nathan Johnson.

At a meeting of the Colored Citizens of this town, in pursuance of public notice held in the Colored Christian Church last evening, Richard C. Johnson was called to the Chair, and John Briggs chosen Secretary.

A committee of five was appointed to prepare resolutions, who retired for the purpose.

A committee of seven was appointed to nominate a list of candidates to be supported as Representatives to the General Court, and instructed to make their report at an adjournment of the meeting.

The committee on Resolutions then came in and reported the following resolutions, which were unanimously adopted.

*Resolved,* That for the purpose of enabling the friends of Liberty to vote consistently, a committee of three be appointed to interrogate all candidates in this County for Legislative officers, as to their views on the following subjects;—1st, Is Liberty by will of the Creator the birthright of all men? does its universal enjoyment tend to promote the general welfare? and is it withheld from any except by a wicked tyranny? 2d, Whether Congress has power to abolish slavery in the District of Columbia; and the territories under the jurisdiction of the United States, and whether such power ought to be immediately exercised for this purpose? 3d, Whether Congress has power to put an end to the internal or domestic slave trade, and whether that trade ought to be immediately abolished? 4th, If they will vote to instruct or request our Senators and Representatives in Congress to use all their influence to preserve to the people inviolate, the freedom of speech and the press, and the right of petition or remonstrance on all subjects?

*Resolved,* That the great objects of impartial Liberty and equal rights, for which we are contending, are far superior to any of the principles or measures which divide the political parties of the present day.

*Resolved,* That as a people oppressed and proscribed, we have not as yet discovered any sincerity in either party, therefore as Abolitionists we deem it our duty to stand aloof from all political parties, and will be careful to vote for no man of any party who will not give his influence in favor of the objects embraced in these Resolutions.

*Voted,* That the proceedings of this meeting be published in the papers of this town.

*The Liberator,* November 17, 1837.

## 74

# THE NEGRO'S RESPONSE TO LOVEJOY'S MARTYRDOM, 1837

On November 7, 1837, Elijah P. Lovejoy was murdered by a pro-slavery mob while attempting to defend the press of the Alton, Illinois *Observer.* No one was punished for this act. *The Colored American* of November 25, 1837 published the following editorial, in black borders, concerning this event. In addition, Negroes met in mass meetings throughout the North to condemn the act, and to raise money for the martyr's widow and children. Typical is a meeting held in New York City on December 18, 1837, in which $60 was raised for the Lovejoys, and the resolutions herewith printed were adopted.

## [a]

AN AMERICAN CITIZEN MURDERED! THE PRESS DESTROYED! ! THE SPIRIT OF
SLAVERY TRIUMPHANT! ! !

Elijah P. Lovejoy, that fearless advocate of the press, has fallen a victim to the fury of a mob, thirsting for his blood, because he dared to lift up his voice against the oppression of the poor slave. . . .

How horrible to contemplate, and how fearfully pregnant with danger to the safety of every institution in our country!

Whither shall we turn our aching eyes? Where shall we look for a redeeming spirit? To the Press? Gracious Heaven! how has it spoken? Read the New-York *Gazette*, the *Courier & Enquirer*, the *Star* and the *Sun*, and then let us hang our heads in shame. To the pulpit? It is recreant to its trust. With a few *noble* and *splendid exceptions* the Pulpit and the Press, have virtually by their silence and actual committal, espoused the side of the oppressor. Truly "on the side of the oppressor there is power."

Who are guilty in this matter? Is it the poor, ignorant, sunken and abandoned wretches who consummate the work planned out by "gentlemen of property and standing?" No! They know not what they do. But the Press, which from the commencement of the Anti-Slavery controversy, has kept alive by base misrepresentations, the worst passions of the human heart, and pointed at Abolitionists as fit subjects for the assassin's dagger—the press—Political and Religious, by baptising itself in all manner of abominations, in order to oppose the progress of pure principles, is guilty of this crime.

The Pulpit, also, standing aloof from the contest, or putting forth its bulls of condemnation, against the efforts making for Emancipation, is guilty. Upon it is the blood of the murdered Lovejoy, and before the gathering wrath of a just God it will stand condemned as recreant to its trust.

### [b]

#### *Resolutions of New York Meeting*

That as American citizens, we the people of color of the city of New York, repose the utmost confidence *in* and respect *for* the character and principles of the Abolitionists, whose steady advocacy of our rights as men gives assurance that they rather desire to plead God than man.

That we condole with the widow of the Rev. Elijah P. J. Lovejoy, who fell a sacrifice to the demon of slavery and a corrupt public sentiment; whose labors in behalf of our oppressed countrymen were indicative of a mind and heart, that nobly sustained the private character of husband and father, as well as the public one of philanthropist and patriot.

That the blood of the martyred Lovejoy calls upon us, an oppressed people, to become more united in sentiment and effort, while two and a half millions of our brethren are dragging out a life of misery and degradation in that most detestable system of slavery which not only reduces its victims to brutes, but threatens slavery and death to those who plead their cause.

That among our rights, we hold none dearer than the freedom of speech and of the press; and that, whilst in the land of the free, we can never relinquish that freedom for the dumb eloquence of the down trodden slave.

That a letter of condolence be forwarded to the widow, expressive of our wish, that the God of the widow and orphan may support her mind through the hours of affliction and sorrow, and lead her to the contemplation of the time when the sorrows of earth shall be exchanged for the joys of heaven.

That we recommend a similar expression of sentiments upon this event to our fellow citizens, in all parts of the country.

*The Liberator*, December 29, 1837.

## 75·

## APPEAL OF FORTY THOUSAND, 1838

The Pennsylvania Constitutional Convention of 1837 provided for the disfranchisement of Negroes. Numerous petitions from Negroes throughout the state had reached this convention in opposition to the provision, but in vain. A great mass meeting of Negroes was held in Philadelphia on March 14, 1838 as part of a futile effort to defeat its ratification. From this meeting issued the following statement, in pamphlet form, filled with valuable information as well as strong emotion.

A very numerous and respectable meeting of the colored citizens of Pennsylvania, was held in the Presbyterian Church, Seventh Street, below Shippen, on the evening of the 14th inst. The meeting was organized by calling John P. Burr to the chair, and appointing Thomas Butler and Stephen H. Gloucester Vice-Presidents, and James Cornish and James Forten, Jr., Secretaries. After an appropriate prayer by the Rev. Charles W. Gardner, the Chairman, with some suitable observations, stated the object of the meeting,—which was to receive the report of a Committee consisting of the following gentlemen: Robert Purvis, James Cornish, J. C. Bowers, Robert B. Forten, J. J. G. Bias, James Needham, and John P. Burr—appointed at a public meeting held prior to the above, in St. Paul's Lutheran Church, Quince Street, to prepare an appeal in behalf of forty thousand citizens, threatened with disfranchisement, to their fellow citizens, remonstrating against the late cruel act of the Reform Convention: Robert Purvis, Chairman of said Committee, presented and read the appeal; it was accepted, and remarks were then made by James Forten, sr., Robert Purvis, J. C. Bowers, F. A. Hinton, Charles W. Gardner, and several others, after which it was adopted with a unanimity and spirit equalled only by the memorable meeting of 1817.

The following resolutions were unanimously adopted:

1. *Resolved*, That our warm and grateful thanks are due those gentlemen who, on the floor of the Convention, stood by us in the hour of need, in the able assertion and advocacy of our rights, and to others who voted

against the insertion of the word "white." Also, that like thanks are due to our Abolition friends for their active though unavailing exertions to prevent the unrighteous act.

2. *Resolved,* That a committee of five be appointed to draw up a remonstrance against the Colonization Society, to be presented to the various Churches, Presbyterys, Conferences, and Conventions. The following persons were appointed:—James Forten, sr., S. H. Gloucester, Robert Douglass, Charles W. Gardner, and Bishop [Morris] Brown.

Thomas Butler    } Vice Presidents              John P. Burr, President
S. H. Gloucester }

James Cornish    } Secretaries
James Forten, jr. }

### APPEAL

FELLOW CITIZENS:—We appeal to you from the decision of the "Reform Convention," which has stripped us of a right peaceably enjoyed during forty-seven years under the Constitution of this commonwealth. We honor Pennsylvania and her noble institutions too much to part with our birthright, as her free citizens, without a struggle. To all her citizens the right of suffrage is valuable in proportion as she is free; but surely there are none who can so ill afford to spare it as ourselves.

Was it the intention of the people of this commonwealth that the Convention to which the Constitution was committed for revision and amendment, should tear up and cast away its first principles? Was it made the business of the Convention to deny "that all men are born equally free," by making political rights depend upon the skin in which a man is born? or to divide what our fathers bled to unite, to wit, TAXATION and REPRESENTATION? We will not allow ourselves for one moment to suppose, that the majority of the people of Pennsylvania are not too respectful of the rights and too liberal towards the feelings of others, as well as too much enlightened to their own interests, to deprive of the right of suffrage a single individual who may safely be trusted with it. And we cannot believe that you have found among those who bear the burdens of taxation any who have proved, by their abuse of the right, that it is not safe in their hands. This is a question, fellow-citizens, in which we plead *your* cause as well as our own. It is the safeguard of the strongest that he lives under a government which is obliged to respect the voice of the weakest. When you have taken from an individual his right to vote, you have made the government, in regard to him, a mere despotism; and you have taken a step towards making it a despotism to all. To your women and children, their inability to vote at the polls may be no evil, because they are united by consanguinity and affection with those who can do it. To foreigners and paupers the want of the right may be tolerable, because a little time or labor will make it theirs. They are candidates for the privilege, and hence substantially enjoy its benefits. But when a distinct class of the community, already sufficiently the objects of prejudice, are wholly, and for ever, disfranchised and excluded, to the remotest posterity, from the possibility of a voice in regard to the laws under which they are to live—it is the same thing as if their abode were transferred to the dominions of the Russian Autocrat, or of the Grand Turk. They have lost their check upon oppression, their wherewith to buy friends, their panoply of manhood; in short, they are thrown upon the mercy of a despotic majority. Like every other despot, this despot majority, will believe in the mildness of its own sway; but who will the more willingly submit to it for that?

To us our right under the Constitution has been more precious, and our deprivation of it will be the more grievous, because our expatriation has come to be a darling project with many of our fellow citizens. Our abhorrence of a scheme which comes to us in the guise of Christian benevolence, and asks us to suffer ourselves to be transplanted to a distant and barbarous land, *because we are a "nuisance" in this,* is not more deep and thorough than it is reasonable. We love our native country, much as it has wronged us; and in the peaceable exercise of our inalienable rights, we will cling to it. The immortal Franklin, and his fellow laborers in the cause of humanity, have bound us to our homes here with chains of gratitude. We are PENNSYLVANIANS, and we hope to see the day when Pennsylvania will have reason to be proud of us, as we believe she has now none to be ashamed! Will you starve our patriotism?

Will you cast our hearts out of the treasury of the commonwealth? Do you count our enmity better than our friendship?

Fellow citizens, we entreat you, in the name of fair dealing, to look again at the just and noble charter of Pennsylvania freedom, which you are asked to narrow down to the lines of caste and color. The Constitution reads as follows:—

"Article 3, paragraph 1. In elections by the citizens, every freeman, of the age of twenty-one years, having resided in the State two years next before the election, and within that time paid a State or county tax, which shall have been assessed at least six months before the election, shall enjoy the rights of an election."

This clause guarantees the right of suffrage to us as fully as to any of our fellow citizens whatsoever, for

1. Such was the intention of the framers. In the original draft reported by a committee of nine, the word "WHITE" stood before "FREEMAN." On

motion of Albert Gallatin it was stricken out, for the express purpose of including colored citizens with the pale of the elective franchise. (See Minutes of the Convention, 1790.)

2. We are CITIZENS. This, we believe, would never have been denied, had it not been for the scheme of expatriation to which we have already referred. But as our citizenship has been doubted by some who are not altogether unfriendly to us, we beg leave to submit some proof, which we think you will not hastily set aside.

We were regarded as CITIZENS by those who drew up the articles of confederation between the States, in 1778. The fourth of the said articles contains the following language:—"The free inhabitants of each of these States, paupers, vagabonds, and fugitives from justice excepted, shall be entitled to all privileges and immunities of free *citizens* in the several States." That we were not excluded under the phrase "paupers, vagabonds, and fugitives from justice," any more than our white countrymen, is plain from the debates that preceded the adoption of the article. For, on the 25th of June, 1778, "the delegates from South Carolina moved the following amendment *in behalf of their* State. In article fourth, between the words *free* inhabitants, insert *white*. Decided in the negative; ayes, two States; nays, eight States; one State divided." Such was the solemn decision of the revolutionary Congress, concurred in by the entire delegation from our own commonwealth. On the adoption of the present Constitution of the United States no change was made as to the rights of citizenship. This is explicitly proved by the Journal of Congress. Take, for example, the following resolution passed in the House of Representatives, December 21, 1803: "On motion; *Resolved,* That the Committee appointed to enquire and report whether any further provisions are necessary for the more effectual protection of American seamen, do enquire into the expediency of granting protections to such American seamen, *citizens of the United States,* as *are free persons of color,* and that they report by bill, or otherwise."

. . . Proofs might be multiplied. In almost every State we have been spoken of, either expressly or by implication; as *citizens.* In the very year before the adoption of the present Constitution, 1789, the "Pennsylvania Society for Promoting the Abolition of Slavery & c," put forth an address, signed by "BENJAMIN FRANKLIN, *President,*" in which they stated one of their objects to be, "to *qualify* those who have been restored to freedom, for the exercise and enjoyment of CIVIL LIBERTY." The Convention of 1790, by striking out the word "WHITE," fixed the same standard of *qualification* for all; and, in fact, granted and guaranteed "civil liberty" to all who possessed that qualification. Are we now to be told, that the Convention did not intend to include colored men, and that BENJAMIN FRANKLIN did not know what he was about, forasmuch as it was impossible for a colored man to become a citizen of the commonwealth?

It may here be objected to us, that in point of fact we have lost by the recent decision of the [Pennsylvania] Supreme Court, in the case of *Fogg* vs. *Hobbs,* whatever claim to the right of suffrage we may have had under the Constitution of 1790; and hence have no reason to oppose the amended Constitution. Not so. We hold our rights under the present Constitution none the cheaper for that decision. The section already cited gives us all that we ask—all that we can conceive it in the power of language to convey. Reject, fellow citizens, the partial, disfranchising Constitution offered you by the Reform Convention, and we shall confidently expect that the Supreme Court will do us the justice and itself the honor to retract its decision. Should it not, our appeal will still be open to the conscience and common sense of the people, who through their chief magistrate and a majority of two-thirds of both branches of the Legislature may make way to the bench of the Supreme Court, for expounders of the Constitution who will not do violence to its most sacred and fundamental principles.

We cannot forbear here to refer you to some points in the published opinion of the Court as delivered by Chief Justice Gibson, which we believe will go far to strip it of the weight and authority ordinarily conceded to the decision of the highest tribunal (save the elections) of this commonwealth.

1. The Court relies much on a decision *said to have been had* "ABOUT" forty-three years ago, the claim of which to a place in the repository of Pennsylvania law is thus set forth by the Court itself:—

"About the year 1795, as I have it from James Gibson, Esq., of the Philadelphia bar, the very point before us was ruled by the High Court of Errors and Appeals, against the right of Negro suffrage. Mr. Gibson declined an invitation to be concerned in the argument, and therefore has no memorandum of the cause to direct us to the record. I have had the office searched for it; but the papers had fallen into such disorder as to preclude a hope of its recovery. Most of them were imperfect, and many were lost or misplaced. *But Mr. Gibson's remembrance of the decision is perfect and entitled to full confidence.*"

Now, suppressing doubt, and supposing such a decision actually to have emanated from the then highest tribunal of the commonwealth, does not the fact that it was so utterly forgotten as not to have regulated the polls within the memory of the present generation; nor to have been brought up against us in the Reform Convention; prove that it was virtually retracted? And if retracted, is it now to be revived to the overthrow of rights enjoyed without contradiction during the average life of man?

2. The Court argues that colored men are not *freemen*, and hence not entitled by the present Constitution to vote, because under laws prior to the Constitution there *might be* individuals who were not slaves, and yet were not *freemen! . . .*

3. Since the argument above referred to, such as it is, does not rest upon color, it is not less applicable to the descendants of Irish and German ancestors than to ourselves. If there ever have been within the commonwealth, men, or sets of men, who though personally free were not technically *freemen*, it is unconstitutional, according to the doctrine of the Court, for their descendants to exercise the right of suffrage, pay what taxes they may, till in "the discretion of the judges," their blood has "become so diluted in successive descents as to lose its distinctive character." Is this the doctrine of Pennsylvania freedom?

4. Lastly, the Court openly rests its decision on the authority of a wrong which this commonwealth so long ago as 1780 solemnly acknowledged, and, to the extent of its power, forever repealed. To support the same *wrong* in *other States*, the Constitution of *this*, when it uses the words "every freeman," must be understood to exclude every freeman of a certain color! The Court is of opinion that the people of this commonwealth had no power to confer the rights of citizenship upon one who, were he in another State, *might be* loaded by its laws with "countless disabilities." Now, since in some of the States men may be found in slavery who have not the slightest trace of African blood, it is difficult to see, on the doctrine of the Court, how the Constitution of Pennsylvania could confer the right of citizenship upon any person; and, indeed, how it could have allowed the emancipation of slaves of any color. To such vile dependence on its own ancient *wrongs*, and on the present *wrongs* of other States, is Pennsylvania reduced by this decision!

Are we then presumptuous in the hope that this grave sentence will be as incapable of resurrection fifty years hence, as is that which the Chief Justice assures us was pronounced *"about* the year 1795?" No. The blessings of the broad and impartial charter of Pennsylvania rights can no more be wrested from us by legal subtlety, than the beams of our common sun or the breathing of our common air.

What have we done to forfeit the inestimable benefits of this charter? Why should tax-paying colored men, any more than other tax-payers, be deprived of the right of voting for their representatives? It was said in the Convention, that this government belongs to the *Whites*. We have already shown this to be false, as to the past. Those who established our present government designed it equally for all. It is for you to decide whether it shall be confined to the European complexion in future. Why should you exclude us from a fair participation in the benefits of the republic? Have we oppressed

the whites? Have we used our rights to the injury of any class? Have we disgraced it by receiving bribes? Where are the charges written down, and who
will swear to them? We challenge investigation. We put it to the conscience
of every Pennsylvanian, whether there is, or ever has been, in the commonwealth, either a political party or religious sect which has less deserved than
ourselves to be thus disfranchised. As to the charge of idleness, we fling it
back indignantly. Whose brows have sweat for our livelihood but our own?
As to vice, if it disqualifies us for civil liberty, why not apply the same rule
to the whites, so far as they are vicious? Will you punish the innocent for
the crimes of the guilty? The execution of the laws is in the hands of the
whites. If we are bad citizens let them apply the proper remedies. We do not
ask the right of suffrage for the inmates of our jails and penitentiaries, but for
those who honestly and industriously contribute to bear the burdens of the
State. As to inferiority to the whites, if indeed we are guilty of it, either by
nature or education, we trust our enjoyment of the rights of freemen will
on that account be considered the less dangerous. If we are incompetent to
fill the offices of State, it will be the fault of the whites only if we are suffered
to disgrace them. We are in too feeble a minority to cherish a mischievous
ambition. Fair protection is all that we aspire to.

We ask your attention, fellow citizens, to facts and testimonies which
go to show that, considering the circumstances in which we have been placed,
our country has no reason to be ashamed of us, and that those have the
most occasion to blush to whom nature has given the power.

By the careful inquiry of a committee appointed by the "Pennsylvania
Society for Promoting the Abolition of Slavery," it has been ascertained that
the colored population of Philadelphia and its suburbs, numbering 18,768
souls, possess at the present time, of real and personal estate, not less than
$1,350,000. They have paid for taxes during the last year $3,252.83, for
house, water, and ground rent, $166,963.50. This committee estimate the
income of the holders of real estate occupied by the colored people, to be
7½ per cent on a capital of about $2,000,000. Here is an addition to the
wealth of their white brethren. But the rents and taxes are not all; to pay
them, the colored people must be employed in labor, and here is another profit
to the whites, for no man employs another unless he can make his labor
profitable to himself. For a similar reason, a profit is made by all the whites
who sell to colored people the necessaries or luxuries of life. Though the aggregate amount of the wealth derived by the whites from our people can
only be conjectured, its importance is worthy of consideration by those who
would make it less by lessening our motive to accumulate for ourselves.

Nor is the profit derived from us counterbalanced by the sums which
we in any way draw from the public treasures. From a statement published

by order of the Guardians of the Poor of Philadelphia, in 1830, it appears that out of 549 out-door poor relieved during the year, only 22 were persons of color, being about four per cent of the whole number, while the ratio of our population to that of the city and suburbs exceeds 8¼ per cent. By a note appended to the printed report above referred to, it appears that the colored *paupers* admitted into the almshouse for the same period, did not exceed four per cent of the whole. Thus it has been ascertained that they pay more than they receive in the support of their own poor. The various "mutual relief" societies of Philadelphia expend upwards of $7,000 annually for the relief of their members when sick or disabled.

That we are not neglectful of our religious interests, nor of the education of our children, is shown by the fact that there are among us in Philadelphia, Pittsburg, York, West Chester, and Columbia, 22 churches, 48 clergymen, 26 day schools, 20 Sabbath schools, 125 Sabbath school teachers, 4 literary societies, 2 public libraries, consisting of about 800 volumes, besides 8,333 volumes in private libraries, 2 tract societies, 2 Bible societies, and 7 temperance societies.

In other parts of the State we are confident our condition will compare very favorably with that in Philadelphia, although we are not furnished with accurate statistics.

Our fathers shared with yours the trials and perils of the wilderness. Among the facts which illustrate this, it is well known that the founder of your capital, from whom it bears the name of Harrisburg, was rescued by a *colored man*, from a party of Indians, who had captured, and bound him to the stake for execution. In gratitude for this act, he *invited colored persons* to settle in his town, and offered them land on favorable terms. When our common country has been invaded by a foreign foe, colored men have hazarded their lives in its defence. Our fathers fought by the side of yours in the struggle which made us an independent republic. . . .

We would have the right of suffrage only as the reward of industry and worth. We care not how high the qualification be placed. All we ask is, that no man shall be excluded on account of his *color*, that the same rule shall be applied to all.

Are we to be disfranchised, lest the purity of the *white* blood should be sullied by an intermixture with ours? It seems to us that our white brethren might well enough reserve their fear, till we seek such alliance with them. We ask no social favors. We would not willingly darken the doors of those to whom the complexion and features, which our Maker has given us, are disagreeable. The territories of the commonwealth are sufficiently ample to afford us a home without doing violence to the delicate nerves of our white brethren, for centuries to come. Besides, we are not intruders here, nor were our ancestors. Surely you ought to bear as unrepiningly the evil consequences of your fathers' guilt, as we those of our fathers' misfortune. Proscription and disfranchisement are the last things in the world to alleviate these evil consequences. Nothing, as shameful experience has already proved, can so powerfully promote the evil which you profess to deprecate, as the degradation of our race by the oppressive rule of yours. Give us that fair and honorable ground which self-respect requires to stand on, and the dreaded amalgamation, if it take place at all, shall be by your own fault, as indeed it always has been. We dare not give full vent to the indignation we feel on this point, but we will not attempt wholly to conceal it.

We ask a voice in the disposition of those public resources which we ourselves have helped to earn; we claim a right to be heard, according to our numbers, in regard to all those great public measures which involve our lives and fortunes, as well as those of our fellow citizens; we assert our right to vote at the polls as a shield against that strange species of benevolence which seeks legislative aid to banish us—and we are told that our white fellow citizens cannot submit to an *intermixture of the races!* Then let the indentures, title-deeds, contracts, notes of hand, and all other evidences of bargain, in which colored men have been treated as *men,* be torn and scattered on the winds. Consistency is a jewel. Let no white man hereafter ask his colored neighbor's *consent* when he wants his property or his labor; lest he should endanger the Anglo-Saxon purity of his descendants? Why should not the same principle hold good between neighbor and neighbor, which is deemed necessary, as a fundamental principle, in the Constitution itself? Why should you be ashamed to act in private business, as the Reform Convention would have you act in the capacity of a commonwealth? But, no! we do not believe our fellow citizens, while with good faith they hold ourselves bound by their contracts with us, and while they feel bound to deal with us only by fair contract, will ratify the arbitrary principle of the Convention, howmuchsoever they may prefer the complexion in which their Maker has pleased to clothe themselves.

We would not misrepresent the motives of the Convention; but we are constrained to believe that they have laid our rights a sacrifice on the altar of slavery. We do not believe our disfranchisement would have been proposed, but for the desire which is felt by political aspirants to gain the favor of the slave-holding States. This is not the first time that northern statesmen have "bowed the knee to the dark spirit of slavery," but it is the first time that they have bowed so low! Is Pennsylvania, which abolished slavery in 1780, and enfranchised her tax-paying colored citizens in 1790, now, in 1838, to get upon her knees and repent of her humanity, to gratify those who disgrace the very name of American Liberty, by holding our brethren as goods and chattels? We freely acknowledge our brotherhood to the slave, and our interest in his welfare. Is this a crime for which we should be ignominiously punished? The very fact that we are deeply interested for our kindred in bonds, shows that we are the right sort of stuff to make good citizens of. Were we not so, we should better deserve a lodging in your penitentiaries than a franchise at your polls. Doubtless it will be well pleasing to the slaveholders of the South to see us degraded. They regard our freedom from chains as a dangerous example, much more our political freedom. They see in every thing which fortifies our rights, an obstacle to the recovery of their fugitive property. Will Pennsylvania go backwards towards slavery, for the better safety of southern slave property? Be assured the South will never be satisfied till the old "Keystone" has returned to the point from which she started in 1780. And since the number of colored men in the commonwealth is so inconsiderable, the safety of slavery may require still more. It may demand that a portion of the white tax-payers should be unmanned and turned into chattels—we mean those whose hands are hardened by daily toil.

Fellow citizens, will you take the first step towards reimposing the chains which have now rusted for more than fifty years? Need we inform you that every colored man in Pennsylvania is exposed to be arrested as a fugitive from slavery? and that it depends not upon the verdict of a jury of his peers, but upon the decision of a judge on summary process, whether or not he shall be dragged into southern bondage? The Constitution of the United States provides that "no person shall be deprived of life, liberty, or property, without due process of law"—by which is certainly meant a TRIAL BY JURY. Yet the act of Congress of 1793, for the recovery of fugitive slaves, authorizes the claimant to seize his victim without a warrant from any magistrate, and allows him to drag him before "any magistrate of a county, city, or town corporate, where such seizure has been made," and upon proving, by "oral testimony or affidavit," to the satisfaction of such magistrate that the man is his slave, gives him a right to take him into everlasting bondage.

Thus may a free-born citizen of Pennsylvania be arrested, tried without counsel, jury, or power to call witnesses, condemned by a single man, and carried across Mason and Dixon's line, within the compass of a single day. An act of this commonwealth, passed 1820, and enlarged and re-enacted in 1825, it is true, puts some restraint upon the power of the claimant under the act of Congress; but it still leaves the case to the decision of a single judge, without the privilege of a jury! What unspeakably aggravates our loss of the right of suffrage at this moment is, that, while the increased activity of the slave-catchers enhances our danger, the Reform Convention has refused to amend the Constitution so as to protect our liberty by a jury trial! We entreat you to make our case your own—imagine your own wives and children to be trembling at the approach of every stranger, lest their husbands and fathers should be dragged into a slavery worse than Algerine—worse than death! Fellow citizens, if there is one of us who has abused the right of suffrage, let him be tried and punished according to law. But in the name of humanity, in the name of justice, in the name of the God you profess to worship, who has no respect of persons, do not turn into gall and wormwood the friendship we bear to yourselves by ratifying a Constitution which tears from us a privilege dearly earned and inestimably prized. We lay hold of the principles which Pennsylvania asserted in the hour which tried men's souls—which BENJAMIN FRANKLIN and his eight colleagues, in name of the commonwealth, pledged their lives, their fortunes, and their sacred honor to sustain: We take our stand upon that solemn declaration; that to protect inalienable rights "governments are instituted among men, deriving their JUST POWERS from the CONSENT of the governed," and pro-claim that a government which tears away from us and our posterity the very power of CONSENT, is a tyrannical usurpation which we will never cease to oppose. We have seen with amazement and grief the apathy of white Pennsylvanians while the "Reform Convention" has been perpetrating this outrage upon the good old principles of Pennsylvania freedom. But however others may forsake these principles, we promise to maintain them on *Pennsylvania soil*, to the last man. If this disfranchisement is designed to uproot us, it shall jail Pennsylvania's fields, valleys, mountains, and rivers; her canals, railroads, forests, and mines; her domestic altars, and her pub-lic, religious and benevolent institutions; her Penn and Franklin, her Rush, Rawle, Wistar, and Vaux; her consecrated past and her brilliant future, are as dear to us as they can be to you. Firm upon our Pennsylvania BILL OF RIGHTS, and trusting in a God of Truth and justice, we lay our claim before you, with the warning that no amendments of the present Constitution can compensate for the loss of its foundation principle of equal rights, nor for the conversion into enemies of 40,000 friends.

In behalf of the Committee,
Robert Purvis, *Chairman*

*Appeal of Forty Thousand Citizens, threatened with disfranchisement, to the people of Pennsylvania* (Phila., 1838).

76

# AN ABOLITIONIST AGITATOR TALKS OF HIS WORK, 1838

The most effective propagandists for Abolitionism were Negro speakers. Among the earliest and most forceful of these was Charles Lenox Remond. As an agent of the American Anti-Slavery Society he toured the free states carrying the word. Some sense of this work may be obtained from the following letter he wrote a fellow Massachusetts Negro Abolitionist, Thomas Cole, from Winthrop, Maine, on July 3, 1838:

My dear Friend:—I take advantage of the earliest opportunity to inform you, that on the third day after bidding you farewell, I met my friend Mr. Codding, at Brunswick, at which place, on the following Sunday afternoon, I addressed the friends a short time and was well received. On Tuesday following, left Brunswick for Alfred, to attend the formation of a County Anti-Slavery Society. There was not much interest taken in the meeting. On the following evening I was invited to address the meeting and complied. On the next day, I was invited to go into the country a short distance. I cut loose from Mr. Codding very reluctantly, and commenced lecturing in my feeble way. Received requests to lecture in four different places on four successive evenings. I consented, and spoke in each place an hour and a half; and although my audiences were generally dark on the subject of prejudice and slavery, I received on every occasion the most marked attention, and assurances of good feeling for the cause, and wishes for the success of our enterprise. At one place, they resolved at the close of the lecture, to form a society and lend their assistance in the great work.

On Wednesday last I went to Saco, to attend the conference meeting of the Congregational denomination. The delegation of ministers was very numerous, and much interest was manifested to every great and good, and benevolent undertaking, save the cause of the poor slave in our own beloved but guilty country. On Thursday evening I was invited to speak on the subject in the Baptist meetinghouse. My audience was almost entirely composed of ministers who were attending the conference, and a good number of interesting and intelligent ladies. At this place they have determined to do something forthwith for the slave, by forming a male and female society, and contributing to the cause. On last Sabbath afternoon, I lectured in the meeting-house in Bowdoin. Nothing special occurred.

I am now at the house of our kind and devoted friend, Rev. David

Thurston, and the feeling manifested on every occasion by his wife and daughters in behalf of human liberty is indeed such as may well make glad the hearts of our brethren in bonds. It is of no use for me to attempt to give you any thing like a description of the change which I believe is now taking place on the subject of slavery and the elevation of the nominally free. We have every thing, friend Thomas, to encourage us. Slavery is trembling, prejudice is falling, and I hope will soon be buried—buried beyond resurrection; and we will write over its grave as over Babylon—"Prejudice, the mother of abominations, the liar, the coward, the tyrant, the waster of the poor, the brand of the white man, the bane of the black man, is fallen! is fallen!"

*The Liberator*, July 20, 1838.

## 77

## RESISTING JIM CROW, 1838

The struggle against segregation has been an individual as well as a collective one. The following letter, dated Boston, October 26, 1838, from Thomas Van Renselaer, a New York Negro Abolitionist, to a white friend, Joshua Leavitt of Boston, is typical of thousands of courageous personal acts of resistance to discrimination.

Dear Brother,—I stepped on board the Steamboat J. W. Richmond, in your city, yesterday afternoon, for Providence. I had previously understood that *this* being an opposition boat, people were treated irrespective of complexion; so, full of hope of a pleasant entertainment, I went to the office and paid $3.50 (fifty cents more than the regular fare,) for my passage and a berth, No. 15, which was assigned me in the after cabin, and obtained my ticket. I walked about until dark, when, feeling chilly, I repaired to the cabin in which my berth was. I had not been there long, before a man came up to me in a very abrupt manner, and said, "Whose servant are you?" I at first gave no answer; he repeated, and I replied, I am my own, Sir. "Well," said he, "you must go on deck." I asked, why so? "Because you ought to know your place." I said, this is my place. Said he, "Go on deck, I tell you." Said I, I cannot go on deck. Said he with an oath, and running upon deck, "I'll make you." He returned in a moment with the captain, who came trembling, and said, "I want you to go on deck immediately." I asked the reason. "Not a word from you, sir." I asked, what offence have I committed? "Not a word, sir," said he, and laid hold of me with violence, and ordered two men to remove me. But when I saw him in such a rage, and fearing that he might do *himself* harm, I retired, and walked the deck till late at night, when I had another talk with the captain. I then told him he had not treated me well, and that an explanation was due from him; but he refused to allow me to go below, or to give me a berth. I then told him I should publish the treatment I had received. He again flew into a passion, and I saw no more of him. Between 11 and 12 o'clock, one of the waiters invited me to occupy a bed which he had prepared. I accepted it, and was rendered comfortable; and feel very grateful to three of the waiters for their sympathy in these trying moments, as well as to some of the passengers. One gentleman in particular, the Rev. Mr. Scudder (Methodist) gave me great consolation by identifying himself with me at the time.

Now dear brother, I have made this communication of facts for the information of the friends of human rights, who, I believe, have patronized *this boat* from principle, that they may act accordingly hereafter.

*The Liberator,* November 30, 1838.

# 78

## FIGHTING THE NEGRO PEW, 1839

We have seen that one of the responses to discrimination practiced by churches was the establishment of all-Negro religious organizations. Another response was agitation within the churches involved, a phase exemplified in the story of Jeremiah Asher's fight against the Negro pew in a Hartford, Connecticut Baptist Church in 1839.

Soon after my return to Hartford, a singular and rather novel circumstance occurred in the Church of which I was a member. In that, as in most of the Baptist, as well as other chapels, they have, as a matter of course, the Negro pew. This was the most objectionable one I had ever seen, though I have been accustomed to sit there with a degree of comfort up to this time. I will give a description of it:—In the first place, it was unlike every thing else in the house except its fellow; for there is usually two, one in each extreme corner of the gallery. The rest of the seats in the house are much like the seats in the Chapels in England. These, however, were about six feet square, with the sides so high it was almost impossible to see the minister or the rest of the congregation; and calculated to accommodate about fifteen or twenty persons. There was one seat in this pew which had, I suppose by general consent been conceded to me ever since my connexion with the church. However, one sabbath morning, it so happened, contrary to my usual practice, I was late, and the seat I was accustomed to occupy was taken; I was obliged to take one of the most objectionable; and that morning I was so tried, (for it is always difficult for me to hear when I cannot see), I resolved I would never go into that place again, and I was as good as my word, for I think I never went in after.

In that city there was, as I have already stated, a place where coloured persons of all denominations were in the habit of meeting for worship, so I resolved hereafter to meet there, the place where the Lord on a former occasion passd by me in the way of mercy; a place (however much there was in doctrine or practice which I deemed to be wrong,) yet dear to me, so I took my seat there for a time. Very soon, enquiries were made for me, and a reason demanded, for this strange conduct. At first I was reluctant about giving an answer, but being somewhat pressed I gave the reason, stating at the same time my determination to stand to my resolution. ·

I was advised to give up my determination; for such a course could not fail to bring me under the discipline of the church. However, I was immoveable; but the enquiry still was among the members of the church, why I had left. I refused to give any information on the subject to any one except the deacons, and finally they communicated my reasons to some of the members, and the subject came up at a subsequent meeting for consideration, and instead of disciplining me they disciplined the Negro pews, for they were arraigned and proved guilty of the charge of making distinction between the members of the body of Christ, condemned and excluded, never more to be admitted. This I regarded as a great triumph in behalf of my coloured brethren and sisters. But to my surprise, I was requested to meet a committee of the church to inform them what would satisfy the coloured members, for they were getting quite out of their place.

I informed these brethren in behalf of my coloured brethren and sisters, that the charge was not true—we were not at all difficult or hard to please— they asked nothing more than what had been already done; there were plenty of unoccupied seats in the gallery, (I did not of course presume that black christians had a right to sit below in their Father's house) on either side; all we asked, was to sit in the seats just as they were, without one penny expense by way of alteration. I contended, that those seats which were made for whites were good enough for blacks; if they did not wish us to mix together, they could give us a certain number of seats expressly for coloured persons. But they were aware that, without some visible distinction, whites coming in would often be sitting in the Negro seat, and their devotions would be frequently disturbed by the pew-opener, who would be obliged to remove them, and regulate all such irregularities. Hence they contended for the necessity of making considerable alterations, said it would be so much better and more respectable, to make some nice seats on purpose for the coloured people. I said they were quite respectable and nice enough; we were quite willing to take sittings in them at the rate of those rented in the gallery; but if they were to be altered, I must decline having anything to do with it—I should neither hire nor occupy one of them, even if they made them the best seats in the house; I would not pay for *proscription* any where, much less in the house of God, and especially in a Baptist Church, after having been welcome to all of the privileges of God's house in that place.

If men will disfranchise and separate me from the rest of my Father's children, they shall do it at their own expense, not mine. I cannot prevent it, but I will not help them to do it. I will lift up my voice against it. However, my counsel was set aside, and it was decided to make some nice seats on purpose for the coloured members; so they proceeded forthwith to carry this plan into execution. When finished, and an expense was incurred of about forty pounds, then it was noticed that these seats would be rented to the coloured people at one dollar a sitting per year. The time came, and I think there was not more than two or three present, and they did not take sittings. Now I was charged with preventing them, which certainly I did not. Matters came to such a crisis, I really thought I should be excluded; I was quite willing to be. At this time I did not attend any of the meetings for business. However, I received a very polite invitation to attend a meeting which was to be held in one of the coloured member's houses, in F. Street, when the pastor and deacons and all the coloured members would be present, and then this troublesome matter must be settled. So I complied with this request, and when the time came attended. I was called upon to open the meeting by prayer, which I at first declined; but as they urged it, I tried to pray, and I have never been sorry since, for the Lord heard my prayer, and I learnt a lesson that day which I have not forgotten since, that is, to call upon God in the day of trouble. After prayer, the pastor presiding, began a kind of inquiry with the members, as to their objections to the nice little seats they had made them. All were inquired of before they interrogated me. I think there was not an objection raised. Then they inquired what I had to say; when I rose up from my seat and addressed them for about twenty or thirty minutes, and if ever I felt the presence of God, it was that day. I was not replied to either by the chair or any one of the assembly. It was agreed to report to the church favourably. The committee were satisfied; the coloured members might sit where they pleased in the galleries, and that was the end of this revolution.

*Incidents in the Life of the Rev. J. Asher, Pastor of Shiloh (Coloured) Baptist Church, Philadelphia, United States, and a concluding chapter of facts illustrating the unrighteous prejudice existing in the minds of American citizens toward their coloured brethren* (London, 1850), pp. 43–47. Copy in Brooklyn Public Library.

79

## THE SPLIT IN THE ABOLITIONIST
## MOVEMENT, 1839-1840

In 1839 divergent tendencies in the Abolitionist movement, centering around the questions of female equality, opposition to all political activity and uncompromising denunciation of all established churches (as advocated particularly by Garrison) precipitated an organizational split resulting in the formation of the American and Foreign Anti-Slavery Society. Negro Abolitionists split, too, on these issues and especially on the question of political action, with men like William C. Nell, James G. Barbadoes, and William P. Powell supporting Garrison, and Samuel Cornish, Christopher Rush (founder and second bishop of the African Methodist Episcopal Zion Church), and Charles B. Ray, then an editor of *The Colored American,* becoming members of the first executive committee of the new society.

Two documents illustrative of these issues and personalities follow. The first is a joint statement dated March 19, 1840 of pro-Garrisonian Boston Negroes such as Barbadoes, Nell and John T. Hilton; the second is a letter dated New York, May 20, 1840, from a new organization supporter, Charles B. Ray, to Henry Stanton and James G. Birney, likewise anti-Garrisonians and delegates to a World Anti-Slavery Convention meeting in London.

### [a]

*Resolved,* That whereas the Massachusetts *Abolitionist* of the 13th inst. contains an article over the signature of a "A Colored Man," charging the old Massachusetts Anti-Slavery Society, and the editor of the *Liberator,* with recreancy to the first principles of abolition; and whereas he claims to give utterance to the sentiments and feelings of the colored population of Boston; therefore we feel called upon, out of respect to ourselves, and to the old society, to whose principles of equal rights, liberty, and humanity, we subscribe, to register our united and unqualified denial of the truth of these unwarranted assertions.

*Resolved,* That the position taken by the author, where he says, "Touch one colored man, and you touch all," would not seem to be true in all cases; for the poor slaves are daily touched, and there are some, we regret to say, among us, who have little or no sympathy for them, if judge them by the scripture standard, "Out of the abundance of the heart, the mouth speaketh." Again—were there no exceptions to this rule, persons might not be sheltered from justice, who are guilty of crimes of the deepest dye, and that simply because they are colored.

*Resolved,* That whereas the same writer has said, that were a meeting called of the colored people to try their votes on the merits of the two societies in question, they would give their hearty amen in favor of the new—we pronounce it a wholesale falsehood, and feel justified in saying, that the spirit which prompted him in penning said article was dictated neither by truth nor self-respect.

*Resolved,* That, so far from our confidence being shaken in the integrity of the Massachusetts Anti-Slavery Society, or that of the veteran editor of the *Liberator,* as stated in the article above alluded to, daily proofs of their real merits increase our attachment, and bind us stronger to them; and of Mr. Garrison we can truly add, that we doubt not that the day will come, when many an emancipated slave will say of him, while weeping over his monument, "This was my best friend and benefactor. I here bathe his tomb with the tears of that liberty, which his services and sufferings achieved for me."

*Resolved,* That to slander Garrison, and pronounce him a hypocrite is certainly the most unkind and ungrateful expression that could ever escape the lips of any colored man, and is what we least expected to hear, after so much toil and suffering in our behalf; and we rejoice that such spirits are few and far between.

*The Liberator,* April 3, 1840.

## [b]

Dear Friends and Coadjutors in the great cause of human Freedom:

I improve the detention of our brethren by a contrary wind, to transmit you a circumstance which I hope may not be called for, but which from evidence received I have reason to think may be. It refers to the results of a meeting held by some of us, on the evening of the 18 instant, and which I am informed our esteemed friend N. P. Rogers intends to use at the worlds convention, to show the effect New Organization has had upon the colored people of our City. My object in writing is to repudiate the idea, and to furnish you with the true state of the case, being rather apprehensive that our friend may be wrongly informed, as to the history of the matter.

On the 17th ultimo, Bro. T. Van Rensalaer between meetings, (it being Sunday) suggested to me the propriety as he thought, of having a meeting of the colored people, to hear an address from our old and tried FRIEND MR. GARRISON, and as he was to leave us the day following for LONDON to attend the worlds convention, to pass some resolutions expressive of our confidence in him, as a delegate, to said convention. I objected to aid him in getting up a meeting for that object alone, on the grounds as I stated to him, that other men had gone, who were dear to us as a *colored community*, and if we were going to express our confidence in one as a delegate, we should do the same to all, and not make such an invidious distinction, which in my opinion was unjust. The Rev. Thomas L. Wright, concurred with my views. Mr. Van Rensalaer deemed them satisfactory and judicious, as we thought, whereupon the House was granted, and I exerted myself to notify the meeting. Three of us, Mr. Van Rensalaer being one, resolved ourselves into a committee, to draft resolutions for the meeting, and were to meet at my office at 4 o'clock. Upon presenting our resolutions in committee, Mr. Van Rensalaer presented but one and that expressive of our views of the Convention to be held, and our confidence in four only, of the delegation; those who were taken up by the AMERICAN SOCIETY, upon the third day of the meeting. We objected to the resolution as perverting the meeting from its avowed object and contrary to the notices given, and a violation of the conditions upon which the House was obtained, and I had consented to cooperate in getting up the meeting, and because it was a negative disapproval of all the other delegates to be present from this country, who were alike entitled to our approbation and love, and as the resolution if passed, would be presented to the convention, it would place those other delegates in awkward position, and be both unfair and unjust. Mr. Van Rensalaer, determined to accept no amendment, we waived the matter until it should be presented to the meeting, informing him, that then, it should be laid aside.

The meeting convened in the Rev. Mr. Wrights church, a very respectable audience both as to number and character. The Rev. Brother Wright in the chair, and myself appointed Secretary.

After an address of some length, from our FRIEND MR. GARRISON, MR. VAN RENSALAER, immediately arose and presented his resolution. Brother H. H. Garnet, of Oneida Institute, seconded the resolution and moved an amendment to insert your names as delegates also virtually appointed by the AMERICAN SOCIETY. This not meeting my objections, Mr. J. Tuille, a clerk in our office, moved an amendment to Mr. Garnet's amendment, and I suggested an improvement to his, so that it should read "we approve of the American delegation, sent out by American Abolitionists" for we knew them all, either personally or by reputation. The whole matter elicited some considerable debate, all excepting Mr. Van Rensalaer, in favour of the amendments. Some however thought we had better take no action upon the matter, and after hearing some remarks from MR. GARRISON in which he objected to have his name associated with yours and Mr. Colver's, remarks which the meeting were very sorry to hear, and which they were not prepared to receive and it now being late, I moved the indefinite postponement of the whole subject, which was carried.

We could easily have passed a resolution, approving of the entire delegation, had it not been so late, but any other invidious resolution, could not have been passed by that meeting, not because we were wanting in any respect of any, but because we had too much real regard for all.

Now this refusal to pass an *illiberal* resolution (taken in its relation to the delegation) expressing our confidence in and approval of a few of the delegation of which Brother Garrison was one, to the rejection of the many, Brother Rogers regards as an alienation of feeling, and respect towards Mr. Garrison and this alienation of affection, as he regards it, Brother Rogers is going to show as he says and as I am informed by Brother Van Rensalaer as one of the fruits of New Organization as though nothing else could effect our minds toward MR. GARRISON if affected at all, but New Organization, a conclusion more unfounded and more unfair, in relation to us, could hardly have been arrived at.

If the colored people of this City, or any section of this country, do manifest less warmth of feeling, than formerly towards *Mr. Garrison* it is in part oweing to our *Friends* having multiplied who are equally active, and equally efficient with *Mr. Garrison,* and as a necessary consequence our good feeling is scattered upon all, instead of being concentrated upon one, as when Mr. Garrison stood alone. But there is another reason, and which I intended to have mentioned to Mr. Garrison personally, but had not the time when I saw him, viz the spirit with which Brother Garrison has conducted his own PAPER since this controversy commenced, especially the repeated use which he made of Brother Wrights letter to yourself.

These things affected some of our intelligent brethren, as they have informed me, and not *New Organization;* however much that may have a tending to alienate feeling from Brother Garrison. I give you this history of the meeting by no means in defence of New Organization but that you may have the facts to prevent any wrong impression that might be made, by Brother Rogers from his want of a knowledge of the true state of the case, and that it might not appear in England that we have forsaken our friends, but are constrained to cleave at all. We look forward to the worlds convention with great interest. We anticipate the happiest results from its proceedings, especially if you do not drag in foreign matters which may God prevent. We are proud in a proper sense, of our American delegation; and no man is an exception. We know you as men having passed through the ordeal that tried men's souls, and now hardly having escaped, you are not going to form an alliance with the enemy. We regret that some more of us cannot be with you. We hope, we pray that the enslaved of the world, those held in a chattel sense, of all colors and of all climes, may be the object of your deliberations, and that the result of them may be to raise up mankind to all the dignity of free men. We hope our American delegation, will meet together in London and although they have differed here, that they will bury the hatchet, and do nothing to reflect upon our holy cause in this our beloved though slavery ridden country. . . .

D. L. Dumond, ed., *Letters of James G. Birney* (2 vols., N.Y., Appleton-Century, 1938), I, pp. 575–79.

## 80

## THE WORLD ANTI-SLAVERY CONFERENCE, 1840

Among the delegates to the London World Anti-Slavery Conference was Charles L. Remond. He, however, excluded himself in protest against the Conference's refusal to seat female delegates. The following letter, dated London, June 30, 1840, is from Remond to Charles B. Ray. In addition to some remarks about the Conference it is indicative of the anti-slavery work conducted abroad by several American Negroes.

Faithful to my promise, although in the midst of engagements, I steal a moment, not to fill this sheet, as my time will not admit, but to inform you of my safe arrival and good health at this time; and that this sheet may meet you with your wife, sisters and friends in possession of the same privilege is my best wish. In referring to the subject of anti-slavery on this side the Atlantic, permit me to say, as a silent listener, I was much interested in the discussions during the sitting of the British and Foreign Anti-Slavery Society, (not World's Convention, as we had fondly and anxiously anticipated, which facts, with many others, forbid my taking a seat, and participating in its deliberations.) That on my arrival I learned with much sorrow of the rejection of the female delegation I need not mention. And in a few instances through life have I met with greater disappointment, especially in view of the fact, that I was almost entirely indebted to the kind and generous members of the Bangor Female Anti-Slavery Society, the Portland Sewing Circle, and the Newport Young Ladies' Juvenile Anti-Slavery Society, for aid in visiting this country. And I can assure you it was among my most happy reflections to know, that in taking my seat in the World's Convention, I should do so, the honored representative of the three female associations, at once most praiseworthy in their object, and efficient in this cooperation. And sure I am, that could the members of these associations have had even a place in the imaginations of those who voted for their exclusion, the decision would have been otherwise, far otherwise.

Thanks be to Providence, I have yet to learn, that the emancipation of the American slave, from the sepulchre of American slavery, is not of more importance than the rejection of females from the platform of any Anti-Slavery Society, Convention, or Conference. In the name of heaven, and in the name of the bleeding, dying slave, I ask, if I shall scruple the propriety of female action, of whatever kind or description. I trust not—I hope not— I pray not, until the bastard system is annihilated, and not a vestige remains to remind the future traveller, that such a system ever cursed our country, and made us a hissing and a by-word in the mouth of every subject of every Monarch, King, Queen, Despot, Tyrant, Autocrat and Czar of the civilized and uncivilized world!

My friend, for thirteen years have I thought myself an Abolitionist; but I had been in a measure mistaken, until I listened to the scorching rebukes of the fearless [Daniel] O'Connell in Exeter Hall, on the 24th June, when before that vast assemblage, he quoted from American publications, and alluded to the American declaration, and contrasted the theory with the practice; then was I moved to think, and feel, and speak; and from his soul-stirring eloquence and burning sarcasm would every fibre of my heart contract in abominating the worse than Spanish Inquisition system in my own, I almost fear, devoted country. Let it suffice to say, the meeting at Exeter Hall more than compensated me for the sacrifice and suffering I experienced in crossing the Atlantic, under circumstances which I shall make known at some future time. Until the facts are known, let no one envy me in my voyage or undertaking.

A few words in relation to slavery's grand handmaid, in the States proclaimed to be non-slaveholding—I mean *prejudice*, that acts the part to slavery of second king at arms, and exercises its authority by assisting in kidnapping the innocent and free at the capital, disfranchises the citizens of Pennsylvania, proscribes the colored man in Rhode Island, abuses and gives him no resting place as a man in New-Hampshire, which murders in Illinois, cries out amalgamation in Maine, mobs him in New York, and stones him in Connecticut. I say this hydra-headed personage, thanks be to God, has but few advocates in this country; if any, I have it to learn; and if you would rouse the honest indignation of the intelligent Englishman, tell him of our school and academy exclusions. If you would enlist the sympathies of the pious, refer him to our Negro pews in the house of worship, and when you tell him of the Jim Crow car, the top of the stage coach, the forward deck of the steamboat, as the only place for colored people to occupy, he at once, turning pale, then red, inquires if this is American republicanism, if this is the fruit of our many religious institutions; and as a West Indian remarked to me yesterday, that liberty in my country was, in its best estate, but the grossest licentiousness. I could not—I dare not contradict him, as my presence in England, at this time, proved too much for his argument. . . .

*P.S.* I will not mail this sheet without saying that, notwithstanding the pleasant circumstances with which I am surrounded, I long to tread again the country of my birth, again to raise my feeble voice in behalf of the suffering, again to unite with you in razing to the ground, the system which is, and ever has proved too faithfully, the fell destroyer of our race and nation.

*The Liberator,* October 16, 1840.

## 81

## NEW YORK STATE CONVENTION OF NEGROES, 1840

State conventions of Negro people became very important instruments of struggle prior to the Civil War. Several examples will be offered in their appropriate place. Below are printed the call to and part of the address of a New York State Convention of Negroes meeting in Albany, August 18–20, 1840. The call, signed by about 100 people, was drafted by a committee consisting of Charles B. Ray, John J. Zuille, Theodore S. Wright, Charles L. Reason and Timothy Seaman, appointed at a New York City meeting on May 29, 1840. The address was written by Alexander Crummell. In attendance at the Convention were 133 delegates from 23 cities and towns. The elected chairman was Austin Steward of Rochester and one of the Secretaries was Henry Highland Garnet, then of Troy.

### [a]

### *A Call*

For A Convention of the Colored Inhabitants of the State of New York.

Fellow citizens,—We issue this call, to invite you to attend a State Convention, to be held in the city of Albany on Tuesday, the 18th day of August next.

The primary object we have, in inviting you to assemble, is, to take into consideration the political condition of our people in this State, and to adopt such measures as can be simultaneously carried out by our brethren in every section of the State, to obtain a relief from those political disabilities under which we labor.

The principal legal disability which affects us, is, our deprivation of the free exercise, in common with other men, of the elective franchise. A free suffrage is the basis of a free government, the safeguard of a free people, the strength of the strong, the defence of the weak, a powerful auxiliary to respectability, wealth, and usefulness; and just in proportion as men are deprived of this, they are shorn of their strength, and are subject to poverty, disgrace, and abuse.

We are convinced, fellow citizens, that not only our political, but our depressed condition in all other respects in the State, owes itself, not in the least sense, to the fact that we are politically weak, not possessing the unrestricted use of the elective franchise. The body politic see in us, therefore, no favors to court, and nothing to fear. It is to them a matter of no concern, what may be the abuses we suffer, or how unhappy our condition.

You are aware, that while other citizens have a free and unrestricted use of the elective franchise, a property qualification is required on our part, in order for us to exercise this right, so important to a free people, and without which, a man cannot be considered, in a democratic sense, a freeman. This invidious requisition to the exercise of a birth-right privilege, weakens our standing as citizens of the State, and subjects us to all the consequent inconveniences. It also degrades our population, because it virtually lowers us in the scale of humanity, and reflects disparagingly upon our character. To seek a removal of this radical evil, is the object of calling you together in convention.

There has been no time so favorable for us to meet for the above object, as the present season. There is evidently a redeeming spirit abroad in our State—an increasing disposition to stand by, and defend the weak against the strong, as the noble acts of the Legislature regarding our protection as citizens, clearly indicate. Ought we not, then, to avail ourselves of this favorable indication, and come together to take some decisive measures to lay before the next Legislature our grievances, with a view to produce further action on their part, for our political disenthralment?

To facilitate the business of the Convention, it will be necessary that statements setting forth the legal and other disabilities of our people in different parts of the State, be presented at the Convention. To further this object, we invite all who expect to be present, to collect such statements, and also statistical accounts of the property, real and personal, public buildings, with their value, &c, owned by our people, and the condition of the people in morals, as compared with former times.

We therefore urge upon colored men in all sections of the State—men in all circumstances—if you possess self-respect, if you love liberty, if you appreciate your own rights, if you wish for political and moral elevation, if you have any interest in the prosperity of our people, if you have any regard for the welfare of your children, for the welfare of the State and of the nation, to assemble at Albany on the 18th of August next.

We call upon the farmer to leave for a while his harvesting, and repair to the assemblage of his brethren. Let the mechanic leave his workshop, to share the toils of a general council. Let the laborer and the working man be seen crowding the avenues that lead to the place of assemblage. Let every portion of our great and growing State, where lives a single object of oppression, be represented. We call upon the people in every city, town, and village to represent themselves in that Convention. Let the aged and the youth—all—all—be found at the above place, on that day. Come up, fellow citizens, from Suffolk to Erie, from Clinton to Steuben, and let us engage together in a common interest.

## [b]

### The Address

. . . We have been deprived of the elective franchise during the last twenty years. In a free country, this is ever a stimulant to enterprise, a means of influence, and a source of respect. The possession of it sends life, vigor, and energy through the entire heart of a people. The want of it in a community, is the cause of carelessness, intellectual inertness, and indolence. Springing above all these depressing circumstances, and exerting ourselves with unwonted alacrity, by native industry, by the accumulation of property, we have helped contribute, to a considerable extent, not only to the means of the State, but likewise to its character and respectability.

We claim, that there is no consideration whatever in existence, on account of which, the odious proscription of which we complain, should be continued. The want of intelligence, our misfortune, and the *crime* of others, which was once urged against us, does not now exist. Again: *we are the descendants of some of the earliest settlers of the State.* We can trace our ancestry back to those who first pierced the almost impenetrable forests that then lifted their high and stately heads in silent grandeur to the skies. When the vast and trackless wilderness, that had alone answered to the fierce roar of the roaming beast, or the whoop of the wild native, spread itself before the earlier settlers, our fathers were among those, who, with sinewy frame and muscular arm, went forth to humble that wilderness in its native pride. Since that time, our fathers, and we ourselves, have lent our best strength in cultivating the soil, in developing its vast resources, and contributing to its wealth and importance. Those who are the least acquainted with the history of the State, cannot but grant, that in this respect we have contributed more than our proportionate part.

In times when patient toil and hardy industry were demanded, it will thus be seen, we have ever been present and active. Not only so. *In times of peril has our aid been called for, and our services as promptly given.* When the country, its interests, its best and most cherished rights and institutions, have been assailed, not unavailingly have we been looked to. When the shrill trumpet-call of Freedom was heard amid the mountains and the rocks, and along the broad fields and pine forests of the South; when the whole country, aroused by the injustice of British policy, arose as one man, for the maintenance of natural and unprescriptable rights; the dark-browned man stood side by side wtih his fairer fellow citizen, with firm determination and indomitable spirit. During that memorable conflict, in severe and trying service, did they contend for those principles of liberty set forth in the Declaration of Independence, which are not of partial or local applicability, but which pertain alike to every being possessed of those high and exalted endowments that distinguish humanity.

Their blood is mingled with the soil of every battle field, made glorious by revolutionary reminiscence; and their bones have enriched the most productive lands of the country. In the late war of 1812, our people were again called upon to defend their country. The splendid naval achievements on Lakes Erie and Champlain, were owing mostly to the skill and prowess of colored men. The fame of Perry was gained at the expense of the mangled bodies and bleeding veins of our disfranchised people. Not inconsiderably is it owing to them, that Americans of the present day can recur with pleasurable emotions, and pride of country, to the battle fields of Plattsburgh and Sacketts Harbor.

*We are Americans.* We were born in no foreign clime. Here, where we behold, the noble rivers, and the rich fields, and the healthful skies, that may be called American; here, amid the institutions that now surround us, we first beheld the light of the impartial sun. We have not been brought up under the influence of other strange, aristocratic, and uncongenial political relations. In this respect, we profess to be American and republican. With the nature, features, and operations of our government, we have been familiarized from youth; and its democratic character is accordant with the flow of our feelings, and the current of our thoughts.

We have thus laid before you, fellow citizens, some considerations why we should never have been deprived of an equal suffrage, and why a just and impartial guarantee of this right, should soon be made.

But bating all these, we lay our claim on still higher ground. We *do* regard the right of our birthdom, our service in behalf of the country, contributing to its importance, and developing its resources, as favorable considerations— considerations adapted to banish all thought of proscription and injustice, from the power-holding body of the country, and to lead them to a hearty and practical acknowledgement of the claims and rights of a disfranchised people.

Yet for these alone, we do not ask for the extension of the elective franchise. We would not, we do not, predicate any right to it from any such a basis. We would not fall into the error of basing rights upon grounds so untenable. We object to others placing our rights upon complexion. We ourselves would not lay our claims to consideration on this or any similar ground.

We can find no system of moral or political ethics in which rights are based upon the conformation of the body, or the color of the skin. We can find no nation that has the temerity to insult the common sense of mankind, by promulgating such a sentiment as part of its creed. However individuals or nations may act, however they may assail the rights of man, or wrest from him his liberties, they all equally and alike *profess* regard for natural rights, the protection and security of which they claim as the object of the formation of their respective systems.

Rights have an existence, aside from conventional arrangements or unnatural partialities. They are of higher origin and of purer birth. They are inferrable from the settled and primary sentiments of man's nature. The high dignities and exalted tendencies of our common humanity, are the original grounds from which they may be deduced. Wherever a being may be found endowed with the light of Reason, and in the exercise of its various exalted attributes, that being is possessed of certain peculiar rights, on the ground of his nature.

We base our claim upon the possession of those common and yet exalted faculties of manhood. WE ARE MEN. 1. Those sympathies which find their natural channel, and legitimate and healthy exercise in civil and political relations, have the same being and nature in us that they have in the rest of the human family. 2. Those yearnings and longings for the exercise of political prerogatives, that are the product of the adaptedness of man's social nature to political arrangements, strive with irrepressible potency within us, from the fact of our disfranchised condition, a prevalent and unreasonable state of caste, and the operation of laws and statutes not proceeding from, yet operating upon us. 3. Those indignities and wrongs which naturally become the portion of a disfranchised class, and gather accumulated potency from an increase and intenseness of proscription, naturally and legitimately revert to us. From possessing like sympathies for civil and political operations with others, and like susceptibilities for evil, when nature is hindered in any of its legitimate exercises—on the ground of our *common humanity,* do we claim equal and entire rights with the rest of our fellow citizens. All that we say here, meets with full sympathy from all connected with the history of the country, the nature of its institutions, the spirit of its Constitution, and the designs and purposes of its great originators.

We have no reason to think that the framers of the Declaration of Independence, in setting forth the doctrines it contains, regarded them as mere dogmas or idle theories. We believe they put full faith in them, as actual truths, and living verities. This they evinced, by pledging to each other their lives, their fortunes, and their sacred honors. This they manifested, by an unswerving opposition to injustice and oppression.

It was in accordance with the views of that great charter of American freedom, that they framed the constitution of the country. Setting aside the stale primogenital fallacies of the blood-dyed political institutions of the old world; repudiating the unnatural assumptions of the feudal system, and exploding the aged and destructive sophism of natural inequalities in the family of man, they clung with undying tenacity to the connecting chain that runs through the whole mighty mass of humanity, recognized the common sympathies and wants of the race, and framed a political edifice of such a nature and character as was congenial with the natural and indestructible principles of man, and as was adapted to secure to all under its broad Aegis, the purest liberty God ever conferred upon him.

That Declaration, and that Constitution, we think, may be considered as more fully developing the primary ideas of American republicanism, than any other documents—each and every one as men, fully capacitated by the Creator, for government and progressive advancement—which capacities, in a natural exercise, are not to be interfered with by government.

Republicanism, in these two documents, has an eye to individual freedom, without lets or hindrances. In her operations, she is impartial. She regards man—all men; and is indifferent to all arbitrary and conventional considerations. This we deem to be the character of the Declaration of Independence—and this, likewise, the character of the Constitution, after which it was modelled. Republicanism was to be the distinguishing feature in its operations.

The Constitution of our own State, as it sprung from the clear head and pure heart of that incomparable patriot, JOHN JAY, in its preamble and several sections, was, in spirit, concordant with it. By this we mean, that although the qualifications for voting, *in general*, were higher than those prevailing at the present, yet the ground of the suffrage enactment was not based upon national peculiarities, or complexional distinctions. It said that *any* man possessed of such and such qualifications, should be a political denizen of the State.

As the State advanced in age, intelligence, and population, augmented in wealth, and extended in resources, the call went forth for the extension of the franchise right. In accordance with the will of the people, thus expressed, a convention was held in the city of Albany in 1821–2.

We beg that it may be remembered, that the convention was called for the purpose of *extending* the suffrage right. We would also call your attention to the fact, that the votes by which many of the delegates were elected to that convention, were cast by colored voters. And more especially would we remind you, that during the proceedings of that convention, in its reports, address, &c., a peculiar deference is ever paid to the republican features of our common country, and its democratic tendencies. Yet in that convention, that portion of the citizens of the State whom we here represent, were shut out from an equal and common participation in the prerogatives of citizenship, in the operations of both State and National Governments, and thus placed under the operation of laws and statutes without our agency, and to which we are subjected without acquiescence.

We, the Colored Citizens of the State, in Convention assembled, representing 50,000 of the population, do ask your earnest attention, your deep reflection, your unbiased and conscientious judgment in this matter. We ask you, as a matter in which you are deeply concerned, to come forward and restore the fountains of political justice in this State to their pristine purity. We ask you to secure to us our political rights. We call upon you to return to the pure faith of your republican fathers. We lift up our voices for the restored spirit of the first days of the republic—for the great principles that then maintained, and that regard for man which revered the characteristic features of his nature, as of more honor and worth than the form and color of the body in which they dwell.

For no vested rights, for no peculiar privileges, for no extraordinary prerogatives, do we ask. We merely put forth our appeal for a republican birthright. We wish to be something more than political serfs and slaves. We fully believe in the fundamental doctrines set forth in the Declaration of Independence. We acquiesce in the sentiment that "governments derive their just powers from the consent of the governed." And we say it is injustice of the most aggrieved character, either to deprive us of a just and legitimate participation in the rights of the State, or to make us bear the burdens, and submit to its enactments, when all its arrangements, plans, and purposes, are framed and put into operation utterly regardless of us, in their incipient state, than if we were nonentities; but which, in their practical operation, act upon us with destructive tendency, eat away our soul, and destroy our life. We ask for a living manifestation of belief in the above doctrine: we know already too much of its dead letter.

Fellow citizens! the Colored Citizens of this State, through us, their representatives, respectfully and earnestly ask at your hands, the speedy adoption of such plans, and the formation of such measures, as may soon lead to the erasure of the odious prospective act of which we complain—we secured an equal suffrage, and the State freed from a stain upon its character.

*Minutes of the State Convention of Colored Citizens, held at Albany, on the 18th, 19th and 20th of August, 1840, for the purpose of considering their political condition.* (New York, 1840). Copy in editor's possession.

## 82

# AFRICAN METHODIST EPISCOPAL CHURCH CONFERENCE, 1840

The church has been a most significant organization in the life of the Negro people, and no particular sect has been more important than the African Methodist Episcopal Church. Indicative of the direction of its efforts are the resolutions adopted at the tenth annual conference, September 5, 1840, of the Pittsburgh or Western district. Twenty delegates representing 2,448 members from Pittsburgh, Cincinnati, Chillicothe, Zanesville, Richmond, Uniontown, Hillsboro and Columbus were at this conference presided over by the Senior Bishop, the Rt. Rev. Morris Brown.

We, the members of this Conference, are fully satisfied that the principles of the gospel are arrayed against all sin, and that it is the duty of all Christians to use their influence and energies against all systems that rudely trample under foot the claims of justice and the sacred principles of revelation. And, whereas, slavery pollutes the character of the church of God, and makes the Bible a sealed book to thousands of immortal beings—Therefore,

*Resolved,* on motion, That we will aid, by our prayers, those pious persons whom God has raised up to plead the cause of the dumb, until every fetter shall be broken and all men enjoy the liberty which the gospel proclaims.

*Resolved,* on motion, That, whereas education is one of the principal means of creating in our minds those noble feelings which prompt us to the practice of piety, virtue, and temperance, and is calculated to elevate us above the condition of brutes, by assimilating us to the image of our Maker, we therefore recommend to all our preachers to enjoin undeviating attention to its promotion, and earnestly request all our people to neglect no opportunity of advancing it, by pledging ourselves to assist them as far as it is in our power.

*Resolved,* on motion, That we hereby recommend to all our preachers, in their labors to promote the cause of temperance, to hold up the principle of total abstinence from (as a beverage) all intoxicating drinks, as the true and safe rule for all consistent friends of temperance to go by, and is in accordance with our discipline and the resolutions of our former annual conferences.

*Resolved,* on motion, That a sermon be preached, quarterly, on all our circuits and stations, by our preachers, on the subjects of temperance and moral reform; and the preacher in charge who neglects to attend to that duty, or see that it is attended to, shall be amenable to the next annual conference.

*Resolved,* on motion, That there be four sermons preached in the year, in all our churches and congregations, for the purpose of encouraging the cause of education and Sabbath schools among our people; and that a collection be taken up, where there are Sabbath schools established, at those times, for the special aid of those schools.

*A.M.E. Church Magazine* (Brooklyn) I, No. 1 (Sept. 1841) pp. 7–8. Copy in library of Dr. W. E. B. Du Bois.

## 83

## A SLAVE AUCTION DESCRIBED BY A SLAVE, 1841

Solomon Northup, kidnapped and held as a slave for twelve years, describes the auctioning of Negroes in the New Orleans of 1841:

In the first place we were required to wash thoroughly, and those with beards to shave. We were then furnished with a new suit each, cheap, but clean. The men had hat, coat, shirt, pants and shoes; the women frocks of calico, and handkerchief to bind about their heads. We were now conducted into a a large room in the front part of the building to which the yard was attached, in order to be properly trained, before the admission of customers. The men were arranged on one side of the room, the women at the other. The tallest was placed at the head of the row, then the next tallest, and so on in the order of their respective heights. Emily was at the foot of the line of women. Freeman [Theophilus Freeman, owner of the slave-pen.] charged us to remember our places; exhorted us to appear smart and lively,—sometimes threatening, and again, holding out various inducements. During the day he exercised us in the art of "looking smart," and of moving to our places with exact precision.

After being fed, in the afternoon, we were again paraded and made to dance. Bob, a colored boy, who had some time belonged to Freeman, played on the violin. Standing near him, I made bold to inquire if he could play the "Virginia Reel." He answered he could not, and asked me if I could play. Replying in the affirmative, he handed me the violin. I struck up a tune, and finished it. Freeman ordered me to continue playing, and seemed well pleased, telling Bob that I far excelled him—a remark that seemed to grieve my musical companion very much.

Next day many customers called to examine Freeman's "new lot." The latter gentleman was very loquacious, dwelling at much length upon our several good points and qualities. He would make us hold up our heads, walk briskly back and forth, while customers would feel of our hands and arms and bodies, turn us about, ask us what we could do, make us open our mouths and show our teeth, precisely as a jockey examines a horse which he is about to barter for or purchase. Sometimes a man or woman was taken back to the small house in the yard, stripped, and inspected more minutely. Scars upon a slave's back were considered evidence of a rebellious or unruly spirit, and hurt his sale.

An old gentleman, who said he wanted a coachman, appeared to take a fancy to me. From his conversation with Burch [Freeman's business associate], I learned he was a resident in the city. I very much desired that he would buy me, because I conceived it would not be difficult to make my escape from New Orleans on some northern vessel. Freeman asked him fifteen hundred dollars for me. The old gentleman insisted it was too much as times were very hard. Freeman, however, declared that I was sound of health, of a good constitution, and intelligent. He made it a point to enlarge upon my musical attainments. The old gentleman argued quite adroitly that there was nothing extraordinary about the Negro, and finally, to my regret, went out, saying he would call again. During the day, however, a number of sales were made. David and Caroline were purchased together by a Natchez planter. They left us, grinning broadly, and in a most happy state of mind, caused by the fact of their not being separated. Sethe was sold to a planter of Baton Rouge, her eyes flashing with anger as she was led away.

The same man also purchased Randall. The little fellow was made to jump, and run across the floor, and perform many other feats, exhibiting his activity and condition. All the time the trade was going on, Eliza was crying aloud, and wringing her hands. She besought the man not to buy him, unless he also bought herself and Emily. She promised, in that case, to be the most faithful slave that ever lived. The man answered that he could not afford it, and then Eliza burst into a paroxysm of grief, weeping plaintively. Freeman turned round to her, savagely, with his whip in his uplifted hand, ordering her to stop her noise, or he would flog her. He would not have such work—such snivelling; and unless she ceased that minute, he would take her to the yard and give her a hundred lashes. Yes, he would take the nonsense out of her pretty quick—if he didn't, might he be d——d. Eliza shrunk before him, and tried to wipe away her tears, but it was all in vain. She wanted to be with her children, she said, the little time she had to live. All the frowns and threats of Freeman, could not wholly silence the afflicted mother. She kept on begging and beseeching them, most piteously, not to separate the three. Over and over again she told them how she loved her boy. A great many times she repeated her former promises—how very faithful and obedient she would be; how hard she would labor day and night, to the last moment of her life, if he would only buy them all together. But it was of no avail; the man could not afford it. The bargain was agreed upon, and Randall must go alone. Then Eliza ran to him; embraced him passionately; kissed him again and again; told him to remember her—all the while her tears falling in the boy's face like rain.

Freeman damned her, calling her a blubbering, bawling wench, and ordered her to go to her place, and behave herself, and be somebody. He swore he wouldn't stand such stuff but a little longer. He would soon give her something to cry about, if she was not mighty careful, and *that* she might depend upon.

The planter from Baton Rouge, with his new purchase, was ready to depart.

"Don't cry, mama. I will be a good boy. Don't cry," said Randall, looking back, as they passed out of the door.

What has become of the lad, God knows. It was a mournful scene indeed. I would have cried myself if I had dared.

Solomon Northup, *Twelve Years A Slave* . . . (Auburn, Buffalo, London, 1853), pp. 78 ff.

## 84

## PENNSYLVANIA STATE CONVENTION OF NEGROES, 1841

On August 23–25, 1841, one hundred and forty-seven delegates gathered in Pittsburgh at a State Convention of Pennsylvania Negroes, under the leadership of John Peck, John B. Vashon and Lewis Woodson. The call, issued July 17, 1841 from Pittsburgh, tells the story of the Convention's purpose:

Freemen: The present Constitution of the Commonwealth of Pennsylvania deprives you of the right of suffrage—a right, paramount in importance to all other political rights . . . Argument to induce you to make one united and powerful effort to obtain this right is useless. Nay, if argument were necessary to induce such effort, it would show that you were undeserving of its enjoyment. Your love of liberty, of your country, of yourselves, and of your posterity, will constitute inducements to effort more powerful than the most eloquent argument which we could devise. You are therefore at once invited to assemble in State Convention, and devise and adopt the best means for its attainment.

The Convention should be a large one. Every county in the state should be represented. Every friend of equal laws and equal rights should be present, either in person or by representation. Every community that can should elect and send on a representation; and those who can elect no representatives should come themselves.

*Proceedings of the State Convention of the Colored Freemen of Pennsylvania, held in Pittsburgh, on the 23d, 24th and 25th of August, 1841, for the purpose of considering their condition, and the means of its improvement.* (Pittsburgh 1841.) Copy in Ridgway Branch, Library Company of Philadelphia.

# 85

## PROSPECTUS OF A PIONEER NEGRO MAGAZINE, 1841

The first general magazine published by Negroes in the United States was the *African Methodist Episcopal Church Magazine*. It was issued in Brooklyn, New York and edited by George Hogarth. The prospectus, taken from its first number, dated September, 1841, follows:

*To the Friends of the African Methodist Episcopal Church:*

BRETHREN,—The clergy of our church, in their conferences, have long contemplated upon the importance and necessity of a Magazine, either monthly or quarterly, published under the immediate supervision of our church, as a circulating medium of intelligence throughout the wide extensive bounds of our connection. Such a work, we consider, if properly conducted, will be of vast importance towards advancing the interests of our general church, and at the same time convey such information periodically through its pages, of the general progress of our church, as every friend and well wisher of our connection naturally desires.

In embarking upon this laudable enterprise, it becomes our duty, in the outset, to inform our friends that such a work cannot be conducted with dignity and honor to our people, unless it meets with ample supply of pecuniary and intellectual means. A fear of failure in obtaining these important contingencies, had, in a great measure, prevented our brethren in their deliberations from coming to any conclusions on this important subject. But, judging from the present aspect cf things, that the times have greatly changed in our favor as a people, light has burst forth upon us, intelligence in a great measure is taking the place of ignorance, especially among the younger portions of our people, opening the avenues to proper Christian feeling and benevolence—our brethren, from these important considerations, came to the conclusion, at our last New York Annual Conference, held in June, in the city of Brooklyn, to order such a work, and lay it before the public for their patronage.

In soliciting the aid of our friends, we would wish it fully understood, that it is far from our intention to close our pages to the respectful communications of any who may at any time be so kind as to contribute to the advancement of our enterprise, as we assure our friends that we shall stand greatly in need of talented contributors to our pages.

Among the prominent objects of our enterprise, which call for our immediate and particular attention, is primitive Christianity, as was understood to exist in the Methodist church in Mr. Wesley's day: a vindication of the rights and privileges of our Church in all its bearings in this country as African Methodists, its episcopacy, and doctrines, holding up to the observance of our Christian brethren, regardless of color, the importance of union among us, not only as Methodists, but as worshippers before the same Lamb in whose blood we are washed: the extension of the Redeemer's kingdom among our brethren of color in this country, who are still perishing for the want of an opportunity of hearing his sacred word to their advantage: the importance of turning the attention of our brethren to the land of our fathers, the millions of souls who are enshrouded in mid-night darkness, under heathenish superstition and idolatry, that the prayers of our brethren may ascend to the ear of the Lord, that he may in mercy raise up some of our young men, and prepare them to carry to Afric's shore the glad tidings of salvation, that the sunbeams of the morning may burst forth with its radiant light upon those benighted regions, and dispel the shades of ignorance, superstition, idolatry and death, that now lays them prostrate in the dust: the necessity of contributing to the education of our pious young men, who may be called of God to the work of the ministry, that they may be able to study unembarrassed to shew themselves approved of God, workmen that need not be ashamed, rightly dividing the word of truth. Sabbath school, and every other religious instruction, shall meet with our most cordial support, that our members, under God, may become remarkable for science and Christian piety and intelligence in this highly-favored land of Christendom. And last, but not least, Moral Reform in all its branches shall command our special attention, as we are fully satisfied that its principles open to the view the avenues to true Christian piety and holiness.

Copy in the library of Dr. W. E. B. Du Bois.

## 86

## ON THE QUESTION OF NEGRO DISUNITY, 1841

In 1840, under the leadership of David Ruggles, a short-lived organization called the American Reformed Board of Disfranchised Commissioners was formed. At the anniversary meeting September 8, 1841, in New York, David Ruggles made some significant remarks on the problem of Negro disunity:

While every man's hand is against us, our every hand is against each other. I speak plainly, because truth will set us free. Are we not guilty of cherishing, to an alarming extent, the sin of sectarian, geographical, and complexional proscription? The spirit abroad is this: Is that brother a Methodist? He is not one of us. A Baptist? He is not one of us. A Presbyterian? He is not one of us. An Episcopalian? He is not one of us. A Roman Catholic? He is not one of us. Does he live above human creeds, and enjoy the religion of the heart? He is of Beelzebub.

Again. Is that brother from the east? He is not of us. From the west? He is not of us. From the north? He is not of us. From the south? He is not of us. From the middle States? He is not of us. Is he a foreigner? He can never be of us. But, forsooth, is that brother of a dark complexion? He is of no worth. Is he of a light complexion? He is of no nation. Such, sir, are the visible lines of distinction, marked by slavery for us to follow. If we hope for redemption from our present condition, we must repent, turn, and UNITE in the hallowed cause of reform.

*The Liberator,* September 24, 1841.

## 87

## CALL TO NEGRO TEACHERS' MEETING, 1841

The great interest of the Negro people in educational opportunities has already been demonstrated in several documents. It is certain that at least as early as 1841 an Association of Colored Teachers existed in New York and that this group had its own organ, called the *New York Journal of Education and Weekly Messenger.* Meetings devoted to their own particular problems were held, as is clear from the following call issued in November, 1841 and signed by sixteen Negro teachers including Samuel V. Berry, Jonathan Mingo, Richard Lustus and W. J. Hodges:

## A Call

To the Colored Freeman of Long Island, for a convention to be held at Jamaica, Queen's County, November 25th, 1841, at 10½ o'clock, A.M., for devising means more effectually to advance the cause of education and temperance, and also for co-operating with our disfranchised brethren throughout the State, in petitioning for the right of suffrage.

—Brethren, come! The cause of Education calls loudly upon you to come. Hundreds of children that are now shut out from the blessings of Education, call loudly upon you to come. If there ever was a time that called for united action, it is now. If there ever was a time for colored freemen to show their love of liberty, their hatred of ignorance, and determination to be free and enlightened, it is now! We want *union* and *action*. The man who draws back, and refuses to give heed to a call for such noble purposes, plainly shows himself to be an enemy to the greatest earthly blessings conferred by the Creator on his creatures. Come, brethren, refuse not the voice that calls you together for such noble purposes. It is the voice of Liberty, of Education, and of Temperance. Inactivity is criminal! Come from old Suffolk! Our noble, active and enterprising brethren of Kings, they must come! They of Queens must not stay at home! Come from the borders of the blue waters of the Atlantic—from the shores of the Long Island Sound! Let a general rally be made, and let there be a delegate from every town and village, and from every society in the Island. Remember that the first county convention held in this State was held on the Island, and the first State convention was appointed by the freemen of the Island; and now let us give an impetus to the cause of Education! Again we say, come! Let none refuse but those who are enemies to the prosperity and happiness of their people.

*The Liberator*, November 26, 1841.

## 88

## A PIONEER STUDY OF A NEGRO COMMUNITY, 1841

One of the first book-length studies of the Negro community within a particular city was the anonymous volume, *Sketches of the Higher Classes of Colored So-*

*ciety in Philadelphia,* published in 1841. Its author signed himself "A Southerner" but within the volume specifically identified himself as a Negro. At the time this work appeared, Philadelphia had the largest Negro population (about 19,000) of any Northern city. Extracts from this volume follow:

The prejudiced reader, I feel well assured, will smile at the designation "higher classes of colored society." The public—or at least the great body, who have not been at the pains to make an examination—have long been accustomed to regard the people of color as one consolidated mass, all huddled together, without any particular or general distinctions, social or otherwise. The sight of one colored man with them, whatever may be his apparent condition; (provided it is any thing but genteel!) is the sight of a community; and the errors and crimes of one, is adjudged as the criterion of character of the whole body. But the first of those considerations is far from being correct; the latter, too openly palpable to command a moment's attention. Compared in conditions, means and abilities, there are as broad social distinctions to be found here, as among any other class of society; aye, and, it may be added, with as much justice, too;—for what are all human distinctions worth, founded otherwise than in virtue? True, it is readily admitted, they have not, to any great extent, the customary grounds which have always obtained, for marking their lines of separation with distinctness; but this is the fault of circumstances—the offspring of exigencies which they had no agency in producing—and which they have never been able to surmount. . . .

Among the very erroneous opinions that are formed, respecting the people of color, is the one that supposes them indifferent to the state of things by which they are surrounded, and that they make little or no effort for their relief. But this arises from the want of closer observance of their situation; and the nature and character of their disabilities. If the truth, which should be the aim of all, is faithfully sought, it will be found in the very reverse of this supposition. Never have any people, in proportion to their means of operation, made greater efforts for their entire enfranchisement. . . . But education possesses its own intrinsic worth, which it imparts to those who enter its pursuits. Of this, colored Philadelphians seem to be fully aware; and as one important avenue towards further advancement and perfection, they have established numerous literary associations, the most prominent of which it is here purposed briefly to notice.

Among the earliest established of these institutions, stands first—"The Philadelphia Library Company of Colored Persons."

This Company was instituted January 1st, 1833. The number of persons present at its formation, and who signed the Constitution, were nine; whose names are here given:—Messrs. Frederick A. Hinton, James Needham (now *Treasurer,* and who kindly furnished these particulars), James Cornish, Robert C. Gordon, Junior, John Depee, William Whipper, J. C. Bowers, Charles Trulier, Robert Douglass, Junior, and James C. Mathews;—who may be considered the founders of the first successful literary institution of this description; established by the colored classes in Philadelphia.

The object of the Company, as its title implies, was the collection of a library of useful works of every description for the benefit of its members. who might there successfully apply, without comparatively any cost, for that mental good which they could not readily obtain elsewhere. This enterprise met with great encouragement, both in the way of donations of books, pamphlets, maps, &c, and otherwise; so that in a short time a large and valuable collection was made. A systematic order of reading was then adopted by the members, to the very great advantage of those who persevered therein. In connexion with this, a system of debates was introduced, for the purpose of stimulating the members to historical and other researches, and for practising them in the arts of elocution and public speaking.

Soon after the establishment of the Library Company—their numbers having greatly augmented—application was made to the Legislature for an act of incorporation. In this they also met with speedy success—corporate existence having been granted them in the early part of 1836. From this period the Company rapidly increased in numbers and usefulness, until at the present time the roll book presents the names of about one hundred (including a number of honorary) members; all of whom have partaken of its benefits.

The debating department has of late greatly improved in regard to the intelligence and ability of those who usually participate therein. Discussions of interesting subjects, take place on Tuesday of each week.

The library at present contains nearly six hundred volumes of valuable historical, scientific and miscellaneous works, among which are several Encyclopoedias, and is a source of great mental profit to the members of the Company. Among those who took an interest in, and contributed towards the collection of the Library, was the late Right Reverend Bishop White, of the Protestant Episcopal Church.

The fee of admission to membership of the institution, is such as to place it within the reach of every one disposed to connect themselves therewith. It is *one dollar;* and the monthly assessment thereafter, *twenty-five cents. . . .*

The progress of this institution has been marked by evidences of the most gratifying character—gratifying to all who delight to witness the progress of knowledge and refinement among their fellow-men. Many a young man of color in this community, who previous to the establishment of "The Philadelphia Library Company of Colored Persons" never dreamed of rising before a public auditory to make an address, or engage in a debate, is now enabled to do so with little or no embarrassment, and in a manner highly creditable.

*Sketches of the Higher Classes of Colored Society in Philadelphia by a Southerner* (Phila., 1841), pp. 13–14, 68–69, 96–100.

## 89

## AGAINST SEGREGATION IN TRAVEL, 1842

Charles Lenox Remond addressed the Legislative Committee of the Massachusetts House of Representatives in support of petitions against segregation in travelling, in February, 1842, as follows:

Mr. Chairman, and Gentlemen of the Committee: In rising at this time, and on this occasion, being the first person of color who has ever addressed either of the bodies assembling in this building, I should, perhaps, in the first place, observe that, in consequence of the many misconstructions of the principles and measures of which I am the humble advocate, I may in like manner be subject to similar misconceptions from the moment I open my lips in behalf of the prayer of the petitioners for whom I appear, and therefore feel I have the right at least to ask, at the hands of this intelligent Committee, an impartial hearing; and that whatever prejudices they may have imbibed, be eradicated from their minds, if such exist. I have, however, too much confidence in their intelligence, and too much faith in their determination to do their duty as the representatives of this Commonwealth, to presume they can be actuated by partial motives. Trusting, as I do, that the day is not distant, when, on all questions touching the rights of the citizens of this State, men shall be considered great only as they are good—and not that it shall be told, and painfully experienced, that, in this country, this State, aye, this city, the Athens of America, the rights, privileges and immunities of its citizens are measured by complexion, or any other physical peculiarity or conformation, especially such as over which no man has any control. Complexion can in no sense be construed into crime, much less be rightfully made the criterion of rights. Should the people of color, through a revolution of Providence, become a majority, to the last I would oppose it upon the same principle; for, in either case, it would be equally reprehensible and unjustifiable—alike to be condemned and repudiated. It is JUSTICE I stand here to claim, and not FAVOR for either complexion.

And now, sir, I shall endeavor to confine my remarks to the same subject which has occupied the attention of the Committee thus far, and to stand upon the same principle which has been so ably and so eloquently maintained and established by my esteemed friend, Mr. [Wendell] Phillips.

Our right to citizenship in this State has been acknowledged and secured by the allowance of the elective franchise and consequent taxation; and I know of no good reason, if admitted in this instance, why it should be denied in any other.

With reference to the wrongs inflicted and injuries received on railroads, by persons of color, I need not say they do not end with the termination of the route, but, in effect, tend to discourage, disparage and depress this class of citizens. All hope of reward for upright conduct is cut off. Vice in them becomes a virtue. No distinction is made by the community in which we live. The most vicious is treated as well as the most respectable, both in public and private.

But it is said we all look alike. If this is true, it is not true that we all behave alike. There is a marked difference; and we claim a recognition of this difference.

In the present state of things, they find God's provisions interfered with in such a way, by these and kindred regulations, that virtue may not claim her divinely appointed rewards. Color is made to obscure the brightest endowments, to degrade the fairest character, and to check the highest and most praiseworthy aspirations. If the colored man is vicious, it makes but little difference; if besotted, it matters not; if vulgar, it is quite as well; and he finds himself as well treated, and received as readily into society, as those of an opposite character. Nay, the higher our aspirations, the loftier our purposes and pursuits, does this iniquitous principle of prejudice fasten upon us, and especial pains are taken to irritate, obstruct and injure. No reward of merit, no remuneration for services, no equivalent is rendered the deserving. And I submit, whether this unkind and unchristian policy is not well calculated to make every man disregardful of his conduct, and every woman unmindful of her reputation.

The grievances of which we complain, be assured, sir, are not imaginary, but real—not local, but universal—not occasional, but continual, every day matter of fact things—and have become, to the disgrace of our common country, matter of history. . . .

There is a marked difference between social and civil rights. It has been well and justly remarked, by my friend Mr. Phillips, that we all claim the privilege of selecting our society and associations; but, in civil rights, one man has not the prerogative to define rights for another. For instance, sir, in public conveyances, for the rich man to usurp the privileges to himself, to the injury of the poor man, would be submitted to in no well regulated society. And such is the position suffered by persons of color. On my arrival home from England, I went to the railway station, to go to Salem, being anxious to see my parents and sisters as soon as possible—asked for a ticket—paid 50 cents for it, and was pointed to the American designation car. Having previously received information of the regulations, I took my seat peaceably, believing it better to suffer wrong than do wrong. I felt then, as I felt on many occasions prior to leaving home, unwilling to descend so low as to bandy words with the superintendents, or contest my rights with conductors, or any others in the capacity of servants of any stage or steamboat company, or rail-road corporation; although I never, by any means, gave evidence that, by my submission, I intended to sanction usages which would derogate from uncivilized, much less long and loud professing and high pretending America.

Bear with me while I relate an additional occurrence. On the morning after my return home, I was obliged to go to Boston again, and on going to the Salem station I met two friends, who enquired if I had any objection to their taking seats with me. I answered, I should be most happy. They took their seats accordingly, and soon afterwards one of them remarked to me—"Charles, I don't know if they will allow us to ride with you." It was some time before I could understand what they meant, and, on doing so, I laughed —feeling it to be a climax to every absurdity I had heard attributed to Americans. To say nothing of the wrong done those friends, and the insult and indignity offered me by the appearance of the conductor, who ordered the friends from the car in a somewhat harsh manner—they immediately left the carriage.

On returning to Salem some few evenings afterwards, Mr. Chase, the superintendent on this road, made himself known to me by recalling bygone days and scenes, and then enquired if I was not glad to get home after so long an absence in Europe. I told him I was glad to see my parents and family again, and this was the only object I could have, unless he thought I should be glad to take a hermit's life in the great pasture; inasmuch as I never felt to loathe my American name so much as since my arrival. He wished to know my reasons for the remark. I immediately gave them, and wished to know of him, if, in the event of his having a brother with red hair, he should find himself separated while traveling because of this difference, he should deem it just. He could make no reply. I then wished to know if the principle was not the same; and if so, there was an insult implied by his question.

In conclusion, I challenged him as the instrument inflicting the manifold injuries upon all not colored like himself to the presentation of an instance in any other Christian or unchristian country, tolerating usages at once so disgraceful, unjust and inhuman. What if some few of the West or East India planters and merchants should visit our liberty-loving country, with their colored wives—how would he manage? Or, if R. M. Johnson, the gentleman who has been elevated to the second office in the gift of the people, should be travelling from Boston to Salem, if he was prepared to separate him from his wife or daughters.* [Involuntary burst of applause, instantly restrained.] †

Sir, it happens to be my lot to have a sister a few shades lighter than myself; and who knows, if this state of things is encouraged, whether I may not on some future occasion be mobbed in Washington Street, on the supposition of walking with a white young lady! [Suppressed indications of sympathy and applause.] †

Gentlemen of the Committee, these distinctions react in all their wickedness—to say nothing of their concocted and systematized odiousness and absurdity—upon those who instituted them; and particularly so upon those who are illiberal and mean enough to practise them.

Mr. Chairman, if colored people have abused any rights granted them, or failed to exhibit due appreciation of favors bestowed, or shrunk from dangers or responsibility, let it be made to appear. Or if our country contains a population to compare with them in loyalty and patriotism, circumstances duly considered, I have it yet to learn. The history of our country must ever testify in their behalf. In view of these and many additional considerations, I unhesitatingly assert their claim, on the naked principle of merit, to every advantage set forth in the Constitution of this Commonwealth.

Finally, Mr. Chairman, there is in this and other States a large and growing colored population, whose residence in your midst has not been from choice (let this be understood and reflected upon), but by the force of circumstances over which they never had control. Upon the heads of their oppressors and calumniators be the censure and responsibility. If to ask at your hands redress for injuries, and protection in our rights and immunities, as citizens, is reasonable, and dictated alike by justice, humanity and religion, you will not reject, I trust, the prayer of your petitioners.

Before sitting down, I owe it to myself to remark, that I was not apprised of the wish of my friends to appear here until passing through Boston, a day or two since; and having been occupied with other matters, I have had

* Colonel Richard M. Johnson, of Kentucky, Vice-President of the United States (1837–1841), lived openly with a Negro woman named Julia Chinn until her death in 1833. With her, Colonel Johnson had two daughters, Imogene and Adaline, both of whom married white men.
† Bracketed words in original.

no opportunity for preparation on this occasion. I feel much obliged to the Committee for their kind, patient, and attentive hearing. [Applause.] *

*The Liberator*, February 25, 1842.


## 90

## ON UNJUST WARS, 1842

One hundred and thirty-four slaves, led by one among them named Madison Washington, rebelled aboard the slave-trader, *Creole*, in 1841 while enroute from Virginia to Louisiana. One of the crew was killed, the rest overpowered and the Negroes sailed into the British port of Nassau in the Bahamas. The United States demanded that Great Britain return the slaves (something that was never done; rather in 1853 she agreed to pay the United States $110,000) and this quarrel was one of several which provoked talk of war between England and the United States in the 1840's. A Negro newspaper editorialized, in March, 1842, as follows:


### *Prospect Of War*

Whilst we look forward with some degree of curiosity to learn in what manner our Secretary of State [Daniel Webster] will sneak out of the bullying position into which his late despatch has placed him, we cannot shut our eyes to the fact, that the decision of the British Parliament, neither to indemnify, nor to deliver up the self-liberated slaves of the *Creole*, may lead to war. And as it is well "in time of peace to prepare for war," let us seriously and solemnly ask our brethren to make up their minds *now*, as to the position they may assume in such a catastrophe.

If war be declared, shall we fight with the chains upon our limbs? Will we fight in defence of a government which denies us the most precious right of citizenship? Shall we shed our blood in defence of the American slave trade? Shall we make our bodies a rampart in defence of American slavery?

We ask these questions, because there is no law in existence which can compel us to fight, and any fighting on our part, must be a VOLUNTARY ACT. The States in which we dwell have twice availed themselves of our *voluntary services*, and have repaid us with chains and slavery. Shall we a third time kiss the foot that crushes us? If so, we deserve our chains. No! let us maintain an organized neutrality, until the laws of the Union and of all the States have made us free and equal citizens.

*The Liberator*, April 1, 1842, quoting the *Colored People's Press* (n.d.).

---

* Bracketed words in original.

## 91

# A NEGRO WRITES OF AN AMERICAN POGROM, 1842

Mass pillage and murder by white mobs in Negro communities have marked American history for over a century. Such an outbreak occurred in Philadelphia late in August, 1842—a year of severe depression—while Negroes were celebrating the anniversary of the emancipation of slaves in the British West Indies. Several people were killed, scores injured and buildings leveled before state troops quelled the violence. An anonymous Negro wrote to the white Abolitionist, Henry C. Wright, from Philadelphia on August 22, 1842:

I am every way disqualified for making proper answers to your interrogatories in reference to one of the most ferocious and bloody-spirited mobs that ever cursed a *Christian* community. I know not where to begin, nor where nor how to end, in a detail of the wantonness, brutality and murderous spirit of the actors in the late riots; nor of the apathy and inhumanity of the whole community, in regard to the matter. Press, church, magistrates, clergymen and devils are against us. The measure of our suffering is full.

"Man's inhumanity to man," indeed makes countless millions mourn.

From the most painful and minute investigation into the feelings, views and acts of this community, in regard to us, I am convinced of our utter and complete nothingness in public estimation. I feel that my life, and those tendrils of my heart, dearer than life to me, would find no change in death, but a glorious riddance of a life, weighed down and crushed by a despotism whose sway makes hell of earth—we the *tormented*, our persecutors the *tormentors*.

But I must stop. I am sick, miserably sick. Every thing around me is as dark as the grave. Here and there, the bright countenance of a true friend is to be seen. Save that, nothing redeeming, nothing hopeful. Despair, black as the pall of death, hangs over us, and the bloody *will* is in the heart of the community to destroy us.

To attempt a reply to your letter, now, is impracticable.

"*I have no feeling—Scarce conscious what I wish.*" Yet never forget my gratitude to you, and all the dear, true and faithful friends in the sacred cause of human freedom.

*The Liberator,* September 9, 1842.

## 92

# PROTESTING MARITIME RESTRICTIONS, 1842

Late in 1822, South Carolina, stimulated by the Vesey conspiracy, passed a law forbidding free Negro seamen to leave their vessels when in her ports. In the ensuing years several other slave states passed similar laws. These evoked many protests from Negro individuals and groups, not only because of the attack this represented against their rights but also because maritime occupations were among the most important followed by Negroes. Typical are the resolutions adopted at a meeting of Boston Negroes held October 27, 1842:

*Resolved,* That the legislative enactments of South Carolina, Georgia, Alabama, Mississippi and Louisiana, prohibiting all free colored citizens of the United States entering those several States under penalty of imprisonment, are manifestly unconstitutional; insomuch as the Constitution declares that the citizens of each State shall be entitled to all the rights and immunities of citizens of the several States.

*Resolved,* That Congress possesses the power to invalidate any State Legislative enactment which tends to restrain the liberties of any portion of the citizens of the United States.

*Resolved,* That the voice of the Massachusetts Legislative should be heard in the Congress of our nation, remonstrating against the unjust and unconstitutional deprivation of the liberties of her citizens. . . .

*Resolved,* Therefore, That we, the colored citizens of Boston, memorialize Congress, and our Legislature, at their next sessions, for their action in this case; especially that on some fitting occasion the point may be carried by this State before the Supreme Court of the United States, in order that such laws may be pronounced unconstitutional by that tribunal.

A committee was appointed to prepare and circulate petitions, and also to correspond with our friends in the several States, to awaken an interest in behalf of their own seamen. Committee as follows, viz: William C. Nell, Victor W. Barker, Robert Wood, Benjamin Weeden, John Thompson, Charles A. Battiste, Eli Cesar.

*The Liberator,* November 4, 1842.

## 93

# FREDERICK DOUGLASS DESCRIBES THE LATIMER CASE, 1842

In October, 1842 one James B. Gray appeared in Boston and claimed as his slave a Negro, George Latimer, who had lived in the city for several years. The Latimer case became the first of several famous Boston fugitive slave cases. Prominent in it was Frederick Douglass, himself a fugitive with only one year's experience behind him in the Abolitionist movement. As the result of the sort of work Douglass describes in the following stirring letter sent to Garrison from Lynn, November 8, 1842, sufficient funds were raised to buy Latimer's freedom. Shortly thereafter, Massachusetts passed a Personal Liberty Law forbidding state officers from participating in the hunting for fugitive slaves.

This letter, incidentally, is the first piece from Frederick Douglass' pen that was published.

The date of this letter finds me quite unwell. I have for a week past been laboring, in company with bro. Charles Remond, in New-Bedford, with special reference to the case of our outraged brother, George Latimer, and speaking almost day and night, in public and in private; and for the reward of our labor, I have the best evidence that a great good has been done. It is said by many residents, that New-Bedford has never been so favorably aroused to her anti-slavery responsibility as at present. Our meetings were characterized by that deep and solemn feeling which the importance of the cause, when properly set forth, is always calculated to awaken. On Sunday, we held three meetings in the new town hall, at the usual meeting hours, morning, afternoon, and evening. In the morning, we had quite a large meeting, at the opening of which, I occupied about an hour, on the question as to whether a man is better than a sheep. Mr. Dean then made a few remarks, and after him, Mr. Clapp, of Nantucket, arose and gave his testimony to the truth, as it is in anti-slavery. The meeting then adjourned, to meet again in the afternoon. I said that we held our meetings at the regular meeting hours. Truth requires me to make our afternoon meeting an exception to this remark. For long before the drawling, lazy church bells commenced sounding their deathly notes, mighty crowds were making their way to the town hall. They needed no bells to remind them of their duty to bleeding humanity. They were not going to meeting to hear as to the best mode of performing water baptism; they were not going to meeting to have their prayers handsomely said for them, or to say them, merely, themselves;

but to pray, not in word, but in deed and in truth; they were not going thither to be worshipped, but to worship, in spirit and in truth; they were not going to sacrifice, but to have mercy; they did not go there to find God; they had found him already. Such I think I may safely say of a large portion of the vast assembly that met in the afternoon. As I gazed upon them, my soul leaped for joy; and, but for the thought that the time might be better employed, I could have shouted aloud.

After a short space, allotted to secret or public prayer, bro. J. B. Sanderson arose and requested the attention of the audience to the reading of a few passages of scripture, selected by yourself in the editorial of last week. They did give their attention, and as he read the solemn and soul-stirring denunciations of Jehovah, by the mouth of his prophets and apostles, against oppressors, the deep stillness that pervaded that magnificent hall was a brilliant demonstration, that the audience felt that what was read was but the reiteration of words which had fallen from the great Judge of the universe. After reading, he proceeded to make some remarks on the general question of human rights. These, too, seemed to sink deep into the hearts of the gathered multitude. Not a word was lost; it was good seed, sown in good ground, by a careful hand; it must, it will bring forth fruit.

After him, rose bro. Remond, who addressed the meeting in his usual happy and deeply affecting style. When he had concluded his remarks, the meeting adjourned to meet again at an early hour in the evening. During the interval, our old friends and the slaves' friends, John Butler, Thomas Jones, Noah White, and others, were engaged in carrying benches from liberty hall to the town hall, that all who came might be accommodated with seats. They were determined to do something for humanity, though by so doing, they should be ranked with sabbath-breakers. Christianity prays for an overwhelming revival of anti-slavery truth, to convert and send forth more just such.

The meeting met according to adjournment, at an early hour. The splendid hall was brilliantly lighted, and crowded with an earnest, listening audience, and notwithstanding the efforts of our friends before named to have them seated, a large number had to stand during the meeting, which lasted about three hours; where the standing part of the audience were, at the commencement of the meeting, there they were at the conclusion of it; no moving about with them; any place was good enough, so they could but hear. From the eminence which I occupied, I could see the entire audience; and from its appearance, I should conclude that prejudice against color was not there, at any rate, it was not to be seen by me; we were all on a level, every one took a seat just where they chose; there were neither men's side, nor women's side; white pew, nor black pew; but all seats were free, and all sides free. When the meeting was fully gathered, I had something to say, and was followed by bro. Sanderson and Remond. When they had concluded their remarks, I again took the stand, and called the attention of the meeting to the case of bro. George Latimer, which proved the finishing stroke of my present public speaking. On taking my seat, I was seized with a violent pain in my breast, which continued till morning, and with occasional raising of blood; this past off in about two hours, after which, weakness of breast, a cough, and shortness of breath ensued, so that now such is the state of my lungs, that I am unfit for public speaking, for the present.

My condition goes harder with me, much harder than it would at ordinary times. These are certainly extraordinary times; times that demand the efforts of the humblest of our most humble advocates of our perishing and dying fellow-countrymen. Those that can but whisper freedom, should be doing even that, though they can only be heard from one side of their short fire place to the other. It is a struggle of life and death with us just now. No sword that can be used, be it never so rusty, should lay idle in its scabbard. Slavery, our enemy, has landed in our very midst, and commenced its bloody work. Just look at it; here is George Latimer a man—a brother—a husband—a father, stamped with the likeness of the eternal God, and redeemed by the blood of Jesus Christ, out-lawed, hunted down like a wild beast, and ferociously dragged through the streets of Boston, and incarcerated within the walls of Leverett-st. jail. And all this is done in Boston—liberty-loving, slavery-hating Boston—intellectual, moral, and religious Boston. And why was this—what crime had George Latimer committed? He had committed the crime of availing himself of his natural rights, in defence of which the founders of this very Boston enveloped her in midnight darkness, with the smoke proceeding from their thundering artillery. What a horrible state of things is here presented!

Boston has become the hunting-ground of merciless men-hunters, and man-stealers. Henceforth we need not portray to the imagination of northern people, the flying slave making his way through thick and dark woods of the South, with white fanged blood-hounds yelping on his blood-stained track; but refer to the streets of Boston, made dark and dense by crowds of professed christians. Take a look at James B. Gray's * new pack, turned loose on the track of poor Latimer. I see the blood-thirsty animals, smelling at every corner, part with each other, and meet again; they seem to be consulting as to the best mode of coming upon their victim. Now they look sad, discouraged;—tired, they drag along, as if they were ashamed of their business, and about to give up the chase; but presently they get a sight of their prey, their eyes brighten, they become more courageous, they approach

* Gray was the legal owner of Latimer.

their victim unlike the common hound. They come upon him softly, wagging their tails, pretending friendship, and do not pounce upon him, until they have secured him beyond possible escape. Such is the character of James B. Gray's new pack of two-legged blood-hounds that hunted down George Latimer, and dragged him away to the Leverett-street slave prison but a few days since.

We need not point to the sugar fields of Louisiana, or to the rice swamps of Alabama, for the bloody deeds of this soul-crushing system, but to the city of the pilgrims. In future, we need not uncap the bloody cells of the horrible slave prisons of Norfolk, Richmond, Mobile, and New-Orleans, and depict the wretched and forlorn condition of their miserable inmates, whose groans rend the air, pierce heaven, and disturb the Almighty; listen no longer at the snappings of the bloody slavedrivers' lash. Withdraw your attention, for a moment, from the agonizing cries coming from hearts bursting with the keenest anguish at the South, gaze no longer upon the base, cold-blooded, heartless slave-dealer of the South, who lays his iron clutch upon the hearts of husband and wife, and, with one mighty effort, tears the bleeding ligaments apart which before constituted the twain one flesh. I say, turn your attention from all this cruelty abroad, look now at home—follow me to your courts of justice—mark him who sits upon the bench. He may, or he may not—God grant he may not—tear George Latimer from a beloved wife and tender infant. But let us take a walk to the prison in which George Latimer is confined, inquire for the turn-key; let him open the large iron-barred door that leads you to the inner prison. You need go no further. Hark! listen! hear the groans and cries of George Latimer, mingling with which may be heard the cry—my wife, my child—and all is still again.

A moment of reflection ensues—I am to be taken back to Norfolk—must be torn from a wife and tender babe, with the threat from Mr. Gray that I am to be murdered, though not in the ordinary way—not to have my head severed from my shoulders, not to be hanged—not to have my heart pierced through with a dagger—not to have my brains blown out. No, no, all these are too good for me. No: I am to be killed by inches. I know not how; perhaps by cat-hauling until my back is torn all to pieces, my flesh is to be cut with the rugged lash, and I faint; warm brine must now be poured into my bleeding wounds, and through this process I must pass, until death shall end my sufferings. Good God! save me from a fate so horrible. Hark! hear him roll in his chains; "I can die, I had rather, than go back. O, my wife! O, my child!" You have heard enough. What man, what Christian can look upon this bloody state of things without his soul swelling big with indignation on the guilty perpetrators of it, and without resolving to cast in his influence with those who are collecting the elements which are to come down in ten-fold thunder, and dash this state of things into atoms?

Men, husbands and fathers of Massachusetts—put yourselves in the place of George Latimer; feel his pain and anxiety of mind; give vent to the groans that are breaking through his fever-parched lips, from a heart immersed in the deepest agony and suffering; rattle his chains; let his prospects be yours, for the space of a few moments. Remember George Latimer in bonds as bound with him; keep in view the golden rule—"All things whatsoever ye would that men should do unto you, do ye even so to them." "In as much as ye did it unto the least of these my brethren ye have done it unto me."

Now make up your minds to what your duty is to George Latimer, and when you have made your minds up, prepare to do it and take the consequences, and I have no fears of George Latimer going back. I can sympathize with George Latimer, having myself been cast into a miserable jail, on suspicion of my intending to do what he is said to have done, viz. appropriating my own body to my use.

My heart is full, and had I my voice, I should be doing all that I am capable of, for Latimer's redemption. I can do but little in any department; but if one department is more the place for me than another, that one is before the people.

I can't write to much advantage, having never had a day's schooling in my life, nor have I ever ventured to give publicity to any of my scribbling before; nor would I now, but for my peculiar circumstances.

*The Liberator*, Nov. 18, 1842.

## 94

## GARNET'S CALL TO REBELLION, 1843

From August 21–24, 1843, a National Negro Convention was held, despite some opposition, in Buffalo, New York. Over seventy delegates from a dozen states were present, including such young and rising figures as Frederick Douglass, William Wells Brown, Charles B. Ray, Charles L. Remond and Henry Highland Garnet. The latter, though but twenty-seven years of age, had already served as editor of a newspaper and was then the pastor of a Presbyterian Church in Troy, New York. He delivered a very militant speech at this convention entitled "An Address to the Slaves of the United States," which attracted national attention, and which failed by one vote of being adopted as the sentiments of the convention. These are his words:

Brethren and Fellow Citizens:—Your brethren of the North, East, and West have been accustomed to meet together in National Conventions, to sympathize with each other, and to weep over your unhappy condition. In these meetings we have addressed all classes of the free, but we have never, until this time, sent a word of consolation and advice to you. We have been contented in sitting still and mourning over your sorrows, earnestly hoping that before this day your sacred liberty would have been restored. But, we have hoped in vain. Years have rolled on, and tens of thousands have been borne on streams of blood and tears, to the shores of eternity. While you have been oppressed, we have also been partakers with you; nor can we be free while you are enslaved. We, therefore, write to you as being bound with you.

Many of you are bound to us, not only by the ties of a common humanity, but we are connected by the more tender relations of parents, wives, husbands, children, brothers, and sisters, and friends. As such we most affectionately address you.

Slavery has fixed a deep gulf between you and us, and while it shuts out from you the relief and consolation which your friends would willingly render, it affects and persecutes you with a fierceness which we might not expect to see in the fiends of hell. But still the Almighty Father of mercies has left to us a glimmering ray of hope, which shines out like a lone star in a cloudy sky. Mankind are becoming wiser, and better—the oppressor's power is fading, and you, every day, are becoming better informed, and more numerous. Your grievances, brethren, are many. We shall not attempt, in this short address, to present to the world all the dark catalogue of this nation's sins, which have been committed upon an innocent people. Nor is it indeed necessary, for you feel them from day to day, and all the civilized world look upon them with amazement.

Two hundred and twenty-seven years ago, the first of our injured race were brought to the shores of America. They came not with glad spirits to select their homes in the New World. They came not with their own consent, to find an unmolested enjoyment of the blessings of this fruitful soil. The first dealings they had with men calling themselves Christians, exhibited to them the worst features of corrupt and sordid hearts; and convinced them that no cruelty is too great, no villainy and no robbery too abhorrent for even enlightened men to perform, when influenced by avarice and lust. Neither did they come flying upon the wings of Liberty, to a land of freedom. But they came with broken hearts, from their beloved native land, and were doomed to unrequited toil and deep degradation. Nor did the evil of their bondage end at their emancipation by death. Succeeding generations inherited their chains, and millions have come from eternity into time, and have returned again to the world of spirits, cursed and ruined by American slavery.

The propagators of the system, or their immediate ancestors, very soon discovered its growing evil, and its tremendous wickedness, and secret promises were made to destroy it. The gross inconsistency of a people holding slaves, who had themselves "ferried o'er the wave" for freedom's sake, was too apparent to be entirely overlooked. The voice of Freedom cried, "Emancipate yourselves." Humanity supplicated with tears for the deliverance of the children of Africa. Wisdom urged her solemn plea. The bleeding captive plead his innocence, and pointed to Christianity who stood weeping at the cross. Jehovah frowned upon the nefarious institution, and thunderbolts, red with vengeance, struggled to leap forth to blast the guilty wretches who maintained it. But all was in vain. Slavery had stretched its dark wings of death over the land, the Church stood silently by—the priests prophesied falsely, and the people loved to have it so. Its throne is established, and now it reigns triumphant.

Nearly three millions of your fellow-citizens are prohibited by law and public opinion, (which in this country is stronger than law,) from reading the Book of Life. Your intellect has been destroyed as much as possible, and every ray of light they have attempted to shut out from your minds. The oppressors themselves have become involved in the ruin. They have become weak, sensual, and rapacious—they have cursed you—they have cursed themselves—they have cursed the earth which they have trod.

The colonists threw the blame upon England. They said that the mother country entailed the evil upon them, and that they would rid themselves of it if they could. The world thought they were sincere, and the philanthropic pitied them. But time soon tested their sincerity.

In a few years the colonists grew strong, and severed themselves from the British Government. Their independence was declared, and they took their station among the sovereign powers of the earth. The declaration was a glorious document. Sages admired it, and the patriotic of every nation reverenced the God-like sentiments which it contained. When the power of Government returned to their hands, did they emancipate the slaves? No; they rather added new links to our chains. Were they ignorant of the principles of Liberty? Certainly they were not. The sentiments of their revolutionary orators fell in burning eloquence upon their hearts, and with one voice they cried, Liberty or Death. Oh what a sentence was that! It ran from soul to soul like electric fire, and nerved the arm of thousands to fight in the holy cause of Freedom. Among the diversity of opinions that are entertained in regard to physical resistance, there are but a few found to gainsay that stern declaration. We are among those who do not. Slavery! How much misery is comprehended in that single word. What mind is there that does not shrink from its direful effects? Unless the image of God be obliterated from the soul, all men cherish the love of Liberty. The nice discerning political economist does not regard the sacred right more than the untutored African who roams in the wilds of Congo. Nor has the one more right to the full enjoyment of his freedom than the other. In every man's mind the good seeds of liberty are planted, and he who brings his fellow down so low, as to make him contented with a condition of slavery, commits the highest crime against God and man. Brethren, your oppressors aim to do this. They endeavor to make you as much like brutes as possible. When they have blinded the eyes of your mind—when they have embittered the sweet waters of life—then, and not till then, has American slavery done its perfect work.

To SUCH DEGRADATION IT IS SINFUL IN THE EXTREME FOR YOU TO MAKE VOLUNTARY SUBMISSION. The divine commandments you are in duty bound to reverence and obey. If you do not obey them, you will surely meet with the displeasure of the Almighty. He requires you to love him supremely, and your neighbor as yourself—to keep the Sabbath day holy—to search the Scriptures—and bring up your children with respect for his laws, and to worship no other God but him. But slavery sets all these at nought, and hurls defiance in the face of Jehovah. The forlorn condition in which you are placed, does not destroy your moral obligation to God. You are not certain of heaven, because you suffer yourselves to remain in a state of slavery, where you cannot obey the commandments of the Sovereign of the universe. If the ignorance of slavery is a passport to heaven, then it is a blessing, and no curse, and you should rather desire its perpetuity than its abolition. God will not receive slavery, nor ignorance, nor any other state of mind, for love and obedience to him. Your condition does not absolve you from your moral obligation. The diabolical injustice by which your liberties are cloven down, NEITHER GOD, NOR ANGELS, OR JUST MEN, COMMAND YOU TO SUFFER FOR A SINGLE MOMENT. THEREFORE IT IS YOUR SOLEMN AND IMPERATIVE DUTY TO USE EVERY MEANS, BOTH MORAL, INTELLECTUAL, AND PHYSICAL THAT PROMISES SUCCESS. If a band of heathen men should attempt to enslave a race of Christians, and to place their children under the influence of some false religion, surely Heaven would frown upon the men who would not resist such aggression, even to death. If, on the other hand, a band of Christians should attempt to enslave a race of heathen men, and to entail slavery upon them, and to keep them in heathenism in the midst of Christianity, the God of heaven would smile upon every effort which the injured might make to disenthral themselves.

Brethren, it is as wrong for your lordly oppressors to keep you in slavery, as it was for the man thief to steal our ancestors from the coast of Africa. You should therefore now use the same manner of resistance, as would have been just in our ancestors when the bloody foot-prints of the first remorseless soul-thief was placed upon the shores of our fatherland. The humblest peasant is as free in the sight of God as the proudest monarch that ever swayed a sceptre. Liberty is a spirit sent out from God, and like its great Author, is no respecter of persons.

Brethren, the time has come when you must act for yourselves. It is an old and true saying that, "if hereditary bondmen would be free, they must themselves strike the blow." You can plead your own cause, and do the work of emancipation better than any others. The nations of the world are moving in the great cause of universal freedom, and some of them at least will, ere long, do you justice. The combined powers of Europe have placed their broad seal of disapprobation upon the African slave-trade. But in the slaveholding parts of the United States, the trade is as brisk as ever. They buy and sell you as though you were brute beasts. The North has done much—her opinion of slavery in the abstract is known. But in regard to the South, we adopt the opinion of the *New York Evangelist*— We have advanced so far, that the cause apparently waits for a more effectual door to be thrown open than has been yet. We are about to point out that more effectual door. Look around you, and behold the bosoms of your loving wives heaving with untold agonies! Hear the cries of your poor children! Remember the stripes your fathers bore. Think of the torture and disgrace of your noble mothers. Think of your wretched sisters, loving virtue and purity, as they are driven into concubinage and are exposed to the unbridled lusts of incarnate devils. Think of the undying glory that hangs around the ancient name of Africa—and forget not that you are native born American citizens, and as such, you are justly entitled to all the rights that are granted to the freest. Think how many tears you have poured out upon the soil which you have cultivated with unrequited toil and enriched with your blood; and then go to your lordly enslavers and tell them plainly, that you *are determined to be free.* Appeal to their sense of justice, and tell them that they have no more right to oppress you, than you have to enslave them. Entreat them to remove the grievous burdens which they have imposed upon you, and to remunerate you for your labor. Promise them renewed diligence in the cultivation of the soil, if they will render to you an equivalent for your services. Point them to the increase of happiness and prosperity in the British West Indies since the Act of Emancipation.

Tell them in language which they cannot misunderstand, of the exceeding sinfulness of slavery, and of a future judgment, and of the righteous retributions of an indignant God. Inform them that all you desire is FREEDOM, and that nothing else will suffice. Do this, and for ever after cease to toil for the heartless tyrants, who give you no other reward but stripes and abuse. If they then commence the work of death, they, and not you, will be responsible for the consequences. You had better all die—*die immediately*, than live slaves and entail your wretchedness upon your posterity. If you would be free in this generation, here is your only hope. However much you and all of us may desire it, there is not much hope of redemption without the shedding of blood. If you must bleed, let it all come at once—rather *die freemen, than live to be slaves*. It is impossible like the children of Israel, to make a grand exodus from the land of bondage. The Pharaohs are on both sides of the blood-red waters! You cannot move *en masse*, to the dominions of the British Queen—nor can you pass through Florida and overrun Texas, and at last find peace in Mexico. The propagators of American slavery are spending their blood and treasure, that they may plant the black flag in the heart of Mexico and riot in the halls of the Montezumas. In the language of the Rev. Robert Hall, when addressing the volunteers of Bristol, who were rushing forth to repel the invasion of Napoleon, who threatened to lay waste the fair homes of England, "Religion is too much interested in your behalf, not to shed over you her most gracious influences."

You will not be compelled to spend much time in order to become inured to hardships. From the first moment that you breathed the air of heaven, you have been accustomed to nothing else but hardships. The heroes of the American Revolution were never put upon harder fare than a peck of corn and a few herrings per week. You have not become enervated by the luxuries of life. Your sternest energies have been beaten out upon the anvil of severe trial. Slavery has done this, to make you subservient, to its own purposes; but it has done more than this, it has prepared you for any emergency. If you receive good treatment, it is what you could hardly expect; if you meet with pain, sorrow, and even death, these are the common lot of slaves.

Fellow men! Patient sufferers! behold your dearest rights crushed to the earth! See your sons murdered, and your wives, mothers and sisters doomed to prostitution. In the name of the merciful God, and by all that life is worth, let it no longer be a debatable question whether it is better to choose *Liberty or death*.

In 1822, Denmark Veazie [Vesey], of South Carolina, formed a plan for the liberation of his fellow men. In the whole history of human efforts to overthrow slavery, a more complicated and tremendous plan was never formed. He was betrayed by the treachery of his own people, and died a martyr to freedom. Many a brave hero fell, but history, faithful to her high trust, will transcribe his name on the same monument with Moses, Hampden, Tell, Bruce and Wallace, Toussaint L'Ouverture, Lafayette and Washington. That tremendous movement shook the whole empire of slavery. The guilty soul-thieves were overwhelmed with fear. It is a matter of fact, that at that time, and in consequence of the threatened revolution, the slave States talked strongly of emancipation. But they blew but one blast of the trumpet of freedom and then laid it aside. As these men became quiet, the slaveholders ceased to talk about emancipation; and now behold your condition today! Angels sigh over it, and humanity has long since exhausted her tears in weeping on your account!

The patriotic Nathaniel Turner followed Denmark Veazie [Vesey]. He was goaded to desperation by wrong and injustice. By despotism, his name has been recorded on the list of infamy, and future generations will remember him among the noble and brave.

Next arose the immortal Joseph Cinque, the hero of the *Amistad*. He was a native African, and by the help of God he emancipated a whole ship-load of his fellow men on the high seas. And he now sings of liberty on the sunny hills of Africa and beneath his native palm-trees, where he hears the lion roar and feels himself as free as that king of the forest.

Next arose Madison Washington that bright star of freedom, and took his station in the constellation of true heroism. He was a slave on board the brig *Creole*, of Richmond, bound to New Orleans, that great slave mart, with a hundred and four [sic] others. Nineteen struck for liberty or death. But one life was taken, and the whole were emancipated, and the vessel was carried into Nassau, New Providence.

Noble men! Those who have fallen in freedom's conflict, their memories will be cherished by the true-hearted and the God-fearing in all future generations; those who are living, their names are surrounded by a halo of glory.

Brethren, arise, arise! Strike for your lives and liberties. Now is the day and the hour. Let every slave throughout the land do this, and the days of slavery are numbered. You cannot be more oppressed than you have been— you cannot suffer greater cruelties than you have already. *Rather die free-men than live to be slaves*. Remember that you are FOUR MILLIONS!

It is in your power so to torment the God-cursed slaveholders that they will be glad to let you go free. If the scale was turned, and black men were the masters and white men the slaves, every destructive agent and element would be employed to lay the oppressor low. Danger and death would hang over their heads day and night. Yes, the tyrants would meet with plagues more terrible than those of Pharaoh. But you are a patient people. You act as though, you were made for the special use of these devils. You act as though your daughters were born to pamper the lusts of your masters and overseers. And worse than all, you tamely submit while your lords tear your wives from your embraces and defile them before your eyes. In the name of God, we ask, are you men? Where is the blood of your fathers? Has it all run out of your veins? Awake, awake; millions of voices are calling you! Your dead fathers speak to you from their graves. Heaven, as with a voice of thunder, calls on you to arise from the dust.

Let your motto be resistance! *resistance!* RESISTANCE! No oppressed people have ever secured their liberty without resistance. What kind of resistance you had better make, you must decide by the circumstances that surround you, and according to the suggestion of expediency. Brethren, adieu! Trust in the living God. Labor for the peace of the human race, and remember that you are FOUR MILLIONS.

*A Memorial Discourse; by Rev. Henry Highland Garnet, delivered in the Hall of the House of Representatives, Washington . . . February 12, 1865, with an introduction by James McCune Smith* (Phila., 1865), pp. 44–51.

## 95

## MICHIGAN NEGRO CONVENTION, 1843

What appears to have been the first state convention of the Negroes of Michigan met with twenty-three delegates in Detroit on October 26 and 27, 1843. The call for this Convention, drafted by a committee headed by William Lambert, was dated September 19, 1843 and captures much of the fighting spirit which characterized the meeting itself:

*Dear Brethren:* Believing the time has come for us to be united in sentiment and action, and to speak out in our own defence upon the great cause of Human Liberty and Equal Rights: we call upon you to cooperate with us in this important movement that we are about to make. For as we are an oppressed people wishing to be free, we must evidently follow the examples of the oppressed nations that have preceded us: for history informs us that the liberties of an oppressed people are obtained only in proportion to their own exertions in their own cause. Therefore, in accordance with this truth, let us come up, and, like the oppressed people of England, Ireland, and Scotland, band ourselves together and wage unceasing war against the high-handed wrongs of the hideous monster Tyranny. Come up brethren, and rally under the banner of Freedom; for since our late National Convention, a new and a bright star has made its appearance in our dark horizon, and has attracted the attention of our oppressors, and caused many to cry out, Go on, thou genius of Liberty, go on! The friends of liberty throughout the civilized world has hailed it, and now stand cheering us to go on.—Then, brethren, shall we not meet together, and consult how we may better our condition? Shall we not infuse into the minds of our young men, and posterity, a disposition to be free, and leave their present low and degraded employment, and endeavor to obtain mechanic arts, and follow agricultural pursuits? Shall we not meet together and endeavor to promote the cause of Education, Temperance, Industry, and Morality among our people; and by our correct, upright and manly stand in the defence of our liberties, prove to our oppressors, and the world, that we are determined to be free?

Yes! yes! let us assemble—let us come together, and pledge ourselves in the name of God and bleeding humanity and posterity, to organize, organize and organize, until the green-eyed monster Tyranny, shall be trampled under the feet of the oppressed, and Liberty and Equality shall embrace each other, and shall have scattered their blessings throughout the length and breadth of our land.

> Then, come, dear brethren,
>   If we would be free,
> We must demand our Liberty,
>   And strike the blow with all our might,
> For Liberty is the Balm of Life.

*Minutes of the State Convention of the Colored Citizens of the State of Michigan, for the purpose of considering their moral & political conditions, as citizens of the State.* (Detroit, 1843). Copy in the Boston Athenaeum.

## 96

## GARNET ON PATRONIZING FRIENDS, 1843

In the temporary absence of Garrison, *The Liberator* was edited by a well-known Abolitionist writer and poet, Mrs. Maria Weston Chapman. This lady condemned the 1843 speech of Garnet (Document 94) in severest but patronizing terms. The latter feature of her remarks drew a sharp rebuke from Garnet in a letter dated Troy, N.Y., November 17, 1843:

Respected Madam: Some time ago you wrote an article in the *Liberator*, condemnatory of the National Convention of colored people, which was held in the city of Buffalo, in the month of August last. I should have sent a reply, ere this time, had I not been engaged so much in the cause of freedom, since the appearance of your article. I must confess that I was exceedingly amazed to find that I was doomed to share so much of your severity, to call it nothing else. And, up to this moment, I have not been able to understand the motives which led you to attack my character as you have in the paper referred to. I am a stranger to you, comparatively, and whatever of my public life has come to your notice, you have seen nothing impeachable.

I was born in slavery, and have escaped, to tell you, and others, what the monster has done, and is still doing. It, therefore, astonished me to think that you should desire to sink me again to the condition of a *slave,* by forcing me to think just as you do. My crime is, that I have dared to think, and act, contrary to your opinion. I am a Liberty party man—you are opposed to that party—far be it from me to attempt to injure your character because you cannot pronounce my shibboleth. While you think as you do, we must differ. If it has come to this, that I must think and act as you do, because you are an Abolitionist, or be exterminated by your thunder, then I do not hesitate to say that your abolitionism is abject slavery. Were I a slave of the Hon. George McDuffie, or John C. Calhoun, I would not be required to do anything more than to think and act as I might be commanded. I will not be the slave of any person or party. I am a Liberty party man from choice. No man ever asked me to join that party; I was the first colored man that ever attached his name to that party, and you may rely upon my word, when I tell you I mean "to stand."

You likewise adopt all that E. M. Marsh, of Buffalo, has said of the Convention and myself.* I shall not attempt to say anything more than this, in regard to him. My friend, Mr. Marsh, is a man of a very unstable mind. He is one thing to-day, and another thing to-morrow. He was once a Liberty man, but he is now a no-church and no-government man. I never saw such an unfair statement penned by a man calling himself a Christian. Every thing that he has written, is either false, or exaggerated. I have no more to say of him—I leave him alone in his glory. But I am sorry that you have echoed his false allegations. I am sorry that all the old organization journals have likewise echoed that libellous report.

But the address to the slaves you seem to doom to the most fiery trials. And yet, Madam, you have not seen that address—you have merely *heard* of it; nevertheless, you criticised it very severely. You speak, at length, of myself, the author of the paper. You say that I "have received bad counsel." You are not the only person who has told your humble servant that his humble productions have been produced by the *"counsel"* of some Anglo-Saxon. I have expected no more from ignorant slaveholders and their apologists, but I really looked for better things from Mrs. Maria W. Chapman, an antislavery poetess, and editor *pro tem.* of the Boston *Liberator.* I can think on the subject of human rights without "counsel," either from the men of the West, or the women of the East. My address was read to but two persons, previous to its presentation at Buffalo. One was a colored brother, who did not give me a single word of counsel, and the other was my wife; and if she

* In *The Liberator,* September 8, 1843, Mr. Marsh published a long and very critical report of the Convention in general and of Mr. Garnet in particular.

did counsel me, it is no matter, for "we twain are one flesh." In a few days I hope to publish the address, then you can judge how much treason there is in it. In the meantime, be assured that there is one black American who dares to speak boldly on the subject of universal liberty.

*The Liberator*, December 3, 1843.

## 91

## A JAILED NEGRO PETITIONS CONGRESS, 1843

The injustices suffered by the Negro people in the capital of the United States prior to the Civil War were many and keen. One such act evoked a petition from the victim, William Jones, to the Congress of the United States dated Washington Jail, December 28, 1843. This was presented to the House by the fiery anti-slavery advocate, Representative Joshua Giddings of Ohio, and provoked two days of bitter debate. The petition was referred to a committee which reported two weeks later and gave Mr. Jones no satisfaction but rather initiated legislation applying the Fugitive Slave Act of 1793 to the District of Columbia.

*To the Congress of the United States:*

The humble petition of William Jones, now a prisoner in the United States jail in Washington city, respectfully represents:

That your memorialist is a free citizen of the United States, born free in the State of Virginia, and has always been an industrious and honest citizen, chargeable with no crime; that, while enjoying his liberty in this city, he was seized, and, without any charge of crime, was thrown into jail, where he has been confined for several weeks, and is now advertised to be sold as a slave by the marshal of the United States to pay the expenses of his imprisonment, unless his owner shall appear; that your petitioner has no owner but his God, and owes no service but to his country; that it is hard for him to be imprisoned without fault, and then sold to pay the expense. He therefore prays that Congress will exert their powers for the protection of the weak, and procure for him that liberty and justice which are his right, and which he has a special claim for in the District, which is under the exclusive legislation of your honorable body.

*Congressional Globe*, Dec. 28, 1843, 25th Cong., 1st Sess., vol. 13, p. 78.

## 98

# MASTER-FUGITIVE SLAVE
# CORRESPONDENCE, 1844

Masters, upon learning the whereabouts of fugitive slaves would occasionally begin a correspondence (generally brief and sharp) with them. An early example of this came in 1844. In February of that year a W. H. Gatewood wrote from Bedford, Kentucky to Henry Bibb who had fled from him. He told his former slave that his mother was well and asked that Bibb give his regards to two other Negroes—King and Jack—who had escaped with him. On March 23, 1844, Henry Bibb replied as follows, from Detroit:

Dear Sir:—I am happy to inform you that you are not mistaken in the man whom you sold as property, and received pay for as such. But I thank God that I am not property now, but am regarded as a man like yourself, and although I live far north, I am enjoying a comfortable living by my own industry. If you should ever chance to be traveling this way, and will call on me, I will use you better than you did me while you held me as a slave. Think not that I have any malice against you, for the cruel treatment which you inflicted on me while I was in your power. As it was the custom of your country, to treat your fellow men as you did me and my little family, I can freely forgive you.

I wish to be remembered in love to my aged mother, and friends; please tell her that if we should never meet again in this life, my prayer shall be to God that we may meet in Heaven, where parting shall be no more.

You wish to be remembered to King and Jack. I am pleased, sir, to inform you that they are both here, well, and doing well. They are both living in Canada West. They are now the owners of better farms than the men are who once owned them.

You may perhaps think hard of us for running away from slavery, but as to myself, I have but one apology to make for it, which is this: I have only to regret that I did not start at an earlier period. I might have been free long before I was. But you had it in your power to have kept me there much longer than you did. I think it is very probable that I should have been a toiling slave on your property today, if you had treated me differently.

To be compelled to stand by and see you whip and slash my wife without mercy, when I could afford her no protection, not even by offering myself to suffer the lash in her place, was more than I felt it to be the duty of a slave husband to endure, while the way was open to Canada. My infant child was also frequently flogged by Mrs. Gatewood, for crying, until its skin was bruised literally purple. This kind of treatment was what drove me from home and family, to seek a better home for them. But I am willing to forget the past. I should be pleased to hear from you again, on the reception of this, and should also be very happy to correspond with you often, if it should be agreeable to yourself. I subscribe myself a friend to the oppressed, and Liberty forever.

*Narrative of the Life and Adventures of Henry Bibb, an American Slave* (N.Y., 1849), pp. 175–78.

## 99

## FACTS CONCERNING FREE NEGROES, 1844

In April, 1844, in the course of official correspondence relative to the *Creole* case (see document 90), the Secretary of State, John C. Calhoun, made exceedingly derogatory remarks concerning Negroes to the British Minister to the United States. As a result, that same month, New York Negroes at a mass meeting empowered a committee consisting of men like James McCune Smith, Theodore S. Wright, Patrick H. Reason, Charles B. Ray, and Philip A. Bell to draft a reply. This was done; the reply, written by Dr. James McCune Smith, was read and approved at another mass meeting, held May 3, 1844, and it was then forwarded, as a memorial, to the Senate of the United States:

The memorial of the undersigned, free colored citizens of the city and county of New York, respectfully showeth, that

*Whereas,* in a letter, addressed to the Right Hon. Richard Pakenham, &c (bearing date April 18th, 1844,) the Hon. John C. Calhoun, Secretary of State for these United States, saith,

*First,* "That in the States which have changed their former relations, (the States which have emancipated their slaves, meaning,) the African race has sunk into vice and pauperism";

*Secondly,* That this "vice and pauperism" is "accompanied by the bodily and mental afflictions incident thereto—deafness, blindness, insanity and idiocy"; and that "the number of deaf, dumb, blind, idiots and insane of the Negroes in the States which have changed the ancient relation between the races is one out of every ninety-six"; and, that, "in the State of Maine, the number of Negroes returned as deaf, dumb, blind, insane and idiots, by the census of 1840, is one out of every twelve";

*Thirdly,* "And the number of Negroes, who are deaf and dumb, blind, idiots, insane, paupers and in prison, in the States that have changed, (the free States, meaning,) is one out of every six";

*Fourthly,* While in all other States that have retained the ancient relations (the slave States, meaning,) between them (the races, meaning,) "they (the slaves, meaning,) have improved greatly in every respect, in number, comfort, intelligence and morals;"

And whereas, in regard to these allegations,

*First,* Your memorialists have great reason to doubt the accuracy of the first; because,

*Secondly,* It appears in regard to the second allegation, which is the particular proof of the first, that in an examination of the census of 1840, it is found to be self-contradictory: to wit, in asserting the existence of the free colored persons insane, blind, deaf, dumb, in certain towns in free States, in which towns, it appears by the same census of 1840, there are no free colored persons whatever of any condition:

For example, in

|  | Insane | Blind | Deaf & Dumb |
|---|---|---|---|
| **MAINE** | | | |
| In 8 towns containing no colored— there are reported, | 27 | 1 | 2 |
| **NEW HAMPSHIRE** | | | |
| 11 towns containing no colored— there are reported, | 12 | 0 | 3 |
| **VERMONT** | | | |
| 2 towns containing no colored— there are reported, | 2 | 2 | 1 |
| **MASSACHUSETTS** | | | |
| 5 towns containing no colored— there are reported, | 10 | 1 | 0 |
| 1 town Worcester, the white insane at the Asylum are returned as colored | 133 | 0 | 0 |
| **NEW YORK** | | | |
| 19 towns containing no colored— there are reported, | 29 | 8 | 5 |
| **PENNSYLVANIA** | | | |
| 11 towns containing no colored— there are reported, | 20 | 6 | 6 |

|  | Insane | Blind | Deaf & Dumb |
|---|---|---|---|
| **OHIO** | | | |
| 33 towns containing no colored— there are reported, | 48 | 9 | 5 |
| **INDIANA** | | | |
| 4 towns containing no colored— there are reported, | 6 | 9 | 7 |
| **ILLINOIS** | | | |
| 9 towns containing no colored— there are reported, | 18 | 0 | 3 |
| **MICHIGAN** | | | |
| 12 towns containing no colored— there are reported, | 12 | 2 | 5 |
| **IOWA** | | | |
| 1 town containing no colored— there are reported, | 2 | 0 | 4 |
| Showing | | | |

|  | Colored Insane | Blind | Deaf & Dumb |
|---|---|---|---|
| Total colored inhabitants—000 | 186 | 38 | 36 |

By the same census, it appears that in the above, and other towns in the free States, there is—

| | |
|---|---|
| An excess of colored insane over colored residents, | 213 |
| Error in the return of colored for white insane at Worcester, Mass. | 133 |
| Total, | 346 |

The whole number of colored insane in the free States being stated to be 1,199 by the census of 1840; if from this number we deduct the 346 shown to be not colored persons, there remains 853 colored insane in the free States, or one in about 200, which your memorialists are satisfied is greatly beyond the actual proportion; because, so far as your memorialists have been able to ascertain, the proportion of the insane among the free colored is not greater than among the white population of the free States. It is stated, for example, by Dr. J. Ray, the physician of the Lunatic Asylum of the State of Maine, that there are not five colored lunatics or insane in that State. In the Lunatic Asylum at Blackwell's Island, in the county of New York, there are but 17 colored insane, or about 1 to 1000 colored inhabitants of this county. In 1837, the same proportion existed in the free colored population of Philadelphia.

In regard to the deaf, dumb and blind, it will be seen that the census is likewise self contradictory, asserting that there are 74 free colored afflicted with these dispensations, in towns which contain no colored inhabitants.

*Thirdly,* In regard to the third allegation, which asserts that one in every six of the free colored in the free States are either "deaf, dumb, blind, insane, or in prison," or, in other words, that there are 30,000 free colored supported at the public charge in the free States, your memorialists humbly think that they have furnished, in answer to the second allegation, sufficient facts to disprove the entire accuracy of this astounding assertion. And your memorialists further believe, that the same errors have crept into the census and other documents based thereon, in regard to the pauperism of the free colored, as they have shown to have crept into the census in regard to the insane, &c. Especially when your memorialists know, from the books of the alms-houses of New York and Philadelphia, there are in these places one colored pauper to about 100 of the colored population, a proportion which is about the same as the pauperism of the free white citizens of these cities; and as these cities contain 37,000, more than one sixth part of the entire colored population of the free States; and as it is known that the proportion of paupers in this as well as in other classes is greatest in large cities, it is a fair inference that the third allegation, at least so much of it as relates to pauperism, cannot be accurate.

*Fourthly,* In relation to the fourth allegation, which is in subtsance, that the slaves have improved in morals, intelligence, comfort and number—reversing the order of the items; your memorialists would observe, that the natural increase of the slaves (which is greater than the natural increase of the whites or of the free colored) is a measure of their relative fecundity, not of their relative condition. Whilst the percentage of longevity, and the ratio of mortality, which are tests of relative condition, are greatly in favor of the free colored, the more remotely they may be removed in time from slavery. For the slaves who live beyond 36 years are only 15.49 per cent, while free colored in the free States who live beyond 36 years are 22.68, showing a balance of 7.19 per cent in favor of the condition of the free colored.

In the cities of New York and Philadelphia, (by the city Inspector's reports,) it appears that a joint population of 37,000 free colored have diminished their ratio of mortality from 1 in 17 in Philadelphia, and 1 in 21 in New York in 1820; to 1 in 40, in both places in 1843, being a distinct improvement in *condition* of at least 100 per cent in 23 years! There are no records of the mortality among slaves!

In regard to *intelligence* there are in the free States, to a total population of 170,000 free colored persons, 40,000 children of an age to go to school, one school to every 543 children, in addition to a large number of children attending white schools, and a number of colored students who are pursuing their studies at Oberlin Western Theological Seminary, and Dartmouth College whilst the children of slaves are forbidden to be taught to read, under heavy penalties, in the States which have not changed the *ancient relations* —*death* being the penalty for the second offence. Your memorialists do not deem it irrelevant to state, in this connexion, that the proportion of adults above 20 years of age, who cannot read or write, is 1 in 1081, in the States which have changed the *ancient relations* (the free States) whilst the number of adults who cannot read and write is 1 in 144, in the States that have not changed the ancient relations (the slave States).

In regard to morals, believing that religion is the only basis of sound morals, your memorialists would state that there are to the 170,000 free colored people of the free States—

| Denominations | Churches |
|---|---|
| Independent Methodists | 2 |
| Baptist Association | 2 |
| Methodist | 284 |
| Baptist | 15 |
| Presbyterian & Congregational | 3 |
| Episcopal | 6 |
| Lutheran | 1 |
| Total | 318 |

Making about one church to every 543 of the free colored of the free States.

At the same time, granting that all the churches in the South are promiscuously attended by the slaves and whites, it appears, taking the eleven cities of Baltimore, Richmond, Petersburgh, Virginia, Norfolk, Charleston, Savannah, Mobile, New Orleans, Louisville, St. Louis and Washington, with a total population, of all classes, of 360,905; these cities contain only 167 churches; or one church to every 2,161 inhabitants; from which it follows that the free colored people of the North have a greater number of churches by nearly four fold, than have the entire population of these slave-holding cities. They have, also, 340 Benevolent societies; and 7 newspapers are printed by the free colored people of the free States.

For all of which reasons, your memorialists would humbly pray—

*1st.* That your honorable body would cause the Census of 1840 to be reexamined, and so far as possible, corrected anew, in the Department of State, in order that the head of that Department may have facts upon which to found his arguments.

*2d.* That your honorable body would establish at Washington, a general office of Registration, with a proper officer at its head, who shall cause to be returned from each county in the United States, a yearly report of the sanitary condition of each class of inhabitants, as well as the births, deaths, and marriages.

*3d.* That your honorable body will cause to be taken, in the Census of 1850, the number of adults who cannot read and write among the whites, the slaves, and the free people of color, in every county of the United States.

And your Memorialists will ever pray.

*New York Tribune,* May 5, 1844, and *The Liberator,* May 31, 1844.

# 100

# STRUGGLE AGAINST JIM CROW SCHOOLS, 1844

For many years Boston Negroes struggled against the segregated pattern of public education in their city. Indicative of this effort are the resolutions adopted by these Negroes on June 24, 1844 after a series of mass meetings held that spring:

*Resolved,* That, impelled by a deep sense of gratitude, we tender to Dr. H. Storer our unfeigned thanks for his successful efforts in instituting the late investigation of affairs connected with the Smith School [for Negroes], and for his unremitting attention to the same from the commencement to the close.

*Resolved,* That we present our most grateful acknowledgements to the Hon. John C. Park, for the late voluntary and disinterested devotion of his time and eminent talents in the cause of the wronged and neglected colored children of this city.

*Whereas,* we, the colored citizens of the city of Boston, have recently sent a petition to the School Committee, respectfully praying for the abolition of the separate schools for colored children, and asking for the rights and privileges extended to other citizens in respect to the common school system—viz. the right to send our children to the schools established in the respective districts in which we reside; and

*Whereas,* the School Committee, at their last meeting, passed a vote saying, in substance, that the prayer of our petition would not be granted, and that the separate schools for colored children would be continued; and

*Whereas,* we believe, and have the opinion of eminent counsel, that the institution and support of separate schools, at the public charge, for any one class of the inhabitants in exclusion of any other class, is contrary to the laws of this Commonwealth; therefore,

*Resolved,* That we consider the late action of the School Committee, in regard to our petition asking for the entire abolition of separate schools for colored children, as erroneous and unsatisfactory.

*Resolved,* That while we would not turn aside from our main object, the abolition of the separate colored schools, we cannot allow this occasion to pass without an expression of our surprise and regret at the recent acquittal by the School Committee of Abner Forbes, Principal of the Smith School, and of our deep conviction that he is totally unworthy of his present responsible station; and that the colored parents of this city are recommended to withdraw their children from the exclusive school established in contravention of that equality of privileges which is the vital principle of the school system of Massachusetts.

*Resolved,* That a copy of the above preamble and resolutions be sent to the Chairman of the School Committee, with a request that the petition heretofore presented may be reconsidered, and that we be allowed a hearing on said petition before them.

*Resolved,* That the heartfelt thanks of the colored citizens of Boston are due to Messrs. George S. Hillard and John T. Sargent for the humane and independent stand recently taken by them in the School Committee, in behalf of the rights and welfare of the colored children.

*Resolved,* That the expression of the sense of this meeting be transmitted to the several gentlemen named in the foregoing resolutions, and be also published in the city papers.

John T. Hilton, President

Henry L. W. Thacker ⎱ Vice Presidents
Jonas W. Clark ⎰

William C. Nell ⎱ Secretaries
Robert Morris ⎰

*The Liberator,* June 28, 1844.

## 101

## FIFTH ANNUAL CONVENTION OF NEW YORK NEGROES, 1844

Indicative of the unflagging efforts of Negroes for full suffrage rights are the following resolutions adopted at the fifth convention of New York Negroes, held in

Schenectady, September 18–20, 1844. Eighteen cities were represented with eighty-four delegates, including several women.

*Whereas,* in a republic its great and distinctive feature is the "consent of the people," they signifying their approbation *for* or their dissent *from* such rules and laws as have being by the exercise of their voting power,—and whereas a numerous minority of the people of the State of New York (viz: the colored portion thereof) are not permitted fairly to vote and are as a consequence governed without their consent, therefore

*Resolved,* That for the completion of that feature of Republicanism in our state government hereabove instanced, we are called upon by every motive of self political emancipation to adopt all lawful and energetic means to secure an equally free exercise of the suffrage; and the majority of the people of the state are bound, in order to be consistent with their professions, to alter that Anti-Republican clause in our constitution which restricts us in the exercise of the franchise, and thereby render the state just and impartial in this essential feature of Democratic governments.

*Resolved,* That our brethren throughout the State be requested to commence immediately circulating petitions, praying the Legislature to extend to the colored citizens of New York the right of equal suffrage.

*Resolved,* That the delegates from each county be a committee to circulate petitions in their districts, and that they forward them to the Legislature at an early period of their session, or to the Central Committee * by the first of January next.

*Minutes of the Fifth Annual Convention of the Colored Citizens of the State of New York,* (Troy, 1844). Copy in Columbia University Library.

## 102

## ANOTHER KIDNAPPING, 1844

William Wells Brown, while touring Ohio for the Abolitionist movement in 1844, came upon the type of scene which served to confirm him and his comrades in their belief in the necessity for persistent and vigorous agitation. He describes it in a letter, dated Mount Pleasant, September 27, 1844, to Sydney H. Gay, then editor of the *National Anti-Slavery Standard:*

I left Cadiz this morning at four o'clock, on my way for Mount Pleasant. Passing through Georgetown at about five o'clock, I found the citizens

* On the central committee were: Henry H. Garnet and William Rich of Troy; Stephen Myers and Richard Thompson of Albany; and John Wendell of Schenectady.

standing upon the corners of the streets, talking as though something had occurred during the night. Upon inquiry, I learned that about ten o'clock at night, five or six men went to the house of a colored man by the name of John Wilkinson, broke open the door, knocked down the man and his wife, and beat them severely, and seized their boy, aged fourteen years, and carried him off into Slavery. After the father of the boy had recovered himself, he raised the alarm, and with the aid of some of the neighbors, put out in pursuit of the kidnappers, and followed them to the river; but they were too late. The villains crossed the river, and passed into Virginia. I visited the afflicted family this morning. When I entered the house, I found the mother seated with her face buried in her hands, weeping for the loss of her child. The mother was much bruised, and the floor was covered in several places with blood. I had been in the house but a short time, when the father returned from the chase of the kidnappers. When he entered the house, and told the wife that their child was lost forever, the mother wrung her hands and screamed out, "Oh, my boy! oh, my boy! I want to see my child!" and raved as though she was a maniac. I was compelled to turn aside and weep for the first time since I came into the State. I would that every Northern apologist for Slavery, could have been present to have beheld that scene. I hope to God that it may never be my lot to behold another such. One of the villains was recognized, but it was by a colored man, and the colored people have not the right of their oath in this State. This villain will go unwhipped of Justice. What have the North to do with Slavery? Ever yours, for the slave.

*National Anti-Slavery Standard* (N.Y.), November 7, 1844.


## 103

## COTTON GROWING VIEWED BY A SLAVE, 1845

Few are the contemporary pictures of cotton plantation work during slavery as viewed by the Negro. One of the best of these comes from the pen of Solomon Northup, a kidnapped Negro, who labored as a slave in Louisiana for twelve years. Conditions on a cotton plantation in 1845 were described by him this way:

He [Edwin Epps] had been a driver and overseer in his younger years, but at this time was in possession of a plantation on Bayou Huff Power, two and a half miles from Holmesville, eighteen from Marksville, and twelve from Cheneyville. It belonged to Joseph B. Roberts, his wife's uncle, and was leased by Epps. His principal business was raising cotton, and inasmuch as some may read this book who have never seen a cotton field, a description of the manner of its culture may not be out of place.

The ground is prepared by throwing up beds or ridges, with the plough—back-furrowing, it is called. Oxen and mules, the latter almost exclusively, are used in ploughing. The women as frequently as the men perform this labor, feeding, currying, and taking care of their teams, and in all respects doing the field and stable work, precisely as do the ploughboys of the North.

The beds, or ridges, are six feet wide, that is, from water furrow to water furrow. A plough drawn by one mule is then run along the top of the ridge or center of the bed, making the drill, into which a girl usually drops the seed, which she carries in a bag hung round her neck. Behind her comes a mule and harrow, covering up the seed, so that two mules, three slaves, a plough and harrow, are employed in planting a row of cotton. This is done in the months of March and April. Corn is planted in February. When there are no cold rains, the cotton usually makes its appearance in a week. In the course of eight or ten days afterwards the first hoeing is commenced. This is performed in part, also, by the aid of the plough and mule. The plough passes as near as possible to the cotton on both sides, throwing the furrow from it. Slaves follow with their hoes, cutting up the grass and cotton, leaving hills two feet and a half apart. This is called scraping cotton. In two weeks more commences the second hoeing. This time the furrow is thrown towards the cotton. Only one stalk, the largest, is now left standing in each hill. In another fortnight it is hoed the third time, throwing the furrow towards the cotton in the same manner as before, and killing all the grass between the rows. About the first of July, when it is a foot high or thereabouts, it is hoed the fourth and last time. Now the whole space between the rows is ploughed, leaving a deep water furrow in the center. During all these hoeings the overseer or driver follows the slaves on horseback with a whip, such as has been described. The fastest hoer takes the lead row. He is usually about a rod in advance of his companions. If one of them passes him, he is whipped. If one falls behind or is a moment idle, he is whipped. In fact, the lash is flying from morning until night, the whole day long. The hoeing season thus continues from April until July, a field having no sooner been finished once, than it is commenced again.

In the latter part of August begins the cotton picking season. At this time each slave is presented with a sack. A strap is fastened to it, which goes over the neck, holding the mouth of the sack breast high, while the bottom reaches nearly to the ground. Each one is also presented with a large basket that will hold about two barrels. This is to put the cotton in when the sack is filled. The baskets are carried to the field and placed at the beginning of the rows.

When a new hand, one unaccustomed to the business, is sent for the first time into the field, he is whipped up smartly, and made for that day to pick as fast as he can possibly. At night it is weighed, so that his capability in cotton picking is known. He must bring in the same weight each night following. If it falls short, it is considered evidence that he has been laggard, and a greater or less number of lashes is the penalty.

An ordinary day's work is two hundred pounds. A slave who is accustomed to picking, is punished, if he or she brings in a less quantity than that. There is a great difference among them as regards this kind of labor. Some of them seem to have a natural knack, or quickness, which enables them to pick with great celerity, and with both hands, while others, with whatever practice or industry, are utterly unable to come up to the ordinary standard. Such hands are taken from the cotton field and employed in other business. . . .

The cotton grows from five to seven feet high, each stalk having a great many branches, shooting out in all directions, and lapping each other above the water furrow.

There are few sights more pleasant to the eye, than a wide cotton field when it is in the bloom. It presents an appearance of purity, like an immaculate expanse of light, new-fallen snow.

Sometimes the slave picks down one side of a row, and back upon the other, but more usually there is one on either side, gathering all that has blossomed, leaving the unopened bolls for a succeeding picking. When the sack is filled, it is emptied into the basket and trodden down. It is necessary to be extremely careful the first time going through the field, in order not to break the branches off the stalks. The cotton will not bloom upon a broken branch. Epps never failed to inflict the severest chastisement on the unlucky servant who, either carelessly or unavoidably, was guilty in the least degree in this respect.

The hands are required to be in the cotton field as soon as it is light in the morning, and, with the exception of ten or fifteen minutes, which is given them at noon to swallow their allowance of cold bacon, they are not permitted to be a moment idle until it is too dark to see and when the moon is full they often times labor till the middle of the night. They do not dare to stop even at dinner time, nor return to the quarters, however late it be, until the order to halt is given by the driver.

The day's work over in the field, the baskets are "toted," or in other words, carried to the gin-house, where the cotton is weighed. No matter how fatigued and weary he may be—no matter how much he longs for sleep and rest—a slave never approaches the gin-house with his basket of cotton but with fear. It it falls short in weight—if he has not performed the full task appointed him, he knows that he must suffer. And if he has exceeded it by ten or twenty pounds, in all probability his master will measure the next day's task accordingly. So, whether he has too little or too much, his approach to the gin-house is always with fear and trembling. Most frequently they have too little, and therefore it is they are not anxious to leave the field. After weighing, follow the whippings; and then the baskets are carried to the cotton house, and their contents stored away like hay, all hands being sent in to tramp it down. If the cotton is not dry, instead of taking it to the gin-house at once, it is laid upon platforms, two feet high, and some three times as wide, covered with boards or plank, with narrow walks running between them.

This done, the labor of the day is not yet ended, by any means. Each one must then attend to his respective chores. One feeds the mules, another the swine—another cuts the wood, and so forth; besides, the packing is all done by candle light. Finally, at a late hour, they reach the quarters, sleepy and overcome with the long day's toil. Then a fire must be kindled in the cabin, the corn ground in a small hand-mill, and supper, and dinner for the next day in the field, prepared. All that is allowed them is corn and bacon, which is given out at the corncrib and smoke-house every Sunday morning. Each one receives, as his weekly allowance, three and a half pounds of bacon, and corn enough to make a peck of meal. That is all—no tea, coffee, sugar, and with the exception of a very scanty sprinkling now and then, no salt. . . .

The softest couches in the world are not to be found in the log mansion of the slave. The one whereon I reclined year after year, was a plank twelve inches wide and ten feet long. My pillow was a stick of wood. The bedding was a coarse blanket, and not a rag or shred beside. Moss might be used, were it not that it directly breeds a swarm of fleas.

The cabin is constructed of logs, without floor or window. The latter is altogether unnecessary, the crevices between the logs admitting sufficient light. In stormy weather the rain drives through them, rendering it comfortless and extremely disagreeable. The rude door hangs on great wooden hinges. In one end is constructed an awkward fire-place.

An hour before day light the horn is blown. Then the slaves arouse, prepare their breakfast, fill a gourd with water, in another deposit their dinner of cold bacon and corn cake, and hurry to the field again. It is an offence invariably followed by a flogging, to be found at the quarters after daybreak. Then the fears and labors of another day begin; and until its close there is no such thing as rest. He fears he will be caught lagging through the day; he fears to approach the gin-house with his basket-load of cotton at night; he fears, when he lies down, that he will oversleep himself in the morning. Such is a true, faithful, unexaggerated picture and description of the slave's daily life, during the time of cotton-picking, on the shores of Bayou Boeuf.

*Twelve Years A Slave—Narrative of Solomon Northup* . . . (Auburn, Buffalo and London, 1854), pp. 163–66, 170–71.

## 104

# DOUGLASS CROSSES THE ATLANTIC, 1845

In 1845 Frederick Douglass carried the message of Abolitionism to Ireland and England. In a letter, dated Dublin, September 1, 1845, he told Garrison of the eventful trip across the Atlantic.

Thanks to a kind Providence, I am now safe in old Ireland, in the beautiful city of Dublin, surrounded by the kind family, and seated at the table of our mutual friend, James H. Webb, brother of the well-known Richard D. Webb. I landed at Liverpool on Thursday morning, 28th August, and took lodgings at the Union hotel, Clayton Square, in company with friend [Arnold] Buffum and our warm-hearted singers, the Hutchinson family. Here we all continued until Saturday evening, the 30th instant, when friend Buffum and myself (with no little reluctance) separated from them, and took ship for this place, and on arrival here, were kindly invited by James, in the temporary absence of Richard D. Webb and family, to make his house our home.

There are a number of things about which I should like to write, aside from those immediately connected with our cause, but of this I must deny myself,—at least under present circumstances. Sentimental letter-writing must give way, when its claims are urged against facts necessary to the advancement of our cause, and the destruction of slavery. I know it will gladden your heart to hear, that from the moment we first lost sight of the American shore, till we landed at Liverpool, our gallant steam-ship was the theatre of an almost constant discussion of the subject of slavery—commencing cool, but growing hotter every moment as it advanced. It was a great time for anti-slavery, and a hard time for slavery;—the one delighting in the sunshine of free discussion, and the other horror-stricken at its God-like approach. The discussion was general. If suppressed in the saloon, it broke out in the steerage; and if it ceased in the steerage, it was renewed in the saloon; and if suppressed in both, it broke out with redoubled energy, high upon the saloon deck, in the open, refreshing, free ocean air. I was happy. Every thing went on nobly. The truth was being told, and having its legitimate effect upon the hearts of those who heard it. At last, the evening previous to our arrival at Liverpool, the slaveholders, convinced that reason, morality, common honesty, humanity, and Christianity, were all against them, and that argument was no longer any means of defence, or at least for a poor means, abandoned their post in debate, and resorted to their old and natural mode of defending their morality by brute force.

Yes, they actually got up a MOB—a real American, republican, democratic, Christian mob,—and that, too, on the deck of a British steamer, and in sight of the beautiful high lands of Dungarvan! I declare, it is enough to make a slave ashamed of the country that enslaved him, to think of it: Without the slightest pretensions to patriotism, as the phrase goes, the conduct of the mobocratic Americans on board the *Cambria* almost made me ashamed to say I *had run away* from such a country. It was decidedly the most daring and disgraceful, as well as wicked exhibition of depravity, I ever witnessed, North or South; and the actors in it showed themselves to be as hard in heart, as venomous in spirit, and as bloody in design, as the infuriated men who bathed their hands in the warm blood of the noble Lovejoy.

The facts connected with, and the circumstances leading to, this most disgraceful transaction, I will now give, with some minuteness, though I may border, at times, a little on the ludicrous.

In the first place, our passengers were made up of nearly all sorts of people, from different countries, of the most opposite modes of thinking on all subjects. We had nearly all sorts of parties in morals, religion, and politics, as well as trades, callings, and professions. The doctor and the lawyer, the soldier and the sailor, were there. The scheming Connecticut wooden clock-maker, the large, surly, New-York lion-tamer, the solemn Roman Catholic bishop, and the Orthodox Quaker were there. A minister of the Free Church of Scotland, and a minister of the Church of England— the established Christian and the wandering Jew, the Whig and the Democrat, the white and the black—were there. There was the dark-visaged Spaniard, and the light-visaged Englishman—the man from Montreal, and the man from Mexico. There were slaveholders from Cuba, and slaveholders from Georgia. We had anti-slavery singing and pro-slavery grumbling; and at the same time that Governor Hammond's * Letters were being read, my Narrative was being circulated.

* James Henry Hammond, of South Carolina, was a leading pro-slavery theoretician.

In the midst of the debate going on, there sprang up quite a desire, on the part of a number on board, to have me lecture to them on slavery. I was first requested to do so by one of the passengers, who had become quite interested. I, of course, declined, well knowing that that was a privilege which the captain alone had a right to give, and intimated as much to the friend who invited me. I told him I should not feel at liberty to lecture, unless the captain should personally invite me to speak. Things went on as usual till between five and six o'clock in the afternoon of Wednesday, when I received an invitation from the captain to deliver an address upon the saloon deck. I signified my willingness to do so, and he at once ordered the bell to be rung and the meeting cried. This was the signal for a general excitement. Some swore I should not speak, and others said I should. Bloody threats were being made against me, if I attempted it. At the hour appointed, I went upon the saloon deck, where I was expected to speak. There was much noise going on among the passengers, evidently intended to make it impossible for me to proceed. At length, our Hutchinson friends broke forth in one of their unrivalled songs, which, like the angel of old, closed the lions' mouths, so that, for a time, silence prevailed. The captain, taking advantage of this silence, now introduced me, and expressed the hope that the audience would hear me with attention. I then commenced speaking; and, after expressing my gratitude to a kind Providence that had brought us safely across the sea, I proceeded to portray the condition of my brethren in bonds. I had not uttered five words, when a Mr. Hazzard from Connecticut, called out, in a loud voice, "That's a lie!" I went on, taking no notice of him, though he was murmuring nearly all the while, backed up by a man from New-Jersey. I continued till I said something which seemed to cut to the quick, when out bawled Hazzard, "That's a lie!" and appeared anxious to strike me. I then said to the audience that I would explain to them the reason of Hazzard's conduct. The colored man, in our country, was treated as a being without rights. "That's a lie!" said Hazzard. I then told the audience that as almost every thing I said was pronounced lies, I would endeavor to substantiate them by reading a few extracts from slave laws. The slaveocrats, finding they were now to be fully exposed, rushed up about me, with hands clenched, and swore I should not speak. They were ashamed to have American laws read before an English audience. Silence was restored by the interference of the captain, who took a noble stand in regard to my speaking. He said he had tried to please all of his passengers— and a part of them had expressed to him a desire to hear me lecture to them, and in obedience to their wishes he had invited me to speak; and those who did not wish to hear, might go to some other part of the ship. He then turned, and requested me to proceed. I again commenced, but was again interrupted—more violently than before. One slaveholder from Cuba shook his fist in my face, and said, "O, I wish I had you in Cuba!" "Ah!" said another, "I wish I had him in Savannah! We would use him up!" Said another, "I will be one of a number to throw him overboard!"

We were now fully divided into two distinct parties—those in favor of my speaking, and those against me. A noble-spirited Irish gentleman assured the man who proposed to throw me overboard, that two could play at that game, and that, in the end, he might be thrown overboard himself. The clamor went on, waxing hotter and hotter, till it was quite impossible for me to proceed. I was stopped, but the cause went on. Anti-slavery was uppermost, and the mob was never of more service to the cause against which it was directed. The clamor went on long after I ceased speaking, and was only silenced by the captain, who told the mobocrats if they did not cease their clamor, he would have them put in irons; and he actually sent for the irons, and doubtless would have made use of them, had not the rioters become orderly.

Such is but a faint outline of an AMERICAN MOB ON BOARD OF A BRITISH STEAM PACKET.

*The Liberator*, September 26, 1845.

## 105

## THE NEW ENGLAND FREEDOM ASSOCIATION, 1845

The Negroes of New England formed a "Freedom Association" late in 1845 to carry on the illegal work of assisting fugitive slaves. Boldly they announced its formation and purpose in the Abolitionist press. The leaders were men and women like Henry Weeden, William C. Nell, Judith Smith, Mary L. Armstead, and Thomas Cummings:

The object of our Association is to extend a helping hand to all who may bid adieu to whips and chains, and by the welcome light of the North Star, reach a haven where they can be protected from the grasp of the man-stealer. An article of the constitution enjoins upon us not to pay one farthing to any slaveholder for the property they may claim in a human being. We believe that to be the appropriate work of those at the North, who contend that the emancipation of the slaves should be preceded by the compensation of the masters. Our mission is to succor those who claim property in themselves, and thereby acknowledge an independence of slavery.

Fugitives are constantly presenting themselves for assistance which we are at times unable to afford, in consequence of the lack of means. Donations of money or clothing, information of places where they may remain for a temporary or permanent season as the case may demand, are the instrumentalities by which we aim to effect our object. We feel it to be a legitimate branch of anti-slavery duty, and solicit, therefore, in the name of the panting fugitive, the countenance and support of all who "remember those in bonds as bound with them." . . . Donations are punctually acknowledged in some of the anti-slavery papers.

*The Liberator*, December 12, 1845.

## 106

## IS IT RIGHT TO BUY ONE'S FREEDOM?, 1846

When, in 1846, it was announced that friends of Frederick Douglass were to raise sufficient funds to purchase from his master, Thomas Auld, his legal emancipation, an Abolitionist, Henry C. Wright, objected. Mr. Wright felt that buying one's freedom tended to recognize the principle of man as property of man. Here is Douglass' reply, dated Manchester, England, December 22, 1846:

Dear Friend:—Your letter of the 12th December reached me at this place, yesterday. Please accept my heartfelt thanks for it. I am sorry that you deemed it necessary to assure me, that it would be the last letter of advice you would ever write me. It looked as if you were about to cast me off for ever! I do not, however, think you meant to convey any such meaning; and if you did, I am sure you will see cause to change your mind, and to receive me again into the fold of those, whom it should ever be your pleasure to advise and instruct.

The subject of your letter is one of deep importance, and upon which, I have thought and felt much; and, being the party of all others most deeply concerned, it is natural to suppose I have an opinion, and ought to be able to give it on all fitting occasions. I deem this a fitting occasion, and shall act accordingly.

You have given me your opinion: I am glad you have done so. You have given it to me direct, in your own emphatic way. You never speak insipidly, smoothly, or mincingly; you have strictly adhered to your custom, in the letter before me. I now take great pleasure in giving you my opinion, as plainly and unreservedly as you have given yours, and I trust with equal good feeling and purity of motive. I take it, that nearly all that can be said against my position is contained in your letter; for if any man in the wide world would be likely to find valid objections to such a transaction as the one under consideration, I regard you as that man. I must, however, tell you, that I have read your letter over, and over again, and have sought in vain to find anything like what I can regard a valid reason *against the purchase of my body or against my receiving the manumission papers, if they are ever presented to me.*

Let me, in the first place, state the facts and circumstances of the transaction which you so strongly condemn. It is your right to do so, and God forbid that I should ever cherish the slightest desire to restrain you in the exercise of that right. I say to you at once, and in all the fulness of sincerity, speak out; speak freely; keep nothing back; let me know your whole mind. "Hew to the line, though the chips fly in my face." Tell me, and tell me plainly when you think I am deviating from the strict line of duty and principle; and when I become unwilling to hear, I shall have attained a character which I now despise, and from which I would hope to be preserved. But to the facts.

I am in England, my family are in the United States. My sphere of usefulness is in the United States; my public and domestic duties are there; and there it seems my duty to go. But I am *legally* the property of Thomas Auld, and if I go to the United States, (no matter to what part, for there is no City of Refuge there, no spot sacred to freedom there,) Thomas Auld, *aided by the American Government,* can seize, bind and fetter, and drag me from my family, feed his cruel revenge upon me, and doom me to unending slavery. In view of this simple statement of facts, a few friends, desirous of seeing me released from the terrible liability, and to relieve my wife and children from the painful trepidation, consequent upon the liability, and to place me on an equal footing of safety with all other anti-slavery lecturers in the United States, and to enhance my usefulness by enlarging the field of my labors in the United States, have nobly and generously paid Hugh Auld, the agent of Thomas Auld, £150—in consideration of which, Hugh Auld (acting as agent) and the Government of the United States agree, that I shall be free from all further liability.

These, dear friend, are the facts of the whole transaction. The principle here acted on by my friends, and that upon which I shall act in receiving the manumission papers, I deem quite defensible.

First, *as to those who acted as my friends, and their actions.* The actuating motive was, to secure me from a liability full of horrible forebodings to myself and family. With this object, I will do you the justice to say, I believe you fully united, although some parts of your letter would seem to justify a different belief.

Then, as to the measure adopted to secure this result. Does it violate a fundamental principle, or does it not? This is the question, and to my mind the only question of importance, involved in the discussion. I believe that, on our part, no just or holy principle has been violated.

Before entering upon the argument in support of this view, I will take the liberty (and I know you will pardon it) to say, I think you should have pointed out some principle violated in the transaction, before you proceeded to exhort me to repentance. You have given me any amount of indignation against "Auld" and the United States, in all which I cordially unite, and felt refreshed by reading: but it has no bearing whatever upon the conduct of myself, or friends, in the matter under consideration. It does not prove that I have done wrong, nor does it demonstrate what is right, or the proper course to be pursued. Now that the matter has reached its present point, before entering upon the argument, let me say one other word; it is this— I do not think you have acted quite consistently with your character for promptness, in delaying your advice till the transaction was completed. You knew of the movement at its conception, and have known it through its progress, and have never, to my knowledge, uttered one syllable against it, in conversation or letter, till now that the deed is done. I regret this, not because I think your earlier advice would have altered the result, but because it would have left me more free than I can now be, since the thing is done. Of course, you will not think hard of my alluding to this circumstance. Now, then, to the main question.

The principle which you appear to regard as violated by the transaction in question, may be stated as follows:—*Every man has a natural and inalienable right to himself.* The inference from this is, "*that man cannot hold property in man*"—*and as man cannot hold property in man, neither can Hugh Auld nor the United States have any right of property in me—and, having no right to sell me, no one has a right to buy me.* I think I have now stated the principle and the inference from the principle, distinctly and fairly. Now, the question upon which the whole controversy turns is, simply, this: does the transaction, which you condemn, really violate this principle? I own that, to a superficial observer, it would seem to do so. But I think I am prepared to show, that, so far from being a violation of that principle, it is truly a noble vindication of it. Before going further, let me state here, briefly, what sort of a purchase would have been a violation of this principle, which, in common with yourself, I reverence, and am anxious to preserve inviolate.

*1st.* It would have been a violation of that principle, had those who purchased me done so, *to make me a slave, instead of a freeman.* And,

*2ndly.* It would have been a violation of that principle, had those who purchased me done so with a view to compensate the slaveholder, for what he and they regarded as his rightful property. In neither of these ways was my purchase effected. My liberation was, in their estimation, of more value than £150; the happiness and repose of my family were, in their judgment, more than paltry gold. The £150 was paid to the remorseless plunderer, not because he had any just claim to it, but to induce him to give up his legal claim to something which they deemed of more value than money. It was not to compensate the slaveholder, but to release me from his power: not to establish my *natural right* to freedom, but to release me from all legal liabilities to slavery. And all this, you and I, and the slaveholders, and all who know anything of the transaction, very well understood. The very letter to Hugh Auld, proposing terms of purchase, informed him that those who gave, *denied his right to it.* The error of those, who condemn this transaction, consists in their confounding the crime of buying men *into slavery,* with the meritorious act of buying men out of slavery, and the purchase of legal freedom with abstract right and natural freedom. They say, "If you BUY, you recognize the right to sell. If you receive, you recognize the right of the giver to give." And this has a show of truth, as well as of logic. But a few plain cases will show its entire fallacy.

There is now, in this country, a heavy duty on corn. The government of this country has imposed it: and though I regard it a most unjust and wicked imposition, no man of common sense will charge me with endorsing or recognizing the right of this government to impose this duty, simply because, to prevent myself and family from starving, I buy and eat this corn.

Take another case:—I have had dealings with a man. I have owed him one hundred dollars, and have paid it; I have lost the receipt. He comes upon me the second time for the money. I know, and he knows he has no right to it; but he is a villain, and has me in his power. The law is with him, and against me. I must pay or be dragged to jail. I choose to pay the bill a second time. To say I sanctioned his right to rob me, because I preferred to pay rather than go to jail, is to utter an absurdity, to which no sane man would give heed. And yet the principle of action, in each of these cases, is the same. The man might indeed say, the claim is unjust—and declare, I will rot in jail, before I will pay it. But this would not, certainly, be demanded by any principle of truth, justice, or humanity; and however much we might be disposed to respect his daring, but little deference could be paid to his wisdom. The fact is, we act upon this principle every day of our lives, and we have an undoubted right to do so. When I came to this country from the United States, I came in the *second* cabin. And why? Not because my natural right to come in the *first* cabin was not as good as that of any other man, but because a wicked and cruel prejudice decided, that the second cabin was the place for me. By coming over in the second, did I sanction or justify this wicked proscription? Not at all. It was the best I could do. I acted from necessity.

One other case, and I have done with this view of the subject. I think you will agree with me, that the case I am now about to put is pertinent, though you may not readily pardon me for making yourself the agent of my illustration. The case respects the passport system on the Continent of Europe. That system you utterly condemn. You look upon it as an unjust and wicked interference, a bold and infamous violation of the *natural* and *sacred* right of locomotion. You hold, (and so do I,) that the image of our common God ought to be a passport all over the habitable world. But bloody and tyrannical governments have ordained otherwise; they usurp authority over you, and decide for you, on what conditions you shall travel. They say you shall have a passport, or you shall be put in prison. Now, the question is, have they a right to prescribe any such terms? and do you, by complying with these terms, sanction their interference? I think you will answer, no; submission to injustice, and sanction of injustice, are different things; and he is a poor reasoner who confounds the two, and makes them one and the same thing. Now, then, for the parallel, and the application of the passport system to my own case.

I wish to go to the United States. I have a natural right to go there, and be free. My natural right is as good as that of Hugh Auld, or James K. Polk; but that plundering government says, I shall not return to the United States in safety—it says, I must allow Hugh Auld to rob me, or my friends, of £150, or be hurled into the infernal jaws of slavery. I must have a "bit of paper, signed and sealed," or my liberty must be taken from me, and I must be torn from my family and friends. The government of Austria said to you, "Dare to come upon my soil, without a passport, declaring you to be an American citizen, (which you say you are not,) you shall at once be arrested, and thrown into prison." What said you to that Government? Did you say that the threat was a villainous one, and an infamous invasion of your right of locomotion? Did you say, "I will come upon your soil; I will go where I please! I dare and defy your government!" Did you say, "I spurn your passports; I would not stain my hand, and degrade myself, by touching your miserable parchment. You have no right to give it, and I have no right to take it. I trample your laws, and will put your constitutions under my feet! I will not recognize them!" Was this your course? No! dear friend, it was not. Your practice was wiser than your theory. You took the passport, submitted to be examined while travelling, and availed yourself of all the advantages of your "passport"—or, in other words, escaped all the evils which you ought to have done, without it, and would have done, but for the tyrannical usurpation in Europe.

I will not dwell longer upon this view of the subject; and I dismiss it, feeling quite satisfied of the entire correctness of the reasoning, and the principle attempted to be maintained. As to the expediency of the measures, different opinions may well prevail; but in regard to the principle, I feel it difficult to conceive of two opinions. I am free to say, that, had I possessed one hundred and fifty pounds, I would have seen Hugh Auld *kicking*, before I would have given it to him. I would have waited till the emergency came, and only given up the money when nothing else would do. But my friends thought it best to provide against the contingency; they acted on their own responsibility, and I am not disturbed about the result. But, having acted on a true principle, *I do not feel free to disavow their proceedings*.

In conclusion, let me say, I anticipate no such change in my position as you predict. I shall be Frederick Douglass still, and once a slave still. I shall neither be made to forget nor cease to feel the wrongs of my enslaved fellow-countrymen. My knowledge of slavery will be the same, and my hatred of it will be the same. By the way, I have never made my own person and suffering the theme of public discourse, but have always based my appeal upon the wrongs of the three millions now in chains; and these shall still be the burthen of my speeches. You intimate that I may reject the papers, and allow them to remain in the hands of those friends who have effected the purchase, and thus avail myself of the security afforded by them, without sharing any part of the responsibility of the transaction. My objection to this is one of honor. I do not think it would be very honorable on my part, to remain silent during the whole transaction, and giving it more than my silent approval; and then, when the thing is completed, and I am safe, attempt to play the *hero*, by throwing off all responsibility in the matter. It might be said, and said with great propriety, "Mr. Douglass, your indignation is very good, and has but one fault, and that is, *it comes too late!*" It would be a show of bravery when the danger is over. From every view I have been able to take of the subject, I am persuaded to receive the papers, if presented,—not, however, as a proof of my right to be free, for *that is self-evident*, but as a proof that my friends have been legally robbed of £150, in order to secure that which is the birth-right of every man. And I will hold up those papers before the world, in proof of the plundering character of the American government. It shall be the brand of infamy, stamping the nation, in whose name the deed was done, as a great aggregation of hypocrites, thieves and liars,—and their condemnation is just. They declare that all men are created equal, and have a natural and inalienable right to liberty, while they rob me of £150, as a condition of my enjoying this natural and inalienable right. It will be their condemnation, in their own hand-writing, and may be held up to the world as a means of humbling that haughty republic into repentance.

I agree with you, that the contest which I have to wage is against the government of the United States. But the representative of that government is the slaveholder, *Thomas Auld*. He is commander-in-chief of the army and navy. The whole civil and naval force of the nation are at his disposal. He may command all these to his assistance, and bring them all to bear upon me, until I am made entirely subject to his will, or submit to be robbed myself, or allow my friends to be robbed, of seven hundred and fifty dollars. And rather than be subject to his will, I have submitted to be robbed, or allowed my friends to be robbed, of the seven hundred and fifty dollars.

*The Liberator,* January 29, 1847.

## 107

## DRED SCOTT SUES FOR FREEDOM, 1847

In July, 1847, a Negro resident of Missouri, Dred Scott, filed suit for his freedom in a Circuit Court. This petition, printed below, started the renowned case on its way through the machinery of the Federal judiciary until the Supreme Court ten years later rendered, through Chief Justice Taney, the critically important Dred Scott decision.

Dred Scott
vs.
Alex. Sandford,
Saml. Russell, and
Irene Emerson
} To the Honorable, the Circuit Court within and for the County of St. Louis.

Your petitioner, Dred Scott, a man of color, respectfully represents that sometime in the year 1835 your petitioner was purchased as a slave by one John Emerson, since deceased, who afterwards, to-wit; about the year 1836 or 1837, conveyed your petitioner from the State of Missouri to Fort Snelling, a fort then occupied by the troops of the United States and under the jurisdiction of the United States, situated in the territory ceded by France to the United States under the name of Louisiana, lying north of 36 degrees and 30′ North latitude, now included in the State of Missouri, and resided and continued to reside at Fort Snelling upwards of one year, and

held your petitioner in slavery at such Fort during all that time in violation of the Act of Congress of 1806 and 1820, entitled An Act to Authorize
the People of Missouri Territory to form a Constitution and State Government, and for the admission of such State into the Union on an equal footing with the original states, and to Prohibit Slavery in Certain Territories.

Your petitioner avers that said Emerson has since departed this life,
leaving his widow Irene Emerson and an infant child whose name is unknown to your petitioner; and that one Alexander Sandford administered
upon the estate of said Emerson and that your petitioner is now unlawfully
held in slavery by said Sandford and by said administrator and said Irene
Emerson claims your petitioner as part of the estate of said Emerson and
by one Samuel Russell.

Your petitioner therefore prays your Honorable Court to grant him leave
to sue as a poor person, in order to establish his right to freedom, and that
the necessary orders may be made in the premises.

Dred Scott.

State of Missouri ⎱
County of St. Louis ⎰ ss.

This day personally came before me, the undersigned, a Justice of the
Peace, Dred Scott, the person whose name is affixed to the foregoing petition, and made oath that the facts set forth in the above petition are true
to the best of his knowledge and belief, that he is entitled to his freedom.
Witness my hand this 1st day of July, 1847.

his<br>Dred  X  Scott<br>mark

Sworn to and subscribed before me this 1st day of July, 1847.

Peter W. Johnstone<br>Justice of the Peace.

Albert B. Hart, Ed., *American History Told by Contemporaries* (N.Y., 1938, Macmil-
lan), IV, pp. 122–23, citing MS Court Records of St. Louis County.

108

# DOUGLASS ON OHIO ANTI-SLAVERY WORK, 1847

A highly informative letter on the progress and techniques of anti-slavery work in
the Ohio region was written by Frederick Douglass from Cleveland, September 17,
1847 and published six days later in the *National Anti-Slavery Standard:*

Mr. Garrison and myself are still pursuing our Western course, and steadily persevering (though much worn with our labours) in the fulfilment of our appointments, which are only like angels' visits in that they are "far between." Our industrious and devoted friend, the general agent, in making our appointments thus far, has studied more the wants of the cause than the weakness of our frames. We have an appointment for every day, and some of these are thirty and forty miles apart. I know that these distances will appear quite paltry to our Eastern friends, in the land of railroads and steamboats. But as the Rev. Bishop Meade says, in his celebrated sermon, on reconciling slaves to *evangelical floggings*, "if you consider it right you must needs think otherwise of it." * We are carried by horses, fed with corn instead of fire—bone instead of iron. And you know, as said a certain rather windy orator, when a locomotive passed the house in which he was holding forth, and completely drowned his voice, "*wind* must yield to the superiority of *steam.*" . . .

The enthusiasm of our friends, out here, is glorious. They cannot wait for our arrival into their towns, but come twenty, thirty, and even forty miles, with their own teams, to meet us. They generally commence their kind communications to us by giving us some idea of the great importance of their locality, and of the importance of being promptly on the ground, and occupying every available moment in the propagation of our principles and measures; and when we are about to leave we are sympathetically informed, sometimes by the same persons, that we are fast wearing ourselves out, and that we ought to stay a day or two longer, omitting some appointment ahead, and thus secure the necessary rest. These speeches, though somewhat inconsistent, are the natural outpourings of kind hearts. Thus far, we have resisted this sort of eloquence, and fulfilled all our appointments. Since the meetings at Medina and Richfield, of both which I believe you have been informed, we have held four meetings at Massillon and four at Leesburgh. Our meetings in these places were not so large as those held in other parts of this State, yet they would appear large in any part of New-York or New England.

This State is very justly called the giant of the West. Everything connected with it is on the most gigantic scale. She is a giant in population, in energy, and in improvement. She possesses, too, those moral elements of greatness which might easily make her the pioneer State, in resisting, successfully, the aggressions of Slavery in the North, and leading the way to the redemption of millions in the South. Her contiguity to a slave State gives her many advantages over States more removed from Slavery. Ohio

---

* William Meade had been Bishop of the Episcopal Church in Virginia. For the speech Douglass quotes, see H. Aptheker, *American Negro Slave Revolts* (N.Y., 1943), p. 57.

may, if she will, abolish Slavery in Kentucky, and Western Virginia. At present her hands are tied,—the fetters of Slavery are on her giant limbs,—she is corrupted by Slavery. The moral pestilence that walketh in darkness along her southern border, has spread blight and mildew over her legislation. Her statute-book is polluted,—she is disgraced by her villainous black laws. Let her repeal those infernal laws—blot them forever from her statute-book, and thus cease to afford impunity to every white ruffian who may desire to insult, or plunder, who may desire to rob, or commit other outrages on her coloured population, and her power to do good would become apparent, and her moral greatness would be equal to her numerical and political strength. Till this is done, she is not in a position to exert much moral influence on the South. Before she can ask freedom for the coloured man of Kentucky, she must do justice to the black man of Ohio.

You are aware that what are called the black laws of this State, disallow and prohibit the testimony of coloured persons against white persons in courts of law. By this diabolical arrangement, law, as a means of protecting the property and persons of the weak, becomes meaningless, since it gives a "Thug" commission to any and every white villain, and permits them to insult, cheat, and plunder coloured persons with the utmost impunity. A score of facts might be mentioned of cases where persons having the fortune to have a white skin, have, in the presence of coloured persons, taken away their property without remuneration, and the guilty persons could not be brought to condign punishment, because their victims were black.

These shameful laws are not the natural expression of the moral sentiment of Ohio, but the servile work of pandering politicians, who, to conciliate the favour of slaveholders, and win their way into political power, have enacted these infernal laws. Let the people of Ohio demand their instant repeal, and the complete enfranchisement of her coloured people, and their gallant State would speedily become the paragon of all the free States, securing the gratitude and love of her coloured citizens, and wiping out a most foul imputation from the character of her white citizens. She might then well boast that *justice* within her borders, like its author in Heaven, is without respect to persons. I may mention that our friends here have it in contemplation to get up an agitation this winter, against those laws, which it is hoped will end in their repeal. Should they succeed, a staggering blow will be given to Slavery in Kentucky. The slaveholders will begin to feel that the North is fast combining against them, and must soon make their calling a bye-word and a hissing throughout all the land. Should Ohio take the step, Indiana may follow; this done and Kentucky is forsaken.

The work must be done soon, or the moral effect will be lost; for the time is coming, when it will be but small work to repeal such laws, even in the slave States. The power to do good, if not embraced, must soon be taken from the North.

Since the above was written, we have held meetings at Salem, New Lisbon, Ravenna, Warren, and Cleveland. Our meeting at Salem was a great one—in some respects the greatest of the series. It was held two days, commencing Saturday morning, and continuing till late Sunday afternoon, deepening in interest to the last. In addition to the lofty appeals and powerful eloquence of Messrs. Garrison and [Stephen S.] Foster, we had with us, James and Lucretia Mott. I have never seen Mrs. Mott under more favourable circumstances. It was admirable to see her rise up in all her elegance and dignity of womanhood—her earnest but tranquil countenance, overshadowed and animated with the inspiration of sincere benevolence—at once arresting attention, dispelling prejudice, and commanding the entire respect of the assembled thousands. A slight pause, and all eyes are fixed, and all ears turned—a deep stillness pervades the audience, and her silvery voice, without effort or vehemence, is distinctly heard, even far beyond the vast multitude. Her truthful words came down upon the audience like great drops of summer rain upon parched ground. Mrs. Mott attended the meetings at Warren, Ravenna, and New Lisbon, and greatly added to the interest of the meetings in all these places. She parted with us at Ravenna, and pursued her course toward Indiana, where she is intending to hold religious meetings. Our meetings in this place have been well attended, and exceedingly spirited, and nothing occurred (as we somewhat feared from intimations thrown out in the [Cleveland] *Plaindealer*) to mar the harmony and beauty of the occasion.

We shall leave here this morning for Buffalo, N.Y. where our next meeting is to be held. But one hasty word before we leave, with respect to western hospitality. Our tour thus far has been made very agreeable and happy by the noble generosity, and the kind and affable deportment of all with whom we have come in contact. There is nothing mean, narrow, or churlish about a true Buckeye—find him where or how you will, rich or poor, in a miserable log cabin, or a magnificent mansion, he is the same open, free, and truly generous man. Agreeing with or differing from you, of the same religious faith and politics, or differing from you in both, it makes no difference. Once make him feel you are an honest man and you are welcomed with all the fullness of genuine hospitality, to his heart and his home.

> "I ask not for his lineage
> I ask not for his birth

If the stream be pure what matters it,
The source from which it burst."

Since we have been in this State, we have been warmly welcomed and as
cordially received at the homes of Liberty party men, as by Old Organiza-
tionists; and so may I say of Whigs, and sometimes Democrats. And in no
case was there unfaithfulness or shunning to declare the whole truth, with
reference to each and all these parties.


## 109


# FIRST NUMBER OF DOUGLASS' *NORTH STAR*, 1847

Notwithstanding discouragement and even bitter attack from elements within the
Abolitionist movement, Frederick Douglass, with Martin R. Delany as co-editor,
launched his own newspaper, *The North Star*, in Rochester, N.Y., on December 3,
1847. From this number are taken the following editorials addressed in the first
instance, to Negroes and, in the second case, to Abolitionists generally:


### [a]

#### *To Our Oppressed Countrymen*

We solemnly dedicate the "North Star" to the cause of our long oppressed
and plundered fellow countrymen. May God bless the undertaking to your
good! It shall fearlessly assert your rights, faithfully proclaim your wrongs,
and earnestly demand for you instant and even-handed justice. Giving no
quarter to slavery at the South, it will hold no truce with oppressors at the
North. While it shall boldly advocate emancipation for our enslaved brethren,
it will omit no opportunity to gain for the nominally free complete enfranchisement. Every effort to injure or degrade you or your cause—originating wheresoever, or with whomsoever—shall find in it a constant, unswerving
and inflexible foe. . . .

Remember that we are one, that our cause is one, and that we must help
each other, if we would succeed. We have drank to the dregs the bitter cup
of slavery; we have worn the heavy yoke; we have sighed beneath our bonds,
and writhed beneath the bloody lash;—cruel mementoes of our oneness are
indelibly marked on our living flesh. We are one with you under the ban
of prejudice and proscription—one with you under the slander of inferiority—one with you in social and political disfranchisement. What you
suffer, we suffer; what you endure, we endure. We are indissolubly united,
and must fall or flourish together. . . .

### [b]

It is scarcely necessary for us to say that our desire to occupy our present position at the head of an Anti-Slavery Journal, has resulted from no unworthy distrust or ungrateful want of appreciation of the zeal, integrity, or ability of the noble band of white laborers in this department of our cause; but, from the sincere and settled conviction that such a Journal, if conducted with only moderate skill and ability, would do a most important and indispensable work, which it would be wholly impossible for our white friends to do for us.

It is neither a reflection on the fidelity, nor a disparagement of the ability of our friends and fellow-laborers, to assert what "common sense affirms and only folly denies," that the man who has *suffered the wrong* is the man to *demand redress,*—that the man STRUCK is the man to CRY OUT—and that he who has *endured the cruel pangs of Slavery* is the man to *advocate Liberty*. It is evident we must be our own representatives and advocates, not exclusively, but peculiarly—not distinct from, but in connection with our white friends. In the grand struggle for liberty and equality now waging, it is meet, right and essential that there should arise in our ranks authors and editors, as well as orators, for it is in these capacities that the most permanent good can be rendered to our cause. . . .

## 110

## DOUGLASS ON THE MEXICAN WAR, 1848

The Treaty of Guadalupe-Hidalgo, was ratified by the U.S. Senate on March 10, 1848, thus officially ending the Mexican War. The opposition to this war, expressed by men like Abraham Lincoln and Thomas Corwin in Congress and Henry David Thoreau and James Russell Lowell in their writings, was repeatedly voiced by the Negro people. Indicative of this was Douglass' editorial, appearing in his *North Star*, March 17, 1848:

#### PEACE! PEACE! PEACE!

The shout is on every lip, and emblazoned on every paper. The joyful news is told in every quarter with enthusiastic delight. We are such an exception to the great mass of our fellow-countrymen, in respect to everything else, and have been so accustomed to hear them rejoice over the most barbarous outrages committed upon an unoffending people, that we find it difficult to unite with them in their general exultation at this time; and for this reason, we believe that by *peace* they mean *plunder*. In our judgment, those who have all along been loudly in favor of a vigorous prosecution of the war, and heralding its bloody triumphs with apparent rapture, and glorifying the atrocious deeds of barbarous heroism on the part of wicked men engaged in it, have no sincere love of peace, and are not now rejoicing over *peace*, but *plunder*. They have succeeded in robbing Mexico of her territory, and are rejoicing over their success under the hypocritical pretence of a regard for peace. Had they not succeeded in robbing Mexico of the most important and most valuable part of her territory, many of those now loudest in their professions of favor for peace, would be loudest and wildest for war—war to the knife. Our soul is sick of such hypocricy. We presume the churches of Rochester will return thanks to God for peace they did nothing to bring about, and boast it as a triumph of Christianity! That an end is put to the wholesale murder in Mexico, is truly just cause for rejoicing; but we are not the people to rejoice, we ought rather blush and hang our heads for shame, and in the spirit of profound humility, crave pardon for our crimes at the hands of a God whose mercy endureth forever.

## 111

## DOUGLASS WRITES HIS FORMER MASTER, 1848

On the tenth anniversary of his flight from slavery, September 3, 1848, Frederick Douglass wrote the following letter to his former master, Thomas Auld:

Sir—The long and intimate, though by no means friendly relation which unhappily subsisted between you and myself, leads me to hope that you will easily account for the great liberty which I now take in addressing you in this open and public manner. The same fact may possibly remove any disagreeable surprise which you may experience on again finding your name coupled with mine, in any other way than in an advertisement, accurately describing my person, and offering a large sum for my arrest. In thus dragging you again before the public, I am aware that I shall subject myself to no inconsiderable amount of censure. I shall probably be charged with an unwarrantable, if not a wanton and reckless disregard of the rights and proprieties of private life. There are those North as well as South who entertain a much higher respect for rights which are merely conventional, than they do for rights which are personal and essential. Not a few there are in our country, who, while they have no scruples against robbing the laborer of the hard earned results of his patient industry, will be shocked by the extremely indelicate manner of bringing your name before the public. Believing this to be the case, and wishing to meet every reasonable or plausible objection to my conduct, I will frankly state the ground upon which I justify myself in this instance, as well as on former occasions when I have thought proper to mention your name in public.

All will agree that a man guilty of theft, robbery, or murder, has forfeited the right to concealment and private life; that the community have a right to subject such persons to the most complete exposure. However much they may desire retirement, and aim to conceal themselves and their movements from the popular gaze, the public has a right to ferret them out, and bring their conduct before the proper tribunals of the country for investigation. Sir, you will undoubtedly make the proper application of these generally admitted principles, and will easily see the light in which you are regarded by me, I will not therefore manifest ill temper, by calling you hard names. I know you to be a man of some intelligence, and can readily determine the precise estimate which I entertain of your character. I may therefore indulge in language which may seem to others indirect and ambiguous, and yet be quite well understood by yourself.

I have selected this day on which to address you, because it is the anniversary of my emancipation; and knowing of no better way, I am led to this as the best mode of celebrating that truly important event. Just ten years ago this beautiful September morning, yon bright sun beheld me a slave—a poor, degraded chattel—trembling at the sound of your voice, lamenting that I was a man, and wishing myself a brute. The hopes which I had treasured up for weeks of a safe and successful escape from your grasp, were powerfully confronted at this last hour by dark clouds of doubt and fear, making my person shake and my bosom to heave with the heavy contest between hope and fear. I have no words to describe to you the deep agony of soul which I experienced on that never to be forgotten morning—(for I left by daylight). I was making a leap in the dark. The probabilities, so far as I could by reason determine them, were stoutly against the undertaking. The preliminaries and precautions I had adopted previously, all worked badly. I was like one going to war without weapons—ten chances of defeat to one of victory. One in whom I had confided, and one who had promised me assistance, appalled by fear at the trial hour, deserted me, thus leaving the responsibility of success or failure solely with myself. You, sir, can never know my feelings. As I look back to them, I can scarcely realize that I have passed through a scene so trying. Trying however as they were, and gloomy as was the prospect, thanks be to the Most High, who is ever the God of the oppressed, at the moment which was to determine my whole earthly career. His grace was sufficient, my mind was made up. I embraced the golden opportunity, took the morning tide at the flood, and a free man, young, active and strong, is the result.

I have often thought I should like to explain to you the grounds upon which I have justified myself in running away from you. I am almost ashamed to do so now, for by this time you may have discovered them yourself. I will, however, glance at them. When yet but a child about six years old, I imbibed the determination to run away. The very first mental effort that I now remember on my part, was an attempt to solve the mystery, Why am I a slave? and with this question my youthful mind was troubled for many days, pressing upon me more heavily at times than others. When I saw the slave-driver whip a slave woman, cut the blood out of her neck, and heard her piteous cries, I went away into the corner of the fence, wept and pondered over the mystery. I had, through some medium, I know not what, got some idea of God, the Creator of all mankind, the black and the white, and that he had made the blacks to serve the whites as slaves. How could he do this and be *good*, I could not tell. I was not satisfied with this theory, which made God responsible for slavery, for it pained me greatly, and I have wept over it long and often. At one time, your first wife, Mrs. Lucretia, heard me singing and saw me shedding tears, and asked of me the matter, but I was afraid to tell her. I was puzzled with this question, till one night, while sitting in the kitchen, I heard some of the old slaves talking of their parents having been stolen from Africa by white men, and were sold here as slaves. The whole mystery was solved at once. Very soon after this my aunt Jinny and uncle Noah ran away, and the great noise made about it by your father-in-law, made me for the first time acquainted with the fact, that there were free States as well as slave States. From that time, I resolved that I would some day run away.

The morality of the act, I dispose as follows: I am myself; you are yourself; we are two distinct persons, equal persons. What you are, I am. You are a man, and so am I. God created both, and made us separate beings. I am not by nature bound to you, or you to me. Nature does not make your existence depend upon me, or mine to depend upon yours. I cannot walk upon your legs, or you upon mine. I cannot breathe for you, or you for me; I must breathe for myself, and you for yourself. We are distinct persons, and are each equally provided with faculties necessary to our individual existence. In leaving you, I took nothing but what belonged to me, and in no way lessened your means for obtaining an *honest* living. Your faculties remained yours, and mine became useful to their rightful owner. I therefore see no wrong in any part of the transaction. It is true, I went off secretly, but that was more your fault than mine. Had I let you into the secret, you would have defeated the enterprise entirely; but for this, I should have been really glad to have made you acquainted with my intentions to leave.

You may perhaps want to know how I like my present condition. I am free to say, I greatly prefer it to that which I occupied in Maryland. I am, however, by no means prejudiced against the State as such. Its geography, climate, fertility and products, are such as to make it a very desirable abode for any man; and but for the existence of slavery there, it is not impossible that I might again take up my abode in that State. It is not that I love Maryland less, but freedom more. You will be surprised to learn that people at the North labor under the strange delusion that if the slaves were emancipated at the South, they would flock to the North. So far from this being the case, in that event, you would see many old and familiar faces back again to the South. The fact is, there are few here who would not return to the South in the event of emancipation. We want to live in the land of our birth, and to lay our bones by the side of our fathers'; and nothing short of an intense love of personal freedom keeps us from the South. For the sake of this, most of us would live on a crust of bread and a cup of cold water.

Since I left you, 1 have had a rich experience. I have occupied stations which I never dreamed of when a slave. Three out of the ten years since I left you, I spent as a common laborer on the wharves of New Bedford, Massachusetts. It was there I earned my first free dollar. It was mine. I could spend it as I pleased. I could buy hams or herring with it, without asking any odds of any body. That was a precious dollar to me. You remember when I used to make seven or eight, or even nine dollars a week in Baltimore, you would take every cent of it from me every Saturday night, saying that I belonged to you, and my earnings also. I never liked this conduct on your part—to say the best, I thought it a little mean. I would not have served you so. But let that pass. I was a little awkward about counting money in New England fashion when I first landed in New Bedford. I like to have betrayed myself several times. I caught myself saying phip, for fourpence; and at one time a man actually charged me with being a runaway, whereupon I was silly enough to become one by running away from him, for I was greatly afraid he might adopt measures to get me again into slavery, a condition I then dreaded more than death.

I soon, however, learned to count money, as well as to make it, and got on swimmingly. I married soon after leaving you: in fact, I was engaged to be married before I left you; and instead of finding my companion a burden, she was truly a helpmeet. She went to live at service, and I to work on the wharf, and though we toiled hard the first winter, we never lived more happily. After remaining in New Bedford for three years, I met with Wm. Lloyd Garrison, a person of whom you have *possibly* heard, as he is pretty generally known among slaveholders. He put it into my head that I might make myself serviceable to the cause of the slave by devoting a portion of my time to telling my own sorrows, and those of other slaves which had come under my observation. This was the commencement of a higher state of existence than any to which I had ever aspired. I was thrown into society the most pure, enlightened and benevolent that the country affords. Among these I have never forgotten you, but have invariably made you the topic of conversation—thus giving you all the notoriety I could do. I need not tell you that the opinion formed of you in these circles, is far from being favorable. They have little respect for your honesty, and less for your religion.

But I was going on to relate to you something of my interesting experience. I had not long enjoyed the excellent society to which I have referred, before the light of its excellence exerted a beneficial influence on my mind and heart. Much of my early dislike of white persons was removed, and their manners, habits and customs, so entirely unlike what I had been used to in the kitchen-quarters on the plantations of the South, fairly charmed me, and gave me a strong disrelish for the coarse and degrading customs of my former condition. I therefore made an effort so to improve my mind and deportment, as to be somewhat fitted to the station to which I seemed almost providentially called. The transition from degradation to respectability was indeed great, and to get from one to the other without carrying some marks of one's former condition, is truly a difficult matter. I would not have you think that I am now entirely clear of all plantation peculiarities, but my friends here, while they entertain the strongest dislike to them, regard me with that charity to which my past life somewhat entitles me, so that my condition in this respect is exceedingly pleasant.

So far as my domestic affairs are concerned, I can boast of as comfortable a dwelling as your own. I have an industrious and neat companion, and four dear children—the oldest a girl of nine years, and three fine boys, the oldest eight, the next six, and the youngest four years old. The three oldest are now going regularly to school—two can read and write, and the other can spell with tolerable correctness words of two syllables: Dear fellows! they are all in comfortable beds, and are sound asleep, perfectly secure under my own roof. There are no slaveholders here to rend my heart by snatching them from my arms, or blast a mother's dearest hopes by tearing them from her bosom. These dear children are ours—not to work up into rice, sugar and tobacco, but to watch over, regard, and protect, and to rear them up in the nurture and admonition of the gospel—to train them up in the paths of wisdom and virtue, and, as far as we can to make them useful to the world and to themselves.

Oh! sir, a slaveholder never appears to me so completely an agent of hell, as when I think of and look upon my dear children. It is then that my feelings rise above my control.

I meant to have said more with respect to my own prosperity and happiness, but thoughts and feelings which this recital has quickened unfits me to proceed further in that direction. The grim horrors of slavery rise in all their ghastly terror before me, the wails of millions pierce my heart, and chill my blood. I remember the chain, the gag, the bloody whip, the death-like gloom overshadowing the broken spirit of the fettered bondman, the appalling liability of his being torn away from wife and children, and sold like a beast in the market. Say not that this is a picture of fancy. You well know that I wear stripes on my back inflicted by your direction; and that you, while we were brothers in the same church, caused this right hand, with which I am now penning this letter, to be closely tied to my left, and my person dragged at the pistol's mouth, fifteen miles, from the Bay side to Easton to be sold like a beast in the market, for the alleged crime of intending to escape from your possession. All this and more you remember, and know to be perfectly true, not only of yourself, but of nearly all of the slaveholders around you.

At this moment, you are probably the guilty holder of at least three of my own dear sisters, and my only brother in bondage. These you regard as your property. They are recorded on your ledger, or perhaps have been sold to human flesh mongers, with a view to filling your own ever-hungry purse. Sir, I desire to know how and where these dear sisters are. Have you sold them? or are they still in your possession? What has become of them? are they living or dead? And my dear old grandmother, whom you turned out like an old horse, to die in the woods—is she still alive? Write and let me know all about them. If my grandmother be still alive, she is of no service to you, for by this time she must be nearly eighty years old—too old to be cared for by one to whom she has ceased to be of service, send her to me at Rochester, or bring her to Philadelphia, and it shall be the crowning happiness of my life to take care of her in her old age. Oh! she was to me a mother, and a father, so far as hard toil for my comfort could make her such. Send me my grandmother! that I may watch over and take care of her in her old age. And my sisters, let me know all about them. I would write to them, and learn all I want to know of them, without disturbing you in any way, but that, through your unrighteous conduct, they have been entirely deprived of the power to read and write. You have kept them in utter ignorance, and have therefore robbed them of the sweet enjoyments of writing or receiving letters from absent friends and relatives. Your wickedness and cruelty committed in this respect on your fellow-creatures, are greater than all the stripes you have laid upon my back, or theirs. It is an outrage upon the soul—

a war upon the immortal spirit, and one for which you must give account at the bar of our common Father and Creator.

The responsibility which you have assumed in this regard is truly awful—and how you could stagger under it these many years is marvellous. Your mind must have become darkened, your heart hardened, your conscience seared and petrified, or you would have long since thrown off the accursed load and sought relief at the hands of a sin-forgiving God. How, let me ask, would you look upon me, were I some dark night in company with a band of hardened villains, to enter the precincts of your elegant dwelling and seize the person of your own lovely daughter Amanda, and carry her off from your family, friends and all the loved ones of her youth—make her my slave—compel her to work, and I take her wages—place her name on my ledger as property—disregard her personal rights—fetter the powers of her immortal soul by denying her the right and privilege of learning to read and write—feed her coarsely—clothe her scantily, and whip her on the naked back occasionally; more and still more horrible, leave her unprotected—a degraded victim to the brutal lust of fiendish overseers, who would pollute, blight, and blast her fair soul—rob her of all dignity—destroy her virtue, and annihilate in her person all the graces that adorn the character of virtuous womanhood? I ask how would you regard me, if such were my conduct? Oh! the vocabulary of the damned would not afford a word sufficiently infernal, to express your idea of my God-provoking wickedness. Yet sir, your treatment of my beloved sisters is in all essential points, precisely like the case I have now supposed. Damning as would be such a deed on my part, it would be no more so than that which you have committed against me and my sisters.

I will now bring this letter to a close; you shall hear from me again unless you let me hear from you. I intend to make use of you as a weapon with which to assail the system of slavery—as a means of concentrating public attention on the system, and deepening their horror of trafficking in the souls and bodies of men. I shall make use of you as a means of exposing the character of the American church and clergy—and as a means of bringing this guilty nation with yourself to repentance. In doing this I entertain no malice towards you personally. There is no roof under which you would be more safe than mine, and there is nothing in my house which you might need for your comfort, which I would not readily grant. Indeed, I should esteem it a privilege, to set you an example as to how mankind ought to treat each other.

I am your fellow man, but not your slave.

*The Liberator,* September 22, 1848.

112

## DOUGLASS ON THE JIM CROWING OF HIS DAUGHTER, 1848

Discrimination practiced against Frederick Douglass' daughter, and supported by one Horatio G. Warner, editor of his home town's daily paper, *The Rochester Courier,* brought the following letter from Douglass to Warner in September, 1848:

Sir:—My reasons—I will not say my apology, for addressing to you this letter, will become evident, by perusing the following brief statement of facts.

About the middle of August of the present year—deeply desiring to give my daughter, a child between nine and ten years old, the advantages of a good school—and learning that "Seward Seminary" of this city was an institution of that character—I applied to its principal, Miss Tracy, for the admission of my daughter into that Seminary. The principal—after making suitable enquiries into the child's mental qualifications, and informing me of the price of tuition per term, agreed to receive the child into the school at the commencement of the September term. Here we parted. I went home, rejoicing that my child was about to enjoy advantages for improving her mind, and fitting her for a useful and honorable life. I supposed that the principal would be as good as her word—and was more disposed to this belief when I learned that she was an Abolitionist—a woman of religious principles and integrity—and would be faithful in the performance of her promises, as she had been prompt in making them. In all this I have been grievously— if not shamefully disappointed.

While absent from home, on a visit to Cleveland, with a view to advance the cause of education and freedom among my despised fellow countrymen, with whom I am in all respects identified, the September term of the "Seward Seminary" commenced, and my daughter was promptly sent to that school. But instead of receiving her into the school according to agreement— and as in honor the principal was bound to do, she was merely thrust into a room separate from all other scholars, and in this prison-like solitary confinement received the occasional visits of a teacher appointed to instruct her. On my return home, I found her still going to school, and not knowing the character of the treatment extended to her, I asked with a light heart, as I took her to my side, well my daughter, how do you get on at the Seminary? She answered with tears in her eyes, *"I get along pretty well, but father, Miss Tracy does not allow me to go into the room with the other scholars because I am colored.*"

Stung to the heart's core by this grievous statement, and suppressing my feelings as well as I could, I went immediately to the Seminary to remonstrate with the principal against the cruelty and injustice of treating my child as a criminal on account of her color—subjecting her to solitary confinement because guilty of a skin not colored like her own. In answer to all that I could say against such treatment, I was answered by the principal, that since she promised to receive the child into school, she had consulted with the trustees, (a body of persons I believe unknown to the public,) and that they were opposed to the child's admission to the school—that she thought at first of disregarding their opposition, but when she remembered how much they had done for her in sustaining the institution, she did not feel at liberty to do so; but she thought if I allowed her to remain and be taught separately for a term or more, that the prejudice might be overcome, and the child admitted into the school with the other young ladies and misses.

At a loss to know what to do for the best interest of the child, I consulted with Mrs. Douglass and others, and the result of the consultation was, to take my child from the Seminary, as allowing her to remain there in such circumstances, could only serve to degrade her in her own eyes, and those of the other scholars attending the school. Before, however, carrying out my determination to withdraw the child from the Seminary, Miss Tracy, the principal, submitted the question of the child's reception to each scholar individually, and I am sorry to say, in a manner well calculated to rouse their prejudices against her. She told them if there was one objection to receiving her, she should be excluded; and said if any of them felt that she had a prejudice, and that that prejudice needed to be strengthened, that they might have time to whisper among themselves, in order to increase and strengthen that prejudice. To one young lady who voted to receive the child, she said, as if in astonishment; "did you mean to vote so? Are you *accustomed* to black persons?" The young lady stood silent; the question was so extraordinary, and withal so ambiguous, that she knew not what answer to make to it. Despite, however, of the unwomanly conduct of the principal, (who, whatever may be her religious faith, has not yet learned the simplest principle of Christianity—do to others as ye would that others should do unto you)—thanks to the uncorruptible virtue of childhood and youth, in the fulness of their affectionate hearts, they welcomed my child among them, to share with them the blessings and privileges of the school; and when asked where she should sit if admitted, several young ladies shouted "By me, by me, by me." After this manifestation of sentiment on the part of the scholars, one would have supposed that all opposition on the part of the principal would have ceased; but this was not the case. The child's admission was subjected to a severer test. Each scholar was then told by the principal, that the question must be submitted to their parents, that if one parent objected, the child would not be received into the school. The next morning, my child went to school as usual, but returned with her books and other materials, saying that one person objected, and that she was therefore excluded from the Seminary.

Now sir, these are the whole facts, with one important exception, and that fact is, that you are the person, the only person of all the parents sending young ladies and misses to that Seminary, who was hardened and mean enough to take the responsibility of excluding that child from school. I say, to you exclusively belongs the honor or infamy, of attempting to degrade an innocent child by excluding her from the benefit of attending a respectable school.

If this were a private affair, only affecting myself and family, I should possibly allow it to pass without attracting public attention to it; but such is not the case. It is a deliberate attempt to degrade and injure a large class of persons, whose rights and feelings have been the common sport of yourself, and such persons as yourself, for ages, and I think it unwise to allow you to do so with impunity. Thank God, oppressed and plundered as we are and have been, we are not without help. We have a press, open and free, and have ample means by which we are able to proclaim our wrongs as a people, and your own infamy, and that proclamation shall be as complete as the means in my power can make it. There is a sufficient amount of liberality in the public mind of Rochester to see that justice is done to all parties, and upon that liberality I rely. The young ladies of the school who saw the child, and had the best means of determining whether her presence in the schoolroom would be offensive or degrading to them, have decided in favor of admitting her, without a dissenting vote. Out of all the parents to whom the question of her admission was submitted, no one, excepting yourself, objected. You are in a minority of *one*. You may not remain so; there are perhaps others, whom you may corrupt, and make as much like yourself in the blindness of prejudice, as any ordinarily wicked person can be.

But you are still in a minority, and if I mistake not, you will be in a *despised minority*. You have already done serious injury to Seward Seminary. Three young ladies left the school immediately after the exclusion of my daughter, and I have heard of three more, who had intended to go, but who have now declined going to that institution, because it has given its sanction to that antidemocratic, and ungodly caste. I am also glad to inform you that you have not succeeded as you hoped to do, in depriving my child of the means of a decent education, or the privilege of going to an excellent school. She had not been excluded from Seward Seminary five hours, before she was welcomed into another quite as respectable and *equally* Christian to the one from which she was excluded. She now sits in a school among children as pure, and as white as you or yours, and no one is offended. Now I should like to know how much better are you than me, and how much better your children than mine? We are both worms of the dust, and our children are like us. We differ in color, it is true, (and not much in that respect,) but who is to decide which color is most pleasing to God, or most honorable among men? But I do not wish to waste words or argument on one whom I take to be as destitute of honorable feeling, as he has shown himself full of pride and prejudice.

*The Liberator,* October 6, 1848.

## 113

## THE FLIGHT OF ELLEN AND WILLIAM CRAFT, 1849

One of the most dramatic moments in the always dramatic history of the Underground Railroad came in January, 1849, with the escape of a young Georgia slave couple, Ellen and William Craft. A Negro Abolitionist, himself a fugitive slave, William Wells Brown, tells of the event, in a letter to Garrison, written at the time:

One of the most interesting cases of the escape of fugitives from American slavery that have ever come before the American people, has just occurred, under the following circumstances:—William and Ellen Craft, man and wife, lived with different masters in the State of Georgia. Ellen is so near white, that she can pass without suspicion for a white woman. Her husband is much darker. He is a mechanic, and by working nights and Sundays, he laid up money enough to bring himself and his wife out of slavery. Their plan was without precedent; and though novel, was the means of getting them their freedom. Ellen dressed in man's clothing, and passed as the *master,* while her husband passed as the *servant.* In this way they travelled from Georgia to Philadelphia. They are now out of the reach of the blood-hounds of the South. On their journey, they put up at the best hotels where they stopped. Neither of them can read or write. And Ellen, knowing that she would be called upon to write her name at the hotels, &c, tied her right hand up as though it was lame, which proved of some service to her, as she was called upon several times at hotels to "register" her name. In Charleston, S.C., they put up at the hotel which Gov. M'Duffie and John C. Calhoun generally make their home, yet these distinguished advocates of the "peculiar institution" say that the slaves cannot take care of themselves. They arrived in Philadelphia, in four days from the time they started. Their history, especially that of their escape, is replete with interest. They will be at the meeting of the Massachusetts Anti-Slavery Society, in Boston, in the latter part of this month, where I know the history of their escape will be listened to with great interest. They are very intelligent. They are young, Ellen 22, and William 24 years of age. Ellen is truly a heroine.

Yours, truly,

William W. Brown

*P.S.* They are now hid away within 25 miles of Philadelphia, where they will remain until the 6th, when they will leave with me for New England. Will you please say in the *Liberator* that I will lecture, in connexion with them, as follows:—

At Norwich, Conn., Thursday evening, January 18
At Worcester, Mass., Friday evening, January 19
At Pawtucket, Mass., Saturday evening, January 20
At New Bedford, Mass., Sunday afternoon and evening, January 28.

*The Liberator,* January 12, 1849.

# 114

# STATE CONVENTION OF OHIO NEGROES, 1849

From January 10 to 13, 1849, a state convention of Ohio Negroes, with forty-one delegates from twelve counties, met in Columbus. Guided by such leaders as Dr. Charles Henry Langston, William Howard Day, David Jenkins and James Poindexter, the deliberations of this convention were of great significance as may be seen by the following extracts from its proceedings:

*Whereas,* we the free colored people of the State of Ohio are cursed by the blighting influence of oppression in this professedly free State, to which many of us have fled for refuge and protection; and

*Whereas,* the history of the political world as well as the history of nations clearly shows that "who would be free, himself must strike the blow," and

*Whereas,* both the old and new worlds are shaken throughout their length and breadth, by the uprising of oppressed millions who are erecting firm foundations and stupendous platforms on which they may unitedly battle for that liberty which God has benignantly given to all his creatures, and which will be wrested from them only by vampire despots, therefore,

*Resolved,* That we adopt the following as our Declaration of Sentiments, as to State and National policy, and in harmony with these we will ever fight, until our rights are regained. It is our purpose,

I.  To sternly resist, by all the means which the God of Nations has placed in our power, every form of oppression or proscription attempted to be imposed upon us, in consequence of our condition or color.

II.  To acknowledge no enactment honored with the name of the law, as binding upon us, the object of which is in any way to curtail the natural rights of man.

III.  To give our earnest attention to the universal education of our people.

IV.  To sustain the cause of Temperance in our midst, and advocate the formation of societies for its promotion.

V.  To leave what are called menial occupations, and aspire to mechanical, agricultural and professional pursuits.

VI.  To respect and love that as the religion of Jesus Christ, and that alone, which, in its practical bearings, is not excitement merely, but that which loves God, loves humanity, and thereby preaches deliverance to the captive, the opening of the prison-doors to them that are bound, and teaches us to do unto others as we would have them do to us.

### RESOLUTIONS.

1.  *Resolved,* That the Convention appoint a committee of three to request the General Assembly of this State to allow a hearing from some member of the Convention before their body, respecting the disabilities of the colored people of Ohio.

2.  *Resolved,* That we the colored citizens of Ohio, in Convention assembled, petition the Legislature now in session, to repeal all laws making distinction on account of color, and that we urge the duty of petitioning upon our brethren throughout the State.

3.  *Resolved,* That we petition Congress to repeal all laws of the United States making distinction on account of color.

4.  *Resolved,* That to elevate ourselves as a people—to toss from our shoulders the dead weight in the way of our religious, political and social elevation, *concerted action* is necessary.

5.  *Resolved,* That the Convention make it obligatory on its members to persuade men to put in practice the acts passed in the Convention.

6.  *Resolved,* That we will never submit to the system of Colonization to any part of the world, in or out of the United States; and we say once for all, to those soliciting us, that all their appeals to us are in vain; our minds are made up to remain in the United States, and contend for our rights at all hazards.

7. *Whereas* we believe it necessary to enlighten the public mind in this State as to our condition, and

*Whereas* the colored people need to be aroused and encouraged, and

*Whereas* the living speaker is a powerful engine to accomplish these ends, therefore

*Resolved,* That we recommend to the different towns and counties of the State, to create a fund to sustain and remunerate a colored man as Lecturer, to traverse the State for the purposes above named.

8. *Resolved,* That a committee of seven be appointed to prepare an Address to the People of this State, and report the same to this Convention as early as possible.

9. *Resolved,* That we the colored citizens of the State of Ohio, hereby declare that whereas the Constitution of our common country gives us citizenship, we hereby, each to each pledge ourselves to support the other in claiming our rights under that Constitution, and in having the laws oppressing us tested.

10. *Resolved,* That we hereby, now and forever, refuse to vote for or support any man for office, who will not go for us and ours in common with others.

11. *Whereas,* we believe with the "Fathers of '76," that taxation and representation ought to go together,

*Resolved,* That we are very much in doubt about paying any tax upon which representation is based, until we are permitted to be represented.

12. *Resolved,* That we still adhere to the doctrine of urging the slave to leave immediately with his hoe on his shoulder, for a land of liberty, and would accordingly recommend that five hundred copies of Walker's Appeal,* and Henry H. Garnet's Address to the Slaves † be obtained in the name of the Convention, and gratuitously circulated.

13. *Resolved,* That we urge all colored persons and their friends to keep a sharp lookout for men-thieves and their abettors, and warn them that no person claimed as a slave shall be taken from our midst without trouble.

14. *Resolved,* That we recommend to the colored inhabitants throughout this State, immediate and energetic action on their part, in aiding our brothers and sisters in fleeing from the prison-house of bondage to the land of freedom; and furthermore we declare that he who would not aid our brothers and sisters in this most glorious cause, should by every community be published to the world as a bitter enemy to the cause of justice and humanity.

15. *Resolved,* That the attempt to establish churches or schools for the benefit of colored persons EXCLUSIVELY, where we can enter either upon equal terms with the whites, is in our humble opinion reprehensible.

* See document 41b.
† See document 94.

16. *Resolved,* That a committee of five be appointed to recommend a school system which may be used until school privileges are granted us in this State.

17. *Resolved,* That we hereby recommend to our people throughout the State to give their children mechanical trades, and encourage them to engage in the agricultural, professional and other elevating pursuits of the day. And furthermore,

*Resolved,* That every Clergyman who feels the importance of this Resolution be hereby requested to read it or lecture upon it once to his congregation.

18. *Resolved,* That we establish a Parent Anti-Slavery Society at this Convention; and appoint State officers, and recommend County Societies as auxiliary to said Parent Society. [For want of time amended by appointing a committee of three to draft a Constitution for the government of a Parent Society—the committee to report at the next Convention.] *

19. *Resolved,* That this Convention take measures to establish a Newspaper, in some of the towns in this State, which paper shall be the organ of the people.

20. *Resolved,* That the Conference of colored men or association that is afraid to speak out against the monster, SLAVERY, when they have an opportunity so to do, and while their own brethren are in bonds, is not only undeserving of our confidence, but deserving of our deepest reprobation. And we further believe that the man, be he white or colored, who wrapped in ecclesiastical dignity, shuts his pulpit against the claims of God's suffering poor, whether these claims be presented in the anti-slavery, temperance or other causes, is not unworthy only of the name of minister, but of the honored appellation, MAN.

21. *Resolved,* That we regard the conduct of that portion of our people who fellowships those men who treat them as things and not as men, or encourage those that do, and who will not encourage in their churches the elevation of the colored people, and who vote for men-stealers to fill the highest offices in the gift of the people, thereby tightening the chain upon three millions of our brethren in the South, as highly detrimental to our elevation, at war with the injunctions of the Bible, and contrary to the progressive light of the age.

22. *Resolved,* That we are determined to consider all colored men who do not treat other colored men on terms of perfect equality with the whites in all cases, as recreant to their dearest cause, and should be esteemed outcasts.

23. *Resolved,* That we consider the treatment of the "Ohio Stage Company" towards colored persons unjust—a species of slavery of the blackest

* Brackets in original.

die—emanating from the blackest hearts—therefore deserving the contempt and reprobation of every colored man and his true friend; and we further believe that the Stage Houses and other hotels in Ohio, that will not accommodate respectable colored persons, ought not to be patronized by our professed friends, where they know of other houses of different principles.

24. *Whereas* the ladies of England, Scotland, Ireland and France have made strenuous efforts in behalf of right, liberty and equality, in giving their burning rebuke to the God-defying institution of American slavery, and protesting against the contemptible conduct of that miserable wretch, H. G. Warner, in excluding from the Seminary in Rochester the child of the far-famed Frederick Douglass,* therefore

*Resolved,* That the conduct of those ladies and gentlemen in this respect has our hearty approbation and united concurrence, and we hail it as an omen of the time when the world of mankind will be engaged on the side of outraged and oppressed humanity.

25. *Resolved,* That a Central Committee of four . . . be appointed, to call a State Convention whenever they in their judgment may deem it expedient.

26. *Resolved,* That the Central Committee be hereby instructed to call a Delegated and not a Mass Convention.

27. *Resolved,* That we hereby recommend that the next National Convention be held in Detroit, Michigan, sometime in the year 1849.

28. *Resolved,* That the Convention elect twenty-three Delegates to attend the National Convention, provided that the National Convention be held before the next State Convention.

29. *Whereas* we believe in the principle that who would be free, himself must strike the blow; and

*Whereas,* Liberty is comparatively worth nothing to the oppressed, without effort on their part, therefore

*Resolved,* That we recommend to our brethren throughout the Union, that they, thanking their white friends for all action put forth in our behalf, pursue an independent course, relying only on the right of their cause and the God of Freedom.

30. *Resolved,* That the course of Messrs. Hale, Giddings, Root and others who have advocated our claims in the United States Congress, merits our sincere thanks and highest approbation.

31. *Resolved,* That we in our efforts for elevation, recognize no such word as FAIL.

32. *Resolved,* That we contemplate with joy the successful career of the *North Star,* thus far, and recommend that the colored people in particular

* See document 112.

and all friends of humanity in general, give it the best support in their power, until the ends for which it is designed shall have been accomplished. . . .

The Chairman of the Business Committee reported the following resolution; submitted by Mrs. Jane P. Merritt.

"Whereas we the ladies have been invited to attend the Convention, and have been deprived of a voice, which we the ladies deem wrong and shameful, therefore

"*Resolved,* That we will attend no more after to-night [January 12] unless the privilege is granted." *

### TO THE CITIZENS OF OHIO

In compliance with the vote of the above noticed Convention of your colored fellow citizens . . . essay to address you in brief upon the great topics in [which?] we and you in this state are or ought to be interested.

The desire of universal man for liberty, your own acts when oppressed by Great Britain, the curse of the Black Laws in this State, and our appreciation of that curse, is our only apology for thus addressing you.

The intelligent and Christian among you admit that you and we have a common origin and a common destiny. That we are children of the same great parent, and heirs of the same immortality. You admit that we are in the same government. That seventy-two years ago you helped to form it, announcing as its primal principle—all men are created equal—endowed by their Creator with certain inalienable rights—among which are life, liberty, and the pursuit of happiness—and that to secure these rights governments are instituted among men, deriving their just powers from the consent of the governed. You here asserted two important principles:—1st. That the object of legislation is to secure rights; and 2. That every one governed, is in the sense of giving or refusing consent, a legislator, and as an inference from these, you say, the government which does not respect these two principles is not just.

In accordance with these principles you framed a United States Constitution. This you claimed as supreme law, and in accordance with it in 1802 framed a constitution for this State. To the principles thus announced we heartily subscribe. We believe them just and equitable. We believe they ought to be enforced as well for us as for you. *Our fathers* helped to rear this temple of Liberty. Their sons, we claim, ought to be inheritors of its blessings. We therefore beg leave to state to you our and your principles, and contrasting the enactments in this state against us, with these, state what ought to be our and your conclusions.

* It was granted.

We believe not only that "liberty is the birth-right of all, and law its defence," but we believe also that *every human being* has rights in common, and that the meanest of those rights is legitimately beyond the reach of legislation, and higher than the claims of political expediency. Do you admit our belief as true? We believe in the fact, the "fixed and unalterable" fact "that *to secure these rights* governments are instituted among men deriving their just powers from the consent of the governed." This you have taught us. Ohio law is a violation of this principle. Now for the proof.

*1st*. We are unrepresented. The elective franchise, one of the dearest privileges of a free people, we are deprived of. For members of the Convention framing the Ohio Constitution, colored men voted without distinction. The question was raised in that Convention whether the colored man should still enjoy the elective franchise, and it was carried in the affirmative by a vote of 19 to 15. But ultimately, by a re-consideration, the casting vote of the President decided it against us, and the illegitimate word "white" became a part of the Ohio State Constitution. We are thus by this one word, strange and inconsistent as it may seem, deprived of all the blessings which flow out from the "free consent of the governed." But,

*2d*. We are taxed, while we are unrepresented. You hire your Governor, Secretaries, Auditor and Treasurer, 108 members of the General Assembly, together with the officers attached, and you filch our property to help pay them. You have built Asylums for the Blind, for the Deaf and Dumb, and for the Lunatic, together with Houses for the Poor, and you not only demand that we should help sustain them equally with you, but deny us the benefits of them. Only last year Governor Bebb endeavored to place a colored child in the Asylum for the Deaf and Dumb, and the child was refused. Until within a short time, colored persons have not been permitted to enter the Lunatic Asylum, even as visitors, and yet colored persons are taxed for its support. We say then, these things are violations of the fundamental principles you yourselves, of your own accord, have laid down. Ohio law ought in this respect then to be a nullity.

Fellow Citizens—the 5th Clause of 1st section of Article 2d of the United States Constitution, recognizes the principle that *natural birth gives citizenship*. Article 4th, section 2d, and 1st clause, claims that the citizens of each State, shall be entitled to all privileges and immunities of citizens of the several States; and the Ohio Bill of Rights, Article 8th, of the Ohio State Constitution, Section 1st, declares, that all men are born equally free and independent, and have certain, natural, inherent, and inalienable rights, among which are the enjoying and defending life and liberty, acquiring, possessing, and protecting property, and pursuing and obtaining happiness and safety . . . therefore we claim that the colored citizens of the State of Ohio have rights equal with the rest of her citizens. And we claim in addition that he who solemnly swears to support the Constitution of the State of Ohio, also solemnly swears to support her Bill of Rights—swears to give "all men," irrespective of any accidental distinction, "the certain natural, inherent and inalienable rights" therein specified.

Article 8th, Section 7th, Ohio State Constitution, announces—That all courts shall be open, and every person, for any injury done him in his lands, goods, person or reputation, shall have remedy, by the dire course of law, and right and justice administered without denial or delay. We hold that the "testimony law," so called, is of this part of the Constitution, if of no other, a direct and shameful violation.

Article 4th, Section 1st, Articles of the Confederation, provides that "the better to secure and perpetuate mutual friendship and intercourse among the people of the different States in this Union, the free inhabitants of each of these States, paupers, vagabonds, and fugitives from justice excepted, shall be entitled to all privileges and immunities of free citizens in the several States; and the people of each State shall have free ingress and regress, to and from any other State, and shall enjoy therein all the privileges of trade and commerce, subject to the same duties, impositions and restrictions, as the inhabitants thereof respectively."

Says the law of Ohio, "No Negro or mulatto person shall be permitted to emigrate into and settle within this State, unless such Negro or mulatto persons shall, within twenty days thereafter, enter into bond with two or more freehold sureties, in the penal sum of five hundred dollars, before the clerk of the court of common pleas of the county in which such Negro or mulatto may wish to reside, (to be approved by the clerk,) conditioned for the good behavior of such Negro or mulatto, and moreover, to pay for the support of such person, in case she, or they should thereafter be found within any township in this State, unable to support themselves. And if any Negro or mulatto person shall migrate into this State, and not comply with the provisions of this act, it shall be the duty of the overseers of the poor of the township where such Negro or mulatto person may be found, to remove immediately such black or mulatto person, in the same manner as required in the case of paupers." We are neither "paupers, vagabonds, or fugitives from justice," therefore we hold this enactment to be in direct opposition to the spirit and principles of the Articles of Confederation of the thirty States of this Union.

Article 8, Section 25, State Constitution, says, that "no law shall be passed to prevent the poor in the several counties and townships within this State, from an equal participation in the schools, academies, colleges, and universities within this State, which are endowed, in whole or in part, from the revenue arising from the donations made by the United States for the support of schools and colleges; and the doors of said schools, academies and universities, shall be open for the reception of scholars, students and teachers, of every grade, without any distinction or preference whatever, contrary to the intent for which the said donations were made." We hold that the actual exclusion of colored inhabitants from the benefit of the school fund is a violation of the principle here announced.

Permit us here to say a word to you on the effect of such a law.

*1st*. It encourages ignorance in your communities. To encourage ignorance is to encourage vice. The vicious character of uneducated communities, both in the direct and indirect influence, is seen the world over, and to prove it we need not to cite you to all past history. Therefore, even if the colored people of Ohio were aliens, your own interest would demand the extending educational privileges to them all; but here we are, born on your soil, and unless your own professed principles be a lie, entitled to all the rights and privileges of all others. Consequently you are doubly bound to act for us as for yourselves.

*2d*. In children, thus divided by law, the most Satanic hate is likely to be engendered. This, no one who has studied human nature will deny. This hate "grows with the growth and strengthens with the strength." What children are in the school-room, they are when manhood has come over them, and what feeling the school-room fosters appears in after life in the shape of a monster called law.

But another thing. We asked what was the "intent for which the said donations were made?" Was it merely for men called *"white?"* We say no. Nor was it left a bone for quibblers by saying "citizens."—nay, verily, but for the "INHABITANTS." With all deference, we ask, who are they?

We wish those in authority to be at least consistent, either by wiping the black laws, (aye *black* enough to merit a birth place other than in the free soil of Ohio,) we say, either by wiping them from her statute book, or else by openly repudiating the free principles which she by agreement is bound to regard as her higher law.

But we appeal not to Constitutions alone. We convict you of inconsistencies by them. But we appeal in the name of Him who presides over the destinies of nations, to the principles of Right and Justice, existing and hoary in their age, long before Constitutions were known, or the United States nation born. We care not then, as far as the actual right is concerned, whether the Constitutions be leagues with death and agreements with hell or no. We appeal from them, (if they be such,) to a higher *judicature*.

Our moral and social elevation we speak of last, but not because we deem them of the least consequence. We speak to you of *political* privileges *first,* for with you is the entire political power. Still you can assist us in attaining a true moral and social position. We ask not that you remove the disabilities under which we labor merely because you pity us. We ask for no such sympathy. We ask for equal privileges, *not* because we would consider it a condescension on your part to grant them—but because we are MEN, and therefore entitled to all the privileges of other men in the same circumstances.

We ask that the "Negro pew" in your churches be removed, and that *character* and not color be the basis of your treatment of colored men, both in those churches and in your families.

We ask for school privileges in common with others, for we pay school taxes in the same proportion.

We ask permission to send our deaf and dumb, our lunatic, blind, and poor to the asylums prepared for each.

We ask for the repeal of the odious enactments, requiring us to declare ourselves "paupers, vagbonds, or fugitives from justice," before we can "lawfully" remain in the State.

We ask that colored men be not obliged to brand themselves liars, in every case of testimony in "courts of justice" where a white person is a party.

We ask that the word "white" in the State Constitution be stricken out at once and forever, and of course that the privileges growing out of such striking out be restored to us.

We ask that we may be one people, bound together by one common tie and sheltered by the same impartial law.

Citizens of Ohio—We have had put into your hands copies of a memorial to the General Assembly, signed by David Christy, Agent of the American Colonization Society, speaking of the increase of the colored people in the West, and especially in the State of Ohio. He urges their increase as a reason why the Legislature should furnish money to transport colored people from this State to "Ohio in Africa." We wish him first to show to candid minds, if he can, that the increase of the colored people in this State, is an evil. He basely hints that we are a nuisance in your midst, and gratuitously informs you that you thus consider us, and that therefore you do not intend to repeal your black enactments. We as gratuitously, and with a better right, inform you, that we independently but humbly beg leave to differ with Mr. Christy and the Colonization Society, and say, we believe you *do* mean to repeal the enactments against us, and also, that whether they are repealed or not, we mean, in the spirit of our resolution, here to remain amid the broken columns of our temple of liberty, and cry, "Repeal, Repeal, Repeal," until that repeal is granted.

To those in this State who have labored in our behalf, we tender our heartfelt thanks: we ask them still to labor: but while they labor we beseech them not to despise us. In the spirit of the heathen slave, and we hope as intelligently, we each say, "Homo sum, atque humani nihil a me alienium puto"—"I am a man, and I think that nothing is estranged from me which pertains to humanity"—and therefore entitled to all the privileges—moral, mental, political and social, to which other men attain. We ask for no more— no less privileges than ye yourselves would desire to enjoy under the same circumstances.

To the Colored Citizens of Ohio, we would echo the voice of the Convention and say, come out, as soon as possible, from situations called degrading— encourage education—be temperance men and women—resist every species of oppression—serve God and humanity. Let us go to work. In our Platform the principles of action are laid down. Let us study them—let us practice them—humbly—independently, and, devising means for sustaining them, thus inform our opposers that we are coming—coming for our rights—coming through the Constitution of our common country—coming through the law—and relying upon God and the justice of our cause, pledge ourselves never to cease our resistance to tyranny, whether it be in the *iron* manacles of the *slave*, or in the unjust *written* manacles of the *free*.

*State Convention of the Colored Citizens of Ohio, convened at Columbus, January 10–13, 1849* (Oberlin, 1849).

# 115

## A DOUGLASS-GARNET DEBATE, 1849

Spirited meetings and heated debates concerning the way in which to attack slavery most effectively were common amongst the Negro population during the pre-Civil War generation. Typical is this account, from a Negro newspaper, of such meetings held in New York in May, 1849:

On Wednesday evening, the colored people held a large and spirited meeting in Prince street, at which Messrs. [Samuel R.] Ward, [Henry] Bibb, and [Henry H.] Garnet were advertised to speak. Messrs. Garnet and Ward on this occasion commented severely on the views of those who are opposed to *Abolitionists* making special efforts to send the Bible to the slaves. At this stage of the meeting, C. L. Remond was called for, who came forward, and in our judgment in less than half an hour demolished the position of the other two gentlemen on this subject, and established beyond all controversy the fallacy of this half-hearted measure. We never saw the position of three such strong men as Ward, Garnet and Bibb so completely demolished as theirs was by Mr. Remond, in so brief a space of time, and this after the audience had given a verdict the other way; and we trust that Mr. Bibb will not venture hereafter to press this subject upon the consideration of colored people.

On Thursday evening, the meeting was held, by adjournment, in Zion's Church, which was crowded to its utmost capacity. Mr. Bibb led off with considerable warmth, and confined himself mostly to the Bible question, and in opposition to the previously expressed views of Remond and Douglass. He was followed by Mr. Ward and Garnet, on the same side of the question, at considerable length; after which, Mr. Douglass obtained the floor, and was again victorious on this question; and concluded by exhorting the vast audience not to give one cent towards this doubtful scheme. It being late in the evening, Mr. Douglass was in the act of retiring from the house, when Mr. Garnet rose to reply to his remarks, and called on Mr. Douglass to stop and answer a question, which he would propound to him. Mr. Douglass left his company, and came forward to answer. Mr. Garnet asked Mr. Douglass if he did not, on Tuesday evening, say that the Bible made slaves unhappy.

*Mr. Douglass*—Yes, but I—

*Mr. Garnet*—That will do. I have the floor.

*Mr. Douglass*—I wish to state the connection in which I said it.

*Mr. Garnet*—I have the floor, and will not yield it.

Great confusion in all parts of the house; some calling for Douglass to explain, others for Garnet to go on. Douglass and his friends insisting upon it that he should be permitted to answer, as he had been called up for that purpose, but Mr. Garnet and his friends refused permission; and thus the confusion continued for an hour and a half. Neither gentleman could be heard, but both kept their feet until the lights were blown out, and it was not known which left the stand first.

We shall abstain from making any comments on this delicate subject, but will leave our readers to draw their own conclusions of the propriety and impropriety of the conduct of the two parties. All we have to say is, that it was an unfortunate occurrence.

On Friday afternoon the great debate took place at the Minerva Room, between Samuel R. Ward and Frederick Douglass. The proposition for debate was affirmed by Mr. Ward, viz: That the United States Constitution, in letter, spirit, and design, is essentially Anti-Slavery. Mr. Ward opened the debate before a highly intelligent audience, and consumed his half hour with considerable clearness and great power. Mr. Douglass consumed an equal amount of time in his opening reply, but appeared to make but little exertion, simply stating the proposition at issue, and the course he should take in sustaining his side of the question. Mr. Ward came forward again, and did himself and the people with whom he is identified great credit. Mr. Douglass closed the debate for the afternoon in one of his best efforts; almost every word was an argument. In the evening, the debate was renewed, and quite equalled the power and eloquence of the afternoon on both sides. Mr. Ward showed great tact and skill in managing the bad side of a question, and Mr. Douglass, with his apparent consciousness of the right, grasped the subject with the power of a lion.

The debate was concluded without taking the question. The discussion was conducted with great ability, courtesy, and urbanity, and the meeting adjourned with the best of feelings.

*New York Ram's Horn*, n.d., in *The Liberator*, June 1, 1849.

## 116

## A CALL TO REBELLION, 1849

In June, 1849, the legislature and governor of Louisiana approved resolutions expressing sympathy towards the revolutionists of Hungary and urging them to maintain the struggle for freedom. This evoked the following editorial from a Negro newspaper—an editorial reminiscent of Garnet's address to the slaves of 1843:

Slaves of the South, Now Is Your Time!

Strike for your freedom *now*, at the suggestion of your enslavers. Governor Johnson, one of the largest slaveholders in Louisiana, encourages you to strike at once. You may be sure of his sympathy for your success in a physical struggle for liberty. What have you to gain by procrastination in a manly struggle for liberty? You have nothing to lose, but every thing to gain. God is with you for liberty. Good men will sympathize for your success, and even slaveholders are ready . . . to cheer you on in the holy cause of freedom. Men will respect you in proportion to the physical efforts you put forth in resisting tyranny and slavery.

We do not tell you to murder the slaveholders; but we do advise you to refuse longer to work without pay. Make up your minds to die, rather than bequeath a state of slavery to your posterity.

Remember that thousands of your friends in the free States, both colored and white, are anxiously waiting for you to make a demonstration of your desire for freedom. The first thing for you to do is to make up your minds deliberately, that you will work no longer, for any living man, without wages. Let this determination be general, and well understood. In the second place, select out your bravest men to go and tell the slaveholders your determination, and make up your minds, as *Christians,* to die rather than submit. By such a course, you will throw the responsibility on them of a resort to physical violence. And in case of a struggle, you will stand justified before the world in your noble struggle for freedom, and will transmit your example to generations yet unborn.

We appeal to you, then, as men, as philanthropists, and as Christians, to act promptly in this glorious cause, while the world is anxiously looking on to see the glorious result, of Liberty and Equality, triumph over Slavery and oppression; and may God prosper the right.

*N.Y. Ram's Horn,* n.d., quoted in *The Liberator,* August 3, 1849.

## 117

# STATE CONVENTION OF CONNECTICUT NEGROES, 1849

The constitution of Connecticut adopted in 1818 disfranchised Negroes. From then, until the adoption of the Civil War constitutional amendments, the Negroes of this State attempted to gain the suffrage. In 1847 a referendum on the question was held and defeated. It was the main business before the State Convention of Connecticut Negroes held in New Haven, September 12–13, 1849, as the following extracts from its address show:

Brethren: It is unnecessary to set forth before your minds the particulars of our political condition in the State of Connecticut. We are wronged; and our wrongs are matter of daily and humiliating experience. We are disfranchised. Our manhood and citizenship are thus assailed at a vital point. And this was done by the authority of the State. When freemen, irrespective of color, had enjoyed on equal terms the elective franchise for one hundred and fifty years, under the charter of a King, a line was drawn proscriptive, unnatural and unjust, under a republican State Constitution. But no authority can sanctify injustice and oppression. The drapery of the law cannot conceal their monstrous forms, nor shield them from the darts of truth! Thirty years have we been disfranchised. But our disfranchisement, odious enough in itself, is the prolific source of other forms of proscription. It is a monster that multiplies itself upon us in each new form increasingly repulsive, obtruding in our very path of enterprise, knowledge, virtue, and religion, until many have turned backward in despair from all the high ways of progress. Two years ago, when Justice uttered her voice throughout Connecticut, and Liberty held her rendezvous in every town, but five thousand heeded the cry, and rallied to the standard.

What then? Shall we despair? Shall we cease all efforts? Shall we heed those who discouragingly say, "You can accomplish nothing"—"It will do no good"? A moment's consideration, and every one must be convinced, that hopelessly to yield the struggle is an unwise and ruinous course . . . They are false to nature, blind to duty, treacherous to the interests of the present, and unmindful of coming generations, who advise us to bear unresistingly the burthen of oppression . . . The question recurs, brethren, what shall we do? We are convinced it will not do to yield to despair. There is no course of "masterly inactivity" profitable or practicable to us in this extremity. Something must be done more effective than bewailing our lot in each other's ears. The conviction of these truths led to the issuing of the call, and finally to the holding of the Convention from which this address emanates, a Convention characterized in an eminent degree by a spirit of harmony, unanimity and enthusiasm. Among the measures advocated there, that of training our youth in the practice of the mechanic arts, met with much favor. This measure strongly commends itself to us as looking to the abandonment of those menial and servile employments, which were the unavoidable lot of the past generations.

The acquisition of property in the soil, homesteads, farms, and the pursuit of agriculture, are measures deserving of serious consideration, as inducing habits of industry and economy. . . .

The deep injuries we have inflicted on ourselves by partaking of the deadly intoxicating draught were not there forgotten . . . Every man should be careful to maintain a proper degree of self-respect, as an infallible method of commanding the respect of others. But let no man think to exalt himself by standing aloof from his people; but, on the contrary everywhere identifying himself with them, and laboring earnestly and patiently for the elevation and welfare of all . . . Let us arise in our might and scatter the living coals of Truth upon the consciences of our fellow-citizens of Connecticut; let us repeat the story of our wrongs in their ears, until it shall affect their hearts, and influence their votes. Let there be no hesitancy to make sacrifices, to sustain and vindicate our cause . . . We need not fear the result. *We must succeed* . . .

*The Liberator*, October 12, 1849.

## 118

# WILLIAM WELLS BROWN ON CITIZENSHIP AND SLAVERY, 1849

William Wells Brown was one of several fugitive slaves who carried the Abolition-ist message to Europe. Two letters from his voluminous correspondence while abroad are here reprinted. Both were sent from London; the first on November 22, 1849, to Wendell Phillips, the second on the next day to Enoch Price of St. Louis, from whom Brown had fled fifteen years before. The letter to Phillips is of interest because of the light it sheds on the ante-bellum Negro's persistent efforts to establish his United States citizenship; the letter to Price illuminates the Negro's feelings concerning slavery.

## [a]

Dear Friend,—I observe in the American papers an elaborate discussion upon the subject of passports for colored men. What must the inhabitants of other countries think of the people of the United States, when they read, as they do, the editorials of some of the Southern papers against recog-nizing colored Americans as citizens? In looking over some of these articles, I have felt ashamed that I had the misfortune to be born in such a country. We may search history in vain to find a people who have sunk themselves as low, and made themselves appear as infamous by their treatment of their fellow men, as have the people of the United States. If colored men make their appearance in the slave States as seamen, they are imprisoned until the departure of the vessel. If they make their appearance at the capital of the country, unless provided with free papers, they are sold for the benefit of the Government. In most of the States we are disfranchised, our children are shut out from the public schools, and embarrassments are thrown in the way of every attempt to elevate ourselves. And after they have degraded us, sold us, mobbed us, and done everything in their power to oppress us, then, if we wish to leave the country, they refuse us passports, upon the ground that we are not citizens. This is emphatically an age of discoveries; but I will venture the assertion, that none but an American slaveholder could have discovered that a man born in a country was not a citizen of it. Their chosen motto, that "all men are created equal," when compared with their treat-ment of the colored people of the country, sinks them lower and lower in the estimation of the good and wise of all lands. In your letter of the 15th ult., you ask if I succeeded in getting a passport from the American Minister in London, previous to going to Paris to attend the Peace Congress. Through the magnanimity of the French Government, all delegates to the Congress were permitted to pass freely without passports. I did not, therefore, apply for one.

But as I intend soon to visit the Continent, and shall then need one, I called a few days since on the American Minister, and was furnished with a passport, of which the following's a copy. If it will be of any service in the discussion upon that subject, you are at perfect liberty to use it.

### Legation of the United States of America in England
*Passport* No. 33

The undersigned, Envoy Extraordinary and Minister Plenipotentiary of the United States of America at the Court of the United Kingdom of Great Britain and Ireland, begs all whom it may concern to allow safely and freely to pass, and in case of need, to give aid and protection to

MR. WILLIAM W. BROWN

a citizen of the United States, going on the Continent.

Given under my signature, and the imprint of the seal of the legation in London, October 31, 1849, the 74th year of the independence of the United States.

For the Minister,
John C. B. Davis
Secretary of Legation.

So you see, my friend, that though we are denied citizenship in America, and refused passports at home when wishing to visit foreign countries, they dare not refuse us a passport when we apply for it in Old England. There is a public sentiment here, that, hard-hearted as the Americans are, they fear. When will the Americans learn, that if they would encourage liberty in other countries, they must practice it at home? . . . I was asked a few days since, at a meeting, if I was not afraid that the Abolitionists would become tired, and give up the cause as hopeless. My answer was, that the slave's cause was in the hands of men and women who intended to agitate and agitate, until the iron hand of slavery should melt away, drop by drop, before a fiery public sentiment.

*The Liberator*, November 30, 1849.

### [b]

To Capt. Enoch Price, of St. Louis, Mo.:

Sir,—When I left you fifteen years ago, I had not the most remote idea that I should ever correspond with you, either publicly or privately. But as this seems to be an age of progression, and reform the order of the day,

I have taken the liberty of addressing you. Since we last parted, the world has made rapid advances in civilization. The principles of human right have been to some extent discussed, and their blessings secured to a great portion of mankind. The amelioration of the condition of the human family seems to be the great idea of the present age. All Christendom is unsettled, and its ocean of mind is heaving and advancing towards the high mark of Christianity. Almost all the nations of the earth are discussing the rights of man. Not only the civilized, but the semi-civilized are acting under the guidance of the clearer light of the nineteenth century, and the higher motives of the present day.

The subject to which I wish to call your attention is one with which you are intimately connected, namely, Chattel Slavery in the United States. The institution of slavery has been branded as infamous by the good and wise throughout the world. It is regarded as an offence in the sight of God, and opposed to the best interests of man. Whatever in its proper tendency and general effect destroys, abridges, or renders insecure, human welfare, is opposed to the spirit and genius of Christianity. There is a proverb, that no man can bind a chain upon the limb of his neighbor, without inevitable fate fastening the other end around his own body. This has been signally verified by the slaveholders of America. While they have been degrading the colored man, by enslaving him, they have become degraded themselves; in withholding education from the minds of their slaves, they have kept their own children in comparative ignorance. The immoralities which have been found to follow in the train of slavery in all countries and all ages, are to be seen in their worst forms in the Slave States of America. This is attributable to the degree of ignorance which is deemed necessary to keep the enslaved in their chains. It is a fact admitted by the American slaveholders themselves, that their slaves are in a worse state of heathenism than any other heathen in the civilized world. There is constant action and reaction—the immoralities of the slave contaminate the master, the immoralities of the master contaminate the slave. The effects of the system are evident in the demeanor of the slaveholders. For example, they are proverbial for their want of courtesy to those who differ from them in opinion. They are noted for their use of the "bowie-knife," an instrument peculiar to the "peculiar institution." Slaveholding parents sending their children to the free States to be educated, frequently find a difficulty in getting boarding places for them, from the mere fact that they have been found to spread their vices among the children with whom they have associated in the free States, to such an extent that parents have often taken their children out of school on the introduction of the children of slaveholders. As deep and malignant as is the prejudice in the free States against the colored people, there are those who would rather have the companionship of colored youths for their children, than the society of the sons of the most distinguished slaveholders in the South.

These are the legitimate results of an institution, which sets at defiance the laws of God and the reason of man. Believe me, sir, it is from no wish of mine to hurt the feelings of yourself, or those with whom you are associated, that I give publicity to these facts. Connected as I am with the slaveholders of America by the blood that courses through my own veins, if I could I would throw the mantle of charity over the disgusting institution, and everything connected with it. But the duty I owe to the slave, to truth, and to God, demands that I should use my pen and tongue so long as life and health are vouchsafed to me to employ them, or until the last chain shall fall from the limbs of the last slave in America and the world.

Sir, you are a slaveholder, and by the laws of God and of nature, your slaves, like yourself, are entitled to "life, liberty, and the pursuit of happiness," and you have no right whatever to deprive them of these inestimable blessings which you claim for yourself. Your slaves have the same right to develop their moral and intellectual faculties that you have; but you are keeping them in a state of ignorance and degradation; and if a single ray of light breaks forth, and penetrates to their souls, it is in despite of your efforts to keep their minds obscured in mental darkness.

You profess to be a Christian, and yet you are one of those who have done more to bring contempt upon Christianity in the United States, by connecting that religion with slavery, than all other causes combined. Were it not for slavery, the United States would be what they have long professed to be, but are not, the "land of the free, and the home of the brave." The millions in Europe, who are struggling for political and religious liberty, have looked in vain to the United States for sympathy. The Americans, busily engaged in spreading slavery over new territory, and thereby forging chains for the limbs of unborn millions, are not in the position to sympathise with the oppressed in other countries. America has her Red Republicans, as well as her black slaves; their hands are crimsoned with the blood of their victims. If the atrocities recently practised upon defenceless women in Austria make the blood run cold through the veins of the humane and good throughout the civilized world, the acts committed daily upon the slave women of America should not only cause the blood to chill, but to stop its circulation.

In behalf of your slaves, I ask you, in the name of the God whom you profess to worship, to take the chains from their limbs, and to let them go free. It is a duty that you owe to God, to the slave, and to the world. You are a husband:—I ask you then to treat the wives of your slaves as you would have your own companion dealt with. You are a father:—I ask you, therefore, to treat the children of your slaves as you would have your own legitimate offspring treated. . . . When you look upon your own parents, sisters and brothers, and feel thankful that you are kept in safety together, think of him who now addresses you, and remember how you, with others, tore from him a beloved mother, an affectionate sister, and three dear brothers, and sold them to the slave trader, to be carried to the far South, there to be worked upon a cotton, sugar or rice plantation, where, if still living, they are now wearing the galling chains of slavery. By your professed love of America, I conjure you to use your influence for the abolition of an institution which has done a thousand times more to blacken the character of the American people, and to render the name of their boasted free republic more odious to the ears of the friends of human freedom throughout the world, than all their other faults combined. I will not yield to you in affection for America, but I hate her institution of slavery. I love her, because I am identified with her enslaved millions by every tie that should bind man to his fellow-man. The United States has disfranchised me, and declared that I am not a citizen, but a chattel: her Constitution dooms me to be your slave. But while I feel grieved that I am alienated and driven from my own country, I rejoice that, in this land, I am regarded as a man. I am in England, what I can never be in America, while slavery exists there.

Sir, you may not be pleased with me for speaking to you in so plain a manner; but in this I have only done my duty. See that you do yours!

*The Liberator*, December 14, 1849.

# 119

# SEGREGATED EDUCATION: TWO VIEWS, 1850

The struggle against segregated education in Boston did not have the unanimous support of the Negro people. The position of those favoring separation is set forth in a letter from one Thomas Paul Smith to Garrison, written early in February, 1850. In April 1850 the Massachusetts Supreme Court rejected a suit by a Negro student, Sarah Roberts, seeking the outlawry of Boston's discriminatory education. The father of this girl, Benjamin F. Roberts, announced the new tactic of the struggle in a communication to the Abolitionist press, dated June 12, 1850. Both documents follow:

## [a]

In perusing the last number of *The Liberator*,* I was exceedingly amused by a strain of characteristic allusions and a certain resolution in a com-

* February 8, 1850.

munication signed by W.[illiam] C. N.[ell]; and that fairness may prevail, you will, I know, allow me a word in defence of those who have not favored the abolition of colored schools in Boston. It is most untrue and unphilosophical, that we should oppose the abolition of colored schools in order to degrade ourselves, or our prosperity. We are colored men, exposed alike to oppression and prejudice; our interests are all identical—we rise or fall together. We believe colored schools to be institutions, when properly conducted, of great advantage to the colored people. We believe society imperatively requires their existence among us. Many of us having children ourselves, for their sakes we are opposed to any measure which would interrupt or retard their elevation. Believing ourselves to be right, and our policy judicious, we laugh at slander, scorn opposition, and rejoice in the approval of our consciences and judgments. It is worthy of remark, however, that while those individuals who profess to desire the abolition of the colored schools claim such an immense majority, they could show on their mass petition only 227 names, according to their own count, even including children as young as three years—and that out of a population of 1950! And furthermore, a petition of 170, at least, was presented against them, including several of our clergymen. To be brief, as the subject has been quite fully discussed elsewhere: We feel from experience (not hearsay) that education among our people requires the existence of schools among us; that from no other source can we obtain so much practical good; and, appreciating the sentiment that "knowledge is power," ay, and liberty and equality too, we feel determined, as we regard the intellectual above the physical, mind above matter, principle above friends to maintain our positions while we know them to be right, for ever true, for ever faithful, and slander may talk itself tired, opposition rage and riot to exhaustion; still we will fearlessly announce the truth, "amid the wreck of matter and the crash of world."

*The Liberator,* February 15, 1850.

## [b]

The undersigned is about to commence a mission to several towns in Massachusetts, for the purpose of obtaining signatures to a petition, asking the Legislature of this Commonwealth to pass a law compelling those who have charge of public instruction for children to make no distinction on account of color, in relation to the admission of children to the schools nearest their residences, and to those to which other children in the several neighborhoods are admitted.

The recent action of the School Commission of the city of Boston, and the subsequent decision of the judges of the Supreme Court, in the case of

Roberts vs. City of Boston, show the great injustice against the colored people perpetrated by those agents in the public service, and demand the serious attention of every citizen of this State.

As it will require means to prosecute this effort, the friends of equal rights are requested to govern themselves accordingly.

BENJAMIN F. ROBERTS

*The Liberator,* June 14, 1850.


## 120


## THE NEGRO LOOKS AT THE FUGITIVE SLAVE LAW, 1850

A fugitive slave act was passed in September, 1850. This law was so heavily weighted against the fugitive that even free Negroes of the North were seriously endangered. The Negro claimed as a fugitive—by a master's affidavit presented before a United States judge or commissioner—was given no jury trial. And the official's fee was ten dollars if he found the Negro to be a fugitive; five dollars if he did not! Moreover, all residents were required by this law to prevent the rescue or escape of the condemned fugitive.

The response of the Negro people to this act was swift and militant. Below are given five examples of this. The first [a] is a "Letter to the American Slaves" adopted by a convention of fugitive slaves held in September, 1850 in Cazenovia, New York; the second [b] consists of resolutions adopted September 17, 1850 at a mass meeting in Springfield, Massachusetts; the third [c] is an editorial by Samuel R. Ward in his newspaper, *Impartial Citizen;* the fourth [d] a speech made by the Rev. J. W. Loguen, a fugitive slave and a leader in the Underground Railroad, at a meeting held in Syracuse, New York on October 4, 1850; the fifth [e] consists of a petition, dated November 27, 1850, signed by fifty-nine Negroes of Iowa and presented to that state's legislature.


[a]

*Afflicted and beloved Brothers:*—The meeting which sends you this letter, is a meeting of runaway slaves. We thought it well, that they, who had once suffered, as you still suffer, that they, who had once drank of that bitterest of all bitter cups, which you are still compelled to drink of, should come together for the purpose of making a communication to you.

The chief object of this meeting is to tell you what circumstances we find ourselves in—that, so, you may be able to judge for yourselves, whether the prize we have obtained is worth the peril of the attempt to obtain it.

The heartless pirates, who compelled us to call them "master," sought to persuade us, as such pirates seek to persuade you, that the condition of those, who escape from their clutches, is thereby made worse, instead of better. We confess, that we had our fears that this might be so. Indeed, so great was our ignorance, that we could not be sure, that the Abolitionists were not the fiends, which our masters represented them to be. When they told us, that the Abolitionists, could they lay hands upon us, would buy and sell us, we could not certainly know, that they spoke falsely; and when they told us, that Abolitionists are in the habit of skinning the black man for leather, and of regaling their cannibalism on his flesh, even such enormities seemed to us to be possible. But owing to the happy change in our circumstances, we are not as ignorant and credulous now, as we once were; and if we did not know it before, we know it now, that slaveholders are as great liars, as they are great tyrants.

The Abolitionists act the part of friends and brothers to us; and our only complaint against them is, that there are so few of them. The Abolitionist, on whom it is safe to rely, are, almost all of them, members of the American Anti-Slavery Society, or of the Liberty Party. There are other Abolitionists; but most of them are grossly inconsistent; and, hence, not entirely trust-worthy Abolitionists. So inconsistent are they, as to vote for anti-Abolitionists for civil rulers, and to acknowledge the obligation of laws, which they them-selves interpret to be pro-slavery.

We get wages for our labor. We have schools for our children. We have opportunities to hear and to learn to read the Bible—that blessed book, which is all for freedom, notwithstanding the lying slaveholders say it is all for slavery. Some of us take part in the election of civil rulers. Indeed, but for the priests and politicians, the influence of most of whom is against us, our condition would be every way eligible. The priests and churches of the North are, with comparatively few exceptions, in league with the priests and churches of the South; and this, of itself, is sufficient to account for the fact, that a caste-religion and a Negro-pew are found at the North, as well as at the South. The politicians and political parties of the North are con-nected with the politicians and political parties of the South; and hence, the political arrangements and interests of the North, as well as its ecclesias-tical arrangements and interests, are adverse to the colored population. But, we rejoice to know, that all this political and ecclesiastical power is on the wane. The spuriousness of American religion, and American democracy, has become glaring; and, every year, multitudes, once deluded by them, come to repudiate them. The credit of this repudiation is due, in a great measure, to the American Anti-Slavery Society, to the Liberty Party, and to anti-sectarian meetings, and conventions. The purest sect on earth is the rival of, instead of one with Christianity. It deserves not to be trusted with a deep and honest and earnest reform. The temptations, which beset the pathway of such a reform, are too mighty for it to resist. Instead of going forward for God, it will slant off for itself. Heaven grant, that soon, not a shred of the current religion, nor a shred of the current politics of this land, may remain. Then will follow, ay, that will itself be, the triumph of Christianity; and then, white men will love black men, and gladly acknowledge that all men have equal rights. Come, blessed day—come quickly.

Including our children, we number in Canada, at least, twenty thousand. The total of our population in the free States far exceeds this. Nevertheless, we are poor, we can do little more to promote your deliverance than pray for it to the God of the oppressed. We will do what we can to supply you with pocket compasses. In dark nights, when his good guiding star is hidden from the flying slave, a pocket compass greatly facilitates his exodus. Besides, that we are too poor to furnish you with deadly weapons, candor requires the admission, that some of us would not furnish them, if we could; for some of us have become non-resistants, and have discarded the use of these weapons: and would say to you: "love your enemies; do good to them, which hate you; bless them that curse you; and pray for them, which despitefully use you." Such of us would be glad to be able to say, that all the colored men of the North are non-resistants. But, in point of fact, it is only a handful of them, who are. When the insurrection of the Southern slaves shall take place, as take place it will unless speedily prevented by voluntary emancipation, the great mass of the colored men of the North, however much to the grief of any of us, will be found by your side, with deep-stored and long-accumulated revenge in their hearts, and with death-dealing weapons in their hands. It is not to be disguised, that a colored man is as much disposed, as a white man, to resist, even unto death, those who oppress him. The colored American, for the sake of relieving his colored brethren, would no more hesitate to shoot an American slaveholder, than would a white American, for the sake of delivering his white brother, hesitate to shoot an Algerine slaveholder. The State motto of Virginia, "Death to Tyrants," is as well the black man's, as the white man's motto. We tell you these things not to encourage, or justify, your resort to physical force; but, simply, that you may know, be it to your joy or sorrow to know it, what your Northern colored brethren are, in these important respects. This truth you are entitled to know, however the knowledge of it may affect you, and however you may act, in view of it.

We have said, that some of us are non-resistants. But, while such would dissuade you from all violence toward the slaveholder, let it not be supposed, that they regard it as guiltier than those strifes, which even good men are wont to justify. If the American revolutionists had excuse for shedding but one drop of blood, then have the American slaves excuse for making blood to flow "even unto the horsebridles."

Numerous as are the escapes from slavery, they would be far more so, were you not embarrassed by your misinterpretations of the rights of property. You hesitate to take even the dullest of your masters' horses—whereas it is your duty to take the fleetest. Your consciences suggest doubts, whether in quitting your bondage, you are at liberty to put in your packs what you need of food and clothing. But were you better informed, you would not scruple to break your masters' locks, and take all their money. You are taught to respect the rights of property. But, no such rights belong to the slaveholder. His right to property is but the robber-right. In every slaveholding community, the rights of property all center in them, whose coerced and unrequited toil has created the wealth, in which their oppressors riot. Moreover, if your oppressors have rights of property, you, at least, are exempt from all obligation to respect them. For you are prisoners of war, in an enemy's country—of a war, too, that is unrivalled for its injustice, cruelty, meanness:—and therefore, by all the rules of war, you have the fullest liberty to plunder, burn, and kill, as you may have occasion to do to promote your escape.

We regret to be obliged to say to you, that it is not every one of the Free States, which offers you an asylum. Even within the last year, fugitive slaves have been arrested in some of the Free States, and replunged into slavery. But, make your way to New York or New England, and you will be safe. It is true, that even in New York and New England, there are individuals, who would rejoice to see the poor flying slave cast back into the horrors of slavery. But, even these are restrained by public sentiment. It is questionable whether even Daniel Webster, or Moses Stuart,* would give chase to a fugitive slave; and if they would not, who would?—for the one is chief-politician and the other chief-priest.

We do not forget the industrious efforts, which are now making to get new facilities at the hands of Congress for re-enslaving those who have escaped from slavery. But we can assure you, that, as to the State of New York and the New England States, such efforts must prove fruitless. Against all such devilism—against all kidnappers—the colored people of these States will "stand for their life"; and, what is more, the white people of these States will not stand against them. A regenerated public sentiment has forever removed these States beyond the limits of the slaveholders' hunting ground. Defeat—disgrace—and it may be death—will be their only reward

---

* The Rev. Moses Stuart (1780–1852) was a leading theologian of the time. His work, *Conscience and the Constitution* . . . (Boston, 1850) was an elaborate defense of Daniel Webster's course in supporting the Compromise of 1850.

for pursuing their prey into this *abolitionized* portion of our country. . . .

There are three points in your conduct, when you shall have become inhabitants of the North, on which we cannot refrain from admonishing you.

*1st*. If you will join a sectarian church, let it not be one which approves of the Negro-pew, and which refuses to treat slaveholding as a high crime against God and man. It were better, that you sacrifice your lives than that by going into the Negro pew, you invade your self-respect—debase your souls—play the traitor to your race—and crucify afresh Him who died for the one brotherhood of man.

*2d*. Join no political party which refuses to commit itself fully, openly, and heartily, in its newspapers, meetings, and nominations, to the doctrine, that slavery is the grossest of all absurdities, as well as the guiltiest of all abominations, and that there can no more be a law for the enslavement of man, made in the image of God, than for the enslavement of God himself. Vote for no man for civil office who makes your complexion a bar to political, ecclesiastical, or social equality. Better die than insult yourself, and insult every person of African blood, and insult your Maker, by contributing to elevate to civil rule, the man who refuses to eat with you, to sit by your side in the House of Worship, or to let his children sit in the school by the side of your children.

*3d*. Send not your children to the school which the malignant and murderous prejudice of white people has gotten up exclusively for colored people. Valuable as learning is, it is too costly, if it is acquired at the expense of such self-degradation.

The self-sacrificing, and heroic, and martyr-spirit, which would impel the colored men of the North to turn their backs on pro-slavery churches, and pro-slavery politics, and pro-slavery schools, would exert a far mightier influence against slavery, than could all their learning, however great, if purchased by concessions of their manhood, and surrenders of their rights, and coupled as it then would be by characteristic meanness and servility.

And now brethren, we close this letter with assuring you that we do not, cannot forget you. You are ever in our minds, our hearts, our prayers. Perhaps you are fearing that the free colored people of the United States will suffer themselves to be carried away from you by the American Colonization Society. Fear it not. In vain is it, that this greatest and most malignant enemy of the African race is now busy devising new plans, and in seeking the aid of Government to perpetuate your enslavement. It wants us away from your side, that you may be kept in ignorance. But we will remain by your side to enlighten you. It wants us away from your side, that you may be contented. But we will remain by your side, to keep you, and make you more discontented. It wants us away from your side to the end, that your unsuccored and conscious helplessness may make you the easier and surer prey of your oppressors. But we will remain by your side to sympathize with you and cheer you, and give you the help of our rapidly swelling numbers. The land of our enslaved brethren is our land, and death alone shall part us.

We cannot forget you, brethren, for we know your sufferings, and we know your sufferings, because we know from experience what it is to be an American slave. So galling was our bondage, that to escape from it, we suffered the loss of all things, and braved every peril, and endured every hardship. Some of us left parents, some wives, some children. Some of us were wounded with guns and dogs, as we fled. Some of us, to make good our escape, suffered ourselves to be nailed up in boxes, and to pass for merchandise. Some of us secreted ourselves in the suffocating holds of ships. Nothing was so dreadful to us as slavery; and hence, it is almost literally true, that we dreaded nothing, which could befall us, in our attempt to get clear of it. Our condition could be made no worse, for we were already in the lowest depths of earthly woe. Even should we be overtaken, and subjected to slavery, this would be but to return to our old sufferings and sorrows; and should death itself prove to be the price of our endeavor after freedom, what would that be but a welcome release to men, who had all their lifetime, been killed every day, and "killed all the day long."

We have referred to our perils and hardships in escaping from slavery. We are happy to be able to say, that every year is multiplying the facilities for leaving the Southern prison house. The Liberty Party, the Vigilance Committee of New York, individuals, and companies of individuals in various parts of the country, are doing all they can, and it is much, to afford you a safe, and a cheap passage from slavery to liberty. They do this, however, not only at great expense of property, but at great peril of liberty and life. Thousands of you have heard, ere this, that within the last fortnight, the precious name of William L. Chaplin * has been added to the list of those who, in helping you gain your liberty, have lost their own. Here is a man, whose wisdom, cultivation, moral worth, bring him into the highest and best class of men:—and yet, he became a willing martyr for the poor, despised, forgotten slave's sake. Your remembrance of one such fact is enough to shed light and hope upon your darkest and most desponding moments.

Brethren, our last word to you is to bid you be of good cheer, and not to despair of your deliverance. Do not abandon yourselves, as have many thousands of American slaves, to the crime of suicide. Live! Live to escape from slavery! Live to serve God! Live till He shall Himself call you into eternity!

* This convention raised a defense fund for Chaplin, an Abolitionist confined in a Washington jail for assisting a slave to flee.

Be prayerful—be brave—be hopeful. "Lift up your heads, for your redemption draweth nigh."

Salem, Ohio, *Anti-Slavery Bugle,* September 28, 1850; published by Helen Boardman in *Common Ground* (Spring 1947) vol. VII.

## [b]

*Whereas,* a Bill entitled the Fugitive Slave Bill has recently passed both Houses of Congress . . .

1. *Resolved,* That in the event of this Bill becoming a law, we, the citizens of Springfield, feel called upon to express, in the most decided manner, and in language not to be misunderstood, our disapprobation of the same, or of any further legislation having a tendency to oppress mankind.

2. *Resolved,* That we will repudiate all and every law that has for its object the oppression of any human being, or seeks to assign *us* degrading positions.

And, *whereas,* we hold to the declaration of the poet, "that he who would be free, himself must strike the blow," and that resistance to tyrants is obedience to God, therefore,

3. *Resolved,* That we do welcome to our doors every one who feels and claims for himself the position of a man, and has broken from the Southern house of bondage, and that we feel ourselves justified in using every means which the God of love has placed in our power to sustain our liberty.

4. And, *whereas,* active vigilance is the price of liberty, we *resolve* ourselves into a Vigilance Association, to look out for the panting fugitive, and also for the oppressor, when he shall make his approach, and that measures be taken forthwith to organize a committee to carry out the object of the Association.

5. *Resolved,* That should the task-master presume to enter our dwellings, and attempt to reclaim any of our brethren whom he may call his slaves, we feel prepared to resist his pretensions.

6. *Resolved,* That as the passage of the Fugitive Slave Bill is an encroachment upon the sovereign rights of the Free States, and as the soil of the State of Massachusetts is thereby made slave-hunting-ground, and her citizens slave-hunters, that it behooves her, as a free Sovereign State, to exercise her legal authority in sustaining herself against being made a participant in so disgraceful an act.

J. N. MARS,
JOHN B. SMITH, }Committee
B. B. YOUNG,

*The Liberator,* October 4, 1850.

[c]

Now, this bill strips us of all manner of protection, by the writ of *habeas corpus*, by jury trial, or by any other process known to the laws of civilized nations, that are thrown as safeguards around personal liberty. But while it does this, it throws us back upon the natural and inalienable right of self-defence—self-protection. It solemnly refers to each of us, individually, the question, whether we will submit to being enslaved by the hyenas which this law creates and encourages, or whether we will protect ourselves, even if, in so doing, we have to peril our lives, and *more than peril the useless and devilish carcasses of Negro-catchers*. It gives us the alternative of dying freemen, or living slaves. Let the men who would execute this bill beware. Let them know that the business of catching slaves, or kidnapping freemen, is an open warfare upon the rights and liberties of the black men of the North. Let them know that to enlist in that warfare is present, certain, inevitable death and damnation. Let us teach them, that none should engage in this business, but those who are ready to be offered up on the polluted altar of accursed slavery. So say the black men of Brooklyn and Williamsburg; so say those who speak through the Portland Convention; so say the brave "Negroes of Philadelphia," . . . and so let all the black men of America say, and we shall teach Southern slavecrats, and Northern doughfaces, that to perpetuate the Union, they must beware how they expose *us* to slavery, and themselves to death and destruction, present and future, temporal and eternal!

*The Impartial Citizen*, quoted in *The Liberator*, October 11, 1850.

[d]

I was a slave; I knew the dangers I was exposed to. I had made up my mind as to the course I was to take. On that score I needed no counsel, nor did the colored citizens generally. They had taken their stand—they would not be taken back to slavery. If to shoot down their assailants should forfeit their lives, such result was the least of the evil. They will have their liberties or die in their defence. What is life to me if I am to be a slave in Tennessee? My neighbors! I have lived with you many years, and you know me. My home is here, and my children were born here. I am bound to Syracuse by pecuniary interests, and social and family bonds. And do you think I can be taken away from you and from my wife and children, and be a slave in Tennessee? Has the President and his Secretary sent this enactment up here, to you, Mr. Chairman,* to enforce on me in Syracuse?—and will you

* The Chairman was the Mayor of Syracuse, Alfred H. Hovey.

obey him? Did I think so meanly of you—did I suppose the people of
Syracuse, strong as they are in numbers and love of liberty—or did I believe
their love of liberty was so selfish, unmanly and unchristian—did I believe
them so sunken and servile and degraded as to remain at their homes and
labors, or, with none of that spirit which smites a tyrant down, to surround
a United States Marshal to see me torn from my home and family, and hurled
back to bondage—I say did I think so meanly of you, I could never
come to live with you. Nor should I have stopped, on my return from Troy,
twenty-four hours since, but to take my family and moveables to a neighborhood which would take fire, and arms, too, to resist the least attempt to
execute this diabolical law among them. Some kind and good friends advise
me to quit my country, and stay in Canada, until this tempest is passed. I
doubt not the sincerity of such counsellors. But my conviction is strong,
that their advice comes from a lack of knowledge of themselves and the case
in hand. I believe that their own bosoms are charged to the brim with qualities that will smite to the earth the villains who may interfere to enslave
any man in Syracuse. I apprehend the advice is suggested by the perturbation
of the moment, and not by the tranquil spirit that rules above the storm, in
the eternal home of truth and wisdom. Therefore have I hesitated to adopt
this advice, at least until I have the opinion of this meeting. Those friends
have not canvassed this subject. I have. They are called suddenly to look at
it. I have looked at it steadily, calmly, resolutely, and at length defiantly,
for a long time. I tell you the people of Syracuse and of the whole North
must meet this tyranny and crush it by force, or be crushed by it. This hellish
enactment has precipitated the conclusion that white men must live in
dishonorable submission, and colored men be slaves, or they must give their
physical as well as intellectual powers to the defence of human rights. The
time has come to change the tones of submission into tones of defiance—and
to tell Mr. Fillmore and Mr. Webster, if they propose to execute this measure
upon us, to send on their blood-hounds. Mr. President, long ago I was beset
by over prudent and good men and women to purchase my freedom. Nay,
I was frequently importuned to consent that they purchase it, and present
it as an evidence of their partiality to my person and character. Generous
and kind as those friends were, my heart recoiled from the proposal. I owe
my freedom to the God who made me, and who stirred me to claim it against
all other beings in God's universe. I will not, nor will I consent, that anybody else shall countenance the claims of a vulgar despot to my soul and
body. Were I in chains, and did these kind people come to buy me out of
prison, I would acknowledge the boon with inexpressible thankfulness. But
I feel no chains, and am in no prison. I received my freedom from Heaven,
and with it came the command to defend my title to it. I have long since
resolved to do nothing and suffer nothing that can in any way, imply that I

am indebted to any power but the Almighty for my manhood and personality.

Now, you are assembled here, the strength of this city is here to express their sense of this fugitive act, and to proclaim to the despots at Washington whether it shall be enforced here—whether you will permit the government to return me and other fugitives who have sought an asylum among you, to the Hell of slavery. The question is with you. If you will give us up, say so, and we will shake the dust from our feet and leave you. But we believe better things. We know you are taken by surprize. The immensity of this meeting testifies to the general consternation that has brought it together, necessarily, precipitately, to decide the most stirring question that can be presented, to wit, whether, the government having transgressed constitutional and natural limits, you will bravely resist its aggressions, and tell its soulless agents that no slave-holder shall make your city and county a hunting field for slaves.

Whatever may be your decision, my ground is taken. I have declared it everywhere. It is known over the State and out of the State—over the line in the North, and over the line in the South. I don't respect this law—I don't fear it—I won't obey it! It outlaws me, and I outlaw it, and the men who attempt to enforce it on me. I place the governmental officials on the ground that they place me. I will not live a slave, and if force is employed to re-enslave me, I shall make preparations to meet the crisis as becomes a man. If you will stand by me—and I believe you will do it, for your freedom and honor are involved as well as mine—it requires no microscope to see that—I say if you will stand with us in resistance to this measure, you will be the saviours of your country. Your decision to-night in favor of resistance will give vent to the spirit of liberty, and it will break the bands of party, and shout for joy all over the North. Your example only is needed to be the type of public action in Auburn, and Rochester, and Utica, and Buffalo, and all the West, and eventually in the Atlantic cities. Heaven knows that this act of noble daring will break out somewhere—and may God grant that Syracuse be the honored spot, whence it shall send an earthquake voice through the land!

*The Rev. J. W. Loguen, As A Slave and As A Freeman. A Narrative of Real Life* (Syracuse, 1859), pp. 391–93. (The first three sentences of this speech are here altered from the third to the first person. By a vote of 395 to 96 Loguen's position was upheld.)

## [e]

To the Honorable The Senate and House of Representatives of the state of Iowa.

The undersigned respectfully ask your Honorable body to instruct our

Senators and request our Representatives in the Congress of the United States to use their endeavors to procure the immediate repeal of the Fugitive Slave law passed at the recent session of Congress.

We your petitioners [feel?] it onnecessary to say anything about the injustus of the Law, or its oppressive influences upon us as Colored Citizens of the United States of America but we will submit it to the honest consideration of your Honorable body ever hoping that the god of heaven may g[u]ide and direct your acts in favor of Justus and opprest humanity.

MS. in folder marked *"Legislative Petitions, Negroes, certain rights of"* in State Historical Building, Des Moines, Iowa.

## 121

## FREDERICK DOUGLASS DISCUSSES SLAVERY, 1850

No one surpassed Douglass in the effectiveness and brilliance of his Abolitionist speeches. As examples are offered fairly full excerpts from lectures he delivered in Rochester, New York on December 1 and 8, 1850.

### [a]

### *December 1, 1850*

More than twenty years of my life were consumed in a state of slavery. My childhood was environed by the baneful peculiarities of the slave system. I grew up to manhood in the presence of this hydra-headed monster—not as an idle spectator—not as the guest of the slaveholder; but as A SLAVE, eating the bread and drinking the cup of slavery with the most degraded of my brother bondmen, and sharing with them all the painful conditions of their wretched lot. In consideration of these facts, I feel that I have a right to speak, and to speak *strongly*. Yet, my friends, I feel bound to speak truly.

Goading as have been the cruelties to which I have been subjected—bitter as have been the trials through which I have passed—exasperating as have been (*and still are*) the indignities offered to my manhood, I find in them no excuse for the slightest departure from truth in dealing with any branch of this subject.

First of all, I will state, as well as I can, the legal and social relation of master and slave. A master is one (to speak in the vocabulary of the Southern States) who claims and exercises a right of property in the person of a fellow man. This he does with the force of the law and the sanction of Southern religion. The law gives the master absolute power over the slave.

He may work him, flog him, hire him out, sell him, and in certain contingencies, *kill* him, with perfect impunity. The slave is a human being, divested of all rights—reduced to the level of a brute—a mere "chattel" in the eye of the law—placed beyond the circle of human brotherhood—cut off from his kind—his name, which the "recording angel" may have enrolled in heaven, among the blest, is impiously inserted in a *master's ledger,* with horses, sheep and swine. In law, the slave has no wife, no children, no country, and no home. He can own nothing, possess nothing, acquire nothing, but what must belong to another. To eat the fruit of his own toil, to clothe his person with the work of his own hands, is considered stealing. He toils that another may reap the fruit; he is industrious that another may live in idleness; he eats unbolted meal, that another may ride in ease and splendor abroad; he lives in ignorance, that another may be educated; he is abused, that another may be exalted; he rests his toil-worn limbs on the cold, damp ground, that another may repose on the softest pillow; he is clad in coarse and tattered raiment, that another may be arrayed in purple and fine linen; he is sheltered only by the wretched hovel, that a master may dwell in a magnificent mansion; and to this condition he is bound down as by an arm of iron.

From this monstrous relation, there springs an unceasing stream of most revolting cruelties. The very accompaniments of the slave system, stamp it as the offspring of hell itself. To ensure good behavior, the slaveholder relies on *the whip;* to induce proper humility, he relies on *the whip;* to rebuke what he is pleased to term insolence, he relies on *the whip;* to supply the place of wages, as an incentive to toil, he relies on *the whip;* to bind down the spirit of the slave, to imbrute and destroy his manhood, he relies on *the whip,* the chain, the gag, the thumb-screw, the pillory, the bowie-knife, the pistol, and the blood-hound. These are the necessary and unvarying accompaniments of the system . . .

It is perfectly well understood at the South that to educate a slave is to make him discontented with slavery, and to invest him with a power which shall open to him the treasures of freedom; and since the object of the slaveholder is to maintain complete authority over his slave, his constant vigilance is exercised to prevent everything which militates against, or endangers the stability of his authority. Education being among the menacing influences, and, perhaps, the most dangerous, is, therefore, the most cautiously guarded against.

It is true that we do not often hear of the enforcement of the law, punishing as a crime the teaching of slaves to read, but this is not because of a want of disposition to enforce it. The true reason, or explanation of the matter is this, there is the greatest unanimity of opinion among the white population in the South, in favor of the policy of keeping the slave in ignorance. There is, perhaps, another reason why the law against education is so seldom violated. The slave is *too* poor to be able to offer a temptation sufficiently strong to induce a white man to violate it; and it is not to be supposed that in a community where the moral and religious sentiment is in favor of slavery, many martyrs will be found sacrificing their liberty and lives by violating those prohibitory enactments.

As a general rule, then, darkness reigns over the abodes of the enslaved and "how great is that darkness!"

We are sometimes told of the contentment of the slaves, and are entertained with vivid pictures of their happiness. We are told that they often dance and sing; that their masters frequently give them wherewith to make merry; in fine, that they have little of which to complain. I admit that the slave *does* sometimes sing, dance, and appear to be merry. But what does this prove? It only proves to my mind, that though slavery is armed with a thousand stings, it is not able entirely to kill the elastic spirit of the bondman. That spirit will rise and walk abroad, despite of whips and chains, and extract from the cup of nature, occasional drops of joy and gladness. No thanks to the slaveholder, nor to slavery, that the vivacious captive may sometimes dance in his chains, his very mirth in such circumstances, stands before God, as an accusing angel against his enslaver.

But *who* tells us of the extraordinary contentment and happiness of the slave? What traveller has explored the balmy regions of our Southern country and brought back "these glad tidings of joy?" Bring him on the platform and bid him answer a few plain questions. We shall then be able to determine the weight and importance that attach to his testimony. Is he a minister? Yes. Were you ever in a slave State, sir? Yes. May I inquire the object of your mission South? To preach the gospel, sir. Of what denomination are you? A Presbyterian, sir. To whom were you introduced? To the Rev. Dr. Plummer. Is he a slaveholder, sir? Yes, sir. Has slaves about his house? Yes, sir. Were you then the guest of Dr. Plummer? Yes, sir. Waited on by slaves while there? Yes, sir. Did you preach for Dr. Plummer? Yes, sir. Did you spend your nights at the great house, or at the quarters among the slaves? At the great house. You had, then, no social intercourse with the slaves? No, sir. You fraternized, then, wholly with the *white* portion of the population while there? Yes, sir. This is sufficient, sir; you can leave the platform.

Nothing is more natural than that those who go into slave States, and enjoy the hospitality of slaveholders, should bring back favorable reports of the condition of the slave. If that ultra republican, the Hon. Lewis Cass, could not return from the Court of France, without paying a compliment to royalty simply because King Louis Phillippe patted him on the shoulder, called him "friend," and invited him to dinner, it is not to be expected that those hungry shadows of men in the shape of ministers, that go South, can escape a contamination even more beguiling and insidious. Alas! for the weakness of poor human nature! "Pleased with a rattle, tickled with a straw!"

Why is it that all the reports of contentment and happiness among the slaves at the South come to us upon the authority of slave-holders, or (what is equally significant) of slave-holders' friends? *Why* is it that we do not hear from the slave direct? The answer to this question furnishes the darkest features in the American slave system.

It is often said, by the opponents of the Anti-Slavery cause, that the condition of the people of Ireland is more deplorable than that of the American slaves. *Far* be it from me to underrate the sufferings of the Irish people. They have been long oppressed; and the same heart that prompts me to plead the cause of the American bondman, makes it impossible for me *not* to sympathize with the oppressed of all lands. Yet I must say that there is no analogy between the two cases. The Irishman is poor, but he is *not* a slave. He *may* be in rags, but he is *not* a slave. He is still the master of his own body, and can say with the poet, "The hand of Douglass is his own."— "The world is all before him, where to choose"; and poor as may be my opinion of the British Parliament, I cannot believe that it will ever sink to such a depth of infamy as to pass a law for the recapture of Fugitive Irishmen! The shame and scandal of kidnapping will long remain wholly monopolized by the American Congress! The Irishman has not only the liberty to emigrate from his country, but he has liberty at home. He can write, and speak, and co-operate for the attainment of his rights and the redress of his wrongs.

The multitude can assemble upon all the green hills and fertile plains of the Emerald Isle—they can pour out their grievances, and proclaim their wants without molestation; and the press, that "swift-winged messenger," can bear the tidings of their doings to the extreme bounds of the civilized world. They have their "Conciliation Hall" on the banks of the Liffy, their reform Clubs, and their newspapers; they pass resolutions, send forth addresses, and enjoy the right of petition. But how is it with the American slave? *Where* may he assemble? *Where* is his Conciliation Hall? Where are his newspapers? Where is his right of petition? Where is his freedom of speech?—his liberty of the press?—and his right of locomotion? He is said to be happy; happy men can speak. But ask the slave—*what* is his condition?—*what* his state of mind?—*what* he thinks of his enslavement?— and you had as well address your inquiries to the *silent dead*. There comes no *voice* from the enslaved. We are left to gather his feelings by imagining what our's would be, were our souls in his soul's stead.

If there were no other fact descriptive of slavery, than that the slave is dumb, this alone would be sufficient to mark the slave system as a grand aggregation of human horrors.

## [b]

### *December 8, 1850*

I hold myself ready to prove that more than a million of women, in the Southern States of this Union, are, by the laws of the land, and through no fault of their own, consigned to a life of revolting prostitution; that, by those laws, in many of the States, if a woman, in defence of her own innocence, shall lift her hand against the brutal aggressor, she may be lawfully put to death. I hold myself ready to prove, by the laws of slave states, that three million of the people of those States are utterly incapacitated to form marriage contracts. I am also prepared to prove that slave breeding is relied upon by Virginia as one of her chief sources of wealth. It has long been known that the best blood of old Virginia may now be found in the slave markets of New Orleans. It is also known that slave women, who are nearly white, are sold in those markets, at prices which proclaim, trumpet-tongued, the accursed purposes to which they are to be devoted. Youth and elegance, beauty and innocence, are exposed for sale upon the auction block; while villainous monsters stand around, with pockets lined with gold, gazing with lustful eyes upon their prospective victims. But I will not go behind the scene further. I leave you to picture to yourselves what must be the state of society where marriage is not allowed by the law, and where *woman* is reduced to a mere *chattel*. To the thoughtful I need say no more. You have already conceived a state of things equalling, in horror and abomination, your worst conceptions of Sodom itself.

Every slaveholder is a party, a guilty party, to this awful wickedness. He owns the house, and is master of the victims. He is therefore responsible. I say again, no matter how high the slaveholder may stand in popular estimation—he may be a minister of religion, or an Hon. member of Congress; but so long as he is a slaveholder, he deserves to be held up before the world as the patron of lewdness, and the foe of virtue. He may not be personally implicated in the wickedness; he may scrupulously maintain and respect the marriage institution for himself and for his family, for all this can be done selfishly; but while he robs any portion of the human family of the right of marriage, and takes from innocent women the protection of the law, no matter what his individual respectability may be, he is to be classed with the vilest of the vile, and with the basest of the base . . .

The northern people have been long connected with slavery; they have been linked to a decaying corpse, which has destroyed the moral health. The union of the government; the union of the North and South, in the political parties; the union in the religious organizations of the land, have all served to deaden the moral sense of the northern people, and to impregnate them with sentiments and ideas for ever in conflict with what as a nation, we call *genius of American institutions.* Rightly viewed, this is an alarming fact, and ought to rally all that is pure, just, and holy in one determined effort, to crush the monster of corruption, and to scatter "its guilty profits" to the winds. In a high moral sense, as well as in a national sense, the whole American people are responsible for slavery, and must share, in its guilt and shame, with the most obdurate men-stealers of the South.

While slavery exists, and the union of these States endures, every American citizen must bear the chagrin of hearing his country branded before the world, as a nation of liars and hypocrites; and behold his cherished national flag pointed at with the utmost scorn and derision. . . .

Let me say again, *slavery is alike the sin and the shame of the American people:* It is a blot upon the American name, and the only national reproach which need make an American hang his head in shame, in the presence of monarchical governments.

With this gigantic evil in the land, we are constantly told to look *at home;* if we say ought against crowned heads, we are pointed to our enslaved millions; if we talk of sending missionaries and Bibles abroad, we are pointed to three millions, now lying in worse than heathen darkness; if we express a word of sympathy for Kossuth and his Hungarian fugitive brethren, we are pointed to that horrible and hell-black enactment "the FUGITIVE SLAVE BILL."

Slavery blunts the edge of all our rebukes of tyranny abroad—the criticisms that we make upon other nations, only call forth ridicule, contempt and scorn. In a word, we are made a reproach, and a by-word to a mocking earth, and we must continue to be so made, so long as slavery continues to pollute our soil.

We have heard much of late of the virtue of patriotism, the love of country, &c., and this sentiment, so natural and so strong, has been impiously appealed to, by all the powers of human selfishness, to cherish the viper which is stinging our national life away. In its name we have been called upon to deepen our infamy before the world, to rivet the fetter more firmly on.the limbs of the enslaved, and to become utterly insensible to the voice of human woe that is wafted to us on every Southern gale. We have been called upon, in its name, to desecrate our whole land by the footprints of slave-hunters, and, even to engage ourselves in the horrible business of kidnapping.

I, too, would invoke the spirit of patriotism; *not* in a narrow and restricted sense, but I trust, with a broad and manly signification; *not* to cover up our national sins, but to inspire us with sincere repentance; *not* to hide our shame from the world's gaze, but utterly to abolish the cause of that shame; *not* to explain away our gross inconsistencies as a nation, but to remove the hateful, jarring and incongruous elements from the land; *not* to sustain an egregious wrong, but to unite all our energies in the grand effort to remedy that wrong . . .

Without appealing to any higher feeling, I would warn the American people, and the American government, to *be wise* in their day and generation. I exhort them to remember the history of other nations; and I remind them that America cannot always sit "as a queen," in peace and repose; that prouder and stronger governments than this have been shattered by the bolts of a just God; that the time *may* come when those they now despise and hate, may be needed; when those whom they now compel, by oppression, to be enemies, may be wanted as friends; what *has* been, *may* be again. There is a point beyond which human endurance cannot go. The crushed worm may yet turn under the heel of the oppressor. I warn them, then, with all solemnity, and in the name of retributive justice, *to look to their ways;* for in an evil hour, those sable arms that have, for the last two centuries, been engaged in cultivating and adorning the fair fields of our country, may yet become the instruments of terror, desolation, and death, throughout our borders. We are told, by the President of the United States, in his recent message to Congress, that the American people are at peace with all the world; and this may be true in the sense in which it is used; but *what* if this may not always be the case? *What* if, by some strange vicissitude, amicable relations with Europe should be interrupted. What if *war* should take the place of diplomacy? And some principle of international law between this and some strong European power should be defeated on the battle-field? *Where,* then, would be our safety? We are told, (by a Southern Statesman) that *a million* of slaves are ready to "strike for freedom," at the first roll of a foreign drum; and I would ask, in his language, "How are you to sustain an assault from England or France, with this cancer in your vitals?" The slaves in our land have reached a number *not* to be despised. They are *three* millions—a fearful multitude to be in chains. The American people numbered *three* millions when they asserted their independence; and although they contended with the strongest power on the globe, they were successful.

It was the sage of the Old Dominion that said, (while speaking of the possibility of a conflict between the slaves and the slaveholders,) "God has no attribute that could take sides with the oppressor in such a contest. I tremble for my country when I reflect that *God* is *just,* and that his justice cannot sleep for ever." Such is the warning voice of Thomas Jefferson; * and every day's experience since its utterance until now, confirms its wisdom, and commends its truth.

*Lectures on American Slavery by Frederick Douglass* (Buffalo, 1851).

122

## THE CONSTITUTION AS SEEN BY NEGROES, 1851

One of the points dividing Abolitionists was that involving different interpretations of the United States Constitution. One group, opposing political action, insisted that the Constitution was in essence and in fact a pro-slavery document; another group, favoring political action, insisted that while the Constitution in fact supported slavery, it, in essence and spirit, was not pro-slavery. As a result the latter group affirmed that political struggle against slavery, within the framework provided by the Constitution, was not only possible but desirable.

A cogent discussion of these points of view occurred during a State Convention of Ohio Negroes held in Columbus, January 15–18, 1851. The three speakers quoted below, each of whom was an outstanding Negro leader, were H. Ford Douglass (not a relative of Frederick Douglass), William Howard Day and Charles H. Langston.

A Resolution was introduced by H. Ford Douglass: "That it is the opinion of this Convention, that no colored man can consistently vote under the United States Constitution."—He spoke for it as follows: Mr. Chairman †— I am in favor of the adoption of the resolution. I hold, sir, that the Constitution of the United States is pro-slavery, considered so by those who framed it, and construed to that end ever since its adoption. It is well known that in 1787, in the Convention that framed the Constitution, there was considerable discussion on the subject of slavery. South Carolina and Georgia refused to come into the Union, without the Convention would allow the continuation of the Slave Trade for twenty years. According to the demands of these two States, the Convention submitted to that guilty contract, and declared that the Slave Trade should not be prohibited prior to 1808. Here

* The exact quotation, from Jefferson's *Notes on Virginia* (1781) reads: "Indeed I tremble for my country when I reflect that God is just; that His justice cannot sleep forever . . . The Almighty has no attribute which can take side with us in such a contest."
† The Chairman was David Jenkins.

we see them engrafting into the Constitution, a clause legalizing and protecting one of the vilest systems of wrong ever invented by the cupidity and avarice of man. And by virtue of that agreement, our citizens went to the shores of Africa, and there seized upon the rude barbarian, as he strolled unconscious of impending danger, amid his native forests, as free as the winds that beat on his native shores. Here, we see them dragging these bleeding victims to the slave-ship by virtue of that instrument, compelling them to endure all the horrors of the "middle passage," until they arrived at this asylum of western Liberty, where they were doomed to perpetual chains. Now, I hold, in view of this fact, no colored man can consistently vote under the United States Constitution. That instrument also provides for the return of fugitive slaves. And, sir, one of the greatest lights now adorning the galaxy of American Literature, declares that the "Fugitive Law" is in accordance with that stipulation;—a law unequaled in the worst days of Roman despotism, and unparalleled in the annals of heathen jurisprudence. You might search the pages of history in vain, to find a more striking exemplification of the compound of all villainies! It shrouds our country in blackness; every green spot in nature, is blighted and blasted by that withering Upas. Every monument of national greatness, erected to commemorate the virtuous and the good, whether its foundation rests upon the hallowed repositories that contain the ashes of the first martyrs in the cause of American Liberty, or lifts itself in solemn and majestic grandeur, from that sacred spot when the first great battle of the Revolution was fought, no matter how sacred the soil, whether fertilized by the blood of a Warren, or signalized by the brilliant and daring feats of Marion! We are all, according to Congressional enactments, involved in that horrible system of human bondage; compelled, sir, by virtue of that instrument, to assist in the black and disgraceful avocation of re-capturing the American Hungarian, in his hurried flight from that worse than Russian or Austrian despotism, however much he may be inspired with that love of liberty which burns eternal in every human heart. Sir, every man is inspired with a love of liberty—a deep and abiding love of liberty. I care not where he may dwell—whether amid the snows of the polar regions, or weltering beneath an African sun, or clanking his iron fetters in this free Republic—I care not how degraded the man—that Promethean spark still lives, and burns, in secret and brilliant grandeur, upon his inmost soul, and the iron-rust of slavery and uninterrupted despotism, can never extinguish it. Did not the American Congress, professing to be a Constitutional body, after nine months' arduous and patriotic legislation, as Webster would have it, strike down in our persons, the writ of *Habeas Corpus,* and *Trial by Jury*—those great bulwarks of human freedom, baptized by the blood, and sustained by the patriotic exertions of our English ancestors?

The gentleman from Franklin, (Mr. [David] Jenkins), alluded to the Free Soil candidate for Governor. I will here state, that I had the pleasure, during the Gubernatorial campaign, to hear Mr. Smith make a speech in opposition to the "Fugitive Law," in which he remarked, that it was humiliating to him to acknowledge that our forefathers did make a guilty compromise with Slavery in order to form this Union; and so far as the validity of that agreement was concerned, he felt that it was not binding upon him as a man, and that he never would obey any law which conflicts with that higher law, that has its seat in the bosom of God, and utters its voice in the harmony of the world.

Mr. Douglass having taken his seat, Mr. Day, of Lorain, obtained the floor, and addressing the President, in substance said:

I cannot sit still, while this resolution is pending, and by my silence acquiesce in it. For all who have known me for years past, know that to the principle of the resolution I am, on principle opposed. The remarks of the gentleman from Cuyahoga (Mr. Douglass), it seems to me, partake of the error of many others who discuss this question, namely, of making the *construction* of the Constitution of the United States, the same as the Constitution itself. There is no dispute between us in regard to the pro-slavery action of this government, nor any doubt in our minds in regard to the aid which the Supreme Court of the United States has given to Slavery, and by their unjust and, according to their own rules, illegal decisions; but *that* is not the Constitution—they are not that under which I vote. We, most of us, profess to believe in the Bible; but men have, from the Bible, attempted to justify the worst of iniquities. Do we, in such a case, discard the Bible, believing, as we do, that iniquities find no shield there?—Or do we not rather discard the false opinions of mistaken men, in regard to it? As some one else says, if a judge make a wrong decision in an important case, shall we abolish the Court? Shall we not rather remove the *Judge,* and put in his place one who will judge righteously? We all so decide. So in regard to the Constitution: In voting, with judges' decisions we have nothing to do. Our business is with the Constitution. If it says it was framed to "establish justice," it, of course, is opposed to injustice; if it says plainly no person shall be deprived of "life, *liberty,* or property, without due process of law,"—I suppose it means it, and I shall avail myself of the benefit of it. Sir, coming up as I do, in the midst of three millions of men in chains, and five hundred thousand only half free, I consider every instrument precious which guarantees to me liberty. I consider the Constitution the foundation of American liberties, and wrapping myself in the flag of the nation, I would plant myself upon that Constitution, and using the weapons they have given me, I would appeal to the American people for the rights thus guaranteed.

Mr. Douglass replied by saying—

The gentleman may wrap the stars and stripes of his country around him forty times, if possible, and with the Declaration of Independence in one hand, and the Constitution of our common country in the other, may seat himself under the shadow of the frowning monument of Bunker Hill, and if the slave holder under the Constitution, and with the "Fugitive Bill," doesn't find you, then there doesn't exist a Constitution.

Yes, resumed Mr. Day, and with the Constitution I will *find* the "Fugitive Bill." You will mark this—the gentleman has assumed the same error as before, and has not attempted to reply to my argument. This is all I need now say.

Mr. C. H. Langston obtained the floor and spoke as follows: Mr. President: I do not intend to make a speech, but merely to define my position on this subject, as I consider it one of no ordinary importance.

I perfectly agree with the gentleman from Cuyahoga, (Mr. Douglass) who presented this resolution, that the United States' Constitution is pro-slavery. It was made to foster and uphold that abominable, vampirish and bloody system of American slavery. The highest judicial tribunals of the country have so decided. Members, while in the Convention and on returning to their constituents, declared that Slavery was one of the interests sought to be protected by the Constitution. It was so understood and so administered all over the country. But whether the Constitution is pro-slavery, and whether colored men "can consistently vote under that Constitution," are two very distinct questions; and while I would answer the former in the affirmative, I would not, like the gentleman from Cuyahoga, answer the latter in the negative. I would vote under the United States Constitution on the same principle, (circumstances being favorable) that I would call on every slave, from Maryland to Texas, to arise and assert their *liberties*, and cut their masters' throats if they attempt again to reduce them to slavery. Whether or not this principle is correct, an impartial posterity and the Judge of the Universe shall decide.

Sir, I have long since adopted as my God, the freedom of the colored people of the United States, and my religion, to do anything that will effect that object—however much it may differ from the precepts taught in the Bible, such as "Whosoever shall smite thee on thy right cheek, turn to him the other also"; or "Love your enemies; bless them that curse you, and pray for them that despitefully use you and persecute you." Those are the lessons taught us by the religion of our white brethren, when they are free and we are slaves; but when their enslavement is attempted, then "Resistance to Tyranny is obedience to God." This doctrine is equally true in regard to colored men as white men. I hope, therefore, Mr. President, that the resolution will not be adopted, but that colored men will vote, or do anything else under the Constitution, that will aid in effecting our liberties, and in securing our political, religious and intellectual elevation.*

*Minutes of the State Convention, of the Colored Citizens of Ohio, convened at Columbus, January 15–18, 1851* (Columbus, 1851).

## 123

## A PIONEER NEGRO HISTORY BOOK, 1851

One of the first extended works devoted to the history of the American Negro was that by the Abolitionist, William C. Nell. Entitled, *Services of Colored Americans in the Wars of 1776 and 1812,* it was issued in 1851 by R. F. Wallcut, an important Boston publisher of that day. A new edition, with an introduction by Wendell Phillips, appeared the next year. Extracts from Nell's preface, dated May, 1851, follow:

There are those who will ask, why make a parade of the *military* services of *Colored* Americans, instead of recording their attention *to* and progress *in* the various other departments of civil, social, and political elevation? To this let me answer, that I yield to no one in appreciating the propriety and pertinency of *every* effort, on the part of Colored Americans, in *all* pursuits, which, as members of the human family, it becomes them to share in; and, among those, *my* predilections are *least* and *last* for what constitutes the pomp and circumstance of War.

Did the limits of this work permit, I could furnish an elaborate list of those who have distinguished themselves as Teachers, Editors, Orators, Mechanics, Clergymen, Artists, Farmers, Poets, Lawyers, Physicians, Merchants, etc., to whose perennial fame be it recorded, that most of their attainments were reached through difficulties unknown to any but those whose sin is the curl of the hair and hue of the skin.

There is now an institution of learning in the State of New York, Central College, which recently employed, as Professor of Belles Lettres, a young Colored man, CHARLES L. REASON, and who, on resigning his chair, dropped his mantle gracefully upon the shoulders of WILLIAM G. ALLEN, another Colored young man as worthy for scholastic abilities and gentlemanly deportment.

These men, as Teachers, especially in Colleges open to all, irrespective of accidental differences, are doing a mighty work in uprooting prejudice. The influences thus generated are already felt. Many a young white man

* The resolution was defeated, 28-2.

or woman who, in early life, has imbibed wrong notions of the Colored man's inferiority, is taught a new lesson by the Colored Professors at McGrawville; and they leave its honored walls with thanksgiving in their hearts for their conversion from Pro-Slavery Heathenism to the Gospel of Christian Freedom; and are thus prepared to go forth as Pioneers in the cause of Human Brotherhood.

But the Orator's voice and Author's pen have both been eloquent in detailing the merits of Colored Americans in these various ramifications of society, while a combination of circumstances have veiled from the public eye a narration of those military services which are generally conceded as passports to the honorable and lasting notice of Americans.

## 124

## BARGAINING FOR THE REDUCTION OF A FAMILY'S SALE PRICE, 1851

Peter Still, who had purchased his own freedom, learned from his former master, a Mr. McKiernan of Alabama, that for $5,000 he might buy the liberty of his wife, daughter and two sons. The letter that follows, dated August 16, 1851, was written by Peter's brother, William Still, director of the Underground Railroad in Philadelphia, to this Mr. McKiernan. Despite the letter the master refused to lower his price. Peter Still thereupon raised the $5,000 in thirty months by personal appeals before thousands of people in scores of communities throughout New England, New York, New Jersey and Pennsylvania. Among those who contributed were Thurlow Weed, Horace Greeley, Harriet Beecher Stowe and Gerrit Smith.

*Sir*—I have received your letter * from South Florence, Ala., under date of the 6th inst. To say that it took me by surprise, as well as afforded me pleasure, for which I feel to be very much indebted to you, is no more than true. In regard to your informants of myself—Mr. Thornton, of Ala., and Mr. Samuel Lewis, of Cincinnati—to them both I am a stranger. However, I am the brother of Peter, referred to, and with the fact of his having a wife and three children in your service I am also familiar. This brother, Peter, I have only had the pleasure of knowing for the brief space of one year and thirteen days, although he is now past forty and I twenty-nine years of age. Time will not allow me at present, or I should give you a detailed account of how Peter became a slave, the forty long years which intervened between the

* This letter is printed in Kate R. Pickard, *The Kidnapped and the Ransomed* (N.Y., 1941), pp. 245–46.

time he was kidnapped, when a boy, being only six years of age, and his arrival in this city, from Alabama, one year and fourteen days ago, when he was re-united to his mother, five brothers and three sisters.

None but a father's heart can fathom the anguish and sorrows felt by Peter during the many vicissitudes through which he has passed. He looked back to his boyhood and saw himself snatched from the tender embraces of his parents and home to be made a slave for life.

During all his prime days he was in the faithful and constant service of those who had no just claim upon him. In the meanwhile he married a wife, who bore him eleven children, the greater part of whom were emancipated from the troubles of life by death, and three only survived. To them and his wife he was devoted. Indeed I have never seen attachment between parents and children or husband and wife, more entire than was manifested in the case of Peter.

Through these many years of servitude, Peter was sold and re-sold, from one State to another, from one owner to another, till he reached the forty-ninth year of his age, when, in a good Providence, through the kindness of a friend and the sweat of his brow, he regained the God-given blessings of Liberty. He eagerly sought his parents and home with all possible speed and pains, when, to his heart's joy, he found his relatives.

Your present humble correspondent is the youngest of Peter's brothers, and the first one of the family he saw after arriving in this part of the country. I think you could not fail to be interested in hearing how we became known to each other, and the proof of our being brothers, etc., all of which I should be most glad to relate, but time will not permit me to do so. The news of this wonderful occurrence, of Peter finding his kindred, was published quite extensively, shortly afterwards, in various newspapers, in this quarter, which may account for the fact of "Miller's" knowledge of the whereabouts of the "fugitives." Let me say, it is my firm conviction that no one had any hand in persuading "Miller" to go down from Cincinnati, or any other place after the family.* As glad as I should be, and as much as I would do for the liberation of Peter's family (now no longer young), and his three "likely" children, in whom he prides himself—how much, if you are a father, you can imagine; yet I would not, and could not, think of persuading any friend to peril his life, as would be the case, in an errand of that kind.

As regards the price fixed upon by you for the family, I must say I do not think it possible to raise half that amount, though Peter authorized me to say he would give you twenty-five hundred for them. Probably he is not as well aware as I am, how difficult it is to raise so large a sum of money from

---

* "Miller" was the pseudonym of the Abolitionist, Seth Conklin, who lost his life in May, 1851, in an unsuccessful attempt to rescue the wife and children of Peter Still from slavery.

the public. The applications for such objects are so frequent among us in the North, and have always been so liberally met, that it is no wonder if many get tired of being called upon. To be sure some of us brothers own some property, but no great amount; certainly not enough to enable us to bear so great a burden. Mother owns a small farm in New Jersey, on which she has lived for nearly forty years, from which she derives her support in her old age. This small farm contains between forty and fifty acres, and is the fruit of my father's toil. Two of my brothers own small places also, but they have young families, and consequently consume nearly as much as they make, with the exception of adding some improvements to their places.

For my own part, I am employed as a clerk for a living, but my salary is quite too limited to enable me to contribute any great amount towards so large a sum as is demanded. Thus you see how we are situated financially. We have plenty of friends, but little money. Now, sir, allow me to make an appeal to your humanity, although we are aware of your power to hold as property those poor slaves, mother, daughter and two sons,—that in no part of the United States could they escape and be secure from your claim— nevertheless, would your understanding, your heart, or your conscience re- prove you, should you restore to them, without price, that dear freedom, which is theirs by right of nature, or would you not feel a satisfaction in so doing which all the wealth of the world could not equal? At all events, could you not so reduce the price as to place it in the power of Peter's relatives and friends to raise the means for their purchase? At first, I doubt not, but that you will think my appeal very unreasonable; but, sir, serious reflection will decide, whether the money demanded by you, after all, will be of as great a benefit to you, as the satisfaction you would find in bestowing so great a favor upon those whose entire happiness in this life depends mainly upon your decision in the matter. If the entire family cannot be purchased or freed, what can Vina and her daughter be purchased for? Hoping, sir, to hear from you, at your earliest convenience, I subscribe myself,

Your obedient servant,<br>WM. STILL.

William Still, *The Underground Railroad. A Record of facts, authentic narratives, letters, etc.* . . . (Phila., 1878), pp. 35–36.

125

## NEGROES BEAT OFF SLAVE-CATCHERS, 1851

A free Negro, William Parker of Christiana, Pennsylvania, was claimed in Sep- tember, 1851 as a fugitive slave by one Edward Gorsuch. The latter with the assistance of others, including a United States Marshal, besieged Parker's home, which was stoutly defended not only by himself but also by several Negro neighbors. Two of the white men, including Gorsuch, were killed, and one, a Marshal, was wounded. Parker escaped, with the help of Frederick Douglass, into Canada. Several Negroes—and two white men who had refused to assist in the attack upon Parker's home—were arrested and tried for treason. Their defense was handled by Thaddeus Stevens and within twenty minutes of deliberation the jury acquitted them. There follows an editorial appearing in a Negro newspaper just after the battle.

### The Christiana Affair

On our first page will be found extracts from several papers, in different sections of the country, in regard to the resistance recently offered to the kidnapping miscreants from Maryland, at Christiana, Pa. Their utter recklessness of truth, and ferocious malignity of sentiment, cannot be paralleled this side the kingdom of Naples. The moral, if a melancholy, may still be an instructive one. It shows how little real faith the popular press of this nation has in the principles upon which its whole action is professedly based. Had a band of Austrian mercenaries attacked Kossuth in Turkey, with the avowed purpose of delivering him into the hands of their government, and had his companions met them with the same sort of resistance which was offered at Christiana, the act would have been trumpeted to every wind as an instance of noble and self-sacrificing heroism, for which no wreath of glory was too bright, no words of panegyric too warm. But the black men of Christiana, whose feelings prompted them to a similar act in the service of their friends—what of them? They must be tried for treason against a Government based upon the principle, that "all men are created equal, and endowed by Nature with certain inalienable rights, among which are life, LIBERTY, and the pursuit of happiness!"

We are glad that among the general recreancy of the press, a few voices are raised in defence of the eternal truths for which Jefferson wrote, and Attucks and Warren bled. The great lesson of the Revolution has not been utterly in vain.

*Impartial Citizen* (N.Y., n.d.) in *The Liberator*, October 3, 1851.

## 126

## NEGROES WELCOME KOSSUTH, 1851

Lajos Kossuth, leader of the 1848 rebellion in Hungary, was brought to the United States from his exile in Turkey by the American battleship, *Mississippi*. On December 9, 1851, five days after reaching New York, he was addressed by George T.

Downing on behalf of a reception committee of the Negro people, including John J. Zuille, James McCune Smith and Philip A. Bell. George T. Downing's remarks are printed below.

Kossuth disappointed the Negro people by refusing to take a stand on American slavery and was denounced therefor by men like Samuel R. Ward and Frederick Douglass. After a whirlwind tour of the country, a reception by the President, an appearance before Congress—all, however, failing to bring American intervention against the Hapsburgs—Kossuth returned to Europe, aboard the steamer, *Africa*, in July, 1852.

We appear before you to pay homage to a great principle, which you announce with so much distinctness, and uphold with so much power, the principle that a man has a right to the full exercise of his faculties and powers in the land which gave him birth; and that it is his first duty to devote all the energies of his being to maintain that right for himself and his compatriots. Around this principle you have thrown a radiance which almost clothes it with the sacredness of a new Evangelist, and from your world's platform have called upon peoples and nations, however weak, to stand up and maintain it against whatever odds oppression and tyranny may have arrayed against it.

In the face of the distinguished example of the Pilgrim Fathers, and the many eminent men who have made this their *exile* home, we have steadily maintained this birth-home right during the last third of a century in this our native land, and will continue to maintain it until its ultimate triumph, "for the first love of man is in his home."

We feel that this great principle is surely gaining ground, and we hail in your person its living Apostle, who has given it voice and expression. We would express the deep sympathy we feel in you, because of the relation you sustain to Liberty. We feel that your mission is a most happy and propitious one. We see in it a part of the special ordering of Providence. The landing of the Pilgrim Fathers; our Declaration of Independence; the Revolutionary struggle, led by Washington; and the later developments of the principles of Liberty, as seen in the struggles now going on in our own country for its further advancement and application to all men, are kindred efforts.

God speed you in your mission! May Hungary be free! And we earnestly pray, that when the resurrection of your country shall indeed take place, she will clothe herself in the true vestment of Democracy, fitly prepared for her when you abolished caste, so that pure Republicanism will in her be vindicated, and every man stand an equal in the eyes of the law. Yes! illustrious patriot, may Hungary be free! May the world rejoice in her speedy disenthralment. May the joy be two-fold in that Hungary shall be redeemed—and not Hungary alone, but with her the world—mankind.

The attention of nations is fixed upon you! At the mention of your name, tyrants tremble, the oppressed rejoice! There is not a principle advocated by you, not a word that escapes your lips, but that is caught up and wafted to every civilized nation. And deep and widespread is the joy felt through Europe, when you proclaim the thrilling and trumpet-toned annunciation, "Ye oppressed nations of Europe, be of good cheer and courage."

God moves in mysterious ways. The result of the late Hungarian struggle will be propitious to the general growth of freedom. But for your imprisonment, the world would not now be so electrified by your eloquence—by the spirit of freedom. Hungary suffers in the ordering of Providence, for the good of the whole—but her destiny is to be free.

Respected Sir, your mission is too high to be allied with party or sect; it is the common cause of crushed, outraged humanity.

May you, when you leave our shores in furtherance of your heaven-high mission, carry with you the sympathy of *all*, the active countenance of *all*.

Be assured, that as you have now our prayers, so when the time comes, we shall give our own "liberty offering," though it may be but the "widow's mite."

*The Liberator*, December 19, 1851.

## 127

## "A NATION WITHIN A NATION . . . ," 1852

Few indeed are the theoretical works dealing with the Negro question, and written by Negroes, prior to the Civil War. One of the most significant of these is the book, *The Condition, Elevation, Emigration and Destiny of the Colored People of the United States, Politically Considered,* by Martin R. Delany (published by the author in Philadelphia in 1852). Delany was the co-founder and assistant editor of Douglass' *North Star.* The feeling of nationality which pervades the work is particularly noteworthy. Below are printed extracts from the book's preface and appendix.

### [a]

### *Preface*

The subject of this work is one that the writer has given thought for years, and the only regret that he has now in placing it before the public is, that his circumstances and engagements have not afforded him such time and opportunity as to do justice to it. But, should he succeed in turning the attention of the colored people, in general, in this direction—he shall have been amply compensated for the labor bestowed. An appendix will be found giving the plan of the author, laid out at twenty-four years of age, but subsequently improved on, for the elevation of the colored race. That plan, of course, as this work will fully show, has been abandoned for a far more glorious one; albeit, we as a race, still lay claim to the project, which one day must be added to our dashing strides in national advancement, successful adventure, and unsurpassed enterprise.

One part of the American people, though living in or near proximity and together, are quite unacquainted with the other; and one of the great objects of the author, is to make each acquainted. Except the character of an individual is known, there can be no just appreciation of his worth; and as with individuals, so it is with classes.

The colored people are not yet known, even to their most professed friends among the white Americans; for the reason, that politicians, religionists, colonizationists, and Abolitionists, have each and all, at different times, presumed to *think* for, dictate to, and *know* better what suited colored people, than they knew for themselves; and consequently, there has been no other knowledge of them obtained, than that which has been obtained through these mediums. Their history—past, present, and future, has been written by them, who, for reasons well known, which are named in this volume, are not their representatives, and, therefore, do not properly nor fairly present their wants and claims among their fellows. Of these impressions, we design disabusing the public mind, and correcting the false impressions of all classes upon this great subject. A moral and mental, is as obnoxious as a physical servitude, and not to be tolerated; as the one may, eventually, lead to the other.

## [b]

### *Appendix*

A project for an Expedition of Adventure, to the Eastern Coast of Africa.

Every people should be the originators of their own designs, the projector of their own schemes, and creators of the events that lead to their destiny— the consummation of their desires.

Situated as we are, in the United States, many, and almost insurmountable obstacles present themselves. We are four-and-a-half millions in numbers, free and bond; six hundred thousand free, and three-and-a-half millions bond.

We have native hearts and virtues, just as other nations; which in their pristine purity are noble, potent, and worthy of example. We are a nation within a nation;—as the Poles in Russia, the Hungarians in Austria; the Welsh, Irish, and Scotch in the British dominions.

But we have been, by our oppressors, despoiled of our purity, and corrupted in our native characteristics, so that we have inherited their vices, and but few of their virtues, leaving us in character, really a *broken people.*

Being distinguished by complexion, we are still singled out—although having merged in the habits and customs of our oppressors—as a distinct nation of people; as the Poles, Hungarians, Irish and others, who still retain their native peculiarities, of language, habits, and various other traits. The claims of no people, according to established policy and usage, are respected by any nation, until they are presented in a national capacity.

To accomplish so great and desirable an end, there should be held, a great representative gathering of the colored people of the United States; not what is termed a National Convention, representing en masse, such as have been, for the last few years, held at various times and places; but a true representation of the intelligence and wisdom of the colored freemen; because it will be futile and an utter failure, to attempt such a project without the highest grade of intelligence.

No great project was ever devised without the consultation of the most mature intelligence, and discreet discernment and precaution.

To effect this, and prevent intrusion and improper representation, there should be a CONFIDENTIAL COUNCIL held; and circulars issued, only to such persons as shall be *known* to the projectors to be equal to the desired object.

The authority from whence the call should originate, to be in this wise:— The originator of the scheme, to impart the contemplated Confidential Council, to a limited number of known, worthy gentlemen, who agreeing with the project, endorse at once the scheme, when becoming joint proprietors in interest, issue a *Confidential Circular,* leaving blanks for date, time, and place of holding the Council, sending them to trusty, worthy and suitable colored freemen, in all parts of the United States, and the Canadas, inviting them to attend; who when met in Council, have the right to project any scheme they may think proper for the general good of the whole people— provided, that the project is laid before them after its maturity.

By this Council to be appointed, a Board of Commissioners, to consist of three, five, or such reasonable number as may be decided upon, one of whom shall be chosen as Principal or Conductor of the Board, whose duty and business shall be, to go on an expedition to the EASTERN COAST OF AFRICA, to make researches for a suitable location on that section of the coast, for the settlement of colored adventurers from the United States, and elsewhere. Their mission should be to all such places as might meet the approbation of the people; as South America, Mexico, the West Indies, &c.

The Commissioners all to be men of decided qualifications; to embody among them, the qualifications of physician, botanist, chemist, geologist, geographer, and surveyor—having a sufficient knowledge of these sciences, for practical purposes.

Their business shall be, to make a topographical, geological, and botanical examination, into such part or parts as they may select, with all other useful information that may be obtained. . . .

The National Council shall appoint one or two Special Commissioners, to England, France, to solicit, in the name of the Representatives of a Broken Nation, of four-and-a-half millions, the necessary outfit and support, for any period not exceeding three years, of such an expedition. Certainly, what England and France would do, for a little nation—mere nominal nation, of five thousand civilized Liberians, they would be willing and ready to do, for five millions; if they be but authentically represented, in a national capacity. What was due to Greece, enveloped by Turkey, should be due to United States, enveloped by the United States; and we believe would be respected, if properly presented. To England and France, we should look for sustenance, and the people of those two nations—as they would have everything to gain from such an adventure and eventual settlement on the EASTERN COAST OF AFRICA—the opening of an immense trade being the consequence. The whole Continent is rich in minerals, and the most precious metals, as but a superficial notice of the topographical and geological reports from that country, plainly show to any mind versed in the least, in the science of the earth . . . The land is ours—there it lies with inexhaustible resources; let us go and possess it. In Eastern Africa must rise up a nation, to whom all the world must pay commercial tribute.

We must MAKE an ISSUE, CREATE an EVENT, and ESTABLISH a NATIONAL POSITION for OURSELVES: and never may expect to be respected as men and women, until we have undertaken, some fearless, bold, and adventurous deeds of daring—contending against every odds—regardless of every consequence.

## 128

## NEGROES AGAIN DENOUNCE COLONIZATION, 1852

In his annual message to the legislature of January, 1852, Governor Hunt of New York proposed that money be appropriated to the American Colonization Society. This drew from the New York State Convention of Colored Citizens, meeting under the chairmanship of the Rev. James W. C. Pennington in Albany's City Hall on January 20, 1852, a vigorous protest. as follows:

*First*—Because the appropriation is unconstitutional. The 10th section of the 7th article of the Constitution states, that "the credit of the State shall not in any manner be given or loaned to, or in aid of any individual association or incorporation." The American Colonization Society is an "association" foreign to the State, and unknown to its laws. By granting no matter what sum to that Society, the good faith of the State would be pledged to the cruel and monstrous doctrines on which that Society is founded—that a man has no right to live in the land of his birth.

*Secondly*—Because such an appropriation is entirely unnecessary. Of the colored population of this State, there are not fifty persons, all told, who desire to emigrate to Africa.

We need no State appropriation. Should it ever occur that we should be called upon to leave our native State, having means of our own, we shall not burthen the public fund in our departure any more than we do while remaining home . . . the road is short to Canada; from whose fertile fields and equal institutions, we might be permitted to witness the prosperity of that State, which, in giving us birth, has entwined in its commonweal every fibre of our being; this would take away half the bitterness of exile, and would leave us the privilege, should peril come to her, of baring the breasts of black men as a shield to whatever blows may be aimed against the heart of the Empire State.

*Thirdly*—We protest against such appropriation, because the American Colonization Society is a gigantic fraud . . . a moulder of, and a profiter by a diseased public opinion, it keeps alive an army of agents who live by plundering us of our good name.

*And lastly*—We protest against this appropriation, because "we remember those that are in bonds as bound with them"; bone of our bone, and flesh of our flesh, may evil betide us when the hope of gain, or the fear of oppression, shall compel or persuade us to forsake them to the rayless gloom of perpetual slavery.

*The Liberator,* March 5, 1852.

## 129

# FREDERICK DOUGLASS DISCUSSES THE FOURTH OF JULY, 1852

As the city's most distinguished resident, Frederick Douglass was requested to address the citizens of Rochester on the Fourth of July celebration in 1852. The speech he delivered, under the title, "What to the Slave is the Fourth of July?", illustrates the great power, insight and integrity of the man.

*Fellow Citizens:* Pardon me, and allow me to ask, why am I called upon to speak here today? What have I or those I represent to do with your national independence? Are the great principles of political freedom and of natural justice, embodied in that Declaration of Independence, extended to us? And am I, therefore, called upon to bring our humble offering to the national altar, and to confess the benefits, and express devout gratitude for the blessings resulting from your independence to us?

Would to God, both for your sakes and ours, that an affirmative answer could be truthfully returned to these questions. Then would my task be light, and my burden easy and delightful. For who is there so cold that a nation's sympathy could not warm him? Who so obdurate and dead to the claims of gratitude, that would not thankfully acknowledge such priceless benefits? Who so stolid and selfish that would not give his voice to swell the halleluiahs of a nation's jubilee, when the chains of servitude had been torn from his limbs? I am not that man. In a case like that, the dumb might eloquently speak, and the "lame man leap like a hare."

But such is not the state of the case. I say it with a sad sense of disparity between us. I am not included within the pale of this glorious anniversary! Your high independence only reveals the immeasurable distance between us. The blessings in which you this day rejoice are not enjoyed in common. The rich inheritance of justice, liberty, prosperity, and independence bequeathed by your fathers is shared by you, not by me. The sunlight that brought life and healing to you has brought stripes and death to me. This Fourth of July is *yours,* not *mine. You* may rejoice, *I* must mourn. To drag a man in fetters into the grand illuminated temple of liberty, and call upon him to join you in joyous anthems, were inhuman mockery and sacrilegious irony. Do you mean, citizens, to mock me, by asking me to speak today? If so, there is a parallel to your conduct. And let me warn you, that it is dangerous to copy the example of a nation whose crimes, towering up to heaven, were thrown down by the breath of the Almighty, burying that nation in irrecoverable ruin. I can today take up the lament of a peeled and woe-smitten people.

"By the rivers of Babylon, there we sat down. Yes! We wept when we remembered Zion. We hanged our harps upon the willows in the midst thereof. For there they that carried us away captive, required of us a song; and they who wasted us, required of us mirth, saying, Sing us one of the songs of Zion. How can we sing the Lord's song in a strange land? If I forget thee, O Jerusalem, let my right hand forget her cunning. If I do not remember thee, let my tongue cleave to the roof of my mouth."

Fellow citizens, above your national, tumultuous joy, I hear the mournful wail of millions, whose chains, heavy and grievous yesterday, are today rendered more intolerable by the jubilant shouts that reach them. If I do forget, if I do not remember those bleeding children of sorrow this day, "may my right hand forget her cunning, and may my tongue cleave to the roof of my mouth!" To forget them, to pass lightly over their wrongs, and to chime in with the popular theme, would be treason most scandalous and shocking, and would make me a reproach before God and the world. My subject, then, fellow citizens, is "American Slavery." I shall see this day and its popular characteristics from the slave's point of view. Standing here, identified with the American bondman, making his wrongs mine, I do not hesitate to declare, with all my soul, that the character and conduct of this nation never looked blacker to me than on this Fourth of July. Whether we turn to the declarations of the past, or to the professions of the present, the conduct of the nation seems equally hideous and revolting. America is false to the past, false to the present, and solemnly binds herself to be false to the future. Standing with God and the crushed and bleeding slave on this occasion, I will, in the name of humanity, which is outraged, in the name of liberty, which is fettered, in the name of the Constitution and the Bible, which are disregarded and trampled upon, dare to call in question and to denounce, with all the emphasis I can command, everything that serves to perpetuate slavery—the great sin and shame of America! "I will not equivocate; I will not excuse"; I will use the severest language I can command, and yet not one word shall escape me that any man, whose judgment is not blinded by prejudice, or who is not at heart a slave-holder, shall not confess to be right and just.

But I fancy I hear some of my audience say it is just in this circumstance that you and your brother Abolitionists fail to make a favorable impression on the public mind. Would you argue more and denounce less, would you persuade more and rebuke less, your cause would be much more likely to succeed. But, I submit, where all is plain there is nothing to be argued. What point in the anti-slavery creed would you have me argue? On what branch of the subject do the people of this country need light? Must I undertake to prove that the slave is a man? That point is conceded already. Nobody doubts it. The slave-holders themselves acknowledge it in the enactment of laws for their government. They acknowledge it when they punish disobedience on the part of the slave. There are seventy-two crimes in the State of Virginia, which, if committed by a black man (no matter how ignorant he be), subject him to the punishment of death; while only two of these same crimes will subject a white man to like punishment. What is this but the acknowledgment that the slave is a moral, intellectual, and responsible being? The manhood of the slave is conceded. It is admitted in the fact that Southern statute-books are covered with enactments, forbidding, under severe fines and penalties, the teaching of the slave to read and write. When you can point to any such laws in reference to the beasts of the field, then I may consent to argue the manhood of the slave. When the dogs in your streets, when the fowls of the air, when the cattle on your hills, when the fish of the sea, and the reptiles that crawl, shall be unable to distinguish the slave from a brute, then I will argue with you that the slave is a man!

For the present it is enough to affirm the equal manhood of the Negro race. Is it not astonishing that, while we are plowing, planting, and reaping, using all kinds of mechanical tools, erecting houses, constructing bridges, building ships, working in metals of brass, iron, copper, silver, and gold; that while we are reading, writing, and cyphering, acting as clerks, merchants, and secretaries, having among us lawyers, doctors, ministers, poets, authors, editors, orators, and teachers; that while we are engaged in all the enterprises common to other men—digging gold in California, capturing the whale in the Pacific, feeding sheep and cattle on the hillside, living, moving, acting, thinking, planning, living in families as husbands, wives, and children, and above all, confessing and worshipping the Christian God, and looking hopefully for life and immortality beyond the grave—we are called upon to prove that we are men?

Would you have me argue that man is entitled to liberty? That he is the rightful owner of his own body? You have already declared it. Must I argue the wrongfulness of slavery? Is that a question for republicans? Is it to be settled by the rules of logic and argumentation, as a matter beset with great difficulty, involving a doubtful application of the principle of justice, hard to understand? How should I look today in the presence of Americans, dividing and subdividing a discourse, to show that men have a natural right to freedom, speaking of it relatively and positively, negatively and affirmatively? To do so would be to make myself ridiculous, and to offer an insult to your understanding. There is not a man beneath the canopy of heaven who does not know that slavery is wrong *for him*.

What! Am I to argue that it is wrong to make men brutes, to rob them of their liberty, to work them without wages, to keep them ignorant of their relations to their fellow men, to beat them with sticks, to flay their flesh with the last, to load their limbs with irons, to hunt them with dogs, to sell them at auction, to sunder their families, to knock out their teeth, to burn their flesh, to starve them into obedience and submission to their masters? Must I argue that a system thus marked with blood and stained with pollution is wrong? No; I will not. I have better employment for my time and strength than such arguments would imply.

What, then, remains to be argued? Is it that slavery is not divine; that God did not establish it; that our doctors of divinity are mistaken? There is blasphemy in the thought. That which is inhuman cannot be divine. Who can reason on such a proposition? They that can, may; I cannot. The time for such argument is past.

At a time like this, scorching irony, not convincing argument, is needed. Oh! had I the ability, and could I reach the nation's ear, I would today pour out a fiery stream of biting ridicule, blasting reproach, withering sarcasm, and stern rebuke. For it is not light that is needed, but fire; it is not the gentle shower, but thunder. We need the storm, the whirlwind, and the earthquake. The feeling of the nation must be quickened; the conscience of the nation must be roused; the propriety of the nation must be startled; the hypocrisy of the nation must be exposed; and its crimes against God and man must be denounced.

What to the American slave is your Fourth of July? I answer, a day that reveals to him more than all other days of the year, the gross injustice and cruelty to which he is the constant victim. To him your celebration is a sham; your boasted liberty an unholy license; your national greatness, swelling vanity; your sounds of rejoicing are empty and heartless; your denunciation of tyrants, brass-fronted impudence; your shouts of liberty and equality, hollow mockery; your prayers and hymns, your sermons and thanksgivings, with all your religious parade and solemnity, are to him mere bombast, fraud, deception, impiety, and hypocrisy—a thin veil to cover up crimes which would disgrace a nation of savages. There is not a nation of the earth guilty of practices more shocking and bloody than are the people of these United States at this very hour.

Go where you may, search where you will, roam through all the monarchies and despotisms of the Old World, travel through South America, search out every abuse and when you have found the last, lay your facts by the side of the every-day practices of this nation, and you will say with me that, for revolting barbarity and shameless hypocrisy, America reigns without a rival.

Alice Moore Dunbar, ed., *Masterpieces of Negro Eloquence* (N.Y., 1914, The Bookery Pub. Co.), pp. 42–47.

## 130

## A KIDNAPPED NEGRO'S WIFE PETITIONS FOR HIS FREEDOM, 1852

A kidnapped free Negro of New York, Solomon Northup, after laboring in the deep South for twelve years as a slave, was finally able, in 1852, to get information of his plight to his wife. She submitted a petition on November 19, 1852, to the

Governor of New York which led, in 1853, to Northup's restitution to freedom. Mrs. Anne Northup's petition follows:

The memorial of Anne Northup, of the village of Glens Falls, in the county of Warren, State aforesaid, respectfully sets forth—

That your memorialist, whose maiden name was Anne Hampton, was forty-four years old on the 14th day of March last, and was married to Solomon Northup, then of Fort Edward, in the county of Washington and State aforesaid, on the 25th day of December, A.D. 1828, by Timothy Eddy, then a Justice of the Peace. That the said Solomon, after such marriage, lived and kept house with your memorialist in said town until 1830, when he removed with his said family to the town of Kingsbury in said county, and remained there about three years, and then removed to Saratoga Springs in the State aforesaid, and continued to reside in said Saratoga Springs and the adjoining town until about the year 1841, as near as the time can be recollected, when the said Solomon started to go to the city of Washington, in the District of Columbia, since which time your memorialist has never seen her said husband.

And your memorialist further states, that in the year 1841 she received information by a letter directed to Henry B. Northup, Esq., of Sandy Hill, Washington county, New-York, and post-marked at New-Orleans, that said Solomon had been kidnapped in Washington, put on board of a vessel, and was then in such vessel in New-Orleans, but could not tell how he came in that situation, nor what his destination was.

That your memorialist ever since the last mentioned period has been wholly unable to obtain any information of where the said Solomon was, until the month of September last, when another letter was received from the said Solomon, post-marked at Marksville, in the parish of Avoyelles, in the State of Louisiana, stating that he was held there as a slave, which statement your memorialist believes to be true.

That the said Solomon is about forty-five years of age, and never resided out of the state of New-York, in which State he was born, until the time he went to Washington city, as before stated. That the said Solomon Northup is a free citizen of the State of New-York, and is now wrongfully held in slavery, in or near Marksville, in the parish of Avoyelles, in the State of Louisiana, one of the United States of America, on the allegation or pretence that the said Solomon is a slave.

And your memorialist further states that Mintus Northup was the reputed father of said Solomon, and was a Negro, and died at Fort Edward, on the 22d day of November, 1829; that the mother of said Solomon was a mulatto, or three quarters white, and died in the county of Oswego, New-

York, some five or six years ago, as your memorialist was informed and believes, and never was a slave.

That your memorialist and her family are poor and wholly unable to pay or sustain any portion of the expenses of restoring the said Solomon to his freedom.

Your excellency is entreated to employ such agent or agents as shall be deemed necessary to effect the restoration and return of said Solomon Northup, in pursuance of an act of the Legislature of the State of New-York, passed May 14th, 1840, entitled "An act more effectually to protect the free citizens of this State from being kidnapped or reduced to slavery." And your memorialist will ever pray.

*Twelve Years a Slave, Narrative of Solomon Northup* . . . (Auburn, Buffalo, London, 1854), pp. 325 ff.

## 131

## POLITICAL ACTION AGAINST SLAVERY, 1852

William C. Nell sent Garrison, in December, 1852, a long letter with significant information concerning Massachusetts Negroes. Of particular interest is the evidence here offered of the near unanimity of the Negro people, quite unlike the divisions among many white Abolitionists, in support of political action to combat slavery.

During the past few weeks of a temporary sojourn in my native city [Boston], I have been somewhat an observer of those events, which, though in many respects but local, are nevertheless connected with the elevation of colored Americans generally; and as such, their record may, I trust, secure an insertion in the *Liberator*.

A series of public meetings has been held, under the auspices of colored citizens ranking with the Free Soil party. These gatherings have been characterized by great enthusiasm, and a willing ear for any citizen or stranger present whose voice could aid, directly or indirectly, the cause of human freedom. Though in the main intended as political meeting, yet every phase of an oppressed people's enlargement had its orator, and fervid, heart-stirring eloquence in the application of home truths, caustic denunciations of known delinquence, and warm approval bestowed upon the faithful, severally struck those chords, which, vibrating among the audience, have not yet ceased to bring forth abundant fruits.

Among the resolutions defining their position in the Presidential and State elections, the following served as a nucleus:

Resolved, That as the Whig and so-called Democratic parties of this country are endeavoring to crush, debase and dehumanize us as a people, any man among us voting for their respective candidates, virtually recognizes the righteousness of their principles, and shall be held up to public reprobation as a traitor, a hissing and a by word, a pest and a nuisance, the offscouring of the earth.

Resolved, That the candidates of the Free Democracy need no eulogy—they stand out in bold relief, as the representatives of principles which command the admiration and support of every lover of Truth, Justice and Humanity. Our hands, our hearts and our votes are theirs.

In discussing the first resolution, much sensitiveness was manifested by a few voters who were still wedded to the two great pro-slavery parties. (Thank God, there were but a few so recreant to their highest duty!) The blended powers of argument and sarcasm were levelled at these men, who semed to think it their duty to espouse the cause by which they eat and drink.

The second resolution concentrated the remarks of many speakers, and when the names of prominent liberty candidates were mentioned, they were received with prolonged and deafening applause. Aside from the associations surrounding them as candidates, there were remembrances of specific acts by certain individuals, which became signals for renewed plaudits. John P. Hale was cheered as the eloquent and gifted advocate for the defence in the trials of the alleged Shadrach rescuers; * Charles Sumner for his elaborate and learned argument before the Supreme bench of Massachusetts, contending for equal school rights of colored children. The old war-horse, Joshua R. Giddings, for his bold defiance of the slave domination in Congress, was gratefully remembered, as were many others. . . .

Regarding the Free Soil party as an offshoot from the old pioneer antislavery tree, the meeting unanimously adopted a resolution of unwavering confidence in the efforts of William Lloyd Garrison, and of sincere gratitude to him and his noble coadjutors, invoking their continued warfare upon American slavery.

Lewis Hayden said he was happy to notice several clergymen present, whose co-operation in this department of anti-slavery labor was in strong contrast with the conduct of the main body of their ministerial brethren among the dominant class. He regretted that truth demanded the confession, that even among colored clergymen were to be found those who

* In February, 1851, a fugitive slave named Shadrach, was forcibly rescued from U.S. custody in Boston by Negroes led by Lewis Hayden, James Scott and Robert Morris. These men, defended by Charles Dana and John Hale, won a hung jury and the case against them was dismissed.

sustain ecclesiastical relations wholly inconsistent with their position as aspiring leaders of an oppressed people.

Robert Morris, Esq., cautioned the people against the proposed plans of the American Colonization Society and the Ebony Line of steamers. He also spoke of the operations of the Fugitive Slave Law, alluding to recent decisions *pro* and *con,* and occasionally indulged in some graphic sketches of the Shadrach rescue.

Robert Johnson expressed his concurrence in the prayer offered at the opening meeting, that every colored man would be sure to pay his taxes, and not forego the opportunity, as he had done for some years after being eligible; but he now rejoiced in the right of a citizen, and would always exercise it. The Free Democratic party, he believed, would exert a powerful influence for the slave's emancipation. Correcting himself, he recalled the appellation. Our brethren at the South should not be called *slaves,* but *prisoners of war.*

Rev. J. B. Smith, of Rhode Island, recounted some incidents of his early life, which he said he held in undying remembrance. He alluded especially to the persevering efforts of his father and uncle to burst the chains of slavery. His father took him by the hand, and on leading him from a master's domain, made him swear that he would never be a slave. They were pursued by an armed posse with bloodhounds, and in attempting to ford a river rather than surrender his liberty, his life was sacrificed by a rifle shot from his merciless pursuers. That scene was even now vividly before him. He believed that resistance to tyrants was obedience to God, and hence, to his mind, the only drawback to the matchless Uncle Tom of Mrs. Stowe was his virtue of submission to tyranny—an exhibition of grace which he (the speaker) did not covet.

William J. Watkins eloquently enforced the duty of every colored voter to sustain the Free Soil party, when the most strenuous exertions of pro-slavery men were lavishly contributed to its defeat. It was recreancy in any colored man to be lukewarm during the contest. It had always been his pride to do battle for the right—a duty he learned from William Lloyd Garrison, who, on his liberation from a Baltimore prison, where he had been confined for his devotion to the anti-slavery cause, met him (the speaker), then a boy five years old, at his father's house, and told him to be always an Abolitionist. In the light of that instruction he had ever endeavored to walk, and hoped to be faithful to the end.

Rev. James E. Crawford, of Nantucket, said he appreciated the importance of remembering the slave at the ballot-box, and cited some instances in his anti-slavery experience where it had been signally efficacious. He would not, however, regard politics as an end, but merely as a means for securing a certain good. He would have them ever keep in mind, that moral power was a more exalted and positive lever for promoting the anti-slavery or any other good cause. He expressed, in substance, the sentiment of Mrs. [Lydia Maria] Child, that he who gives his mind to politics sails on a stormy sea, with a giddy pilot. He informed the audience that he dated his conversion to anti-slavery from October 21st, 1835, when, landing from shipboard, and walking up State street, Boston, he suddenly encountered that mob of "gentlemen of property and standing," who, with a rope around Mr. Garrison's neck, were bent upon his destruction. On learning that it was for words and deeds in behalf of the enslaved colored man, his heart and soul at that moment became fully committed to the cause for which our noble advocate was so near sacrificing his life.

Wm. C. Nell remarked, that in behalf of 428,000 nominally free colored Americans, and nearly four millions of chattel slaves in these United States, he could not but commend those who exercised the elective franchise in favor of liberty. Remembering that in Pennsylvania that right had been stolen from her 52,000 colored citizens, and that in several States, falsely termed free, it was restricted to property qualification, and in others absolutely denied, he rejoiced that today it was our untrammeled right, in the old Bay State, and that its influences were felt not only in commingling with other citizens at the polls, but in every sphere of society.

But there were other ways of advancing the anti-slavery cause than at the ballot-box; and he concurred with other speakers in reference to the women, who he regretted were yet denied their right to vote, but their means of appeal to husbands, father and brothers, intelligently directed, were various and all-powerful. The emancipation of 800,000 slaves in the British West Indies was mostly attributable to the women's petition, two miles and a quarter long, which, as declared by members of parliament, could no longer be resisted.

Among our white fellow-citizens participating, Dr. James W. Stone and Hon. Anson Burlingame were most prominent. The latter created much enthusiasm by his eloquent effort. He thought that the heroic, courageous and romantic escape of William and Ellen Craft from slavery had not its analogy in history; and that their refusal to retreat from the city, when hunted by the hounds of power, that others might be inspired by their example, was worthy of everlasting praise. He expressed the hope that when Thomas Sims * should again fly for freedom, thousands of others might find it with him. After submitting an instructive narrative of the power wielded by the slave oligarchy over the tame and subservient North, he besought

* Sims, a 17 year old Negro lad, was seized in Boston in 1851 as a fugitive from Georgia. Despite efforts at his liberation he was returned to his master.

the colored citizens to remember that they too were a power on earth here in Massachusetts.

The first opportunity of hearing Rev. J. W. Loguen, of Syracuse, occurred at the conclusion of these meetings, and it was a treat which will long be remembered. His recital of the Jerry escape, and the reciprocal expressions between him and some of the *lookers-on* at the Shadrach rescue, elicited responsive cheers which made the welkin ring, and constituted a scene which slaveholding Commissioners would have groaned in spirit to witness.

Boston has indeed figured rather conspicuously in the history of fugitive slave cases. August 4th, 1836, two slaves of John B. Morris, of Baltimore, were spirited from the Supreme Court in Boston—mainly through the prowess of a few colored women; the memory of which deed is sacredly cherished and transmitted to posterity. Sheriff Sumner—the honored father of Charles Sumner, whose impulses for freedom are a choice inheritance—was severely censured because he did not prevent their escape; an undertaking which those who were present knew he could not accomplish if he would, and believe he would not if he could. The stirring events connected with the Latimer war, the hunting of William and Ellen Craft, the escape of Shadrach from the lion's den, and the unparalleled excitement of Thomas Sims's arrest, are each so many eloquent themes of appeal for renewed exertions in freedom's cause.

Charles Lenox Remond followed, in one of his felicitous speeches, during which—though careful to note the improving signs of the times—he felt called upon to enumerate various short-comings on the part of residents in Boston, the capital of the old Bay State, who, considering that fact, did not occupy so high an anti-slavery position as the emergency loudly demanded.

Other voices helped to augment the interest of these meetings, but the foregoing must suffice.

The position of the colored citizens of Boston is in many features a peculiar one; for while with truth it can be said that they enjoy certain facilities denied to their brethren in nearly all other sister cities, yet the extremes of equality and proscription meet in their case, as indicated by the pro-slavery School Committee Board. While in every other city and town in the State, colored children have free access to the district schools, here they are debarred that right. To such an extent have the feelings of a large majority been outraged in this matter, that Boston is fast losing many of her intelligent, worthy, aspiring citizens, who are becoming tax payers in adjoining localities, for the sole advantage of equal school rights. These rights are fully appreciated, and with a result which the annual report of the Cambridgeport School Committee of last year testifies to as follows:

"In the Broadway Primary School, a singular fact was noticed; namely, the mixture of four different races amongst the pupils—the Anglo-Saxon, Teutonic, Celtic and African. But by the influence of the teachers and of habit, there exists perfect good feeling among them, and there is no apparent consciousness of a difference of race or condition."

Two independent schools are now supported by parents in the city, rather than send their children to the Smith School, upheld as it is against their long-continued protest. How much longer such a state of things will exist, who can tell?

But though *this* incubus yet bears upon the progress of society, there are many visible signs of improvement in other departments. A few evenings since, it was my privilege to meet a company where happened to be present, one young man upon whom had been conferred the degree of Master of Arts, he having passed through a course of theology, and being now engaged in reading law, with a prospect of an early admssion to the bar of one of the Western States. In conversation with him were two young physicians, one just graduated from Dartmouth College, the other a student at Bowdoin, having perfected his medical education by three years' attendance at the hospitals in Paris. These gratifying features are multiplying much faster than many believe. In various cities and towns may now be found those Home Circles, where mental and moral worth, genius and refinement lend their charms, in giving to the world assurance that, despite accidental differences of complexion, here you behold a man, there a woman, competent to fill any station in civilized society.

It was my intention to have alluded to the vocal and instrumental concerts of the Excelsior Glee Club, and to the elocutionary and musical juvenile exhibitions, under the management of Miss Washington; also, to the interest manifested in a recent course of physiological lectures, volunteered by Dr. Archibald Miles; but enough has been detailed to show that the colored citizens of Boston are improving in some degree, though not so fast as their most sanguine friends could desire.

*The Liberator,* Dec. 10, 1852.

# 132

## THE NATIONAL NEGRO CONVENTION, 1853

The most representative of the pre-Civil War National Negro Conventions was that held in Rochester, New York, July 6–8, 1853. It was attended by one hundred and fourteen delegates and its officers were: President, James W. C. Pennington of New York; Vice-Presidents, William H. Day of Ohio, Amos G. Beman of Connecticut, William C. Nell of Massachusetts, Frederick Douglass of New York, James C. McCrummell and John B. Vashon of Pennsylvania, and John Jones of Illinois; Secretaries, Peter H. Clarke of Ohio, Charles B. Ray and Henry M. Wilson of New York and Charles Reason of Pennsylvania.

Four documents issued by this convention are reproduced here: the call to the convention; the convention's address to the American people—prepared by a committee consisting of Frederick Douglass, J. M. Wagoner, the Rev. A. N. Freeman and George B. Vashon; the plan for a National Council, as presented by Dr. James McCune Smith and amended and adopted by the delegates; and the report on a Manual Labor School submitted by a committee consisting of Charles Reason, George B. Vashon and Dr. Charles H. Langston.

## [a]

### Call for the Convention

Fellow Citizens:—In the exercise of a liberty which we hope, you will not deem unwarrantable, and which is given us, in virtue of our connection and identity with you, the undersigned do hereby, most earnestly and affectionately, invite you, by your appropriate and chosen representatives, to assemble at ROCHESTER, N.Y., on the 6th of July, 1853 under the form and title of a National Convention of the free people of color of the United States.

After due thought and reflection upon the subject, in which has entered a profound desire to serve a common cause, we have arrived at the conclusion, that the time has now fully come when the free colored people from all parts of the United States, should meet together, to confer and deliberate upon their present condition, and upon principles and measures important to their welfare, progress and general improvement.

The aspects of our cause, whether viewed as being hostile or friendly, are alike full of argument in favor of such a Convention. Both reason and feeling have assigned us to a place in the conflict now going on in our land between liberty and equality on the one hand, and slavery and caste on the other—a place which we cannot fail to occupy without branding ourselves as unworthy of our natural post, and recreant to the cause we profess to love. Under the whole heavens, there is not to be found a people which can show better cause for assembling in such a Convention than we.

Our fellow-countrymen now in chains, to whom we are united in a common destiny demand it; and a wise solicitude for our own honor, and that of our children, impels us to this course of action. We have gross and flagrant wrongs against which, if we are men of spirit we are bound to protest. We have high and holy rights, which every instinct of human nature and every sentiment of manly virtue bid us to preserve and protect to the full extent of our ability. We have opportunities to improve—difficulties peculiar to our condition to meet—mistakes and errors of our own to correct—and therefore we need the accumulated knowledge, the united character, and the combined wisdom of our people to make us (under God) sufficient for these things.

The Fugitive Slave Act, the most cruel, unconstitutional and scandalous outrage of modern times—the proscriptive legislation of several States with a view to drive our people from their borders—the exclusion of our children from schools supported by our money—the prohibition of the exercise of the franchise—the exclusion of colored citizens from the jury box—the social barriers erected against our learning trades—the wily and vigorous efforts of the American Colonization Society to employ the arm of government to expel us from our native land—and withal the propitious awakening to the fact of our condition at home and abroad, which has followed the publication of "Uncle Tom's Cabin"—call trumpet-tongued for our union, cooperation and action in the premises.

Convinced that the number amongst us must be small, who so far miscalculate and undervalue the importance of united and intelligent moral action, as to regard it as useless, the undersigned do not feel called upon here for an argument in its favor. Our warfare is not one where force can be employed; we battle against false and hurtful customs, and against the great errors [of] opinion which support such customs. Nations are more and more guided by the enlightened and energetically expressed judgment of mankind. On the subject of our condition and welfare, we may safely and properly appeal to that judgment. Let us meet, then, near the anniversary of this nation's independence, and enforce anew the great principles and self-evident truths which were proclaimed at the beginning of the Republic.

Among the matters which will engage the attention of our Convention will be a proposition to establish a NATIONAL COUNCIL of our people with a view to permanent existence. This subject is one of vast importance, and should only be disposed of in the light of a wise deliberation. There will come before the Convention matters touching the disposition of such funds as our friends abroad, through Mrs. Harriet Beecher Stowe, may appropriate to the cause of our progress and improvement. In a word, the whole field of our interests will be opened to enquiry, investigation and determination.

That this be done successfully, it is desirable that each delegate to the Convention should bring with him an accurate statement as to the number of colored inhabitants in his town or neighborhood—the amount of property owned by them—their business or occupation—the state of education— the extent of their school privileges and the number of children in attendance, and any other information which may serve the great purposes of the Convention.

It is recommended that all colored churches, literary and other societies, banded together for laudable purposes, proceed at once to the appointment of at least one, and not more than three, delegates to attend the National Convention. Such persons as come from towns, villages or counties, where no regular delegate may have been chosen, shall be received and enrolled as honorary members of the Convention.

## [b]

### ADDRESS, of the Colored National Convention to the People of the United States

Fellow Citizens: Met in convention as delegates, representing the Free Colored people of the United States; charged with the responsibility of inquiring into the general condition of our people, and of devising measures which may, with the blessing of God, tend to our mutual improvement and elevation; conscious of entertaining no motives, ideas, or aspirations, but such as are in accordance with truth and justice, and are compatible with the highest good of our country and the world, with a cause as vital and worthy as that for which (nearly eighty years ago) your fathers and our fathers bravely contended, and in which they gloriously triumphed—we deem it proper, on this occasion, as one method of promoting the honorable ends for which we have met, and of discharging our duty to those in whose name we speak, to present the claims of our common cause to your candid, earnest, and favorable consideration.

As an apology for addressing you, fellow-citizens! we cannot announce the discovery of any new principle adapted to ameliorate the condition of mankind. The great truths of moral and political science, upon which we rely and which we press upon your consideration, have been evolved and enunciated by you. We point to your principles, your wisdom, and to your great example for the full justification of our cause this day. That "ALL MEN ARE CREATED EQUAL": that "LIFE, LIBERTY, AND THE PURSUIT OF HAPPINESS" ARE THE RIGHT OF ALL; that "TAXATION AND REPRESENTATION" SHOULD GO TO-GETHER; that GOVERNMENTS ARE TO PROTECT, NOT TO DESTROY, THE RIGHTS OF MANKIND; that THE CONSTITUTION OF THE UNITED STATES WAS FORMED TO ESTABLISH JUSTICE, PROMOTE THE GENERAL WELFARE, AND SECURE THE BLESSING OF LIBERTY TO ALL THE PEOPLE OF THIS COUNTRY; THAT RE-SISTANCE TO TYRANTS IS OBEDIENCE TO GOD—are American principles and maxims, and together they form and constitute the constructive elements of the American government. From this elevated platform, provided by the Republic for us, and for all the children of men, we address you. In doing so, we would have our spirit properly discerned. On this point we would gladly free ourselves and our cause from all misconception. We shall affect no especial timidity, nor can we pretend to any great boldness. We know our poverty and weakness, and your wealth and greatness. Yet we will not attempt to repress the spirit of liberty within us, or to conceal, in any wise, our sense of justice and the dignity of our cause.

We are Americans, and as Americans, we would speak to Americans. We address you not as aliens nor as exiles, humbly asking to be permitted to dwell among you in peace; but we address you as American citizens asserting their rights on their own native soil. Neither do we address you as enemies, (although the recipients of innumerable wrongs;) but in the spirit of patriotic good will. In assembling together as we have done, our object is not to excite pity for ourselves, but to command respect for our cause, and to obtain justice for our people. We are not malefactors imploring mercy; but we trust we are honest men, honestly appealing for righteous judgment, and ready to stand or fall by that judgment. We do not solicit unusual favor, but will be content with rough-handed "fair play." We are neither lame nor blind, that we should seek to throw off the responsibility of our own existence, or to cast ourselves upon public charity for support. We would not lay our burdens upon other men's shoulders; but we do ask, in the name of all that is just and magnanimous among men, to be freed from all the unnatural burdens and impediments with which American customs and American legislation have hindered our progress and improvement. We ask to be disencumbered of the load of popular reproach heaped upon us—for no better cause than that we wear the complexion given us by our God and our Creator.

We ask that in our native land, we shall not be treated as strangers, and worse than strangers.

We ask that, being friends of America, we should not be treated as enemies of America.

We ask that, speaking the same language, and being of the same religion, worshipping the same God, owing our redemption to the same Savior, and learning our duties from the same Bible, we shall not be treated as barbarians.

We ask that, having the same physical, moral, mental, and spiritual wants, common to other members of the human family, we shall also have the same means which are granted and secured to others to supply those wants.

We ask that the doors of the school-houses, the work-shop, the church, the college, shall be thrown open as freely to our children as to the children of other members of the community.

We ask that the American government shall be so administered as that beneath the broad shield of the Constitution, the colored American seaman, shall be secure in his life, liberty and property, in every State in the Union.

We ask that as justice knows no rich, no poor, no black, no white, but, like the government of God, renders alike to every man reward or punishment, according as his works shall be—the white and black may stand upon an equal footing before the laws of the lands.

We ask that (since the right of trial by jury is a safeguard of liberty, against the encroachments of power, only as it is a trial by impartial men, drawn indiscriminately from the country) colored men shall not, in every instance, be tried by white persons; and that colored men shall not be either by custom or enactment excluded from the jury-box.

We ask that (inasmuch as we are, in common with other American citizens, supporters of the State, subject to its laws, interested in its welfare, liable to be called upon to defend it in time of war, contributors to its wealth in time of peace) the complete and unrestricted right of suffrage, which is essential to the dignity even of the white man, be extended to the Free Colored man also.

Whereas, the colored people of the United States have too long been retarded and impeded in the development and improvement of their natural faculties and powers, ever to become dangerous rivals to white men, in the honorable pursuits of life, liberty and happiness; and whereas, the proud Anglo-Saxon can need no arbitrary protection from open and equal competition with any variety of the human family; and whereas, laws have been enacted limiting the aspirations of colored men, as against white men—we respectfully submit that such laws are flagrantly unjust to the man of color, and plainly discreditable to white men; and for these and other reasons, such laws ought to be repealed.

We especially urge that all laws and usages which preclude the enrollment of colored men in the militia, and prohibit their bearing arms in the navy, disallow their rising, agreeable to their merits and attainments—are unconstitutional—the constitution knowing no color—are anti-Democratic, since Democracy respects men as equals—are unmagnanimous, since such laws are made by the many, against the few, and by the strong against the weak.

We ask that all those cruel and oppressive laws, whether enacted at the South or the North, which aim at the expatriation of the free people of color, shall be stamped with national reprobation, denounced as contrary to the humanity of the American people, and as an outrage upon the Christianity and civilization of the nineteenth century.

We ask that the right of pre-emption, enjoyed by all white settlers upon the public lands, shall also be enjoyed by colored settlers; and that the word "*white*" be struck from the pre-emption act. We ask that no appropriations whatever, state or national, shall be granted to the colonization scheme; and we would have our right to leave or to remain in the United States placed above legislative interference.

We ask that the Fugitive Slave Law of 1850, that legislative monster of modern times, by whose atrocious provisions the writ "of habeas corpus," the "right of trial by jury," have been virtually abolished, shall be repealed.

We ask, that the law of 1793 be so construed as to apply only to apprentices, and others really owing service or labor; and not to slaves, who can *owe* nothing. Finally, we ask that slavery in the United States shall be immediately, unconditionally, and forever abolished.

To accomplish these just and reasonable ends, we solemnly pledge ourselves to God, to each other, to our country, and to the world, to use all and every means consistent with the just rights of our fellow men, and with the precepts of Christianity.

We shall speak, write and publish, organize and combine to accomplish them.

We shall invoke the aid of the pulpit and the press to gain them.

We shall appeal to the church and to the government to gain them.

We shall vote, and expend our money to gain them.

We shall send eloquent men of our own condition to plead our cause before the people.

We shall invite the co-operation of good men in this country and throughout the world—and above all, we shall look to God, the Father and Creator of all men, for wisdom to direct us and strength to support us in the holy cause to which we this day solemnly pledge ourselves.

Such, fellow-citizens are our aims, ends, aspirations and determinations. We place them before you, with the earnest hope, that upon further investigation, they will meet your cordial and active approval.

And yet, again, we would free ourselves from the charge of unreasonableness and self-sufficiency.

In numbers we are few and feeble; but in the goodness of our cause, in the rectitude of our motives, and in the abundance of argument on our side, we are many and strong.

We count our friends in the heavens above, in the earth beneath, among good men and holy angels. The subtle and mysterious cords of human sympathy have connected us with philanthropic hearts throughout the civilized world. The number in our own land who already recognize the injustice of our cause, and are laboring to promote it, is great and increasing.

It is also a source of encouragement, that the genuine American, brave and independent himself, will respect bravery and independence in others. He spurns servility and meanness, whether they be manifested by nations or by individuals. We submit, therefore, that there is neither necessity for, nor disposition on our part to assume a tone of excessive humility. While we would be respectful, we must address you as men, as citizens, as brothers, as dwellers in a common country, equally interested with you for its welfare, its honor and for its prosperity.

To be still more explicit: we would, first of all, be understood to range ourselves no lower among our fellow-countrymen than is implied in the high appellation of *"citizen."*

Notwithstanding the impositions and deprivations which have fettered us—notwithstanding the disabilities and liabilities, pending and impending—notwithstanding the cunning, cruel and scandalous efforts to blot out that right, we declare that we are, and of right we ought to be *American citizens*. We claim this right, and we claim all the rights and privileges, and duties which, properly, attach to it.

It may, and it will, probably, be disputed that we are citizens. We may, and probably shall be denounced for this declaration, as making an inconsiderate, impertinent and absurd claim to citizenship; but a very little reflection will vindicate the position we have assumed, from so unfavorable a judgement. Justice is never inconsiderate; truth is never impertinent; right is never absurd. If the claim we set up be just, true and right, it will not be deemed improper or ridiculous in us to declare it. Nor is it disrespectful to our fellow-citizens, who repudiate the aristocratic notions of the old world that we range ourselves with them in respect to all the rights and prerogatives belonging to American citizens. Indeed, we believe, when you have duly considered this subject, you will commend us for the mildness and modesty with which we have taken our ground.

By birth, we are American citizens; by the principles of the Declaration of Independence, we are American citizens; within the meaning of the United States Constitution, we are American Citizens; by the facts of history, and the admissions of American statesmen, we are American citizens; by the hardships and trials endured; by the courage and fidelity displayed by our ancestors in defending the liberties and in achieving the independence of our land, we are American citizens. In proof of the justice of this primary claim, we might cite numerous authorities, facts and testimonies,—a few only must suffice . . .* We hope you will now permit us to address you in the plainness of speech becoming the dignity of American citizens.

Fellow-citizens, we have had, and still have, great wrongs of which to complain. A heavy and cruel hand has been laid on us.

As a people, we feel ourselves to be not only deeply injured, but grossly

* Here appear four pages of historical evidence of the citizenship of free Negroes following so closely the material in William Yates' pamphlet, *Rights of Colored Men to Suffrage, Citizenship and Trial by Jury* (Philadelphia, 1838), as to make it certain that the committee was familiar with this valuable work.

misunderstood. Our white fellow-countrymen do not know us. They are strangers to our character, ignorant of our capacity, oblivious of our history and progress, and are misinformed as to the principles and ideas that control and guide us as a people. The great mass of American citizens estimate us as being a characterless and purposeless people; and hence we hold up our heads, if at all, against the withering influence of a nation's scorn and contempt.

It will not be surprising that we are so misunderstood and misused when the motives for misrepresenting us and for degrading us are duly considered. Indeed, it will seem strange, upon such consideration, (and in view of the ten thousand channels through which malign feelings find utterance and influence) that we have not even fallen lower in public estimation than we have done. For, with the single exception of the Jews, under the whole heavens, there is not to be found a people pursued with a more relentless prejudice and persecution, than are the Free Colored people of the United States.

Without pretending to have exerted ourselves as we ought, in view of an intelligent understanding of our interest, to avert from us the unfavorable opinions and unfriendly action of the American people, we feel that the imputations cast upon us, for our want of intelligence, morality and exalted character, may be mainly accounted for by the injustice we have received at your hands. What stone has been left unturned to degrade us? What hand has refused to fan the flame of popular prejudice against us? What American artist has not caricatured us? What wit has not laughed at us in our wretchedness? What songster has not made merry over our depressed spirits? What press has not ridiculed and contemned us? What pulpit has withheld from our devoted heads its angry lightning or its sanctimonious hate? Few, few, very few; and that we have borne up with it all—that we have tried to be wise, though denounced by all to be fools—that we have tried to be upright, when all around us have esteemed us as knaves—that we have striven to be gentlemen, although all around us have been teaching us its impossibility—that we have remained here, when all our neighbors have advised us to leave, proves that we possess qualities of head and heart such as cannot but be commended by impartial men. It is believed that no other nation on the globe could have made more progress in the midst of such an universal and stringent disparagement. It would humble the proudest, crush the energies of the strongest, and retard the progress of the swiftest. In view of our circumstances, we can, without boasting, thank God, and take courage, having placed ourselves where we may fairly challenge comparison with more highly favored men.

Among the colored people we can point, with pride and hope, to men of education and refinement, who have become such, despite of the most un-favorable influences, we can point to mechanics, farmers, merchants, teach-ers, ministers, doctors, lawyers, editors, and authors against whose progress the concentrated energies of American prejudice have proved quite un-availing. Now, what is the motive for ignoring and discouraging our im-provement in this country? The answer is ready. The intelligent and upright free man of color is an unanswerable argument in favor of liberty, and a killing condemnation of American slavery. It is easily seen that, in propor-tion to the progress of the free man of color in knowledge, temperance, industry, and righteousness, in just that proportion will he endanger the stability of slavery; hence, all the powers of slavery are exerted to prevent the elevation of the free people of color.

The force of fifteen hundred million dollars is arrayed against us; hence, the press, the pulpit, and the platform, against all the natural promptings of uncontaminated manhood, point their deadly missiles of ridicule, scorn and contempt at us; and bid us, on pain of being pierced through and through, to remain in our degradation.

Let the same amount of money be employed against the interest of any other class of persons, however favored by nature they may be, the result could scarcely be different from that seen in our own case. Such a people would be regarded with aversion; the money-ruled multitude would heap contumely upon them, and money-ruled institutions would proscribe them. Besides this money consideration, fellow-citizens, an explanation of the erroneous opinions prevalent concerning us is furnished in the fact, less creditable to human nature, that men are apt to hate most those whom they injure most. Having despised us, it is not strange that Americans should seek to render us despicable; having enslaved us, it is natural that they should strive to prove us unfit for freedom; having denounced us as in-dolent, it is not strange that they should cripple our enterprise; having as-sumed our inferiority, it would be extraordinary if they sought to surround us with circumstances which would serve to make us direct contradictions to their assumption.

In conclusion, fellow-citizens, while conscious of the immense disad-vantages which beset our pathway, and fully appreciating our own weakness, we are encouraged to persevere in efforts adapted to our improvement, by a firm reliance upon God, and a settled conviction, as immovable as the ever-lasting hills, that all the truths in the whole universe of God are allied to our cause.

## [c]

### *Plan for National Council*

For the purpose of improving the character, developing the intelligence, maintaining the rights, and organizing a Union of the Colored People of the Free States, the National Convention does hereby ordain and institute the "NATIONAL COUNCIL OF THE COLORED PEOPLE."

*Article 1*—The Council shall consist of two members from each State, represented in this Convention, to be elected by this Convention, and two other members from each State to be elected as follows: On the 15th day of November next, and biennially thereafter, there shall be held in each State, a Poll, at which each colored inhabitant * may vote who pays ten cents as a poll-tax; and each State shall elect, at such election, delegates to State Councils, twenty in number from each State, at large. The election to be held in such places and under such conditions as the public meetings in such localities may determine. The members of the National Council in each State shall receive, canvass and declare the result of such vote. The State Council thus elected, shall meet to select a location in the State designated by the National Council, to erect buildings, appoint or dismiss instructors in the literary or mechanical branches. There shall be a farm attached to the School. . . . .

*Article 4*—The Committee on Protective Union, shall institute a Protective Union for the purchase and sale of articles of domestic consumption, and shall unite and aid in the formation of branches auxiliary to their own.

*Article 5*—The Committee on Business Relations, shall establish an office, in which they shall keep a registry of colored mechanics, artizans and business men throughout the Union. They shall keep a registry of all persons willing to employ colored men in business, to teach colored boys mechanical trades, liberal and scientific professions, and farming; and, also, a registry of colored men and youth seeking employment or instruction. They also shall report upon any avenues of business or trade which they deem inviting to colored capital, skill or labor. Their reports and advertisements to be in papers of the widest circulation. They shall receive for sale or exhibition, products of the skill and labor of colored people.

*Article 6*—The Committee on Publication shall collect all facts, statistics and statements, all laws and historical records and biographies of the Colored People, and all books by colored authors. They shall have for the safe keeping of these documents, a Library, with a Reading Room and

* Note that this does not say "male."

Museum. The Committee shall also publish replies to any assaults, worthy of note, made upon the character or condition of the Colored People.

*Article 7*—Each Committee shall have absolute control over its special department; shall make its own by-laws, and in case of any vacancy occurring, shall fill up the same forthwith, subject to the confirmation of the Council. Each Committee shall meet at least once a month or as often as possible; shall keep a minute of its proceedings, executive and financial, and shall submit a full statement of the same, with the accounts audited, at every regular meeting of the National Council.

*Article 8*—The National Council shall meet at least once in six months, to receive the reports of the Committees, and to consider any new plan for the general good, for which it shall have power, at its option, to appoint a new Committee, and shall be empowered to receive and appropriate donations for the carrying out of the objects of the same. At all such meetings, eleven members shall constitute a quorum. In case any Committee neglect or refuse to send in its report, according to article 8th, then the Council shall have power to enter the bureau, examine the books and papers of such Committee; and in case the Committee shall persist in its refusal or neglect, then the Council shall declare their offices vacant, and appoint others in their stead.

*Article 9*—In all cases of the meetings of the National Council, or the Committees, the travelling expenses (if any) of the members shall be paid out of their respective funds.

*Article 10*—The Council shall immediately establish a bureau in the place of its meeting; and the same rooms shall, as far as possible, be used by the several Committees for their various purposes. The Council shall have a clerk, at a moderate salary, who shall keep a record of their transactions, and prepare a condensed report of the Committees for publication; and also a registry of the friends of the cause.

*Article 11*—The expenses of the Council shall be defrayed by the fees of membership of sub-societies or Councils, to be organized throughout the States. The membership fee shall be one cent per week.

*Article 12*—A member of the Council shall be a member of only one of the Committees thereof.

*Article 13*—All officers holding funds, shall give security in double the amount likely to be in their hands. This security to be given to the three first officers of the Council.

*Article 14*—The Council shall have power to make such By-Laws as are necessary for their proper government.

## [d]

### *Manual Labor School*

The aim and the end of a right culture, is primarily to develop power, and to turn that power into a proper channel. Educational Institutions ought therefore to be so modeled and so conducted as to draw out thought, incite useful inquiry, and give such aid and strength to the individual as will enable him to be something in the world, in addition to the mere scholar. Every person is here not merely to enjoy, but to work; and schools are only valuable in their teachings, as they assist in making both thinker and worker. They may saturate men with the learning of every age—yet, except they strive to make them something more than literary flowers, they sin greatly against the individual and humanity also. The hungry world asks for grain, and those growths that give nutriment. Not by floral beauty is the physical being builded up. Not by mere word study do the races grow intellectually strong. Not by eloquent abstract preaching, do the nations prove Christianity. The elements of truth, the principles of industrial advancement, of national greatness, that lie in questionable shapes amid the knowledge of the schools, must be separated from the useless materials that surround them; and made as chyle to the human body, the givers of nutriment, the restorers of expended energy.

And as in the human body, the richness of the digested food goes to make up bone, and muscle, and flesh, and the various tissues of vessels of the system—in like manner schools ought so to be fashioned, as to deposit here and there on the surface of society, artizan and merchant, mechanic and farmer, linguist and mathematician—mental power in every phase, and practical science in as many as may be. The truth of this view is virtually acknowledged in part already. Where men know beforehand what kind of knowledge their duties in life will require, they avail themselves of Institutions whose course of study is specific and well digested. Hence exist our Law-Schools, and Military Academies, and Medical Colleges. And these are necessary, even amid a class of people whose position enables them to make the most of a *general* course of study, by the application of some of the specialties of such course, to any avocation, that, in after life, they may choose to pursue. When *we* are called upon to consider the subject of Education with reference to ourselves, and to ask what kind of an Institution would best befit *us*, the answer comes in the light of the announced doctrine, namely, one that would develop *power;* and that kind of power most essential to our elevation. If after submitting to a general system of instruction, according to the provisions of the colleges of the land, *we* can add the store of knowledge gained to any pursuit in life *we* please, as so much starting capital, then we might not need to ask the establishing of Institutions different from those already erected. But this is not the case. We have, indeed, a few literary colleges accessible to those of us who can pay; two Manual Labor Colleges with the system partially carried out; besides an academy of the same kind established in Southern Ohio.

Between these two varieties of schools, there need be no hesitation in deciding as to which is best adapted to our special wants. Under any circumstance, Manual Labor Establishments commend themselves to the patronage of all classes. The long entertained beliefs that mental effort may be made and continued without any reference to physical exercise, are rapidly passing away. And with them, also, those more injurious and unfriendly views of true gentility and scholarship, that hitherto have held labor in contempt. Literature has too long kept itself aloof from the furrowed field, and from the dust and bustle of the work-shop. The pale, sickly brow and emaciated form have been falsely shown to the world as the ripeness of mental discipline; and sun-burnt and brawny muscular arms, have been among the majority of students synonymous with dulness of parts, and ignorant vulgarity. Thanks, however, to true views of the dignity of human nature, and an appreciation of the correct laws of physical development; labor has received the anointing of the highest refinement, and healthy frames are proven to be the best accompaniment to high intellectual power.

Moreover, with regard to ourselves, a consideration of our position in this country, teaches us that our inheritance is one that can only be ameliorated by the combination of practical art, with literary preparation. Hitherto our educated youth have found no corresponding channel to their academic equipment, and so they have failed to make their mark on society and the age. The work-shops, as a general thing, are closed to them, while at the same time they are reproached for lack of inventive or industrial talent. We know that we cannot form an equally useful part of any people without the ability to contribute our full share to the wealth, activity, social comforts, and progress of such people. If, then, the necessary education to fit us to share in these responsibilities, cannot be generally had, by reason of the prejudices of the country, where best they can be taught, namely in the work-shops and counting-houses, and the other varied establishments of the land, that have to do with the machinery of activities carried on around us; we must needs consider the importance of making our Literary Institutions contribute by a change of form to filling up this want in our midst.

The agricultural life, standing pre-eminent, and looming in importance above all others, would demand a prominent place among the internal arrangements of such a school. Farming, as a scientific system, ought to be a part of the course of every scholar, and especially of that class of students whose highest interests would be benefited by leaving the cities, for the freer and no less noble life in the country. No professorship in any college can claim more on the score of usefulness than that of agriculture. In none of the Institutions thus far open to us, has labor in this department been at all regularized on scientific principles. Literary preparation has absorbed most of the attention of students, because of the order and beauty infused into that phase of college life. The department of labor has ever remained crude and unseemly-subordinate in position and outline to the other, and, therefore unable to provide that extensive field for industry, as to warrant the title assumed by them of Manual Labor Institutions. We make no complaint against the incompleteness of any of the existing schools, in order to detract from their usefulness in other ways. We only believe it desirable, that a more thorough plan be established that will combine the literary course of the schools, scientific agricultural knowledge, theoretic mechanics and engineering, and, what is a feature we hope to see engrafted on the plan, a series of work-shops under systematic and skilful instruction. Not simply as a means of furnishing poor students with the facilities of continuing under instruction, but to remedy also as far as may be the disadvantages under which we labor in acquiring a knowledge of the mechanical arts.

To this end we advise the maturing of a plan by some other suitable Committee for erecting in some locality, central as to population, a school of a high intellectual grade, having incorporated an Agricultural Professorship, or an equivalent thereto, a professorship to superintend the practical application of mathematics and natural philosophy to surveying, mechanics and engineering, the following branches of industry: general smithing, turning, wheel-wrighting and cabinet-making; and a general workshop in which may be combined such application of skill in wood, iron, and other material as to produce a variety of saleable articles,* with suitable buildings and machinery for producing the same. These superintended by competent workmen, under pay precisely as other teachers, would give students a foundation for after self-support in life, and break down the distinctions that never ought to exist between the study and the work-shop. The above industrial pursuits are named, not because others more desirable perhaps, or more difficult to secure, might not have had a place given them in this imperfect report; but, because it seemed wise to choose some

---

* A work-shop of this kind is, we believe, now in operation in Ohio, connected with the State Penitentiary. It produces stirrups, buckles, harness frames, saw-handles, &c, &c. [Footnote in original.]

which are primary to most others in general usefulness, and at the same time, such as whose products have an extensive marketable demand. In establishing work-shops, it must be remembered that the introducing of any large part of the very useful or lucrative branches is an utter impossibility. All that can be aimed at in the beginning, is to elevate labor to its own true standard—vindicate the laws of physical health, and at the same time, as a repaying benefit, make the work done as intrinsic and *profitable*, a part of education as a proficiency in Latin, mathematics or medicine.

As to the *means* by which such an Institution may be erected and carried on, we advise the issuing of joint stock under proper Directors, to the amount of $50,000 in shares of $10 each, or a less number of a larger amount, if considered advisable. The Committee are of opinion that $50,000 used in the purchase of land and the erecting and fitting up of buildings, will be fully enough, to warrant the beginning of a thorough Manual Labor School, on the plan suggested.

The sale of scholarships, at judicious rates, and the contributions of the liberal and the philanthropic, ought to give an additional $100,000 as an endowment, which sum properly invested, would be a guarantee, that the liabilities and expense of the Institution would be faithfully met.

The Department of Industry for Females, the Committee cannot, in the short time given them, intelligently settle upon, except in outline. We are of opinion, that looms could be erected for the weaving of carriage and other trimmings; for bindings of various kinds; that the straw hat business in some of its branches, paper box making, and similar occupations, might from time to time be connected.

The shareholders, if such a plan be approved, would compose the college association; and would have a right to appoint the Trustees of the School, said Trustees being citizens of the State wherein such Institution shall be located.

Such is the rough outline of a plan which we think would be, in judicious hands, and so modified as to conform to the proper school laws, feasible and fraught with unbounding good.

In the past, the misfortune has been that our knowledge has been much distributed. We have had educated *heads* in one large division among us, and educated *hands* in another. We do not concede in this remark, that the mind worker is not a benefactor or a creator. The inventing, the directing intellect produces the demand for mechanical labor; but we believe, that, the instances of the marriage, so to speak, of thoroughly educated mind with manual labor, are lamentably rare among us. All over the land, our earnest youth have gone asking to be cared for by the work-shops of the country, but no acknowledgement has been made of their human relationships; their mental, and bodily fitness, have had the same contumely heaped upon them, as is received by those unfortunate beings who in social life bear upon their persons the brand of illegitimacy. As a consequence, we have grown up too large an extent—mere scholars on one side and muscular giants on the other. We would equalize these discrepancies. We would produce a harmonious development of character. In the sweat of their brows, we would have every mother dedicate her child to the cause of freedom; and then, in the breeze wafted over the newly plowed field, there will come encouragement and hope; and the ringing blows of the anvil and the axe, and the keen cutting edge of the chisel and the plane, will symbolize on the one hand human excellence is rough hewn by self-exertion, and on the other, fashioned into models of beauty by reflection and discipline.

Let us educate our youth in such wise, as shall give them means of success, adapted to their struggling condition; and ere long following the enterprise of the age, we may hope to see them filling everywhere positions of responsibility and trust, and, gliding on the triple tide of wealth, intelligence and virtue, reach eventually, to a sure resting place of distinction and happiness.

*Proceedings of the Colored National Convention, held in Rochester, July 6th, 7th, and 8th, 1853* (Rochester, 1853, printed at office of Frederick Douglass' paper).

# 133

# NEGROES SEEK TO ENTER A STATE MILITIA, 1853

The Army of the United States banned Negroes as soldiers from the end of the War of 1812 to the middle years of the Civil War. Northern Negroes during this period formed private military companies and made persistent efforts to gain admission into the state militias. Indicative of these efforts is a petition, dated August 1, 1853, signed by William C. Nell and many other Negroes, which was presented to the Massachusetts Constitutional Convention.

*To the Convention for revising and amending the Constitution of Massachusetts:*—

The undersigned, acknowledged citizens of this Commonwealth, (notwithstanding their complexional differences) and therefore citizens of the United States, with the feeling and spirit becoming freemen, and with the deepest solicitude, respectfully submit—

That having petitioned your honorable body for such a modification of the laws as that no able-bodied male citizen shall be forbidden or prevented from serving, or holding office or commission, in the militia, on account of his color, their petition was duly referred and considered, but not granted, and therefore they are still a proscribed and injured class. The reason assigned for the rejection of their request, in the report submitted by the Committee to whom the subject was referred, was, "that this Convention cannot incorporate into the Constitution of Massachusetts, any provision which shall conflict with the laws of the United States." In the course of the debate that ensued upon this report, the Attorney General of Massachusetts said—"You can raise no colored regiment, or part of a regiment, that shall be of the militia of the United States—none whatever . . .

"It is certain that, if they were to go upon parade, and to *win Bunker Hills*, yet they never can be part of the militia of the United States . . . Nay, more—he did not see how he could do anything for *this colored race,* by putting them in one of the high places of the Commonwealth, with weapons in their hands, and allow our glorious banner to throw around them all the pomp and parade and condition of war; *the color cleaves to them there,* and on parade is only the more conspicuous."

Another distinguished member of the Convention said, "If Massachusetts should send a colored commander-in-chief at the head of her Militia, the United States *would not recognize his authority, and would at once supersede him.*"

Your petitioners feel bound to protest, (in behalf of the colored citizens of Massachusetts) that all such opinions and declarations constitute—

(1) A denial of their quality as citizens of this Commonwealth, and are clearly at variance with the Constitution of this State, which knows nothing of the complexion of the people, and which asserts (Article I) that "all men are born free and EQUAL, and have certain natural, essential and inalienable rights: among which may be reckoned the right of enjoying and DEFENDING their lives and liberties; that of acquiring, possessing and protecting property; in fine, that of seeking and obtaining their safety and happiness." It would be absurd to say, that the General Government, or that Congress, has the constitutional right to declare, if it think proper, that the white citizen of Massachusetts shall not be enrolled in the militia of the country; and it is not to be supposed, for a moment, that, if such proscriptive edict were to be issued, it would be tamely submitted to. It is, surely, just as great an absurdity, just as glaring an insult, to assume that colored citizens may be legally excluded from the national militia.

(2) In the Constitution of the United States, not a sentence or a syllable can be found, recognizing any distinctions among the citizens of the States, collectively or individually, but they are all placed on the same equality. Article IV, Section 2d, declares—"The citizens of each State shall be entitled to all the privileges and immunities of citizens in the several States."

It is not possible to make a more unequivocable recognition of the equality of all citizens; and, therefore, whatever contravenes or denies it, in the shape of legislation, is manifestly unconstitutional. Whatever may have been the compromises of the Constitution, in regard to those held in bondage as chattel slaves, none were ever made, or proposed, respecting the rights and liberties of citizens.

(3) It is true, that, by the United States Constitution, Congress is empowered "to provide for organizing, arming and disciplining the militia"; it is also true, that Congress, in "organizing" the militia, has authorized none but "white" citizens to be enrolled therein; nevertheless, it is not less true, that the law of Congress, making this unnatural distinction, is, in this particular, unconstitutional, and therefore ought to exert no controlling force over the legislation of any of the States. To organize the militia of the country is one thing; to dishonor and outrage a portion of the citizens, on any ground, is a very different thing. To do the former, Congress is clothed with ample constitutional authority; to accomplish the latter, it has no power to legislate, and resort must be had, and has been had, to usurpation and tyranny.

Your petitioners, therefore, earnestly entreat the Convention, by every consideration of justice and righteousness, not to adjourn without asserting and vindicating the entire fitness and equal right of the colored citizens of Massachusetts to be enrolled in the national militia; or, if this be not granted, then they respectfully ask that this protest may be placed on the records of the Convention, and published with the official proceedings, that the stigma may not rest upon their memories, of having tamely acquiesced in a proscription, equally at war with the American Constitution, the Massachusetts Bill of Rights, and the claims of human nature.

*The Liberator*, August 5, 1853.


## 134

# A LOCAL BATTLE AGAINST JIM CROW, 1853

An incident in the centuries-long struggle against Jim Crow is told by Robert Purvis in a letter, dated November 4, 1853, addressed to the Philadelphia tax collector. Mr. Purvis is protesting against the all-white character of the city's public school system.


You called yesterday for the tax upon my property in this Township, which I shall pay, excepting the "School Tax." I object to the payment of this tax, on the ground that my rights as a citizen, and my feelings as a man and a parent, have been grossly outraged in depriving me, in violation of law and justice, of the benefits of the school system which this tax was designed to sustain. I am perfectly aware that all that makes up the character and worth of the citizens of this township look upon the proscription and exclusion of my children from the Public School as illegal, and an unjustifiable usurpation of my right. I have borne this outrage ever since the innovation upon the usual practice of admitting *all* the children of the Township into the Public Schools, and at considerable expense, have been obliged to obtain the services of private teachers to instruct my children, while my school tax is greater, with a single exception, than that of any other citizen of the township. It is true, (and the outrage is made but the more glaring and insulting,) I was informed by a *pious Quaker* director, with a sanctifying grace, imparting, doubtless, an unctuous glow to his *saintly* prejudices, that a school in the village of Mechanicsville was appropriated for *"thine."* The miserable shanty, with all its appurtenances, on the very line of the township, to which this *benighted* follower of George Fox alluded, is, as you know, the most flimsy and ridiculous sham which any tool of a skin-hating aristocracy could have resorted to, to cover or protect his servility. To submit by voluntary payment of the demand is too great an outrage upon nature, and, with a spirit, thank God, unshackled by this, or any other wanton and cowardly act, I shall resist this tax, which, before the unjust exclusion, had always afforded me the highest gratification in paying. With no other than the best feeling towards yourself, I am forced to this unpleasant position, in vindication of my rights and personal dignity against an encroachment upon them as contemptibly mean as it is infamously despotic.

*Pennsylvania Freeman,* n.d., in *The Liberator,* December 16, 1853.

## 135

## THE SOUTHERN END OF THE UNDERGROUND RAILROAD, 1853

Late in 1853 a fugitive slave, J. H. Hill, sent a letter to William Still, Underground Railroad leader in Philadelphia, containing hard-to-get information on the operation of this railroad at its point of origin.

Nine months I was trying to get away. I was secreted for a long time in a kitchen of a merchant near the corner of Franklyn and 7th streets, at Richmond, where I was well taken care of, by a lady friend of my mother. When I got Tired of staying in that place, I wrote myself a pass to pass myself to

Petersburg, here I stopped with a very prominent Colored person, who was a friend to Freedom—stayed here until two white friends told other friends if I was in the city to tell me to go at once, and stand not upon the order of going, because they had heard a plot. I wrote a pass, started for Richmond, Reached Manchester, got off the Cars walked into Richmond, once more got back into the same old Den, Stayed here from the 16th of Aug. to 12th Sept. [1853]. On the 11th of Sept. 8 o'clock P.M. a message came to me that there had been a State Room taken on the steamer City of Richmond for my benefit, and I assured the party that it would be occupied if God be willing. Before 10 o'clock the next morning, on the 12th, a beautiful Sept. day, I arose early, wrote my pass for Norfolk left my old Den with a many a good bye, turned out the back way to 7th St., thence to Main, down Main behind 4 night waich to old Rockett's and after about 20 minutes of delay I succeed in Reaching the State Room. My Conductor was very much Excited, but I felt as Composed as I do at this moment, for I had started from my Den that morning for Liberty or for Death providing myself with a Brace of Pistels.

William Still, *Underground Railroad* . . . , pp. 191–92.

136

AN ARGUMENT FOR INDUSTRIAL EDUCATION,
1854

The idea of industrial education was broached by leading Negroes very frequently in the nineteenth century. A cogent argument in its favor was offered by a Negro teacher, Charles Reason, in 1854.

The Abolitionist of to-day is the Iconoclast of the age, and his mission is to break the idolatrous images set up by a hypocritical Church, a Sham Democracy, or a corrupt public sentiment, and to substitute in their stead the simple and beautiful doctrine of a common brotherhood. He would elevate every creature by abolishing the hinderances and checks imposed upon him, whether these be legal or social—and in proportion as such grievances are invidious and severe, in such measure does he place himself in the front rank of the battle, to wage his emancipating war.

Therefore it is that the Abolitionist has come to be considered the especial friend of the Negro, since *he*, of all others, has been made to drink deep from the cup of oppression.

The free-colored man at the North, for his bond-brother as for himself, has trusted hopefully in the increasing public sentiment, which, in the multiplication of these friends, has made his future prospect brighter. And, to-day, while he is making a noble struggle to vindicate the claims of his entire class, depending mainly for the accomplishment of that end on his own exertions, he passes in review the devotion and sacrifices made in his behalf: gratitude is in his heart, and thanks fall from his lips. But, in one department of reformatory exertion he feels that he has been neglected. He has seen his pledged allies throw themselves into the hottest of the battle, to fight for the Abolition of Capital Punishment—for the Prohibition of the Liquor Traffic—for the Rights of Women, and similar reforms,—but he has failed to see a corresponding earnestness, according to the influence of Abolitionists in the business world, in opening the avenues of industrial labor to the proscribed youth of the land. This work, therefore, is evidently left for himself to do. And he has laid his powers to the task. The record of his conclusions was given at Rochester, in July [1853], and has become already a part of history.*

Though shut out from the workshops of the country, he is determined to make self-provision, so as to triumph over the spirit of caste that would keep him degraded. The utility of the Industrial Institution he would erect, must, he believes, commend itself to Abolitionists. But not only to them. The verdict of less liberal minds has been given already in its favor. The usefulness, the self-respect and self-dependence,—the combination of intelligence and handicraft,—the accumulation of the materials of wealth, all referable to such an Institution, present fair claims to the assistance of the entire American people.

Whenever emancipation shall take place, immediate though it be, the subjects of it, like many who now make up the so-called free population, will be in what Geologists call, the "Transition State." The prejudice now felt against them for bearing on their persons the brand of slaves, cannot die out immediately. Severe trials will still be their portion—the curse of a "taunted race" must be expiated by almost miraculous proofs of advancement; and some of these miracles must be antecedent to the great day of Jubilee. To fight the battle on the bare ground of abstract principles, will fail to give us complete victory. The subterfuges of pro-slavery selfishness must *now* be dragged to light, and the last weak argument—that the Negro can never contribute anything to advance the national character, "nailed to the counter as base coin." To the conquering of the difficulties heaped up in the path of his industry, the free-colored man of the North has pledged himself. Already he sees, springing into growth, from out his foster *work-school*, intelligent young laborers, competent to enrich the

* See Document Number 132.

world with necessary products—industrious citizens, contributing their proportion to aid on the advancing civilization of the country—self-providing artizans vindicating their people from the never-ceasing charge of a fitness for servile positions.

Abolitionists ought to consider it a legitimate part of their great work, to aid in such an enterprise—to abolish not only chattel slavery, but that other kind of slavery, which, for generation after generation, dooms an oppressed people to a condition of dependence and pauperism. Such an Institution would be a shining mark, in even this enlightened age; and every man and woman, equipped by its discipline to do good battle in the arena of active life, would be, next to the emancipated bondman, the most desirable *"Autograph for Freedom."*

Julia Griffiths, ed., *Autographs for Freedom* [vol. II] (Auburn, Rochester, 1854), pp. 12–15.

## 137

## A NEGRO EMIGRATION CONVENTION, 1854

Within the Abolitionist movement a major point at issue, as we have seen, was whether or not the constitution of the United States was inherently and irrevocably a pro-slavery document. This question divided Negroes as well as whites, and those Negroes who considered the document as a "covenant with the devil" tended to look with favor upon plans of voluntary emigration and colonization.

The outstanding convention of those holding this viewpoint occurred in Cleveland, Ohio, August 24–26, 1854. One hundred and two delegates attended, led by two distinguished churchmen, William C. Munroe of Michigan (president of the Convention), and William Paul Quinn of Indiana (its first vice-president) and by Dr. Martin R. Delany. Notable, too, were several women delegates, including the convention's second vice-president, Mrs. Mary E. Bibb of Canada.

Printed below are the platform of the convention and extracts from a speech delivered at the convention by H. Ford Douglass, a free Negro originally from Louisiana (no relation to Frederick Douglass). Noteworthy in this convention was the expression of a feeling of and a yearning for Negro nationality.

### [a]

*Platform: or Declaration of Sentiments of the Cleveland Convention*
Whereas, for years the Colored People of the United States have been looking, hoping and waiting in expectation of realizing the blessings of Civil Liberty; and Whereas, during this long, tedious and anxious period, they have been depending upon their white fellow-countrymen to effect for them

this desirable end but instead of which they have met with disappointment, discouragement and degradation; and Whereas, no people can ever attain to the elevated position of freemen, who are totally or partially ignorant of the constituent elements of Political Liberty; and

Whereas, in the multitude of Conventions heretofore held by our fathers and contemporaries among the colored people of the United States, no such principles as a basis have ever been adduced or demonstrated to us as a guide for action; and

Whereas, no people can maintain their freedom without an interested motive and a union of sentiment, as a rule of action and nucleus to hold them together; and

Whereas, all of the Conventions heretofore held by the whites in this country, of whatever political pretensions—whether Democrat, Whig, or Free Democracy—all have thrown themselves upon the declaration: "To sustain the Constitution as our forefathers *understood* it, and the *Union as they formed it;*" all of which plainly and boldly imply, unrestricted liberty to the whites, and the right to hold the blacks in slavery and degradation.

Therefore, as the Declaration of Sentiments and Platform of the Convention, be it—

*Resolved,*

1.—That we acknowledge the natural equality of the Human Race.

2.—That man is by nature free, and cannot be enslaved, except by injustice and oppression.

3.—That the right to breathe the Air and *use* the Soil on which the Creator has placed us, is co-inherent with the birth of man, and coeval with his existence; consequently, whatever interferes with this sacred inheritance, is the joint ally of Slavery, and at war against the just decree of Heaven. Hence, man cannot be independent without *possessing* the land on which he resides.

4.—That whatever interferes with the natural rights of man, should meet from him with adequate resistance.

5.—That, under no circumstances, let the consequences be as they may, will we ever submit to enslavement, let the power that attempts it, emanate from whatever source it will.

6.—That no people can have political liberty without the sovereign right to exercise a freeman's will.

7.—That no individual is politically *free* who is deprived of the right of self representation.

8.—That to be a freeman *necessarily* implies the right of the elective franchise. . . . .

10.—That the elective franchise necessarily implies *eligibility to every position* attainable; the indisputable right of being chosen or elected as the representative of another, and otherwise than this the term is the sheerest imposition and delusion.

11.—That a people who are *liable*, under any pretext or circumstances whatever, to enslavement by the laws of a country, cannot be free in that country, because the rights of a freeman necessarily are sacred and inviolable.

12.—That, as men and equals, we demand every political right, privilege and position to which the whites are eligible in the United States, and we will either attain to these, or accept of nothing.

13.—That, as colored people, in whatever part of the country we may be located, we will accept of no political rights nor privileges but such as shall be impartial in their provisions; nor will we acknowledge these, except extended alike to each and every colored person in such State or territory.

14.—That the political distinctions in many of the States, made by the whites, and accepted of by the colored people, comprise, in many instances, our greatest social curses, and tend more than any thing else to divide our interests and make us indifferent to each others' welfare.

15.—That we pledge our integrity to use all honorable means, to unite us, as one people, on this continent.

16.—That we have no confidence in any political party nor politician—by whatever name they may be styled, or whatever their pretensions—who acknowledges the right of man to hold property in his fellow man—whether this right be admitted as a "necessary" part of the National Compact, the provisions of the Missouri Compromise, the detestably insulting and degrading Fugitive Slave Act, or the more recent contemptible Nebraska-Kansas Bill.

17.—That the Act of Congress of 1850, known as the Fugitive Bill, we declare to be a general law, tending to the virtual enslavement of every colored person in the United States; and consequently we abhor its existence, dispute its authority, refuse submission to its provisions and hold it in a state of the most contemptuous abrogation.

18.—That, as a people, we will never be satisfied nor contented until we occupy a position where we are acknowledged a necessary *constituent* in the *ruling element* of the country in which we live.

19.—That no oppressed people have ever obtained their rights by voluntary acts of generosity on the part of their oppressors.

20.—That it is futile hope on our part to expect such results through the agency of moral goodness on the part of our white American oppressors.

21.—That all great achievements by the Anglo-Saxon race have been accomplished through the agency of self-interest.

22.—That the liberty of a people is always insecure who have not absolute control of their own political destiny.

23.—That if we desire liberty, it can only be obtained at the price which others have paid for it.

24.—That we are willing to pay that price, *let the cost be what it may.*

25.—That according to the present social system of civilized society, the equality of persons is only recognized by their equality of attainments,—as with individuals, so is it with classes and communities;—therefore, we impress on the colored races throughout this Continent and the world, the necessity of having their children and themselves properly qualified in *every* respectable vocation pertaining to the Industrial and Wealth accumulating occupations; of arts, science, trades and professions; of agriculture, commerce and manufactures, so as to equal in *position* the leading characters and nations of the earth, without which we cannot, at best, but occupy a position of subserviency.

26.—That the potency and respectability of a nation or people, depends entirely upon the position of their women, therefore, it is essential to our elevation that the female portion of our children be instructed in all the arts and sciences pertaining to the highest civilization.

27.—That we will forever discountenance all invidious distinctions among us.

28.—That no people, as such, can ever attain to greatness who lose their identity, as they must rise entirely upon their own native merits.

29.—That we shall ever cherish our identity of origin and race, as preferable, in our estimation, to any other people.

30.—That the relative terms Negro, African, Black, Colored and Mulatto, when applied to us, shall ever be held with the same respect and pride; and synonymous with the terms, Caucasion, White, Anglo-Saxon and European, when applied to that class of people.

31.—That, as a people determined to be free, we individually pledge ourselves to support and sustain, on all occasions, by every justifiable effort, as far as possible, the declarations set forth in this bill of sentiments.

*Proceedings of the National Emigration Convention of Colored People; held at Cleveland, Ohio . . . 24–26 August, 1854* (Pittsburgh, 1854).

[b]

### Speech of H. Ford Douglass

I suppose that the enemies of this Convention have been highly gratified at the bombastic outpouring of the gentleman from Ohio, (Mr. J. M.

Langston,*) who, in the abundance of his wisdom, has thought it proper to enlighten us on the many mistakes of his past life, all of which he very modestly attributes to his "youthful enthusiasm."

Not content with exposing the instability of "human nature," as exhibited in himself, he undertakes to correct what he conceives to be the errors of others, by assailing the aims and objects of this Convention and the principles which we have come here to advocate . . .

But to be serious, Sir, our degraded condition needs something more substantial than fine rhetoric, or Latin maxims. These things cannot arrest the biting lash of the soul driver nor better the condition of three millions of slaves. The time has come when colored men must cease to build their castles of hope upon the ideal sands of a sickly sentimentality, the effect will only be to hush within us the "still sad music of Humanity." The mingled tones of sorrow and woe which come up upon every breeze from the deep and damning hell of Negro slavery speaks a common language to each and every individual, no matter how humble he may be, reminding him that he too has a duty to perform in this world as well as the gifted and the great. A truth told by a patrician would be no less the truth when told by a plebian. Because Mr. [Frederick] Douglass, Mr. [J. McCune] Smith or Mr. [J. Mercer] Langston tell me that the principles of emigration are destructive to the best interests of the colored people in this country, am I to act the part of a "young robin," and swallow it down without ever looking into the merits of the principles involved? No! Gentlemen. You must show some more plausible reason for the faith which is within you . . .

Is not the history of the world, the history of emigration? . . . The coming in and going out of nations, is a natural and necessary result . . . Let us then be up and doing. To stand still is to stagnate and die . . . Shall we then refuse to follow the light which history teaches, and be doomed, like our "fathers," to perish in the dark wilderness of oppression?

No! In spite of the vapid anathemas of "Eastern Stars," who have become so completely dazzled by their own supposed elevation, that they can scarcely see any of the dark realities below; or the stale commonplace of "Western satellites" the expediency of a "COLORED NATIONALITY," is becoming self-evident to Colored men more and more every day . . .

It is not our "little faith," that makes us anxious to leave this country or that we do not believe in the ultimate triumph of the principles of FREEDOM, but that the life-sustaining resources which slavery is capable of commanding may enable the institution to prolong its existence to an

* John Mercer Langston, though not a delegate, had been invited to address the Convention.

indefinite period of time. You must remember that slavery is not a foreign element in this government nor is it really antagonistic to the feelings of the American people. On the contrary, it is an element commencing with our medieval existence, receiving the sanction of the early Fathers of the Republic, sustained by their descendants through a period of nearly three centuries, deep and firmly laid in our organization. Completely interwoven into the passions and prejudices of the American people. It does not constitute a local or sectional institution as the generous promptings of the great and good [Charles] Sumner would have it, but is just as national as the Constitution which gives it an existence . . .

I can hate this Government without being disloyal, because it has stricken down my manhood, and treated me as a saleable commodity. I can join a foreign enemy and fight against it, without being a traitor, because it treats me as an ALIEN and a STRANGER, and I am free to avow that should such a contingency arise I should not hesitate to take any advantage in order to procure indemnity for the future . . .

When I remember that from Maine to Georgia, from the Atlantic waves to the Pacific shore, I am an alien and an outcast, unprotected by law, proscribed and persecuted by cruel prejudice, I am willing to forget the endearing name of home and country, and as an unwilling exile seek on other shores the freedom which has been denied me in the land of my birth.

*Speech of H. Ford Douglass, in reply to Mr. J. M. Langston before the Emigration Convention, at Cleveland, Ohio. Delivered on the evening of the 27th of August, 1854* (Chicago, 1854).

## 138

## ANTHONY BURNS TELLS HIS STORY, 1855

Perhaps the most renowned of all fugitive slave cases was that of Anthony Burns which rocked Boston in May and June, 1854. Burns' own account of his return to and rendition from slavery comes from two documents; the first a report of a speech he delivered at a Negro church in New York in February, 1855, the second a letter Burns wrote, in November, 1855, to the Baptist Church in Union, Virginia after learning it had excommunicated him:

### [a]

### *Anthony Burns in New York*

"My friends, I am very glad to have it to say, have it to *feel*, that I am once more in the land of liberty; that I am with those who are my friends. Until my tenth year I did not care what became of me; but soon after I began to learn that there is a Christ who came to make us free; I began to hear about a North, and to feel the necessity for freedom of soul and body. I heard of a North where men of my color could live without any man daring to say to them, 'You are my property;' and I determined by the blessing of God, one day to find my way there. My inclination grew on me, and I found my way to Boston.

"You see, I didn't want to make myself known, so I didn't tell who I was; but as I came to work, I got employment, and I worked hard; but I kept my own counsel, and didn't tell anybody that I was a slave, but I strove for *myself* as I never had an opportunity to do before. When I was going home one night I heard some one running behind me; presently a hand was put on my shoulder, and somebody said: 'Stop, stop; you are the fellow who broke into a silversmith's shop the other night.' I assured the man that it was a mistake, but almost before I could speak, I was lifted from off my feet by six or seven others, and it was no use to resist. In the Court House I waited some time, and as the silversmith did not come, I told them I wanted to go home to supper. A man then came to the door; he didn't open it like an honest man would, (laughter) but kind of slowly opened it, and looked in. He said, 'How do you do, Mr. Burns?' and I called him, as we do in Virginia, 'master!'

"He asked me if there would be any trouble in taking me back to Virginia, and I was brought right to a stand, and didn't know what to say. He wanted to know if I remembered the money that he used to give me, and I said 'Yes, I do recollect that you used to give me twelve and a half cents at the end of every year I worked for you.' He went out and came back next morning. I got no supper nor sleep that night. The next morning they told me that my master said that he had the right to me, and as I had called him 'master,' having the fear of God before my eyes, I could not go from it. Next morning I was taken down, with the bracelets on my wrists—not such as you wear, ladies, of gold and silver—but iron and steel, that wore into the bone. [He showed the marks which his irons had made.] *

"The lawyers insisted that I should have counsel, but I told them I didn't think it would do any good, for what I had first said had crushed me, and I could not deny the truth, and my only hope was in the assistance of Heaven." † He proceeded to relate how the officers were armed in the court room; how the United States officials told him that Dana, Ellis, Phillips and the rest were d——d sons of b——s of Abolitionists; that he would be freed when he got back to Virginia, and advised him to have nothing to do with

* Bracketed words in original.
† From here on, the reporter summarizes Burns' remarks.

those who pretended to befriend him while they made his case worse. He replied that they worked for him manfully, and if they did not succeed it was not their fault. He said he saw in a newspaper that he had said he wished to go back to Virginia. Had the Devil himself said it, he could have told no greater lie.

He then described the scene of his rendition; how he, a poor fugitive was made a great lion, and escorted out of the free city of Boston, and on board of the revenue cutter, amid troops of men armed to the teeth. How they (the law and order men) promised to purchase him when he got to Virginia, and when he got to Norfolk they clapped him into jail, and put irons on his wrists, and kept him in a room without bed or seat, and with but scanty food, for two days. He was taken to Richmond, where he was kept in a little pen in the Traders' Jail for four months, with irons on his wrists and ankles, so tight that they wore the flesh through to the bone, and during the month of August they gave him a half-pailful of water every two days.

From this cell he was not allowed to come out once during four months; at the end of that time he was sold for $905 to one David McDaniel, who took him to North Carolina.

The remainder of his story is short: hearing of his situation the money was raised, and his purchase effected by Mr. Grimes.*

N.Y. *Tribune,* n.d., in *The Liberator,* March 9, 1855.

## [b]

### Anthony Burns to the Baptist Church

In answer to my request by mail, under date July 13, 1855, for a letter of dismission in fellowship and of recommendation to another church, I have received a copy of the *Front Royal Gazette,* dated Nov. 8, 1855, in which I find a communication addressed to myself and signed by John Clark, as pastor of your body, covering your official action upon my request, as follows:—

The Church Of Jesus Christ, At Union, Fauquier Co., Virginia.
*To all whom it may concern:*
Whereas, Anthony Burns, a member of this church, has made application to us, by a letter to our pastor, for a letter of dismission, in fellowship, in order that he may unite with another church of the same faith and order; and whereas, it has been satisfactorily established before us, that the said

* The sum of $1,300 was raised under the leadership of a Negro minister, the Reverend Leonard A. Grimes.

Anthony Burns absconded from the service of his master, and refused to return voluntarily—thereby disobeying both the laws of God and man, although he subsequently obtained his freedom by purchase, yet we have now to consider him only as a *fugitive from labor* (as he was before his arrest and restoration to his master), have therefore

*Resolved,* Unanimously, that he be excommunicated from the communion and fellowship of this church.

Done by order of the church, in regular church meeting, this twentieth day of October, 1855.

Wm. W. West, *Clerk.*


Thus you have excommunicated me, on the charge of "disobeying both the laws of God and men," "in absconding from the service of my master, and refusing to return voluntarily."

I admit that I left my master (so called), and refused to return; but I deny that in this I disobeyed either the law of God, or any real *law* of men.

Look at my case. I was stolen and made a slave as soon as I was born. No man had any right to steal me. That manstealer who stole me trampled on my dearest rights. He committed an outrage on the law of God; therefore his manstealing gave him no right in me, and laid me under no obligation to be his slave. God made me a *man*—not a *slave;* and gave me the same right to myself that he gave the man who stole me to himself. The great wrongs he has done me, in stealing me and making me a slave, in compelling me to work for him many years without wages, and in holding me as merchandize,—these wrongs could never put me under obligation to stay with him, or to return voluntarily, when once escaped.

You charge me that, in escaping, I disobeyed God's law. No, indeed! That law which God wrote on the table of my heart, inspiring the love of freedom, and impelling me to seek it at every hazard, I obeyed, and, by the good hand of my God upon me, I walked out of the house of bondage.

I disobeyed no law of God revealed in the Bible. I read in Paul (Cor. 7:21), "But, if thou mayest be made free, use it rather." I read in Moses (Deut. 23:15, 16), "Thou shalt not deliver unto his master the servant which is escaped from his master unto thee. He shall dwell with thee, even among you in that place which he shall choose in one of thy gates, where it liketh him best; thou shalt not oppress him." This implies my right to flee if I feel myself oppressed, and debars any man from delivering me again to my professed master.

I said I was stolen. God's Word declares, "He that stealeth a man and selleth him, or if he be found in his hand, he shall surely be put to death." (Ex. 21:16.) Why did you not execute God's law on the man who stole me from my mother's arms? How is it that you trample down God's law against the *oppressor,* and wrest it to condemn me, the *innocent* and *oppressed?* Have you forgotten that the New Testament classes "manstealers" with "murderers of fathers" and "murderers of mothers" with "manslavers and whoremongers?" (1 Tim. 1:9, 10.)

The advice you volunteered to send me, along with this sentence of ex-communication, exhorts me, when I shall come to preach like Paul, to send every runaway home to his master, as he did Onesimus to Philemon. Yes, indeed I would, *if you would let me.* I should love to send them back *as he did,* "NOT NOW AS A SERVANT, but *above a servant:*—A BROTHER—a brother beloved—both in *the flesh* and in the Lord;" both a brother-man, and a brother-Christian. Such a relation would be delightful—to be put on a level, in position, with Paul himself. "If thou count me, therefore, a *partner,* receive him as *myself."* I would to God that every fugitive had the privilege of returning to such a condition—to the embrace of *such a Christianity*— "not now as a servant, but above a servant,"—a "partner,"—even as Paul himself was to Philemon!

You charge me with disobeying the *laws of men.* I utterly deny that those things which outrage all right are laws. To be real laws, they must be founded in equity.

You have thrust me out of your church fellowship. So be it. You can do no more. You cannot exclude me from heaven; you cannot hinder my daily fellowship with God.

You have used your liberty of speech freely in exhorting and rebuking me. You are aware that I too am now where I may think for myself, and can use great freedom of speech, too, if I please. I shall therefore be only returning the favor of your exhortation if I exhort you to study carefully the golden rule, which reads, "All things whatsoever ye would that men should do to you, do ye even so to them; for this is the law and the prophets." Would you like to be *stolen,* and then *sold?* and then worked without wages? and forbidden to read the Bible? and be torn from your wife and children? and then, if you were able to make yourself free, and should, as Paul said, *"use it rather,"* would you think it quite right to be cast out of the church for this? If it were done, so wickedly, would you be afraid God would indorse it? Suppose you were to put your soul in my soul's stead; how would *you* read the law of love?

Charles Emery Stevens, *Anthony Burns A History* (Boston, 1856), pp. 280–83. To this letter Stevens appended: "In reply to a note which I addressed to Anthony, respecting this letter, he informed me that while he had some little assistance in its preparation, it was for substance his own."

## 139

# FIRST CALIFORNIA NEGRO CONVENTION, 1855

The first state convention of the approximately 6,000 Negroes of California was held in the Colored Methodist Church of Sacramento from November 20th to 22nd, 1855. Forty-nine delegates from ten counties were present under the chairmanship of William H. Yates of San Francisco.

The proceedings make clear that the leadership of this convention was not Abolitionist and even a proposal that an account of the proceedings be sent to *The Liberator* and to Frederick Douglass' newspaper was rejected. Published below are the key resolutions adopted by this gathering and the address to the people of California written by J. H. Townsend of San Francisco, as well as an undated letter dealing with the tactics behind the convention written by Jeremiah B. Sanderson, teacher in the San Francisco Colored Public School to William C. Nell, of Boston.

## [a]

### *The Resolutions*

*Whereas,* We the colored people of the State of California, believing that the laws of this State, relating to the testimony of colored people in the courts of justice, recorded in 394th section of chapter 3d of an act entitled "an act for regulating proceedings in the court practice of the courts of this State," as follows: *"And persons having one-half or more of Negro blood,* shall not be witnesses in an action or proceeding to which a white person is a party"—to be unjust in itself and oppressive to every class in the community; that this law was intended to protect white persons from a class whose intellectual and social condition was supposed to be so low as to justify the depriving them of their testimony.

*And, whereas,* We believe that careful inquiries into our social, moral, religious, intellectual, and financial condition, will demonstrate that, as a class, allowing for the disabilities under which we labor, we compare favorably with any class in the community.

*And, whereas,* We believe that petitions to the Legislature, to convene in January, praying for the abrogation of this law will meet with a favorable response; believing, as we do, that it cannot be sustained on the ground of sound policy or expediency . . .

*Resolved,* That we memorialize the Legislature at its approaching session, to repeal the third and fourth paragraphs of section three hundred and ninety-four of an Act passed April 20th, 1851, entitled, "An Act to regulate proceeding in civil cases, in the Courts of Justice of this State," and also for the repeal of sections fourteen of an Act entitled "An Act concerning Crimes and Punishments," passed April 6th, 1850.

*Resolved,* That a State Executive Committee be appointed by the Convention, with full powers to adopt such measures as may be deemed expedient to accomplish the object in view.

*Resolved,* That we recommend the organization of a State Association, with auxiliaries in every county, for the purpose of collecting statistical and other evidences of our advancement and prosperity; also to encourage education, and a correct and proper deportment in our relations towards our white fellow citizens and to each other.

*Resolved,* That we regret and reprobate the apathy and timidity of a portion of our people, in refusing to take part in any public demonstration, having for its object the removal of political and other disabilities, by judicious and conservative action.

*Resolved,* That we recommend the creation of a contingent fund of twenty thousand dollars, to be controlled by a Committee having discretionary powers, to enable us to carry forward any measure that has for its object the amelioration of our condition.

## [b]

### *Address to the People of California*

The colored citizens of this Commonwealth, would respectfully represent before you, their state and condition; and they respectfully ask a candid and careful investigation of facts in relation to their true character.

Our population numbers about 6,000 persons, who own capital to the amount of near $3,000,000. This has been accumulated by our own industry, since we migrated to the shores of the Pacific.

Most of us were born upon your soil; reared up under the influence of your institutions; become familiar with your manners and customs; acquired most of your habits, and adopted your policies. We yield allegiance to no other country save this. With all her faults we love her still.

Our forefathers were among the first who took up arms and fought side by side with yours; poured out their blood freely in the struggle for American independence. They fought, as they had every reason to suppose, the good fight of liberty, until it finally triumphed.

In the war of 1812, in which you achieved independence and glory upon the seas, the colored men were also among the foremost to engage in the conflict, rendering efficient service in behalf of their common country. Through a long series of years have we been always ready to lay down our lives for the common weal, in defense of the national honor. On the other hand, instead of treating us as good and loyal citizens, you have treated us as aliens; sought to degrade us in all walks of life; proscribed us in Church and State as an ignorant and debased class, unworthy the sympathy and regard of men; without examining into our true character, you have allowed yourselves to become bitterly prejudiced against us. When we have spoken of the wrongs inflicted upon us, you have turned a deaf ear to our representations and entreaties, or spurned us from you.

We again call upon you to regard our condition in the State of California. We point with pride to the general character we maintain in your midst, for integrity, industry, and thrift. You have been wont to multiply our vices, and never to see our virtues. You call upon us to pay enormous taxes to support Government, at the same time you deny us the protection you extend to others; the security for life and property. You require us to be good citizens, while seeking to degrade us. You ask why we are not more intelligent? You receive our money to educate your children, and then refuse to admit our children into the common schools. You have enacted a law, excluding our testimony in the Courts of justice of this State, in cases of proceedings wherein white persons are parties; thus openly encouraging and countenancing the vicious and dishonest to take advantage of us; a law which while it does not advantage you, is a great wrong to us. At the same time, you freely admit the evidence of men in your midst, who are ignorant of the first principles of your Government—who know not the alphabet. Many colored men, who have been educated in your first colleges, are not allowed to testify! And wherefore? our Divine Father has created us with a darker complexion.

People of California! we entreat you to repeal that unjust law.* We ask it in the name of humanity, in the enlightened age in which we live, because of the odium it reflects upon you as a free and powerful people; we ask you to remove it from your civil code; we ask it, that our homes and firesides may be protected; we ask it, that our just earnings as laborers may be secured to us, and none offered impunity, in withholding from us our just hire; that justice may be meted out to all, without respect to complexion; the guilty punished; the innocent protected; the shield of wise, and wholesome and equal laws, extended over all in your great State; upon her mountains, in her valleys and deep ravines; by her winding streams; may your State

* As late as 1862 a bill—the McClay Negro Testimony Bill—whose provisions would have equalized the position of the Negro as a witness in California's courts, was defeated.

be a model, even to the elder sister States, in respect of your just laws; may your growth, prosperity and happiness, be bounded only by time and immortality.

*Proceedings of the First State Convention of the Colored Citizens of the State of California . . .* (Sacramento, 1855).

### [c]

### *Sanderson's Letter to Nell*

We have got among our young men here the right material for devising and carrying out plans for our general good. We anticipated opposition from the press, and this is apt to stir up the baser sort to indulge in some excess. Those papers, however, which spoke, did so calmly, and encouragingly in regard to the objects of the Convention, (which was mainly to get the right of testimony in the courts,) and though we heard distant grumbling and dark threats, it passed off.

One of our city papers, (Know-Nothing,) the *Daily Tribune,* liberally reported our proceedings from day to day. This did us good, and certainly did them good, as they were obliged to strike off many extra copies, to supply the very general demand. There has been a general desire here among the whites to know what we were doing—and that is what we want they should know.

In what we are trying to do, in order to get the right of testimony, very many of the best and most influential men of the State are with us— Southern as well as Northern. *This* right secured, and then "the next thing will be something else," as we used to say.

The School Question still remains in *status quo,* and is likely to be for the present. We have got an ordinance from the Common Council, through much tribulation, for a separate school. Here we are in the condition to take the half loaf; we have "Hobson's choice." The only difficulty now is, "no money in the city treasury."

*The Liberator,* January 25, 1856.

## 140

## BOSTON'S JIM CROW SCHOOL IS CLOSED, 1855

The long struggle of Boston Negroes against Jim Crow schooling was won in September, 1855. On December 17 of that year a dinner in honor of William C. Nell for his efforts in this regard was held under the auspices of John T. Hilton,

Robert Morris, Dr. J. V. DeGrasse, Dr. John S. Rock and Lewis Hayden. In the course of the dinner Mr. Nell made the following remarks:

In the year 1829 while a pupil in the basement story of the Belknap-street church, Hon. Harrison Gray Otis, then Mayor of the city, accompanied Hon. Samuel T. Armstrong to an examination of the colored school. It chanced that Charles A. Battiste, Nancy Woodson and myself were pronounced entitled to the highest reward of merit. In lieu of Franklin Medals, legitimately our due, Mr. Armstrong gave each an order on Dea. James Loring's Bookstore for the *Life of Benjamin Franklin*. This is the copy I received! The white medal scholars were invited guests to the Faneuil Hall dinner. Having a boy's curiosity to be spectator at the "feast of reason and the flow of soul," I made good my court with one of the waiters, who allowed me to seem to serve others as the fee for serving myself, the physical being then with me subordinate. Mr. Armstrong improved a prudent moment in whispering to me, "*You* ought to be here with the other *boys.*" Of course, the same idea had more than once been mine, but his remark, while witnessing the honors awarded to white scholars, only augmented my sensitiveness all the more, by the intuitive inquiry which I eagerly desired to express—"If you think so, why have you not taken steps to bring it about?"

The impression made on my mind, by this day's experience, deepened into a solemn vow that, God helping me, I would do my best to hasten the day when the color of the skin would be no barrier to equal school rights. While I would not in the smallest degree detract from the credit justly due the *men* for their conspicuous exertions in this reform, truth enjoins upon me the pleasing duty of acknowledging that to the *women,* and the *children* also, is the cause especially indebted for success.

In the dark hours of our struggle, when betrayed by traitors within and beset by foes without, while some men would become lukewarm and indifferent, despairing of victory; then did the women keep the flame alive, and as their hopes would weave bright visions for the future, their husbands and brothers would rally for a new attack upon the fortress of colorphobia. Yes, Sir, it was the *mothers* (God bless them!) of these little bright-eyed boys and girls, who, through every step of our progress, were executive and vigilant, even to that memorable Monday morning (September 3, 1855) the trial hour, when the colored children of Boston went up to occupy the long-promised land. It was these mothers who accompanied me to the various school-houses, to residences of teachers and committee-men, to see the laws of the Old Bay State applied in good faith . . .

On the morning preceding their advent to the public schools, I saw from my window a boy passing the exclusive Smith School, (where he had been a pupil) and, raising his hands, he exultingly exclaimed to his companions, *"Good bye forever, colored school! Tomorrow we are like other Boston boys!"*

*The Liberator,* December 28, 1855. For a good account of this whole struggle, see Rabbi Louis Ruchames, "Race and Education in Massachusetts," in *The Negro History Bulletin,* December, 1949.

# 141

# A SECRET ORGANIZATION FOR FREEDOM, 1856

A remarkable story of secret revolutionary organization culminating in 1856, after a decade of work, is told by the Rev. Moses Dickson. He was born in Ohio in 1824 and as a very young man traveled for three years through the South in the capacity of a barber. In August, 1846, according to his own story, he and eleven others— John Patton and Henry Wright of South Carolina, James Bedford and Silas W. Green of Mississippi, Irving Hodges of Alabama, Peter Coleman and Willis Owens of Virginia, James Orr of Louisiana, Miles Graves of North Carolina, Henry Simpson of Georgia, and Lewis Williams of Tennessee—met in St. Louis and formed the Twelve Knights of Tabor. This organization was active in the Underground Railroad; its other plans and activities through 1857 are told in Dickson's own words below.

Dickson himself was a minister of the African Methodist Episcopal Church from 1867 to his death in 1901. He was a militant fighter for civil rights in Missouri, a leading post-Civil War Republican and a founder of Lincoln Institute, now Lincoln University, in Jefferson City, Missouri.

The organization of the Order of Twelve that was made in Galena, Ill., in 1856, was made to perpetuate the names of the Twelve Knights of Tabor, who were so successful in enrolling the 47,000 Knights of Liberty, for the purpose of aiding in breaking the bonds of our slavery. This secret organization of the Knights of Liberty was one of the strongest and most secret of any organization ever formed by men. The question of giving the history of this organization to the world is one that has had my most earnest thoughts for several years. There are so many families of the old men of renown, both in this country and England, that are now living and hold high positions, that they might be injured by revealing the secrets of the Knights of Liberty and giving the names of their fathers. I had almost decided to let this part of our history rest in the grave, more especially since God found other means to give us our manhood and freedom; but the names of the *twelve* men who were instruments in God's hands in preparing and organizing 47,000 men of undoubted courage to do battle for our freedom shall be perpetuated. God fixed the time, and every man was at his post. In their death struggles they gave us the boon of liberty. Precious be their memory . . .

This organization [Knights of Liberty] was known among its members by the name of Knights of Tabor—a name that gave the members Courage. That God was with Barak and Deborah, in Israel's great battle with the immense army of Sisera; they, with only ten thousand men, assembled on Tabor, to fight Jabin's army, and if possible, win the victory and break the bondage of the Israelites. God was with Israel, and gave the victory to the bondsmen, though they were opposed by twenty times their number. Our cause was just, and we believed in the justice of the God of Israel and the rights of man. Under the old name of Tabor we resolved to make full preparation to strike the blow for liberty. We felt sure that the Lord God was on the side of right and justice, our faith and trust was in him, and that he would help us in our needy time.

From the very origin of the organization of the Knights of Liberty, the necessity of secrecy was impressed on each member. Let not your right hand know what your left hand does; trust no one and test every man before he is admitted to membership. A part of the oath was: "We can die, but we can't reveal the name of a member or make known the organization and its objects." It was absolutely a secret organized body. We know of the failure of Nat Turner and others, the Abolitionist in the North and East. The underground railroad was in good running order, and the Knights of Liberty sent many passengers over the road to freedom.

We feel that we have said enough on this subject. If the War of the Rebellion had not occurred just at the time it did, the Knights of Liberty would have made public history.

They were fully prepared to enter the conflict, and to do battle for the freedom of the bondmen. The year 1856 found them well drilled, with ample arms and ammunition. Wealthy friends, both in this country and England, had provided money to get supplies of all kinds; these were safely hid away near the camps of the Knights. The plans were carefully made, and the leaders of companies and divisions were instructed in the line of march from their various headquarters to Atlanta, Ga., where the entire army was to unite. In the month of July, 1857, orders were received at every camp to hold themselves in readiness to march at any time that the Chief gave the command. It was a gigantic, desperate movement, and demanded the closest study of every move that was to be made. We expected to arrive at Atlanta with at least 150,000 well-armed men. The Chief's positive orders were to spare women and children, and to parole non-combatants; capture all of the arms and ammunition found anywhere; treat their prisoners well.

March, fight, and conquer was the command, or leave their bodies on the battle-field. It was a death-struggle for freedom, and God is just. He will give us the victory. The flag under which the Knights of Liberty were to fight, the bars were green, red, and blue; in the center were twelve stars in the form of a cross. The time for each company and division to report at Atlanta was fixed, and from there circumstances were to shape their future movements. The South was taking it easy over a slumbering volcano; a word from one man would have started the eruption to rolling. Death and destruction would have marked its way through the Southland at the command of one man. . . .

The Chief was almost ready to give the command to move forward in July, 1857, but he paused and scanned the signs that were gathering over the Union. The North and South were having a terrible struggle for mastery on the slave question. The Chief called a halt and notified the Knights that it was plainly demonstrated to him that a higher power was preparing to take a part in the contest between the North and South. . . .

Moses Dickson, *Manual of the International Order of Twelve of Knights and Daughters of Tabor containing general laws; regulations, ceremonies, drill and landmarks* (10th ed., Glasgow, Mo., 1918 [copyright, 1891], Moses Dickson Pub. Co.), pp. 16–21. Copy in University of Minnesota library.

## 142

## OHIO CONVENTION OF NEGRO MEN, 1856

A state convention representing the Negro men of Ohio met in the Columbus City Hall, January 16–18, 1856. Present were forty delegates, prominent among whom were the Langston brothers—J. Mercer and Charles H.—David Jenkins, James Poindexter, John J. Gaines, Peter H. Clarke, John Booker and John Malvin. A moving address to these men from the Ladies' Anti-Slavery Society of Delaware, Ohio—all of whose members were Negroes—is printed below as representative of the Negro woman's militance; following this appears the Convention's address to the Ohio State legislature.

### [a]

*Address of the Ladies' Anti-Slavery Society of Delaware, Ohio*

*To the Convention of Disfranchised Citizens of Ohio:*

Gentlemen:—Convened as you are in the Capital City of our State—A State great in wealth, power, and political influence, an avowed devotee of Freedom, and a constituent part of a Christian Democratic Confederacy—to concoct measures for obtaining those rights and immunities of which unjust legislation has deprived you, we offer this testimonial of our sympathy and interest in the cause in which you are engaged—a cause fraught with infinite importance—and also express our earnest hope that such determination and invincible courage may be evinced by you in assembly as are requisite to meet the exigencies of the times.

Truth, Justice and Mercy, marshaling their forces, sound the tocsin which summons the warrior in his burnished armor to the conflict against Error and Oppression. On earth's broad arena—through Time's revolving cycles—this warfare has been continuous; and now here, in this most brilliant star in the galaxy of nations, where Christianity and civilization, with their inestimable accompaniments and proclivities, have taken their abode and add their benign light to her stellate brightness—bands of her offspring, in very truth her own, despised, persecuted and crushed, assemble in scattered fragments to take the oath of fealty to Freedom, and swear eternal enmity to Oppression; to enter into a bond sacred and inviolable, ever to wage interminable intellectual and moral war against the demon, and to demand the restoration of their birthright, *Liberty*—kindred of Deity. Nor is the path to victory strewn with flowers; obstacles formidable, and apparently insurmountable, arise ominously before even the most hopeful and ardent.

As the Alpine avalanche sweeps tumultously adown the mountain, overwhelming the peasant and his habitation, so the conglomeration of hatred and prejudice against our race, brought together by perceptible accumulation, augmented and fostered by religion and science united, sweeps with seeming irresistible power toward us, menacing complete annihilation. But, should these things exercise a retarding influence upon our progressive efforts? Let American religion teach adoration to the demon Slavery, whom it denominates God: at the end, the book of record will show its falsity or truth. Let scientific research produce elaborate expositions of the inferiority and mental idiosyncrasy of the colored race; one truth, the only essential truth, is incontrovertible:—The Omnipotent, Omniscient God's glorious autograph—the seal of angels—is written on our brows, that immortal characteristic of Divinity—the rational, mysterious and inexplicable soul, animates our frames.

Then press on! Manhood's prerogatives are yours by Almighty fiat. These prerogatives American Republicanism, disregarding equity, humanity, and the fundamental principles of her national superstructure, has rendered a nonentity, while on her flag's transparencies and triumphal arches, stood beautifully those great, noble words: Liberty and Independence—Free Government—Church and State! And still they stand exponents of American character—her escutcheon wafts them on its star-spangled surface, to every clime—each ship load of emigrants from monarchical Europe, shout the words synonymous with Americans, their first paean in "the land of the free." Briery mountain, sparkling river, glassy lake, give back the echoes, soft and clear as if the melody was borrowed from the harps of angels. But strange incongruity! As the song of Freedom verberates and reverberates through the northern hills, and the lingering symphony quivers on the still air and then sinks away into silence, a low deep wail, heavy with anguish and despair, rises from the southern plains, and the clank of chains on human limbs mingles with the mournful cadence.

What to the toiling millions there, is this boasted liberty? What to us is this organic body—this ideal reduced to reality—this institution of the land?—A phantom, shadowy and indistinct—a disembodied form, impalpable to our sense or touch. In the broad area of this Republic there is no spot, however small or isolated, where the colored man can exercise his God-given rights. Genius of America! How art thou fallen, oh Lucifer, son of the morning how art thou fallen!

In view of these things, it is self-evident, and above demonstration that we, as a people, have every incentive to labor for the redress of wrongs. On our native soil, consecrated to freedom, civil liberties are denied us, and we are by compulsion subject to an atrocious and criminal system of political tutelage deleterious to the interest of the entire colored race, and antagonistical to the political axioms of this Republic.

Intuitively, then, we search for the panacea for the manifold ills which we suffer. One, and only one, exists; and when each individual among us realizes the absolute impossibility for him to perform any work of supererogation in the common cause, the appliances will prove its own efficacy; it is embodied in one potent word—ACTION. Let unanimity of action characterize us; let us reject the absurd phantasy of non-intervention; let us leave conservatism behind, and substitute a radical, utilitarian spirit, let us cultivate our moral and mental faculties, and labor to effect a general diffusion of knowledge, remembering that "ascendancy naturally and properly belongs to intellectual superiority."

Let "Excelsior" be our watchword; it is the inspiration of all great deeds, and by the universal adoption of this policy we will soon stand triumphantly above that ignorance and weakness of which slavery is the inevitable concomitant—will soon reach that apex of civilization and consequent power to which every earnest, impassioned soul aspires.

Continued and strenuous effort is the basis of all greatness, moral, intellectual, and civil. "Work, man," says Carlyle, "work! work! thou hast all eternity to rest in."

To you, gentlemen, as representatives of the oppressed thousands of

Ohio, we look hopefully. This convening is far from being nugatory or un-important. "Agitation of thought is the beginning of truth," and further-more, by pursuing such a line of policy as you in your wisdom may deem expedient, *tending toward that paramount object*, the results may transcend those attending similar assemblies which have preceded it. Sure, you are numerically small; but the race is not always gained by the swift, nor the battle by the strong, and it has become a truism that greatness is the legiti-mate result of labor, diligence, and perseverance.

It was a Spartan mother's farewell to her son, "Bring home your shield or be brought upon it." To you we would say, be true, be courageous, be stead-fast in the discharge of your duty. The citadel of Error must yield to the unshrinking phalanx of truth. In our fireside circles, in the seclusion of our closets, we kneel in tearful supplication in your behalf. As Christian wives, mothers and daughters, we invoke the blessing of the King, Eternal and Immortal, "who sitteth upon the circle of the earth, who made the heavens with all their host," to rest upon you, and we pledge ourselves to exert our influence unceasingly in the cause of Liberty and Humanity.

Again we say, be courageous; be steadfast; unfurl your banner to the breeze—let its folds float proudly over you, bearing the glorious inscription, broad and brilliant as the material universe: *"God and Liberty!"*

SARA G. STALEY,

*In behalf of the Delaware Ladies' Anti-Slavery Society.*

## [b]

*Address, to the Senate and House of Representatives of the State of Ohio:*

Gentlemen:—We, the disfranchised Colored Citizens of Ohio, assembled in General Convention, feeling deeply the grievous wrongs unjustly imposed upon us by the prohibitions implied in the first Section of the fifth Article of the Constitution of the State and knowing "the people have the right to assemble together, in a peaceful manner to counsel for their common good, and petition the General Assembly for a redress of grievances;" and, believ-ing it to be a solemn duty we owe to ourselves, our posterity, and the honor and dignity of the free State of Ohio, to use every constitutional means which the law-makers of Ohio have left in our power, to remove from our necks the burdens too grievous to be borne; we do, therefore, most earnestly, in the name of our common humanity, in the name of the Declaration of Inde-pendence and the Bill of Rights of the State of Ohio, ask your Honorable Body, to take the necessary constitutional steps to strike the word "white" from the section before referred to, and all other places in which it occurs in the Constitution, and thereby abrogate the unwise and unjust distinction therein made between the citizens of the State on account of the accident of color. The section referred to is couched in the following language: "Article V, Section 1. Every *white* male citizen of the United States, of the age of twenty-one years, who shall have been a resident of the State one year next preceding the election, and of the county, township, or ward in which he resides, such times as may be provided by law, shall have the qualifications of an elector, and be entitled to vote at all elections."

The first reason we will assign for the removal of this odious word from the Constitution of a professedly free State, is, that we are MEN. This, to our minds, seems an all-sufficient plea. Human rights are not to be graduated by the shades of color that tinge the cheeks of men. Any being, however low in the scale of civilization, that yet preserves the traits that serve to distinguish humanity from the brutes, is endowed with all rights that can be claimed by the most cultivated races of men.

That we are men, we will not insult your intelligence by attempting to prove. The most bitter revilers and oppressors of the race admit this, even in the enactments by which they wrong us. Statutes and ordinances are not necessary for the regulation and control of animals, but men, reasoning men, who can understand and obey, or plot to overthrow. The section of which we complain, by defining that *white* men may exercise the right of franchise, virtually admits that there are black men who are by the rule prohibited from voting. We ask any who doubt our manhood, Hath not the *Negro* eyes? Hath not the *Negro* hands, organs, dimensions, senses, affections, passions?—fed with the same food—hurt with the same weapons—subject to the same diseases—healed by the same means—warmed and cooled by the same summer and winter as the *white man* is? If you prick us, do we not bleed? If you tickle us, do we not laugh? If you poison us, do we not die?

We ask you to ponder the danger of circumscribing the great doctrines of human equality, which our fathers promulgated and defended at the cost of so much blood and treasure, to the narrow bounds of races or nations. All men are by nature equal, and have inalienable rights, or none have. We beg you to reflect how insecure your own and the liberties of your posterity would be by the admission of such a rule of construing the rights of men. Another nation or race may displace you, as you have displaced nations and races; and the injustice you teach, they may execute; perchance they may better the instruction. Remember, in your pride of race and power, "That we are all, children of one Father, and all ye are brethren!"

But the principles upon which our Government is founded, condemns the practice of excluding colored men from the advantages of the ballot box. To uphold the principle that taxation and representation should go together, the union between Great Britain and the American Colonies was broken, and a desolating war of seven years' duration was waged. As proof of the correctness of the principle, we have the declaration and actions of our fathers, and your own declarations. If the sentiment was so true in 1776, what new concatenation of circumstances has arisen to render it false in 1856? None whatever.

It is one of those immutable truths that change not with time or circumstances. They are emanations from the eternal foundation of truth, which we all worship—the Deity Himself. Yet, in nearly every county of our State, colored tax-payers are found, who are unrepresented, and can only be heard in your halls as a matter of favor. We are aware that difference of race is urged by our enemies as a reason for our disfranchisement; but we submit that we are not Africans, but Americans, as much so as any of your population. Here then is a great injustice done us, by refusing to acknowledge our right to the appellation of Americans, which is the only title we desire, and legislating for us as if we were aliens, and not bound to our country by the ties of affection which every human being must feel for his native land; which makes the Laplander prefer his snows and skins to the sunny skies and silken garb of Italy; which makes the colored American prefer the dear land of his birth, even though oppressed in it, to any other spot on earth.

But admit, for argument, that there is an irradicable difference between us and the whites of our land. That very difference unfits them to represent us. Our wants and feelings are unknown or unappreciated by them; or can any one presume to represent us whom we have not aided to select. In our government, every citizen should be represented in the legislative councils, and this can only be attained by permitting each one a voice in the selection of representatives. No class of the white population would be willing to concede to any other class, however honest and enlightened, the custody of their rights. To demand such a thing, would be deemed monstrous; and the injustice is not lessened when the demand is made upon black men instead of white men.

Our want of intelligence is urged as a reason against our admission to equal citizenship. The assumption that we are ignorant is untrue; but, even if it were true, it really affords an argument for the removal of the disabilities that cramp our energies, destroy that feeling of self respect, so essential to form the character of a good citizen. Give us the opportunity of elevating ourselves:—It can do you no harm, and may do us much good; and if we fail, upon us be the blame. We would bring to your recollection that, by a decision of your Supreme Court, a large portion of our people are already in the possession of the elective franchise.* These men are not above the average

* The Court had ruled that Negroes with predominantly white ancestry might vote.

of colored men in intelligence or morals. They are educated under the same depressing social influences with the rest of us, and are no better fitted to exercise the right of voting than their brethren. Yet, by an accident of color, they are enfranchised. What good reason can be adduced for permitting the father to vote and not the son, or the son and not the father, as is frequently the case? The most obtuse intellect can at once perceive the utter folly and injustice of such distinctions. But the folly and injustice is equally as great when the difference is made between white and colored men.

We are aware that it has been recently asserted by a high political personage, that this is a government of white men. This we cannot admit. In addition to the arguments we have already advanced, touching the doctrine of the universality of human rights, we submit that the assertion casts an imputation upon the veracity and good faith of our fathers, who claimed the sympathy and aid of the world on the ground that they were contending for principles of universal application, and desired to found a government in which the doctrine of human equality would be reduced to practice.

The Bill of Rights of the State of Ohio sets forth "That all men are created equal and independent, and have inalienable rights, among which are enjoying and *defending* life, and liberty, acquiring, possessing, and *protecting* property, and seeking and obtaining happiness and safety."

Now, admitted that we are men, how are we to *defend* and protect life, liberty and property? The whites of the State, through the ballot-box, can do these things peacefully; but we, by the organic law of the State, are prevented from defending those precious rights by any other than violent means. For the same document that asserts our right to defend life, liberty and property, strips us of the power to do so otherwise than by violence. We ask you gentlemen, in the name of justice, shall this stand as the judgment of the State of Ohio?

We are *aware* that deference to the opinions and institutions of the States tolerating slavery, to whom we are bound by the federal compact, may induce some to oppose this our application for equal rights. But those States, of all others, are the most tenacious of their rights as sovereign States, and reprobate all attempts to influence their domestic policy by the action of public opinion in other States. We pray you, therefore, to do us justice; and, in doing right, imitate the independence they display in doing wrong. Our rights are as high and precious as theirs; and they can have no right to complain of any act of the people of Ohio, improving the condition of any class of her citizens.

We do not ask you to countenance any change destructive to your form of government. The principles we ask you to indorse are recognized by the wise and good of your own and other lands. It will be but the legitimate result of a proper appreciation of the Declaration of Independence and our Bill of Rights. Already five States of the Union have admitted colored men to vote; and we have yet to hear that the action has been followed by any other than beneficial results.

The arguments we have advanced are equally applicable to the statutory enactments which inflict such grievous disabilities upon us as a people.

The inestimable privilege and protection of a trial by a jury of our peers, we are deprived of, and to our great damage. Every legal gentleman in your body must be aware of the facility with which convictions are obtained against colored men.

Admission to your infirmaries and other benevolent institutions, is demanded by the spirit of the age. It is a shame to your civilization and humanity that decrepit age, the helplessly maimed, drivelling idiots and raving maniacs, are turned into the streets to die, as has been done in the metropolis of your State. In your public schools, too, needless and injurious distinctions are made.* The duty of the State is the same to all her children. None are so insignificant as to be forgotten; none so important as to be preferred before others. The interests of the State demand that all should be educated alike.

In conclusion, we will call your attention to the duties incumbent on you as legislators—to pass such laws as will increase the happiness, prosperity and security of the people of the State; to remove all just causes of dissatisfaction.

Many may indulge the hope that the colored population is destined to pass away from your midst, and so refuse our prayer. But the hope is a delusion. We are a part of the American people, and we and our posterity will forever be a constituent part of your population. If we are deprived of education, of equal political privileges, still subjected to the same depressing influences under which we now suffer, the natural consequences will follow; and the State, for her planting of injustice, will reap her harvest of sorrow and crime. She will contain within her limits a discontented population— dissatisfied, estranged—ready to welcome any revolution or invasion as a relief, for they can lose nothing and gain much. A contrary course of policy will enable us to keep step with our white fellow citizens in the march of improvement, disaffection will cease, and our noble State stand securely defended by the loving hearts of all her sons.

*Proceedings of the State Convention of Colored Men, Held in the City of Columbus, Ohio, January 16th, 17th, and 18th, 1856* (n.p., n.d.).

---

* Ohio excluded Negroes from schools in 1829 and twenty years later instituted segregated—and very inadequate—schools for Negroes.

## 143

# NEGRO VOTERS ENDORSE THE REPUBLICAN TICKET, 1856

A very early instance of Negro support of the Republican Party—characteristically expressed in guarded terms—appears in the resolutions adopted by Boston Negroes at a meeting held August 26, 1856. Prominent in this gathering were Dr. John S. Rock, Coffin Pitts, George L. Ruffin and Robert Johnson.

Resolved, That we, the colored citizens of Boston, will support with our voices and our votes, John C. Frémont, of California, as President of the United States, and William L. Dayton, of New Jersey, as Vice President.

Resolved, That while we regard the Republican party as the people's party, the resolve in the Republican platform endorsing the Kansas free State Constitution, which prohibits colored men from going into that territory, and the determination of the Republican press to ignore the colored man's interest in the party, plainly shows us that it is not an anti-slavery party; and while we are willing to unite with them to resist the aggressions of the Slave Power, we do not pledge ourselves to go further with the Republicans than the Republicans will go with us.

*The Liberator*, September 5, 1856.

## 144

# THE UNDERGROUND RAILROAD AS SEEN BY NEGROES, 1856–57

Various aspects of the working of America's most adventuresome organization—the Underground Railroad—are portrayed in the following four letters written from March, 1856 to March, 1857 and addressed to William Still, Negro director of the key Philadelphia station on that Railroad.

[a]

Hamilton [Canada], March 25th, 1856.
Mr. Still:—Sir and Friend—I take the liberty of addressing you with these few lines hoping that you will attend to what I shall request of you.
I have written to Virginia and have not received an answer yet. I want

to know if you can get any one of your city to go to Richmond for me. If you can, I will pay the expense of the whole. The person that I want the messenger to see is a white girl.* I expect you know who I allude to, it is the girl that sent me away. If you can get any one to go, you will please write right away and tell me the cost, &c. I will forward the money and a letter. Please use your endeavors.

Yours Respectfully,

John Hall.

Direct yours to Mr. Hill.

[b]

Havana, August 11, 1856, Schuykill Co., N.Y.

Mr. Wm. Still—Dear Sir: I came from Virginia in March, and was at your office the last of March. My object in writing you, is to inquire what I can do, or what can be done to help my wife to escape from the same bondage that I was in. You will know by your books that I was from Petersburg, Va., and that is where my wife now is. I have received two or three letters from a lady in that place and the last one says, that my wife's mistress is dead, and that she expects to be sold. I am very anxious to do what I can for her before it is too late, and beg of you to devise some means to get her away. Capt. the man that brought me away, knows the colored agent at Petersburg, and knows he will do all he can to forward my wife. The Capt. promised, that when I could raise one hundred dollars for him that he would deliver her in Philadelphia. Tell him that I can now raise the money, and will forward it to you at any day that he thinks that he can bring her. Please see the Captain and find when he will undertake it, and then let me know when to forward the money to you. I am at work for the Hon. Charles Cook, and can send the money any day. My wife's name is Harriet Robertson, and the agent at Petersburg knows her.

Please direct your answer, with all necessary directions, to N. Coryell, of this village, and he will see that all is right.

Very respectfully,

Daniel Robertson.

[c]

Syracuse [New York], Oct. 5, 1856.

Dear Friend Still:—I write to you for Mrs. Susan Bell, who was at your city some time in September last. She is from Washington city. She left her dear

* The girl's name was Mary Weaver. Shortly after John Hall's escape she left Richmond and joined him in Canada where the two were married.

little children behind (two children). She is stopping in our city, and wants to hear from her children very much indeed. She wishes to know if you have heard from Mr. Biglow, of Washington city. She will remain here until she can hear from you. She feels very anxious about her children, I will assure you. I should have written before this, but I have been from home much of the time since she came to our city. She wants to know if Mr. Biglow has heard anything about her husband. If you have not written to Mr. Biglow, she wishes you would. She sends her love to you and your dear family. She says that you were all kind to her, and she does not forget it. You will direct your letter to me, dear brother, and I will see that she gets it.

Miss F. E. Watkins left our house yesterday for Ithaca, and other places in that part of the State. Frederick Douglass, Wm. J. Watkins and others were with us last week; Gerritt Smith with others. Miss Watkins is doing great good in our part of the State. We think much indeed of her. She is such a good and glorious speaker, that we are all charmed with her.* We have had thirty-one fugitives in the last twenty-seven days; but you, no doubt, have had many more than that. I hope the good Lord may bless you and spare you long to do good to the hunted and outraged among our brethren.

Yours truly,

J. W. Loguen

Agent of the Underground Rail Road.

[d]

Camden, Del., March 23d, 1857.

Dear Sir;—I tak my pen in hand to write you, to inform you what we have had to go throw for the last two weaks. Thir wir six men and two woman was betraid on the tenth of this month, thea had them in prison but thea got out was conveyed by a black man, he told them he wood bring them to my hows, as he wos told, he had ben ther Befor, he has com with Harrett,† a woman that stops at my hous when she pases two and throw yau. You don't no me I supos, the Rev. Thomas K. Kennard dos, or Peter Lowis. He road Camden Circuit, this man led them in dover prisin and left them with a whit man; but tha tour out the winders and jump out, so cum back to Camden. We put them throug, we hav to carry them 19 mils and cum back the sam night wich maks 38 mils. It is tou much for our littel horses. We must do the bes we can, ther is much Bisness dun on this Road. We hav to go throw dover

---

\* This young Negro Abolitionist later gained greater prominence as Mrs. Frances Ellen Watkins Harper, essayist and poet.

† It is probable this refers to the magnificent Harriet Tubman, greatest of all Underground Railroad agents.

and smerny, the two wors places this sid of mary land lin. If you have herd or sean them ples let me no. I will Com to Phila be for long and then I will call and se you. There is much to do her. Ples to wright, I Remain your frend,

WILLIAM BRINKLY.

Remember me to Thom. Kennard.

William Still, *Underground Railroad Records*, pp. 74, 158, 252, 331.


## 145

## A PRO-SLAVERY NEGRO AND HOW NEGROES GREETED HIM, 1857

In the Spring of 1857 papers like the New York *Independent* and the *Cleveland Leader* reported pro-slavery lectures in the West by one Rev. Dr. Ross, a free Negro (with a white father) from Alabama. In June a public meeting was held by the Negroes of Cleveland, led by John Malvin and the Rev. Robert Johnson, to express their sentiments concerning the Rev. Dr. Ross' conduct.

Whereas, one Rev. Dr. Ross has taken such extraordinary grounds on the subject of slavery, we, the colored people of the city of Cleveland, feel it to be our duty to express our feelings in relation to his position on the inferiority of the colored race; and whereas, we have received intelligence, from public prints, that the said Dr. Ross is of African descent, and, from his complexion and general appearance, we believe the above statement to be correct; therefore

Resolved, That while we are not surprised to hear colored men advocate the principle of slavery, we are greatly surprised to hear one of that class argue the inferiority of his own race.

Resolved, That in viewing the position taken by Dr. Ross, in saying that the emancipation of the slave would equal infidelity, we deprecate it as a crime against God and humanity, as "uttering the most diabolical sentiment coming up from hell" [quoting Dr. Ross' words].

Resolved, That the Doctor remarked that he was loved by all, and especially by the slaves and the Abolitionists, but we do not love him, but hate him as an apostate from the religion of Jesus Christ, and a traitor and disgrace to his people.

*The Liberator*, July 3, 1857.

146

# THE DRED SCOTT DECISION, 1857

The Supreme Court's Dred Scott decision of March, 1857—opening all Federal territory to slavery and denying the citizenship of the Negro—evoked a storm of protest from the Negro people. Typical reactions came from a packed meeting held in Israel Church, Philadelphia, on April 3, 1857. The remarks that follow were made by Robert Purvis and Charles L. Remond at that meeting.

### Robert Purvis:

*Whereas,* The Supreme Court of the United States has decided in the case of Dred Scott, that *people of African descent are not and cannot be citizens of the United States, and cannot sue in any of the United States courts;* and whereas, the Court in rendering its decision has declared that "this unfortunate class have, with the civilized and enlightened portion of the world, for more than a century, been regarded as being of an inferior order, and unfit associates for the white race, either socially or politically, having no rights which white men are bound to respect;" and whereas, this Supreme Court is the constitutionally approved tribunal to determine all such questions; therefore,

*Resolved,* That this atrocious decision furnishes final confirmation of the already well known fact that under the Constitution and Government of the United States, the colored people are nothing, and can be nothing but an alien, disfranchised and degraded class.

*Resolved,* That to attempt, as some do, to prove that there is no support given to Slavery in the Constitution and essential structure of the American Government, is to argue against reason and common sense, to ignore history and shut our eyes against palpable facts; and that while it may suit white men who do not feel the iron heel, to please themselves with such theories, it ill becomes the man of color whose daily experience refutes the absurdity, to indulge in any such idle phantasies.

*Resolved,* That to persist in supporting a Government which holds and exercises the power, as distinctly set forth by a tribunal from which there is no appeal, to trample a class under foot as an inferior and degraded race, is on the part of the colored man at once the height of folly and the depth of pusillanimity.

*Resolved,* That no allegiance is due from any man, or any class of men, to a Government founded and administered in iniquity, and that the only duty the colored man owes to a Constitution under which he is declared to be an inferior and degraded being, having no rights which white men are bound to respect, is to denounce and repudiate it, and to do what he can by all proper means to bring it into contempt.

Mr. Purvis's speech in support of these resolutions was brief but earnest. He scouted the idea of colored people taking comfort from the pretence that this decision of the Supreme Court was unconstitutional. The Supreme Court, he said, was the appointed tribunal, and what it said was constitutional, was constitutional to all *practical* intents and purposes. There was nothing new in this decision; it was in perfect keeping with the treatment of the colored people by the American Government from the beginning to this day. Mr. Purvis was asked by one of the audience if he had not been acknowledged and treated as an American citizen. He said he had been, and that by the Cabinet of General Jackson. He stated that, intending to embark on a voyage to Europe, he applied to the Secretary of State for a passport, and an informal ticket of leave sort of paper was sent him in return.

He showed this to Mr. Robert Vaux, father of the present Mayor, who was so indignant that he wrote to Washington on the subject, and as a result, a formal passport, giving him the protection of the Government, as a citizen of the United States, was sent to him.* But, said Mr. Purvis, I was indebted for this not to the American Constitution or to the spirit of the American Government, but to the generous impulses of General Andrew Jackson, who had on more occasions than one in the then late war publicly tendered his gratitude to colored citizens for their brave assistance in the defence of the country.

Mr. Purvis was followed by C. L. Remond, of Salem, Mass., who, in reply to the same interrogation, stated that his father, being an immigrant from the West Indies, was formally naturalized as a citizen of the United States, but, like Mr. Purvis, he considered this no proof that the Supreme Court was not vested with power to declare that people of African descent could not be citizens of the United States. Mr. Remond then offered the following resolutions, with a view, as he said, of making the expression contained in those of Mr. Purvis more complete:—

*Resolved,* That though many of our fathers and some of us have, in time past, exercised the right of American citizenship; this was when a better spirit pervaded the land, and when the patriotic services of colored men in the defence of the country were fresh in the minds of the people; but that

* Among the papers of Robert Vaux, in the library of the Historical Society of Pennsylvania, is a letter to Vaux from Arnold Buffum, dated Philadelphia, 5 Mo., 16, 1834, appealing for Vaux's aid in getting Robert Purvis a bona fide passport.

the power to oppress us lurked all the time in the Constitution, only waiting to be developed; and that now when it suits the slave oligarchy to assert that power, we are made to feel its grinding weight.

*Resolved,* That what little remains to us of political rights in individual States, we hold, as we conceive, only by sufferance; and that when it suits the purposes of the slave power to do so, they will command their obedient dough-faced allies at the North to take these rights away from us, and leave us no more room under the State Government, than we have under the Federal.

*Resolved,* That we rejoice that slave holding despotism lays its ruthless hand not only on the humble black man, but on the proud Northern white man; and our hope is, that when our white fellow slaves in these so called free States see that they are alike subject with us to the slave oligarchy, the difference in our servitude being only in degree, they will make common cause with us, and that throwing off the yoke and striking for impartial liberty, they will join with us in our efforts to recover the long lost boon of freedom.

Mr. Remond spoke at length and with much fervor. He considered that for colored people, after this, to persist in claiming citizenship under the United States Constitution would be mean-spirited and craven. We owe no allegiance to a country which grinds us under its iron hoof and treats us like dogs. The time has gone by for colored people to talk of patriotism: He used to be proud that the first blood shed in the American Revolution (that of Attucks, who fell in Boston) was that of a colored man. He used to be proud that his grandfather, on his mother's side, fought for liberty in the Revolutionary war. But that time had passed by. The liberty purchased by the Revolutionary men was used to enslave and degrade the colored man, and, as a colored man, he loathed and abhorred the government that could perpetrate such outrages. He repudiated, he denounced the American Union in strong terms. People might talk to him of "patience." He had no patience to submit quietly to chains and oppression. Let others bare their backs to the lash, and meekly and submissively wear their chains. That was not his idea of duty, of manhood, or of self-respect.

Mr. Remond made many remarks on other subjects, as did also Mr. Purvis, who again took the floor. When the resolutions came to be put, some opposition was made, and a rambling and somewhat personal debate ensued; the end of which was, that the question was taken on the resolutions as a whole, and the chair pronounced them carried.

*The Liberator,* April 10, 1857.

## 147

## NEGRO BUSINESSMEN AND TAXATION WITHOUT REPRESENTATION, 1857

Two Negro partners, Mifflin Gibbs and John Lester, proprietors of a general merchandise store in San Francisco, voiced their protest against taxation without representation in the following open letter, of April, 1857, to that state's press:

During a residence of seven years in California, we, with hundreds of other colored men, have cheerfully paid city, State and county taxes on real estate and merchandise, as well as licenses to carry on business, and every other species of tax that has been levied from time to time for the support of the government, save only the "poll-tax"—that we have persistently refused. On the day before yesterday, the Tax Collector called on us, and seized and lugged off twenty or thirty dollars' worth of goods, in payment, as he said, of this tax.

Now, while we cannot understand how a "white" man can refuse to pay each and every tax for the support of government, under which he enjoys every privilege—from the right to rob a Negro up to that of being Governor of the State—we can perceive and feel the flagrant injustice of compelling "colored men" to pay a special tax for the enjoyment of a special privilege and then break their heads if they attempt to exercise it. We believe that every voter should pay poll-tax, or every male resident who has the privilege of becoming a voter; but regard it as low and despicable, the very quintessence of meanness, to compel colored men to pay it, situated as they are politically. However, if there is no redress, the great State of California may come around annually, and rob us of twenty and thirty dollars' worth of goods, as we will never willingly pay three dollars as poll-tax as long as we remain disfranchised, oath-denied, outlawed colored Americans.

*The Liberator,* July 3, 1857.

## 148

## WISCONSIN NEGROES DEMAND THE SUFFRAGE, 1857

Wisconsin disfranchised its Negro residents in 1849. Thereafter a continual effort was made by the Negroes of the state to reverse this act. Typical is this numerously signed petition presented to the Wisconsin legislature in September, 1857.

We the undersigned, colored inhabitants of the State of Wisconsin, would once more exercise the *right,* which is guaranteed to *all the people,* peaceably to assemble, and petition the Government for a redress of grievances. We complain of Article 3d, Section 1st of the Constitution of the State of Wisconsin. We now ask your honorable body to regard our feeble request, and remove this *heel of oppression* and disability which rests upon us, as contained in the Article and Section referred to, and thereby give us an opportunity to become respected citizens of the State. We complain of that part of the Section which disallows to us the right of franchise, and at the same time grants it to others who immigrate from foreign lands, and who do not understand the Constitution, Government and Laws as well as ourselves. We do not *say,* neither do we *believe,* that men of foreign birth, immigrating to this asylum of the oppressed, should be deprived of any of the rights and blessings which this government has confirmed upon them; but we *do* say, that the same rights and blessings should be extended to us. In addition to all this, is it not proper to submit to your honorable body to say if it be right, justice, or *common sense,* that we should be subject to taxation without representation?

*The Liberator,* October 23, 1857.

149

## BUYING THE LIBERTY OF A SON AND A NIECE, 1857

Below are two letters chronicling the efforts of Negroes in the task of purchasing the freedom of dear ones. The first is from Mrs. Earro Weems to William Still of Philadelphia and is dated Washington, D.C., September 19, 1857; the second, from an anonymous Negro lady is addressed to the Rev. Mr. Crawford of Nantucket and is dated New Bedford, Mass., December 20, 1857.

[a]

I have just sent for my son Augustus, in Alabama. I have sent eleven hundred dollars which pays for his body and some thirty dollars to pay his fare to Washington. I borrowed one hundred and eighty dollars to make out the eleven hundred dollars. I was not very successful in Syracuse. I collected only twelve dollars, and in Rochester only two dollars. I did not know that the season was so unpropitious. The wealthy had all gone to the springs. They must have returned by this time. I hope you will exert yourself and help me get a part of the money I owe, at least. I am obliged to pay it by the 12th of next month. I was unwell when I returned through Philadelphia, or I should have called. I have been from home five weeks.

My son Augustus is the last of the family in Slavery. I feel rejoiced that he is soon to be free and with me, and of course feel the greatest solicitude about raising the one hundred and eighty dollars I have borrowed of a kind friend, or who has borrowed it for me at bank. I hope and pray you will help me as far as possible. Tell Mr. Douglass to remember me, and if he can, to interest his friends for me.

You will recollect that five hundred dollars of our money was taken to buy the sister of Henry H. Garnet's wife. Had I been able to command this I should not be necessitated to ask the favors and indulgences I do.

I am expecting daily the return of Augustus, and may Heaven grant him a safe deliverance and smile propitiously upon you and all kind friends who have aided in his return to me.

Be pleased to remember me to friends, and accept yourself the blessing and prayers of your dear friend.

Wm. Still, *Underground Railroad Records*, pp. 186–87.

### [b]

Dear Brother:

I deeply sympathize with you, knowing the strong ties of nature. Though born in a boasted land of liberty, and having all my relatives born free, I forget not my brothers and sisters in bonds.

In hearing that sad, but O, too true narrative, last evening, of that beautiful girl, fettered in thought and limb, I could but weep. But weeping alone won't do. Bearing in mind that in judgment, God will not accept me for my weeping and praying, but, "inasmuch as ye have done it unto one of these, the least of my little ones, ye have done it unto me," within I enclose the small sum of five dollars. Would to the Lord I could give more.

Now, dear brother, do not stop to thank me, for do I want to be thanked for freeing my sister, or for doing my duty? Accept it, and while it is put with the rest to free that dear niece of yours, and sister of mine, I will pray that God will break the heart of that cruel oppressor; pray that God will kill him, and make him alive in Jesus. I believe in prayer.

Pardon me for thus writing so freely, but my soul is stirred within.

God speed you! Put your trust in him, for all things are his. Do not get discouraged, but look up!

Your sister in the Lord.

*The Liberator*, January 15, 1858.

150

# NEW YORK NEGROES APPEAL FOR BETTER SCHOOLS, 1857

The New York Society for the Promotion of Education Among Colored Children —a Negro organization with Charles B. Ray as president and Philip A. White as secretary—presented on Dec. 28, 1857, a carefully documented paper supporting requests for improvement in the education of Negro children to a special commission appointed by the Governor to investigate the city's schools. This document was published in the New York Negro magazine, *The Anglo-African*, in July, 1859 (I, pp. 222–24) with the following note appended to it: "Although nearly two years old, it is of intrinsic value as a record of what Caste Schools are, when left to the tender mercies of a Board of Education, whose members feel themselves little if at all responsible to colored voters. It is, nevertheless, one of the most effective documents ever issued by an association of colored men, for since it was written, and mainly in consequence of it, the School-house in Thomas street has been removed to the corner of Hudson and Franklin street, one of the finest locations in the fifth ward; the school-house in Mulberry street has been taken down, to be replaced immediately by a new and elegant structure, replete with all the modern furniture and equipments; and a handsome sum has been appropriated to re-model the school-house in Laurens street. Yet there are men among the colored people who say, that we cannot do anything in this land!"

The following statement in relation to the colored schools in said city and county is respectfully presented by the New York Society for the Promotion of Education among Colored Children:

1. The number of colored children in the city and county of New York (estimated in 1855 from the census of 1850), between the ages of 4 and 17 years         3,000

    a. Average attendance of colored children at public schools in 1855       913

        Average do. in corporate schools supported by school funds (Colored Orphan Asylum)       240

                                       1,153

    b. Proportion of average attendance in public schools of colored children to whole number of same is as 1 to 2.60

2. The number of white children in the city of New York in 1855 (estimated as above), between the ages of 4 and 17 years       159,000

    a. Average attendance of white children in public schools in 1855       43,858

Average attendance of do. in corporate schools
supported by public funds                                    2,826
                                                                    ———
                                                                    46,684

b. Proportion of average attendance of white children in public schools to whole number of the same is as 1 to 3.40

3. From these facts it appears that colored children attend the public schools (and schools supported by public funds in the city of New York) in the proportion of 1 to 2.60, and that white children attend similar schools in said city in the proportion of 1 to 3.40; that is to say, nearly 25 per cent more of colored children than of white children attend the public schools, and schools supported by public funds in the city of New York.

4. The number of colored children attending private schools in the city of New York, 125.

a. The number of white children attending private schools in 1850, census gave 10,175, which number has since been increased by the establishment of Catholic parochial schools, estimated in 1856, 17,560.

b. The proportion of colored children attending private schools to white children attending same, is as 1 to 140.

c. But the average attendance of colored children in all schools is about the same as that of white in proportion, that is to say, as many colored children attend the public schools as do whites attend both public and private schools, in proportion to the whole number of each class of children.

### Locality, capability, &c., of colored schools.

1. a. The Board of Education, since its organization, has expended in sites and buildings for white schools $1,600,000.

b. The Board of Education has expended in sites and buildings for colored schools (addition to building leased 19 Thomas) $1,000.

c. The two school-houses in possession of the Board now used for colored children were assigned to same by the Old Public School Society.

2. The proportion of colored children to white children attending public schools is as 1 to 40.

a. The sum expended on school-buildings and sites of colored and white schools by the Board of Education is as 1 to 1,600.

3. a. School-house No. 1, for colored children, is an old building, erected in 1820 by the New York Manumission Society as a school for colored children, in Mulberry street, in a poor but decent locality. It has two departments, one male and one female; it consists of two stories only, and has two small recitation rooms on each floor, but as primary as well as grammar

children attend each department, much difficulty and confusion arises from the want of class room for the respective studies. The building covers only part of the lot, and as it is the best attended, and among the best taught of the colored schools, a new and ample school building, erected in this place, would prove a great attraction, and could be amply filled by children.

b. School-house No. 2, erected in Laurens street more than twenty years ago for colored children by the Public School Society, is in one of the lowest and filthiest neighborhoods, and hence, although it has competent teachers in the male and female departments, and a separate primary department, the attendance has always been slender, and will be until the school is removed to a neighborhood where children may be sent without danger to their morals.

c. School No. 3 for colored children, in Yorkville, is an old building, is well attended, and deserves, in connection with School house No. 4, in Harlem, a new building between the present localities.

d. School-house No. 5, for colored children, is an old building, leased at No. 19 Thomas street, a most degraded neighborhood, full of filth and vice; yet the attendance in this school, and the excellence of its teachers, earn for it the need of a new site and new building.

e. School-house No. 6, for colored children, is in Broadway, near 37th street, in a dwelling house leased and fitted up for a school, in which there is always four feet of water in the cellar. The attendance good. Some of the school-officers have repeatedly promised a new building.

f. Primary school for colored children, No. 1, is in the basement of a church on 15th street, near 7th avenue, in a good location, but premises too small for the attendance; no recitation rooms, and is perforce both primary and grammar school, to the injury of the progress of all.

g. Primary schools for colored children, No. 2 and 3, are in the rear of Church, in 2d street, near 6th avenue; the rooms are dark and cheerless, and without the needful facilities of sufficient recitation rooms, &c.

From a comparison of the school-houses with the splendid, almost palatial edifices, with manifold comforts, conveniences and elegancies which make up the school-houses for white children in the city of New York, it is evident that the colored children are painfully neglected and positively degraded. Pent up in filthy neighborhoods, in old and dilapidated buildings, they are held down to low associations and gloomy surroundings.

Yet Mr. Superintendent Kiddle, at a general examination of colored schools held in July last, (for silver medals awarded by the society now addressing your honorable body) declared the reading and spelling equal to that of any schools in the city.

The undersigned enter their solemn protest against this unjust treatment of colored children. They believe with the experience of Massachusetts, and especially the recent experience of Boston before them, there is no sound reason why colored children should be excluded from any of the common schools supported by taxes levied alike on whites and blacks, and governed by officers elected by the vote of colored as well as white voters.

But if in the judgment of your honorable body common schools are not thus common to all, then we earnestly pray you to recommend to the Legislature such action as shall cause the Board of Education of this city to erect at least two well appointed modern grammar schools for colored children on suitable sites, in respectable localities, so that the attendance of colored children may be increased, and their minds be elevated in like manner as the happy experience of the honorable the Board of Education has been in the matter of white children.

In addition to the excellent impulse to colored youth which these new grammar schools would give, they will have the additional argument of actual economy; the children will be taught with far less expense in two such schoolhouses than in the half dozen hovels into which they are now driven. It is a costly piece of injustice which educates the white scholar in a palace at $10 per year, and the colored pupil in a hovel at $17 or $18 per annum.

### Taxes, &c., of colored population of the city.

No proposition can be more reasonable than that they who pay taxes for schools and school-houses should be provided with schools and school-houses. The colored population of this city, in proportion to their numbers, pay their full share of the general and therefore of the school-taxes. There are about nine thousand adults of both sexes; of these over three thousand are householders, rent-payers, and therefore tax-payers, in that sense of the word in which owners make tax-payers of their poor tenants. The colored laboring man, with an income of $200 per year, who pays $72 per year for a room and bedroom, is really in proportion to his means a larger tax-payer than the millionaire whose tax-rate is thousands of dollars.

But directly, also, do the colored people pay taxes. From examination carefully made, the undersigned affirm that there are in the city at least 1,000 colored persons who own and pay taxes on real estate

| Taxed real estate in the city of New York owned by colored persons | $1,400,000 |
|---|---|
| Untaxed by colored persons (Churches) | 250,000 |
| Personal estate | 710,000 |
| Money in savings banks | 1,121,000 |
| | $3,481,000 |

These figures indicate that in proportion to their numbers, the colored population of this city pay a fair share of the school-taxes, and that they have been most unjustly dealt with. Their money has been used to purchase sites and erect and fit up school-houses for white children, whilst their own children are driven into miserable edifices in disgraceful localities. Surely the white population of the city are too able, too generous, too just, any longer to suffer this miserable robbing of their colored fellow-citizens for the benefit of white children.

## 151

# COMPARING WHITE AND NEGRO AMERICANS, 1858

Dr. John S. Rock, a distinguished Negro Abolitionist, physician and lawyer of Boston (he was the first Negro attorney admitted to the bar of the United States Supreme Court), is a singularly neglected figure. He had, nevertheless, one of the most brilliant minds and sharpest tongues of any pre-Civil War orator. Indicative of his prowess is the following speech delivered at Boston, March 5, 1858, at a meeting commemorating the Boston Massacre and also addressed by Theodore Parker, Charles L. Remond, William Lloyd Garrison and Wendell Phillips.

White Americans have taken great pains to try to prove that we are cowards. We are often insulted with the assertion, that if we had had the courage of the Indians or the white man, we would never have submitted to be slaves. I ask if Indians and white men have never been slaves? The white man tested the Indian's courage here when he had his organized armies, his battle-grounds, his places of retreat. with everything to hope for and everything to lose. The position of the African slave has been very different. Seized a prisoner of war, unarmed, bound hand and foot, and conveyed to a distant country among what to him were worse than cannibals; brutally beaten, half-starved, closely watched by armed men, with no means of knowing their own strength or the strength of their enemies, with no weapons, and without a probability of success. But if the white man will take the trouble to fight the black man in Africa or in Hayti, and fight him as fair as the black man will fight him there—if the black man does not come off victor, I am deceived in his prowess. But, take a man, armed or unarmed, from his home, his country, or his friends, and place him among savages, and who is he that would not make good his retreat? "Discretion is the better part of

valor," but for a man to resist where he knows it will destroy him, shows more
foolhardiness than courage. There have been many Anglo-Saxons and Anglo-
Americans enslaved in Africa, but I have never heard that they successfully
resisted any government. They always resort to running indispensables.

The courage of the Anglo-Saxon is best illustrated in his treatment of the
Negro. A score or two of them can pounce upon a poor Negro, tie and beat
him, and then call him a coward because he submits. Many of their most
brilliant victories have been achieved in the same manner. But the greatest
battles which they have fought have been upon paper. We can easily account
for this; their trumpeter is dead. He died when they used to be exposed for
sale in the Roman market, about the time that Cicero cautioned his friend
Atticus not to buy them, on account of their stupidity. A little more than
half a century ago, this race, in connection with their Celtic neighbors, who
have long been considered (by themselves, of course,) the bravest soldiers
in the world, so far forgot themselves, as to attack a few cowardly, stupid
Negro slaves, who, according to their accounts, had not sense enough to go
to bed. And what was the result? Why, sir, the Negroes drove them out from
the island like so many sheep, and they have never dared to show their faces,
except with hat in hand.

Our true and tried friend, Rev. Theodore Parker, said, in his speech at
the State House, a few weeks since, that "the stroke of the axe would have
settled the question long ago, but the black man would not strike." Mr.
Parker makes a very low estimate of the courage of his race, if he means that
one, two or three millions of these ignorant and cowardly black slaves could,
without means, have brought to their knees five, ten, or twenty millions of intelligent, brave white men, backed up by a rich oligarchy. But I know of no
one who is more familiar with the true character of the Anglo-Saxon race
than Mr. Parker. I will not dispute this point with him, but I will thank him
or any one else to tell us how it could have been done. His remark calls to
my mind the day which is to come, when one shall chase a thousand, and
two put ten thousand to flight. But when he says that "the black man *would
not strike,*" I am prepared to say that he does us great injustice. The black
man is not a coward. The history of the bloody struggles for freedom in
Hayti, in which the blacks whipped the French and the English, and gained
their independence, in spite of the perfidy of that villainous First Consul,
will be a lasting refutation of the malicious aspersions of our enemies. The
history of the struggles for the liberty of the United States ought to silence
every American calumniator. . . .

The white man contradicts himself who says, that if he were in our
situation, he would throw off the yoke. Thirty millions of white men of this
proud Caucasian race are at this moment held as slaves, and bought and sold

with horses and cattle. The iron heel of oppression grinds the masses of all the European races to the dust. They suffer every kind of oppression, and no one dares to open his mouth to protest against it. Even in the Southern portion of this boasted land of liberty, no white man dares advocate so much of the Declaration of Independence as declares that "all men are created free and equal, and have an inalienable right to life, liberty," &c.

White men have no room to taunt us with tamely submitting. If they were black men, they would work wonders; but, as white men, they can do nothing. "O, Consistency, thou art a jewel!"

Now, it would not be surprising if the brutal treatment which we have received for the past two centuries should have crushed our spirits. But this is not the case. Nothing but a superior force keeps us down. And when I see the slaves rising up by hundreds annually, in the majesty of human nature, bidding defiance to every slave code and its penalties, making the issue Canada or death, and that too while they are closely watched by paid men armed with pistols, clubs and bowie-knives, with the army and navy of this great Model Republic arrayed against them, I am disposed to ask if the charge of cowardice does not come with ill-grace . . .

I do not envy the white American the little liberty which he enjoys. It is his right, and he ought to have it. I wish him success, though I do not think he deserves it. But I would have all men free. We have had much sad experience in this country, and it would be strange indeed if we do not profit by some of the lessons which we have so dearly paid for. Sooner or later, the clashing of arms will be heard in this country, and the black man's services will be needed: 150,000 freemen capable of bearing arms, and not all cowards and fools, and three quarter of a million slaves, wild with the enthusiasm caused by the dawn of the glorious opportunity of being able to strike a genuine blow for freedom, will be a power which white men will be "bound to respect." Will the blacks fight? Of course they will. The black man will never be neutral. He could not if he would and would not if he could. Will he fight for this country, right or wrong? This the common sense of every one answers; and when the time comes, and come it will, the black man will give an intelligent answer. Judge Taney may outlaw us; Caleb Cushing * may show the depravity of his heart by abusing us; and this wicked government may oppress us; but the black man will live when Judge Taney, Caleb Cushing and this wicked government are no more. White men may despise, ridicule, slander and abuse us; they may seek as they always have done to divide us, and make us feel degraded; but no man shall cause me to turn my back upon my race. With it I will sink or swim.

* Cushing was a leading Massachusetts Democrat. He was Attorney-General of the United States from 1853 to 1857.

The prejudice which some white men have, or affected to have, against my color gives me no pain. If any man does not fancy my color, that is his business, and I shall not meddle with it. I shall give myself no trouble because he lacks good taste. If he judges my intellectual capacity by my color, he certainly cannot expect much profundity, for it is only skin deep, and is really of no very great importance to any one but myself. I will not deny that I admire the talents and noble characters of many white men. But I cannot say that I am particularly pleased with their physical appearance. If old mother nature had held out as well as she commenced, we should, probably, have had fewer varieties in the races. When I contrast the fine tough muscular system, the beautiful, rich color, the full broad features, and the gracefully frizzled hair of the Negro, with the delicate physical organization, wan color, sharp features and lank hair of the Caucasian, I am inclined to believe that when the white man was created, nature was pretty well exhausted—but determined to keep up appearances, she pinched up his features, and did the best she could under the circumstances. (Great laughter.)

I would have you understand, that I not only love my race, but am pleased with my color; and while many colored persons may feel degraded by being called Negroes, and wish to be classed among other races more favored, I shall feel it my duty, my pleasure and my pride, to concentrate my feeble efforts in elevating to a fair position a race to which I am especially identified by feelings and by blood. . . .

In this country, where money is the great sympathetic nerve which ramifies society, and has a ganglia in every man's pocket, a man is respected in proportion to his success in business. When the avenues to wealth are opened to us, we will then become educated and wealthy, and then the roughest looking colored man that you ever saw, or ever will see, will be pleasanter than the harmonies of Orpheus, and black will be a very pretty color. It will make our jargon, wit—our words, oracles; flattery will then take the place of slander, and you will find no prejudice in the Yankee whatever. We do not expect to occupy a much better position than we now do, until we shall have our educated and wealthy men, who can wield a power that cannot be misunderstood. Then, and not till then, will the tongue of slander be silenced, and the lip of prejudice sealed. Then, and not till then, will we be able to enjoy true equality, which can exist only among peers.

*The Liberator*, March 12, 1858.

## 152

# A PUBLIC DISCUSSION OF INSURRECTION, 1858

A State Convention of Massachusetts Negroes met in the New Bedford City Hall during the first week of August, 1858. The presiding officer was William Wells Brown and among those present were Charles L. Remond, Robert Morris, Lewis Hayden, William C. Nell, and Josiah Henson. The spirited nature of the discussion may be seen from the following largely verbatim report of the proceedings of August 2:

Mr. Morris then came out with great strength on the school question: "When we wanted our children to go to the Public Schools in Boston," said he, "they offered them schools, and white teachers; but no, we wouldn't have them. Then they offered to give us colored teachers; no, we wouldn't stand that neither. Then the School Committee said—'Well, if you won't be satisfied either way, you shall have them as we choose.' So we decided on a desperate step, but it turned out to be a successful one. We went round to every parent in the city, and had all the children removed from the Caste Schools; we made all our people take their children away. And in six months we had it all our own way—and that's the way we always should act. Let us be bold, and they'll have to yield to us. Let us be bold, if any man flies from slavery, and comes among us. When he's reached us, we'll say, he's gone far enough. If any man comes here to New Bedford, and they try to take him away, you telegraph to us in Boston, and we'll come down three hundred strong, and stay with you; and we won't go until he's safe. If he goes back to the South, we'll go with him. And if any man runs away, and comes to Boston, we'll send to you, if necessary, and you may come up to us three hundred strong, if you can—come men, and women too."

C. L. Remond regretted that he was obliged to ask for rights which every pale-faced vagabond from across the water could almost at once enjoy. He did not go so far as Uncle Tom, and kiss the hand that smote him. He didn't believe in such a Christianity. He didn't object to the [Dred Scott] "decision," and the slave bill, any more than to the treatment of the colored race in Iowa and Kansas. The exodus for the colored men of this country is over the Constitution and through the Union. He referred to parties, and asked what either of them had done for freedom. The free-soil and republican parties had, alike, been false. We must depend upon our own self-reliance. If we recommend to the slaves in South Carolina to rise in rebellion, it would work greater things than we imagine. If some black Archimedes does not soon arise with his lever, then will there spring up some black William Wallace with his claymore, for the freedom of the black race. He boldly proclaimed himself a traitor to the government and the Union, so long as his rights were denied him for no fault of his own. Our government would disgrace the Algerines and Hottentots. Were there a thunderbolt of God which he could invoke to bring destruction upon this nation, he would gladly do it. . . .

Mr. Remond moved that a committee of five be appointed to prepare an address suggesting to the slaves at the South to create an insurrection. He said he knew his resolution was in one sense revolutionary, and in another, treasonable, but so he meant it. He doubted whether it would be carried. But he didn't want to see people shake their heads, as he did see them on the platform, and turn pale, but to rise and talk. He wanted to see the half-way fellows take themselves away, and leave the field to men who would encourage their brethren at the South to rise with bowie-knife and revolver and musket.

Father Henson doubted whether the time had come for the people of Massachusetts to take any such step. As for turning pale, he never turned pale in his life. [Father Henson is a very black man.] * He didn't want to fight any more than he believed Remond did. He believed that if the shooting time came, Remond would be found out of the question: As he didn't want to see three or four thousand men hung before their time, he should oppose any such action, head, neck and shoulders. If such a proposition were carried out, everything would be lost. Remond might talk, and then run away, but what would become of the poor fellows that must stand? And then the resolution was ridiculous for another reason. How could documents be circulated among the Negroes at the South? Catch the masters permitting that, and you catch a weasel asleep. However, they had nothing to fight with at the South—no weapons, no education. "When I fight," said Father Henson, "I want to whip somebody."

Mr. Troy, of Windsor, Canada, wanted to see the slaves free, for he had relatives who were the property of Senator Hunter, of Virginia; but he knew no such step as was now proposed could help them at all. He hoped the Convention would vote the thing down.

Captain Henry Johnson concurred with the last two speakers. It was easy to talk, but another thing to act. He was opposed to insurrection. In his opinion, those who were the loudest in their professions, were the first to run. The passage of the resolution would do no good. It would injure the cause. If we were equal in numbers, then there might be some reason in the proposition. If an insurrection occurred, he wouldn't fight.

* The bracketed words appear in the original report.

Mr. Remond expressed himself as quite indifferent whether his motion was carried or not. He was in collusion with no one, and he cared nothing if no one supported him. It had been intimated that he would skulk in the time of danger. The men who said so, judged of him by themselves. Some had said the address could not be circulated at the South; in that case, its adoption could certainly do no harm. Others had said, many lives would be lost if an insurrection should come about. He had counted the cost. If he had one hundred relations at the South, he would rather see them die to-day, than to live in bondage. He would rather stand over their graves, than feel that any pale-faced scoundrel might violate his mother or his sister at pleasure. He only regretted that he had not a spear with which he could transfix all the slaveholders at once. To the devil with the slaveholders! Give him liberty, or give him death. The insurrection could be accomplished as quick as thought, and the glorious result would be instantaneously attained.

A vote was taken, and the motion was lost. This was by far the most spirited discussion of the Convention.

*The Liberator,* August 13, 1858.

# 153

## NEGROES DEAL WITH A BETRAYER, 1858

On September 6, 1858 William C. Nell wrote to Garrison from Southfield, Michigan, concerning highly dramatic events revolving about the betrayal, by a Negro, of two fugitive slaves resident in Detroit. The letter speaks for itself.

The papers have already, I presume, informed you somewhat of the recent kidnapping case, and the consequent excitement in Cincinnati. I happened to be in Detroit, where the betrayer and his two victims (all colored men) resided, and when the news reached there, you can easily imagine the effect produced upon the colored men and women, many of whom were acquainted with all the parties.

Miss Frances E. Watkins already had a meeting announced for Thursday evening, Sept. 2d, in the Croghan Street Baptist Church, but the arrival of Rev. Henry H. Garnet, fresh from Cincinnati, prompted an attempt to secure the City Hall for a large gathering of the citizens to protest against kidnapping in Detroit; but the Buchanan Democratic Convention being held there, was of itself sufficient to put a veto upon any hope of ingress for an anti-Fugitive-Slave Law demonstration.

The Colored Methodist Conference adjourned its evening session, and thus augmented the numbers which crowded the meeting. The exercises commenced at an early hour by Mr. Garnet's reading the appropriate hymn of Mr. Follen, commencing, "What mean ye that ye bruise and bind?" This was sung with thrilling effect; after which a fervent prayer was offered by Rev. J. P. Campbell, in which every reference to the traitor, his deserved punishment, his victims and their sad fate, elicited heart-moving responses from various parts of the house.

Rev. Mr. Davis, Chairman, then introduced Rev. H. H. Garnet, who in a graphic and eloquent manner detailed the history of the kidnapping case, tracing Brodie's connection with it under written instructions from the slaveholders, until the imprisonment of the two captives in the jail at Covington, Ky. They had accepted Brodie's pledge to assist their return to the South, with a view to secure the liberation of some of their relatives from slavery. Instead of this blissful realization of their hopes, they were delivered into the hands of their self-styled owners, and by the very man in whom they had most implicitly trusted, receiving each one hundred lashes, and ordered to be sold further South, expressly to cut off all future chance of escape to the North. Mr. Garnet exhibited a pair of manacles, such as were worn by them on their way to jail, and a bull whip, as used in their severe flogging.

The young men of Cincinnati, on learning the facts, with that "eternal vigilance" which is "the price of liberty," succeeded in getting possession of the traitor, and instituted measures for his trial. This occupied two hours, during most of which time Mr. Garnet was present, and it was mainly owing to his intercession that Brodie was not torn limb from limb. He escaped with life, after the infliction of three hundred blows with a paddle—one blow for each dollar of blood money which he had received for doing the infamous work of these Kentucky hunters of men. Two white men, in sympathy with the right, though pretending otherwise to him, acted as police men, and removed him from immediate danger of being killed. He breathed vengeance upon the colored people, threatened to expose the operations of the Underground Railroad, &c. &c.; but when a committee of colored men started for the purpose of hurrying him from Cincinnati, it was found that his gold had bribed the white men, who were endeavoring to screen him from further molestation. But the colored men were determined, and his whereabouts was made known. Brodie delivered himself into the hands of the authorities, who put him in jail to save his life.

It has since turned out that the slaveholding influences united for his defence. State warrants have been issued for the arrest of several colored men charged with participating in his trial and punishment; and the day I left Detroit, some of them had arrived there, to avoid that liability.

But to return to the meeting. Miss Watkins, in the course of one of her very best outbursts of eloquent indignation, charged the treachery of this colored man upon the United States Government, which is the arch traitor to liberty, as shown by the Fugitive Slave Law and the Dred Scott decision. A discussion ensued on the pertinent question, submitted by Mr. Garnet, What shall be done with the traitor on his arrival in Detroit? A resolution embodying their detestation of the man was passed, and at a late hour, the meeting adjourned.

One of these betrayed men has left a wife in Detroit, and a babe born since his departure. A committee of ladies have called to administer to her wants, and to do what in them lies to save her from the clutches of the kidnapper.

*The Liberator,* September 11, 1858.

## 154

## SUPPORTING THE NEW REPUBLICAN PARTY, 1858

A New York Negro Suffrage Convention, with 37 delegates from a score of towns and cities, met in Troy on September 14, 1858, to discuss the current gubernatorial campaign. The following resolutions express the majority opinion of the members of this convention.

Resolved, That we are more than ever convinced of the necessity of intelligent and consolidated action on the part of the colored men themselves, for the security of the rights guaranteed to them, as a part of *"the people,"* in the Constitution of the United States. We have a great work between liberty and despotism; and, duly appreciating the duties and responsibilities devolving upon us, we should so act that our influence, as a political power, should be felt among the ranks of the people. . . .

Resolved, That we are *citizens* of the State of New York and, consequently, of the United States, and should enjoy all the rights and immunities of other citizens, the edict of Judge Taney to the contrary notwithstanding.

Resolved, That we will never cease our efforts to procure the repeal of the property qualification clause [for the suffrage] in our State Constitution, until success shall crown our efforts. . . .

Resolved, That in the ensuing gubernatorial election, it becomes us to act with special reference to securing the elective franchise. We can accomplish nothing in this direction save over the defeat and ruin of the so-called Democratic party, our most inveterate enemy. In order to secure this defeat, it is absolutely necessary to consolidate the strength of the opposition to said party. And we regard the Republican party, all things considered, as more likely than any other to effect this desirable end, and advise the eleven thousand colored voters of this State to concentrate their strength upon the Republican ticket for Governor &c, now before the people.

Resolved, That in so doing, we do not for a moment endorse all the political tenets of that party; we are Radical Abolitionists, and shall ever remain so; but we regard the nomination made by them at Syracuse as calculated to give aid and comfort to the enemy, by electing the Democratic candidate.

*The Liberator,* October 1, 1858.

## 155

## OHIO NEGROES SPEAK THEIR MINDS, 1858

Over fifty Negro leaders met in a State Convention of Ohio Colored Men in Cincinnati November 23–26, 1858. The elected president was Charles H. Langston; others prominent here were John I. Gaines, John Mercer Langston, John Malvin, Peter H. Clarke, David Jenkins, William H. Day, William J. Watkins and John Booker. The convention's resolutions best summarize its sentiments:

*Whereas,* The right to assemble and petition for a redress of grievances, is one of the few rights left to the colored people of the United States, therefore, we, the colored people of Ohio, deem it fit to represent to our fellow citizens the disabilities under which we labor, and for which we seek redress:

We have to complain that, in a country professing to realize in its Government, the grand principles of the Declaration of 1776, millions of our brethren are publicly sold, like beasts in the shambles, that they are robbed of their earnings, denied the control of their children, forbidden to protect the chastity of their wives and daughters, debarred an education and the free exercise of their religion; and if they escape by flight from so horrible a condition, they may be hunted like beasts from city to city, and dragged back to the hell from which they had fled—the Government which should protect them, prostituting its powers to aid the villains who hunt them.

Notwithstanding the rights and immunities of the citizens of the several States, are guaranteed to citizens of all the States, we can not visit large portions of our country in pursuit of health, business or pleasure, without danger of being sold into perpetual slavery, the shores of neighboring States being more inhospitable, than the bleakest or most savage shore that excites the mariner's dread.

To crown all, the highest tribunal of the land, solemnly denies that the great principles of Liberty and Equality which are the boast of our nation, were intended to apply to us and our unfortunate brethren, the slaves. It decides the colored American sailor, or traveler, can receive no protection from his Government; that the National Courts are closed to us; that we have fewer rights in our own native country than aliens, for the aliens may claim and receive justice; from the tribunal before which we may not appear as suitors.

Furthermore, in our own State of Ohio, while we are permitted a partial freedom, we are subjected to iniquitous and burdensome legislation. We are refused the right to vote; we are refused a fair trial by jury; we are refused participation in the emolument and honors of office; we are denied equal education; those of us who are reduced to pauperism, or afflicted with lunacy, are thrust into the cells of the felon's jail, all of which is unjust, tending to destroy those sentiments of self-respect, enterprise and patriotism, which it would be wisdom to foster in the people of the State. Therefore be it

*Resolved* (1), That if it is the province of governments to protect their subjects against unjust seizure and imprisonment, violence, robbery, murder, rape and incest; if they should encourage and sustain industry, marriage, the parental relation, education and religion; if it is their duty to honor God by respecting and protecting the rights of humanity, then should the American government immediately and unconditionally abolish that essence of infernalisms—American Slavery.

*Resolved* (2), That if the Dred Scott dictum be true exposition of the law of the land, then are the founders of the American Republic convicted by their descendants of base hypocrisy, and colored men absolved from all allegiance to a government which withdraws all protection.

*Resolved* (3), That we rejoice at the declension of the Democratic Party in the North, and hope that its defeat presages the downfall of Slavery, of which accursed system it has been a firm supporter.

*Resolved* (4), That we say to those who would induce us to emigrate to Africa or elsewhere, that the amount of labor and self-sacrifice required to establish a home in a foreign land, would if exercised here, redeem our native land from the grasp of slavery; therefore we are resolved to remain where we are, confident that "truth is mighty and will prevail."

*Resolved* (5), That we recommend to our people, in addition to the education they are so generally seeking to give their children, to train them in habits of useful industry.

*Resolved* (6), That a combination of labor and capital will in every field of enterprise, be our true policy. Combination stores of every kind, combination workshops, and combination farms, will, if everywhere established, greatly increase our wealth; and with it our power.

*Resolved* (7), That a State which Taxes a portion of its inhabitants without allowing them a representation, excludes them from offices of honor and trust, refuses them an impartial trial by Jury, refuses an equal education to their youth, disparages their patriotism by refusing to enroll them in her militia, allows them to be hunted through her cities, confined in her jails, and dragged thence to hopeless slavery, consigns their lunatics and paupers to the common jail, forfeits her claim to be called Christian or Republican.

*Resolved* (8), That in the vigorous and unceasing exercise of the rights of petition, we recognize a potent instrument of elevation, and we recommend the people of every city and school district to petition the Legislature to repeal all such laws, and to take the proper steps to expunge from the Constitution all traces of distinction on account of color.

*Resolved* (9), That a committee of three be appointed to prepare a petition * for general circulature.

*Proceedings of a convention of the Colored Men of Ohio, held in the city of Cincinnati, on the 23d, 24th, 25th and 26th days of November, 1858* (Cincinnati, 1858).

156

## POLICY STATEMENT OF *THE ANGLO-AFRICAN*, 1859

An excellent pre-Civil War publication, edited and published by a New York Negro, Thomas Hamilton, was *The Anglo-African Magazine* whose first number was dated January, 1859. Its editorial statement of policy, or "apology," follows, in part:

The publisher of this Magazine was "brought up" among Newspapers, Magazines, &c. The training of his boyhood and the employment of his manhood have been in the arts and mysteries which pertain to the neighborhood of Spruce and Nassau streets in the city of New York. . . . To become a Publisher, was the dream of his youth (not altogether a dream, for, while yet a boy he published, for several months, the *People's Press*, a not unnoticed

* The recommended petition read as follows: *"To the Honorable the General Assembly of the State of Ohio:* Your petitioners, citizens of              county, state of Ohio, respectfully ask your honorable body to take the steps necessary to strike, from the Constitution, the word 'white,' wherever it occurs; and to repeal all laws, or parts of laws, making distinction on account of color or race."

weekly paper,) and the aim of his manhood. He understands the business thoroughly, and intends, if the requisite editorial matter can be furnished, to make this Magazine "one of the Institutions of the country."

He would seem to be the right man in the right place; for the class of whom he is the representative in Printing House Square, sorely need an independent voice in the *"fourth estate."* Frederick Douglass has said that "the twelve millions of blacks in the United States and its environs must occupy the notice and the care of the Almighty:" these millions, in order to assert and maintain their rank as men among men, must speak for themselves; no outside tongue, however gifted with eloquence, can tell their story; no outside eye, however penetrating, can see their wants; no outside organization, however benevolently intended, nor however cunningly contrived, can develop the energies and aspirations which make up their mission.

The wealth, the intellect, the Legislation, (State and Federal,) the pulpit, and the science of America, have concentrated on no point so heartily as in the endeavor to write down the Negro as something less than a man: yet at the very moment of the triumph of this effort, there runs through the marrow of those who make it, an unaccountable consciousness, an aching dread, that this *noir faineant*, this great black sluggard, is somehow endowed with forces which are felt rather than seen, and which may in "some grim revel,"

"Shake the pillars of the commonweal!"

And there is indeed reason for this "aching dread." The Negro is something more than mere endurance; he is a force. And when the energies which now imbrute him exhaust themselves—as they inevitably must—the force which he now expends in resistance will cause him to rise: his force can hardly be measured to-day; the opinions regarding him are excessive; his foes estimate him too low—his friends, perhaps, too high: besides, there is not a-wanting among these latter, in spite of their own good feelings, that "tribe idolatry" which regards him as "not quite us." Twenty-five years ago, in the heat of the conflict which terminated in the Emancipation Act of Great Britain, there was held an anti-slavery meeting in the City of Glasgow, at which a young black made a speech of such fashion that it "brought down the house." He was followed by the eccentric but earnest and eloquent William Anderson, a minister of the Relief denomination: Dr. Wardlaw, with silver tongue had spoken, and George Thompson had revelled in his impetuous eloquence. Rev. Mr. Anderson's subject was a minor one in the programme, a sort of side dish; yet he began, continued, and ended in one of the most extraordinary bursts of eloquence, wit and sarcasm ever heard in Dr. Wardlaw's chapel; people were carried away: at the end of the meeting a friend congratulated Mr. Anderson, and casually asked how it was that he had got off such a grand speech? "Hoch mon!" said Mr. Anderson, "d'ye think I was gaen to be beaten by a black?"

But although we cannot fairly estimate the forces of the Negro, we may approximate them. A handful of English subdued Ireland, and English rule rather than English arms have so impenetrated the Celtic mind with oppression, that the only resistance to this oppression in the middle of the 19th century culminates in Smith O'Brien, Thomas F. Meagher, and John Mitchell! Compare these with Sam Ward, Frederick Douglass, or those who fought at Christiana, or the man who suffered himself to be scourged to death in Tennessee rather than betray his associate insurrectionists.*

The Negro under the yoke of slavery has increased, without additions made by immigration, as rapidly during the last forty years, as have the whites in the whole country, aided by an immense immigration and the increase of the immigrants; and this increase of the Negro in America, unlike that of the Irish in Ireland, is of a strong, healthy, durable stock. Now, let the European immigration diminish, and the African slave trade revive—both which events are in *esse*—and the next forty years will present us with the slave States containing ten millions of whites, and nearly fifteen millions of slaves; and the proportion of the blacks to the whites in the United States, which is now one-seventh, will be nearly one-half. In that event, it requires no prophet to foresee that the Underground Railroad, and the Christian Religion—the two great safety-valves for the restless and energetic among the slaves—will be utterly incompetent to put off that event which was brought about by bloodshed in Hayti, and by timely legislation in the British West Indies. . . .

In addition to an exposé of the condition of the blacks, this Magazine will have the aim to uphold and encourage the now depressed hopes of thinking black men, in the United States—the men who, for twenty years and more have been active in conventions, in public meetings, in societies, in the pulpit, and through the press, cheering on and laboring on to promote emancipation, affranchisement and education; some of them in, and some of them past the prime of life, yet see, as the apparent result of their work and their sacrifices, only Fugitive Slave laws and Compromise bills, and the denial of citizenship on the part of the Federal and State Governments, and, saddest of all, such men as Seward and Preston King insulting the rights of their black constituents by voting to admit Oregon as a state with a constitution denying to black men even an entrance within its borders.

It is not astonishing that the faith of such should grow weak, or that they

---

* On the Tennessee episode see the letter dated Clarkville, December 3, 1856, originally in the N.Y. *Times*, reprinted in *The Liberator*, Dec. 19, 1856.

should set up a breast-work in distant regions; yet it is clear that they are wrong to despond, wrong to change the scene of the contest. The sterner and fiercer the conflict, the sterner and steadier should be the soldiers engaged in it . . .

Neither can it aid our cause to found an empire in Yoruba; they might as well have built a battery at Gibraltar to destroy Sevastopol. The guns won't reach. Our cause is something higher, something holier than the founding of states. Any five hundred men with thews and sinews, and a moderate share of prudence, can found a state; it is nothing new nor wonderful to do. And after we had founded such a state, our work in the United States would remain to be done by other hands. Our work here, is, to purify the State, and purify Christianity from the foul blot which here rests upon them.

All articles in the Magazine, not otherwise designated, will be the products of the pens of colored men and women, from whom we earnestly solicit contributions, which, when used, will be paid for, according to the means of the publisher.*

## 157

## CALIFORNIA SCHOOLS AND THE NEGRO, 1859

An informative discussion of the efforts of Negroes in California to achieve equal educational opportunities for their children came from the pen of J. Holland Townsend, a Negro resident of that State, in March, 1859.

The struggles for our rights, in the Common Schools of the State of California, have been attended also with many interesting incidents. In the village of Grass Valley, Nevada Co., a school was opened in the year 1854. The supervisors, after taking the census of the children, found that three of the white children had colored parents; but as these children were as white as themselves, they very wisely determined to leave them in the school. This action greatly offended the feelings of some of the parents, who petitioned the supervisors to remove these children from the school. But they refused to do so, informing these sensitive parents that there were no colored children in the school, and that they intended to keep all the children that were at present there, until they should see good reason to expel them.

* In the issue of December, 1859 (I, p. 400) the editor wrote: "The contributors to this Magazine have performed a labor of love—the publisher has not been able to pay them —for which we present our loving thanks."

These F.F.Vs. finding themselves thwarted in their attempts to deprive these poor unfortunate children of the benefits of the common school, applied to the State Superintendent, who immediately ordered the supervisors to exclude these children, or he would deprive them of the State Funds belonging to that District; but all honor to the people of Grass Valley, who refused to obey the mandate of a man who would compel our children to grow up in ignorance. The Common Council of Sacramento City, in the year 1855 made as appropriation for the education of colored children. Hon. J. L. English, who was Mayor at the time, vetoed the Bill upon the ground that a majority of the inhabitants of that city were Southerners, and opposed to the education of colored children; yet the Common Council, satisfied of the justice of the ordinance passed the Bill over the Mayor's veto, and it became law.

The first Public School for colored children in the State of California, was established in the city of San Francisco in 1855.

Hon. C. K. Garrison was at that time Mayor of the city, and Wm. O. Grady, Esq., Superintendent of Public Schools. To the latter gentleman we are mostly indebted for the deep interest manifest in behalf of the education of our children. Rev. John J. Moore was appointed teacher, and $150 per month was appropriated for the school.

The character and rank was that of a mixed school for colored children. Prosperity attended the inauguration of this new enterprise, and the average attendance was about 40 scholars, yet a school of this grade was not destined to meet the wants of a flourishing and an increasing community, like San Francisco; families continued to migrate from the East, with their children who had received the advantages of the common schools, and were far in advance of the studies pursued in a mixed school. The result was that a few of the more advanced children were admitted into the Grammar Schools, in the Districts where they resided. One of these pupils, an interesting young lady, from the City of Brotherly Love, the daughter of a respectable merchant, standing at the head of the list as a scholar, in one of the Grammar Schools, was after examination by a committee of the Board of Education, admitted to the High School, where she soon distinguished herself as one of the first scholars in the institution, and by her amiable disposition and lady-like deportment, gained the goodwill and esteem of both teachers and scholars, as well as the Board of Education.

This was too much for a pro-slavery public sentiment, like that of California, quietly to submit to; the fact was soon heralded forth through the political press, that the children of the Negro were admitted into the Grammar, and even into the High School of San Francisco. The Board of

Education were denounced and stigmatized as Abolitionists, and called upon to exclude these children from the schools to which they had been assigned on account of their superior scholarship; all the lower and baser passions were appealed to by a corrupt political newspaper, remonstrances were sent to the Board, signed by the modern chivalry for the abatement of that great nuisance, the education of colored children in the same schools with the white ones. . . . The pressure soon became so great that the Board were obliged to come out and define their position on the question. A resolution was adopted by that body which "directed all colored children to attend the school provided for them in San Francisco." Another resolution was then proposed, directing the superintendent to carry out the first resolution. But the Board voted to lay it on the table, by a decided majority, thus leaving the whole matter stand as it was. F.F.Vs. being now thwarted in attempts to deprive our children of the advantages of education, for which we had paid in common with others, appealed to the State Superintendent of Public Instruction, a Tennessee gentleman, but he wisely declined, informing them that the people of San Francisco had elected a Board of Education to manage the affairs of Common Schools according to their own judgment, and he could not interfere with them in the discharge of their duties.

While this contest was going on, we were encouraged by the people who resided in the 12th District of San Francisco, who presented a petition to the Board of Education to admit into the Grammar School of that District, the children of all persons who resided within the District, without reference to their complexions.

Notwithstanding all these disabilities, we are rapidly progressing both in intelligence and wealth, in this new State of the far West; soon it is expected that the iron horse will thunder through the defiles of the Rocky Mountains, and hasten away to the Pacific. California, Oregon, Washington, and New Caledonia, already send upon air the hum and tread of their busy thousands. China and the Isles of the Sea, hover like a dream in the western horizon. America will soon become the mid-way of the earth, the center and heart of the world, and with a common school system that shall educate all of her sons and daughters alike, her dominion shall be like that of "Julius"—terminate her boundaries by the ocean, and her fame by the stars.

*The Anglo-African,* March, 1859, I, pp. 80–83. Copy in Brooklyn, N.Y., Public Library.

## 158

# LETTERS FROM SOUTHERN NEGRO UNDERGROUND AGENTS, 1859–1860

Two typical letters from the greatest heroes of an organization of heroes, the Southern Negro agents of the Underground Railroad, are printed below. Both letters were sent to William Still of Philadelphia; the first was dated Baltimore, April 16, 1859; the second was dated Petersburg, Virginia, October 17, 1860.

### [a]

Dear Brother i have taken the opportunity of writing you these few lines to inform you that i am well an hoping these few lines may find you enjoying the same good blessing please to write me word at what time was it when israel went to Jerico i am very anxious to hear for thare is a mighty host will pass over and you and i my brother will sing hally luja i shall notify you when the great catastrophe shal take place No more at the present but remain your brother

N. L. J.

### [b]

*Dear Sir*—I am happy to think, that the time has come when we no doubt can open our correspondence with one another again. Also I am in hopes, that these few lines may find you and family well and in the enjoyment of good health, as it leaves me and family the same. I want you to know, that I feel as much determined to work in this glorious cause, as ever I did in all of my life, and I have some very good hams on hand that I would like very much for you to have. I have nothing of interest to write about just now, only that the politics of the day is in a high rage, and I don't know of the result, therefore, I want you to be one of those wide-a-wakes as is mentioned from your section of country now-a-days, &c. Also, if you wish to write to me, Mr. J. Brown will inform you how to direct a letter to me.

No more at present, until I hear from you; but I want you to be a wide-awake.

Yours in haste,<br>HAM & EGGS.

Wm. Still, *Underground Railroad Records*, pp. 41, 48.

159

# FREDERICK DOUGLASS DESCRIBES THE LIFE
# OF A NEGRO TAILOR, 1859

A biographical account of Thomas L. Jennings was written by Frederick Douglass when Jennings died, at the age of 68, on February 11, 1859. It is of interest not only because of the specific information which it contains, but also because of the light it throws upon the career of a modest and very useful Negro resident of New York City.

Mr. Jennings was a native of New York, and in his early youth was one of the bold men of color who, in this then slave State, paraded the streets of the metropolis with a banner inscribed with the figure of a black man, and the words, "AM I NOT A MAN AND A BROTHER?" He was one of the colored volunteers who aided in digging trenches on Long Island in the war of 1812. He took a leading part in the celebration of the abolition of slavery in New York in 1827. He was one of the founders of the Wilberforce Society. When in 1830 Wm. Lloyd Garrison came on from Baltimore, Mr. Jennings was among the colored men of New York, Wm. Hamilton, Rev. Peter Williams, Thomas Sipkins, and others, who gave him a cordial welcome and God-speed, and subscribed largely to establish the *Liberator*, and to aid in the publication of "Garrison's Thoughts on Colonization. . . ."

He was a leading member of the first, second and third of the National Conventions of colored men of the United States, held in New York and Philadelphia in 1831–4. He was one of the originators of the Legal Rights' Association in New York city, and President thereof at the time of his death. His suit against the Third Avenue Railroad Company for ejecting his daughter from one of its cars on Sabbath day, led to the abolition of caste in cars in four out of the five city railroads. He was one of the founders, and during many years a trustee of the Abyssinian Baptist Church.

In his boyhood, Mr. Jennings served an apprenticeship with one of the most celebrated of the New York tailors. Soon after reaching manhood, he entered business on his own account, and invented a method of renovating garments, for which he obtained letters patent from the United States. Although it was well known that he was a black man of "African descent," these letters recognize him as a "citizen of the United States." This document, in an antique gilded frame, hangs above the bed in which Mr. Jennings breathed his last, and is signed by the historic names of John Quincy Adams and William Wirt, and bears the broad seal of the United States of America.

For many years Mr. Jennings conducted a successful business as Clothier, in Nassau and Chatham streets.

Mr. Jennings had a large family, whom he educated carefully and successfully, both in intellectual and moral training. He taught all his children some useful trades, and accustomed them betimes to rely on themselves for their support. His son William died twenty years ago, a successful business man in Boston; Thomas was until lately, one of the most skilful dentists in New Orleans; his daughter Matilda is one of the best dress makers in New York City, and Elizabeth the most learned of our female teachers in the city of New York, having obtained mainly through her own labor, the honor of a diploma from the Board of Education of said city.

This is a noble picture of a noble man. Born in a slave state, and of a race held in slavery, living in the midst of all the crushing influences which human prejudice and caste could heap upon him, he yet fulfilled all the purposes of an upright man, a useful citizen, and a devoted Christian; on no occasion in his long life did he bate one hair's breath of the rights and dignities pertaining to his manhood. He upheld society by an active, earnest and blameless life, and by contributing thereto children carefully trained to conduce to the general good. Not gifted with extraordinary talents or endowments, he made full use of such as it had pleased God to give him.

Mr. Jennings was one of that large class of earnest, upright colored men who dwell in our large cities. He was not an exception, but a representative of his class, whose noble sacrifices, and unheralded labors are too little known to the public, even to the real friends of freedom, the class of whom even our honest friend Gerrit Smith has written, that "the mass of them are ignorant and thriftless." It is a strange ignorance which is manifested by the attendance of 25 per cent more of colored than of white children in the Public Schools of New York City; a strange thriftlessness which shows a smaller proportion of colored than of white persons supported at the Alms-Houses and other charities in New York and Philadelphia. We know that in making such statement, Mr. Smith reluctantly wrote what he believed to be the truth; his view, however, was syllogistic rather than the result of a study of the facts: "while there are a few noble exceptions," said he, "the mass of the blacks are ignorant and thriftless." And he reasoned thus, "the mass of the blacks are poor, and live in the large cities; all poor who crowd large cities are ignorant and thriftless; therefore," &c., &c.

Now the facts happen to be, that, of the free blacks of the free States, a little more than one-third live in the large cities, and the portion who do live in large cities have more wealth (general) and larger intelligence than the proportion who live in the country. We are not defending city dwelling on the part of this class—we state facts. And, in view of them, and while we proudly cast our mite on the cairn of Thomas L. Jennings, we call upon the Hon. Gerrit Smith, in the name of our departed brother, to wipe off the stigma which he has cast upon him and his like, by withdrawing, as publicly as he made it, his unfortunate statement in regard to the mass of the blacks.

*The Anglo-African,* April, 1859, I, pp. 126–28.


## 160

# A PLEA AGAINST MERE MONEY-MAKING, 1859

Segments among professional and middle-class Negroes have been attracted to the idea that their own salvation—if not that of all Negroes—lay in accepting the tenets and mores of the rich. An early argument against this came from the pen of Frances Ellen Watkins in May, 1859.


When we have a race of men whom this blood-stained government cannot tempt or flatter, who would sternly refuse every office in the nation's gift, from a president down to a tide-waiter, until she shook her hands from complicity in the guilt of cradle plundering and man stealing, then for us the foundations of an historic character will have been laid. We need men and women whose hearts are the homes of a high and lofty enthusiasm, and a noble devotion to the cause of emancipation, who are ready and willing to lay time, talent and money on the altar of universal freedom. We have money among us, but how much of it is spent to bring deliverance to our captive brethren? Are our wealthiest men the most liberal sustainers of the Anti-slavery enterprise? Or does the bare fact of their having money, really help mould public opinion and reverse its sentiments? We need what money cannot buy and what affluence is too beggarly to purchase. Earnest, self sacrificing souls that will stamp themselves not only on the present but the future. Let us not then defer all our noble opportunities till we get rich. And here I am, not aiming to enlist a fanatical crusade against the desire for riches, but I do protest against chaining down the soul, with its Heaven endowed faculties and God given attributes to the one idea of getting money as stepping into power or even gaining our rights in common with others. The respect that is only bought by gold is not worth much. It is no honor to shake hands politically with men who whip women and steal babies. If this government has no call for our services, no aim for our children, we have the greater need for them to build up a true manhood and womanhood for ourselves. The important lesson we should learn and be able to teach, is how to make every gift, whether gold or talent, fortune or genius, subserve the cause of crushed humanity and carry out the greatest idea of the present age, the glorious idea of human brotherhood.

*The Anglo-African*, May, 1859, I, p. 160.


## 161

## THE OBERLIN-WELLINGTON RESCUE CASE,
### 1858–59

John Price, a recaptured fugitive slave, was forcibly freed by Negroes and whites in Oberlin, Ohio in September, 1858. This, and the resulting trials of those involved, formed one of the most publicized events in the anti-slavery struggle. The full story, including the moving speech of Charles H. Langston, a Negro defendent, is given in the following article by his brother, John Mercer Langston, a lawyer, a leading Abolitionist, later professor of law at Howard University, American Minister to Haiti, and Congressman from Virginia.

The speech itself was widely reprinted at the time both in pamphlet form and in newspapers, including such very broadly circulated papers as the Columbus, Ohio, *State Journal* and the Cleveland *Leader*.


The 13th day of September, 1858 is at once, the darkest and the brightest day in the Calendar of Oberlin. It is the darkest day because it was then, that heartless and cruel Negro-catchers desecrated the sanctity of this community by their shameless presence, and perpetrated one of those black and devilish acts which render the kidnapper so hateful and despicable. The foul betrayal of John Price into the hands of the kidnappers Lowe, Davis, Mitchell, and Jennings, was accomplished through the agency of Shakespeare Boynton, a fast young lad, about fourteen years of age, the son of a prominent Democrat of Russia Township, and a man particularly distinguished for his utter want of honor and honesty. It is not wonderful that the son of such a father could be influenced and hired, for the paltry sum of twenty dollars, to assist in doing the base deed of *kidnapping a man*. Indeed, it is the opinion of very many excellent and judicious persons, that the father himself gave "aid and comfort," counsel and assistance, to these traitors to humanity. It is very positively asserted, by Lewis D. Boynton, the father of this lad, however, that he knew nothing of his son's having been employed to betray John Price, till several hours after the deed had been done. And yet, Anderson Jennings, the man who employed Shakespeare, very emphatically stated under oath, when under examination as a witness, that he gave Mr. Boynton full information in regard to his intention of securing the services of his son. Whether Boynton be truthful in his assertion and Jennings false, or Jennings be truthful in his and Boynton false, it is not in our power to determine. For the sake of humanity, it is to be hoped, that Boynton knew nothing of this collusion with his son till after its development. That father is indeed base, who can allow his child to do a mean thing for hire. The youthfulness of this lad and his want of suitable training would lead us to excuse his conduct as a boyish though calamitous indiscretion; while the father, intelligent and full of years of observation and experience, can find no forgiveness at our hands, if he be guilty of aiding in this nefarious procedure.

But the 13th day of September, 1858, is the brightest day in the Calendar of Oberlin, because on that day the noble and true men of this place, by their brave and manly conduct in the rescue of John Price, vindicated their determination not to allow the humblest human being "to be deprived of life, liberty, or property, without due process of law," when in their power to prevent it. And on that day, too, Oberlin, with fresh vigor, gave another and more glorious exhibition of her purpose to stand firm in favor of Justice and Christianity, the Declaration and the Constitution, Law and Order, and against Injustice and Atheism, Despotism and Slavery, Mob-violence and Misrule. Indeed, that day and the deeds that distinguish it shall never be forgotten. Posterity, shall regard it as the *bright and glorious* day in the history of this "Gibraltar of Freedom," and shall deem it worthy of the most sacred remembrance.

The manner in which John Price was captured, deserves, in this connection, but a passing notice. It is already well understood. Without attempting the slightest minuteness of detail, then, it is enough to say that he was ensnared by the huge and monstrous falsehood of young Boynton, who came to him with a friendly appearance, but with a heart bent upon his ruin. He knew that this poor fugitive belonged to the class of the energetic, the industrious, and the faithful. He knew, too, that for several months past, Price had suffered extremely under the most excruciating bodily disorder, and that, in consequence of his protracted sickness, he had been driven to the last extremity of want; and, now that he was convalescing, he was anxious to secure employment, that he might replenish his exhausted revenue. Therefore, he came to this poor man—poor in body and in purse—saying, "My father has sent me here to tell you that he wants you to come out and dig potatoes for him, and that he will pay you for your services one dollar and twenty-five cents per day." But Price was still in such feeble health that he dared not undertake such laborious service. Not suspecting anything wrong—not knowing the devil that lurked in the heart of this youthful but arch deceiver—he undertook the kind and neighborly task of pointing out the dwelling-place of another industrious and faithful fugitive whose services Mr. Boynton could secure. This man lived about two miles from the village of Oberlin, and to reach his house it was necessary to pass over an unfrequented road. As they rode along in their buggy, having gone about half the distance, they were suddenly, and unexpectedly to John Price, overtaken by Deputy U.S. Marshals Lowe, Davis, and Mitchell. These Negro-catchers rode in a fine double-seated carriage. They were armed with Bowie-knives and revolvers. As soon as they overtook young Boynton and Price, seizing Price, they dragged him from the buggy in which he was riding, and forced him into the carriage in which they rode. This they did without making exhibition of the process, or giving any account of the authority in accordance with which they acted. Thus, having secured their prey, by an untravelled route, in the most expeditious manner, they hurried off towards Wellington. Meantime, Shakespeare Boynton returned to Oberlin to find Anderson Jennings, of whom he was to receive compensation for his dirty work. He found Jennings, reported that the Negro had been captured, and received his reward. This ended his connection with this black and infamous drama. After having learned of this miscreant what had been done, Jennings left Oberlin, and joined his comrades and co-workers in iniquity at Wellington.

But before these ruffian Negro-catchers arrived at Wellington, fortunately for the kidnapped man and for the Anti-Slavery cause, the report of their doings reached Oberlin, and thrilled and aroused our community, already intensely agitated by villainous deed done within a few days prior to this time by these hunters of men, under the cover of night. Now one purpose only animated the hearts of the people. Old men and young men, old women and maidens, all expressed in looks and voice their determination to rescue this stolen man. At once, men of strong heart and moral nerve—men of stalwart arms and prowess such as knows no fear—with wondrous determination pictured in their faces, were seen hurrying off in buggies, carriages, wagons, and some on horse-back, and others on foot, towards Wellington, a place yet to be celebrated in story and in verse, in forensic address and judicial record, as the scene of the rescue of John Price, a stolen and kidnapped man, from his cowardly and brutal captors.

It is not fit that this rescue be dwelt upon with too great particularity at this time. Names must not be mentioned. The conduct of particular individuals must not be described. It is enough for us to know, just now, that the brave men who came together in hot haste, but with well-defined intention, returned as the shades of night came on bringing silence and rest to the world, bearing in triumph to freedom the man who, but an hour before, was on the road to the fearful doom of Slavery. Today John Price walks abroad in his freedom, or reposes under his own vine and fig-tree, with no one to molest him or make him afraid. But for this boon—this glorious boon—he must be ever grateful to the courageous men who jeopardized their lives, their property, and their liberty to secure his release, for, according to the Fugitive Slave Law of 1850, those who rescue a man under such circumstances, or who aid, assist, and abet in the rescue, are to be indicted, convicted, imprisoned, and fined. It matters not if its victim be born in freedom and reared under its benign influences, and it be thus distinctly understood that he is a free man. It matters not if he be kidnapped. In this sense the law is no respecter of persons. Nor does it make any complexional discriminations. And still it subjects to pains and penalties most severe and cruel all who oppose its execution, whether the opposition be violent, legal, or only such as find an expression in prayerful ejaculations in behalf of the captured. If this statement be doubted, let the incredulous peruse with thoughtfulness and care, the unreasonable, the blasphemous, and the atheistic charge delivered by Judge Wilson to the Grand Jury that found bills of indictment against thirty-seven citizens of Lorain county, charging some with rescuing, and others with aiding and abetting in the rescue of John Price. If the incredulous are still unmoved in their unbelief, they would read with edification and profit the charges of the same Judge delivered to the traverse Jurors before whom Bushnell and Langston were tried and convicted. All these charges harmonize with, and strikingly illustrate this Fugitive Slave Law. It is under such a Congressional enactment—an enactment whose soul is not unreasonableness, but injustice and wrong—an enactment whose horrid features are seen in its unconstitutionality, in its denial of the free exercise of religion, in its subversion of State Sovereignty and individual rights, and in its overthrow of all the ancient bulwarks of liberty and law— that the philanthropic and Christian men who are now confined in the jail of Cuyahoga county, together with those of the noble thirty-seven who have been already released from their confinement, were indicted by a packed and partizan Grand Jury, of which Lewis D. Boynton was an influential member.

Of the persons thus indicted, only two have as yet been tried. Both were found guilty and sentenced. Mr. Simeon M. Bushnell, the first one tried, is a man of true nobility of soul and Christian fortitude. A man of very small physical endurance, he has a heart capable of the boldest endeavor and the most unshrinking purpose in the discharge of duty. After his conviction, when ordered to stand up and receive his sentence, Judge Wilson, seeking to extort some word of humiliation and contrition, asked him if he had anything to say why sentence should not be pronounced upon him. In a clear and manly voice, he answered, "I have not." But the Judge was not satisfied with this stern reply; so he asked him if he had no regrets to offer for his conduct. To this, Mr. Bushnell, conscious of the rectitude of his intentions and satisfied with the part he had played in the rescue, with great emphasis and point, replied again, "I have not." Because Mr. Bushnell had no regrets to offer—because he exhibited the spirit of a man of dignity and courage, and none of the disposition of the poltroon and the coward, he was sentenced by this unjust Judge to sixty days' confinement in the county jail, and to pay a fine of six hundred dollars and the costs of the prosecution. And to-day, he, a white man, an American citizen, is in the common jail, serving out his time, for doing nothing other than giving succor to an oppressed and outraged brother.

Mr. Charles H. Langston, the other person who has been tried, convicted, and sentenced, needs no eulogistic words from my humble pen. He is widely known as a devoted and laborious advocate of the claims of the Negro to liberty and its attendant blessings. Indeed, his entire life has been a free offering to the Anti-Slavery cause. Discreet and far-seeing, uncompromising and able, he has labored most efficiently in behalf of the slave and the disfranchised American. But in no position has he demanded himself with greater propriety and wisdom, with greater decision and courage, and with greater efficiency, than when he stood before Judge Wilson, and, as the representative of the Negro Race, in the most beautiful and powerful tones, told him why sentence should not be pronounced upon him. He spoke as follows: "I am for the first time in my life before a court of Justice, charged with the violation of law, and am now about to be sentenced. But before receiving that sentence, I propose to say one or two words in regard to the mitigation of that sentence, if it may be so construed. I cannot of course, and do not expect, that which I may say, will, in any way, change your pre-determined line of action. I ask no such favor at your hands.

"I know that the courts of this country, that the laws of this country, that the governmental machinery of this country, are so constituted as to oppress and outrage colored men, men of my complexion. I cannot then, of course, expect, judging from the past history of the country, any mercy from the laws, from the constitution, or from the courts of the country.

"Some days prior to the 13th day of September, 1858, happening to be in Oberlin on a visit, I found the country round about there, and the village itself, filled with alarming rumors as to the fact that slave-catchers, kid-nappers, Negro-stealers were lying hidden and skulking about, waiting some opportunity to get their bloody hands on some helpless creature to drag him back—or for the first time, into helpless and life-long bondage. These reports becoming current all over that neighborhood, old men and innocent women and children became exceedingly alarmed for their safety. It was not un-common to hear mothers say that they dare not send their children to school, for fear they would be caught and carried off by the way. Some of these people had become free by long and patient toil at night, after working the long, long day for cruel masters, and thus at length getting money enough to buy their liberty. Others had become free by means of the good will of their masters. And there were others who had become free—by the intensest exercise of their God-given powers;—by escaping from the plantations of their masters, eluding the bloodthirsty patrols and sentinels so thickly scattered all along their path, outrunning blood-hounds and horses, swimming rivers and fording swamps, and reaching at last, through incredible difficulties, what they, in their delusion, supposed to be free soil. These three classes were in Oberlin, trembling alike for their safety, because they well knew their fate, should those men-hunters get their hands on them.

"In the midst of such excitement the 13th day of September was ushered in—a day ever to be remembered in the history of that place, and I presume no less in the history of this Court—on which those men, by lying devices, decoyed into a place where they could get their hands on him—I will not say a slave, for I do not know that—but a *man,* a *brother,* who had a right to his liberty under the laws of God, under the laws of Nature, and under the Declaration of American Independence.

"In the midst of all this excitement, the news came to us like a flash of lightning that an actual seizure under and by means of fraudulent pretenses had been made!

"Being identified with that man by color, by race, by manhood, by sympathies, such as God had implanted in us all, I felt it my duty to go and do what I could toward liberating him. I had been taught by my Revolutionary father—and I say this with all due respect to him—and by his honored associates, that the fundamental doctrine of this government was that *all* men have a right, to life and liberty, and coming from the Old Dominion I brought into Ohio these sentiments, deeply impressed upon my heart; I went to Wellington, and hearing from the parties themselves by what authority the boy was held in custody, I conceived from what little knowledge I had of law, that they had no right to hold him. And as your Honor has repeatedly laid down the law in this Court, a man is free until he is proven to be legally restrained of his liberty, and I believed that upon the principle of law those men were bound to take their prisoner before the very first magistrate they found, and there establish the facts set forth in their warrant, and that until they did this, every man should presume that their claim was unfounded, and to institute such proceedings for the purpose of securing an investigation as they might find warranted by the laws of this State. Now, sir, if that is not the plain, common sense and correct view of the law, then I have been misled by your Honor, and by the prevalent received opinion.

"It is said that they had a warrant. Why then should they not establish its validity before the proper officers? And I stand here to-day, sir, to say that with an exception of which I shall soon speak, *to procure such a lawful investigation of the authority under which they claimed to act, was the part I took in that day's proceedings, and the only part.* I supposed it to be my duty as a citizen of Ohio—excuse me for saying that, sir—as an *outlaw of the United States* (much sensation), to do what I could to secure at least this form of Justice to my brother whose liberty was in peril. *Whatever more than that has been sworn to on this trial, as an act of mine, is false, ridiculously false.* When I found these men refusing to go, according to the law, as I apprehended it, and subject their claim to an official inspection, and that nothing short of a *habeas corpus* would oblige such an inspection, I was willing to go even thus far, supposing in that county a Sheriff, might, perhaps, be found with nerve enough to serve it. In this I again failed. Nothing then was left me, nothing to the boy in custody, but the confirmation of my first belief that the pretended authority was worthless, and the employment of those means of liberation which belong to us. With regard to the part I took in the forcible rescue, which followed, I have nothing to say, further than I have already said. The evidence is before you. It is alleged that I said, 'We will have him anyhow.' *This I never said.* I did say to Mr. Lowe, what I honestly believed to be the truth, that the crowd were very much excited, many of them averse to longer delay, and bent upon a rescue at all hazards; and that he being an old acquaintance and friend of mine, I was anxious to extricate him from the dangerous position he occupied, and therefore advised that he urge Jennings to give the boy up. Further than this I did not say, either to him or any one else.

"The law under which I am arraigned is an unjust one, one made to crush the colored man, and one that outrages every feeling of humanity, as well as every rule of right. I have nothing to do with its constitutionality; about that I care but little. I have often heard it said by learned and good men that it was unconstitutional; I remember the excitement that prevailed throughout all the free States when it was passed; and I remember how often it has been said by individuals, conventions, legislatures, and even *Judges,* that it never could be, never should be, and never was meant to be enforced. I had always believed, until contrary appeared in the actual institution of proceedings, that the provisions of this odious statute would never be enforced within the bounds of this State.

"But I have another reason to offer why I should not be sentenced, and one that I think pertinent to the case. I have not had a trial before a jury of my peers. The common law of England—and you will excuse me for referring to that, since I am but a private citizen—was that every man should be tried before a jury of men occupying the same position in the social scale with himself. That lords should be tried before a jury of lords; that peers of the realm should be tried before peers of the realm; vassals before vassals, and *aliens before aliens,* and they must not come from the district where the crime was committed, lest the prejudices of either personal friends or foes should affect the accused. The Constitution of the U.S. guarantees, not merely to its citizens, but *to all persons,* a trial before an *impartial* jury. I have had no such trial.

"The colored man is oppressed by certain universal and deeply fixed *prejudices.* Those jurors are well known to have shared largely in these prejudices, and I therefore consider that they were neither impartial, nor were they a jury of my peers. . . .

"I was tried by a jury who were prejudiced; before a Court that was prejudiced; prosecuted by an officer who was prejudiced, and defended, though ably, by counsel that were prejudiced. And therefore, it is, your Honor, that I urge by all that is good and great in manhood, that I should not be subjected to the pains and penalties of this oppressive law, when I have *not* been tried, either by a jury of my peers, or by a jury that were impartial.

"One more word, sir, and I have done. I went to Wellington, knowing that colored men have no rights in the United States, which white men are bound to respect; that the Courts had so decided; that Congress had so enacted; that the people had so decreed.

"There is not a spot in this wide country, not even by the altars of God, nor in the shadow of the shafts that tell the imperishable fame and glory of the heroes of the Revolution; no, nor in the old Philadelphia Hall, where any colored man may dare to ask a mercy of a white man. Let me stand in that Hall and tell a United States Marshal that my father was a Revolutionary soldier; that he served under Lafayette, and fought through the whole war, and that he fought for *my* freedom as much as for his own; and he would sneer at me, and clutch me with his bloody fingers, and say he has a *right* to make me a slave! And when I appeal to Congress, they say he has a right to make me a slave; when I appeal to your Honor, *your Honor* says he has a right to make me a slave, and if any man, white or black, seeks an investigation of that claim, they make themselves amenable to the pains and penalties of the Fugitive Slave Act, for BLACK MEN HAVE NO RIGHTS WHICH WHITE MEN ARE BOUND TO RESPECT. (Great Applause.) I, going to Wellington with the full knowledge of all this, knew that if that man was taken to Columbus, he was hopelessly gone, no matter whether he had ever been in slavery before or not. I knew that I was in the same situation myself, and that by the decision of your Honor, if any man whatever were to claim me as his slave and seize me, and my brother. being a lawyer, should seek to get out a writ of *habeas corpus* to expose the falsity of the claim, he would be thrust into prison under one provision of the Fugitive Slave Law, for interfering with the man claiming to be in pursuit of a fugitive, and I, by the perjury of a solitary wretch, would by another of its provisions be helplessly doomed to life-long bondage, without the possibility of escape.

"Some may say that there is no danger of free persons being seized and carried off as slaves. No one need labor under such a delusion. Sir. *four* of the eight persons who were first carried back under the act of 1850, were afterwards proved to be *free men*. They were free persons, but wholly at the mercy of the oath of one man. And but last Sabbath afternoon, a letter came to me from a gentleman in St. Louis, informing me that a young lady who was formerly under my instructions at Columbus, a free person, is now lying in the jail at that place, claimed as the slave of some wretch who never saw her before, and waiting for testimony from relatives at Columbus to establish her freedom. I could stand here by the hour and relate such instances. In the very nature of the case they must be constantly occurring. A letter was not long since found upon the person of a counterfeiter when arrested, addressed to him by some Southern gentleman, in which the writer says:

" 'Go among the Negroes; find out their marks and scars; make good descriptions and send to me, and I'll find masters for 'em.'

"That is the way men are carried 'back' to slavery.

"But in view of all the facts, I say that if ever again a man is seized near me, and is about to be carried southward as a slave, before any legal investigation has been had, I shall hold it to be my duty, as I held it that day, to secure for him, if possible, a legal inquiry into the character of the claim by which he is held. And I go further: I say that if it is adjudged illegal to procure even such an investigation, then we are thrown back upon those last defences of our rights which cannot be taken from us, and which God gave us that we need not be slaves. I ask your Honor, while I say this, to place yourself in my situation, and you will say with me that if your brother, if your friend, if your wife, if your child, had been seized by men who claimed them as fugitives, and the law of the land forbade you to ask any investigation and precluded the possibility of any legal protection or redress, then you will say with me, that you would not only demand the protection of the law, but you would call in your neighbors and your friends, and would ask them to say with you that these, your friends, *could not* be taken into slavery.

"And now I thank you for this leniency, this indulgence, in giving a man unjustly condemned by a tribunal before which he is declared to have no rights, the privilege of speaking in his own behalf. I know that it will do nothing towards mitigating your sentence, but it is a privilege to be allowed to speak, and I thank you for it. I shall submit to the penalty, be it what it may. But I stand here to say, that if, for doing what I did on that day at Wellington, I am to go in jail six months and pay a fine of a thousand dollars, according to the Fugitive Slave Law—and such is the protection the laws of this country afford me—I must take upon myself the responsibility of self-protection; when I come to be claimed by some perjured wretch as his slave, I shall never be taken into slavery. And as in that trying hour I would have others do to me, as I would call upon my friends to help me, as I would call upon you, your Honor, to help me, as I would call upon you (to the District Attorney) to help me, and upon you (to Judge Bliss), and upon you (to his counsel), *so help me* God I stand here to say that I will do all I can for any man thus seized and held, though the inevitable penalty of six months' imprisonment and one thousand dollars fine for each offence hangs over me! We have all a common humanity, and you all would do that; your manhood would require it, and no matter what the laws might be, you would honor yourself for doing it, while your friends and your children to all generations would honor you for doing it, and every good and honest man would say you had done *right!*" (Great and prolonged applause, in spite of the efforts of Court and Marshal.)

This terse, argumentative and eloquent speech so touched the sensibility of the Judge that he sentenced Mr. Langston to confinement in the county jail for but twenty days, to pay a fine of one hundred dollars and costs of the prosecution. He has already served out his time, and is now in his office in Cleveland, discharging his duties as Recording Secretary of the Ohio State Anti-Slavery Society.

How the United States officials will collect the fines imposed upon these men it is impossible to tell. They are said to be destitute of lands, and all manner of personal property. It is reported that they are very poor. Then blessed be nothing!

There still remain in jail awaiting their trial, Prof. Henry E. Peck, John Watson, Henry Evans, J. M. Fitch, David L. Watson, Ralph Plumb, Wilson Evans, A. W. Lyman, John H. Scott, Robert Winsor, and William E. Lincoln. These are all men of indomitable purpose. The terrible penalties of the Fugitive Slave Law cannot drive them from their firm position in favor of Liberty and Right. Nor are they men who will fear and tremble before a tyrannical Judge. The ruffian threats of a Government Prosecutor cannot deter them. These are men, too, whose lives are not marked by acts of selfishness, but by deeds of benevolence and charity. Some of them are distinguished by their scholarly attainments; all of them are distinguished by their deep and consistent devotion to the welfare of humanity. The large circle of friends and acquaintances who daily and hourly express their sympathy for these good and noble men, feel confident that they will conduct themselves in such manner while they remain in jail and when they are brought before the Court for trial, as to further the interests of the Anti-Slavery cause.

It is a fact worthy of particular mention, that in this rescue the colored men played an important and conspicuous part. Twelve of them were indicted; four of them have not yet been taken into custody; two have been discharged; one is now at large upon his own recognizance, and five are still in jail. For the heroic conduct of these worthy men and their white co-laborers, they deserve and shall receive our hearty thanks and lasting gratitude.

Upon the conduct of the Court before which Bushnell and Langston have been tried, and before which the rest of the indicted are to be tried—upon the behavior of the Prosecutor, who has shown himself so anxious and determined to convict these men—upon the character of the Jurors called in the cases already tried, and upon the testimony of the witnesses on the part of the Government, it is needless to say a single word. The Court, the Prosecutor, the Jurors, and the witnesses, with one or two exceptions, are Pro-Slavery and Democratic in their connections and associations. It is well known, then, what we may expect. And, so far, we have not been disappointed.

But the object of this prosecution can never be accomplished. The free spirit of the Western Reserve cannot be "crushed out." Our deep love of liberty, our intelligent veneration for the precepts of Christianity, and our abiding determination to obey God rather than man, no prosecution, however oppressive, no irksome confinement in gloomy dungeons, no illegal and unjust confiscation of our property, can ever overthrow and destroy. And this prosecution, so far, has only tended to deepen and strengthen this conviction.

*The Anglo-African,* July, 1859, I, pp. 209–216.


## 162

# NEW ENGLAND COLORED CITIZENS' CONVENTION, 1859

A meeting of many Negroes occurred in Boston, August 1–2, 1859, under the title New England Colored Citizens' Convention. In attendance, however, were men and women from New York, New Jersey, Pennsylvania, Illinois and Canada as well as New England. The chairman was George T. Downing while others taking a leading part were J. Sella Martin, Amos G. Beman, William Still, Mrs. Ruth Rice Remond and Mrs. Eliza Logan Lawton. The most significant resolutions adopted at this convention follow:

*Resolved,* That in view of the fact, that in several States of the Union where the Republican party is in the ascendant, the elective franchise of colored citizens is denied or its privileges abridged, we would earnestly call upon the party to take a manly position upon this and co-relative questions, that they may deserve what they would undoubtedly receive—the suffrages of all voters who love the cause of freedom.

*Resolved,* That this Convention would recommend colored voters to press these claims upon the Republican party, that if defeated, it may not be by any fault of theirs . . .

*Resolved,* That though our brethren of Connecticut, in their long-continued efforts for the elective franchise, have experienced many defeats, we would exhort them to "pick their flints, and try again," feeling assured that the onward march of reform is their guaranty of freedom.

*Resolved,* That while we deeply regret that there can be found in the State of Rhode Island any colored persons disposed to throw obstacles in the path that leads to the equal school rights of their children, we feel proud to note the intelligent zeal and perseverance which others have exhibited during the protracted and complicated struggle for justice and equality.

*Resolved,* That great as is our joy in view of the recent release from jail of the gallant and unflinching Oberlin rescuers, that joy is modified by the fact, that while some of their number were punished as criminals, the actual kidnappers escaped a trial. Yet, as the plea of *nole contendere* was offered by the government, the result is to be accepted as a virtual defeat of the Slave Power, and the triumph of Oberlin Higher Law.

*Resolved,* That notwithstanding the studied misrepresentation of the pro-slavery American press with regard to the island of Hayti, we know that the Haytians are the only people who achieved their independence by the sword, unaided by other nations; and that they have maintained it to the present hour, through their various revolutions, (which have been progressive steps towards Republicanism,) is full confirmation of their capacity for self-government.

*Resolved,* That we agree in the sentiment expressed by one who had been a slave, that "the minister who can preach and pray twelve months without speaking for the slave must be college made, money called, and devil sent." . . .

*Resolved,* That this Convention appoint a Committee, who shall immediately confer with prominent men of color in every town and city in the free States, and whose duty it shall be to get the signatures of the colored people of those States to petitions which shall be sent to Congress, praying that body to remove the disabilities under which we now labor, on account of the unrighteous Dred Scott decision.

*Resolved,* That in consideration of the many difficulties that surround those colored men who attempt to enter into trade, the mechanic arts, and the liberal professions, it is our duty as an oppressed people struggling to elevate ourselves, to give as much of our patronage as we can to those who are laboring in their various departments to elevate themselves and their race.

*The Liberator,* August 19 and 26, 1859.

## 163

# A NEGRO PARTICIPANT TELLS OF JOHN BROWN'S RAID, 1859

Of John Brown's original party which struck a daring blow against slavery in Harper's Ferry, Virginia (now West Virginia), five were Negroes: Shields Green, Dangerfield Newby, Sherrard Lewis Leary, John A. Copeland and Osborne P. Anderson. The last alone escaped and he published the story soon after in a volume entitled *A Voice from Harper's Ferry* (Boston, 1861). From this book is taken the following account of the effort by Brown and his comrades.

As stated in a previous chapter, the command of the rifle factory was given to Captain Kagi. Under him were John Copeland, Sherrard Lewis Leary, and three colored men from the neighborhood. At an early hour, Kagi saw from his position the danger in remaining, with our small company, until assistance could come to the inhabitants. Hence his suggestion to Captain Brown, through Jeremiah Anderson, to leave. His position being more isolated than the others, was the first to invite an organized attack with success; the Virginians first investing the factory with their hordes, before the final success at the engine house. From the prisoner taken by us who had participated in the assault upon Kagi's position, we received the sad details of the slaughter of our brave companions. Seven different times during the day they were fired upon, while they occupied the interior part of the building, the insurgents defending themselves with great courage, killing and wounding with great precision. At last, overwhelming numbers, as many as five hundred, our informant told us, blocked up the front of the building, battered the doors down and forced their way into the interior. The insurgents were then forced to retreat the back way, fighting, however, all the time. They were pursued, when they took to the river, and it being so shallow, they waded out to a rock, mid-way, and there, made a stand, being completely hemmed in, front and rear. Some four or five hundred shots, said our prisoner, were fired at them before they were conquered. They would not surrender into the hands of the enemy, but kept on fighting until every one was killed, except John Copeland. Seeing he could do no more, and that all his associates were murdered, he suffered himself to be captured. The party at the rifle factory fought desperately till the last, from their perch on the rock. Slave and free, black and white, carried out the special injunction of the brave old Captain, to make sure work of it. The unfortunate targets for so many bullets from the enemy, some of them received two or three balls. There fell poor Kagi, the friend and adviser of Captain Brown in his most trying positions, and the cleverest man in the party; and there also fell Sherrard Lewis Leary, generous-hearted and companionable as he was, and in that and other difficult positions, brave to desperation. There fought John Copeland, who met his fate like a man. But they were all "honorable" men, noble, noble fellows, who fought and died for the most holy principles. John Copeland was taken to the guard-house, where the other prisoners afterwards were, and thence to Charlestown jail. His subsequent mockery of a trial and execution, with his companion Shields Green, on the 16th of December—are they not part of the dark deeds of this era, which will assign their perpetrators to infamy, and cause after generations to blush at the remembrance? . . .

Of the various contradictory reports made by slaveholders and their satellites about the time of the Harper's Ferry conflict, none were more untruthful than those relating to the slaves. There was seemingly a studied attempt to enforce the belief that the slaves were cowardly, and that they were really more in favor of Virginia masters and slavery, than of their freedom. As a party who had an intimate knowledge of the conduct of the colored men engaged, I am prepared to make an emphatic denial of the gross imputation against them. They were charged specially with being unreliable, with deserting Captain Brown the first opportunity, and going back to their masters; and with being so indifferent to the work of their salvation from the yoke, as to have to be forced into service by the Captain, contrary to their will.

On the Sunday evening of the outbreak, when we visited the plantations and acquainted the slaves with our purpose to effect their liberation, the greatest enthusiasm was manifested by them—joy and hilarity beamed from every countenance. One old mother, white-haired from age, and borne down with the labors of many years in bonds, when told of the work in hand, replied: "God bless you! God bless you!" She then kissed the party at her house, and requested all to kneel, which we did, and she offered prayer to God for His blessing on the enterprise, and our success. At the slaves' quarters, there was apparently a general jubilee, and they stepped forward manfully, without impressing or coaxing. In one case only, was there any hesitation. A dark-complexioned freeborn man refused to take up arms. He showed the only want of confidence in the movement, and far less courage than any slave consulted about the plan. In fact, so far as I could learn, the free blacks South are much less reliable than the slaves, and infinitely more fearful. In Washington City, a party of free colored persons offered their services to the Mayor, to aid in suppressing our movement. Of the slaves who followed us to the Ferry, some were sent to help remove stores, and the others were drawn up in a circle around the engine-house, at one time, where they were, by Captain Brown's order, furnished by me with pikes, mostly, and acted as a guard to the prisoners to prevent their escape, which they did.

As in the war of the American Revolution, the first blood shed was a black man's, Crispus Attucks, so at Harper's Ferry, the blood shed by our party, after the arrival of the United States troops, was that of a slave. In the beginning of the encounter, and before the troops had fairly emerged from the bridge a slave was shot. I saw him fall. Phil, the slave who died in prison, with fear, as it was reported, was wounded at the Ferry, and died from the effects of it. Of the men shot on the rocks, when Kagi's party were compelled to take to the river, some were slaves, and they suffered death before they would desert their companions, and their bodies fell into the waves beneath. Captain Brown, who was surprised and pleased by the promptitude with which they volunteered, and with their manly bearing at the scene of violence, remarked to me, on that Monday morning, that he was agreeably disappointed in the behavior of the slaves; for he did not expect one out of ten to be willing to fight. The truth of the Harper's Ferry "raid," as it has been called, in regard to the part taken by the slaves, and the aid given by colored men generally, demonstrates clearly: First, that the conduct of the slaves is a strong guarantee of the weakness of the institution, should a favorable opportunity occur; and, secondly, that the colored people, as a body, were well represented by numbers, both in the fight, and in the number who suffered martyrdom afterward.

## 164

# FREDERICK DOUGLASS ON JOHN BROWN'S RAID, 1859

Rumors concerning the role of Frederick Douglass in Brown's raid—many of them quite fantastic—appeared as soon as the event was reported. Some of this misinformation persists to this day, notwithstanding the fact that Douglass told the story in a letter dated Canada West, October 31, 1859, which was published in *The Liberator*, November 11, 1859. This letter follows:

I notice that the telegraph makes Mr. Cook (one of the unfortunate insurgents at Harper's Ferry, and now in the hands of the thing calling itself the Government of Virginia, but which in fact is but an organized conspiracy by one party of the people against the other and weaker,) denounce me as a coward—and to assert that I promised to be present at the Harper's Ferry Insurrection. This is certainly a very grave impeachment, whether viewed in its bearings upon friends or upon foes, and you will not think it strange that I should take a somewhat serious notice of it.

Having no acquaintance whatever with Mr. Cook, and never having exchanged a word with him about the Harper's Ferry insurrection, I am induced to doubt that he could have used the language concerning me which the wires attribute to him. The lightning, when speaking for itself, is among the most direct, reliable and truthful of things; but when speaking for the terror-stricken slaveholders at Harper's Ferry, it has been made the swiftest of liars. Under their nimble and trembling fingers, it magnified seventeen men into seven hundred—and has since filled the columns of the New York *Herald* for days with interminable contradictions.

But, assuming that it has told only the simple truth, as to the sayings of Mr. Cook in this instance, I have this answer to make to my accuser: Mr. Cook may be perfectly right in denouncing me as a coward. I have not one word to say in defence or vindication of my character for courage. I have always been more distinguished for running than fighting—and, tried by the Harper's Ferry insurrection test, I am most miserably deficient in courage —even more so than Cook, when he deserted his old brave captain, and fled to the mountains. To this extent Mr. Cook is entirely right, and will meet no contradiction from me or from anybody else. But wholly, grievously, and most unaccountably wrong is Mr. Cook, when he asserts that I promised to be present in person at the Harper's Ferry insurrection. Of whatever other imprudence and indiscretion I may have been guilty, I have never made a promise so rash and wild as this. The taking of Harper's Ferry was a measure never encouraged by my word or by my vote, at any time or place; my wisdom, or my cowardice has not only kept me from Harper's Ferry, but has equally kept me from making any promise to go there. I desire to be quite emphatic here—for all guilty men, he is the guiltiest who lures his fellow-men to an undertaking of this sort, under promise of assistance, which he afterwards fails to render. I therefore declare that there is no man living, and no man dead, who if living, could truthfully say that I ever promised him or anybody else, either conditionally or otherwise, that I would be present in person at the Harper's Ferry insurrection. My field of labor for the abolition of slavery has not extended to an attack upon the United States arsenal. In the teeth of the documents already published, and of those which hereafter may be published, I affirm no man connected with that insurrection, from its noble and heroic leader down, can connect my name with a single broken promise of any sort whatever. So much I deem it proper to say negatively.

The time for a full statement of what I know, and of *all* I know, of this desperate but sublimely disinterested effort to emancipate the slaves of Maryland and Virginia, from their cruel taskmasters, has not yet come, and may never come. In the denial which I have now made, my motive is more a respectable consideration for the opinions of the slave's friends, than from my fear of being made an accomplice in the general *conspiracy* against Slavery. I am ever ready to write, speak, publish, organize, combine, and even to conspire against Slavery, when there is a reasonable hope for success. Men who live by robbing their fellow-men of their labor and liberty, have forfeited their right to know anything of the thoughts, feelings, or purposes of those whom they rob and plunder. They have by the single act of slaveholding voluntarily placed themselves beyond the laws of justice and honor, and have become only fitted for companionship with thieves and pirates—the common enemies of God and of all mankind. While it shall be considered right to protect oneself against thieves, burglars, robbers and assassins, and to slay a wild beast in the act of devouring his human prey, it can never be wrong for the imbruted and whip-scarred slaves, or their friends, to hunt, harass and even strike down the traffickers in human flesh. If anybody is disposed to think less of me on account of this sentiment; or because I may have had a knowledge of what was about to occur, and did not assume the base and detestable character of an informer, he is a man whose good or bad opinion of me may be equally repugnant and despicable. Entertaining this sentiment, I may be asked, why I did not join John Brown—the noble old hero whose one right hand has shaken the foundation of the American Union, and whose ghost will haunt the bedchambers of all the born and unborn slaveholders of Virginia through all their generations, filling them with alarm and consternation! My answer to this has already been given, at least, impliedly given: "The tools to those that can use them." Let every man work for the abolition of Slavery in his own way. I would help all, and hinder none. My position in regard to the Harper's Ferry insurrection may be easily inferred from these remarks, and I shall be glad if those papers which have spoken of me in connection with it would find room for this brief statement.

I have no apology for keeping out of the way of those gentlemanly United States Marshals, who are said to have paid Rochester a somewhat protracted visit lately, with a view to an interview with me. A government recognizing the validity of the *Dred Scott* decision, at such a time as this, is not likely to have any very charitable feelings towards me; and if I am to meet its representatives, I prefer to do so, at least, upon equal terms. If I have committed any offence against Society, I have done so on the soil of the State of New York, and I should be perfectly willing *there* to be arraigned before an impartial jury; but I have quite insuperable objections to being caught by the hands of Mr. Buchanan, and *"bagged"* by Gov. Wise. For this appears to be the arrangements. Buchanan does the fighting and hunting, and Wise *"bags"* the game.

Some reflections may be made upon my leaving on a tour to England, just at this time. I have only to say, that my going to that country has been rather delayed than hastened by the insurrection at Harper's Ferry. All knew that I had intended to leave here in the first week of November.

165

# THE NEGRO'S RESPONSE TO BROWN'S MARTYRDOM, 1859

Letters, resolutions, meetings and demonstrations were some of the ways in which Negroes responded to John Brown's conviction and execution. Three examples follow in the form of a letter from Frances Ellen Watkins to Brown dated Kendallville, Indiana, November 25, 1859; the communication to Brown from a meeting of Negro women in Brooklyn held the next day; and the resolutions of a memorial meeting of New Bedford, Massachusetts Negroes held December 4, 1859, two days after the Old Man was hanged.

[a]

### *From Frances Ellen Watkins*

*Dear Friend:* Although the hands of Slavery throw a barrier between you and me, and it may not be my privilege to see you in your prison-house, Virginia has no bolts or bars through which I dread to send you my sympathy. In the name of the young girl sold from the warm clasp of a mother's arms to the clutches of a libertine or a profligate,—in the name of the slave mother, her heart rocked to and fro by the agony of her mournful separations,—I thank you, that you have been brave enough to reach out your hands to the crushed and blighted of my race. You have rocked the bloody Bastille; and I hope that from your sad fate great good may arise to the cause of freedom. Already from your prison has come a shout of triumph against the giant sin of our country. The hemlock is distilled with victory when it is pressed to the lips of Socrates. The Cross becomes a glorious ensign when Calvary's page-browed sufferer yields up his life upon it. And, if Universal Freedom is ever to be the dominant power of the land, your bodies may be only her first stepping stones to dominion. I would prefer to see Slavery go down peaceably by men breaking off their sins by righteousness and their iniquities by showing justice and mercy to the poor; but we cannot tell what the future may bring forth. God writes national judgments upon national sins; and what may be slumbering in the storehouse of divine justice we do not know.

We may earnestly hope that your fate will not be a vain lesson, that it will intensify our hatred of Slavery and love of Freedom, and that your martyr grave will be a sacred altar upon which men will record their vows of undying hatred to that system which tramples on man and bids defiance to God. I have written to your dear wife, and sent her a few dollars, and I pledge myself to you that I will continue to assist her. May the ever-blessed God shield you and your fellow-prisoners in the darkest hour. Send my sympathy to your fellow-prisoners; tell them to be of good courage; to seek a refuge in the Eternal God, and lean upon His everlasting arms for a sure support. If any of them, like you, have a wife or children that I can help, let them send me word.

Yours in the cause of freedom.

James Redpath, *Echoes of Harper's Ferry* (Boston, 1860) pp. 418–19.

[b]

*From The Colored Women Of Brooklyn*

*In behalf of the colored women of Brooklyn.* Dear Sir: We, a portion of the American people, would fain offer you our sincere and heartfelt sympathies in the cause you have so nobly espoused, and that you so firmly adhere to. We truly appreciate your most noble and humane effort, and recognize in you a Saviour commissioned to redeem us, the American people, from the great National Sin of Slavery; and though you have apparently failed in the object of your desires, yet the influence that we believe it will eventually exert, will accomplish all your intentions. We consider you a model of true patriotism, and one whom our common country will yet regard as the greatest it has produced, because you have sacrificed all for its sake. We rejoice in the consciousness of your perfect resignation. We shall ever hold you dear in our remembrance, and shall infuse the same feelings in our posterity. We have always entertained a love for the country which gave us birth, despite the wrongs inflicted upon us, and have always been hopeful that the future would augur better things. We feel now that your glorious act for the cause of humanity has afforded us an unexpected realization of some of our seemingly vain hopes. And now, in view of the coming crisis which is to terminate all your labors of love for this life, our mortal natures fail to sustain us under the trying affliction; but when we view it from our religious standpoint, we feel that earth is not worthy of you, and that your spirit yearneth for a higher and holier existence. Therefore we willingly give you up, and submit to His will "who doeth all things well."

James Redpath, *op. cit.*, p. 419.

## [c]

### *New Bedford Meeting*

*Resolved,* That this meeting do fully endorse and heartily approve of the spirit manifested by Captain John Brown and his associates, but deeply regret that the plans so well laid did not succeed. Yet we believe that, under God, the greatest good to the cause of our enslaved brethren will result from the mad career of the slaveholders in sacrificing the lives of their victims, as that act will do more to hasten the downfall of slavery than the liberation of a thousand slaves.

*Resolved,* That we return thanks to the clergy who have had manly independence enough to speak bold words for John Brown, and also to those trustees that complied with the request to allow the use of their bells to be tolled on that mournful occasion, and we hereby acknowledge our want of belief in the Christian virtues of the trustees of such churches as refused the application; as our religion teaches us to do unto others as we would that they should do unto us.

*Resolved,* That the memory of John Brown shall be indelibly written upon the tablets of our hearts, and when tyrants cease to oppress the enslaved, we will teach our children to revere his name, and transmit it to the latest posterity, as being the greatest man in the 19th century.

*Resolved,* That the Committee appointed at a previous meeting be requested to correspond with Captain Avis, the jailor, at Charlestown, Virginia, relating to the condition of the colored men, Green and Copeland, and to endeavor to ascertain whether they have families, and report the same at another meeting to be called as soon as information is obtained.

*Resolved,* That the same Committee be authorized to adopt necessary means to inaugurate the 2d day of December, and to make arrangements to celebrate the day in an appropriate manner.

*The Liberator,* December 16, 1859.

166

# LAST WORDS OF A NEGRO WHO DIED WITH JOHN BROWN, 1859

Mention has already been made of the fact that one of the Negroes in John Brown's original company was John A. Copeland, fugitive slave and resident of Oberlin, Ohio. Upon conviction he was sentenced to be hanged on December 16, 1859. Two of his letters written in the Charlestown jail—one dated December 10 and addressed to a brother, the other written a few hours prior to his execution and addressed to his parents, three brothers and two sisters—are printed below.

The Baltimore *Sun* reported that on his way to the gallows Copeland remarked: "If I am dying for freedom, I could not die for a better cause—I had rather die than be a slave!" Professor James Monroe of Oberlin—a member-elect of the Ohio State Senate—was sent to Virginia in an unsuccessful attempt to bring Copeland's body back to his town and his family.

## [a]

Dear Brother: . . . It was a sense of the wrongs which we have suffered that prompted the noble but unfortunate Captain John Brown and his associates to attempt to give freedom to a small number, at least, of those who are now held by cruel and unjust laws, and by no less cruel and unjust men. To this freedom they were entitled by every known principle of justice and humanity, and for the enjoyment of it God created them. And now, dear brother, could I die in a more noble cause? Could I, brother, die in a manner and for a cause which would induce true and honest men more to honor me, and the angels more readily to receive me to their happy home of everlasting joy above? I imagine that I hear you, and all of you, mother, father, sisters and brothers, say—"No, there is not a cause for which we, with less sorrow, could see you die." Believe me when I tell you, that though shut up in prison and under sentence of death, I have spent some very happy hours here. And were it not that I know that the hearts of those to whom I am attached by the nearest and most enduring ties of blood-relationship—yea, by the closest and strongest ties that God has instituted—will be filled with sorrow, I would almost as lief die now as at any time, for I feel that I am now prepared to meet my Maker . . .

## [b]

Dear Father, Mother, Brothers Henry, William and Freddy and Sisters Sarah and Mary:

The last Sabbath with me on earth has passed away. The last Monday, Tuesday, Wednesday and Thursday that I shall ever see on this earth, have now passed by. God's glorious sun, which he has placed in the heavens to illuminate this earth—whose warm rays make man's home on earth pleasant—whose refulgent beams are watched for by the poor invalid, to enter and make as it were a heaven of the room in which he is confined—I have seen declining behind the western mountains for the last time. Last night, for the last time, I beheld the soft bright moon as it rose, casting its mellow light into my felon's cell, dissipating the darkness, and filling it with that soft pleasant light which causes such thrills of joy to all those in like circumstances with myself. This morning, for the last time, I beheld the glorious sun of yesterday rising in the far-off East, away off in the country where our Lord Jesus Christ first proclaimed salvation to man; and now, as he rises higher and his bright light takes the place of the pale, soft moonlight, I will take my pen, for the last time, to write you who are bound to me by those strong ties, (yea, the strongest that God ever instituted,) the ties of blood and relationship. *I am well, both in body and in mind.* And now, dear ones, if it were not that I knew your hearts will be filled with sorrow at my fate, I could pass from this earth without a regret. Why should you sorrow? Why should your hearts be wracked with grief? Have I not everything to gain, and nothing to lose by the change? I fully believe that not only myself, but also all three of my poor comrades who are to ascend the same scaffold—(a scaffold already made sacred to the cause of freedom by the death of that great champion of human freedom—Captain John Brown) are *prepared* to meet our God.

I am only leaving a world filled with sorrow and woe, to enter one in which there is but one lasting day of happiness and bliss. I feel that God, in his mercy, has spoken peace to my soul, and that all my numerous sins are forgiven.

Dear parents, brothers and sisters, it is true that I am now in a few hours to start on a journey from which no traveler returns. Yes, long before this reaches you, I shall, as I sincerely hope, have met our brother and sister who have for years been worshiping God around his throne—singing praises to him and thanking him that he gave his Son to die that they might have eternal life. I pray daily and hourly that I may be fitted to have my home with them, and that you, one and all, may prepare your souls to meet your God, that so, in the end, though we meet no more on earth, we shall meet in heaven, where we shall not be parted by the demands of the cruel and unjust monster Slavery.

But think not that I am complaining, for I feel reconciled to meet my fate. *I pray God that his will be done, not mine.*

Let me tell you that it is not the mere fact of having to meet death, which I should regret, (if I should express regret I mean,) but that such an unjust institution should exist as the one which demands my life, and not my life only, but the lives of those to whom my life bears but the relative value of zero to the infinite. I beg of you, one and all, that you will not grieve about me; but that you will thank God that he spared me to make my peace with him.

And now, dear ones, attach no blame to any one for my coming here, for not any person but myself is to blame.

I have no antipathy against any one. I have freed my mind of all hard feelings against every living being, and I ask all who have any thing against me to do the same.

And now, dear Parents, Brothers and Sisters, I must bid you to serve your God, and meet me in heaven.

I must with a very few words close my correspondence with those who are the most near and dear to me: but I hope, in the end, we may again commune never more to cease.

Dear ones, he who writes this will, in a few hours, be in this world no longer. Yes, these fingers which hold the pen with which this is written will, before today's sun has reached his meridian, have laid it aside forever, and this poor soul have taken its flight to meet its God.

And now, dear ones, I must bid you that last, long, sad farewell. Good by, Father, Mother, Henry, William and Freddy, Sarah and Mary! Serve your God and meet me in heaven.

Your Son and Brother to eternity,

JOHN A. COPELAND

*The Liberator*, January 13, 1860.

## 167

# AN APPEAL TO THE WORLD BY NEGRO REFUGEES, 1860

In the years immediately preceding the Civil War several southern states enacted laws giving free Negroes the choice of exile or re-enslavement. Typical was the action of Arkansas whose law, passed in February, 1859, required all free Negroes to act on this choice by January 1, 1860. Since many northern states had passed laws barring the entry of free Negroes, those choosing exile had a particularly difficult time. In January, 1860, twelve Negro refugees from Arkansas issued the following "Appeal to Christians throughout the World":

In consequence of a law passed by the Legislature of Arkansas, compelling the Free Colored People either to leave the State or to be enslaved, we, a number of exiles, driven out by this inhuman statute, who reached Ohio on the 3d of January, 1860, teeling a deep sense of the wrong done us, make this Appeal to the Christian World.

We appeal to you, as children of a common Father, and believers in a crucified Redeemer. To-day we are exiles, driven from the homes of our childhood, the scenes of our youth, and the burial places of our friends. We are exiles; not that our hands have been stained with guilt, or our lives accused of crime. Our fault, in a land of Bibles and Churches, of baptisms and prayers, is, that in our veins flows the blood of an outcast race; a race oppressed by power, and proscribed by prejudice; a race cradled in wrong, and nurtured in oppression.

In the very depth of winter, we have left a genial climate of sunny skies, to be homeless strangers in the regions of the icy North. Some of the exiles have left children, who are very dear; but, to stay with them, was to involve ourselves in a life-time of slavery. Some left dear companions; they were enslaved, and we had no other alternative than slavery, or exile. We were weak; our oppressors were strong. We were feeble, scattered, peeled; they being powerful, placed before us slavery or banishment. We chose the latter. Poverty, trials, and all the cares incident to a life of freedom, are better, far better, than slavery.

From this terrible injustice we appeal to the moral sentiment of the world. We turn to the free North; but even here oppression tracks our steps. Indiana shuts her doors upon us. Illinois denies us admission to her prairie homes. Oregon refuses us an abiding place for the soles of our weary feet. And even Minnesota has our exclusion under consideration. In Ohio we found kind hearts; hospitality opened her doors; generous hands reached out a warm and hearty welcome. For this, may the God of the fatherless ever defend and bless them.

And now, Christians, we Appeal to you, as heirs of the same heritage, and children of the same Father, to PROTEST against this gross and inhuman outrage, which has been committed beneath the wing of the American Eagle, and in the shadow of the American Church. We ask you, by the love, the pity, and the mercy, in the religion of Jesus Christ, that you will raise your voices and protest against this sin.

Editors of Newspapers, formers of public opinion, conductors of intelligence and thought; we entreat you to insert this appeal in your papers; and unite your voices against this outrage which disgraces our land, and holds it up to shame before the nations of the earth. We entreat you to move a wave of influence, which will widen, and spread through all the earth, and roll back and wash away this stain.

Christian mothers, by our plundered cradles and child bereft hearts, we appeal to you, and ask your protest.

Christian fathers, by all the sacred associations that cluster around the name, father, we appeal to you, to swell the tide of indignation, against our shameful wrongs.

We appeal to the church of Christ among all nations, kindreds, tongues, and people to protest against the inhumanity that has driven us from our homes and our kindred.

Members of all political parties, we ask *your* protest, in the name of a common humanity, against this cruel act of despotism.

Christian Ministers, we appeal to you, in the name of Him, who came "to preach good tidings to the meek, to bind up the broken hearted; to proclaim liberty to the captive; and the opening of the prison, to them that are bound," to lay before your congregations, the injustice done us; and the wickedness of a system that tramples on the feeble, and crushes out the rights of the helpless.

And we APPEAL to the God of the fatherless and the Judge of the widow, that He will remember His word "Inasmuch as ye have done it to one of the least of these—ye have done it unto me"; that He will move the hearts of His children every where to *unite* their testimony against this unequalled iniquity that writes "property" on man; that chattelizes the immortal mind; and makes merchandise of the deathless soul. We APPEAL to Him who does not permit a sparrow to fall to the ground unnoticed, to plead the cause of the poor and needy to set him at rest from him that puffeth at him.

Signed: Eliza Ann West, Ann Eliza West, Elizabeth Taylor West, Agnes West, Landy Waggoner of Redfork, Desha County, Arkansas; and Rachel Love, William H. Newcomb, Henry McGrath of Napoleon, Arkansas; Polly Taylor, Caroline Parker, Jane Thomson and Nelly Grinton of Little Rock, Arkansas.

*The Principia* (N.Y.), Feb. 11, 1860, I, pp. 101–02.


## 168

# A NEGRO PIONEER DEFENDS HIS LAND CLAIM.
## 1860

On the basis of the non-citizenship of Negroes, an attempt was made to deny the validity of land claims staked out by them in the West. An example of this and the facts concerning it appear in the petition to Congress of Sylvester Gray which was referred, on March 23, 1860, to the Committee on Public Lands of the U.S. Senate.

To the Senate and House of Representatives:

The petition of Sylvester Gray, a free man of color, respectfully showeth: That on the seventh day of August, 1856, he settled upon the North-West quarter of Section 14, Township 48, Range 13, of lands of the U.S. subject to sale at the Land Office at Superior, Wisconsin; that, under the pre-emption act of 1841, he filed his declaratory statement, on the 14th of August, 1856, at the said Land Office, and upon the 20th of June, 1857, located the said tract, containing 160 acres, with Military Bounty Land Warrant No. 39,006, issued under the act of 1855, and received from the Register at Superior a certificate of land location.

Your petitioner further alleges that, in erecting a dwelling place, clearing land, and other labor and improvements upon said tract, he expended the sum of two hundred and twenty three dollars (see memorandum herewith); * which expenses and improvements were made with a view to making said tract a home for himself and family; it having been the practice of the General Land Office to allow entries or locations by persons of his description, under the pre-emption act aforesaid.

But your petitioner has been recently informed, by a letter from the Commissioner of the General Land Office, that on the 27th of January, 1860, his said location was cancelled, for the reason that he is a "man of color"; and his warrant has been returned to him.

Your petitioner begs leave to state that he has understood that the action of the General Land Office in his case was had in pursuance of the decision of the Supreme Court, in Dred Scott's case, that persons of African descent could not be considered as citizens of the United States.

But your petitioner further begs leave to call the attention of your honorable body to the fact that his settlement and improvements, as aforesaid, were made prior to the date of that decision; for which reason, and that he may not be compelled to sustain the loss which would otherwise result to him, he respectfully asks that a law may be passed, directing that a patent be issued to him for the land before described, upon his surrendering to the Commissioner of the General Land Office the warrant aforesaid.

The National Archives, Washington, D.C.

---

* The memorandum reads as follows:

| | Cost of Claim |
|---|---|
| Original expence of building | $ 65.00 |
| "       "     " clearing land | 48.00 |
| Subsequent expence of various improvements & labour | 110.00 |
| | $223.00 |

169

# ETHICS: VIEWS OF SLAVE AND MASTER, 1860

The exchange between a slave owner, Mrs. Sarah Logue of Tennessee, and her fugitive slave, the Rev. J. W. Loguen of Syracuse, New York, illuminates how closely related are one's class position and his morality. "Plainly," remarked Abraham Lincoln, in 1864, "the sheep and the wolf are not agreed upon a definition of the word liberty."

Mrs. Logue's letter is dated Feb. 20, 1860; Mr. Loguen's reply, March 28, 1860:

## [a]

### *The Slaveholder's Letter*

To Jarm:—I now take my pen to write you a few lines, to let you know how we all are. I am a cripple, but I am still able to get about. The rest of the family are all well. Cherry is as well as common. I write you these lines to let you know the situation we are in,—partly in consequence of your running away and stealing Old Rock, our fine mare. Though we got the mare back, she never was worth much after you took her;—and, as I now stand in need of some funds, I have determined to sell you, and I have had an offer for you, but did not see fit to take it. If you will send me one thousand dollars, and pay for the old mare, I will give up all claim I have to you. Write to me as soon as you get these lines, and let me know if you will accept my proposition. In consequence of your running away, we had to sell Abe and Ann and twelve acres of land; and I want you to send me the money, that I may be able to redeem the land that you was the cause of our selling, and on receipt of the above-named sum of money, I will send you your bill of sale. If you do not comply with my request, I will sell you to some one else, and you may rest assured that the time is not far distant when things will be changed with you. Write to me as soon as you get these lines. Direct your letter to Bigbyville, Maury County, Tennessee. You had better comply with my request.

I understand that you are a preacher. As the Southern people are so bad you had better come and preach to your old acquaintances. I would like to know if you read your Bible. If so, can you tell what will become of the thief if he does not repent? and, if the blind lead the blind, what will the consequence be? I deem it unnecessary to say much more at present. A word to the wise is sufficient. You know where the liar has his part. You know that we reared you as we reared our own children; that you was never abused, and that shortly before you ran away, when your master asked if you would like to be sold, you said you would not leave him to go with anybody.

## [b]

### *The Fugitive Slave's Reply*

Mrs. Sarah Logue: Yours of the 20th of February is duly received, and I thank you for it. It is a long time since I heard from my poor old mother, and I am glad to know that she is yet alive, and, as you say, "as well as common." What that means, I don't know. I wish you had said more about her.

You are a woman; but, had you a woman's heart, you never could have insulted a brother by telling him you sold his only remaining brother and sister, because he put himself beyond your power to convert him into money.

You sold my brother and sister, Abe and Ann, and twelve acres of land, you say, because I ran away. Now you have the unutterable meanness to ask me to return and be your miserable chattel, or in lieu thereof, send you $1000 to enable you to redeem the *land,* but not to redeem my poor brother and sister! If I were to send you money, it would be to get my brother and sister, and not that you should get land. You say you are a *cripple,* and doubtless you say it to stir my pity, for you knew I was susceptible in that direction. I do pity you from the bottom of my heart. Nevertheless, I am indignant beyond the power of words to express, that you should be so sunken and cruel as to tear the hearts I love so much all in pieces; that you should be willing to impale and crucify us all, out of compassion for your poor *foot* or *leg.* Wretched woman! Be it known to you that I value my freedom, to say nothing of my mother, brothers and sisters, more than your whole body; more, indeed, than my own life; more than all the lives of all the slaveholders and tyrants under heaven.

You say you have offers to buy me, and that you shall sell me if I do not send you $1000, and in the same breath and almost in the same sentence, you say, "You know we raised you as we did our own children." Woman, did you raise your *own children* for the market? Did you raise them for the whipping-post? Did you raise them to be driven off, bound to a coffle in chains? Where are my poor bleeding brothers and sisters? Can you tell? Who was it that sent them off into sugar and cotton fields, to be kicked and cuffed, and whipped, and to groan and die; and where no kin can hear their groans, or attend and sympathize at their dying bed, or follow in their funeral? Wretched woman! Do you say *you* did not do it? Then I reply, your husband did, and *you* approved the deed—and the very letter you sent me shows that your heart approves it all. Shame on you!

But, by the way, where is your husband? You don't speak of him. I infer, therefore, that he is dead; that he has gone to his great account, with all his sins against my poor family upon his head. Poor man! gone to meet the spirits of my poor, outraged and murdered people, in a world where Liberty and Justice are *Masters.*

But you say I am a thief, because I took the old mare along with me. Have you got to learn that I had a better right to the old mare, as you call her, than Mannasseth Logue had to me? Is it a greater sin for me to steal his horse, than it was for him to rob my mother's cradle, and steal me? If he and you infer that I forfeit all my rights to you, shall not I infer that you forfeit all your rights to me? Have you got to learn that human rights are mutual and reciprocal, and if you take my liberty and life, you forfeit your own liberty and life? Before God and high heaven, is there a law for one man which is not a law for every other man?

If you or any other speculator on my body and rights, wish to know how I regard my rights, they need but come here, and lay their hands on me to enslave me. Did you think to terrify me by presenting the alternative to give my money to you, or give my body to slavery? Then let me say to you, that I meet the proposition with unutterable scorn and contempt. The proposition is an outrage and an insult. I will not budge one hair's breadth. I will not breathe a shorter breath, even to save me from your persecutions. I stand among a free people, who, I thank God, sympathize with my rights, and the rights of mankind; and if your emissaries and venders come here to re-enslave me, and escape the unshrinking vigor of my own right arm, I trust my strong and brave friends, in this city and State, will be my rescuers and avengers.

*The Liberator,* April 27, 1860.


## 170

## ROBERT PURVIS ON AMERICAN "DEMOCRACY" AND THE NEGRO, 1860

On the occasion of the 27th anniversary of the American Anti-Slavery Society, Robert Purvis of Philadelphia delivered a burning indictment of the American government for its subjugation of the Negro people. The speech was made in New York City on May 8, 1860; about half of it is printed below:

What is the attitude of your boasting, braggart republic toward the 600,000 free people of color who swell its population and add to its wealth? I have already alluded to the dictum of Judge Taney in the notorious Dred Scott decision. That dictum reveals the animus of the whole government; it is a fair example of the cowardly and malignant spirit that pervades the entire policy of the country. The end of that policy is, undoubtedly, to destroy the colored man, as a man, to prevent him from having any existence in the land except as a "chattel personal to all intents, constructions and purposes whatsoever." With this view, it says a colored man shall not sue and recover his lawful property; he shall not bear arms and train in the militia; he shall not be a commander of a vessel, not even of the meanest craft that creeps along the creeks and bays of your Southern coast; he shall not carry a mail-bag, or serve as a porter in a post-office; and he shall not even put his face in a United States court-room for any purpose, except by the sufferance of the white man.

I had occasion, a few days since, to go to the United States court-room in the city of Philadelphia. My errand was a proper one; it was to go bail for one of the noble band of colored men who had so bravely risked their lives for the rescue of a brother man on his way to eternal bondage. As I was about entering the door, I was stopped, and ordered back. I demanded the reason. "I have my orders," was the reply. What orders? "To keep out all colored people." Now, sir, who was the man that offered me this indignity? It was Deputy-Marshal Jenkins, the notorious slave-catcher. And why did he do it? Because he had his orders from pious, praying, Christian Democrats, who hold and teach the damnable doctrine that the "black man has no rights that the white man is bound to respect." It is true that Marshal Yost, to whom I indignantly appealed, reversed this man's orders, and apologized to me, assuring me that I could go in and out at my pleasure. But, sir, the apology made the matter worse; for, mark you, it was not me personally that was objected to, *but the race* with which I stand identified. Great God! who can think of such outrages, such meanness, such dastardly, cowardly cruelty, without burning with indignation, and choking for want of words with which to denounce it? And in the case of the noble little band referred to, the men who generously, heroically risked their lives to rescue the man who was about being carried back to slavery; look at their conduct; you know the circumstances. We recently had a slave trial in Philadelphia—no new thing in the city of *"Brotherly Love."* A victim of Virginia tyranny, a fugitive from Southern injustice, had made good his escape from the land of whips and chains to Pennsylvania, and had taken up his abode near the capital of the State. The place of his retreat was discovered; the bloodhounds of the law scented him out, and caught him; they put him in chains and brought him before Judge Cadwallader—a man whose pro-slavery antecedents made him a fitting instrument for the execution of the accursed Fugitive Slave Law.

The sequel can easily be imagined. Brewster, a leading Democrat—the man, who, like your O'Conor of this city, has the unblushing hardihood to defend the enslavement of the black man upon principle—advocated his return. The man was sent into life-long bondage. While the trial was going on, slaveholders, Southern students and pro-slavery Market-street salesmen were freely admitted; but the colored people, the class most interested, were carefully excluded. Prohibited from entering, they thronged around the door of the court-house. At last the prisoner was brought out, handcuffed and guarded by his captors; he was put into a carriage which started off in the direction of the South. Some ten or twelve brave black men made a rush for the carriage, in hopes of effecting a rescue; they were overpowered, beaten, put under arrest and carried to prison, there to await their trial, before this same Judge Cadwallader, for violating the Fugitive Slave law! Mark you, they may go into the court-room as *prisoners,* but not as *spectators!* They may not have an opportunity of hearing the law expounded, but they may be punished if they make themselves chargeable with violating it!

Sir, people talk of the bloody code of Draco, but I venture to assert, without fear of intelligent contradiction, that, all things considered, that code was mild, that code was a law of love, compared with the hellish laws and precedents that disgrace the statute-books of this modern Democratic, Christian Republic! I said that a man of color might not be a commander of the humblest craft that sails in your American waters. There was a man in Philadelphia, the other day, who stated that he owned and sailed a schooner between that city and different ports in the State of Maryland—that his vessel had been seized in the town of Easton, (I believe it was,) or some other town on the Eastern Shore, on the allegation that, contrary to law, there was no white man on board. The vessel constituted his entire property and sole means of supporting his family. He was advised to sue for its recovery, which he did, and, after a long and expensive litigation, the case was decided in his favor. But by this time the vessel had rotted and gone to wreck, and the man found himself reduced to beggary. His business in Philadelphia was to raise $50 with which to take himself and family out of this cursed land, to a country where liberty is not a mockery, and freedom a mere idle name! . . .

But, sir, narrow and proscriptive as, in my opinion, is the spirit of what is called Native Americanism, there is another thing I regard as tenfold more base and contemptible, and that is your American Democracy—your piebald and rotten Democracy, that talks loudly about equal rights, and at the same time tramples one-sixth of the population of the country in the dust, and declares that they have "no rights which a white man is bound to respect." And, sir, while I repudiate your Native Americanism and your bogus Democracy, allow me to add, at the same time, that I am not a Republican. I could not be a member of the Republican party if I were so disposed; I am disfranchised; I have no vote; I am put out of the pale of political society. The time was in Pennsylvania, under the old Constitution, when I could go to the polls as other men do, but your modern Democracy have taken away from me that right. Your Reform Convention, your Pierce Butlers—the man who, a year ago, put up nearly four hundred human beings on the block in Georgia, and sold them to the highest bidder—your Pierce Butlers disfranchised me, and I am without any political rights whatever. I am taxed to support a government which takes my money and tramples on me. But, sir, I would not be a member of the Republican party if it were in my power. How could I, a colored man, join a party that styles itself emphatically the "white man's party!?" How could I, an Abolitionist, belong to a party that is and must of necessity be a pro-slavery party? The Republicans may be, and doubtless are, opposed to the extension of slavery, but they are sworn to support, and they *will* support, slavery where it already exists.

*The Liberator*, May 18, 1860.

## 171

## APPEAL OF NEW YORK NEGROES FOR EQUAL SUFFRAGE RIGHTS, 1860

The special property qualification placed upon the Negro's right to vote in New York in 1821 was consistently fought by them. Finally, this effort, reinforced by the agitation of the Abolitionist movement as a whole, resulted, in 1860, in the holding of a referendum on whether or not the discrimination should be removed. The New York City and County Suffrage Committee of Colored Citizens, under the leadership of Dr. James McCune Smith, James P. Miller and John J. Zuille, issued, in September, 1860, the following tract on "The Suffrage Question." The electorate voted against the reform.

Under the provisions of the first Constitution of the State of New York, which was adopted on the 20th of April, 1777, during the first year of the Revolutionary War—that Constitution having embodied, as part and parcel thereof, the Declaration of Independence passed at Philadelphia by Congress—*all* male inhabitants, without restriction of color or place of birth, who were then inhabitants of this State, and paid rent to the value of forty shillings ($5) were made voters for Assemblymen; and freeholders to the amount of one hundred pounds ($250) voted for members of the Senate, and continued to vote on the same basis, until the Adoption of the Amended Constitution of 1821; when the property qualification was removed from White voters, but retained in regard to colored voters.

The present Constitution of the State of New York was framed and adopted in 1846. "Article II, Section 1—Every male citizen of the age of twenty-one years, who shall have been a citizen for ten days, and an inhabitant of this State for one year next preceding any election; for the last four months a resident of the county where he may offer his vote, shall be entitled to vote at such election in the election-district of which he shall at the time be a resident, and not elsewhere, for all offices that now are or hereafter may be elective by the people." It provides further that no man of color shall have a right to vote unless possessed of $250 worth of real estate, and shall have been three years a citizen of the state, and one year resident in the district in which he claims a vote.

In accordance with the provision of the Constitution for its own amendment, the last Legislature have provided that the inspectors at each poll, at the election for Governor, to be held on the 6th of November, 1860, shall provide a box to receive the ballots of citizens in relation to the proposed Amendment for restoring the equal right of suffrage to the colored people, and that the ballot shall be in one of the following forms:—

*"For the proposed Amendment in relation to Suffrage,"*

or

*"Against the proposed Amendment in relation to Suffrage,"*

and shall be so folded as to conceal the contents, and shall be indorsed on the outside as follows:

October 20, 1860—

"Proposed Amendment in relation to Suffrage."

If a majority of these ballots be cast "for the proposed amendment in relation to Suffrage," then the right to vote on an equal basis with other citizens will be restored to the colored citizens of New York; the Empire State will become a free State indeed—free like Maine and New Hampshire and Vermont and Massachusetts and Rhode Island.

FELLOW CITIZENS: We have had, and still have, great wrongs of which to complain. A heavy and cruel hand has been laid upon us. As a people, we feel ourselves to be not only deeply injured, but grossly misunderstood. Our white countrymen do not know us. They are strangers to our characters, ignorant of our capacity, oblivious to our history and progress, and are misinformed as to the principles and ideas that control and guide us, as a people. The great mass of American citizens estimate us as being a characterless and purposeless people; and hence we hold up our heads, if at all, against the withering influence of a nation's scorn and contempt.

It will not be surprising that we are so misunderstood and misused, when the motives for misrepresenting us and for degrading us are duly considered. Indeed, it will seem strange, upon such consideration (and in view of the ten thousand channels through which malign feelings find utterance and influence), that we have not fallen even lower in public estimation than we have done; for, with the exception of the Jews, under the whole heavens there is not to be found a people pursued with a more relentless prejudice and persecution, than are the free colored people of the United States.

What stone has been left unturned to degrade us? What hand has refused to fan the flame of popular prejudice against us? What American artist has not caricatured us? What wit has not laughed at us in our wretchedness? What songster has not made merry over our depressed spirits? What press has not ridiculed and condemned us? Few, few, very few; and that we have borne up with it all—that we have tried to be wise, though pronounced by all to be fools—that we have tried to be upright, when all around us have esteemed us to be knaves—that we have striven to be gentlemen, although all around us have been teaching us its impossibility—that we have remained here, when all our neighbors have advised us to leave, proves that we possess qualities of head and heart, such as cannot but be commended by impartial men.

It is believed that no other nation on the globe could have made more progress in the midst of such an universal and stringent disparagement. It would humble the proudest, crush the energies of the strongest, and retard the progress of the swiftest.

In view of our circumstances, we can, without boasting, thank God and take courage, having placed ourselves where we may fairly challenge comparison with more highly favored men.

During thirty-three years, colored children, especially in the large cities, have attended public schools. In 1856, according to the Report of the Superintendent of Schools in the City of New York, the average attendance of white children at the Common Schools was 1 in 3.40; the average attendance of colored children at the Common Schools was 1 in 2.60; that is, twenty-five per cent more colored than white children in proportion to the relative population, attended Common Schools. And New York City contains one third of the entire colored population of the State.

The colored people have not only taken good care of themselves in this State, notwithstanding the prejudice of color which limits their sphere of occupation, by amassing real and personal estate of large amount, but they are no greater, if so great a burden to the State in almshouses and prisons than other classes of citizens. In New York City, for example, it is ascertained that they own Real and Personal Estate to the value of nearly four millions of dollars, and the following from the Report for 1859 of the Governors of the Almshouses shows the relative proportions of Colored and White paupers and criminals; and it should be taken into consideration that, from their lack of political influence, colored persons committing any, even the slightest misdemeanors, are arrested; while it is notorious that the whites, who all vote, enjoy a comparative immunity from arrest and even from punishment for crime.

| | *White* | | *Colored* |
|---|---|---|---|
| Children at Randall's Island | 1142 | Colored Orphan Asylum | 180 |
| Almshouse department | 1770 | Colored Home | 323 |
| Bellevue Hospital | 1033 | | None |
| Lunatic Asylum | 696 | | 15 |
| Out-door Children Receiving Money-aid | 7785 | | 117 |
| Out-door Adults Receiving Money-aid | 4949 | | 127 |
| Out-door Adults receiving coal-aid | 44663 | | 1244 |
| Inmates of Workhouse | 5760 | | None |
| Total poor | 67998 | | 2006 |
| Inmates of Penitentiary in all 1859 | 2079 | | 165 |
| Inmates of City Prisons | 41036 | | 971 |
| | 111,113 | | 3,142 |

Principles of justice to the individuals who compose the State, and thereby of justice to the State itself, require that the basis of voting should be equal to all. No one class can be depressed and made unequal without injury to the other classes, and to the whole State. And are not these patriotic, industrious, provident, exemplary citizens deserving equal right at the ballot-box?

Is it not a shame for our State, that in 1777, when it was perilous to life to be a citizen of New York, she made colored men citizens, and that afterwards, in 1821, when it was safe and honorable to be a citizen, she disfranchised her colored citizens? Let us entreat you, remove this reproach from the fair fame of our noble State.

Gratitude is one of the virtues which the veriest hater of the colored man has never denied him; and this sentiment will never be called into such full exercise, as when the last shackle, the last emblem of degradation, shall be removed from the man of color:

> "Oh, yield him back his privilege! No sea
> Swells like the bosom of a man set free!"

We respectfully request you voters of the State of New York, irrespective of party, that you will give your attention to the proposed Amendment to the Constitution. The question is one, not of party, but humanity and right. We appeal with equal confidence to Democrats and Republicans. We feel assured that if you will examine the question in the light of reason and justice and Christianity, you will not hesitate to vote for the proposed Amendment in relation to the Suffrage.

*The Principia,* Oct. 20, 1860, I, pp. 385–86. Copy in Columbia University Library.

# IV

# The Civil War

---

## 172

### SEEKING THE RIGHT TO FIGHT:
### PRIVATE EFFORTS, 1861–1862

As soon as a desperate slaveholding class precipitated the American Civil War by firing upon Fort Sumter on April 12, 1861, the Negro people saw in the conflict the seeds of their own emancipation. To assure and hasten this event they immediately offered their services as soldiers. These offers were not accepted until the summer of 1862 when other agitational pressures, the rising casualty rates, and the necessities of combat, finally led to the enlistment, originally under discriminatory provisions, of Negroes within the Union Army.

Six examples of such offers, from various areas and dating from April, 1861 through August, 1862, are given below. The first five documents were found in the manuscript collection entitled "The Negro in the Military Service of the United States," in the War Records Office, National Archives, Washington. The sixth document [f] is taken from *The Cleveland Leader*, n.d., as republished in *The Liberator*, September 12, 1862.

### [a]

Washington, April 23d, 1861

Hon. Simon Cameron,
Secretary of War
Sir: I desire to inform you that I know of some three hundred of reliable colored free citizens of this City, who desire to enter the service for the defence of the City.

I have been three times across the Rocky Mountains in the service of the Country with Frémont and others.

I can be found about the Senate Chambers, as I have been employed about the premises for some years.

> Yours respectfully,
> Jacob Dodson,
> (Coloured)

## [b]

> Battle Creek [Michigan]
> Oct. 30th. 1861

Hon. Simon Cameron,
Secy of War

Dear Sir: Having learned that in your instructions to Gen. Sherman you authorized the enrollment of colored persons * I wish to solicit the privilege of raising from five to ten thousand free men to report in sixty days to take any position that may be assigned us (sharpshooters preferred). We would like white persons for superior officers.

If this proposition is not accepted we will, if armed and equipped by the government, fight as guerrillas.

Any information or instructions that may be forwarded to me immediately will be thankfully received and implicitly obeyed.

A part of us are half-breed Indians and legal voters in the State of Michigan. We are all anxious to fight for the maintenance of the Union and the preservation of the principles promulgated by President Lincoln and we are sure of success if allowed an opportunity. In the name of God answer immediately.

> Yours fraternally,
> G. P. Miller, M.D.

## [c]

> Cleveland, Ohio, 15th November, 1861

Hon. Simon Cameron
Secretary of War

Sir: The following particulars, hereafter mentioned, have been laid before the Hon. S. P. Chase, Secretary of the Treasury and his reply to us is that we apply to you direct, and therefore we would humbly and respectfully state that we are colored men (legal voters); all voted for the present administration.

The question now is will you allow us the poor privilege of fighting, and, if

* The writer misread the instructions.

need be, dying, to support those in office who are our own choice? We believe that a regiment of colored men can be raised in this State, who, we are sure, would make as patriotic and good soldiers as any other.

What we ask of you is that you give us the proper authority to raise such a regiment, and it can and shall be done.

We could give you a thousand names, as either signers or references, if required. We would, however, refer you to the Hon. General Crowell, Hon. R. G. Riddle, M.C., and Robert Paine, Esq., District Attorney.

W. T. Boyd<br>J. T. Alston

P.S. We wait your reply.

## [d]

London, Canada West<br>May 7th, 1862

Hon. Edwin Stanton
Secretary of War
Dear Sir: Please indulge me the liberty of writing you a few lines upon a subject of grave importance to your and my country.

It is true I am now stopping in Canada for a while, but it is not my home; and before I proceed further I must inform you of your humble correspondent: My name is G. H. White, formerly the servant of Robert Toombs, of Georgia. Mr. William H. Seward knows something about me. I am now a minister and am called upon by my people to tender to your Honor their willingness to serve as soldiers in the Southern parts during the Summer season, or longer if required. . . .

Your most obedient servant,<br>G. H. White

## [e]

Pittsburgh, Penna.<br>May 13, 1862

Secretary of War Stanton
Dear Sir: I see that it is your intention to garrison the Southern forts with colored soldiers,* and if such be the fact I hereby tender you the "Fort Pitt Cadets" of the city of Pittsburg for duty. The Fort Pitt Cadets have been organized for some two years and are quite proficient in military discipline. I can furnish you with satisfactory reference, &c. I will also pledge myself

* This was based on the enrollment of Negroes by the Abolitionist, General David Hunter, in South Carolina. The War Department repudiated the act.

to recruit two hundred men within thirty days after you shall have given authority or placed an officer in the City for recruiting. The men whom I shall recruit will be able-bodied and of unquestionable loyalty to the United States of America. You will please be kind enough to give this your attention.

> I am your obedient servant
> Rufus Sibb. Jones
> Captain Fort Pitt Cadets

### [f]

Cleveland, August 7, 1862

*To His Excellency David Tod, Governor of the State of Ohio:*

Honorable Sir: I hope you will pardon the often-made overtures to you from the colored citizens or men of Ohio, and more particularly those of Cleveland and this county, wishing to render their services to you, and for the benefit of the country, to suppress the great calamity which now threatens the peacefulness of this great Republic; and knowing that there has been a direct repudiation of our services rendered both on the part of the Government of Ohio and of the government of the United States, notwithstanding, knowing that you have at Camp Chase and Sandusky two or more regiments of well-drilled men, and knowing that their services could be used for better purposes than guarding rebel prisoners, therefore we heartily offer to you two or more regiments of colored men for that purpose, and we will assure you that no one of them shall escape; and we will discharge any duty imposed upon us as soldiers and appertaining to camp duty. And, in our judgment, we could not offer any more severe rebuke to the rebel master, and no more than has been practiced upon our Union men in New Orleans; and, therefore, we pray your consideration and reply.

Respectfully yours,

W. E. AMBUSH.

## 173

## SEEKING THE RIGHT TO FIGHT: PUBLIC EFFORTS, 1861–1862

The Negro people did not confine themselves to letters to public officials in their efforts to fully participate in the suppression of the Confederate assault. On the contrary, through correspondence in the press, mass meetings, petitions and public addresses they made the points that slavery was the main force behind that assault, that the sooner the Federal government conducted its military efforts in accordance with this truth the quicker would come victory, and that to help gain such a victory the strength of the Negro must be harnessed.

Five documents illustrative of this type of activity follow. The first [a] is an anonymous letter, dated Boston, April 19, 1861, which first appeared in that city's *Daily Atlas and Bee;* the second [b] is a petition presented May 15, 1861 to the Massachusetts legislature and signed by the Rev. J. Sella Martin and twenty-five other Negroes; the third [c] consists of resolutions adopted by a mass meeting of Negroes held in Boston on May 20, 1861; the fourth [d] is a speech by John S. Rock delivered on January 23, 1862 at the annual meeting of the Massachusetts Anti-Slavery Society; the fifth [e] is a speech by William Wells Brown, delivered May 6, 1862 at the annual meeting in New York of the American Anti-Slavery Society.

[a]

*To the Editors of the [Boston] Daily Atlas and Bee*

I am of that class not dominant in the land against whom a prejudice exists; and therefore I feel that there is more than the common necessity for being discreet, but withal, manly and honest. In the exercise of that discretion, I have told those colored persons with whom I have any influence, to avoid a too immediate active identity with the movements now directed against the slaveholders of the South,—that the blindness, the madness of slaveholders as to the best policy for them to have pursued to the end of enjoying all *possible* security under the circumstances for slavery, is illustrative of the expression: "Those whom the gods would destroy, they first make mad"; which madness would, in time, call us into the field.

Though the colored American has had but little inducement, so far as the policy of the national government is concerned, to be patriotic, he is, nevertheless, patriotic; he loves his native land; he feels for "the glory and the shame" of his country; his blood, as in revolutionary times—in the times of old Sam Adams, and of Crispus Attucks the black—boils, ready to flow in its defence; not as a black man, but as an American—he will fight for his country's defence, for her honor, and asks only for his rights as an equal fellow-countryman. This Massachusetts has given him—*he will stand by her*—she has but to make her demands.

Colored men calculate upon being yet in the midst of the fight *as soldiers.* We feel that our services will be needed: they will be forthcoming; but we must be discreet. They will be forthcoming when most needed. The colored man will fight,—not as a tool, but as an American patriot. He will fight most desperately, because he will be fighting against his enemy, slavery, and because he feels that among the leading claims he has to your feelings as fellow-countrymen, is, that in the page of facts connected with the battles for liberty which his country has fought, his valor—the valor of black men—

*challenges comparison;* and because he feels that those facts have weight in causing his countrymen to award to him all his rights as an American citizen.

The colored man will go where duty shall call him, though not because he is colored. He will stand by the side of his white brave fellow-countrymen. They will together, if needs be, make "a great sacrifice of life"; they will together occupy, if needs be, "the yellow fever posts in the enemy's country, during the summer months." Yes, all this for freedom, their common country, and the right. This he will do without price; but he would have his rights.

*The Boston Daily Atlas and Bee,* n.d., in *The Liberator,* May 10, 1861.

## [b]

### *Petition to Massachusetts Legislature*

We, the undersigned, colored citizens of Boston, respectfully pray your honorable body to remove the word "white" from that part of the statutes of the Commonwealth known as the militia law.

We make this prayer, first, because such a distinction is anomalous to the spirit of justice and equality pervading all the other laws of this Commonwealth; secondly, because we desire to be recognized by the laws as competent to and worthy of defending our homes and the government that protects these homes—

*The Liberator,* May 24, 1861. The petition was rejected.

## [c]

### *Resolutions of Negro Mass Meeting*

*Whereas,* the traitors of the South have assailed the United States Government, with the intention of overthrowing it for the purpose of perpetrating slavery; and,

*Whereas,* in such a contest between the North and South—believing, as we do, that it is a contest between liberty and despotism—it is as important for each class of citizens to declare, as it is for the rulers of the Government to know, their sentiments and position; therefore,

*Resolved,* That our feelings urge us to say to our countrymen that we are ready to stand by and defend the Government as the equals of its white defenders—to do so with "our lives, our fortunes, and our sacred honor," for the sake of freedom and as good citizens; and we ask you to modify your laws, that we may enlist—that full scope may be given to the patriotic feelings burning in the colored man's breast—and we pledge ourselves to raise an army in the country of fifty thousand colored men.

*Resolved,* That more than half of the army which we could raise, being natives of the South, knowing its geography, and being acquainted with the character of the enemy, would be of incalculable service to the Government.

*Resolved,* That the colored women would go as nurses, seamstresses, and warriors, if need be, to crush rebellion and uphold the Government.

*Resolved,* That the colored people, almost without an exception, "have their souls in arms, and all eager for the fray," and are ready to go at a moment's warning, if they are allowed to go as soldiers.

*Resolved,* That we do immediately organize ourselves into drilling companies, to the end of becoming better skilled in the use of fire-arms; so that when we shall be called upon by the country, we shall be better prepared to make a ready and fitting-response.

*The Liberator,* May 31, 1861.

## [d]

### *Speech by John S. Rock*

Ladies and Gentlemen,—I am here not so much to make a speech as to add a little more *color* to this occasion. (Laughter.)

I do not know that it is right that I should speak, at this time, for it is said that we have talked too much already; and it is being continually thundered in our ears that the time for speech-making has ended, and the time for action has arrived. Perhaps this is so. This may be the theory of the people, but we all know that the active idea has found but little sympathy with either of our great military commanders, or the National Executive; for they have told us, again and again, that "patience is a cure for all sores," and that we must wait for the "good time" which, to us, has been long a-coming. (Applause.)

It is not my desire, neither is it the time for me to criticise the Government, even if I had the disposition so to do. The situation of the black man in this country is far from being an enviable one. To-day, our heads are in the lion's mouth, and we must get them out the best way we can. To contend against the Government is as difficult as it is to sit in Rome, and fight with the Pope. (Laughter.) It is probable, that, if we had the malice of the Anglo-Saxon, we would watch our chances and seize the first opportunity to take our revenge. If we attempted this, the odds would be against us, and the first thing we should know would be—nothing! (Laughter.) The most of us are capable of perceiving that the man who spits against the wind, spits in his own face! (Laughter.)

While Mr. Lincoln has been more conservative than I had hoped to find him, I recognize in him an honest man, striving to redeem the country from the degradation and shame into which Mr. Buchanan and his predecessors have plunged it. (Applause.)

This nation is mad. In its devoted attachment to the Negro, it has run crazy after him, (laughter,) and now, having caught him, hangs on with a deadly grasp, and says to him, with more earnestness and pathos than Ruth expressed to Naomi, "Where thou goest, I will go; where thou lodgest, I will lodge; thy people shall be my people, and thy God my God." (Laughter and Applause.) . . .

The educated and wealthy class despise the Negro, because they have robbed him of his hard earnings, or, at least, have got rich off the fruits of his labor; and they believe if he gets his freedom, their fountain will be dried up, and they will be obliged to seek business in a new channel. Their "occupation will be gone." The lowest class hate him because he is poor, as they are, and he is a competitor with them for the same labor. The poor ignorant white man, who does not understand that the interest of the laboring classes is mutual, argues in this wise: "Here is so much labor to be performed,—that Negro does it. If he was gone, I should have his place." The rich and the poor are both prejudiced from interest, and not because they entertain vague notions of justice and humanity. While uttering my solemn protest against this American vice, which has done more than any other things to degrade the American people in the eyes of the civilized world, I am happy to state that there are many who have never known this sin, and many others who have been converted to the truth by the "foolishness of anti-slavery preaching," and are deeply interested in the welfare of the race, and never hesitate to use their means and their influence to help break off the yoke that has been so long crushing us. I thank them all, and hope the number may be multiplied, until we shall have a people who will know no man save by his virtues and his merits. (Loud applause.)

Now, it seems to me that a blind man can see that the present war is an effort to nationalize, perpetuate and extend slavery in this country. In short, slavery is the cause of the war: I might say, is *the* war itself. Had it not been for slavery, we should have had no war! Through two hundred and forty years of indescribable tortures, slavery has wrung out of the blood, bones and muscles of the Negro hundreds of millions of dollars, and helped much to make this nation rich. At the same time, it has developed a volcano which has burst forth, and, in a less number of days than years, has dissipated this wealth and rendered the Government bankrupt! And, strange as it may appear, you still cling to this monstrous iniquity, notwithstanding it is daily sinking the country lower and lower! (Hear, hear.) Some of our ablest and best men have been sacrificed to appease the wrath of this American god. (Hear, hear.) . . .

The Government wishes to bring back the country to what it was before. This is possible; but what is to be gained by it? If we are fools enough to retain the cancer that is eating out our vitals, when we can safely extirpate it, who will pity us if we see our mistake when we are past recovery? (Hear, hear.) The Abolitionists saw this day of tribulation and reign of terror long ago, and warned you of it; *but you would not hear!* You now say that it is their agitation, which has brought about this terrible civil war! That is to say, your friend sees a slow match set near a keg of gunpowder in your house and timely warns you of the danger which he sees is inevitable; you despise his warning, and, after the explosion, say, if he had not told you of it, it would not have happened! (Loud applause.)

Now, when some leading men who hold with the policy of the President, and yet pretend to be liberal, argue, that while they are willing to admit that the slave has an undoubted right to his liberty, the master has an equal right to his property; that to liberate the slave would be to injure the master, and a greater good would be accomplished to the country in these times, by the loyal master's retaining his property, than by giving to the slave his liberty,—I do not understand it so. Slavery is treason against God, man and the nation. The master has no right to be a partner in a conspiracy which has shaken the very foundation of the Government. Even to apologize for it, while in open rebellion, is to aid and abet in treason. The master's right to his property in human flesh cannot be equal to the slave's right to his liberty.

To-day, when it is a military necessity, and when the safety of the country is dependent upon emancipation, our humane political philosophers are puzzled to know what would become of the slaves if they were emancipated! The idea seems to prevail that the poor things would suffer, if robbed of the glorious privileges they now enjoy! If they could not be flogged, half-starved, and work to support in ease and luxury those who have never waived an opportunity to outrage and wrong them, they would pine away and die! Do you imagine that the Negro can live outside of slavery? Of course, now, they can take care of themselves and their masters too; but if you give them their liberty, must they not suffer? (Laughter and applause.) Have you never been able to see through all this? Have you not observed that the location of this organ of sympathy is in the pocket of the slaveholder and the man who shares in the profits of slave labor? Of course you have; and pity those men who have lived upon their ill-gotten wealth. You know, if they do not have somebody to work for them, they must leave their gilded *salons,* and take off their coats and roll up their sleeves, and take their chances among the *live* men of the world. This, you are aware, these respectable gentlemen will not do, for they have been so long accustomed to live by robbing and cheating the Negro, that they are sworn never to work while they can·live by plunder. (Applause.)

Can the slaves take care of themselves? What do you suppose becomes of the thousands who fly ragged and pennyless from the South every year, and scatter themselves throughout the free States of the North? Do they take care of themselves? I am neither ashamed nor afraid to meet this question. Assertions like this, long uncontradicted, seem to be admitted as established facts. I ask your attention for one moment to the fact that colored men at the North are shut out of almost every avenue to wealth, and yet, strange to say, the proportion of paupers is much less among us than among you! (Hear, hear.) Are the beggars in the streets of Boston colored men? (Cries of "No, no!") In Philadelphia, where there is a larger free colored population than is to be found in any other city in the free States, and where we are denied every social privilege, and are not even permitted to send our children to the schools that we are taxed to support, or to ride in the city horse cars, yet even there we pay taxes enough to support our own poor, and have a balance of a few thousand in our favor, which goes to support those "poor whites" who "can't take care of themselves." (Laughter and loud applause.)

Many of those who advocate emancipation as a military necessity seem puzzled to know what is best to be done with the slave, if he is set at liberty. Colonization in Africa, Hayti, Florida and South America are favorite theories with many well-informed persons. This is really interesting! No wonder Europe does not sympathize with you. You are the only people, claiming to be civilized, who take away the rights of those whose color differs from your own. If you find that you cannot rob the Negro of his labor and of himself, you will banish him! What a sublime idea! You are certainly a great people! What is your plea? Why, that the slaveholders will not permit us to live among them as freemen, and that the air of Northern latitudes is not good for us! Let me tell you, my friends, *the slaveholders are not the men we dread!* (Hear, hear.) They do not desire to have us removed. The Northern pro-slavery men have done the free people of color ten-fold more injury than the Southern slave-holders. (Hear, hear.) In the South, it is simply a question of dollars and cents. The slaveholder cares no more for you than he does for me. They enslave their own children, and sell them, and they would as soon enslave white men as black men. The secret of the slaveholder's attachment to slavery is to be found in the dollar, and *that* he is determined to get without working for it. There is no prejudice against color among the slaveholders. Their social system and one million of mulattoes are facts which no arguments can demolish. (Applause.) If the slaves were emancipated, they would remain where they are. Black labor in the South is at a premium. The free man of color there has always had the preference over the white laborer. Many of you are aware that Southerners will do a favor for a free colored man, when they will not do it for a white man in the same condition in life. They believe in their institution because it supports them. . . .

When the orange is squeezed, we throw it aside. (Laughter.) The black man is a good fellow while he is a slave, and toils for nothing, but the moment he claims his own flesh and blood and bones, he is a most obnoxious creature, and there is a proposition to get rid of him! He is happy while he remains a poor, degraded, ignorant slave, without even the right to his own offspring. While in this condition, the master can ride in the same carriage, sleep in the same bed, and nurse from the same bosom. But give this same slave the right to use his own legs, his hands, his body and his mind, and this happy and desirable creature is instantly transformed into a miserable and loathsome wretch, fit only to be colonized somewhere near the mountains of the moon, or eternally banished from the presence of all civilized beings. You must not lose sight of the fact that it is the emancipated slave and the free colored man whom it is proposed to remove—not the slave: this country and climate are perfectly adapted to Negro slavery; it is the free black that the air is not good for! What an idea! A country good for slavery, and not good for freedom! . . .

I do not regard this trying hour as a darkness. The war that has been waged on us for more than two centuries has opened our eyes and caused us to form alliances, so that instead of acting on the defensive, we are now prepared to attack the enemy. This is simply a change of tactics. I think I see the finger of God in all this. Yes, *there* is the hand-writing on the wall: *I come not to bring peace, but the sword. Break every yoke, and let the oppressed go free. I have heard the groans of my people, and am come down to deliver them!* (Loud and long-continued applause.) . . .

This rebellion for slavery means something! Out of it emancipation must spring. I do not agree with those men who see no hope in this war. (Hear, hear.) There is nothing in it but hope. (Applause.) Our cause is onward. As it is with the sun, the clouds often obstruct his vision, but in the end we find there has been no standing still. (Applause.) It is true the Government is but little more anti-slavery now than it was at the commencement of the war; but while fighting for its own existence, it has been obliged to take slavery by the throat, and sooner or later *must* choke her to death. (Loud applause.) . . .

*The Liberator*, Feb. 14, 1862; indications of the audience's reactions are from this source.

[e]

*Speech by William Wells Brown*

. . . All I demand for the black man is, that the white people shall take their heels off his neck, and let him have a chance to rise by his own efforts. (Applause.) One of the first things that I heard when I arrived in the free States—and it was the strangest thing to me that I heard—was, that the slaves cannot take care of themselves. I came off without any education. Society did not take me up; I took myself up. (Laughter.) I did not ask society to take me up. All I asked of the white people was, to get out of the way, and give me a chance to come from the South to the North. That was all I asked, and I went to work with my own hands. And that is all I demand for my brethren of the South to-day—that they shall have an opportunity to exercise their own physical and mental abilities. Give them that, and I will leave the slaves to take care of themselves, and be satisfied with the result.

Now, Mr. President, I think that the present contest has shown clearly that the fidelity of the black people of this country to the cause of freedom is enough to put to shame every white man in the land who would think of driving us out of the country, provided freedom shall be proclaimed. I remember well, when Mr. Lincoln's proclamation went forth, calling for the first 75,000 men, that among the first to respond to that call were the colored men. A meeting was held in Boston, crowded as I never saw a meeting before; meetings were held in Rhode Island and Connecticut, in New York and Philadelphia, and throughout the West, responding to the President's call. Although the colored men in many of the free States were disfranchised, abused, taxed without representation, their children turned out of the schools, nevertheless, they went on, determined to try to discharge their duty to the country, and to save it from the tyrannical power of the slaveholders of the South. But the cry went forth—"We won't have the Negroes; we won't have anything to do with them; we won't fight with them; we won't have them in the army, nor about us." Yet scarcely had you got into conflict with the South, when you were glad to receive the news that contrabands brought. (Applause.) The first telegram announcing any news from the disaffected district commences with—"A contraband just in from Maryland tells us" so much. The last telegram, in to-day's paper, announces that a contraband tells us so much about Jefferson Davis and Mrs. Davis and the little Davises. (Laughter.) The nation is glad to receive the news from the contraband. We have an old law with regard to the mails, that a Negro shall not touch the mails at all; and for fifty years the black

man has not had the privilege of touching the mails of the United States
with his little finger; but we are glad enough now to have the Negro bring
the mail in his pocket! The first thing asked of a contraband is—"Have you
got a newspaper?—what's the news?" And the news is greedily taken in,
from the lowest officer or soldier in the army, up to the Secretary of War.
They have tried to keep the Negro out of the war, but they could not keep
him out, and now they drag him in, with his news, and are glad to do so.
General Wool says the contrabands have brought the most reliable news.
Other Generals say their information can be relied upon. The Negro is taken
as a pilot to guide the fleet of General Burnside through the inlets of the
South. (Applause.) The black man welcomes your armies and your fleets,
takes care of your sick, is ready to do anything, from cooking up to
shouldering a musket; and yet these would-be patriots and professed lovers
of the land talk about driving the Negro out!

*The Liberator*, May 16, 1862; audience's reactions as in this source.

## 174

# THE NEGRO ON LINCOLN'S COLONIZATION
# PLANS, 1862

Abraham Lincoln proposed various Negro colonization schemes—always, however,
opposing compulsory deportation—during the Civil War. The law emancipating
the slaves of the District of Columbia, enacted April, 1862, provided $100,000 for
such colonization.

On August 14, 1862, Lincoln invited a Negro delegation to hear his views on
this subject. After these were expressed, the Negro people responded on the whole
in their traditional manner of opposition towards all suggestions of colonization.
Typical of this are the two documents presented below. The first consists of the
resolutions adopted at a mass meeting of Negroes held on August 20, 1862, in
Newtown, Long Island; the second consists of a published *Appeal* very numerously
signed by Philadelphia Negroes and dispatched to Lincoln in the same month.

## [a]

### *The Newtown Meeting*

We, the colored citizens of Queen's County, N.Y., having met in mass meet-
ing, according to public notice, to consider the speech of Abraham Lincoln,
President of the United States, addressed to a committee of Free Colored
Men, called at his request at the White House in Washington, on Thursday,
August 14, 1862, and to express our views and opinions of the same; and
whereas, the President desires to know in particular our views on the subject

of being colonized in Central America or some other foreign country, we will take the present opportunity to express our opinions most respectfully and freely, since as loyal Union colored Americans and Christians we feel bound to do so.

*First*. We rejoice that we are colored Americans, but deny that we are a "different race of people," * as God has made of one blood all nations that dwell on the face of the earth, and has hence no respect of men in regard to color, neither ought men to have respect to color, as they have not made themselves or their color.

*Second*. The President calls our attention particularly to this question—"Why should we leave this country?" This, he says, is perhaps the first question for proper consideration. We will answer this question by showing why we should remain in it. This is our country by birth, consequently we are acclimated, and in other respects better adapted to it than any other country. This is our native country; we have as strong attachment naturally to our native hills, valleys, plains, luxuriant forests, flowing streams, mighty rivers, and lofty mountains, as any other people. Nor can we fail to feel a strong attachment to the whites with whom our blood has been commingling from the earliest days of this country. Neither can we forget and disown our white kindred. This is the country of our choice, being our fathers' country.

*Third*. Again, we are interested in its welfare above every other country; we love this land, and have contributed our share to its prosperity and wealth. This we have done by cutting down forests, subduing the soil, cultivating fields, constructing roads, digging canals . . .

*Fourth*. Again, we believe, too, we have the right to have applied to ourselves those rights named in the Declaration of Independence . . . While bleeding and struggling for her life against slaveholding traitors, and at this very time, when our country is struggling for life, and one million freemen are believed to be scarcely sufficient to meet the foe, we are called upon by the President of the United States to leave this land . . . But at this crisis, we feel disposed to refuse the offers of the President since the call of our suffering country is too loud and imperative to be unheeded . . . Our answer is this: There is no country like our own. Why not declare slavery abolished, and favor our peaceful colonization in the rebel States, or some portion of them?

We would cheerfully return there, and give our most willing aid to deliver our loyal colored brethren and other Unionists from the tyranny of rebels to our Government.

* The quoted words are Lincoln's. The entire speech may be conveniently consulted in Carl Sandburg, *Lincoln The War Years* (N.Y., 1939), I, pp. 574–76.

In conclusion, we would say that, in our belief, the speech of the President has only served the cause of our enemies, who wish to insult and mob us, as we have, since its publication, been repeatedly insulted, and told that we must leave the country.

Hence we conclude that the policy of the President toward the colored people of this country *is a mistaken policy.*

*The Liberator,* September 12, 1862.

### [b]

### *The Philadelphia Appeal*

In the purity and goodness of your heart, and as we believe, through a willingness to serve the cause of humanity, you have been pleased to hold an audience with a Committee of colored men,* brethren of ours—kindred in race.

The object was to acquaint them with the fact that a sum of money had been appropriated by Congress for the purpose of Colonization, a cause which you were inclined to favor, and dear to the hearts of many good men.

Among the prominent reasons given for colonizing us, is the one most common throughout our enslaved country, that of color. Admitting this distinction to be of great disadvantage to us, the cause of many tears and much anguish, as we pass along this rugged life of ours; yet, we believe that most of this prejudice grows out of the Institution of Slavery.

Benighted by the ignorance entailed upon us, oppressed by the iron-heel of the master who knows no law except that of worldly gain and self-aggrandizement, why should we not be poor and degraded?

If, under the existing prejudices, adverse laws, and low degree of general education, a few become respectable and useful citizens, there is truly hope for the many. We pray for a more liberal and enlightened public policy. We regret the ignorance and poverty of our race. We find, however, in this great city a parallel in the white, and however degraded a part of us may be, there is, under the circumstances surrounding each, a deeper degradation still. Our fathers were not, of their own free will and accord, transferred to this, our native land. Neither have we, their descendants, by any act of ours, brought this country to its present deplorable condition. If there is in the heart of any, claiming by virtue of their color and predominance, a desire to persecute and oppress, no such unhallowed motives govern us.

We can find nothing in the religion of our Lord and Master, teaching us that color is the standard by which He judges his creatures, either in this

---

* The holding of such an audience by a President was, up to that time, unprecedented.

life nor the life which is to come. He created us and endowed us with the faculties of man, giving us a part of the earth as an habitation, and its products for our sustenance. He also made it sufficient in compass and fruitfulness to provide for the wants of all, and has nowhere taught us to devour each other, that even life itself might be sustained.

Thus, humbly, have we presented our cause in some of its moral aspects.

Permit us, in further response to your generous efforts in our behalf, to present another, and possibly, a more selfish view, embracing pecuniary and political matters, not more important to ourselves than to others.

We know that the problem of American Slavery has been a difficult one to solve; that statesmen hesitate, politicians ignore, and the people even now evade the serious reality of a most bloody war, caused solely by the dealers in our flesh. We have not sought such a solution, nor asked a sacrifice so great, without being willing to drink of the same bitter cup.

The blood of millions of our race cries from the ground, while millions more are yet enslaved.

They have produced much of the wealth of this country. Cotton, the product of their labor, while it should have proven a blessing to mankind, has well nigh overthrown the Nations dependent upon it, and is now denominated "King."

Thus has the master of the slave enslaved the world. While colonization, in many of its features might be advantageous to our race, yet were all of us to be sent out of the country, the population of the United States would be reduced nearly one-sixth part. It is doubtful whether the people seriously desire a depletion of this kind, however much they may wish to separate from us.

If statistics prove anything, then we constitute, including our property qualifications, almost the entire wealth of the Cotton States, and make up a large proportion of that of the others. Many of us, in Pennsylvania, have our own houses and other property, amounting, in the aggregate, to millions of dollars. Shall we sacrifice this, leave our homes, forsake our birth-place, and flee to a strange land, to appease the anger and prejudice of the traitors now in arms against the Government, or their aiders and abettors in this or in foreign lands? Will the country be benefitted by sending us out of it, and inviting strangers to fill our places?

Will they make better citizens, prove as loyal, love the country better, and be as obedient to its laws as we have been? If God has so ordained it, we shall yet be free. In His providence, He may gather us together in States, by ourselves, and govern us in accordance with His laws. Will the white man leave us alone, when so gathered?

We believe that the world would be benefitted by giving the four millions of slaves their freedom, and the lands now possessed by their masters. They have been amply compensated in our labor and the blood of our kinsmen. These masters "toil not, neither do they spin." They destroy, they consume, and give to the world in return but a small equivalent. They deprive us of "life, liberty, and the pursuit of happiness."

They degrade us to the level of the brute. They amalgamate with our race, and buy and sell their own children. They deny us the right to gain knowledge or hold property; neither do they allow us to have the avails of our own industry.

They requite our labor by stripes, manacles and torture. They have entailed upon the poor whites of the South a despotism almost equaling that inflicted upon us. By unjust and arbitrary laws they have driven honest white men from their midst, or imprisoned them in their dungeons.

By falsehood and political cunning they have corrupted the politics of the people in all the States. Finally, they have rebelled against their Government.

Having set all laws, both human and divine, at naught, what does a just Government owe them in return? Would it be too great a penalty to deprive them of the labor of their slaves, and compel them to earn their own subsistence by honest means; to permit us to be free, to enjoy our natural rights, to have the avails of our own industry; to live with and have our own wives and children; to have the benefit of the school, the church, and salutary laws, that we may become better men and more valuable citizens; to give the slave an opportunity to increase the wealth of the people, while he consumes the more of the world's products? All of this is not too much to ask. We would reciprocate by increasing commerce, and proving to the world that we were worthy of being freemen.

Beyond this, our humble appeal, we are almost powerless in our own great cause.

God, in his providence, has enlisted in our behalf some of the most noble men of the age. May their efforts be crowned with success. In the President of the United States we feel and believe that we have a champion, most able and willing to aid us in all that is right. We ask, that by the standard of justice and humanity we may be weighed, and that men shall not longer be measured by their stature or their color.

That the Ruler over all, in his infinite mercy and goodness, will keep and protect you, and cause your administration to triumph, in justice, over all its enemies, is the prayer of the Colored men of Philadelphia.

*An Appeal from the Colored Men of Philadelphia to the President of the United States* (Phila., 1862). Copy in Boston Athenaeum.

175

## WAITING FOR THE EMANCIPATION PROCLAMATION, DECEMBER 31, 1862

The integral relationship between the existence of the United States as a nation and the freedom of the Negro people was formally recognized with the issuance of the Emancipation Proclamation on midnight of the last day of 1862. The document, confiscating by executive action millions of dollars worth of legally recognized property, was necessarily a war measure applicable only to areas dominated by the Confederates, but its promulgation symbolized the fact that the war to save the union had become a war to free the slaves since in this freedom lay that salvation.

Scores of meetings of Negro people and their friends were held on this evening throughout the land. One such, held in Boston, is described by Frederick Douglass:

An immense assembly convened in Tremont Temple to await the first flash of the electric wires announcing the "new departure." Two years of war, prosecuted in the interests of slavery, had made free speech possible in Boston, and we were now met together to receive and celebrate the first utterance of the long-hoped-for proclamation, *if* it came, and if it did *not* come, to speak our minds freely; for, in view of the past, it was by no means certain that it would come.

The occasion, therefore, was one of both hope and fear. Our ship was on the open sea, tossed by a terrible storm; wave after wave was passing over us, and every hour was fraught with increasing peril . . .

Every moment of waiting chilled our hopes, and strengthened our fears. A line of messengers was established between the telegraph office and the platform of Tremont Temple, and the time was occupied with brief speeches from Hon. Thomas Russell of Plymouth, Miss Anne E. Dickinson (a lady of marvelous eloquence), Rev. Mr. [Leonard] Grimes, J. Sella Martin, William Wells Brown, and myself.

But speaking or listening to speeches was not the thing for which the people had come together. The time for argument was passed. It was not logic, but the trump of jubilee, which everybody wanted to hear. We were waiting and listening as for a bolt from the sky, which would rend the fetters of four millions of slaves; we were watching, as it were, by the dim light of the stars, for the dawn of a new day; we were longing for the answer to the agonizing prayers of centuries. Remembering those in bonds as bound with them, we wanted to join in the shout for freedom, and in the anthem of the redeemed.

Eight, nine, ten o'clock came and went, and still no word. A visible shadow seemed falling on the expecting throng, which the confident utterances of the speakers sought in vain to dispel. At last, when patience was well-nigh exhausted, and suspense was becoming agony, a man (I think it was Judge Russell) with hasty step advanced through the crowd, and with a face fairly illumined with the news he bore, exclaimed in tones that thrilled all hearts, "It is coming!" "It is on the wires!"

The effect of this announcement was startling beyond description, and the scene was wild and grand. Joy and gladness exhausted all forms of expression, from shouts of praise to sobs and tears. My old friend Rue, a Negro preacher, a man of wonderful vocal power, expressed the heartfelt emotion of the hour, when he led all voices in the anthem, "Sound the loud timbrel o'er Egypt's dark sea, Jehovah hath triumphed, his people are free."

About twelve o'clock, seeing there was no disposition to retire from the hall, which must be vacated, my friend Grimes (of blessed memory), rose and moved that the meeting adjourn to the Twelfth Baptist church, of which he was pastor, and soon the church was packed from doors to pulpit, and this meeting did not break up till near the dawn of day. It was one of the most affecting and thrilling occasions I ever witnessed, and a worthy celebration of the first step on the part of the nation in its departure from the thraldom of ages.

*Life and Times of Frederick Douglass, written by himself* (N.Y., 1941, Pathway Press), pp. 387–89.


# 176

# "MEN OF COLOR, TO ARMS!"

With the Federal government committed to a policy of emancipation and permitting Negroes to enlist in the Army, Negro leaders played a decisive role in gaining such enlistments. Indicative of this is the editorial by Frederick Douglass in his Rochester newspaper on March 2, 1863, entitled "Men of Color, To Arms!" and a letter from Martin R. Delany to Secretary of War Stanton, dated Chicago, December 15, 1863. Delany was later commissioned a Major in the Quartermaster Corps of the Union Army.

## [a]

### *Frederick Douglass*

When first the rebel cannon shattered the walls of Sumter and drove away its starving garrison, I predicted that the war then and there inaugurated would not be fought out entirely by white men. Every month's experience during these weary years has confirmed that opinion. A war undertaken and brazenly carried on for the perpetual enslavement of colored men, calls logically and loudly for colored men to help suppress it. Only a moderate share of sagacity was needed to see that the arm of the slave was the best defense against the arm of the slaveholder. Hence with every reverse to the national arms, with every exulting shout of victory raised by the slaveholding rebels, I have implored the imperiled nation to unchain against her foes, her powerful black hand.

Slowly and reluctantly that appeal is beginning to be heeded. Stop not now to complain that it was not heeded sooner. That it should not, may or it may not have been best. This is not the time to discuss that question. Leave it to the future. When the war is over, the country is saved, peace is established, and the black man's rights are secured, as they will be, history with an impartial hand will dispose of that and sundry other questions. Action! Action! not criticism, is the plain duty of this hour. Words are now useful only as they stimulate to blows. The office of speech now is only to point out when, where, and how to strike to the best advantage.

There is no time to delay. The tide is at its flood that leads on to fortune. From East to West, from North to South, the sky is written all over, "Now or Never." "Liberty won by white men would lose half its luster." "Who would be free themselves must strike the blow." "Better even die free, than to live slaves." This is the sentiment of every brave colored man amongst us.

There are weak and cowardly men in all nations. We have them amongst us. They tell you this is the "white man's war"; that you will be no "better off after than before the war"; that the getting of you into the army is to "sacrifice you on the first opportunity." Believe them not; cowards themselves, they do not wish to have their cowardice shamed by your brave example. Leave them to their timidity, or to whatever motive may hold them back.

I have not thought lightly of the words I am now addressing you. The counsel I give comes of close observation of the great struggle now in progress, and of the deep conviction that this is your hour and mine. In good earnest then, and after the best deliberation, I now for the first time during this war feel at liberty to call and counsel you to arms.

By every consideration which binds you to your enslaved fellow-countrymen, and the peace and welfare of your country; by every aspiration which you cherish for the freedom and equality of yourselves and your children; by all the ties of blood and identity which make us one with the brave black men now fighting our battles in Louisiana and in South Carolina, I urge you to fly to arms, and smite with death the power that would bury the government and your liberty in the same hopeless grave.

I wish I could tell you that the State of New York calls you to this high honor. For the moment her constituted authorities are silent on the subject. They will speak by and by, and doubtless on the right side; but we are not compelled to wait for her. We can get at the throat of treason and slavery through the State of Massachusetts. She was first in the War of Independence; first to break the chains of her slaves; first to make the black man equal before the law; first to admit colored children to her common schools, and she was first to answer with her blood the alarm cry of the nation, when its capital was menaced by rebels. You know her patriotic governor, and you know Charles Sumner. I need not add more.

Massachusetts now welcomes you to arms as soldiers. She has but a small colored population from which to recruit. She has full leave of the general government to send one regiment to the war, and she has undertaken to do it. Go quickly and help fill up the first colored regiment from the North. I am authorized to assure you that you will receive the same wages, the same rations, the same equipments, the same protection, the same treatment, and the same bounty, secured to the white soldiers. You will be led by able and skillful officers, men who will take especial pride in your efficiency and success. They will be quick to accord to you all the honor you shall merit by your valor, and see that your rights and feelings are respected by other soldiers. I have assured myself on these points, and can speak with authority.

More than twenty years of unswerving devotion to our common cause may give me some humble claim to be trusted at this momentous crisis. I will not argue. To do so implies hesitation and doubt, and you do not hesitate. You do not doubt. The day dawns; the morning star is bright upon the horizon! The iron gate of our prison stands half open. One gallant rush from the North will fling it wide open, while four millions of our brothers and sisters shall march out into liberty. The chance is now given you to end in a day the bondage of centuries, and to rise in one bound from social degradation to the plane of common equality with all other varieties of men.

Remember Denmark Vesey of Charleston; remember Nathaniel Turner of Southampton; remember Shields Green and Copeland, who followed noble John Brown, and fell as glorious martyrs for the cause of the slave. Remember that in a contest with oppression, the Almighty has no attribute which can take sides with oppressors.

The case is before you. This is our golden opportunity. Let us accept it, and forever wipe out the dark reproaches unsparingly hurled against us by our enemies. Let us win for ourselves the gratitude of our country, and the best blessings of our posterity through all time. The nucleus of this first regiment is now in camp at Readville, a short distance from Boston. I will undertake to forward to Boston all persons adjudged fit to be mustered into the regiment, who shall apply to me at any time within the next two weeks.

*Life and Times of Frederick Douglass* (N.Y., 1941), pp. 373–76.

## [b]

### Martin R. Delany

The subject and policy of black troops have become of much interest in our country, and the effective means and method of raising them, is a matter of much importance. In consideration of this, sir, I embrace the earliest opportunity of asking the privilege of calling the attention of your department to the fact, that as a policy in perfect harmony with the course of the President, and your own enlightened views, that the agency of intelligent, competent, black men adapted to the work must be the most effective means of obtaining black troops; because knowing and being of that people as a race, they can command such influences as is required to accomplish the object. I have been successfully engaged as a recruiting agent of black troops, first as a recruiting agent for Massachusetts, 54th Regiment, and from the commencement as the managing agent in the West and Southwest, for Rhode Island Heavy Artillery, which is now nearly full; and now have the contract from the State authorities of Connecticut, for the entire West and South-West, in raising colored troops to fill her quota. During these engagements, I have had associated with me, Mr. John Jones, a very respectable and responsible business colored man of this city, and we have associated ourselves permanently together in an agency for raising black troops for all parts of the country. We are able sir, to command all the effective black men, as agents, in the United States, and in the event of an order from your department, giving us the authority to recruit colored troops in any of the southern or seceded States, we will be ready and able to raise a regiment, or brigade, if required, in a shorter time than can be otherwise effected. With the belief sir, that this is one of the measures in which the claims of the black man may be officially recognized, without seemingly infringing upon those of other citizens, I confidently ask sir, that this humble request may engage your early notice. All satisfactory references will be given by both of us.

MS. in War Records Office, National Archives, Washington, D.C.

## 177

# NEGRO FIGHTERS FOR FREEDOM AND UNITY, 1863–1865

During the Civil War about 200,000 Negroes enlisted in the Union Army and 30,000 in the Navy. Another quarter of a million Negro men and women labored for that Army and Navy as teamsters, nurses, cooks, pilots, fortification-builders and pioneers, while many more served as guides, spies and scouts. Through this direct participation the Negro people contributed, directly and decisively, towards the maintenance of the American Republic and their own liberation from chattel slavery.

The eight documents that follow are presented in an attempt to provide a succinct view of this activity which involved not only meeting the enemy in physical combat, but also struggle against discrimination.

The first document [a] is a letter from Frederick Douglass' son, Lewis, to his betrothed, dated Morris Island, S.C., July 20, 1863, written just after the young man had participated with his regiment, the 54th Massachusetts Infantry Regiment (Volunteers), in its heroic, but unsuccessful, storming of Fort Wagner.

The second document [b] is also a letter from a member of the 54th Massachusetts. It was written by 26-year-old Corporal James Henry Gooding, originally a mariner from New Bedford, Mass., to President Lincoln and is dated Morris Island, S.C., September 28, 1863.

The third document [c] is a letter also written at Morris Island, on October 13, 1863, to Col. M. S. Littlefield, then commanding the 54th Massachusetts. Its author was Sgt. William H. Carney, of that regiment, one of nine Negroes to be awarded the Congressional Medal of Honor during the Civil War.

The fourth document [d], signed "S.J.R." was dated Folly Island, S.C., January 18, 1864, and was addressed to William Lloyd Garrison. Its author was a member of the 55th Massachusetts Infantry Regiment (Volunteers). This letter concerns itself largely with the demand for Negro officers, as does the fifth document [e], addressed to William C. Nell by an anonymous sergeant of the 54th Massachusetts, and dated Morris Island, S.C., August 26, 1864.

The sixth and seventh documents [f, g], dated Nashville, January 3, 1865, and Chattanooga, February 3, 1865, respectively, were written to Major J. H. Cochrane, commanding the 44th U.S. Colored Infantry, by two enlisted men of the regiment, Pvt. Joseph Howard and Sgt. John S. Leach. Both men were escaped war prisoners and their letters describe their experiences while held by the Confederates.

The last document [h] is a contemporaneous account of the battle experiences of the 29th Connecticut Colored Infantry from February through April, 1865. The author was J. J. Hill, orderly for Col. W. B. Wooster, commanding the regiment. In the latter month Richmond was taken and the first troops to enter the Confederacy's capital were the Negroes of the 29th Connecticut.

## [a]

### Lewis Douglass

My Dear Amelia:

I have been in two fights, and am unhurt. I am about to go in another I believe to-night. Our men fought well on both occasions * . . . I escaped unhurt from amidst that perfect hail of shot and shell. It was terrible. I need not particularize, the papers will give a better [account] than I have time to give. My thoughts are with you often, you are as dear as ever, be good to remember it as I no doubt you will. As I said before we are on the eve of another fight and I am very busy and have just snatched a moment to write you. I must necessarily be brief. Should I fall in the next fight killed or wounded I hope I fall with my face to the foe . . .

This regiment has established its reputation as a fighting regiment, not a man flinched, though it was a trying time. Men fell all around me. A shell would explode and clear a space of twenty feet, our men would close up again, but it was no use we had to retreat, which was a very hazardous undertaking. How I got out of that fight alive I cannot tell, but I am here. My Dear girl I hope again to see you. I must bid you farewell should I be killed. Remember if I die I die in a good cause. I wish we had a hundred thousand colored troops we would put an end to this war.

Good Bye to all. Your own loving—Write soon—

LEWIS

C. G. Woodson, ed., *The Mind of the Negro* . . . , p. 544.

## [b]

### James Henry Gooding

Your Excellency, Abraham Lincoln:

Your Excellency will pardon the presumption of an humble individual like myself, in addressing you, but the earnest solicitation of my comrades in arms besides the genuine interest felt by myself in the matter is my excuse, for placing before the Executive head of the Nation our Common Grievance.

On the 6th of the last Month, the Paymaster of the Department informed us, that if we would decide to receive the sum of $10 (ten dollars) per month, he would come and pay us that sum, but that, on the sitting of Congress, the

---

* The two occasions were the battle of James Island, S.C. on July 16, and that of Fort Wagner on July 18, 1863. In the latter assault the 54th Mass. sustained 250 casualties out of a total of 600 men. When Fort Wagner finally surrendered, in September, 1863, the Negro regiment was the first to enter its works.

Regt. would, in his opinion, be allowed the other 3 (three).* He did not give us any guarantee that this would be, as he hoped; certainly he had no authority for making any such guarantee, and we cannot suppose him acting in any way interested.

Now the main question is, are we Soldiers, or are we Laborers? We are fully armed, and equipped, have done all the various duties pertaining to a Soldier's life, have conducted ourselves to the complete satisfaction of General Officers, who were, if anything, prejudiced against us, but who now accord us all the encouragement and honors due us; have shared the perils and labor of reducing the first strong-hold that flaunted a Traitor Flag; and more, Mr. President, to-day the Anglo-Saxon Mother, Wife, or Sister are not alone in tears for departed Sons, Husbands and Brothers. The patient, trusting descendant of Afric's Clime have dyed the ground with blood, in defence of the Union, and Democracy. Men, too, your Excellency, who know in a measure the cruelties of the iron heel of oppression, which in years gone by, the very power their blood is now being spilled to maintain, ever ground them in the dust.

But when the war trumpet sounded o'er the land, when men knew not the Friend from the Traitor, the Black man laid his life at the altar of the Nation,—and he was refused. When the arms of the Union were beaten, in the first year of the war, and the Executive called for more food for its ravenous maw, again the black man begged the privilege of aiding his country in her need, to be again refused.

And now he is in the War, and how has he conducted himself? Let their dusky forms rise up, out of the mires of James Island, and give the answer. Let the rich mould around Wagner's parapets be upturned, and there will be found an eloquent answer. Obedient and patient and solid as a wall are they. All we lack is a paler hue and a better acquaintance with the alphabet.

Now your Excellency, we have done a Soldier's duty. Why can't we have a Soldier's pay? You caution the Rebel chieftain, that the United States knows no distinction in her soldiers. She insists on having all her soldiers of whatever creed or color, to be treated according to the usages of War.†️ Now if the United States exacts uniformity of treatment of her soldiers

---

* In July, 1863, the War Department ruled that all Negro troops were to be classed, in pay, with hired fugitive slaves (the so-called "contrabands") and were to receive ten dollars per month—with three dollars deducted for clothing—rather than the thirteen dollars paid white troops. As an additional insult, this ruling was interpreted to mean that all Negro troops, regardless of rank, were to receive the same pay. In protest against this the men of the 54th Mass. fought for eighteen months without accepting any pay whatsoever!

† The writer has reference here to the fact that the Confederacy announced that it would not treat captured Negro Union troops as prisoners of war, but rather as escaped slaves or insurrectionists.

from the insurgents, would it not be well and consistent to set the example herself by paying all her soldiers alike?

We of this Regt. were not enlisted under any "contraband" act. But we do not wish to be understood as rating our service of more value to the Government than the service of the ex-slave. Their service is undoubtedly worth much to the Nation, but Congress made express provision touching their case, as slaves freed by military necessity, and assuming the Government to be their temporary Guardian. Not so with us. Freemen by birth and consequently having the advantage of thinking and acting for ourselves so far as the Laws would allow us, we do not consider ourselves fit subjects for the Contraband act.

We appeal to you, Sir, as the Executive of the Nation, to have us justly dealt with. The Regt. do pray that they be assured their service will be fairly appreciated by paying them as American Soldiers, not as menial hirelings. Black men, you may well know, are poor; three dollars per month, for a year, will supply their needy wives and little ones with fuel. If you, as Chief Magistrate of the Nation, will assure us of our whole pay, we are content. Our Patriotism, our enthusiasm will have a new impetus, to exert our energy more and more to aid our Country. Not that our hearts ever flagged in devotion, spite the evident apathy displayed in our behalf, but we feel as though our Country spurned us, now we are sworn to serve her. Please give this a moment's attention.*

MS., War Records Office, National Archives, Washington, D.C.

[c]

*William H. Carney*

Dear Sir—Complying with your request, I send you the following history, pertaining to my birth, parentage, social and religious experience and standing; in short, a concise epitome of my life. I undertake to perform it in my poor way:

I was born in Norfolk, Va., in 1840; my father's name was William Carney; my mother's name before her marriage was Ann Dean; she was the property of one Major Carney, but, at his death, she, with all his people, was by his will made *free*. In my fourteenth year, when I had no work to

* Pressure of the nature of this letter finally moved Congress, in July, 1864, to equalize the pay of Negro and white soldiers. In September, 1864, by special act of Congress, the men of the 54th Mass. received $170,000 in full payment of all their back wages since May, 1863, at the same rate as that paid white troops. Corporal James Henry Gooding, however, received none of this money. On February 20, 1864 he was severely wounded at the battle of Olustee, Florida, and was made a prisoner. He died on July 19, 1864 while a prisoner at the notorious camp in Andersonville, Georgia.

do, I attended a private and secret school kept in Norfolk by a minister. In my fifteenth year I embraced the gospel; at that time I was also engaged in the coasting trade with my father.

In 1850, I left the sea for a time, and my father set out to look for a place to live in peace and freedom. He first stopped in Pennsylvania—but he rested not there; the black man was *not secure* on the soil where the Declaration of Independence was written. He went far. Then he visited the empire State—great New York—whose chief ambition seemed to be for commerce and gold, and with her unceasing struggle for supremacy she heard not the slave; she only had time to spurn the man with a sable skin, and make him feel that he was an alien in his native land.

At last he set his weary feet upon the sterile rocks of "Old Massachusetts." The very air he breathed put enthusiasm into his spirit. O, yes, he found a refuge from oppression in the old Bay State. He selected as his dwelling-place the city of New Bedford, where "Liberty Hall" is a sacred edifice. Like the Temple of Diana which covered the virgins from harm in olden time, so old Liberty Hall in New Bedford protects the oppressed slave of the 19th Century. After stopping a short time, he sent for his family, and there they still dwell. I remained in the city with the family, pursuing the avocation of a jobber of work for stores, and at such places as I could find employment. I soon formed connection with a church under charge of the Rev. Mr. Jackson, now chaplain of the 55th Mass. Volunteers.

Previous to the formation of colored troops, I had a strong inclination to prepare myself for the ministry; but when the country called for *all persons,* I could best serve my God by serving my country and my oppressed brothers. The sequel is short—*I enlisted for the war.*

I am your humble and obedient servant,

WILLIAM H. CARNEY
*Sergeant Co. C, 54th Mass. Vols.*

*The Liberator,* November 6, 1863.

[d]

## "S. J. R."

Sir,—After an absence of several months in the field, I feel it my duty to inform you of some facts in regard to our regiment. We are here on Folly Island. . . . Since we have been here, our duty has been fatigue, almost continually.

The first thing that suggests itself to me is the kindness of the State of Massachusetts in offering to make up to us the amount which we enlisted for, and which is withheld from us by the United States. We earnestly hope that it will not be thought, by the State of Massachusetts, that we refused the money for any motive other than that we desire, at this crisis, the recognition of our rights as men and soldiers.* Sorry am I to say, that we have been considered incapable of acting for ourselves long enough; and as it stands, we are even now not equalized with other troops in the field—as is seen in the taking of officers, or rather sergeants for white regiments, and making them captains, lieutenants, &c over us, when there are large numbers of our men who are more capable, even in every respect, to be commissioned officers, than those, or a great portion of those who are coming in continually. I do not state this as mere hearsay, for I know it to be a fact; and, sir, we think and hope that these matters, however small they may appear to some, will be looked into. We, as a race, have been trodden down long enough. Are we, who have come into the field of bloody conflict, and left our quiet homes the same as white men, for the sake of our country, and to beat down the rebellion—are we to be put down lower than these, many of whom have not enlisted with as good motives as we have? If we have men in our regiments who are capable of being officers, why not let them be promoted the same as other soldiers?

I hope, sir, that you will urge this matter, as I am well aware that you are on our side, and always have done for us all in your power to help our race.

*The Liberator,* January 29, 1864.

## [e]

### *The Anonymous Sergeant*

Charleston is not ours yet, but no doubt will soon be. And why? Because the country needs an important victory, and somehow it is a religious or superstitious belief with me that this country will be saved to us (black men) yet. I say I believe this; but it is not a mere blind belief. I know that we shall have to labor hard, and put up with a great deal before we are allowed to participate in the government of this country. I am aware that we in the army have done about all we can do, and that to you civilians at home falls the duty of speaking out for all—as we have done the fighting and marching, and suffered cold, heat and hunger, for you and all of us.

My friend, we want black commissioned officers; and only because we want men we can understand, and who can understand us. We want men whose hearts are truly loyal to the rights of man. We want to be represented in courts martial, where so many of us are liable to be tried and sentenced. We want to demonstrate our ability to rule, as we have demonstrated our

---

* In November, 1863, Massachusetts appropriated money with which to pay the men of the 54th and 55th the difference in their pay and that of white troops. The men rejected the offer, with thanks, as violating their principle.

willingness to obey. In short, we want simple justice. I will try to be plainer: there are men here who were made sergeants at Camp Meigs, (Reidville,) who have had command of their companies for months. Can these men feel contented when they see others, who came into the regiment as second lieutenants, promoted to captaincy, and a crowd of incompetent civilians and non-commissioned officers of other regiments sent here to take their places? . . .

*The Liberator*, October 7, 1864.

## [f]

### Joseph Howard

I was taken prisoner at the surrender of Athens, Alabama, September 20th, 1864. We were marched to Mobile, Alabama, stopping at various places on the route. We were twelve days going to Mobile. After we were captured, the rebels robbed us of everything we had that they could use; they searched our pockets, took our clothing, and even cut the buttons off what little clothing they allowed us to retain. After arriving at Mobile, we were placed at work on the fortifications there, and impressed colored men who were at work when we arrived were released, we taking their places. We were kept at hard labor and inhumanly treated; if we lagged or faltered, or misunderstood an order, we were whipped and abused; some of our own men being detailed to whip others. They gave as a reason for such harsh treatment, that we knew very well what they wanted us to do, but that we feigned ignorance; that if we were with the Yankees, we could do all they wanted, &c. For the slightest cause we were subjected to the lash. We were very poorly provided with food, our rations being corn-meal and mule-meat, and occasionally some poor beef. On the 7th of December, I stole a skiff and went down Mobile River to the Bay, and was taken on board of one of our Gun-boats. Was taken to Fort Morgan on the Gun-boat, and reported to the commanding officer, who, after hearing my story, furnished me with a pass and transportation to New Orleans; from there I was sent to Cairo, thence to Louisville, and from there here.

MS., War Records Office, National Archives, Washington, D.C.

## [g]

### John S. Leach

I have the honor to submit the following statement: I, with the regiment, was captured at Dalton, Georgia, October 13th, 1864. The enlisted men of the regiment were compelled by the rebels to tear up the railroad track in that vicinity. We, the captured men of the 44th U.S. Colored Infantry were marched from Dalton to Corinth, Mississippi, at which place we were compelled to labor on railroads. The number of men of the 44th who labored on these roads I estimated about three hundred and fifty. During the time I was in the hands of the rebels there were about two hundred and fifty men of the 44th delivered to their former masters, or men who claimed to own them, thereby returning these men to slavery. The 44th arrived at Corinth, Mississippi, and commenced labor on or about the 1st of December, 1864, at which labor I remained until I effected my escape, about the 25th of December, 1864, and arrived at Memphis, Tennessee, and from thence I reported to my command at Chattanooga, Tennessee.

When I left the rebels there were about one hundred and twenty-five men of the 44th still laboring on these railroads; the remainder either been sent to hospitals to die, or turned over to civilians as slaves, or effected their escape. While with them our ration consisted of one pint of corn meal per day and a small portion of fresh beef once or twice per week.

MS., War Records Office, National Archives, Washington, D.C.

## [h]

### J. J. Hill

At 10 A.M. on the 29th inst. we moved from the breastworks on the left of Fort Harrison to the hill in the centre, where we built a tower overlooking the rebel works into Richmond. We remained there four weeks, and on the 27th of March we moved again. Part of the 29th rested in Fort Harrison and the 2d Brigade in the white house, known as General Birney's head-quarters. All was quiet here until the 1st of April, when all was in readiness, and the order was given to strike tents and move on to Richmond. During Sunday night the brigade was out in line of battle, and at three o'clock in the morning the rebels blew up three gun boats and commenced vacating their works in our front. At 5 A.M. the troops commenced to advance on the rebel works—the 29th taking the advance, the 9th U.S.C.[olored] troops next. Soon refugees from the rebels came in by hundreds. Col. W. B. Wooster passed them about, and made them go before the regiment and dig up the torpedoes that were left in the ground to prevent the progress of the Union army. They were very numerous, but to the surprise of officers and men, none of the army were injured by them. On our march to Richmond, we captured 500 pieces of artillery, some of the largest kind, 6,000 stand of small arms, and the prisoners I was not able to number. The road was strewed with all kinds of obstacles, and men were lying all along the distance of seven miles. The main body of the army went up the New Market road. The 29th skirmished all the way, and arrived in the city at 7 A.M., and were the first infantry that entered the city; they went at double quick most of the way. When Col. Wooster came to Main st. he pointed his sword at the capitol, and said "Double quick, march," and the company charged through the main street to the capitol and halted in the square until the rest of the regiment came up. Very soon after the arrival of the white troops the colored troops were moved on the outskirts of the city, and as fast as the white troops came in the colored troops were ordered out, until we occupied the advance. The white troops remained in the city as guards. We remained on the outpost.

The 3d instant President Lincoln visited the city. No triumphal march of a conqueror could have equalled in moral sublimity the humble manner in which he entered Richmond. I was standing on the bank of the James river viewing the scene of desolation when a boat, pulled by twelve sailors, came up the stream. It contained President Lincoln and his son . . . In some way the colored people on the bank of the river ascertained that the tall man wearing the black hat was President Lincoln. There was a sudden shout and clapping of hands. I was very much amused at the plight of one officer who had in charge fifty colored men to put to work on the ruined buildings; he found himself alone, for they left work and crowded to see the President. As he approached I said to a woman, "Madam, there is the man that made you free." She exclaimed, "Is that President Lincoln?" My reply was in the affirmative. She gazed at him with clasped hands and said, "Glory to God. Give Him the praise for his goodness," and she shouted till her voice failed her.

When the President landed there was no carriage near, neither did he wait for one, but leading his son, they walked over a mile to Gen'l. Weitzel's headquarters at Jeff. Davis' mansion, a colored man acting as guide. Six soldiers dressed in blue, with their carbines, were the advanced guards. Next to them came President Lincoln and son, and Admiral Porter, flanked by the other officers right and left. Then came a correspondent, and in the rear were six sailors with carbines. Then followed thousands of people, colored and white. What a spectacle! I never witnessed such rejoicing in all my life. As the President passed along the street the colored people waved their handkerchiefs, hats and bonnets, and expressed their gratitude by shouting repeatedly, "Thank God for his goodness; we have seen his salvation." The white soldiers caught the sound and swelled the numbers, cheering as they marched along. All could see the President, he was so tall. One woman standing in a doorway as he passed along shouted, "Thank you, dear Jesus, for this sight of the great conqueror." Another one standing by her side clasped her hands and shouted, "Bless the Lamb—Bless the Lamb." Another one threw her bonnet in the air, screaming with all her might, "Thank you, Master Lincoln." A white woman came to a window but turned away, as if it were a disgusting sight. A few white women looking out of an elegant mansion waved their handkerchiefs. President Lincoln walked in silence, acknowledging the salute of officers and soldiers, and of the citizens, colored and white. It was a man of the people among the people. It was a great deliverer among the delivered. No wonder tears came to his eyes when he looked on the poor colored people who were once slaves, and heard the blessings uttered from thankful hearts and thanksgiving to God and Jesus. They were earnest and heartfelt expressions of gratitude to Almighty God, and thousands of colored men in Richmond would have laid down their lives for President Lincoln. After visiting Jeff. Davis' mansion he proceeded to the rebel capitol and from the steps delivered a short speech, and spoke to the colored people as follows:

"In reference to you, colored people, let me say God has made you free. Although you have been deprived of your God-given rights by your so-called masters, you are now as free as I am, and if those that claim to be your superiors do not know that you are free, take the sword and bayonet and teach them that you are—for God created all men free, giving to each the same rights of life, liberty and the pursuit of happiness."

The gratitude and admiration amounting almost to worship, with which the colored people of Richmond received the President must have deeply touched his heart. He came among the poor unheralded, without pomp or pride, and walked through the streets, as if he were a private citizen more than a great conqueror. He came not with bitterness in his heart, but with the olive leaf of kindness, a friend to elevate sorrow and suffering, and to rebuild what had been destroyed.

J. J. Hill, *A Sketch of the 29th Regiment of Connecticut Colored Troops* (Baltimore, 1867), pp. 25–27.

## 178

# THE BALLOT, THE SCHOOL, THE LAND,
## 1862–1865

The following four documents are indicative of the desires most fervently expressed by the Southern Negro, once emancipation was certain—to acquire land and to gain the ballot and an education.

The first document is a letter dated St. Helena's Island, S.C., November 20, 1862, written by Charlotte Forten, granddaughter of James Forten of Philadelphia.

This young lady had been educated at State Normal School, in Salem, Massachusetts, and was one of the scores of devoted women, Negro and white, who went South during and immediately after the War to serve as teachers.

The second document consists of resolutions adopted by a mass meeting of Memphis Negroes held on the first anniversary, January 1, 1864, of the Emancipation Proclamation.

The third document is a petition, with over a thousand signatures, from Louisiana Negroes, dated New Orleans, January 5, 1864. Two representatives of the petitioners, J. B. Roudanez and Arnold Bertonneau, presented this memorial to President Lincoln in person on March 10, 1864.

The last document consists of the minutes of a remarkable interview held at the headquarters of Major-General Sherman in Savannah on January 12, 1865. Participating were General Sherman, Secretary of War Stanton and E. D. Townsend, Assistant Adjutant-General of the Army (who certified to the exactness of the document) and twenty Negro ministers and church officials of Savannah. One of the Negroes, James Lynch, had been born free in Baltimore and had been in the South for only two years. All the others were Southern Negroes, four of them freeborn and fifteen, slaves. Of those who had been slaves, two had purchased their freedom. The eldest of the Negroes, 67-year-old Garrison Frazier, a minister, who had been born a slave in North Carolina until buying his freedom in 1857, served as their spokesman.

### [a]

### *Charlotte Forten*

St. Helena's Island, on which I am, is about six miles from the mainland of Beaufort. I must tell you that we were rowed hither from Beaufort by a crew of Negro boatmen, and that they sung for us several of their own beautiful songs. There is a peculiar wildness and solemnity about them which cannot be described, and the people accompanying the singing with a singular swaying motion of the body, which seems to make it more effective. How much I enjoyed that row in the beautiful, brilliant southern sunset, with no sounds to be heard but the musical murmur of the water, and the wonderfully rich, clear tones of the singers! But all the time I did not realize that I was actually in South Carolina! And indeed I believe I do not quite realize it now. But we were far from feeling fear,—we were in a very excited, jubilant state of mind, and sang the John Brown song with spirit, as we drove through the pines and palmettos. Ah! it was good to be able to sing that *here*, in the very heart of Rebeldom!

There are no white soldiers on this island. It is protected by gunboats, and by Negro pickets who do their duty well. These men attacked and drove back a boat-load of rebels who tried to land here one night, several weeks ago. General [Rufus] Saxton is forming a colored regiment at Beaufort, and many of the colored men from this and the adjacent islands have joined it. The General is a noble-hearted man, who has a deep interest in the people here, and he is generally loved and trusted by them. I am sorry to say that some other officers treat the freed people and speak of them with the greatest contempt. They are consequently disliked and feared.

As far as I have been able to observe—and although I have not been here long, I have seen and talked with many of the people—the Negroes here seem to be, for the most part, an honest, industrious, and sensible people. They are eager to learn; they rejoice in their new-found freedom. It does one good to see how *jubilant* they are over the downfall of their "secesh" masters, as they call them. I do not believe there is a man, woman, or even a child that is old enough to be sensible, that would submit to being made a slave again. There is evidently a deep determination in their souls that *that* shall never be. Their hearts are full of gratitude to the Government and to the "Yankees." . . .

My school is about a mile from here, in the little Baptist church . . . There are two ladies in the school beside myself—Miss T. and Miss M., both of whom are most enthusiastic teachers. They have done a great deal of good here. At present, our school is small,—many of the children on the island being ill with whooping cough,—but in general it averages eighty or ninety. I find the children generally well-behaved, and eager to learn; yea, they are nearly all most eager to learn, and many of them make most rapid improvement. It is a great happiness to teach them. I wish some of those persons at the North, who say the race is hopelessly and naturally inferior, could see the readiness with which these children, so long oppressed and deprived of every privilege, learn and understand.

I have some grown pupils—people on our own plantation—who take lessons in the evenings. It will amuse you to know that one of them—our man-of-all work—is named *Cupid*. (Venuses and Cupids are very common here.) He told me he was "feared" he was almost too old to learn; but I assured him that was not the case, and now he is working diligently at the alphabet. One of my people—Harry—is a scholar to be proud of. He makes most wonderful improvement. I never saw any one so determined to learn. I enjoy having him and Cupid talk about the time that the rebels had to flee from this place. The remembrance of it is evidently a source of the most exquisite happiness and amusement. There are several families living here, and it is very pleasant to visit their cabins and talk with them. They are very happy now. They never weary of contrasting their present with their former condition, and they work for the Government now, and receive wages and rations in return. I am very happy here, but wish I was able to do a great deal more. I wish some one would write a little Christmas hymn for our children to sing. I want to have a kind of festival for them on Christmas, if we can. The children have just learned the John Brown song, and next week they are going to learn the song of the "Negro Boatman." The little creatures love to sing. They sing with the greatest enthusiasm. I wish you could hear them.

*The Liberator*, December 12, 1862.

## [b]

### *Memphis Mass Meeting*

*Resolved*, That we hail with feelings of joy and gratitude to Almighty God, that we have the exalted privilege of meeting together, for the purpose of offering tribute and honor to one of the most magnanimous and brilliant chapters written in the nineteenth century.

*Resolved*, That we greet the dawn of this beautiful and ever memorable day; and we trust that our children will cherish it until truth, and honor shall cease to be revered among the civilized nations of the earth.

*Resolved*, That the respect to his excellency, the President of the United States, and the admiration we cherish for the gallant army and navy that have borne their glittering arms, backed by their courageous hearts, in triumph over hundreds of battle-fields, call upon us to-day to pledge ourselves as colored men to fill the ranks made vacant by our colored brothers, who have fallen so bravely upon the various fields of strife.

*Resolved*, That we recommend every colored man, capable of performing military duty, both North and South, to enlist forthwith in the army and navy of the United States, where he can successfully perform his duty to his God, his country, and his fellow-men.

*Resolved*, As this is our country, and we are citizens of the United States, in the eloquent language of Attorney-General Bates; * therefore we are willing to defend them with life and limb; and after protecting them with our guns, we humbly pray God that there may be generosity enough left to protect us in our native land.

*Resolved*, That we recommend the colored people everywhere in the United States to stand by the Government, to be true to the stars and stripes.

*Resolved*, That we recommend the benevolent associations of the North to send us teachers, who are known to be our true and devoted friends.

*Resolved*, That we recommend the teachers to bring their tents with them, ready for erection in the field, by the roadside, or in the fort, and not to wait for magnificent houses to be erected in time of war. . . .

*The Liberator*, January 29, 1864.

---

* In an opinion rendered November 29, 1862.

[c]

*Petition of Louisiana Negroes*

*To His Excellency Abraham Lincoln, President of the United States, and to the Honorable the Senate and House of Representatives of the United States of America in Congress assembled:*

The undersigned respectfully submit the following:

That they are natives of Louisiana, and citizens of the United States; that they are loyal citizens, sincerely attached to the Country and the Constitution, and ardently desire the maintenance of the national unity, for which they are ready to sacrifice their fortunes and their lives.

That a large portion of them are owners of real estate, and all of them are owners of personal property; that many of them are engaged in the pur- ;uits of commerce and industry, while others are employed as artisans in various trades; that they are all fitted to enjoy the privileges and immunities belonging to the condition of citizens of the United States, and among them may be found many of the descendants of those men whom the illustrious Jackson styled "his fellow citizens" when he called upon them * to take up arms to repel the enemies of the country.

Your petitioners further respectfully represent that over and above the right, which, in the language of the Declaration of Independence, they possess to liberty and the pursuit of happiness, they are supported by the opinion of just and loyal men, especially by that of Hon. Edward Bates, Attorney-General, in the claim to the right of enjoying the privileges and immunities pertaining to the condition of citizens of the United States; and, to support the legitimacy of this claim, they believe it simply necessary to submit to your Excellency, and to the Honorable Congress, the following considerations, which they beg of you to weigh in the balance of law and justice. Notwithstanding their forefathers served in the army of the United States, in 1814–15, and aided in repelling from the soil of Louisiana the haughty enemy, over-confident of success, yet they and their descendants have ever since, and until the era of the present rebellion, been estranged, and even repulsed-excluded from all franchises, even the smallest . . . During this period of forty-nine years, they have never ceased to be peaceable citizens, paying their taxes on an assessment of more than fifteen millions of dollars.†

At the call of General Banks, they hastened to rally under the banner

* Prior to the Battle of New Orleans in January, 1815.
† When presenting this petition to Lincoln, another memorial, calling for the enfranchisement of *freed* Negroes, was also submitted.

of Union and Liberty; they have spilled their blood, and are still pouring it out for the maintenance of the Constitution of the United States; in a word, they are soldiers of the Union, and they will defend it so long as their hands have strength to hold a musket.

While General Banks was at the seige of Port Hudson, and the city threatened by the enemy, his Excellency, Governor Shepley, called for troops for the defence of the city, and they were foremost in responding to the call, having raised the 1st regiment in the short space of forty-eight hours.

In consideration of this fact, as true and as clear as the sun which lights this great continent—in consideration of the services already performed, and still to be rendered by them to their common country, they humbly beseech your Excellency and Congress to cast your eyes upon a loyal population; awaiting, with confidence and dignity, the proclamation of those inalienable rights which belong to the condition of citizens of the great American Republic.

Theirs is but a feeble voice claiming attention in the midst of the grave questions raised by this terrible conflict; yet confident of the justice which guides the action of the Government, they have no hesitation in speaking what is prompted by their hearts—"We are men; treat us as such."

Mr. President and Honorable members of Congress: The petitioners refer to your wisdom the task of deciding whether they, loyal and devoted men, who are ready to make every sacrifice for the support of the best Government which man has been permitted to create, are to be deprived of the right to assist in establishing a civil government in our beloved State of Louisiana, and also in choosing their Representatives, both for the Legislature of the State and for the Congress of the nation.

Your petitioners aver that they have applied in respectful terms to Brig. Gen. George F. Shepley, Military Governor of Louisiana,* and to Major Gen. N. P. Banks, commanding the Department of the Gulf, praying to be placed upon the registers as voters, to the end that they might participate in the reorganization of civil government in Louisiana, and that their petition has met with no response from those officers, and it is feared that none will be given; and they therefore appeal to the justice of the Representatives of the nation, and ask that all the citizens of Louisiana of African descent, born free before the rebellion, may be, by proper orders, directed to be inscribed on the registers, and admitted to the rights and privileges of electors.

And your petitioners will ever pray.

*The Liberator*, April 1, 1864.

---

* This petition, very similar to the one here reprinted, was submitted on Nov. 5, 1863.

## [e]

### *The Interview*

*First.* State what your understanding is in regard to the Acts of Congress, and President Lincoln's Proclamation, touching the condition of the colored people in the rebel States.

*Answer.* So far as I understand President Lincoln's Proclamation to the rebellious States, it is, that if they would lay down their arms and submit to the laws of the United States before the 1st of January, 1863, all should be well, but if they did not, then all the slaves in the rebel States should be free, henceforth and forever; that is what I understood.

*Second.* State what you understand by slavery, and the freedom that was to be given by the President's Proclamation.

*Answer.* Slavery is receiving by irresistible power the work of another man, and not by his consent. The freedom, as I understand it, promised by the Proclamation, is taking us from under the yoke of bondage, and placing us where we could reap the fruit of our own labor, and take care of our-selves, and assist the Government in maintaining our freedom.

*Third.* State in what manner you think you can take care of yourselves, and how you can best assist the Government in maintaining your freedom.

*Answer.* The way we can best take care of ourselves is to have land, and turn in and till it by our labor—that is, by the labor of the women, and children, and old men—and we can soon maintain ourselves and have something to spare; and to assist the Government, the young men should enlist in the service of the Government, and serve in such manner as they may be wanted—(the rebels told us that they piled them up, and made batteries of them, and sold them to Cuba; but we don't believe that). We want to be placed on land until we are able to buy it, and make it our own.

*Fourth.* State in what manner you would rather live, whether scattered among the whites, or in colonies by yourselves.

*Answer.* I would prefer to live by ourselves, for there is a prejudice against us in the South that will take years to get over; but I do not know that I can answer for my brethren. [*Mr. Lynch* says he thinks they should not be separated, but live together. All the other persons present being questioned, one by one, answer that they agree with "brother *Frazier.*"] *

*Fifth.* Do you think that there is intelligence enough among the slaves of the South to maintain themselves under the Government of the United States, and the equal protection of its laws, and maintain good and peace-able relations among yourselves and with your neighbors?

* Bracketed words in original.

*Answer.* I think there is sufficient intelligence among us to do so.

*Sixth.* State what is the feeling of the black population of the South towards the Government of the United States; what is the understanding in respect to the present war, its causes and object, and their disposition to aid either side; state fully your views.

*Answer.* I think you will find there is thousands that are willing to make any sacrifice to assist the Government of the United States, while there is also many that are not willing to take up arms. I do not suppose there is a dozen men that is opposed to the Government. I understand, as to the war, that the South is the aggressor. President Lincoln was elected President by a majority of the United States, which guaranteed him the right of holding the office, and exercising that right over the whole United States. The South, without knowing what he would do, rebelled. The war was commenced by the rebels before he came into office. The object of the war was not, at first, to give the slaves their freedom, but the sole object of the war was, at first, to bring the rebellious States back into the Union, and their loyalty to the laws of the United States. Afterwards, knowing the value that was set on the slaves by the rebels, the President thought that his Proclamation would stimulate them to lay down their arms, reduce them to obedience, and help to bring back the rebel States; and their not doing so has now made the freedom of the slaves a part of the war. It is my opinion that there is not a man in this city that could be started to help the rebels one inch, for that would be suicide. There was two black men left with the rebels, because they had taken an active part for the rebels, and thought something might befall them if they staid behind, but there is not another man. If the prayers that have gone up for the Union army could be read out, you would not get through them these two weeks.

*Seventh.* State whether the sentiments you now express are those only of the colored people in the city, or do they extend to the colored population through the country, and what are your means of knowing the sentiments of those living in the country.

*Answer.* I think the sentiments are the same among the colored people of the State. My opinion is formed by personal communication in the course of my ministry, and also from the thousands that followed the Union army, leaving their homes and undergoing suffering! I did not think there would be so many; the number surpassed my expectation.

*Eighth.* If the rebel leaders were to arm the slaves, what would be the effect? *

---

* A proposal to this effect was then being discussed by Confederate leaders. In March, 1865 a law providing for the enlistment of slaves was passed but it was not really implemented and no slave fought against the Union.

*Answer.* I think they would fight as long as they were before the bayonet, and just as soon as they could get away they would desert, in my opinion.

*Ninth.* What, in your opinion, is the feeling of the colored people about enlisting and serving as soldiers of the United States, and what kind of military service do they prefer?

*Answer.* A large number have gone as soldiers to Port Royal to be drilled and put in the service, and I think there is thousands of the young men that will enlist; there is something about them that, perhaps, is wrong; they have suffered so long from the rebels, that they want to meet and have a chance with them in the field. Some of them want to shoulder the musket, others want to go into the Quartermaster or the Commissary's service.

*Tenth.* Do you understand the mode of enlistment of colored persons in the rebel States, by State agents, under the act of Congress? If yea, state what your understanding is.

*Answer.* My understanding is that colored persons enlisted by State agents are enlisted as substitutes, and give credit to the States, and do not swell the army, because every black man enlisted by a State agent leaves a white man at home; and, also, that larger bounties are given or promised by the State agents than are given by the States. The great object should be to push through this rebellion the shortest way, or there seems to be something wanting in the enlistment by State agents, for it don't strengthen the army, but takes one away for every colored man enlisted.

*Eleventh.* State what, in your opinion, is the best way to enlist colored men for soldiers.

*Answer.* I think, sir, that all compulsory operation should be put a stop to. The ministers would talk to them, and the young men would enlist. It is my opinion that it would be far better for the State agents to stay at home, and the enlistments to be made for the United States under the direction of General Sherman.

*The Liberator,* February 24, 1865.

<br>

# 179

# THE NORTHERN ARENA DURING THE WAR,
## 1862–1865

While the heart of the Negro's struggle was in the South, there was no lack of activity in the North during the years of war. Ever present were Jim-Crowism, disfranchisement and violence.

Eleven documents illustrative of these conditions follow. The first [a] is a petition to Congress dated Hartford, Conn., December 17, 1862, from two Negro businessmen, T. P. Saunders and P. H. B. Saunders. This represents a protest against taxation without representation and was submitted on January 5, 1863 by Charles Sumner to the Senate which referred it to the Committee on Finance where it died.

The second document [b] is a description by a Negro eyewitness of the first of the major organized attacks upon entire Negro communities which blotched the record of several Northern cities in 1863. The one described occurred in Detroit on March 6.

The third and fourth documents [c, d] deal with the Negroes' fight to be permitted to ride in the city cars of Philadelphia—a fight lasting several years and achieving success in 1866.

The fifth document [e] in this group is a letter dated New York, April 24, 1865, from J. Sella Martin to the *Evening Post*. Mr. Martin's letter is one of protest against the decision of the City Council to exclude Negroes from the funeral procession for Abraham Lincoln. Only a telegram from the Assistant Secretary of War, Charles A. Dana, to General Dix, in command, reversed this decision and on April 25, 1865, about 2,000 Negroes made up the end of the long procession of marchers behind the Emancipator's coffin.

The sixth document [f] is a petition presented, in printed form, to Congress in February, 1864. This was distributed by the Israel Lyceum, a potent Negro organization of Washington, D.C., headed by Thomas H. C. Hinton. It appealed for the enfranchisement of all Negro men.

The seventh document [g] represents another suffrage appeal in the form of a handwritten petition from fifty-seven of the leading Negroes of Washington, D.C. This petition reached Congress in April, 1864, and among its signers were John F. Cook and Jacob Dodson.

The eighth document [h] is a multiple one. It consists of material directly connected with the great "National Convention of Colored Citizens of the United States" which met early in October, 1864, in Syracuse, New York, just before the momentous November elections. One hundred and forty-four delegates were present from eighteen states, including seven Southern ones (Virginia, North Carolina, South Carolina, Florida, Mississippi, Louisiana and Tennessee). Most of the great names in the Negro's struggles during the fifteen or twenty years preceding the Civil War were present. Frederick Douglass was the convention's president, while in attendance were William Wells Brown, Henry Highland Garnet, Peter H. Clark, George L. Ruffin, Robert Hamilton, William Howard Day and George T. Downing. And many who were to play key roles during Reconstruction were delegates, also, like John M. Langston, Jonathan C. Gibbs, William Keeling and A. H. Galloway.

Printed below are the Call for this convention, issued in August, 1864, and the Resolutions of the Convention, its "Declaration of Wrongs and Rights," its "Address to the People of the United States" (written by Douglass), and the preamble and first section of the Constitution of the National Equal Rights League formed at this convention.

The ninth document [i] consists of an appeal "To the Colored People of the United States" from the Executive Board of the National Equal Rights League, calling for the formation of state branches of the League. The "Appeal," dated

Philadelphia, November 24, 1864, was signed by the League's president, John Mercer Langston.

The tenth document [j] typifies the type of action evoked by Langston's appeal. It consists of the resolutions adopted by a convention of Ohio Negroes, held in Xenia, January 10–12, 1865. Fifty-six delegates from twenty-nine cities and villages of Ohio were present and an Ohio branch of the Equal Rights League was founded.

The eleventh document [k] exemplifies the type of petitions with which Northern Negroes were bombarding their state legislatures even prior to the end of hostilities. This particular one was presented by 102 Wisconsin Negroes to their State legislature on January 24, 1865 and requested the right to vote.

## [a]

### *The Saunders Brothers*

We beg leave respectfully to represent that we are carrying on the business of Merchant Tailors in the City of Hartford in the State of Connecticut, and that we are natives of said State—that our Grandfather fought and suffered much in the War of the Revolution, which was professedly waged against the principle of "Taxation without Representation"—that we have commingled in our veins the blood of the Negro, Anglo-Saxon, and the Indian—that by the Constitution of Connecticut because of our Negro blood, and for no other reason we are deprived of the right of Suffrage and of the privilege of taking any part whatever in matters of Government, both State and National—that by Statute of said State as a sort of compensation for disfranchisement (and a very poor compensation it is) we are exempted from taxation—that a heavy burden is imposed on us by the act of the last Congress entitled an act to provide internal revenue to support the Government and to pay interest on the public debt—that besides procuring a manufacturers license we are required to pay from our little business about one hundred dollars per month for the support of a Government we have no voice in administering and for the payment of a public debt which we had no agency in contracting.

The undersigned pray your Honourable body in some way to correct this manifest wrong—and as we are denied the privilege of taking the Oath of Allegiance to either the State in which we are domiciled, or to the United States, we claim exemption from the burden of taxation, which Connecticut so consistently recognizes as a principle be applied to us—and as in duty bound we shall ever pray.

Records of the U.S. Senate, 37th Cong., 3rd Sess., The National Archives, Washington, D.C.

## [b]

### *The Detroit Outbreak*

The present state of affairs in relation to the colored people is one of great perplexity, and is not only so on account of the South, but also in the North.

There certainly is something mysterious about them. On the one hand they are being mobbed, and everything that is sacred to a people to make a country or home dear are denied them, in many of the large Northern cities. And on the other hand they are marching off to the call of the Government as if they were sharing all the blessings of the most favored citizens!

And it is equally mysterious to see the bitter opposition that a class of men, professing loyalty to the Government of the United States, should have against the colored soldier going out and facing the cannon's mouth in defence of a Government that appears to be unable to give them any protection from the rage of the *r*ebels in the South, or their enemies in the North.

But one thing the colored man knows, that the class of men of the same politics as those South are doing the mobbing North; so they are not only ready to suffer, but to die in the cause that promises over three millions of their race liberty.

Whatever, therefore, our treatment may be, so far as the rage of the enemies of freedom may be; whatever, through cowardice, a ruthless mob of men may inflict upon our people, they will not be deterred from the duty they owe to their God, themselves and posterity, to do all they possibly can to undo the heavy burdens and let the oppressed go free! At the first blast the clarion of emancipation may give to call them forth in the irrepressible conflict, though their houses be sacked, their wives and children turned out of doors naked and destitute, they too well know that the way to glory is the way of suffering; therefore they desire to bear a good part in the battlefield rather than to be always exposed to such outrages as slavery entails, on any class it has in its dominion.

The mob, in its first appearance to me, was a parcel of fellows running up Lafayette street after two or three colored men. They then returned back, and in a short time I saw a tremendous crowd coming up Croghan street on drays, wagons, and foot, with kegs of beer on their wagons, and rushed for the prison. Here they crowded thick and heavy. After this, while I was standing on the corner, with half a dozen other gentlemen, a rifle ball came whistling over our heads. After which we heard several shots, but only one ball passing us. In a short time after this there came one fellow down saying, "I am shot in the thigh." And another came with his finger partly shot off. A few minutes after that another ruffian came down, saying: "If we are got to be killed up for Negroes then we will kill every one in this town." A very little while after this we could hear them speaking up near the jail, and appeared to be drinking, but I was unable to hear what they said. This done, they gave a most fiendish yell and started down Beaubien street. On reaching Croghan street, a couple of houses west on Beaubien street, they commenced throwing, and before they reached my residence, clubs, brick, and missiles of every description flew like hail. Myself and several others were standing on the side-walk, but were compelled to hasten in and close our doors, while the mob passed my house with their clubs and bricks flying into my windows and doors, sweeping out light and sash!

They then approached my door in large numbers, where I stood with my gun, and another friend with an axe, but on seeing us, they fell back. They approached four times determined to enter my door, but I raised my gun at each time and they fell back. In the meantime part of the mob passed on down Beaubien street. After the principle part had passed, I rushed up my stairs looking to see what they were doing, and heard the shattering of windows and slashing of boards. In a few moments I saw them at Whitney Reynolds, a few doors below Lafayette street. Mr. Reynolds is a cooper; had his shop and residence on the same lot, and was the largest colored cooper establishment in the city—employing a number of hands regular.

I could see from the windows men striking with axe, spade, clubs, &c., just as you could see men thrashing wheat. A sight the most revolting, to see innocent men, women, and children, all without respect to age or sex, being pounded in the most brutal manner.

Sickened with the sight, I sat down in deep solicitude in relation to what the night would bring forth; for to human appearance it seemed as if Satan was loose, and his children were free to do whatever he might direct without fear of the city authority.

[Thomas Buckner] *A Thrilling Narrative from the Lips of the Sufferers of the Late Detroit Riot* . . . (Detroit, 1863, pub. by the author; reprinted by The Book Farm, Hattiesburg, Miss., 1945). Copy in Wisconsin State Library, Madison.

## [c]

### Philadelphia Cars

*To The Board of Managers of the various City Passenger Cars:*

The Colored Citizens of Philadelphia suffer very serious inconveniences and hardships daily, by being excluded from riding in the City Passenger Cars. In New York City, and in all the principal Northern cities, except

Philadelphia, they ride; even in New Orleans, (although subject to some proscription,) they ride in the cars; why then should they be excluded in Philadelphia, in a city standing so preeminently high for its Benevolence, Liberality, Love of Freedom and Christianity, as the City of Brotherly Love?

Colored people pay more taxes here than are paid by the same class in any other Northern city. The members of the *"Social and Statistical Association,"* although numbering less than fifty members, pay annually about *Five Thousand Dollars* into the Tax Collector's office.

Therefore, the undersigned respectfully petition that the various Boards of the City Passenger Cars rescind the rules indiscriminately excluding colored persons from the inside of the cars.

The petition was accompanied by the following appeal:

*To The Board of Presidents of the City Passenger Railroads:* Gentlemen: The undersigned Committee, appointed by the Social, Civil and Statistical Association of the Colored People of Pennsylvania, who appeared before you, something over two years ago, with a petition, signed by three hundred and sixty highly respectable citizens of Philadelphia, praying that the rules indiscriminately excluding colored people from the inside of the cars be rescinded, would most respectfully again urge the claims of their cause by re-presenting the same petition, with an additional appeal annexed thereto.

We have never understood that the matter was finally disposed of by your Body, but simply postponed. Hence we trust our earnest efforts at this time will not be regarded by you as unduly obtrusive, especially when you shall have considered such facts as we are about to bring before you.

Since our petition was first presented, New York has removed every vestige of proscription from all her city passenger cars, although the rules of their roads, long before this final change, carried colored people generally without proscription, excepting two roads. In these exceptional cases, they could ride in cars especially designated by the words "Colored people are allowed, &c."

Can it be possible that there is more prejudice, and less humanity, in Philadelphia than in New York? We cannot think so, and our experience in this very matter of procuring signatures to the petition now under consideration fully justifies us in assuming this ground.

We applied to men who had never rendered themselves publicly obnoxious by advocating anti-slavery or abolition views; men filling the highest positions in the churches, in the legal profession, in the mercantile calling, and in the editorial vocations, and to our great gratification we rarely applied in vain.

Amongst the signatures may be found a number of Episcopal clergymen.

Not a man of that order to whom we applied hesitated a moment about signing it, but all freely gave their names.

Also among the names may be found the pastors of nearly all the leading Methodist churches in this city, who, with one accord, cheerfully furnished their names of the names of the churches over which they presided, to give additional weight thereto. Every Baptist clergyman also to whom it was presented gave his name, and unqualified approval of the measure.

Other denominations to whom it was presented signed with equal freedom, so far as they were called upon. Hence we take it for granted that, so far as the public are concerned, should the oppressive and proscriptive rules be changed to-day, the great majority of the citizens of Philadelphia would acquiesce in the change.

And, we would further add in this connection, we are fully persuaded that if the Board should feel inclined to test this question by allowing any ordinarily decent woman to ride on any one of the roads, by an impromptu vote of the passengers, two-thirds would side with the women, as often as the trial might be made.

But, you may ask, "Will not the vulgar and the lower order of society rebel against colored people riding?" We reply, no. No sooner here than in New York, Washington or New Orleans.

The truth is, the colored people, in meeting with insult and vulgar epithets from the vulgar, cannot fail to observe that these abuses are, in a great degree, traceable to severe and inhuman rules of this kind.

Nobody insults a colored man or woman in the Tax Receiver's office, however full it may be. Nobody insults a colored man or woman in entering a store, even though it may be the most fashionable in the city. Why, then, should the fear exist that the very people who are meeting colored people in various other directions, without insulting them, should instantly become so intolerably incensed as to indicate a terrible aspect in this particular? They say, fearless of successful gainsaying, that the rules of which the colored people of Philadelphia complain, in point of severity stand un- paralleled, compared with the legislation of any other large city. The fifteen hundred soldiers who lay in pain at the Summitt and Satterlee hospitals a few weeks since, received but few visits from their colored brethren, simply because the rules enforced in these cars would not allow decent colored people to ride; and eight or nine dollars per day, the usual charge for carriage hire, was beyond the means of the masses to pay. Yet we repeat, by the regulations of the City Passenger Railways, not one mother, wife or sister could be admitted, even to see a United States soldier, a relative, although the presence and succor of such mother, wife or sister might save a life. It is well known that through the efforts of the Supervisory Committee of this city, ten or eleven regiments of colored men have been raised for the United States service; and not a few of those men have already won imperishable honor on the battle-field. Nevertheless, thrice the number that has been thus raised for the defence of the country are daily and hourly compelled to endure all the outrages and inconveniences consequent upon rules so severe and inexorable as those which have hitherto governed the roads of Philadelphia.

In conclusion, permit us to express the earnest hope that our efforts will this time meet with a more favorable result than before, and that many weeks or months shall not have passed, ere such change will be made as shall remove the cause of complaint for the future.

Yours respectfully,
William Still,
Isaiah C. Wears,
S. M. Smith,
I. C. Gibbs,
*Committee.*

*The Liberator,* December 23, 1864.

## [d]

### *To the* Philadelphia Press

We, the undersigned, have a sad story to publish by your permission. We have not been drafted, however, but we have had to pass through a more horrible ordeal, as horrid as that may be, and the indelible impressions made upon our minds constrain us to lay our grievances before the enlightened and christianized citizens of Philadelphia. To come to the facts of the case they are as follows. On last Saturday afternoon about 5 o'clock, during a pelting cold rain, we three having an order to attend to in the eastern part of the city, were naturally impressed with the idea that just now, when the impartial draft is making no distinction of color, and when, too, the tax-collectors come to our places of business as readily as to those of white persons, we might be permitted and did enter a car of the Walnut and Chestnut street lines (to avoid the severity of the weather). But scarcely had we reached the threshold ere we were told by the conductor, "You cannot ride in this car." "Why can we not?" one of us asked. "Because you are not allowed," answered the conductor. "You can draft us in the service, and why can we not ride?" "I do not care for that: you have to go out of this car." "We do not mean to go out; you can put us out if you choose. We came from Boston; we could ride in the cars there; we cannot see why we should not ride here," one of us remarked. In the meantime a passenger in an excited manner and with harsh language said: "You know you are not allowed to ride in here." "If we are offensive to the passengers we will get up and go out," we said. "You are offensive to these ladies," he responded, in a rage. The ladies rose, (but two were in the car) and said emphatically, "They are not offensive, but we want no disturbance." At this juncture, the conductor called a policeman, who said, "You must leave the car, or be locked up." "Is it against the law for us to ride in here?" we asked. "It is," said the policeman. "Then we will go out," one of us remarked. Another, not agreeable to this mandate, said, "It is *not* against the law, and you may lock me up." "Then I will take you first," said the officer, grabbing him by the collar roughly. "Do you want assistance?" asked the man who first interfered. "Yes," said the officer. At this moment, a regular assault was made upon us by the opposing party, whose numbers had been swelled from without by those who evidently would rather sustain slavery and prejudice than freedom and justice.

Feeling ourselves, however, to be men and not dogs, one of us determined to suffer risk of personal injury and the lock-up rather than run. He came in for more than a due proportion of blows, as fists and the billy were applied freely to his person, the head not being spared. We confess that in the excitement of the moment, we felt unwilling to endure the outrage without resentment, and at least one of us dealt a few blows in return. But we were overpowered and taken before an alderman. Here insult was, as it were, added to injury, for grave charges were made against us; and we soon found that we should be sent to the lock-up unless bail could be procured. For the time being, our minds were so much absorbed by reflection upon the outrages heaped upon us that we were not in a condition to think of this; hence we were incarcerated, as threatened, and remained so until a friend kindly came and procured our release. These, Mr. Editor, are the simple facts of the case, as they occurred. Without comment, we present them for the consideration of the public.

We try to forget, sir, but we remember that the Democratic cities of New York, Baltimore, Washington, and even New Orleans, do not object to respectable colored persons riding in the cars, while the Republican city of Philadelphia excludes all of her own citizens for color alone.

Miles R. Robinson
James Wallace
R. C. Marshall

Philadelphia *Press*, n.d., in *The Liberator*, March 24, 1865.

## [e]

### *Abraham Lincoln's Funeral*

A committee, consisting of some of the most respectable colored citizens, was appointed to wait on the Committee of Arrangements of the Common Council, to have a place assigned the body which they represented; and after two visits they were compelled to leave the Common Council Committee without an answer, and therefore without any assignment of a place in the procession. Supposing that the Citizens' Committee was an associate, and not a subordinate committee, another committee on behalf of the colored citizens waited on Mr. Moses Taylor this morning, to see if arrangements could not be made for us to join the procession from Union Square, but the Committee was informed by Mr. Taylor that the committee which he represented did not wish to come in conflict with the Common Council, and he gave it as his opinion that the Citizens' Committee was subordinate to that of the Common Council. Mr. Taylor, however, referred the committee waiting on him to a gentleman whom they were unable to see.

The prospect, therefore, is, that every man with a colored face will be refused the much-coveted though melancholy satisfaction of following the corpse of the best public benefactor the country had ever given them . . . The last public words of Mr. Lincoln leave no doubt that had he been consulted, he would have urged, as a dying request, that the representatives of the race which had come to the nation's rescue in the hour of peril, and which he had lifted by the most solemn official acts to the dignity of citizens and defenders of the Union, should be allowed the honor of following his remains to the grave. . . .

*The Liberator*, May 5, 1865.

## [f]

### *Israel Lyceum Petition*

AN APPEAL IN BEHALF OF THE ELECTIVE FRANCHISE TO COLORED PEOPLE OF THE UNITED STATES OF AMERICA.

To the Honorable Senate and House of Representatives:

Gentlemen, Greeting: Prejudice and misinformation have, for a long series of years, been fostered with unremitting assiduity by those interested in upholding the slave system—a party whose corrupt influence has enabled them to gain possession of the public ear, and to abuse public credulity to an extent not generally appreciated in an age otherwise so marked for civilization and improvement. We can only account for the indifference of benevolence manifested towards our race—that they are supposed to be, in reality, destined only for a servile condition, entitled neither to liberty nor the legitimate pursuit of happiness. We do not think that the Almighty has poured the tide of life through our breasts, animating us with a portion of His own spirit; and at the same time struck us off the list of rational beings. Our present purpose is not to enter into a recital of slavery's horrors, but to present a just, judicious, humane and well understood claim.

Amid one of the most foul conspiracies against law and obligation known to the civilized world—a civil war in which slavery attempts to assert her sway over liberty, momentous issues present themselves for human determination. The enemy of man is goaded on to barbarous desperation, to deal death and destruction in its every track. We live, and have a being, and feel a lively interest in all these revolutions of party, principle, prejudice and power. The Government of the United States has called loudly on all of her subjects to rally to her support in this her hour of struggle and trial. The Executive of the nation, your Honorable bodies, respectively each, all have felt their country's call, and each held it to be right and reasonable to use every proper means in their power, or that could be brought into power, to subjugate the rebels in martial array against the Government, and to bring about a permanent peace and settlement of the distracted question—was might to rule over right, or have all men a right to personal liberty, so far as they act in keeping with law and order, and to decide that a human being has rights another human being is bound to respect.

We, the undersigned colored citizens, then, of the United States of America, assert that we regard it to be our duty to act with all who are desirous of putting down the rebellion, "in all ways and means," and under all circumstances, for which we claim at your hands a friendly recognition, and an equal portion of justice, as is meted out to the most favored of our country's subjects. We are thankful for what we now enjoy and receive, or have received, or may receive, tendering our humble thanks to your Honors for discharging your debt of duty towards us so nobly; yet, notwithstanding all this, we claim your especial attention in behalf of the following prayers:

Prayer 1st. That if your Honors believe one of this country's strengths exists with its enlightened citizens, of all classes, that are clearly honest, willing, and patriotic in action, then be it, by the foregoing acknowledgment, understood that all who do thus in concert act, are entitled to all the rights, immunities and privileges accruing thereto.

Prayer 2d. And be it further known, that if your Honors believe, not as a question, but as a fact, that all classes should be liable to the laws of the

land, and for a violation of which all are susceptible to punishment, irrespective of color, class, or clime; then we do hold that any right, any liberty,
any pursuit of happiness otherwise taken from us than for a violation of
such law and order, is a gross violation of justice, a mockery upon our humanity, and a glaring impeachment of an American born person's claim to
enlightened citizenship, and a complete annihilation of all natural human
rights.

Prayer 3d. In conclusion, we . . . ask, in the name of our blood, sweat,
suffering, and constancy to our country, the United States of America, this
thirty-eighth Congress to give the UNCONDITIONAL right of the colored male
citizen to the ballot box, believing, from experience, that in this is the power
and virtue of a free people; that at the ballot box a man confirms his manhood; and defends, supports and preserves his country; and with his right
to vote, have a voice in the weal or woe of his country; and when in the
enjoyment of this right he is a strength and a help, and not until then. We ask
to be clothed with this right, that we may serve our country fully. In the name
of our fathers, brothers, and sons now breathing the red flame of war on the
battle field, in defense of a common country and a common civilization, and
in the name of common justice, and a common God and Father of all men,
having one destiny, we must respectfully ask you to extend to us the sacred
rights and privileges of the elective franchise, in all national and local affairs.
We will ask God, the Father, to watch over and guide you in the right to
universal freedom, in which, and only which, we feel rests the complete
glory of our national pride and renown.

Records of the United States Senate, 38th Cong., 1st Sess., National Archives, Washington.

### [g]

#### Negroes of the District of Columbia

The undersigned Colored Citizens & Tax-payers of the District of Columbia
do respectfully memorialize Your Honorable Body in their behalf to the following effect.

The undersigned would press upon your attention a principle universally
admitted by Americans; namely, that Governments derive their just power
from the consent of the governed. The Colored American Citizens of the Dist.
of Columbia are denied the benefits of this conceded principle in being refused
the right of suffrage in the District, and therefore appeal to you for this
franchise.

They respectfully submit to Your Honorable Body that a large portion of the colored citizens of the District are property holders, that they pay no inconsiderable amount of taxes to the District, but unlike other tax-payers they have no voice in the disposition of the proceeds of their labor.

They are intelligent enough to be free; to be amenable to the same laws and punishable alike with others for infractions of said laws. They sustain as fair a character in the Record of Crime and the Statistics of Pauperism as any other class. They are intelligent enough to be industrious, to have accumulated property, and to build and sustain Churches. They are educating their children without the aid of any school fund, and they have been furnishing—as they thought unjustly—a portion of the means to educate the white children of this District.

The experience of the Past teaches that all reforms have their opponents; but a like experience teaches that apprehensions of evils arising from reforms founded in justice are scarcely if ever realized. The undersigned would offer as an illustration, the just Act of the last Congress, the abolishment of Slavery in the District. The opponents of this measure prophesied the most dire results to the community and to the party whose liberation was proposed. There has been no realization of their predictions of evil; on the contrary, the happy results accruing to all parties from this just measure are now patent, and conceded by all.

Experience likewise teaches that a *complete* debasement is more humane than a partial one. Enjoying what liberty they do makes them the more miserable in contemplating the denial of other just rights.

They have honorable aspirations, they cherish hopes and fond desires in connection with their country, and they ask you respectfully to regard them, to give encouragement to their patriotism.

Their loyalty has never been questioned, their patriotism is unbounded, for in all their Country's trials they have responded voluntarily and with alacrity, *pay or no pay, bounty or no bounty, promotion or no promotion.*

They have in the field two complete regiments of colored men from the District; a third is in course of formation; this too, out of a population according to the Census of 1860, of less than fifteen thousand inhabitants. On the other hand, the white citizens of the District have only one regiment and a battalion out of a population of upwards of sixty thousand.

These principles and considerations are the bases upon which they predicate their claims for suffrage and total affranchisement, and for which they will ever pray.

Records of the U.S. Senate, 38th Cong., 1st Sess., in The National Archives, Washington.

## [h]

### *The Syracuse National Negro Convention*

a) The Call:

Fellow-Citizens: The present state of our country, together with the claims of humanity and universal freedom, and the favorable developments of the Providence of God, pointing to the liberation and enfranchisement of our race, demand of us to be united in council, labor and faith.

The nation and the age have adjudged that the extinction of slavery is necessary to the preservation of liberty and republicanism, and that the existence of the Government itself is contingent upon the total overthrow of the slaveholders' oligarchy and the annihilation of the despotism which is inseparably connected with it.

Brethren, the present time is immeasurably more favorable than any other period in our history to unite and act for our own most vital interests. If we are to live and grow, and prove ourselves to be equal to the exigencies of the times, we must meet in council, and labor together for the general welfare of the people. Sound morality must be encouraged; education must be promoted; temperance and frugality must be exemplified, and industry, and thrift, and everything that pertains to well-ordered and dignified life, must be exhibited to the nation and the world. Therefore, the strong men of our people, the faithful and the true, are invited to meet in a National Convention, for the advancement of these objects and principles, on Tuesday, the 4th day of October, A.D. 1864, at 7 o'clock, P.M. in the city of New York [sic]. The progressive and liberty-loving people of the loyal States are invited to send delegates, properly and regularly chosen. Let them come from the cities, towns, hamlets and districts of every section of the country, and lay the foundation of a super-structure, broad and deep, which in the future shall be a stronghold and defence for ourselves and our posterity.

*The Liberator*, September 9, 1864.

b) The Resolutions:

1. Resolved, That a petition be sent to the Congress of the United States, in the name of this Convention, asking them respectfully, but most earnestly, to use every honorable endeavor that they may, to have the rights of the country's colored patriots now in the field respected, without regard to their complexion; and that our Government cease to set an example to rebels, in arms against it, by making invidious distinctions, based upon color, as to pay, labor, and promotion.

2. Resolved, That the unquestioned patriotism and loyalty of the colored men in the United States—as shown in the alacrity with which, shutting their eyes to the past, and looking steadfastly to the future, at the call of the country, without pay, without bounty, without prospect of promotion, without the protection of the Government, they have rallied to the defence of "Liberty and Union"—vindicate our manhood, command our respect, and claim the attention and admiration of the civilized world.

3. Resolved, That we hereby assert our full confidence in the fundamental principles of this Government, the force of acknowledged American ideas, the Christian spirit of the age, and the justice of our cause; and we believe that the generosity and sense of honor inherent in the great heart of this nation will ultimately concede us our just claims, accord us our rights, and grant us our full measure of citizenship, under the broad shield of the Constitution.

4. Resolved, That, should an attempt be made to reconstruct the Union with slavery, we should regard such a course as a flagrant violation of good faith on the part of the Government, false to the brave colored men who have fallen in its defence, unjust to the living who are perilling their lives for its protection, and to be resisted by the whole moral power of the civilized world.

5. Resolved, That we extend the right hand of fellowship to the freedmen of the South, and express to them our warmest sympathy, and our deep concern for their welfare, prosperity, and happiness; and desire to exhort them to shape their course toward frugality, the accumulation of property, and, above all, to leave untried no amount of effort and self-denial to acquire knowledge, and to secure a vigorous moral and religious growth. We desire, further, to assure them of our co-operation and assistance; and that our efforts in their behalf shall be given without measure, and be limited only by our capacity to give, work and act.

6. Resolved, That we recommend to colored men from all sections of the country to settle, as far as they can, on the public lands.

7. Resolved, That, as Congress has exclusive control over the elective franchise in the District of Columbia, we earnestly pray that body to extend the right of suffrage to the colored citizens of said District.

8. Resolved, That the President of the United States, his Cabinet, and the Thirty-seventh Congress, are hereby tendered our warmest and most grateful thanks,—

For revoking the prohibitory law in regard to colored people carrying the mails;

For abolishing slavery in the District of Columbia;

For recognizing the National Independence of Liberia and Hayti;

For Military Order 252, retaliating for the unmilitary and barbarous treatment of the colored soldiers of the Union army by the rebels.

The Convention further tenders its thanks to Senator Sumner, for his noble efforts to cleanse the statute-books of the nation from every stain of inequality against colored men.

And also to Gen. Butler, for the course he has taken in suggesting a way for lifting the slaves first to the condition of contrabands, and then to the position of freedmen.

And to all other noble workers, both in our legislative halls and elsewhere, who have contributed to bring about the improved state in which, as colored men, we find ourselves to-day.

9. Resolved, That we witness, with the most grateful emotions, the generous and very successful efforts that have been made, and are still in operation, by the "National Freedmen's Relief Association," the "American Missionary Society," the "African Civilization Society," and their auxiliary and kindred bodies, for the mental and moral instruction, and the domestic improvement, of the colored people in our Southern States, who have hitherto been the victims of that impious slaveholding oligarchy, that is now in open rebellion against our American Republic . . .

10. Resolved, That we view with pride, and heartily indorse, the efforts of the gentlemen composing the faculties and executive boards of the "Institute for Colored Youth" at Philadelphia; the "Avery College" at Alleghany City, Penn.; the "Wilberforce University" at Xenia, O.; and the "Albany Enterprise Academy" at Albany, O., to develop the intellectual powers of our youth, and for opening a field for the honorable employment of those powers.

11. Resolved, That we are indebted to the publishers of the *Anglo-African, Christian Recorder,* and *Colored Citizen,* for the manifestation of intellectual energy and business tact which they have shown to the American people by the publication of those journals; the contents of which are complimentary to the heads and hearts of their conductors, and the people whom they represent.

The official *Proceedings* of the Convention, published in Syracuse in 1864, a copy of which is in the library of Dr. W. E. B. Du Bois. The remaining items from this convention are from the same source.

c) Declaration of wrongs and rights:

1st. As a branch of the human family, we have for long ages been deeply and cruelly wronged by people whose might constituted their right; we have been subdued, not by the power of ideas, but by brute force, and have been unjustly deprived not only of many of our natural rights, but debarred the privileges and advantages freely accorded to other men.

2d. We have been made to suffer well-nigh every cruelty and indignity possible to be heaped upon human beings; and for no fault of our own.

3d. We have been taunted with our inferiority by people whose statute-books contained laws inflicting the severest penalties on whomsoever dared teach us the art of reading God's word; we have been denounced as incurably ignorant, and, at the same time, have been, by stern enactments, debarred from taking even the first step toward self-enlightenment and personal and national elevation; we have been declared incapable of self-government by those who refused us the right of experiment in that direction, and we have been denounced as cowards by men who refused at first to trust us with a musket on the battle-field.

4th. As a people, we have been denied the ownership of our bodies, our wives, homes, children, and the products of our own labor; we have been compelled, under pain of death, to submit to wrongs deeper and darker than the earth ever witnessed in the case of any other people; we have been forced to silence and inaction in full presence of the infernal spectacle of our sons groaning under the lash, our daughters ravished, our wives violated, and our firesides desolated, while we ourselves have been led to the shambles and sold like beasts of the field.

5th. When the nation in her trial hour called her sable sons to arms, we gladly went to fight her battles: but were denied the pay accorded to others, until public opinion demanded it; and then it was tardily granted. We have fought and conquered, but have been denied the laurels of victory. We have fought where victory gave us no glory, and where captivity meant cool murder on the field, by fire, sword, and halter; and yet no black man ever flinched.

6th. We are taxed, but denied the right of representation. We are practically debarred the right of trial by jury; and institutions of learning which we help to support are closed against us.

We submit to the American people and world the following Declaration of our Rights, asking a calm consideration thereof:

1st. We declare that all men are born free and equal; that no man or government has a right to annul, repeal, abrogate, contravene, or render inoperative, this fundamental principle, except it be for crime; therefore we demand the immediate and unconditional abolition of slavery.

2d. That, as natives of American soil, we claim the right to remain upon it: and that any attempt to deport, remove, expatriate, or colonize us to any other land, or to mass us here against our will, is unjust; for here were we born, for this country our fathers and our brothers have fought and here we hope to remain in the full enjoyment of enfranchised manhood, and its dignities.

3d. That, as citizens of the Republic, we claim the rights of other citizens. We claim that we are, by right, entitled to respect; that due attention should be given to our needs; that proper rewards should be given for our services, and that the immunities and privileges of all other citizens and defenders of the nation's honor should be conceded to us. We claim the right to be heard in the halls of Congress; and we claim our fair share of the public domain, whether acquired by purchase, treaty, confiscation, or military conquest.

4th. That, emerging as we are from the long night of gloom and sorrow, we are entitled to, and claim, the sympathy and aid of the entire Christian world; and we invoke the considerate aid of mankind in this crisis of our history, and in this hour of sacrifice, suffering, and trial.

Those are our wrongs; these a portion of what we deem to be our rights as men, as patriots, as citizens, and as children of the common Father. To realize and attain these rights, and their practical recognition, is our purpose. We confide our cause to the just God, whose benign aid we solemnly invoke. To him we appeal.

d) Address to the People of the United States:

. . . In surveying our possible future, so full of interest at this moment, since it may bring to us all the blessings of equal liberty, or all the woes of slavery and continued social degradation, you will not blame us if we manifest anxiety in regard to the position of our recognized friends, as well as that of our open and declared enemies; for our cause may suffer even more from the injudicious concessions and weakness of our friends, than from the machinations and power of our enemies. The weakness of our friends is strength to our foes. When the *Anti-Slavery Standard*, representing the American Anti-Slavery Society, denies that that society asks for the enfranchisement of colored men, and the *Liberator* apologizes for excluding the colored men of Louisiana from the ballot-box, they injure us more vitally than all the ribald jests of the whole proslavery press.

Again: had, for instance, the present Administration, at the beginning of the war, boldly planted itself upon the doctrine of human equality as taught in the Declaration of Independence; proclaimed liberty to all the slaves in all the Slave States; armed every colored man, previously a slave or a freeman, who would or could fight under the loyal flag; recognized black men as soldiers of the Republic; avenged the first act of violence upon colored prisoners, in contravention of the laws of war; sided with the radical emancipation party in Maryland and Missouri; stood by its antislavery generals, instead of casting them aside,—history would never have had to record the scandalous platform adopted at Chicago, nor the immeasurable horrors of Fort Pillow.* The weakness and hesitation of our friends, where promptness and vigor were required, have invited the contempt and rigor of our enemies. Seeing, that, while periling every thing for the protection and security of our country, our country did not think itself bound to protect and secure us, the rebels felt a license to treat us as outlaws. Seeing that our Government did not treat us as men, they did not feel bound to treat us as soldiers. It is, therefore, not the malignity of enemies alone we have to fear, but the deflection from the straight line of principle by those who are known throughout the world as our special friends. We may survive the arrows of the known Negro-haters of our country; but woe to the colored race when their champions fail to demand, from any reason, equal liberty in every respect!

We have spoken of the existence of powerful reactionary forces arrayed against us, and of the objects to which they tend. What are these mighty forces? and through what agencies do they operate and reach us? They are many; but we shall detain by no tedious enumeration. The first and most powerful is slavery; and the second, which may be said to be the shadow of slavery, is prejudice against men on account of their color. The one controls the South, and the other controls the North. Both are original sources of power, and generate peculiar sentiments, ideas, and laws concerning us.

The agents of these two evil influences are various: but the chief are, first the Democratic party; and, second, the Republican party. The Democratic party belongs to slavery; and the Republican party is largely under the power of prejudice against color. While gratefully recognizing a vast difference in our favor in the character and composition of the Republican party, and regarding the accession to power of the Democratic party as the heaviest calamity that could befall us in the present juncture of affairs, it cannot be disguised, that, while that party is our bitterest enemy, and is positively and actively reactionary, the Republican party is negatively and passively so in its tendency. What we have to fear from these two parties,— looking to the future, and especially to the settlement of our present national troubles,—is, alas! only too obvious. The intentions, principles, and policy of both organizations, through their platforms, and the antecedents and the recorded utterances of the men who stand upon their respective plat-

---

* On April 12, 1864, the Union garrison of 600 men at Fort Pillow, Tenn.—about half Negro and half white (the white men being members of the 13th Tennessee Cavalry)— was forced to surrender to 6,000 men under the command of Major-General Nathan Bedford Forrest. The troops under Forrest—a Memphis real-estate dealer, slave-trader and cotton-planter of particular ferocity—massacred, after surrender, about 300 Negro troops, some of them wounded, several Negro women and children in the Fort, and some of the Union white troops.

forms, teach us what to expect at their hands, and what kind of a future they are carving out for us, and for the country which they propose to govern.

Without using the word "slavery," or "slaves," or "slaveholders," the Democratic party has none the less declared, in its platform, its purpose to be the endless perpetuation of slavery. Under the apparently harmless verbiage, "private rights," "basis of the Federal Union," and under the language employed in denouncing the Federal Administration for "disregarding the Constitution in every part," "pretence of military necessity," we see the purpose of the Democratic party to restore slavery to all its ancient power, and to make this Government just what it was before the rebellion,— simply an instrument of the slave-power. "The basis of the Federal Union" only means the alleged compromises and stipulations, as interpreted by Judge Taney, by which black men are supposed to have no rights which white men are bound to respect; and by which the whole Northern people are bound to protect the cruel masters against the justly deserved violence of the slave, and to do the fiendish work of hell-hounds when slaves make their escape from thraldom. The candidates of that party take their stand upon its platform; and will, if elected,—which Heaven forbid!—carry it out to the letter. From this party we must look only for fierce, malignant, and unmitigated hostility. Our continued oppression and degradation is the law of its life, and its sure passport to power. In the ranks of the Democratic party, all the worst elements of American society fraternize; and we need not expect a single voice from that quarter for justice, mercy, or even decency. To it we are nothing; the slave-holders every thing. We have but to consult its press to know that it would willingly enslave the free colored people in the South; and also that it would gladly stir up against us mob-violence at the North,—re-enacting the sanguinary scenes of one year ago in New York and other large cities. We therefore pray, that whatever wrath, curse, or calamity, the future may have in store for us, the accession of the Democratic party to the reins of power may not be one of them; for this to us would comprise the sum of all social woes.

How stands the case with the great Republican party in question? We have already alluded to it as being largely under the influence of the prevailing contempt for the character and rights of the colored race. This is seen by the slowness of our Government to employ the strong arm of the black man in the work of putting down the rebellion: and in its unwillingness, after thus employing him, to invest him with the same incitements to deeds of daring, as white soldiers; neither giving him the same pay, rations, and protection, nor any hope of rising in the service by meritorious conduct. It is also seen in the fact, that in neither of the plans emanating from this party for reconstructing the institutions of the Southern States, are colored men, not even those who had fought for the country, recognized as having any political existence or rights whatever.

Even in the matter of the abolition of slavery . . . there is still room for painful doubt and apprehension. It is very evident, that the Republican party, though a party composed of the best men of the country, is not prepared to make the abolition of slavery, in all the Rebel States, a consideration precedent to the re-establishment of the Union. However antislavery in sentiment the President may be, and however disposed he may be to continue the war till slavery is abolished, it is plain that in this he would not be sustained by his party. A single reverse to our arms, in such a war, would raise the hands of the party in opposition to their chief. The hope of the speedy and complete abolition of slavery, hangs, therefore, not upon the disposition of the Republican party, not upon the disposition of President Lincoln; but upon the slender thread of Rebel power, pride, and persistence. In returning to the Union, slavery has a fair chance to live; out of the Union, it has a still better chance to live; but, fighting against the Union, it has no chance for anything but destruction. Thus the freedom of our race and the welfare of our country tremble together in the balance of events.

This somewhat gloomy view of the condition of affairs—which to the enthusiastic, who have already convinced themselves that slavery is dead, may not only seem gloomy, but untruthful—is nevertheless amply supported, not only by the well-known sentiment of the country, the controlling pressure of which is seriously felt by the Administration; but it is sustained by the many attempts lately made by the Republican press to explain away the natural import of the President's recent address "To Whom it may concern," in which he makes the abolition of Slavery a primary condition to the restoration of the Union; and especially is this gloomy view supported by the remarkable speech delivered only a few weeks ago at Auburn, by Hon. William H. Seward, Secretary of State. Standing next to the President in the administration of the government, and fully in the confidence of the Chief Magistrate, no member of the National Cabinet is better qualified than Mr. Seward to utter the mind and policy of the Administration upon this momentous subject, when it shall come up at the close of the war. Just what it will do in the matter of slavery, Mr. Seward says,—

"When the insurgents shall have disbanded their armies, and laid down their arms, the war will instantly cease; and all the war measures then existing, including those which affect slavery, will cease also; and all the moral, economical, and political questions, as well affecting slavery as others, which shall then be existing between individuals and States and the Federal Government, whether they arose before the civil war began, or whether they grew out of it, will, by force of the Constitution, pass over to the arbitrament of courts of law, and the counsels of legislation."

These, fellow-citizens, are studied words, full of solemn and fearful import. They mean that our Republican Administration is not only ready to make peace with the Rebels, but to make peace with slavery also; that all executive and legislative action launched against the slave-system, whether of proclamation or confiscation, will cease the instant the Rebels shall disband their armies, and lay down their arms. The hope that the war will put an end to slavery, has, according to this exposition, only one foundation; and that is, that the courts and Congress will so decree. But what ground have we here? Congress has already spoken, and has refused to alter the Constitution so as to abolish slavery. The Supreme Court has yet to speak; but what it will say, if this question shall come before it, is very easily divined. We will not assert positively what it will say; but indications of its judgment are clearly against us. What then have we? Only this, as our surest and best ground of hope; namely, that the Rebels, in their madness, will continue to make war upon the Government, until they shall not only become destitute of men, money, and the munitions of war, but utterly divested of their slaves also. . . .

Do you, then, ask us to state, in plain terms, just what we want of you, and just what we think we ought to receive at your hands? We answer: First of all, the complete abolition of the slavery of our race in the United States. We shall not stop to argue. We feel the terrible sting of this stupendous wrong, and that we cannot be free while our brothers are slaves. The enslavement of a vast majority of our people extends its baleful influence over every member of our race; and makes freedom, even to the free, a mockery and a delusion: we therefore, in our own name, and in the name of the whipped and branded millions, whose silent suffering has pleaded to the humane sentiment of mankind, but in vain, during more than two hundred years for deliverance, we implore you to abolish slavery. In the name of your country, torn, distracted, bleeding, and while you are weeping over the bloody graves of more than two hundred thousand of your noblest sons, many of whom have been cut down, in the midst of youthful vigor and beauty, we implore you to abolish slavery. In the name of peace, which experience has shown cannot be other than false and delusive while the rebellious spirit of Slavery has an existence in the land, we implore you to abolish slavery. In the name of universal justice, to whose laws great States not less than individuals are bound to conform, and the terrible consequences of whose violation are as fixed and certain as the universe itself, we implore you to abolish slavery; and thus place your peace and national welfare upon immutable and everlasting foundations.

Why would you let slavery continue? What good thing has it done, what evil thing has it left undone, that you should allow it to survive this dreadful war, the natural fruit of its existence? Can you want a second war from the same cause? Are you so rich in men, money, and material, that you must provide for future depletion? Or do you hope, to escape the consequences of wrong-doing? Can you expect any better results from compromises in the future, than from compromises with slavery in the past? If the South fights desperately and savagely to-day for the possession of four millions of slaves, will she fight less savagely and desperately when the prize for which she fights shall become eight instead of four millions? and when her ability to war upon freedom and free institutions shall have increased twofold?

Do you answer, that you have no longer anything to fear? that slavery has already received its death-blow? that it can only have a transient existence, even if permitted to live after the termination of the war? We answer, So thought your Revolutionary fathers when they framed the Federal Constitution; and to-day, the bloody fruits of their mistake are all around us. Shall we avoid or shall we repeat their stupendous error?

Be not deceived. Slavery is still the vital and animating breath of Southern society. The men who have fought for it on the battle-field will not love it less for having shed their blood in its defence. Once let them get Slavery safely under the protection of the Federal Government, and ally themselves, as they will be sure to do, to the Democratic party of the North; let Jefferson Davis and his Confederate associates, either in person or by their representatives, return once more to their seats in the halls of Congress,— and you will then see your dead slavery the most living and powerful thing in the country. To make peace, therefore, on such a basis as shall admit slavery back again in the Union, would only be sowing the seeds of war; sure to bring at last a bitter harvest of blood! The sun in the heavens at noonday is not more manifest, than the fact that slavery is the prolific source of war and division among you; and that its abolition is essential to your national peace and unity. Once more, then, we entreat you—for you have the power—to put away this monstrous abomination. You have repeatedly during this wanton slaveholding and wicked Rebellion, in the darkest hours of the struggle, appealed to the Supreme Ruler of the universe to smile upon your armies, and give them victory: surely you will not stain now your souls with the crime of ingratitude by making a wicked compact and a deceitful peace with your enemies. You have called mankind to witness that the struggle on your part was not for empire merely; that the charge that it was such was a gross slander: will you now make a peace which will justify what you have repeatedly denounced as a calumny? Your antislavery professions have drawn to you the sympathy of liberal and generous minded men throughout the world, and have restrained all Europe from recognizing the Southern Confederacy, and breaking up your blockade of Southern ports. Will you now proclaim your own baseness and hypocrisy by making a peace which shall give the lie to all such professions? You have over and over again, and very justly, branded slavery as the inciting cause of this Rebellion; denounced it as the fruitful source of pride and selfishness and mad ambition; you have blushed before all Europe for its existence among you; and have shielded yourselves from the execrations of mankind, by denying your constitutional ability to interfere with it. Will you now, when the evil in question has placed itself within your constitutional grasp, and invited its own destruction by its persistent attempts to destroy the Government, relax your grasp, release your hold, and to the disappointment of the slaves deceived by your proclamations, to the sacrifice of the Union white men of the South who have sided with you in this contest with slavery, and to the dishonor of yourselves and the amazement of mankind, give new and stronger lease of life to slavery? We will not and cannot believe it.

There is still one other subject, fellow-citizens,—one other want,—looking to the peace and welfare of our common country, as well as to the interests of our race; and that is, political equality. We want the elective franchise in all the States now in the Union, and the same in all such States as may come into the Union hereafter. We believe that the highest welfare of this great country will be found in erasing from its statute-books all enactments discriminating in favor or against any class of its people, and by establishing one law for the white and colored people alike. Whatever prejudice and taste may be innocently allowed to do or to dictate in social and domestic relations, it is plain, that in the matter of government, the object of which is the protection and security of human rights, prejudice should be allowed no voice whatever. In this department of human relations, no notice should be taken of the color of men; but justice, wisdom, and humanity should weigh alone, and be all-controlling.

Formerly our petitions for the elective franchise were met and denied upon the ground, that, while colored men were protected in person and property, they were not required to perform military duty. Of course this was only a plausible excuse; for we were subject to any call the Government was pleased to make upon us, and we could not properly be made to suffer because the Government did not see fit to impose military duty upon us. The fault was with the Government, not with us.

But now even this frivolous though somewhat decent apology for excluding us from the ballot-box is entirely swept away. Two hundred thousand colored men, according to a recent statement of President Lincoln, are now in the service, upon field and flood, in the army and the navy of the United States; and every day adds to their number. They are there as volunteers, coming forward with other patriotic men at the call of their imperilled country; they are there also as substitutes filling up the quotas which would otherwise have to be filled up by white men who now remain at home; they are also there as drafted men, by a certain law of Congress, which, for once, makes no difference on account of color: and whether they are there as volunteers, as substitutes, or as drafted men, neither ourselves, our cause, nor our country, need be ashamed of their appearance or their action upon the battle-field. Friends and enemies, rebels and loyal men,—each, after their kind,— have borne conscious and unconscious testimony to the gallantry and other noble qualities of the colored troops.

Your fathers laid down the principle, long ago, that universal suffrage is the best foundation of Government. We believe as your fathers believed, and as they practised; for, in eleven States out of the original thirteen, colored men exercised the right to vote at the time of the adoption of the Federal Constitution. The Divine-right Governments of Europe, with their aristo-cratic and privileged classes of priests and nobles, are little better than cunningly devised conspiracies against the natural rights of the people to govern themselves.

Whether the right to vote is a natural right or not, we are not here to determine. Natural or conventional, in either case we are amply supported in our appeal for its extension to us. If it is, as all the teachings of your Declaration of Independence imply, a natural right, to deny to us its exercise is a wrong done to our human nature. If, on the other hand, the right to vote is simply a conventional right, having no other foundation or significance than a mere conventional arrangement, which may be extended or contracted, given or taken away, upon reasonable grounds, we insist, that, even basing the right upon this uncertain foundation, we may reasonably claim a right to a voice in the election of the men who are to have at their command our time, our services, our property, our persons, and our lives. This command of our persons and lives is no longer theory, but now the positive practice of our Government. We say, therefore, that having required, demanded, and in some instances compelled, us to serve with our time, our property, and our lives, coupling us in all the obligations and duties imposed upon the more highly favored of our fellow-citizens in this war to protect and defend your country from threatened destruction, and having fully established the precedent by which, in all similar and dissimilar cases of need, we may be compelled to respond to a like requisition,—we claim to have fully earned the elective franchise; and that you, the American people, have virtually contracted an obligation to grant it, which has all the sanctions of justice, honor, and magnanimity, in favor of its prompt fulfilment. Are we good enough to use bullets, and not good enough to use ballots? May we defend rights in time of war, and yet be denied the exercise of those rights in time of peace? Are we citizens when the nation is in peril, and aliens when the nation is in safety? May we shed our blood under the star-spangled banner on the battle-field, and yet be debarred from marching under it to the ballot-box? Will the brave white soldiers, bronzed by the hardships and exposures of repeated campaigns, men who have fought by the side of black men, be ashamed to cast their ballots by the side of their companions-in-arms? May we give our lives, but not our votes, for the good of the republic? Shall we toil with you to win the prize of free government, while you alone shall monopolize all its valued privileges? Against such a conclusion, every sentiment of honor and manly fraternity utters an indignant protest. . . .

But, again, why are we so urgent for the possession of this particular right? We are asked, even by some Abolitionists, why we cannot be satisfied, for the present at least, with personal freedom; the right to testify in courts of law; the right to own, buy, and sell real estate; the right to sue and be sued. We answer, Because in a republican country, where general suffrage is the rule, personal liberty, the right to testify in courts of law, the right to hold, buy, and sell property, and all other rights, become mere privileges, held at the option of others, where we are excepted from the general political liberty. What gives to the newly arrived emigrants, fresh from lands governed by kingcraft and priestcraft, special consequence in the eyes of the American people? It is not their virtue, for they are often depraved; it is not their knowledge, for they are often ignorant; it is not their wealth, for they are often very poor: why, then, are they courted by the leaders of all parties? The answer is, that our institutions clothe them with the elective franchise, and they have a voice in making the laws of the country. Give the colored men of this country the elective franchise, and you will see no violent mobs driving the black laborer from the wharves of large cities, and from the toil elsewhere by which he honestly gains his bread. You will see no influential priest, like the late Bishop Hughes, addressing mobocrats and murderers as "gentlemen"; and no influential politician, like Governor Seymour, addressing the "misguided" rowdies of New York [in 1863] as his "friends." The possession of that right is the keystone to the arch of human liberty: and, without that, the whole may at any moment fall to the ground; while, with it, that liberty may stand forever,—a blessing to us, and no possible injury to you. If you still ask why we want to vote, we answer, Because we don't want to be mobbed from our work, or insulted with impunity at every corner. We are men, and want to be as free in our native country as other men.

Fellow-citizens, let us entreat you, have faith in your own principles. If freedom is good for any, it is good for all. If you need the elective franchise, we need it even more. You are strong, we are weak; you are many, we are few; you are protected, we are exposed. Clothe us with this safeguard of our liberty, and give us an interest in the country to which, in common with you, we have given our lives and poured out our best blood. You cannot need special protection. Our degradation is not essential to your elevation, nor our peril essential to your safety. You are not likely to be outstripped in the race of improvement by persons of African descent; and hence you have no need of superior advantages, nor to burden them with disabilities of any kind. Let your Government be what all governments should be,—a copy of the eternal laws of the universe; before which all men stand equal as to rewards and punishments, life and death, without regard to country, kindred, tongue, or people.

But what we have now said, in appeal for the elective franchise, applies to our people generally. A special reason may be urged in favor of granting colored men the right in all the rebellious States.

Whatever may be the case with monarchial governments; however they may despise the crowd, and rely upon their prestige, armaments, and standing armies, to support them,—a republican government like ours depends largely upon the friendship of the people over whom it is established, for its harmonious and happy operation. This kind of government must have its foundation in the affections of the people: otherwise the people will hinder, circumvent, and destroy it. Up to a few years of the rebellion, our government lived in the friendship of the masses of the Southern people. Its enemies were, however, numerous and active; and these at last prevailed, poisoned the minds of the masses, broke up the government, brought on the war. Now, whoever lives to see this rebellion suppressed at the South, as we believe we all shall, will also see the South characterized by a sullen hatred towards the National Government. It will be transmitted from father to son, and will be held by them "as sacred animosity." The treason, mowed down by the armies of Grant and Sherman, will be followed by a strong undergrowth of treason which will go far to disturb the peaceful operation of the hated Government.

Every United States mail-carrier, every custom-house officer, every Northern man, and every representative of the United States Government, in the Southern States, will be held in abhorrence; and for a long time that country is to be governed with difficulty. We may conquer Southern armies by the sword; but it is another thing to conquer Southern hate. Now what is the natural counterpoise against this Southern malign hostility? This it is: give the elective franchise to every colored man of the South who is of sane mind, and has arrived at the age of twenty-one years, and you have at once four millions of friends who will guard with their vigilance, and, if need be, defend with their arms, the ark of Federal Liberty from the treason and pollution of her enemies. You are sure of the enmity of the masters,—make sure of the friendship of the slaves; for, depend upon it, your Government cannot afford to encounter the enmity of both.

If the arguments addressed to your sense of honor, in these pages, in favor of extending the elective franchise to the colored people of whole country, be strong, that which we are prepared to present to you in behalf of the colored people of rebellious States can be made tenfold stronger. By calling them to take part with you in the war to subdue their rebellious masters, and the fact that thousands of them have done so, and thousands more would gladly do so, you have exposed them to special resentment and wrath; which, without the elective franchise, will descend upon them in unmitigated fury. To break with your friends, and make peace with your enemies; to weaken your friends, and strengthen your enemies; to abase your friends, and exalt your enemies; to disarm your friends, and arm your enemies; to disfranchise your loyal friends and enfranchise your disloyal enemies,—is not the policy of honor, but of infamy.

But we will not weary you. Our cause is in some measure before you. The power to redress our wrongs, and to grant us our just rights, is in your hands. You can determine our destiny,—blast us by continued degradation, or bless us with the means of gradual elevation. We are among you, and must remain among you; and it is for you to say, whether our presence shall conduce to the general peace and welfare of the country, or be a constant cause of discussion and of irritation,—troubles in the State, troubles in the Church, troubles everywhere.

To avert these troubles, and to place your great country in safety from them, only one word from you, the American people, is needed, and that is JUSTICE: let that magic word once be sounded, and become all-controlling in all your courts of law, subordinate and supreme; let the halls of legislation, state and national, spurn all statesmanship as mischievous and ruinous that has not justice for its foundation; let justice without compromise, without curtailment, and without partiality, be observed with respect to all men, no class of men claiming for themselves any right which they will not grant to another,—then strife and discord will cease; peace will be placed upon enduring foundations; and the American people, now divided and hostile, will dwell together in power and unity.

e) From the Constitution of the National Equal Rights League:

Whereas, The purposes entertained by the callers of this Convention, and those who have responded to that call, can be best promoted by a close union of all interested in the principles of justice and right sought to be established; therefore, be it—

Resolved, That we proceed to organize an association, to be called the National Equal-Rights League, with auxiliaries and subordinate associations in the different States.

Resolved, That, in the establishment of the Colored Men's National League, we do not seek to disorganize or in any way interfere with any existing society or institution of a benevolent or other character; but, believing that the interests of colored men generally will be best subserved and advanced by a union of all energies and the use of all our means in a given direction, we therefore invite the co-operation of such societies in the advancement of the objects of the League.

SECTION 1. The objects of this League are to encourage sound morality, education, temperance, frugality, industry, and promote every thing that pertains to a well-ordered and dignified life; to obtain by appeals to the minds and conscience of the American people, or by legal process when possible, a recognition of the rights of the colored people of the nation as American citizens. . . .

[i]

*Appeal from Executive Board National Equal Rights League*

*To the Colored People of the United States:*

In our late National Convention, held in Syracuse, N.Y., we formed a National Equal Rights League. The objects to be accomplished through the League are set forth in the first section of its Constitution . . . These objects, as well as the mode of their attainment and the advantageous results which must follow, are worthy most certainly of your serious attention and consideration. The mode of achieving these objects, as recommended by our National Convention, is two-fold.

We have the National Equal Rights League, with its officers and Executive Board. The province and work of this branch of our organization are altogether national. Its jurisdiction is commensurate with and bounded only by the limits of our country. The language of the 5th section of the Constitution, in defining the duties of the Executive Board, is: "They (the Executive Board) shall hire an agent or agents who shall visit the different States of the nation, accessible to them, and call the people of the States together in Convention or otherwise, and urge them to take the steps necessary to secure the rights and improvements for the attainment of which this League is formed." The other branch of our organization is the State Leagues auxiliary to the National League, together with their subordinate organizations. In regard to these, the 7th section of the Constitution contains the following words: "Persons in the different States friendly to the purposes of this League, (the National,) may form State Leagues auxiliary to this, with such subordinate organizations as they may deem proper, provided that no distinction on account of color or sex shall be permitted in such auxiliaries or subordinate organizations. Such leagues may at their discretion employ agents, and issue such documents as they may deem conducive to the ends for which this League is formed. They shall collect and pay into the treasury of the National Equal Rights League such sums as may be assessed upon them by vote of the majority at the annual meeting and shall co-operate with that Association in all movements which it shall inaugurate for the accomplishment of the purposes for which it was formed."

Thus it will be seen that the two great branches of our national organizations are the National League of the State Leagues, together with their subordinate organizations auxiliary thereto.

The life and power of the national branch of our organization depend upon the formation of State Leagues, while the State branch depends upon the inclination, the purpose, and the action of the people in the various States.

To you, then, the people of the country, belong the duty and responsibility of carrying forward on its errand of justice, humanity and freedom the great national enterprise, inaugurated at our late National Convention.

Shall the National Equal Rights League be sustained?

Shall we labor, concentrating our influence and our means in this organization to achieve the objects and purposes which it contemplates? All will agree that we need such an organization among us. All must acknowledge the importance and necessity of doing all in our power, by united and persistent action, to obtain a full recognition of our rights as American citizens. And all must admit that this, more than all other periods in our history, is the time to enter upon some well defined, energetic and manly course of action looking to the attainment of a full recognition by the General and State governments of equality for us before American law.

To-day two hundred thousand choice colored men are clothed in the uniform of the American Union; and already by the brave and gallant use of the musket and sword on many bloody battle-fields, have they challenged the admiration of mankind as they have fought side by side with their white fellow countrymen, to maintain the integrity of the Union and the authority of the government.

While the devotion, the gallantry, and the heroism displayed by our sons, brothers, and fathers at Port Hudson, Fort Wagner, Petersburg, New Market Heights are fresh in the minds of the American people, let us spare no pains, let us not fail to make every effort in our power to secure for ourselves and our children all those rights, natural and political, which belong to us as men and as native-born citizens of America. This we owe to ourselves—certainly, we owe it to our children. Let not theirs be an inheritance of degradation. And who shall say that we do not owe it to the noble men who represent us in the American army and navy? Shall they return, after weary months and years of laborious service, as soldiers and sailors, bearing the scars of hard-earned victories, to tread again the old ways of degradation and wrong! It must not be.

It may not be amiss, in this connection, to remind you that our fathers were not behind other men in the Revolutionary war and the war of 1812, in exhibitions of patriotism and courage in the defence of this country. . . .

It is true that these men and their descendants, if for no other reason, certainly on account of the gallantry, the courage, and the loyalty displayed by them, deserved not only the grateful acknowledgement of the nation, but a full and practical recognition of their rights.

But we know too well by our bitter experience of wrong and degradation, how they were treated after those wars. Wisdom, then, dictates that we should profit by this lesson.

When this our present war shall have ended, it will be our duty to see to it that we have indeed a standing place under American law.

Let us, therefore, proceed at once to call State Conventions and form State Leagues, and with vigor and purpose enter upon the work of accomplishing the objects of our National League. Let our friends and brothers of the Atlantic States vie with those of the far off West in this glorious work. Let New York, Pennsylvania, Ohio, Illinois, Indiana, and Michigan lead the way in the prompt and energetic formation of State Leagues, through which we may bring to bear upon the people and legislatures of those States, by appeal and argument and memorial, our united and earnest protest against a further continuance of legislative proscription founded on color.

*The Liberator*, December 23, 1864.

### [j]

#### *Resolutions Adopted by the Ohio Convention*

1. *Resolved,* That we are in favor of our Government and the Union, against all enemies, at home or abroad, that our fathers fought to establish, and we will fight to maintain them; that we will not hesitate in the prompt performance of our duty to the nation in this, its dreadful hour of peril, but will prove with our blood that we deserve to be treated as American citizens.

2. *Resolved,* That in the opinion of this Convention the day is near at

hand, when that unmitigated horror, that crime against God and humanity, that sum of all villainies, that hell-born, heaven-defying institution, American slavery, hated of men everywhere, will cease to exist in the United States.

3. *Resolved,* That we hail the event with joy and thanksgiving, as turning a bright page in the history of progressive civilization; a triumph of just principles, a practical assertion of the fundamental truths laid down in the great charter of Republican liberty, the Declaration of Independence.

4. *Resolved,* That while we rejoice in its overthrow as a system, there are serious reasons to fear that we will, in another form, remain its victims so long as we are helpless subjects of arbitrary legislation; and having been pronounced citizens by the judicial advisers of the Government; having been taxed for its support, required to hazard and sacrifice our lives in its defense, we do, therefore, solemnly ask, in the name of justice that there shall remain no laws, State or National, making distinction on account of color.

5. *Resolved,* That the safety of the Republic demands that, in the Territories, in the rebel States, when reorganized, and throughout the entire nation, colored men shall exercise the elective franchise, and be otherwise fully clothed with the rights of American citizens.

6. *Resolved,* That there still remain upon the statute books of Ohio, laws unjustly making distinction on account of color, and we earnestly protest against them, and demand of our Legislature the laws be purified, and made to conform to the requirements of Republican justice.

7. *Resolved,* That we view with pride, the generous ardor of our fellow citizens, men of color, who have rushed to the standard of their country, and have, in so many bloody fights, maintained the honor of their race, their State, and their country.

8. *Resolved,* That justice demands that the path of promotion should be opened to them, and that they should have the same incentives to honorable exertion as are presented to the white soldier.

9. *Resolved,* That we extend to our newly emancipated brothers and sisters of the South, just emerging from their night of slavery, our right hand of fellowship and most cordial God-speed, and advise them to enter upon their new and free life with an earnest determination to cultivate among themselves education, temperance, frugality and morality, together with all other things "that pertain to a well ordered and dignified life," and we pledge to these, our brothers and sisters, a constant and manly endeavor, on our part, to secure to them, and ourselves, complete freedom and enfranchisement in this, our native land and under American laws.

10. *Resolved,* That we do also advise our newly emancipated brothers and sisters who have lived together as husbands and wives, according to slave-

holding usages, while slaves, as soon as practicable to be married according to law, and thus legalize their marriages and legitimate their children.

Whereas, It is the opinion of the Convention that it is through Divine Agency that the present war is thrust upon the American Government, as a just retribution for its insults to justice and its inhumanity to the colored people of the United States, and

Whereas, We believe it to be the duty of every colored man to yield a cheerful obedience to that Divine Agency, and

Whereas, we are convinced that it can be most effectually complied with by giving the Union Army service and support, therefore

11. *Resolved,* That in our petitions to the authorities of the Government, asking all the rights of American citizens, that we do not mean to include such as have illegally evaded, or refused in any way, to assist the Federal Army to subdue the rebellion.

12. *Resolved,* That we hail with joy the emancipation of slaves in the State of Missouri,* and also the re-election of Abraham Lincoln, and the installation of S. P. Chase as the Chief Justice of the United States Supreme Court.

13. *Resolved,* That as fathers and brothers of the brave colored troops in the Army of the James, this Convention express our deep gratitude to Major-General Butler for his fatherly and impartial treatment of the colored soldiers under his command.

14. *Resolved,* That it is the opinion of this Convention that the colored man or woman who will not do for a colored person, the circumstances being the same, what they would do for a white person, is unworthy of our respect and confidence.

Whereas, Many of our rural districts are not thoroughly informed as to their rights and privileges under the State school laws, and

Whereas, In many cases said districts are deliberately deprived of said rights by Boards of Education; therefore be it

15. *Resolved,* That the executive Board shall compile, in a circular all laws and parts of laws bearing on the educational interests of the colored people of Ohio, and circulate the same where needed.

16. *Resolved,* That this Convention, in view of its very high appreciation of the conduct of our brothers in arms, feel called upon to inquire of the General Government what direct action, if any, has yet been taken to release our brave soldiers and sailors now prisoners in the hands of rebels. And that we ask of the authorities prompt retaliation for any wrongs done them.

* Accomplished in January, 1865.

17. *Resolved,* That we appoint a committee of three persons, whose duty it shall be to ascertain the number of men from the State of Ohio who are filling regiments credited to other States; also the number of such men who have been killed, wounded or captured by the enemy, and for the sake of such killed, wounded or captured soldiers, or their families, seek to have the bounty pay or pension due them paid to them, and, if possible, to have such men credited to the State of Ohio.

18. Whereas, We believe great injustice has been done to colored recruits and substitutes by colored and white bounty brokers, acting as recruiting agents, who practice deception upon them, and take advantage of their ignorance, we feel that such men are not worthy of our confidence and respect, and they meet our most hearty disapprobation.

19. *Resolved,* That the delegates of this Convention be and they are hereby requested to use, in their several localities, their best endeavor to procure signatures to petitions asking the Legislature of this State to adopt such measures as will secure the repeal of all laws making distinctions on account of color; said petitions to be first forwarded to the President of the League at Cincinnati.

20. *Resolved,* That we view with pride and heartily endorse the efforts of the gentlemen composing the Faculties and Executive Boards of the Wilberforce University at Xenia, O.; the Albany Enterprise at Albany, O.; the Oberlin College at Oberlin, Lorain Co., O.; and the Iberia College in Morrow Co., O., to develop the intellectual powers of our youth, and for opening a field for the honorable employment of those powers.

21. *Resolved,* That we recommend to the patronage of the colored people of the State of Ohio, as the best family periodicals, the *Anglo-African, Christian Recorder,* and *Colored Citizen:*

22. *Resolved,* That this Convention return thanks to D. Jenkins, Esq., for his untiring efforts to effect the passage of the law securing to the families of our brave soldiers and sailors their rights, and also the passage of an amendment to the school law.

23. *Resolved,* That we do most respectfully recommend to the Executive Board of the State Equal Right's League, as a suitable person to act as an agent on behalf of the colored people of this State, with members of our State Legislature, to secure our rights according to law, David Jenkins, Esq., of Columbus, Ohio.

*Proceedings of a Convention of the Colored Men of Ohio, held in Xenia, on the 10th, 11th, and 12th days of January, 1865; with the Constitution of the Ohio Equal Rights League.* Printed by order of the Convention (Cincinnati, 1865).

## [k]

### Petition of Wisconsin Negroes

To the Honorable, the Senate and Assembly of the State of Wisconsin, at Madison Assembled.

The undersigned Colored Citizens of the State of Wisconsin, respectfully petition your Honorable bodies, and ask that the necessary legal steps be taken, and provision made in accordance with the Constitution of this State, to submit the question of granting the right of suffrage to Colored men of the age of twenty-one years, to the voters of this State at the next general election. We respectfully submit that by Law we are taxed and liable to military Duty as other men. It seems to us but justice that we should have a voice in determining how the taxes should be expended, and how and when our services shall be rendered.

MS., Memorial No. 151A, Petitions 1865, file #322, Legislative Papers, State Historical Society Library, Madison, Wisconsin.